Degrees of Courage

Degrees of Courage

Shari Vester

Mill City Press

Mill City Press, Inc.
212 3rd Avenue North, Suite 290
Minneapolis, MN 55401
612.455.2294
www.millcitypublishing.com

The events and characters portrayed in this book apart from well-known historical figures and the Zachar, Kontra, and Callmeyer families are fictitious or are used fictitiously, and any similarities to real persons, living or dead, is purely coincidental and not intended by the author.

ISBN-13: 978-1-938223-23-5
LCCN: 2012936535

Cover Design by Alan Pranke

Printed in the United States of America

To all my family
Close, Extended, Distant, or Unknown,
past, present, and future generations

CHAPTER ONE

1900 - 1914

Angela

THE MORNING OF JULY 31, 1901, was just the beginning of another day as the sun rose over the European continent and filled the sky with its presence. Only in Sopron, a small gem of a mid-size town on the border where Austria and Hungary mingled together did the sun decide it was not a day for it to shine. The sky, laden with rain-threatening clouds, seemed more appropriate to reflect the somber mood of mourners filing into old St. Mihaly Church. They came to pay their last respects to Theresia Bohaczek, a loving wife, devoted mother, and beloved friend.

A young life cut short is always lamentable, but for the nine children she left behind, her untimely death was truly a tragedy. She was only thirty-nine years old but her body, drained of all reserves from frequent childbirth, could no longer tolerate another pregnancy. She lost her last baby half into term, and a few days later she lost her life, too. The little boy she carried must have sensed that he would be destined to a life without ever knowing the tender love only a mother can give, and this he refused.

His brothers and sisters had no such choice. They were all there, sitting in the front pew, a more pitiable sight hardly imaginable: Angela, the oldest at eighteen, holding her fifteen-month-old baby sister Mitzie in her lap; next to her, Rezie, sixteen, and Gertie, fourteen, with three-year-old Lizzie sitting between them; then came the boys, Henrich, twelve; Franz, ten; Jozsef, seven; and Miska, five. Their grief-stricken father, shoulders sagging and head bent, sat at the end.

Friends, neighbors, and acquaintances filled the rest of the church, their hearts heavy with sadness as they listened to the eulogies, remembering the woman they all loved and respected. At the end of the service they passed by the casket to say a silent personal farewell to Theresia, then walked to the cemetery behind the church to wait for the graveside ceremony. They stood around talking quietly, but grew silent as they noticed the funeral procession approaching the gate. First to enter came a pink-faced altar boy holding up a large cross, with Father Henrich, the young Benedictine priest walking closely behind. His face reflected a profound sadness that was beyond the sorrow he felt each time he stood at an open grave reciting the prayer for the dead. As a priest he trusted God blindly, yet he couldn't keep his mind from questioning the Divine Wisdom in taking this woman when her death meant leaving behind nine motherless orphans. Who would care for them?

It was the question everyone asked. Sure, the children still had their father, but a father who had to work long hours to put bread on the table and rarely got involved with their upbringing. Even when the family was smaller he left that solely to his wife, and now that she was gone, they would need someone to take her place. Unfortunately there was no one, no aunts, or grandparents, not one relative who could step in and help looking after them.

With deep-felt pity the mourners watched the children as they walked behind their mother's coffin, a somber sight that affected everyone present. How young they were, from barely a year old to eighteen! And how well they were holding up, although now that they had reached the grave, the gaping hole seemed to frighten the younger children. They started whimpering, and while their older brothers and sisters held their tears a little longer, they too began to sob when the pallbearers slid the casket onto the boards across the grave. Only their father, a hopelessly broken man, remained dry-eyed. He had no more tears to shed, no will to fight the terrible pain tearing at his heart, and although he must go on living, it was only acting the part. Inside, he was dying too.

Seeing him standing alone apart from his children, people began to wonder, shouldn't he be with them, comforting them? But then, he was always like this, never at his wife's side when she took the children out for a Sunday stroll. It would be easier to understand his aloofness if the children were unruly, hard to control, but they were all well-mannered and respectful, thanks to Theresia's care and guidance. His strangely distant attitude was often subject to speculation: what made him so indifferent toward them? While men usually refrained from passing judgment, women clucked their tongues in disapproval, if not in condemnation. After all, he didn't mind creating those children, did he now! It was to his credit that he supported them financially, but couldn't he also love them a little, be the father these children needed and deserved? Couldn't he show some fatherly pride and praise them now and then when praise was due?

Jozsef Bohaczek knew all about the criticism, how people talked about him, and he admitted, they were right. Yet he was not always like this. He grew lethargic as the children kept arriving, each birth loosening the unique tie that held him and his cherished wife together. He resented the loss of the carefree, happy times they used to share as the attention she lavished on him at the beginning slowly shifted to the children. The extra hours he had to work to support his family also added to his growing bitterness. Oh, he knew they blamed him for not limiting his family, but to suggest birth control to Theresia was utterly futile. He would have been happy if they never had children, but she wanted as many as God would give her. No amount of reasoning could stand up against her Catholic beliefs and deep devotion to the teaching of the Church. Nor would she listen to warnings from doctors and well-meaning friends that too many pregnancies could jeopardize her health. It was all in vain. She stubbornly refused to believe that her life could be in danger, and there was nothing he could do but keep hoping that this sad day would never come.

His tormented mind looked for someone to blame, anyone—even God, who commanded her to bear all these children—when his thoughts were suddenly interrupted by the priest's voice leading in prayers. He bent his head, not in pious acceptance, but in bitter surrender to the finality of the moment, as he listened to the words mingled with the muffled sobs of his children. The three little ones didn't really know what was happening, but the tears of the others sprang from true anguish.

Even Angela lost control and broke down under the weight of relentless pain and sorrow. During her mother's illness she had tried to prepare herself for today, to show strength and courage, but how could she when she had neither? She was only a young girl, grieving over the loss of her mother and scared of the future that would put awesome responsibilities on her shoulders. What would she do? What would her life be when forced to step into her mother's shoes? At eighteen she was at an age when girls usually looked forward to a whirl of social activities, going to parties, dancing at balls, all aimed at catching a husband. Was she to be denied all that now? Was she expected to spend her most opportune young years bringing up children that were not hers, sacrifice her entire future for the sake of her siblings? And what would happen after they were grown and on their own? Was she to be left an old maid, never to know the joy of holding her own child?

The baby squirming in her arms brought Angela back to the moment. How could she let herself wallow in self-pity, awash with anguish over what would become of her, when she was standing at her mother's grave? She quickly wiped her tears and turned her attention to the child trying to free herself, kicking her little feet and arching her back. Angela didn't realize just how tightly she was pressing the baby to her chest, but as she relaxed her hold, little Mitzie calmed down and snuggled against her neck. Her sweet nestling touched something in Angela's heart, a humble acceptance that her little sister would depend entirely on her for the love, care, and nurturing she needed. And in that moment, with her eyes closed, she made a silent promise to her mother that she would always take care of her, and the others, too, look after them, keep them together, because this was all that mattered, not her own future, or what she would miss. And when she looked up again, she was a little less afraid of what was to come.

Vaguely she heard the priest's voice reciting the closing prayer for Theresia's soul, intoning the mournful words "Ashes to ashes and dust to dust." The dreaded moment was at hand when the helpers began lowering the casket to commit her body to the deep. There was hardly a dry eye among the mourners as the children, one following the other and each holding a white carnation, their mother's favorite flower, stepped up to the grave and with tears that always accompany final goodbyes, dropped the flowers on top of the slowly descending casket. Angela, holding the baby and carrying two carnations was the last one, but she just stood there, staring into the gaping blackness, unable to toss the flowers, as if by refusing she could delay the closing of the grave. She only let them fall when Mrs. Karner, a close friend of the family, lifted the child from her and helped her step back to let her father approach the grave.

He walked with a forced steadiness, an obvious effort to maintain a semblance of dignity, carrying twenty-two red roses, one for each year that he and Theresia were married. His expression was a mixture of profound sadness and defiance, a mask that hid the inner battle he fought with the demons that urged him to join his wife and end it all. Their time together was not enough! To the devil with "Death do us part"! But of course, that was impossible. Theresia would send him to eternal damnation if he gave in and abandoned their children. For the sake of being with her in the afterlife, he must accept this temporary separation and go on with his life, even though it no longer held any meaning for him. It was the only way to ensure that she would be waiting for him when his time on earth finally ran out. And so, listening to the sound of rhythmic pounding, the dirt hitting the top of the casket, he willed himself to hold on to his sanity and accept the finality that she was truly gone.

By noon the grave was closed, covered by a forest of flowers, and people were slowly turning to leave. Those close to the family surrounded the children, whispering condolences, reassuring them that they would always be there to help. Only the father, alone in his deep sorrow, remained at the grave. He didn't hear Father Henrich approaching to offer consolation and encouragement for the difficult days ahead.

"Trust in God and in his compassion," he said gently touching his arm. "He knows what you are going through and feels your suffering, but he can also ease your pain if you just let him help you."

Such words always brought comfort to the grieving, but this time they failed, as Jozsef Bohaczek shook his arm free and shot back with a voice full of contempt. "You can save your preaching about your kind and compassionate God! A God who commands to bring children into this world then takes their mother away could only be called cruel and heartless!"

Father Henrich lowered his head. "I know you are heartbroken now, and your words come from the depths of despair. We are only human and do not understand God's design, why he called Theresia back to him. When we grieve it is easy to doubt, but I am sure, given time —"

But Jozsef did not let him finish. "You want me to believe that God had a reason to call my wife, the mother of nine children to his side, and expect me not to question him? Well Father, I can't do that, I can't accept what seems to be your answer to everything, to trust in God's wisdom. It will not do for me because I want an answer why is she lying in that grave. If he were such a loving, passionate God, he could not allow this to happen! He might be your God, but he is not mine anymore!"

The bitter tirade took the young priest aback. He understood the man was distraught, but his attack on God was beyond reason. He hesitated. Should he go on and risk another rebuke by trying to convince him that the deeper his anger was, the more he needed God's help? Perhaps it was best to give him time to recover and talk to him later. He would be more receptive when his state of mind was more rational.

"I pray you find peace, Jozsef," he said, making the sign of the cross, then turned and walked to the group clustering around the children. He would visit the family soon and see what he could do to help, not only spiritually but also in any other way possible.

"Is Father coming?" Angela asked him, but when told that he wished to remain by the grave a while longer, people from her neighborhood gladly offered to help escorting the children home. Nobody expected a feast for the mourners—they all knew Angela couldn't do it alone and there was no one to help making the arrangements—so the ladies in the group decided on the way to the house to take over and hold a small reception. They were soon back, bringing a variety of simple dishes, loaves of bread, some fruits and sweets, and made themselves home in the kitchen, brewing coffee and boiling water for tea, while others kept busy setting up the table. There would be a wake after all, a gathering of friends to reminisce about Theresia, trading little stories, personal recollections, that in their heart would keep her memory alive. The older children knew their mother was well liked by everyone, but that afternoon, listening to these tales of kindness, they also learned just how special she was, helping others in time of need and accepting help graciously when she herself needed a helping hand.

Each hour on the hour the large ornamental clock on the wall chimed, but no one took notice until the sound of a church bell drifted in from the street, reminding everyone that it was time for evening prayers. Most of the ladies got up to attend service, while the less devoted took it as a signal to leave.

Left alone, the girls were clearing the table when their father walked through the door. Having no appetite, he waved aside the plate Angela offered him then, seeing that everything was in order, household chores done and the babies looked after, he mumbled a few praises for holding up so bravely on this difficult day, then headed for the bedroom. In his tortured mind anything more—a comforting word, a warm hug, or a gentle touch—would be excessive.

His children would have to learn to cope without coddling, just like he must live out his days in desolate loneliness.

Angela and the older girls continued to put away the leftovers and wash the dishes, while the little ones sat quietly, their eyes following their sisters' every move. They did not cry, did not ask for their mother; somehow they understood that something had drastically changed today. The toys were left untouched; there was no tickling, no chasing around the table, no begging to go outside.

As evening shadows slowly descended over the city, Angela lit the kerosene lamps and prepared the children for bedtime. She felt exhausted, both physically and emotionally. The funeral and the sleepless nights she had spent at her mother's bedside during her illness had left her worn out and weary. She badly needed a good night's rest to meet the demands of the new day, and a clear mind to live up to what was now expected of her. From this day forward it will be up to her to keep their large household running, look after the children, and stand strong against challenges still waiting in the future. It will not be easy to bear up to her new responsibilities, but she didn't let it discourage her. She said her evening prayers and when she finally laid her head on her pillow, her resolve to do her utmost in caring for her family was as strong as when she made that solemn promise at her mother's grave.

Angela stirred as shafts of the early morning sunlight poked through the scalloped curtains. Her eyelids flickered for a moment, and then she was awake. Sitting up, she stretched, gearing up to start the day, but as she glanced around the room a sudden sense of nostalgia swept over her. Memories of the happy years she had spent between these walls came flooding back, although she quickly discarded them as sentimental nonsense. So what if it was the last time she slept in this room? It was big enough to share it with Rezie and Gertie, but not anymore, not since she brought in the two baby cribs during her mother's illness. To have more space they would change places with their father today; they would move into the big master bedroom, while he would be quite comfortable in this smaller bedroom. Only the curtains would have to be replaced; he wouldn't stand those girlish, lacy frills. She'd put up something else.

As for the rest of the house, there was no need for other rearrangements. The boys would stay in their room; it was spacious enough to accommodate all four of them. Structurally the house was typical of those built in Sopron around the middle of the 19th century. From the street a heavy double door opened into a covered cobblestone court, beyond which was a fenced-in yard with a playground for the children and a storage shed in the back. At the right side of the covered court was the entrance to the house itself, where a long hallway split the living quarters into two: three bedrooms on the left with windows to the backyard, and a parlor and large dining room facing the street on the right. The kitchen and the bathroom were located at the opposite ends of the hallway, albeit both without running water, since Sopron, as most of the provincial towns at the turn of the century, had no electricity or plumbing.

Running the household, Theresia always enlisted the children as young as eight to pitch in doing light chores around the house, the girls sweeping the floors, dusting the furniture, and watching their younger siblings, while the boys ran errands, collected the garbage and fetched water from the pump in front of the house. No one ever complained, but now that their mother was gone, all began to change. As Angela tried to assert her authority to enforce the rules, her efforts met with resistance, especially from Rezie and Gertie. The two girls considered themselves equal to her and were reluctant to do her bidding. "You are not my mother" was their favorite motto, and picking up on it, the boys soon started mouthing back to her the same way. Their attitudes improved only when Angela adopted a different approach; instead of telling them what to do, she made it a challenge to prove they could handle responsibilities. It made them feel important and more willing to help.

Lacking parenting skills, it was an enormous task for this eighteen-year-old to step into her mother's shoes and raise her siblings, especially since she had no one to turn to for help and advice. She was completely alone, left only to fall back on remembering what her mother did. Theresia, as did most mothers in her social standing, focused on preparing the girls to be proper wives, teaching them to cook, keep a clean house and use the needle—all necessary skills for marriageable young ladies. As for the boys, they were brought up to become responsible and hardworking individuals. If they showed an aptitude for higher learning, they had to study hard during their eight-year mandatory schooling to earn a scholarship; otherwise they would learn a trade.

The girls also finished school, but for them it was just as important to acquire the necessary social graces. They took music lessons and later in their teens were sent to dance schools, a good place to establish social contacts that brought invitations to balls and parties. Playing a musical instrument and knowing how to slide across the dance floor gracefully always helped to catch the eye of an eligible young man, but without knowing how to run a household, their chances to channel that interest into a proposal were drastically reduced.

Angela went through the entire process and already attracted several young men by the time her mother died. Although she was not beautiful in the classical sense, she was attractive, with a piquant little nose, high cheekbones, and wide-set eyes. Her ash blond hair framing her face in gentle waves was caught and tied with a ribbon at the back of her neck. She was petite, but her figure was nicely proportioned, outlined with pleasing curves.

She was popular, never lacking partners when her mother took her to dances. At the closing hour there were always plenty of young men vying to escort her home, putting their best foot forward in hopes of earning her mother's approval and gain permission to call on Angela later. Most of them were just starting out in life, working as policemen, teachers, clerks in government service, or perhaps in a family trade. At the turn of the century men in such positions were considered highly acceptable, even sought-after, as future husbands for girls in the lower middle classes like Angela. They were ready to settle down, not like their counterparts in the higher social circles, where boys left home for universities or military academies, or simply traveled to see the world.

Parents warmly welcomed these steady, homegrown boys into their families, and Theresia, too, readily opened her home to Angela's suitors. Visits were always conducted under strict supervision and consisted of polite conversations interwoven with subtle probing to find out more about the young man's character, background, and tendencies. Further invitations followed if he was found worthy of consideration.

With her mother's untimely death, these social activities came to a halt for Angela. During the first weeks following the funeral, her suitors came by to express condolences, but subsequently the calls became fewer until they stopped altogether. It hurt her in the beginning, but she consoled herself that with the amount of work now facing her, there would be very little time for idle socializing. There was no end to her day. She started with rushing to the open market early enough to find the freshest produce before it's picked over. On the way home she'd make several stops to pick up goods at the dairy, the baker and the butcher. Back in the house she set about making breakfast, while Rezie and Gertie helped to get the younger children ready, seeing to it that they were washed and dressed. It was one chore they didn't mind doing—they actually enjoyed bossing over them—but after breakfast, as soon as the dishes were put away and the beds made up, they usually managed to disappear, leaving the rest of the workload to Angela.

And that was just in the morning. Lunch had to be served at one o'clock, the time their father came home for a two-hour siesta. It was their most important meal of the day, consisting of soup, a main dish, and salad. Angela was familiar with the recipes, or could always resort to her mother's cookbook, so her problem was not cooking itself, but to do it for ten people. Recipes were not written for such a crowd, and simply multiplying the suggested ingredients never seemed to produce the desired result. It was frustrating, but what made it worse was her father's criticism. There was always something not to his liking. "Didn't you learn anything from your mother? This food has no taste!" he would say, or worse, just slam down his napkin and leave the table without a word.

She pleaded for more patience and understanding, often on verge of tears, that she was doing her best under the circumstances. She tried to appeal to his sympathy that she needed time to learn the many things her mother knew how to do, but it only fell on deaf ears. Seeing him pushing his food aside, the children soon followed his example and began fussing over their food, too. If they did not like what was on their plate and refused to touch it, saying their father did not eat it either, Angela scolded them, even though it was meant for her father when she said that she hoped their appetites would improve by supper, because they would get the same thing. It was unthinkable to throw out perfectly good food just because it did not taste as it used to. And if the food remained untouched at night too, it would be on the table again the next day. The big block of ice in her tin-lined wooden box kept leftovers safe for a day.

When lunch was over she always took Mitzie in her lap, playing with her until she was ready for her afternoon nap. But even during this quiet time her mind was fast at work, running through the list of things to do later. After washing the dishes and mopping the kitchen floor, there was always the laundry and the mending. Ever since her mother's illness, she had neglected her sewing, but by now it couldn't be put aside any longer. Luckily, she didn't mind working with thread and needle; she was very good at it. Her mother noticed early on that she had talent in this field and enrolled her in pattern making and dress designing courses. Angela never missed her classes, as if sensing that what she was learning would become her livelihood one day.

Busy as she was, she also squeezed in a little time each day to play with the smaller children, if nothing more than building some sandcastles or tossing a ball in the backyard. But she promised herself that once she settled more into her new role, she'd take them out to the park, as her mother always did. She remembered as a child what fun it was to ride the seesaw, play hide and seek between the trees, or just chase after each other with no one to complain about their boisterous shrieks. They were not cooped up during the winter, either. At the first snow Theresia bundled them up and off they'd go with their sleds, the three girls sitting on one holding each other by the waist, and the boys pulling their own sled, pitching snowballs at anyone nearby. Angela would need time, but she would continue those outings; she would see to it that her younger sisters and brothers would not be deprived of such fun.

As her day was winding to a close, Angela could finally sit down, exhausted, and wondering how her mother still managed to read a book or write a letter before retiring. She could hardly wait to put her head down, hoping that the two babies would let her sleep without much interruption.

"Papa, we have leftovers tonight, but I can fix you some omelet with sausage if you'd like," Angela offered when their father came home one night. He liked simple food with lots of spice, and nothing was better than the plump, seasoned Hungarian sausages. He nodded in agreement, and taking a glass of wine walked into the parlor to wait until the food was ready. It was a warm evening with the windows wide open, a gentle breeze rippling through the curtains. He picked up the newspaper and sipped his wine, the only alcohol he drank besides beer. He didn't smoke cigarettes either, only a pipe, and never inside the house, since Theresia wouldn't allow it around the children.

Without any bad habits, friends often teased him that he should develop a vice or two to keep life more interesting. "It must be dull to work all day then go home to your wife every night. There are other things a man can do besides making babies, you know!" they'd taunt him, but he just laughed at the idea that life could be dull with Theresia! What did they know, how could they even guess, what bliss it was to love a woman the way he loved Theresia, and be loved back with equal passion? Nothing made him more content than to sit together with her late at night when all was quiet, the children put to bed, and feel the special closeness that bound them together from the very start. Why did it have to end? Why? The question never left his mind; it was lurking there in the morning when he got out of his lonely bed and was still there, still unanswered, when he put his head down at night.

He ate his supper in silence and was ready to retire when he heard someone knocking on the door. It was still during social hours, but he was annoyed that some caller should interrupt his evening. He would have preferred not to answer the door at all, but after a minute or so got up and opened it to see Father Henrich standing on the threshold.

"Good evening, Mr. Bohaczek, I hope I am not intruding on you," he apologized. "I know it's a bit late, but I was in the neighborhood and thought I would stop by and see how you and your family are doing. I know you work long hours, and I wanted to make sure I find you at home. You see, I have some thoughts I would like to discuss with you."

Jozsef Bohaczek, hardly able to hide his reluctance, waved him inside. To be polite, he offered something to drink and exchanged a few pleasantries, but then asked the priest point-blank what was on his mind.

"Well, I know from your blessed wife that your family has no relatives to rely on for help during these difficult days and I thought, with your permission, I could enlist some of the ladies in my parish to chip in with the housework. They'd be more than glad to lend a hand."

Jozsef Bohaczek dipped his head slightly. "It's kind of you Father, but we don't need charity. We will manage. Angela can handle what needs to be done."

"But she is just a child, still in her teens, Mr. Bohaczek. Surely you don't expect her to take care of the house and the children without help?"

"And why not? She might be young, but my wife was about the same age when I married her, and she has done a good job all by herself. Angela already learned a lot from her, and she'll figure out how to organize her time. Her sisters are helping her, and the boys pitch in too, so thank you, but we won't need any outside help."

Father Henrich looked at the frail figure of Angela and felt his heart overflow with deep empathy for her.

"Mr. Bohaczek, I know you are a proud man, and I don't want you to interpret my offer as charity. These ladies gladly volunteer their time to give a hand when help is needed, and I don't know a better case for that than nine children left without a mother. Just look at them. Don't you think that Angela is too young to do all that work without risking a breakdown? Please, let me line up some help, at least for a while, until the girls work out a routine."

"I don't know how else to tell you, Father, that we can get along just fine without assistance," Jozsef answered barely able to mask his irritation. "My girls might look fragile to you, but they are strong. You need not worry about them. It's mighty nice of your volunteer ladies wanting to help, but I am sure there are plenty of poor deserving families in this town who need them more. Thank them for us, but we are just not in that category."

There was no use further arguing with this maddeningly stubborn, insensible man who would not let his pride accept help, not even for the sake of his children. Such an attitude bordered on cruelty. It was admirable how much he loved his wife, but had he no love for his children? The priest saw that pressing the issue would only aggravate the situation and stopped his pleading, but he knew he would do something, even against his wishes.

"Well, I see your mind is made up, and I am truly sorry I could not convince you to take my suggestion as a well-intended gesture. You seem to have all the confidence in Angela, and I hope she won't break trying to live up to it. But Mr. Bohaczek, if you don't mind, I'd like to come by from time to time. I won't bring up the subject of the volunteers anymore, but perhaps I can give you and the children some spiritual help in coping with the difficult adjustment you and your family face. What would be the most convenient time for you to let me visit?"

"You can come anytime; I don't need to be here. In fact, I'd prefer that you come during the day while I am at work. I am tired by the time I get home and would rather have my evenings to myself. So unless it is something important for me to know, just talk to Angela; she might need some encouragement in the beginning."

"Is that right, Angela? You won't mind?" Father Henrich turned to her.

"No, of course not, Father, it would be so nice if you'd visit us. And even if I am out on an errand, just come in and spend some time with the children, please," she blurted out in one breath.

"I will, I promise, and very soon," he smiled at the girl, wishing he could do more for her. He was keenly aware that with their mother gone and a father lacking compassion, these children needed someone to show them a little kindness, to let them know that someone cared.

A week went by before the young priest called again. He picked an early afternoon hour, knowing that it was around that time of the day when homemakers could usually take a short break. But his timing could not have been worse for Angela. She had just finished putting the babies down for a nap and was gathering the dirty laundry when she heard the knock on the door. *Not now, whoever it is please, not today,* she sighed, holding the bundle. Tomorrow was her washday, which meant she had to cook today for two days; doing laundry took up most of the day, leaving no room to prepare their meals. But when the knocking continued, she dropped the clothes and opened the door to find Father Henrich standing there. Forgetting about the pile on the floor she smiled and ushered him into the parlor with proper formalities.

"Please, make yourself comfortable Father," she motioned toward the sofa and was about to sit down too, when she remembered the dirty laundry she left at the door. Excusing herself for a moment she hurried to put it out of sight, and at the same time rounded up Rezie to keep the children quiet. Then, with a quick look in the hall mirror, she smoothed down her hair and rushed back to the parlor.

"May I bring you something to drink?" she asked the priest. "I baked some muffins this morning, if you'd like some."

"That would be nice, Angela, thank you," he smiled at her, and when she returned with the tray and he took a bite of the muffin, he complimented her generously.

"These are delicious; you are an excellent cook, Angela. Your mother would be so proud of you! The way you handle the household and take care of the children is truly commendable. God will reward you one day for your hard work. I know it's not easy for you, and that's why I want you to know that if coping becomes too difficult, you can always come to the parish and talk to me, instead of waiting until I visit next."

"It's good to know, Father, thank you. I truly appreciate your kindness, and the way you tried to help me the other day. I wish others would see as you do that I could never fill my mother's shoes! No matter how hard I try, I can never do everything the way she used to. I don't mean to complain, but whatever I do, it's never good enough . . ." She stopped, her voice trailing to a sigh.

"You are talking about your father, Angela, aren't you?"

"He expects too much from me, Father! I want to please him but he constantly compares me to Mother and that's not fair! Doesn't he know that I could never be like her?" The words tumbled out of her mouth in sheer frustration. "All I get is criticism. Why must he be so mean to me?"

Angela was fighting tears by now and to hold them back she pressed her fingers hard against her eyes. When they spilled out anyway, the young priest pulled out his handkerchief and, prying her hands away, dabbed awkwardly at her face.

"Now, now, Angela, dear girl, it's all right," he said trying to comfort her. "You have all the right to cry, and I am not trying to stop you. Tears sometimes help to wash away despair; crying cleanses, it brings relief—perhaps that is why God gave man the ability to weep."

His words made her cry even more, and to hide her misery she bent forward, dropping her head. The move loosened a few strands of her hair and the priest reached out and smoothed them back behind her ear, then let his fingers slide along her jaw. He was about to lift her chin, when suddenly she grabbed his hand and covered it with kisses.

"What . . . Angela, you must not do this!" he cried out in surprise and pulled his hand away. He sat up straight and for a moment was lost for words.

Angela lifted her head, her eyes brimming with gratitude. "You are so good to me, Father! You understand how I feel, how much I need a little kindness, a little praise! Tell me, is it too much to ask? Am I vain to feel that I deserve it?"

Looking at her lovely, tear-soaked face, Father Henrich felt such an overwhelming compassion for this young girl, so needy, so starved for affection, that on impulse he reached out and pulled her onto his shoulder. Stroking her hair, he spoke to her in a hushed, soothing voice. "Of course you are not vain Angela, you are just human. Don't we all need acknowledgment, a little encouragement to go on? Especially you, losing your mother so early and left alone to carry such a load that would be a challenge for any woman twice your age. No wonder you feel downhearted. It's only natural. But you must find strength through faith. You must trust God and accept that there is a reason he has chosen this role for you. Perhaps he is preparing you for something you will need later in life. Only he has the answer, and you must not question him. I will be here to help you along, and I promise, together we'll find a way to make things better for you."

By then he had completely regained his composure and pulling away, sat at a respectful distance from her. Seeing a faint smile returning to Angela's lips, he patted her hand.

"Well now, feeling a little better? And you know what? I already have an idea how to make that beautiful smile of yours even brighter. When I came in I could not help noticing that you were getting ready to do the laundry. How would you like a little help with that, huh? Mrs. Szalai down the street would be glad to give you a hand; she is one of the volunteers at the parish and she already spoke to me about wanting to help you. So what if I arrange for it? Wouldn't this give you more time to do your other chores?"

Angela's face lit up, but a second later her smile vanished. She rolled her eyes and waved a hand through the air in resignation. "Oh, but it wouldn't work; Papa would never allow it." With disappointment clearly written on her face she added, "But please tell Mrs. Szalai that I am very grateful, and that it is not me who would not accept her kind offer. I will thank her in person the next time I see her."

Now it was Father Henrich's turn to smile. "Angela, your father need not know about this," he said. "It can be our secret. Mrs. Szalai knows your father, how proud and stubborn he is about things. She could pick up your bundle, do the laundry at her house instead of here, and bring it back the next day, so your little sisters and brothers wouldn't innocently babble about it to your father. Rezie and Gertie will know, but I think you'll agree, they will be more than happy to keep from telling on you if it means that they will have more free time on their hands on washdays, is not that so?"

Angela's lips curled into a sly little smile. "Our secret, Father?" She tipped her head to the side, looking up at him from under her lashes. She held out a hand and when the priest took it, the handshake became a bond between two conspirators. That moment he became her partner, an understanding friend who would stand by her, someone she could trust and rely on.

"Well, it's all settled then," the priest said. "I'll stop by Mrs. Szalai, then you two can work out the details. And this is just the start Angela; together we'll find more ways to help you. But remember what I said earlier. God loves you and will not abandon you if you put your trust in him. Ask for his guidance; give yourself up to him and you'll see how your life will change."

With that he stood up and drew a cross with his thumb on Angela's forehead, ready to leave. On his way out he stopped to greet the other children noisily playing in the yard. Seeing his black-clad figure all horseplay ceased, but only until he put them at ease by picking up the baby and twirling her around to her happy shrieks. After putting her down he reached into his pocket for some candy he brought along, and handing it out reminded them to be good and always listen to their big sister.

Angela waited until the gate closed behind him then rushed to the window and watched him cross the street. Hidden behind curtains, she pressed her hand against her mouth, as if fighting the urge to blow a kiss after him. Her heart overflowing with gratitude, she remained there until he was out of sight, already counting the days when she would see him again.

Her feelings grew stronger each time Father Henrich enlisted another "secret helper" to make her life a little easier. They were running daily errands for her, do the shopping at the various stores, and helped with major house cleaning, until gradually Angela began to learn how to manage her time better. And as people saw how well she was coping, the pity they felt for her in the beginning turned into deep respect, even admiration, especially at her dedication in taking care of the children.

It was hard to believe that the family had no relatives anywhere near, but it was true. Jozsef, a civil servant, and Theresia were originally from Bohemia and came to Hungary in 1881 when he was transferred to Sopron. The Imperial Court in Vienna could easily relocate government employees—and routinely did so—to any country within the Austro-Hungarian Empire, because the official language of the Monarchy was German. When Jozsef received his reassignment, Theresia tried to persuade some of her relatives to come with them, but no one was willing to pull up roots to go and live in a backward country like Hungary. It was not easy for her to cope without help as her family grew, but she found the strength, as did Angela now.

With every passing week she became better organized and more efficient, and with it came a newfound confidence, a certain pride that accomplishment brings. She no longer felt overburdened and talked less and less about problems during Father Henrich's visits, until one day she stopped complaining altogether. From there on, their conversations took on a lighter tone, with Angela hanging on the priest's every word, imagining the places he had been, as he occasionally talked about growing up with vacations at the Adriatic Sea and skiing in the Alps. Without noticing, their relationship became more relaxed, less formal, and with familiarity came easy laughter. His visits became the highlight of her weeks. She took special care that the house was in the best order when he came, and that she, too, looked her prettiest, not because she expected any compliments—she didn't even know if he noticed; she only hoped he did.

He still talked about God and his mysterious ways, how everything happens according to His will, and slowly Angela became convinced that all the recent twists and turns in her life happened for one reason: it was God's design to put Father Henrich in her path. He sent him to her rescue when she was close to despair, and she was forever grateful to Him for that. But she felt equally indebted to the priest, for without his patience and loving guidance she would have been lost. She loved them both with equal passion: God from the depth of her soul, and the priest with all her heart.

The beginning of the new school year in September brought a slight relief in Angela's busy life. Lizzie had just started pre-school and Miska was in kindergarten, while the rest of the children were sitting in classes varying from first grade through the eighth. Rezie, at sixteen, had already completed her schooling but was taking classes in sewing and pattern making, as Angela did a few years back. She didn't have the zeal or the talent Angela had for dressmaking; she only kept going to get out of the house and away from doing chores.

With only the baby at home, it was the first time that Angela was completely alone when Father Henrich came to visit. As always, he greeted her with a beaming smile.

"And how is the young lady of the house doing today? You must have had an easy week to look as lovely as you do today," he teased her playfully, expecting an equally cheerful response.

But instead of ushering him in and chatting about last week's events, Angela just stood there, rooted to the floor, nervously glancing from his face to the door and back. She nudged her head toward the empty house behind her.

"The children are all at school, Father. I can't get used to the quiet, not that I am complaining," she said with a smile, trying to sound nonchalant, but the forced tone of her voice betrayed her edginess. "I thought we could go for a walk; it's a shame to stay cooped up inside on such a beautiful day," she added, still standing in the same spot. "It will only take me a minute to put Mitzie in her pram."

Not waiting for an answer, she turned and started toward the bedroom to fetch the baby, but the priest caught her by the arm. He saw how tense she was and guessed right away what made her so jumpy. Pulling her back and turning her around to face him, he placed his hands firmly on her shoulders to make her stand still.

"Angela, we will go for a walk if that's what you want, but not because the weather is nice. I think I know the real reason. You are afraid of staying here alone with me, because of what people might think or say. But my sweet girl, you have no cause to worry, and let me tell you why. First, I am a priest, and I do what priests do, which includes visiting people who need help, and believe me, everyone in this town, except your father, knows that you need help. These people know me, but more importantly, they know you. They hold you in the highest regard; don't you know that? Whether we are alone or not, trust me, they know we are not doing anything wrong; our conscience is clear, and if I had any doubt about that, I wouldn't be here."

He eased his hold on her shoulders but didn't release her. Sliding his hands down the length of her arms, he took her hands in his and squeezed them gently. "It's true that things have changed between us since my first visits. We both realize that by now I am not only a spiritual counselor to you, but a friend as well, and you, dearest Angela—you are like a beloved sister to me. We became close, but the relationship we have is innocent and above suspicion. If I did not wear this robe, if I were not a priest, I might have different feelings for you because you are a beautiful girl, inside and out. But even then, I would never do anything to compromise you. You must know that!"

"I know, Father, of course I know; it's just that I've never been alone with a man before, someone was always around. I was taught that a girl should not be in the company of a man without a chaperone, that's what my mother pressed on me, and the nuns, too; it is simply not permitted." She stopped, looking uncertain, then added, "Perhaps it's different if the man is a priest. They didn't say anything about that. Is it?"

Father Henrich still holding her hands felt them tremble, her eyes searching his, waiting for a reply. She wanted to hear him say again that they were just trusted friends and nothing more, because she was not sure of her own feelings, a mixture of overwhelming gratitude, admiration, and a physical attraction she could no longer deny. She couldn't help the way she felt about him. From the moment he took up her cause against her father and helped her to go on after her mother's death, he became her shining knight who would never let her down. He could have stopped visiting when her life finally began to take shape, but he didn't. As busy as he was, he cared enough to continue seeing her, finding her worthy of his friendship and affection. Yes, they became friends, but then he said something else a minute ago! Did she hear him right? Did he really say that he might feel different about her if he were not in God's service? Could she mean more to him than a friend or a sister? Oh, only if it were true, she would care less what people would think!

Looking into her eyes, the priest saw the yearning, the need to hear that his feelings for her went beyond the boundaries of pious friendship. He knew they were at a crossroad, and that much depended on what he did next, but where duty, reason, and a cool head should have prevailed, it was the rapid quickening of his heart that answered Angela. A tiny gasp escaped from the back of her throat when he took her hand and placed it over his pounding heart. It told her more clearly than words ever could that he loved her, too. In spite of his priestly robe and aside from their innocent friendship, he also loved her as a woman!

With infinite relief she closed her eyes and offered her lips in breathless anticipation as she felt Henrich pulling her into his embrace. She'd been kissed before but it had never made her heart race with such urgency as now, in his arms. And when she felt his mouth touching hers, first haltingly, barely savoring the sweetness of their first kiss, then probing deeper, it ignited a fire, a fierce, unstoppable, all-consuming desire that drew them helplessly toward the sexual unknown. All their hitherto pent-up, repressed feelings burst upon them with a force that carried them past denial and beyond control. Time and place no longer mattered. They gave themselves up to the moment of miraculously rapturous first-time lovemaking, not thinking of the consequences that would change their lives forever.

. . . .

It was little Mitzie making baby noises in her crib that awakened them from the afterglow of lovemaking. Suddenly remembering there was a world beyond what they had just discovered, Angela sat at the edge of the bed, too self-conscious to stand up naked in the brightness of the sunlit room. She was eyeing her garments strewn around the floor, hoping to retrieve them without getting up, but it was impossible. Trying to pull the heavy bedspread to cover her backside didn't work either; it was too tangled up to give. There was nothing she could do but get up and pick up her clothes piece by piece.

"Henrich, please close your eyes until I get dressed, this is too embarrassing," she pleaded.

He did as she asked, turning his face away, but at the same time kept talking to her in a soft, reassuring voice. "I feel the same way my angel, getting up naked in front of you to put on my robe. It's only natural to feel awkward; this is all new to us, but you should never feel ashamed! What happened between us was so beautiful that it took my breath away. I want to be with you Angela, always, and I say it in all seriousness, not just in the heat of passion. It won't be easy, and it will take time, but I promise, I will make it right for us. We can't go back to yesterday. Nothing can be as before. What we discovered has changed everything. My mind is still reeling at this moment, but when I drop back to earth and can think more clearly, I will know what to do so we can be together. I will find a way."

Angela was dressed by then and was standing at the crib reaching for the baby. "You really think it's possible?" she asked, looking over her shoulder. "I thought religious vows could never be broken!"

The doubt in her voice hung in the air as she carried the child out of the room. Closing the door, she went about taking care of the baby, but her mind was in turmoil. The reality of what they just did came crashing down on her. She felt guilty for having given into her passion, but more than that, the knowledge that she was capable of such abandonment scared her. Was she a sinful creature? She should never have let it happen! But then, how could she not?

The priest had no such qualms. That he gave in so easily to what the Church called "the weakness of the flesh" convinced him of what he had felt vaguely for some time now—that he was not meant for the priesthood, after all. He was too young, just an impressionable boy, when he fell under the spell of the Church. His teachers, all Benedictine priests, became his idols. Serving as an altar boy, a reluctant duty to some of the other boys, was an honor to him and he would attend to it with utter devotion. His desire to join the Order grew stronger with each year, and by age eighteen, the time he graduated from the *gimnazium*—an eight-year European college preparatory school from age 10 to 18 with emphasis on the academics—he was determined to become a priest. His parents were dead against it, but they couldn't sway him. They were frantic at losing him, their only son to carry on the family name, but no amount of argument, plea, or tears would change his mind.

The Benedictines, an order established around the middle of the sixth Century, became famous for providing the best teachers and educators for Catholic schools. Young men entering the Order spent the first two years as novices, learning scholastic philosophy before entering the seminary to study theology for the next four years. During this period they had two choices. They could become teachers with very limited rights in regard to administering sacraments, or choose to become priests in the more traditional sense, performing regular priestly duties. There was one special requirement for the latter though: strong vocal chords and a good ear for music in order to sing during the celebration of High Mass. Submerged in liturgy, they would conduct Holy Mass, hear confessions, perform weddings and baptisms, administer last rites, and officiate at funerals. As much as Henrich admired his teachers, he felt he could serve God better as an ordained priest, and after he took his vows at the seminary in Vienna, he was sent to Sopron to replace the old retiring parish priest of St. Mihaly Church.

Henrich was only twenty-six years old when Angela's mother died and he began visiting the family. It never entered his mind that coming to see Angela would develop into anything more than what it was intended to be, helping a young girl in a very difficult situation. He knew she had no one to turn to, couldn't rely on her own father for emotional support, and when he saw how she struggled under the staggering weight that fell on her shoulders, he felt it was his duty to step in and give support.

At first the customary formalities due to a priest were strictly observed. Angela's attentiveness meant nothing more to him than expression of gratitude. It was only natural that as they got to know each other more, their relationship deepened into a warm appreciation on her part and a profound satisfaction in Henrich that he could make her life easier, her burden lighter. From the start they were bound by an innocent alliance that later grew into genuine affection for each other. In time the formalities dropped away and they became friends, feeling at ease in each other's company when a lingering touch of hand conveyed trusting familiarity without the slightest feeling of discomfort. If Angela harbored some vague romantic notions, she never let it show, and if Henrich sensed that her feelings were changing, he did nothing to encourage it. But underneath it all, more powerful emotions were developing, which they either chose to ignore or simply didn't recognize until it was too late. It was almost inevitable that these deeply buried feelings would ignite, and after reaching a boiling point would burst open with a force that swept away all barriers, leaving them stranded where there was no turning back to the comfort of the past.

How simple his life had been until now, dedicated to God, his future secured within the Church. He had always adhered to his vow of chastity and fulfilled his duties toward his parishioners, earning their trust and respect. But all had changed today. Today he left the straight line he had walked all these years and stepped onto a different path, one strewn with unknown obstacles. Others might still find a way back to the old familiar grounds, but for him there was no other choice than to follow this unfamiliar new road wherever it would lead him.

. . . .

Henrich left the bedroom to look for Angela. They needed to talk, but there was little time before the children would be arriving home from school. He wanted to tell her about the decision he made, what he must do, and why. He found her in the kitchen, and seeing her feeding the baby, sat down opposite her, waiting patiently until she finished. After she let the child down, he reached across the table and took her hands into his.

"Angela, I want you to know how lucky I feel that you came into my life, and because you are in my life now, everything will change. I meant every word when I said I want to be with you always; I can't give you up, not after what we found in each other. I want us to be together, but to do that I will have to seek dispensation from the Church, a lengthy process, since the Church does not take these things lightly. I'll be faced with strong objections, and we will be separated, could be for years, but it is all worth to me. The question is, do you want me, too? Are you willing to wait for me?"

He paused, but when Angela said nothing he continued. "I have to leave Sopron immediately and go back to Vienna to put things in motion. I will try to let you know what I am doing, but it is possible that I won't be able to do so for a good while. Please don't let it discourage you. Just know that I will not change my mind and let the Church persuade me to remain in their fold. Say you believe me that I will do everything to come for you as a free man!"

When Angela still sat there with a blank stare, he squeezed her hands and gave them a small tug. "Angela, are you listening to what I am saying? I must know what you are thinking. Will you wait for me?"

"You know my answer, Henrich; I wait for you as long as it will take," she finally spoke, her voice low, but firm. "I am a little scared of all that happened and what is to come, but I'll be all right. There is so much running through my mind right now, questions without answers. How did we get here? The only thing I know is that I will never regret what happened. From the beginning you brought me nothing but joy and now love, and I will never let it slip from my heart. Never. I know you must leave, and I hate the thought of not seeing you and holding you for a while, but I understand, it must be done. Separation will be hard, but it won't change my feelings; you will be in my heart and mind just as you are here with me now."

With all the strange new emotions surging through her, she felt the tears swelling, but she swallowed them to show that she was strong. She wanted to tell him that she believed when he said he loved her and would come back for her, and that her faith in him was absolute, but there was no time; the sound of children's laughter coming from the street cut her short. Any minute her siblings would be walking through the door.

"You have to go, Henrich; we must say goodbye now," Angela rose and rushed into his arms just as they heard the gate opening. "I will miss you more than I can say," she said looking into his eyes, "but you must not worry about me. I'll be waiting. I know you will do your best to come for me."

"Until then, my angel, until I can hold you again," all Henrich could say, lifting both her hands to his lips. There was no priestly blessing bestowed on her this time; they were saying goodbye as man and woman.

The next minute, the children burst in the room, chattering excitedly about their day in school, but the priest didn't stay to listen as usual. It didn't feel right to pretend that nothing had changed, so after a few minutes he quietly left. Angela walked him to the gate with only a few words passing between them, a whispered promise to come back, a pledge to wait. Then, with a final touch of hands, he stepped into the street and was gone.

Angela closed the door feeling confused and utterly alone. So much happened to her today! She was happier than ever before and miserable at the same time thinking of the long wait ahead and not knowing where it would lead her.

The waiting

WEEKS AND MONTHS went by without hearing from Henrich, but Angela never lost faith that the day would come when they would be together again. It was only a matter of time. The hardest thing for her was to keep everything to herself. There was no one she could talk to about her feelings—a relative, a friend, a confidant she could turn to for advice and encouragement. She had so many questions, but no one to ask. She was dying to find out about church rules concerning priests leaving the order; it would give her at least a vague idea of how long it would take for Henrich to obtain his freedom. Her confessor could tell, but she did not dare to ask; it would only raise suspicion. And of course, she could never reveal Henrich's identity to anyone. She was alone with her secret, with only her blind faith to sustain her in the lonely wait ahead.

At home she was as busy as ever, although it helped that lately she could rely more on her two sisters, especially on Rezie. She was now seventeen, just beginning to receive social invitations, and knowing full well that she would need Angela to escort her to balls and other outings, she was more willing to cooperate. She was an attractive girl with honey blond hair, green eyes, and a fun-loving nature, blessed with endless energy and a cheerful attitude. She made friends easily and was popular, so it did not come as a surprise that soon suitors started calling at the house. Within a year she was married to Jozsef Balzer, a young man from a small town less than a half hour train ride from Sopron.

This strip of land on Hungary's western frontier with Sopron as its only city was called Burgenland, literally the Land of Forts, a name befitting the historical role Burgenland played in protecting Austria. It served as a buffer zone to halt invaders from the East, just as Hungary became the shield for the whole of Europe against attackers during numerous crucial times in her thousand-year existence. Because of the proximity to Austria, a large segment of Burgenland's population spoke only German, most of its people working as farmers and wine growers. They grew the best beans in the land, which gave them the moniker *bonenziehter* (bean grower), or p*onzickter* as it was pronounced in the heavy local dialect. This accent, similar to that of the Viennese, was considered semi-foreign and almost impossible to understand by anyone speaking *Hochdeutsch*, the elite German tongue.

Schools taught proper diction, and that's what the Bohaczek children used in front of their father, but they would easily lapse into the local dialect when talking with most of their friends and amongst themselves. Angela also switched between the two forms in her budding new enterprise as a seamstress and dressmaker, using either precise German or the Burgenland dialect, depending on the sophistication level of her customers. A few months back, after she finally got a handle on managing her time better, she started taking in alterations, a small homegrown business at first that soon grew beyond the neighborhood by simple word-of-mouth. Ladies satisfied with her work began to trust her with more elaborate projects and brought their friends and others as new clients.

As busy as Angela was, Henrich was constantly on her mind. During the past year she had heard from him only a few times, always saying the same thing: that his feelings for her were as strong as ever, and although problems mounted with the Church, eventually he would be free. It took another year before she saw the first ray of hope to see him again when he wrote that he had become friends with a young couple sympathetic to their situation, and they could meet at their apartment if she could come to Vienna. Just send them a note a few days before she would arrive, and he would be at the train station waiting for her.

For days after reading his letter Angela floated on air. Finally, she would see him in real life, not just in her dreams. She only had to find an excuse to travel to Vienna. The opportunity came when the daughter of one of her well-to-do clients became engaged and they asked her to create a wedding gown that would be the talk of the town. She suggested that she could visit the fashion salons in Vienna, check out the latest designs, and bring back several sketches to look over. Once they made their choice she would go back to purchase the material, and their daughter would have a dress just like the original but at a fraction of the cost. They readily agreed, and she congratulated herself for coming up with such a clever plan that would allow her to see Henrich twice. She immediately sent a note to his newfound friends with the date and time of her arrival, and made arrangements for Mrs. Szalai to watch the children until she got back later in the day.

It was a beautiful September morning when she boarded the train for the hour-long trip. She wore a smart traveling suit and a matching hat with a cloud-like veil that covered half her face down to the tip of her nose. She took a window seat in restless anticipation of seeing him the minute the train pulled into the station. She was sure of her own feelings, but felt nervous about what Henrich's reaction would be at seeing her after such a long time. She had changed so much in the past two years. She was no longer the confused, desperately needy teenage girl he kissed goodbye, but a confident young woman with an established home-run business, respected by everyone in town. There were only a few who criticized her for being too choosy when she turned down every eligible young man who tried courting her. Catty comments sprang up behind her back after each refusal. "What is the matter with her? What is she waiting for? She is not that young to be so picky! A couple of years and she'll be an old maid, then she'll be sorry," tongues would wag. But those who knew her to be friendly and sociable took it that she was just too busy raising her siblings and working at her dressmaking business; she simply had no time to bother with suitors.

They all guessed wrong, of course, but only she alone knew the real reason: she was waiting for the only man she loved. And now it was just a little more time before she would be with him again.

Her thoughts were interrupted by the conductor's voice announcing the next stop, Vienna. She pulled a small compact from her purse and made a quick check of her face, rubbing her lips together to give them more color. As the train slowed and the wheels came to a screeching halt, Angela was on her feet to get a better view of the platform. Her heart skipped when she spotted him standing near the back wall, and the next instant she was out of the compartment, pushing toward the exit to be the first off the train. But then she stopped. What if the steam bursting from beneath the train should ruin her carefully arranged appearance? Better to wait if she wanted to look beautiful for Henrich.

And that she was, when after a few minutes she stood at top of the steps, sparkling with excitement, waving her hand at Henrich. She needn't have; he already saw her and was elbowing his way through the crowd. The second her feet touched the ground she was in his arms, forgetting time and place as they stood locked in a fiercely possessive embrace, unaware of the noise, the people, the swirling commotion around them. How long had it been? It didn't matter. The sweetness of her kiss took his breath away the same as that first time.

It was Angela who found the strength to pull away. She wanted to look at him, to see if love was still in his eyes. "It's been so very long! Tell me that I am not dreaming, and that this is real," she said, touching her fingers to his face.

"It's hard to believe, isn't it, my angel!" Henrich said, drawing her close again, unwilling to loosen his hold. He was finally forced to release her when people started bumping them in their rush to the exit. "Let's get out of here; I can't wait to be alone with you! I have a carriage waiting outside," he said, offering his arm.

But Angela didn't move; she stood there staring at him, her eyes wide with surprise. In her excitement she never noticed until now that instead of his black robe Henrich was wearing a tweed jacket, shirt and tie and a pair of gray slacks. Her heart jumped. Could this mean that he was no longer tied to the Church? Was it possible that her long wait was over? Was this why he asked her to come, to tell her the good news?

"Why, Henrich, you are not wearing your habit!" she exclaimed. "Does this mean . . . could it be that you . . ." she stammered, as the words stuck in her throat, unable to ask straightforward if he had left the Church.

He smiled down at her and teasingly touched his index finger to the tip of her nose. "I will tell you about it later, my darling, when we are alone."

She could hardly contain her impatience, but she took his arm with a smile and followed him to the outside, where carriages lined the curb waiting for hire. Henrich led her to an open barouche, helped her into her seat, and gave the address to the driver.

It was not her first visit to Vienna but now, sitting beside Henrich, holding his hand and feeling happy and excited, everything seemed to be brighter, more beautiful than she remembered. Leaving the train station, they rode along busy Mariahilfertrasse with its many shops and restaurants, until they reached the Ringstrasse, the avenue that encircled the inner city, the oldest part of Vienna. There the horses pulling their carriage clip-clopped their way through the narrow cobblestone streets leading to Michaelerplatz, a rather small square dominated by the magnificent Hofburg, the Imperial Winter Palace of the Habsburgs. From there they rode under a large freestanding archway to Josef Square with its world famous Spanish Riding School, the home of the magnificent Lipizzaners. Except for members of the Imperial House, and of course the trainers, no one was allowed to ride these purebred Arabian horses, taught to execute stylized jumps and other intricate movements that called for precision stepping in various prescribed patterns.

There was so much more to see along the way, buildings that made the city famous: the Stefan's Kirche (St. Stephen's Cathedral), the great 12th century Gothic cathedral in the heart of the city, its steeped roof set with colorful mosaic-like tiles; the Museum of Fine Arts, one of the great museums of the world; the State Opera House, built to resemble the Italian Renaissance; and the neo-classic Parliament building with its gleaming marble colonnade and a richly decorated fountain in the foreground, out of which rose the imposig statue of Pallas Athena, the Greek Goddess of Wisdom. In the distance loomed the recently built Riesenrad, a giant 213-foot high Ferris wheel, that took thirty minutes to complete a turn, with a longer stop at the peak to allow a good view of the entire city and the woods beyond. And to connect all the sites were the wide boulevards of Vienna, lined with wild chestnut trees planted a hundred years ago.

Angela wished they could spend all day riding around, but then she remembered she'd better visit the bridal salons; it was still mid-morning, but she couldn't risk running out of time. Turning to Henrich, she explained what she must do, and why was it important to take care of her business. If she succeeded in getting the order for the wedding gown, their next meeting was virtually guaranteed. He was a little disappointed to have their time together cut short, but lightened up at the prospect of seeing her again so soon. They turned around, and on the way back to the business district he pointed out a tavern near the salons where he would be waiting for her.

After dropping off Angela, he sat down at an outdoor table of the tavern, listening to the faint sound of music coming from a nearby park. With nothing better to do, he watched the people on the street, out to enjoy the glorious sunny day: nannies pushing baby carriages, ladies stopping to greet friends and exchange the latest gossip, and couples, young and old, strolling leisurely with their arms linked, while young men stood around the corner newsstand reading today's paper. He could almost hear their discussion about the upcoming races, weighing the odds, listening to tips about which horses to pick.

By one o'clock Angela had a dozen sketches in hand, the best of the many presented by the models. With business behind her, she was now free to spend the rest of the day with Henrich. But she must hurry; every precious moment counted in the short time left before she must return to Sopron. In contrast to the locals' firm belief that nothing was so important that couldn't wait until later, she picked up her skirt and dashed headlong in a very un-Viennese fashion toward their meeting place. She got there half out of breath, gasping, her cheeks flushed.

"I came as fast as I could" she managed to say, halting between words.

"My darling, do you know that you just broke the most important Viennese rule never to rush?" Henrich greeted her, grinning as he pulled a chair for her. "Though I am glad you did! I hope everything went as well as you expected."

"More than well, I got some beautiful sketches and I am sure our next meeting is assured," Angela said with a confident little wink at Henrich.

"Well then, I hope you worked up an appetite. But first, it's time for a toast! I ordered some champagne to celebrate," he said as he signaled for the waiter. Their sleek crystal flutes clinked merrily as they toasted everything they could think of—togetherness, the future, success, love, happiness, the sun in the sky, until they ran out of subjects and champagne.

It was already well past two when Henrich signaled for a coach and gave instructions to the driver for the shortest way to get to his friends' apartment. By then the sights of Vienna no longer captured Angela's interest. This was their time together, alone, no children to interrupt them. With eyes closed, she snuggled against Henrich's neck, taking in the smell of his skin to recall later when the day ended and her waiting began again. Feeling his arm around her shoulders, she wanted to lock every precious moment in her mind, enough to fill the dreams in the lonely hours of her nights.

Henrich held her close, brushing his lips against her forehead, but his mind was not at ease. He must tell her about his situation, but when? Should he tell her the discouraging news as soon as they arrived and risk spoiling their time together just when neither of them could think of anything else but falling into each other's arms? Or would it be better to put it off until later, even though it might bring accusations that he purposefully postponed telling her the truth for fear that she would turn around and walk away? He struggled with that decision long before she came and still didn't know what he would do.

His mental tug-of-war ended in the minute they stepped inside the little apartment and he took her into his arms. The question of fairness lost its importance; his mind ceased to ponder whether she would misjudge his motives as he carried her to bed. Nothing mattered anymore as they rushed at each other, urged on by a swirling, dizzying kaleidoscope of emotions. Their long-held passion bursting free, they rode a wave of uncontainable desire, a yearning to please and be pleased, to possess each other body and soul, not satisfied until they reached the crest of total fulfillment.

Spent and happily exhausted, they lingered blissfully in a warm afterglow of lovemaking when every tender caress, each whispered love word was a testimony that their feelings for one another went deeper than the physical. Floating in a haze of happy oblivion, the chiming of a clock brought them back to reality, rudely reminding them that time does not stand still.

Angela bolted up and pressed her hands against her ears, blocking the sound she didn't want to hear. "Oh, go away! Henrich, please make it stop. I don't care what time it is! I don't want to know!"

"Well, well, someone has a temper!" Henrich laughed pulling her into his lap.

"It's not that. I just hate to leave! I want to stay here with you! I want this to last forever!" She dropped her head, letting her hair fall across her face.

"Darling, I hate it too, but we must be patient until the time comes when you don't have to leave ever again." Then suddenly he let go of her and swung his legs over the edge of the bed. "How much time we have left? What time is your train leaving?"

"At 5:45," she said sliding next to him. "It's plenty of time for a repeat performance," she added peeking into his face with a teasing glint in her eye.

"You are a naughty girl, Angela," Henrich wagged a finger at her and made a playful move to grab her, but then stopped. "Sweetheart, we better not," he said turning serious. "Not that I wouldn't love to go on making love to you, but we have to talk; there are things you must know."

Ah-ha, Angela thought, *he wants to tell me why he was in civilian clothes!* She had almost forgotten about it. "Of course we have to talk, I want to hear everything you have to say," she said, tickling his chest, still in a teasing mood, then added, "except first you have to show me where the bathroom is." This time there was no embarrassment, no reaching for cover, she simply got up and, grabbing Henrich's extended hand, followed him out to the hall.

With a pat on her behind, he pointed to one of the doors, then went back to the bedroom, got dressed, and straightened the bed, pulling up the bedspread. Next he went into the kitchen, poured two glasses of lemonade, and carried them to the front room. He was back in the kitchen putting some sandwiches on a platter when he heard Angela closing the bathroom door and heading toward the bedroom.

"Sweetheart, there is lemonade on the table in the front room and I have some snacks for us in a minute," he called after her. By then she saw the hastily made-up bed and felt a pang of disappointment. Yes, Henrich had things to tell her but couldn't they talk lying in bed? All she wanted was to be close to him a little longer, to snuggle up to his warm body, postpone the end to their day. What could be so important that it couldn't be discussed unless fully dressed?

Such formality! Still piqued a little but realizing that their time together was slipping away, she sighed, put on her dress, and went to hear the news from Henrich.

He was waiting for her and from the worried look on his face Angela guessed that what he was about to say was not what she expected.

"Sit down, Angela, please, and hear me out. You might not like what I have to say, but I really believe I have found a solution to our problem." He took a sip of his drink and ran a hand through his hair. "You know how much I want us to be together, to settle down, have children, and grow old with you. You also knew from the start that it would not be easy for me to leave the Church; it would take time before I would be free to marry you. After I left you, I immediately submitted a petition for my release and later had several interviews with my superiors, including the bishop. Of course, they brought up the usual arguments why I shouldn't leave, that I am acting on impulse and that I will regret my decision later. They tried to convince me that what we have is nothing more than a fling, a fleeting thing that will pass, and pressed me hard that it is not worth giving up my life and future in the Church."

He paused and nervously took another sip before continuing. "When they couldn't change my mind they threw me a question that hit me quite out of the blue, simply because, to tell you the truth, I had not thought of it before: how am I going to support a family if I leave? They must have sensed that they hit a target, because they started pleading with me to take a retreat, do some soul-searching, and pray for guidance. God would surely help me to come to the right decision, for who is to know better about the power of temptation? Anyway, they kept the pressure on me to reconsider."

He glanced at Angela to see her reaction, but there was none. She sat stoically, as if she found nothing alarming about what he had said so far. Henrich took a deep breath, then posed a question. "Before I go into more details, let me ask you, how much do you know about the Benedictines? Do you have any idea what it takes to join their order?"

"Not really; all I know is that they have the best teachers, but that's about it."

"You are right, they do have excellent teachers, but as you know, I am not one of them. I am ordained to hold Mass, baptize babies, and so on. That is all I am qualified to do. And that is exactly why that question had such a profound effect on me. It got me thinking, how am I supposed to make a living when I leave the Church? I have no profession or trade, I have no money of my own, and you know why? Because when we join the Church, we pledge to them all we possess, money, property, including any future inheritance or endowment. It is an irrevocable gift; it is theirs to keep whether we stay in the Church or not. Can you see my problem? What am I to do? What can I do, when I am twenty-eight years old, an ex-priest without funds and no prospects? I doubt if I could even get a clerical job anywhere. Who would hire me when I tell them that I left the Church? It's not the best character recommendation in a Catholic country as ours. I spent sleepless nights thinking about this. What kind of future can I offer you?"

Slumped in his chair, he fell silent and lowered his eyes to avoid looking at Angela. He wasn't finished yet; there was more he had to tell her, but before he could go on Angela reached over and put her hand on Henrich's arm. "Darling, I think you are too pessimistic about this." The confidence in her voice made him look up.

She could see how nervous Henrich was and how difficult it was for him to talk about his situation. The bishop was apparently doing a good job of scaring him! Of course, there was uncertainty about their future, but it was not as bleak as Henrich saw it. She was not concerned. Perhaps it was just not in her nature to despair, but instead to grab the bull by the horns when faced with difficulties. Time had taught her to look for solutions, and she already had one.

"I know you are worried and doubtful, and no wonder; you are at a cross-road, making decisions that will affect not only your life but mine, as well. We are tied together in this and if we want a future together we must help each other. I've told you that I am making some money with my sewing, and my clientele is growing. I could help you financially to go to school and learn something—"

"Angela, stop!" Henrich cut her off, raising a hand and shaking his head in total denial.

"But why? It would work, Henrich, if you'd just listen to me, please," she reached across the table grabbing both his wrists. "It is a realistic solution, we could easily do it!" But when she looked into his face all she saw was rejection.

"No Angela, I can't let you do that!" he said with finality. "It's wonderful that you are doing so well, and I am very proud of you! You deserve every bit of success. But what makes me even more proud is that you have the generosity of heart to offer help, a gift that unfortunately I cannot accept, not now, not ever. You have your family, your brothers, and sisters to think about. How can you expect me to take away anything from them?"

"But you are wrong," Angela retorted. "Father provides for us; the money I make is mine to do with as I please, and nothing would please me more than using it to help build a future for us!"

"I know you mean well, my darling, but what you propose is totally unacceptable to me. I couldn't look you in the eye if I took money from you, no matter how sincere you are. No, this is my problem, I must deal with it alone, and I have; I am already doing something about it."

Henrich cleared his throat and made a nervous little gesture with his hand. "I was going to tell you about it before you interrupted that after countless sleepless nights I came up with an idea that would get me out of my predicament. It's really simple, and I think it will work. I'll tell you what it is but you must listen closely, because after you heard what I have to say, you will have some decisions to make. You might not agree with my choice of action, but it was the only way I could think of to start our life on solid grounds and secure a future for us. I only ask you one thing, that after you heard everything you'd tell me if you are willing to stand by me, even if it means more waiting?"

"You know I will," she said without a second thought. "Time can never come between us."

"I hoped you'd say that, because I am afraid we are in for another long wait. You see, biding our time would allow me to offer you the life you deserve, a comfortable life, a respectable life as the wife of a teacher. And I am already on my way to become one. This is what I did. I went on a retreat as the bishop suggested, and afterward told him that I took his advice to heart and would withdraw my petition under one condition: if they allowed me to leave the parish and return to the seminary so I could study to become a teacher. When they asked for an explanation I told them that perhaps I was not suited to be a parish priest. Their mission is to deal with people and their problems with compassion but without getting involved in a more personal and emotional level, something I don't seem to handle well. I confessed that this is how our affair started, and that I was afraid it could happen again if I remained at the parish.The only way to avoid it was to leave the Church, or stay, get a degree, and teach in one of their parochial schools. It took a while for them to consider my proposal, but at the end they said yes, I could begin my studies right here in Vienna. And so I did. As we sit here, I am more than halfway through in getting my diploma as a math and physics teacher—not my favorite subjects, but I guess they wanted to punish me some way," he said with a chuckle. "It means that by early 1906 I will have the key to our future in my hand, Angela; we can start building our life together!"

"Building our life together? But how, Henrich?" Angela stared at him. "You will still be a priest!"

"But not for long, my darling girl! As soon as I have my diploma, I can quit! Once the threat that I can't make a living outside the Church is removed, there is nothing to hold me back. It shouldn't take long after that to get my release, then we can move to a new place, I'll find a job and start our life, you and I and the children we will have! Not only that, but your two little sisters could also come to live with us, especially Mitzie; I know how much that little girl means to you. Gertie will be almost twenty by then, and the boys, too, will be in their teens. It will all work out, don't you think? The price we have to pay is another couple of years of separation, but isn't it worth the wait?"

Henrich leaned forward, confident that Angela would see the logic in what he said. He expected validation, but instead she startled him with a question.

"You are right to say that there is a price to pay, but it's not just the waiting, Henrich. It's more than that. What about honor, doing the right thing? Aren't you concerned about that?"

"Of course, I thought about that Angela. I had some misgivings, but I feel that I am entitled to use some of the money they got from my parents when I joined the order. It was not some pittance either, if I may say so; they will have more than enough left after deducting the cost of my keep from the first day on as a novice until I finish my studies."

"Well, looking at it that way, you could be right," Angela said, still with lingering reservation. "All I can say is that since I have no idea how much you gave to the Church and can only guess the cost of your education, I must leave it up to your conscience to judge what is fair to both you and the Church. I trust you will find a good balance."

"You don't have to worry about that Angela; the Church will not be short-changed! But you didn't say yet if you are willing to wait. Are you?"

"You know my answer, Henrich. I'd wait for you longer than forever," she said without the slightest hesitation. "My commitment to you is for life. I waited two years without seeing you or hearing much from you; at least now I know that in another two years the waiting will be over. And this time we'll have some beautiful interruptions, won't we?" she winked at Henrich with a mischievous smile. "I will come up to see you as often as I can. Just let me know when you are free for the day and I'll try to be here. But use a fictitious name when you write, like it was someone from the salons. Let's see now, how does Henrietta sound to you?"

They both laughed, Henrich more so from the sheer relief that he finally told her what to expect and that Angela agreed to stand by him. She really had no choice. With the truth now out in the open they spent the remaining time talking excitedly about the possibilities of their future life. They didn't notice the time until they heard the clock chiming again. No matter how much Angela hated that cursed noisemaker, if she wanted to catch her train she could no longer ignore the warning that it was getting late. She made it on time to board the train, promising to meet again soon.

Left alone, Henrich's thoughts returned to what Angela said about right and wrong and honor. He was convinced that getting his diploma on Church expense then quitting the order was justifiable, but if it was wrong, so was the Church's practice to take money and property from priests and keep it even if they should decide to leave. He knew this was defensive thinking, but there were plenty of others who shared his view.

During the past years, even before his affair with Angela began, he was slowly losing his spiritual connection to the Church, but now he saw clearly how right his parents were in arguing that he was too young to know what dedicating his life to God meant when he knew so very little about life itself. He entered the seminary as an idealistic eighteen-year-old, imagining he would embark on a safe and blessed journey, guided and protected by the Church, totally unprepared for the sharp turn the road he was traveling took and where it ultimately led him. Perhaps putting Angela in his path was God's way to make him see that he was not meant for the priesthood.

From the day their affair began and during the separation that followed he had one single goal: to leave the Church, and do it in a way that was to his best advantage. Focusing on it single-mindedly kept him from thinking much of anything else, leaving him blissfully blind to the complexity of his situation. The scheming never bothered his conscience, nor did his secret liaisons with Angela. The thrill of their clandestine lovemaking and the sexual intimacy he had never experienced before outweighed all thoughts of problems that sooner or later were bound to surface.

Only one thing made him squirm from the start: having to confess the breaking of his vow of chastity. He lived for the day when he would make love to Angela, but dreaded the moment when he had to kneel in the confessional. He even debated if he should confess it at all, but he quickly dismissed the thought. Taking the sacrament with a mortal sin on his conscience would put his soul in such an unholy state that he would be risking eternal damnation, a threat he didn't dare to dismiss. So he confessed his sin and promised to change, knowing too well that he would break that promise over and over again. The confessor's pledge of secrecy protected him from being exposed, but to live with such duplicity began to unravel him, and by the fall of 1905 it became intensely troubling. It began to affect his mental and physical well-being. He was increasingly nervous and irritable and found concentrating on his studies more and more difficult. He used to console himself that his predicament was temporary, and soon all that disturbed him would be over and forgotten, but it no longer worked.

Angela knew nothing about his inner conflict and its debilitating effect on him. He could never talk to her about the burden he carried, the sense of guilt that gradually engulfed him about their affair and for staying in the Church when in his heart he already left it. How could he explain to her and make her understand that he loved her, yet their involvement was the core of his torment that pitted guilt and shame against his love for her? There was no doubt in his mind that she would end their relationship, if for no other reason than to free him from living with his deception. She must never know! But hiding his anxiety was not easy, and it soon became noticeable. He did not laugh as much as before, and often when they talked he became distant, focusing on something beyond Angela.

She only knew that Henrich was under pressure; she noticed a few strands of gray appearing around his temples and some newly formed lines across his forehead, but since he obviously didn't want to talk about it, she didn't pry. Whenever she sensed tension creeping between them, she pretended not to notice. Her heart ruled her head, and typically, instead of pressing for answers, she only showered him with more love and affection. He'd feel better next time, she told herself; she just had to be patient. A few more months and all this will be over, he would be free to take control of his life, and once they were married, she would be able to share whatever problems plagued him.

The years of waiting did not change Angela's looks. At twenty-two she was as youthful and attractive as ever, with a decided maturity adding to her appeal. The successful way she managed her family and built her business gave her a glow of self-confidence. She was in her prime, smart, radiant, and respected by everyone.

As her sewing business grew and more and more of her younger customers clamored to keep up with the latest Viennese fashion trends, she was able to travel to Vienna more often. She built up extensive contacts with the various fashion salons there, rarely missing any of their important shows. The fact that the children were getting older and no longer required her strict supervision also made it easier for her to get away. Mrs. Szalai was always willing to watch them, while her sister Gertie would step in and handle the customers. She was not as talented as Angela, but was quite good with the sewing machine, which allowed Angela to concentrate more on designing and pattern making. That's where she excelled and what distinguished her from other seamstresses. Her income rose, and when in 1905 Gertie fell in love and got married, Angela had enough money to buy another machine and hire two girls to help with the work. She hung a sign on their gate advertising her business as "Mode a la Vienna."

With her growing bank account, she looked into making some investments and decided to purchase a strip of land in the Loever, the city's lovely garden belt. She leased it out to a local farmer for a reasonable fee, plus a percentage of the harvest from the fruits and vegetables he produced. In the fall of 1905 she collected her first share of crops that included some delicious Jonathan apples. Remembering that they were Henrich's favorite, she decided to take a basketful on her next visit, which was to celebrate the start of his final semester. Five more months and their never-ending wait would be over!

Arriving in Vienna, Henrich was waiting for her at the station in an obviously joyous mood, smiling broadly, happy to see her. He surprised her with a new look, sporting a neatly trimmed mustache. It suited him well and made him look very distinguished, Angela thought; she even liked the tickling sensation when they kissed.

The early September weather was warm and sunny and they both felt euphoric knowing that their seemingly endless wait was coming to an end. They finally could see the light at the end of the tunnel! By early next year their long separation would be over: no more hiding, no more lying, they could be together openly for the whole world to share in their happiness.

After taking care of her business with the salons they had a bite to eat, talked about what they did since they last saw each other, then hurried to spend the afternoon at their hideaway. They rushed into each other's arms, their lovemaking more ardent, more demanding than usual. Only a few more months, a few more furtive visits, and they would leave their double life behind to stand proudly as man and wife.

When it came to saying goodbye, they parted with promises to meet again soon. They never let more than six weeks pass between visits unless illness or something important prevented her from coming. As always, Henrich waited until Angela's train began to move, waving to her, while she blew him a kiss from the window, not knowing how their lives changed forever on that warm autumn day.

In the weeks following her last visit Angela often caught herself daydreaming. In her mind she could already see herself standing at the altar, picture-perfect in the glorious wedding gown she would design, her veil spread around her shoulders, as she had imagined it a thousand times before. Wedding plans filled her head; there was so much to do, decisions to make and details to work out, if she wanted everything to be exactly as she envisioned. How was she going to do it all with the busy holiday season approaching? Only if her mother could be here! How happy she would be to take charge of all the arrangements. It made her misty-eyed to think of her big day without having her mother there to share her excitement and watch her walking down the aisle.

As much as she missed her, she would not let sadness creep in and stop her from taking full measure of the happiness she so well deserved. Not even the prospect of telling her father about Henrich's identity could dampen her mood. Of course, she worried about how her family, her friends, probably the whole town would react when they found out that she was marrying their former priest! She knew the stunned disbelief it would create and the malicious speculations that would follow, and that she must find some way to mitigate the expected tongue-wagging. She spent long hours thinking of ways how to tell their story in the best possible light—not the whole truth, of course, but a story that was believable, convincing, and acceptable. Perhaps she could tell them that they met during one of her trips to Vienna and how, after she found out that Henrich left the Church, romance blossomed between them. They would believe her; after all, everybody knows how schoolgirls have crushes on their teachers and how women fall in love with their doctors, so is it so strange that she, too, fell in love with the man who comforted her when she so desperately needed a shoulder to cry on? They would believe her, because true love and romance always softened the hearts, even her father's, she hoped.

She knew that whatever story she told would invite more questions. People would want more details: how they fell in love, how did Henrich leave the priesthood, and God knows what else. To protect him and downplay the secrecy behind their relationship she would have to work on the answers and make sure they revealed as little as possible. She must also coordinate it with Henrich so they'd tell the same. Oh, she swore to herself, this will be the last time they would be forced to lie! Next year would bring closure to all these deceptions! The hiding and cover-ups of the past years would be over! No more fear of being caught!

Still, as the weeks rolled by, the uncertainty of people's reaction to their story kept her on edge. Until now her reputation was intact, they trusted her, but the way she kept everyone in the dark could change all that. Her news was sure to raise some eyebrows, or even start someone to dig a little deeper. It made her nervous to the point that she couldn't keep her food down. She ate heartily, but her stomach would easily turn upside down. Some smells made her particularly nauseous. She couldn't understand what was wrong. There were times in the past when she was tense or worried, but she never had this kind of reaction. No, it must be something else. Perhaps a nasty virus got into her system, causing havoc in her belly. It couldn't be really serious, though, since she had no fever, and so she dismissed it, hoping she'd get better soon.

But she didn't; if anything, the wooziness has gotten worse, especially in the mornings. Normally, it was her best time of the day, when she felt most energetic, but not anymore. The nausea made her weak and exhausted, and when she missed her period for the second time, she blamed that too on the illness. She tried every home remedy, but when nothing worked, she knew she should see their doctor; perhaps it was a bug that was making the rounds and he was already treating others with the same symptoms.

She wrote a short note to Henrich telling him without going into details that she was under the weather and had to postpone her next trip. Henrich didn't worry; the cold and flu season probably arrived a little earlier this year in Sopron. In a way it was thoughtful of Angela to stay away until she got better, as he couldn't afford to catch anything from her and lose a week's time just when he was preparing for the upcoming exams. There was no room for failure; he needed all his resources to pass his finals and also to gear up to what he must do afterwards.

Angela was still dragging her feet to go and see their family doctor. After all, she was not the type to complain about every little ache and pain, but finally she ran out of excuses the day she was forced to leave in the middle of Sunday Mass because the incense fumes made her sick. After she described her symptoms, the doctor told her to remove her underwear for a pelvic examination. At first she was appalled by the request; she had never been through such intimate probing before, and asked why would it be necessary? She came because of her stomach problems, and that got nothing to do with her private parts. She only complied when the doctor insisted, saying that from what he heard he was quite sure of what was wrong with her.

Feeling extremely embarrassed and nervous, she was vastly relieved when the doctor told her to get dressed then come into his office. Sitting across from each other, Angela couldn't wait any longer.

"Doctor, please, what's wrong with me? I hope it's nothing serious and that there is a quick remedy for whatever I have."

"Well, Angela, the answer is yes and no. Yes, it's nothing serious; you are not ill, but no, there is no remedy for what you have. To put it simply, you are going to have a baby. I guess that you are about three months along." He moved around some papers in front of him, adjusted his glasses, and peeking over the rims, looked straight at Angela. "Frankly, I am surprised that you didn't know it. Women your age are usually familiar with these symptoms; you should have recognized your condition and come to see me sooner. Of course, I know you lost your mother when you were young, but somebody should have told you about the facts of life. Anyway, my congratulations; I hope you are happy about the baby and that the father will do the right thing and accepts his responsibility."

Angela sat dumbfounded, trying to absorb what the doctor had just said. It was true, she knew next to nothing about conception and the biological changes that occur during the early stages of pregnancy. Mothers at the turn of the 20th century were steeped in Victorian morals and found the subject much too delicate to discuss with young daughters. When Angela first started her period her mother only said that it had to do with becoming a woman, then handed her a book that would tell her all she needed to know. It contained veiled references to what takes place between a man and a woman in married life; there were no illustrations, and only a brief mention of babies and birth, and how conception is the result of certain private acts between a husband and wife.

Angela did not understand much of it then, and when her intimate relationship began with Henrich, she had no one to ask the relevant questions. She just relied on his assurances that he knew how to prevent a pregnancy. And it worked for all this time, so how was it possible that she was now going to have a baby? They did not do anything different. At least not that she noticed. Perhaps Henrich would have the answer.

Finally, she pulled herself together and smiled at the doctor.

"Oh yes, I am very happy! And my fiancé will be, too! We were planning to get married in the spring; we just have to move the wedding to an earlier date. Everything will be fine. And you are right, I am ignorant about pregnancies, but once I have the baby I will know what to do. I have lots of experience in nursing and caring for babies! Should I be doing anything different until the baby is born?"

"Drink lots of milk, Angela; it will give your child strong bones and good teeth. Eat fruits and vegetables, they are just as important. But other than that, just go on and do what you have been doing. The nausea should stop soon and you'll be feeling better. Come to see me when you first feel the baby move."

"Thank you, Doctor, I will do as you say. Just one more thing, can you tell me the baby's due date?"

The doctor could only say that it should be about 280 days, or 40 weeks from conception, and it was up to Angela to calculate the date accordingly. There was nothing further to say, but before she left she asked him to keep her condition confidential until she was married.

"How could you think otherwise?" the doctor looked at her indignantly. "You have nothing to worry about, Angela. The important thing is that you take good care of yourself and everything will be fine. Don't lift anything heavy. And if you have any questions, or God forbid, something should go wrong, come to see me right away. Good luck and congratulations again."

Angela left with such mixed feelings about the startling news that she needed a quiet place to collect herself. She stepped inside the nearest church and knelt down at the side altar dedicated to the Virgin Mary. It was mid-afternoon with hardly anyone there, and in the cool quiet she tried to recall what the doctor said. He guessed she was about three months along, which meant it happened during the first week in September when they were last together. Counting the days from there, her due date then should be sometime in May. There was no outward sign of her pregnancy yet; she could easily get by without showing until the New Year. By then Henrich would have his diploma, and given a few more weeks to get his release from the Church, they could get married around the end of January. She would have to redesign her wedding gown to hide her condition, but that is all. And if people noticed it anyway and began to talk, so be it. She would just ignore it; soon there would be other things to gossip about and once the baby is born, all would be forgotten. Feeling a little calmer, a dreamy look appeared on her face: would she have a boy or a little girl? What would Henrich wish for?

But she snapped out of her musing the moment she thought of him. It immediately brought to mind another word the doctor mentioned during her visit: responsibility. The word kept ricocheting in her head, stubbornly refusing to be silenced. Would Henrich do the honorable thing and marry her? But he must, he loved her, he couldn't abandon her now! He might have turned his back on the Church without thinking twice, but he wouldn't desert her and their child! Lifting her eyes to the large altar painting of the Holy Mother holding her infant son, she sought encouragement from her that they won't be forsaken. She would hear her prayers and understand her doubts, for she, too, as a young girl, although innocent of sin, found herself with child outside the sanctity of marriage.

With unshakable faith Angela believed in the power of prayer; it always eased her mind, as it did now, rising from her knees with a confident heart that she had nothing to fear. Henrich would stand by her.

But he must be told without delay! She would write him immediately and press that they must talk as soon as possible. Regardless of the urgency, she would never consider breaking the news in a letter, she could only tell him in person. She began to wonder how would he react when she told him about the baby. Would he be happy? She could only hope. She must trust him and believe that nothing would change between them. And yet, he was still a priest; what if something happened, another delay, some obstacle that would prevent him from leaving the Church? They couldn't wait another year, not this time! With the baby on the way, no matter what, he would have to find a way out; there was no other choice.

All during her trip to Vienna, Angela sat on the edge of her seat. She knew she should relax; she wanted to be calm when she told Henrich about her condition, but the jitters wouldn't leave her.

He was at the station when the train pulled in, greeting her with a barrage of questions.

"My angel, how dare you to get sick and stay away for so long? I missed you and worried about you! How do you feel? What did the doctor say? I hope it's nothing serious, but you do look a little pale!" His concern was genuine; this was the longest time that year they went without seeing each other.

"I will tell you everything, my darling, but first let's get a carriage; I am a little tired. I have no business with the salons today so we can go directly to your friends' place and on the way you can tell me about yourself. I am dying to hear what you've been doing all these weeks." She looked up into his handsome face and with a tender hand smoothed out an unruly lock of hair. "I missed you too; you don't know how much!"

He offered his arm and walked her to the waiting carriage. "I've been studying pretty hard and beginning to feel the pressure to make it through the finals," he said in a voice devoid of enthusiasm. "The prospect of confrontation with the bishop does not help, either. I just wish all this would be over and we could get on with our lives."

Seeing him so discouraged she hated burdening him further with her news, but what could she do? It simply couldn't be put off, he must be told.

When they arrived, Henrich pulled her close and kissed her gently on the lips. "Now sit down darling, make yourself comfortable. Is it warm enough for you here? Let me get you something to drink, then you can tell me all about your illness. It really must have been a nasty bug, because you are still a bit green around the edges. What would you like me to bring—tea, lemonade, a glass of water?"

"It can wait, Henrich. We must talk. Now."

The urgency in her voice made him stop. Still standing, she reached for his hand and, pulling him close, placed it over her stomach. "There is nothing wrong with my health," she said, looking up into his face. "It's only our baby here giving out some rather unpleasant signals that I misread. I didn't know what was happening until I went to see the doctor. We are to have a baby sometime in May."

Her eyes never left him, watching for his reaction. As expected, he showed utter surprise, if not bewilderment. He turned his head, looking to one side, then to the other, as if holding out for time to digest what he just heard. Finally, he looked at Angela.

"A baby? You are going to have a baby? Are you sure? Is the doctor sure?"

She smiled nodding her head. "There is no doubt; we are going to be parents. Isn't it wonderful?" Not waiting for an answer, words were now tumbling out of Angela's mouth. "And look how everything is falling into place! With the diploma virtually in your hand and the problem with the Church soon behind you, we can get married just as we planned, except we have to move up the date a little. We could just have a civil ceremony instead of a church wedding and save the three weeks the Church needs to announce the banns. I know it's rushing a bit, but we have a late start Henrich; it is like we are making up for lost time!"

He stood there, still stunned, but when the reality of what Angela said finally got through to him, his mind began to race. He was going to be a father! But how did that happen? He was always so careful! Well, of course there is never a guarantee, it can happen. He knew that. Still, it was a shock. Yes, they talked about having children; after all, they were not getting any younger, but not just yet. This was so out of the blue! All the stress he was going through, and now this!

He was reeling but looking at Angela, anxiety clearly written on her face, he could not tell her how hard the news hit him. "Phew," he let out a long-held breath, "so I am going to be a papa! This is some news all right!"

"You are not upset then? You can see how it will all work out?"

"Well, I am surprised, but upset? No, of course not. It's just so unexpected. And did you say May?"

"Yes, sometime in the middle of May, I think. We have plenty of time to get over the hurdles before the baby comes."

"Ah, yes, well, the hurdles," his voice trailed off. "What is it now, December? Let's see, if all goes well, I should receive my credentials in January, and it won't take long after that to get my dispensation from the Church. It might even help that you are expecting. We probably could get married around February."

He took another big breath and blew it out through puffed cheeks. "Wow, this is some surprise," he kept saying. Then he suddenly broke into a grin. "You know, I am used to being called Father, but never in this sense! At least I have six months to make the mental adjustment!"

It broke the tension between them. Angela was ecstatic at seeing that he took the news so well and even could crack a joke about it! She threw her arms around his neck and clung to him with all her being.

"Oh, I love you so much! You'll be the most wonderful father in the whole world!" She covered his face with a hundred kisses. "We will have a beautiful life together, my darling, you'll see, and it's because we earned it. If all the separation, all the wait, all the difficulties could not change our feelings for each other, nothing ever will!"

He was caught up in her obvious joy. There was no doubt that she loved him totally, with all her heart. He took her hands from around his neck, and kissed them tenderly. "I love you just as much, if not more," he said with loving sincerity. Then stepping back, still holding her hands, he looked her up and down. "You look beautiful, Angela, it's no wonder that I fell in love with you, but even when you are big and fat, I will still love you."

"Tell me that in May! Maybe then I'll believe you," she said with a pout.

"Nothing can change the way I feel about you," he drew her into his arms. But then, realizing that they were still standing in the front room, he nudged his head toward the bedroom. "Talking about changes, any restriction in that direction?"

"You don't have to worry about that, at least not for a while. The doctor said we could and should do everything as before until the next time I see him."

Without another word Henrich picked her up and carried her to the open bed. His lovemaking was so gentle that she took it upon herself to show him that she was as strong and able a partner as ever.

Reaffirmed in their love, they drifted into a light sleep with Angela snuggling in Henrich's arms. When they woke up they both felt relaxed and in a lighthearted mood. He stroked her tummy and caressed her slightly enlarged breasts.

"Hmm, nice," he mumbled. "Will they grow in the same proportion as that tiny little thing inside you?"

"You wish, you little sex maniac!" she said in mock indignation, covering her chest. "You wouldn't think it so much fun if you'd had to tote these expanding bulges for months on end."

"As much as I'd love to, I am afraid I won't be able to help you with that," Henrich laughed, pulling off the cover and brushing his lips against her nipples.

By then it was getting late and Angela was hungry. They stopped for dinner, all the while talking about the baby. They both agreed it would be nice to have a boy first, a girl next time. They picked names and teased each other about what he or she would look like. She warned him to expect to see more of her from now on—more pregnant, that is. It was a good thing that winter was coming and she could camouflage her growing belly under a heavy coat.

At the train station she still kept up her upbeat, cheerful banter, but it was only a pretense. She dreaded to leave him; she knew he could get discouraged under pressure, and that must not be allowed. So much depended on what happened in the next few weeks. No matter what, he must finish his studies! If she just could stay with him, she could give him support, a little push he might need to get through. But of course it was impossible. When she kissed him goodbye she could only promise to come once more before the holidays.

Henrich

AFTER THE INITIAL shock wore off and Henrich had time to absorb the news about the baby, he found himself pleasantly surprised at the prospect of fatherhood. He had always loved children, and under normal circumstances he would have been long married with a growing family by now. At first, Angela's unexpected pregnancy didn't depress him; on the contrary, it brought into focus the importance of getting his degree so he could immediately seek his release from the Church.

He debated whether to tell the bishop about the baby when the time came to reveal his past deceptions. It might help his case; they most likely would let him go without delay. On the other hand, it could raise the level of their indignation to the point where they could make it very difficult for him to find work. Not only would they deny giving him a recommendation, but most likely they'd also let everyone know about his dishonesty. And without credentials and with his honor and reputation ruined, who was going to hire him? His earlier confidence that he could easily obtain a teaching position was rapidly eroding, yet he knew he must find a way around the problem fast, he'd soon have a family to support!

He worried endlessly, trying to figure out how to present himself favorably when applying for a job. Conjuring up ideas only to discard them one after the other kept him awake at night, robbing him of sleep when he needed a good rest to be ready for the upcoming difficult days. Then one day it suddenly hit him. There was a simple solution! If he could get his hands on a few blank letterheads from the bishop's office, he could write his own recommendation! The first thought of forging a paper brought pangs of guilt; it was bordering on fraud, but what difference would one more lapse make? Anyway, soon he was leaving that part of his life behind. Right now he must concentrate his energies on the future; he had Angela and the baby to think of. His true character would be judged by how he kept his promises to them.

In spite of all the excuses he made to justify what he had done and still would have to do to outsmart the Church, subconsciously he knew it was inexcusably wrong. The guilt feeling was constant and it was getting the better of him. How did he get here? He was a good priest; why did God have to test him by pushing him into Angela's arms and forcing him to make a choice? Stressed and confused, Henrich felt lost and gave up searching for answers. If God had orchestrated his life so far, he would also take care of his future.

Over the next weeks he spent every waking hour in intense studying. He tried to concentrate on the immediate tasks facing him: passing his exams and gathering strength to face the bishop, but at times the pressure to succeed drove him to the point of exhaustion. With nerves stretched thin, there were moments when he was ready to throw in the towel. Why must he go through this, and for what? But then his mind cleared and he forced himself back to his books. Again and again he found himself in this vicious cycle, from self-doubt and fear of the future to a blind trust that somehow it would all work out. The thought that he'd be a free man in charge of his life always brightened his mood, but then his optimism evaporated as soon as the picture of Angela and the baby drifted into the foreground, reminding him of the responsibilities awaiting him. Why did it have to happen so soon, just when he would be starting out? The fact that there was nothing he could do to change things worried him day and night and began pushing him toward the edge of depression.

If that was not enough, in the middle of December he caught the flu that was spreading throughout the city. His resistance already weakened by stress and dark mood swings, it struck him harder than usual. Wracked by a severe cough and burning with high fever, he still refused to stay in bed and kept to his books until the doctor finally ordered him to the ward. Before he checked himself in, he quickly wrote a note to Angela that he was ill and in the hospital. He lamented about wasting time in a sickbed when he should be studying, and suggested that because he would have to make up for lost time when he got back on his feet, it would be best if she postponed coming until the finals were over, hopefully in mid-January.

Angela worried about him, but she did not really mind putting off her visit. Christmas was the busiest time of the year; besides finishing holiday orders for her customers, it was shopping for gifts, decorating the tree, baking cookies, and planning the holiday meals. These few weeks would fly by quickly, then what a joy it would be to see him in January with all his troubles behind, all the hurdles cleared, and nothing standing in the way to start their new life together.

. . . .

By the holidays Henrich's condition had improved somewhat; he was still coughing, less severely but without letup, and had a consistent low temperature that made him weak and sweaty during the night. Upon his insistence, the doctor released him from the hospital but wanted to see him again in two weeks.

Ignoring the fever and chills, he went back to his studies and with sheer willpower got through his finals. He passed, but at a price. At the end he was left totally drained both mentally and physically, without any strength, a condition that put him back in the hospital. He underwent a series of tests that confirmed what the doctor already suspected: Henrich had contracted tuberculosis. It was not in an advanced stage, or life-threatening, but it frightened him enough to realize that if he wanted to regain his health, he must follow doctor's orders, stay in bed, take the prescribed medication, and keep to a special diet. He was even prepared to drink a concoction made of puréed calf liver, if that would help him recover faster.

Then, two days later, his world came crashing down on him. He was told that on closer examination they found his condition more serious than first thought, and he'd be transferred to a clinic near the Swiss border where they specialized in treating patients with lung and heart diseases. Henrich's reaction was near panic. They couldn't do this to him! Put him away for God knows how long, just when he was standing on the threshold of freedom! What would happen to poor Angela and the baby? With a child born out-of-wedlock her reputation would be ruined! Why was he cursed this way? He was losing control, and started to shout that he would not go, they couldn't force him, and when the doctor tried to calm him, he grabbed his smock, screaming in his face that there must be another way! His angry shouts brought the nurse rushing in with a tranquilizer needle in hand.

Sedated, he spent the night in blissful oblivion and woke the next morning calmer and better composed. He apologized to the doctor when he came to check on him, but still tried to fight the transfer to the clinic until the doctor convinced him that refusal could cost his life. As for the length of his confinement, the doctor could only say it depended on his response to the treatment, but he could count on a minimum of six months. Could he expect a complete recovery? By all means yes, the doctor assured him, he would be as good as new. How much time did he have before they moved him? He was told that they had already made arrangements with the sanatorium—another good night's rest, and he could be transported.

So that was it. He was given no other choice. But as he brooded over his situation, a thought began to form in his mind. This illness could work to his advantage! True, for the time being Angela would be left alone to handle her dilemma and he felt sorry about that, but the disease gave him the opportunity to avoid revealing to the bishop any of his past deceptions! It could be the key to his freedom, since the Church considered poor health as one of the acceptable grounds for release. He would walk away with his reputation intact, his honor unblemished.

He was bubbling with enthusiasm. What a stroke of genius! Just thinking about it gave him newfound energy. There would be no need to reveal to the Church the double life he had led for so long, or the scam that enabled him to get his teaching degree, and he wouldn't have to steal blank letterheads, either! The Church would not only give him an excellent recommendation, but would even help him to get a job! No guilty feeling for any of his past deeds; he was clean in the eye of the Church; he was home free!

His euphoria dampened only when his thoughts returned to Angela. She had no idea of what was in store for her. What if they shipped him out the next day? He wouldn't have a chance to let her know what happened, how everything changed for them! He couldn't just write to her about it; he must tell her in person before they transferred him, but how? He needed time! Ironically, it was the doctor who solved the problem by asking him if he'd like to go home for a few days to tell his family about his illness and the treatment he needed.

He immediately rushed a note to Angela asking to meet him in two days at his parents' house in Kismarton, a small town in Burgenland. The message gave no details other than it was important for her to come. Reading it filled Angela with happy anticipation. This could only mean one thing: that all went well with his finals and he was ready to introduce her to his family! They were just a step away from tying the knot!

Adrenaline kept her on edge as her train pulled into the station in Kismarton and she stepped down into Henrich's arms. In the first rush of joy in seeing him she did not notice the pallor of his skin, but caught her breath when she took a closer look.

"My darling, you look so pale, and thin—are you all right?"

"Oh don't worry about me, I know I am still a little green, that nasty bug really got me down. All I need is a little more rest. I'll tell you all about it later, but first I want you to meet my parents and my sister. They know about us, and the baby; I told them everything. They can't wait to meet you."

He was ready to go, but when Angela still stood scrutinizing his face, not at all convinced about his recovery, to divert her attention, he held her at arm's length and looked her up and down in feigned surprise. "Say, where are you hiding that baby of ours? I don't see any change in you," he said teasingly and it worked; her face lit up and laughing together, they fell into step.

Reaching the house, he ushered her inside where his family was waiting. Seeing Angela, Henrich's mother unceremoniously opened her arms to her. "So you are Angela! I am so glad we could finally meet," she said with genuine affection. "Henrich told us so much about you. We want you to know that you are most welcome in our family."

When she released her, she noticed Angela blinking away a tear. "Is anything wrong, my dear? Are you all right?" she asked as Angela fumbled in her purse for a handkerchief. Unable to speak, she just shook her head, then quickly dried her eyes and blew her nose. It gave her time to regain her composure and find her voice.

"Please forgive me; I am really not a crybaby. It's just that it has been so long since I felt such a warm, welcoming embrace," she said with a shy, almost embarrassed glance at Mrs. Pollinger. "I almost forgot how wonderful it feels." Her simple words touched everyone; they knew that she lost her mother at a young age.

Mrs. Pollinger showed Angela to a comfortable chair while Henrich's sister Katie brought in refreshments. They sat around chatting, trying to get to know her, and while she was attentive, inside she was dying to find out if Henrich really brought her here to propose. Would he be asking that all-important question she longed so much to hear? She looked for an encouraging sign from him, but he didn't seem to take notice. *The rascal, he just wants to keep me in suspense, but this is trying my nerves,* Angela thought, although there was nothing she could do but resign to wait until he was ready with his announcement.

By the time lunch came around she felt quite comfortable around her future in-laws, as if already a part of the family. No wonder! They went out of their way to make her feel loved and accepted; after all, she was the reason they were getting their son back, and that they could now look forward to the pleasure of having grandchildren. They could thank her for giving back the hope they thought was lost forever when Henrich decided to become a priest.

Katie, too, was openly thrilled to have Angela in the family. From the minute they met, she was drawn to her and it showed through her every smile, every touch. She was a little older than Angela, and like her, suffered emotional setbacks in her young life. She lost her husband to a sudden illness shortly after they were married and it left her devastated. She was very much in love and looked forward to raising a family, and it almost killed her when it was so cruelly taken away from her. At her parents' insistence she moved back home but never stopped mourning the loss of what might have been. She would never have children of her own, but now, with Angela's baby, she would have a little niece or nephew to dote on and spoil. The anticipation made her almost as anxious as Angela to hear Henrich's formal proposal.

Finally, lunch was over, and after clearing the table they all sat back in smug expectation of hearing the good news. Katie winked at Angela with an encouraging smile and her parents exchanged knowing glances as they waited for their son to speak. But the first words coming out of his mouth, saying that he was ill with tuberculosis, and must go away for treatment, shocked everyone into stunned silence. Their first reaction was total disbelief, a refusal to accept what they just heard. It was simply impossible! It took time until reality began to sink in, but once denial and confusion gave way to deep concern, they all rushed to his side with comforting words.

All, except Angela; unable to move, she was staring blankly, all color drained from her face as the terrifying word tuberculosis kept reverberating through her head. Did she hear him right, that her beautiful, strong Henrich was ill with that dreadful disease? It couldn't be true, her mind screamed! There must be a mistake, or the Church caught up with Henrich's scheming and this is their way to punish him: make up the illness and lock him away!

She imagined one possibility after another, but finally came to realize that it was useless; she must face the awful truth. Then suddenly her heart stopped. Wasn't tuberculosis contagious? Wasn't it transmitted by saliva? She remembered learning in school that the illness usually develops over time; people don't come down with it from one day to the next. What if she caught it from kissing Henrich? She, too, might be infected! And the baby! The doctor warned her that babies are very vulnerable in the first few months of development. Could it be that in this very moment they were both carrying the disease? She felt panic creeping up. She must leave right now and see her doctor immediately; she would not rest until she saw the test results.

But of course she remained slumped in her chair, still numb, vaguely hearing Henrich's voice as if coming from a distance, comprehending but little of what he was saying about a faraway sanatorium, lengthy treatments, and a delay in their marriage. Her mind still battling the onrush of fear, she needed time to absorb the meaning of those words, but as the minutes passed and the impact of the initial shock began to wane, gradually, painfully, it dawned on her what his illness meant for her and their baby. She would be condemned for having a child out-of-wedlock, her reputation ruined, and her baby would be illegitimate, a bastard, branded with that awful, degrading word that stigmatizes innocent children born to unwed mothers. She knew very well about the small town mentality, the sure-to-come tongue-wagging and speculations about who the father was. That, of course, must remain a secret. She must keep silent to protect Henrich's identity until he recovered. And recover he would, he must! Yes, she was facing a difficult time, but it wouldn't last forever. Henrich was young, and under doctor's care he would be cured and would come back to marry her, just like they planned before the illness struck.

She began to rally, the dark thoughts turning a shade lighter, as her natural optimism surfaced. She wouldn't let a momentary setback ruin their future. She might grind her teeth but would stand her ground until Henrich was well again and all that went wrong was righted. Thank God, she had her family to rely on; they would support her and see her through this ordeal.

Eventually, as the emotional turmoil Henrich's disheartening news caused among the family started to abate, everyone's attention shifted to Angela. Seeing her so pale and distraught, they turned to her with deep concern and heartfelt empathy. All of them were painfully aware what it meant for her to lose Henrich at such a crucial time. They showered her with encouragement, that while the wedding must be postponed, she was now a member of the family and could count on their help and support.

Henrich was at her side, holding her hand, promising to do everything to get well. He was profoundly sorry for this unexpected setback, and for leaving Angela alone to suffer the unfortunate consequences. The thought that he couldn't be there to hold his newborn child filled him with infinite sadness. Even if his condition improved somewhat by then the clinic wouldn't let him leave, the risk of infecting the baby was too great. He managed to cheer her a little by telling that the illness gave him a simple and sure way to leave the

Church, and do it with his reputation intact. They would be free to marry as soon as he was released from the clinic.

Angela put up a brave face during the rest of the afternoon as they talked of the difficulties ahead. To keep in touch they decided it would be best to correspond through his parents. It would protect her from speculation that letters from a place near Switzerland could only come from the father of her child. As for Henrich, until he obtained his dispensation he must still pretend that their affair ended a long time ago, and since writing directly to Sopron could be traced, it might lead the Church to find out the truth.

He assured her over and over that as soon as he was back on his feet he would come for her and the baby, and nothing would ever again keep them apart. Yes, this latest misfortune meant more delays, but they would overcome. In the meantime she must take good care of herself and their child, and not forget that his family would stand by her every step of the way.

When the hour came for Henrich to return to Vienna, it was in this spirit they said their goodbyes. They clung to each other for the longest time without words or a parting kiss. There was only a final caress, the brush of his lips on her forehead, and he was gone. And she would never see him again.

Angela alone

DURING ANGELA'S RIDE back to Sopron, the reality of her situation hit her in full force. She was alone, nearly four months into her pregnancy that already started to show. So far she managed to cover it up, but given another month, it would be impossible to hide her condition anymore.

Otherwise she was fine; she was over her cravings and morning sickness, and if her tuberculosis test turned out negative, she could carry on with her household chores and continue her sewing business without difficulty until the birth of her baby. It also helped that caring for her siblings was much easier by now. The oldest boy, sixteen-year-old Henrich, was already apprenticed to a shoemaker, and although her younger brothers, Franz, Jozsef and Miska, ages fourteen, eleven and nine, were still in school, they could do more or less without her fussing over them. Little Mitzie in kindergarten, and Lizzie in first grade still needed looking after, but they never gave her any problem. As the children were growing older, her clients often teased her about what would she do after they all flew the nest and she was left with an empty house? They probably imagined Angela in her late thirties or early forties as a matronly figure, surrounded by nieces and nephews, a sort of substitute grandmother. Well, they were in for a surprise once the truth came out about her situation, Angela thought and shuddered, her spirits sinking further and deeper with each passing day.

But what she dreaded most was the confrontation with her father, when she must tell him about her predicament. He did not have a forgiving nature and although he never raised a hand to strike any of his children, he could mete out punishments much too harsh to fit the wrongdoing. She knew he would react violently, and there would be ranting and accusations for bringing shame on the family. It was futile to count on him being sentimental about the birth of his first grandchild when he was never much of a father to his own children.

She stalled for time trying to muster up courage she'd need to fend against his anticipated angry response, until one clear, crisp February morning, getting dressed she looked in the mirror and realized she could no longer postpone the face-off with her father. Her clothes did not fit anymore, and the holidays were too long gone to take the blame for the extra pounds she put on. It was time to come clean and have that dreaded talk with her father. Before he left for work she asked him to make time for her in the evening so they can talk about something important. She spent all day thinking what would be the best way to approach him, but at the end she decided there was only one way, and that was to come straight to the point.

Hoping to put him in a good mood, she prepared his favorite dish, and he did look pleased after finishing his supper. He remained at the table and asked what she wanted to discuss.

"We need to talk in private, Father, please."

"What's the big secrecy?" he asked, raising an eyebrow, but got up and followed her into her room. Angela pulled a chair for him, bracing for what was to come.

"Papa, what I am about to tell you will shock you, I know, but tell it I must. I am going to have a baby in May, and because of special circumstances it is impossible for me to marry the father of the child until later, after the birth. What makes it more—"

"You are what?" her father cut her short, leaning out of his chair, his face dark with stunned disbelief. "You are pregnant? Is that what you are telling me?" he roared, his voice rising with each word.

"Papa, please, I don't want the children to hear us! They should not be involved in this."

"But they are going to be involved if what you are saying is true! Innocent as they are, they will be involved!" He was on his feet by now, shouting and punching the air with angry gestures.

"Please Papa, calm down and let me tell you about my situation."

"All I want to hear form you is the name of the man who did this to you and where he lives!"

"I can't tell you that, but I am sure, once you hear me out you will understand better and—"

"The only thing I could possibly understand is if somebody forced himself on you, which can happen to any woman in today's loose world. If that's the case, you just leave everything to me. I need all the information you can give me so I can take it to our office for investigation. We will do everything to find the scoundrel and he will pay for what he did to you, believe me, he will pay! You should have come to me with this right away; it would have given us a better chance to catch him, and enough time to do away with the unfortunate result!" He had already convinced himself that this was what happened and was seemingly regaining his composure.

Angela stood there in numb disbelief. Her father could justify her pregnancy if it was the result of rape, and would have subjected her to an abortion as the best solution to her problem? She knew he was not the most loving father, but he could not be this heartless! Perhaps she should tell him the truth, but how could she? It would only make things worse. She could only try to explain why the marriage had to be postponed.

"It's nothing like that father; I was not raped! I fell in love with a man, and we love each other very much. We made a pledge to marry, it's just unfortunate that he fell ill and we must—"

"He fell ill? Now isn't that convenient!" he punctuated each word with a voice full of sarcasm. "And you believe him, you foolish girl? Don't you know that this is one of the oldest excuses men use to get out of a commitment? It comes especially handy when a child is on the way! How stupid, how gullible can you be?"

"You can call me names, Father, but it won't change anything. We love each other and will marry as soon as he is well again."

"And when is that supposed to be? When you are fifty? Face it, he is feeding you a lie, and you apparently swallowed every word of it. Well, I see what I can do about all this. Just tell me who the man is and where can I find him. I will tell him to his face that he can snowball you but I see through his chicanery, and when I am through with him, he will marry you, and do it now, not sometime in the future! Hah! What a joke!" he spit out the words contemptuously. "Ill, is he? Indeed! But should he be really sick, I will drag him out of his sickbed by the ears, long enough to say, 'I do.' I know how to deal with his type!"

Angela shook her head slowly. "You are not listening, Papa. I've told you, I can't do that, not yet, and when the time comes for the two of you to meet, you will understand why. What I can tell you is that he is an honorable man and that he loves me and will come for the baby and me when he is released from the hospital. He has tuberculosis, Papa; he needs good care and lots of rest and it will take a while before he gets well, but he will come for us, I know he will."

"Tuberculosis?" The word stopped him cold as he paced the room. Grabbing Angela by the shoulders, he shook her hard. "He has tuberculosis? What do you know about that disease? Do you know that it is contagious? That he could have passed it to you? You could be infected! And the rest of the children, too! How long have you known this man? When did you find out that he has TB?"

"I've known him a long time, Papa, but it was only in Vienna where I met him again and that's when we fell in love. He got sick just recently, and you don't have to worry, I've seen the doctor, and I tested negative."

"Well at least some good news in all the mess you are in," he said sarcastically. He was still angry but seemed to be cooling down, which made Angela think that the worst was over. But she was wrong; he was not through with her. The worst was yet to come.

"So now I find out that he is not from around here. I suppose all those trips to Vienna had nothing to do with fashion salons either! I bet you thought it pretty clever to fool everybody that you had business in Vienna, and all the while you used it as an excuse to run up there to sleep with him. You are nothing but a slut and a liar!"

The hurtful words hit Angela hard, but she knew that part of the accusation was true. If only it did not sound so dirty! She made an effort to defend herself, but her voice faltered and all she could say was, "I am not a slut, Papa, I lied to you, yes, but I am not a slut. If you only let me explain why I—"

"There is nothing to explain," he sneered at her. "You brought disgrace to yourself, to my name, to the family, and nothing you could say would excuse that. What makes it worse is that you refuse to tell who this man is. I just don't understand—why are you protecting him?" He was shouting again, walking back and forth, but then he stopped suddenly, turned slowly, and lowering his voice jabbed a finger into his daughter's face. "Oh, but I think I do! I think I know exactly why you won't tell me his name! Because you can't! Because you don't really know who got you in trouble! I don't believe that it was just this one man you were sleeping with! The shame of it! You are nothing but a whore! The worst kind! Thank heaven your Mother did not live to see this!"

He turned away in disgust, took a few steps, and then came at her again. "You have any idea how this will reflect on the family? What people will say when they find out about you? No, I don't think you know or care. But I do, and I also know what I have to do to protect your sisters' reputation. You shamed us all, but others need not know about it, not if you leave town. And soon is not soon enough. You will leave here and I don't care where you go. You brought this on yourself; you deal with the consequences."

Angela could take the painful insults her father hurled at her, but ordering her out of their home and the city shocked her to the core. "You can't kick me out," she shouted, losing her composure. "It's my home! Where would I go? And the children! Who will look after them? I am like a mother to Mitzie and Lizzie and I won't leave them! You are just angry, and rightly so, and it's the anger and disappointment that makes you say things that you don't really mean!"

"But I do mean it," he said with icy coldness in his voice. "I can't let you stay and expose those girls, and the boys too, to the spectacle of bringing a bastard in this house. You don't belong here anymore. You will have to go. And don't pretend that you care what happens to your brothers and sisters! You should have thought about them before you started your whoring ways! Mitzie and Lizzie are not babies anymore; I'll see to it that they will be taken care of."

Angela now turned to pleading. "Papa, please don't do this to me! We've been through difficult times before, but we always took care of each other, and we can do it again! You know how young I was when Mother died, how hard it was for me to learn to take care of the house and children. I tried the best I could, and maybe if you had been more understanding, more caring, shown a little love, things might have turned out differently."

"Now I've heard everything! You have the nerve to blame me for your troubles? I don't have the time to coddle the bunch of you. I worked and worked hard all these years to support you so you can all have a decent life. And this is what I get for it? Accusations from my slut of a daughter! I hope someday you will get the same treatment from your little bundle of joy."

He felt insulted, cheated, and he was through arguing. Turning his back on Angela, he headed for the door.

"Papa, please, I am sorry if I hurt your feelings," she cried after him. "I didn't mean it that way. And what you said about me leaving—maybe it can be done. I could go away and have the baby and come back after I am married."

Shaking his head, he laughed in her face. "You just don't get it, do you? Still thinking he is going to marry you?"

Angela ignored the scorn. "All right, even then, if something happens and I am not able to marry him, we could still do something. I could leave the baby with Gertie to care for; they don't have children, and I know she would be glad to raise my child as her own. It will break my heart to be called an aunt instead of mother, but even if it puts me in an early grave, I will find the strength to bear it. Please Father, we could work this out." She was swallowing hard to force back the tears. "I'll do anything, and I promise, your reputation will not suffer . . ."

By then her father was at the door, his hand on the knob as he spoke over his shoulder. "That's enough, Angela. Your little schemes won't work; people can't be fooled so easily." He turned to face her one more time. "You are the biggest disappointment in my life. You will be out of here, and that's final. We are through."

He did not slam the door; he was too wounded to be dramatic. He went straight to his room but hardly slept that night. What did he do to deserve this? How much more could he endure? First losing his beloved wife and now the daughter he trusted and respected the most turned out to be nothing but a disgrace!

Henrich and Franz, the two older boys in the next room, became alarmed by the loud argument. They hovered close to the door and when they heard their father's footsteps receding in the hallway, they rushed in to find Angela slumped to the floor. Kneeling at her side, they called her name and patted her face until she began to stir, and when she finally opened her eyes they helped her up and into the bed.

"Are you all right, Angela? What's wrong? What happened to you?"

She looked into their fearful young faces and started to cry with great heaving sobs that frightened her brothers even more. She rolled onto her side, away from them to hide her face, and lay there, knees drawn against her chest, her body racked with spasms. Unable to stop her crying, she tugged at the bedcover, pulling it up and jamming it into her mouth to muffle the sound. Franz ran out and brought a glass of water, urging her to drink it, all the while pleading with her to stop the crying. Lost at what to do, they kept patting her on the back and calling her name, until slowly, gradually, her fits of convulsive shuddering began to subside. When it finally stopped and Angela regained some composure, she pulled herself up against the headboard, took a sip of water, and after putting the glass down, sat on the edge of the bed, motioning for the boys to sit beside her. She took their hands into hers and with a great effort to keep from crying again, told them what happened.

"Papa is very angry with me for something I did and he can't find it in his heart to forgive me. You are too young to understand the reason why, but he ordered me out of the house. I tried pleading with him, begged him to let me stay, but you know him—once he makes up his mind, that's it. He insists that I go, so I must leave here, and perhaps for a long time. I don't know if he'll ever let me come back. It breaks my heart because I love you all so much, and I will miss you terribly . . ." She had to stop; her throat closed up again and the tears were flooding back. By then the boys were also in tears. After losing their mother, would they lose her too? An aura of deep sadness enveloped them as they huddled together, heads bent, shoulders sagging, an image that would touch anyone's heart, except their father's.

The boys asked if they should talk to him; perhaps he'd listen to them better, but Angela knew it wouldn't change anything. He was an obstinate man who grew more stubborn when opposed. All she asked them was to keep from telling the younger children what happened until she could decide what to do, where to go. There was no need to alarm them; it would be difficult enough to tell them when the time came for her to leave.

Her brothers kept their secret, although it was not easy for them. Angela, too, maintained a cheerful facade when around the children, no matter how wretched she felt. Only when alone did she give way to her grief and an overwhelming fear of what would become of her. Banished from home and visibly pregnant, what would she do, where would she go? Should she ask her married sisters Rezie or Gertie to take her in, or perhaps Henrich's parents? But they all lived too close to Sopron to keep her secret safe. She might as well stay in town. She needed more distance; move to a place where people didn't know her and gossip wouldn't carry back to the embarrassment of her family. And she must also think of the baby and the pending birth. She needed a good doctor she could trust, and in case something went wrong, quick access to emergency facilities.

Forcing herself to look at the possibilities more calmly, her mind soon settled on a place she knew and liked, one that was far enough from Sopron, and also had the best doctors: Vienna. Why didn't she think of it in the first place? It was a big city where no one would pay attention to her; she would be safe there.

Making that first decision became a turning point in how Angela looked at her situation. The anguish over leaving her brothers and sisters still tore at her heart, but she began to come to terms with the inevitable, that she must say goodbye to them and make a new life for herself and her baby. Thank God, she had enough money in the bank to last until Henrich got well and they could tie the knot. And even if there were further complications, more setbacks, she could always fall back on her dressmaking skills; she could find work through her contacts with the salons and support herself and the baby, even Henrich, if he would just accept her help.

The next day she took the train to Vienna looking for a place to live, and soon found a small, furnished apartment on Landstrasse near the inner city. The flat was on the second floor of a four-story building and had two rooms and a kitchen, but no bathroom or running water. Most apartment houses in cities, even as large as Vienna, had no plumbing, only a common faucet installed in the outside hallway, and one commode down the hall shared by the tenants on the same floor. She rented it as Frau Bohaczek, the wife of a sailor in the Imperial Navy currently serving on the Adriatic Sea. She hated lying, but she felt justified for the sake of her baby. If it took a little white lie to protect her child from the prevailing prejudices, then so be it. She immediately wrote to Henrich about her changed circumstances and the reason why she was forced to leave home. She sent the letter through his parents with a similar note to them explaining her move.

Returning home, she took down her Mode a la Vienna sign that hung on the gate and let her two seamstresses go, then began packing her belongings including her sewing paraphernalia. She was planning to leave on Sunday, but before that Angela tried one more time to speak with her father. She told him where she was going, then asked what he intended to do with the children. Who would take care of them? In her heart of hearts she still hoped that faced with the finality of her leaving, he might relent and let her stay. It was not to be. He looked at her coldly and said the children were no longer her concern.

"But they are! I have the right to know what will happen to them!" Angela snapped back, her tone of voice sharp. This time she wouldn't be dismissed so easily. "I promised Mother that I would keep the family together and look after the children. You've seen to it that I can no longer fulfill that promise. At least tell me what arrangements you made for them."

Reminded of the deathbed promise he himself made, he backed down a bit and told her that Mitzie was going to stay with Gertie and her husband, and Lizzie would be sent to live with Rezie and her family. Both would be in good hands. The boys were to remain at home; he already found a woman to come every day and do the cooking and cleaning.

"So, there you have it; all is taken care of. We'll still be a family, just not under the same roof."

"Is that how you see it, Father? Don't you realize that you are tearing this family apart? Don't you care what this will do to your children? It was not enough that they lost their mother; you are exposing them to another crisis, the loss of a stable home life. I can't believe that you don't know how much pain and harm your heartless decision will cause them! Henrich and Franz might be strong enough to get through without much damage; even Jozsef and Miska will have their older brothers to rely on, but Mitzie and Lizzie sent away from home will wonder if they were being punished for something they did not do! They will be the ones who suffer the most! How can you sleep at night with that on your conscience?"

"There you go again, all these dramatics, trying to blame me. I thought you learned by now that it doesn't work. And you know why? Because we both know whose irresponsible, thoughtless action brought this whole situation about. You talk about my conscience? You should examine yours! So let's just leave it at that. The children will get used to the change, they'll be fine."

He was finished with her, and without a goodbye or a grudging good-luck wish, he turned his back and walked away, not caring if he would ever see her again.

Angela had no more tears to shed. She stood there, defeated, feeling weary to the bone, her last hope for staying crushed. Now she must gear up to tell the younger children that she was leaving; how she would do it, she didn't know, she only hoped that her strength would not desert her. She would tell them, but not yet, not today, not tomorrow; she would wait until the last hour to say good-bye, then run as fast as she could, before her heart broke into pieces.

After church on Sunday, the day started out as usual, with Angela preparing breakfast, and their father soon leaving for a soccer game. Young Jozsef was also heading for the door, but Angela called him back. The boy protested that his friends were waiting, they had a game planned, and stayed only reluctantly when Angela drew him close and asked to humor her just this one time.

"I am sorry to keep you all here, but I have something important to tell you, and because it is very difficult for me to say what I must, I need your help and support," she started as she gathered the children around her.

Little Lizzie, always ready to help, moved closer to Angela. "I will help you, just tell me what you want me to do."

"Here, you can hold my hand, darling," she said and gave her a kiss. "You know how much I love you, each and every one of you, and that I'd do anything to stay here forever. I also know that you love me back the same way, and this is why it is so hard for me to tell you that I have to go away for a while. I am not leaving you; I want you to know that. I will come back, but until that time we won't be able to see each other. I won't be here as I am now, but in my thoughts I'll be with you just the same."

Mitzie climbed into Angela's lap. "You mean like Mama, when she went to heaven? You are going away but you will be watching us from where you are going?"

"Exactly! See how smart you are? You understood me right away. And I have good news for you and Lizzie. So you won't have time to miss me, Papa will send you to visit Gertie and Rezie, and won't that be fun? It will be like a vacation!"

"What about us? Are we going somewhere too?" the youngest boy, Miska, asked.

"No, you boys are needed here to look after Father and see that the house is kept in order. Papa will have someone to cook for you, you don't have to clean house or do the laundry, but it's your responsibility to help in every other way. Keep your rooms tidy, set the table for meals, put the dishes in the sink, make sure that the water is brought in every day. And most importantly, look after yourselves. Never forget to brush your teeth and wash regularly, necks too! Keep your clothes clean, and if anything needs mending, let Papa know. Of course, I don't even have to tell you how important it is to keep your grades up in school; you will promise to study hard, won't you?" Raising an eyebrow, she turned to each boy and waited until they nodded before she continued. "Your father will be here to help you. Go to him if you have a question or problem; he will know what to do. Always do what he tells you, because he loves you and wants what's best for you. You must also look after one another! Try to get along, no fighting, so I can be proud of you. I will miss you every day I am away and I can hardly wait for the day when I come back again."

The children listened solemnly, taking her every word to heart, and making promises to behave. Angela saw with relief that her news didn't upset them. None of them cried; they seemed to accept the fact that she must leave for a while. They asked her where she was going and for how long, and seemed to be satisfied with her answer that she would be in Vienna, and will try to come back as soon as she could.

At the sound of the hired coach approaching the house, she stood up and pulled each child into her arms for a final hug and farewell kiss. They clung to her but she wouldn't let them come out to see her off. The weather was too cold, she said, but in truth, it made it easier for her to walk out alone. It would spare her the pain of seeing them waving goodbye to her as the carriage took her away.

Being forced out of her home and leaving her family behind was very hard on Angela, but as she began to adjust to her new life alone, she came to realize that the move actually afforded her a calmer, more peaceful existence. Here she could go on without the slightest shame or embarrassment about her pregnancy and concentrate on the healthy development of her baby. Living in Vienna protected her from the contempt her condition would have surely elicited in Sopron, and as pressures melted away, even her father's debilitating scorn seemed less hurtful.

With a sense of liberation she set about exploring her new neighborhood, where to go for the freshest produce, which bakery kept yesterday's bread off the shelves, or what butcher used loaded weights on the scale. At home she read books, knitted little baby booties, and wrote letters to Henrich almost every day, always with the most fervent hope to have him back soon and in the best of health. She also wrote to Rezie and Gertie explaining what happened and asking for their understanding and moral support. She thanked them for taking in Mitzie and Lizzie, and tucked some bills into the envelopes to cover a few little extras for the girls.

But Angela was not a creature to stay idle for long. She was not used to sitting around doing nothing and letting the days dwindle down to daydreaming. After a few weeks, she decided to visit the fashion salons and offer to take in sewing she could do in her own home. When the proprietors saw her condition, she cheerfully explained that she was now married and living in Vienna; her husband, a Navy man, was a distant cousin on her father's side, hence the same last name, and while he was at sea she felt bored and wanted to do something useful. The salons knew how reliable she was, and soon she found herself busy with assignments. Material was delivered to her and the finished work picked up within a given time, a smooth arrangement that suited both parties.

Angela only took in what she could finish, making sure that she always had time for walks in the nearby park and that she got plenty of rest. The baby was growing, apparently a very energetic little being who often woke her at night with its vigorous activity. In her letters to Henrich she described her feelings, what it meant to know that their child was alive and well, and how much she prayed that he'd be well enough to come back for the baby's birth. She had a good obstetrician who assured her that all was well; he did not foresee any problems with the delivery. He suggested having her baby in Vienna's main hospital, the Allgemeine Krankenhouse, but Angela would not hear of it. Every mother knew the danger in giving birth in a hospital; just thinking of it terrified her.

This general fear was not all midwives' tales; its roots went back to the days when young mothers ran a high risk of dying if giving birth in a hospital. It had much improved by the turn of the century, four decades after Dr. Ignaz Semmelweis, a Hungarian-born Viennese surgeon first recognized the major cause of the fatalities: doctors using unwashed hands and instruments without sterilization during delivery. At the time of his discovery in 1847 his colleagues ridiculed his finding as childish and much too simplistic, and mothers and infants kept dying from childbed fever, a form of septicemia, where toxins get in the bloodstream. To prove his theory Dr. Semmelweis divided expectant mothers into two separate groups; in one group doctors delivered babies the customary way, sometimes without washing their hands when coming directly from an autopsy, while Dr. Semmelweis used his methods for the other group. The result was undeniably clear: mortality among mothers under his care was three times lower. Yet, ignoring the evidence, the rigid, set-in-stone mentality of the Viennese medical corps refused to accept his hypothesis that hygiene could make such difference, and to further disgrace him, they barred him from practicing. The refusal, coupled with humiliation, and the remorse over his demonstration that involved intentionally sacrificing young mothers to prove his colleagues wrong, drove him into a deep depression that ended in madness. He died in 1865 at age forty-seven in a mental asylum.

At the time of his death another doctor, English surgeon Dr. Joseph Lister, was also working on the same idea of using carbolic acid before surgery, and found similar resistance among his colleagues. He published his findings in 1877 backed by scientific research, and by 1879 his principle of antiseptic surgery gained widespread acceptance. In that same year Louis Pasteur also developed the germ theory of disease. Still, it was Dr. Semmelweis who became known as the "Savior of Mothers" and the pioneer of antiseptic procedures. It was to his credit that by the end of the century, as younger doctors coming into the profession accepted his teaching and began practicing it, the fatality rate in maternity wards dropped drastically. Yet women were not convinced. Believing it safer, they chose to give birth at home with the help of a midwife, rather than in a hospital. Angela felt the same way. She only asked the doctor to recommend a good midwife in her neighborhood, and got the name of Frau Muller, a well-qualified nurse with a list of references.

With all the important things arranged, Angela now waited for the birth of her child. The letters from Henrich were encouraging, that with medication, rest, and diet, he was conquering the disease. He praised the fresh Alpine air in helping him along the road to recovery, but also wrote that receiving his diploma deserved credit too; it freed him from the stress that had weighed on him for so long. He was also optimistic that his release from the Church would be approved soon; he was just a step away from being a free man.

As Henrich was undergoing treatment, he had time to look back on his life and he came to see, not without bitterness, that he had never known real freedom. He was always subjected to restrictions, first by his parents then by the Church. But that would soon be over. The time was near when he would be in control of his life, with no one to tell him what to do and when to do it. There was a new world waiting for him, a world with dimensions far beyond that of a compassionate priest whose duty was to give all and take nothing. It offered a future full of opportunities wide open for a well-educated and independent-minded young man like himself; all he needed was to stand up and claim his rightful place.

The vivid image of this bright new world, however, faded quickly when he realized that his vision did not include Angela and the baby. It jolted him back to reality. How could he forget them, even for a moment? It made him feel remorseful and ashamed that he could so easily overlook their existence. He must stop this fantasizing! He might be free from the Church, but he was still bound by the promises he made to Angela.

His momentary euphoria flattened like a deflated balloon at the thought of his commitment to her. He lay in bed, eyes shut, trying to think of nothing, yet certain words, such as duty, must, obligation, kept flashing behind his lids. At first he tried to ignore their nagging presence, but they wouldn't leave him alone. They crept around inside his head, their voices persistent and increasingly louder, reminding him day and night that he was not free at all! Another kind of domination, however loving and gentle it might be, was looming over him just when he was on the threshold of endless possibilities. He was so close to taking control, and it was slipping out of his hands!

Gripped by bitter disappointment, he wallowed in self-pity over the loss of what he might have achieved if he were allowed to soar, and it began to erode the progress he made in his recovery. His health suffered a setback, his fever flared up again, and the hacking cough returned. The doctor, noticing the relapse, talked to him about the importance of keeping his mind free of worry and suggested he spend a few hours outdoors, hoping that the sheer beauty of the surrounding Alps might help him to relax. The majesty of the soaring mountains edged against an azure blue sky was known to have such powers. And so, weather permitting, the nurses bundled him up each morning and put him in a lounge chair out on the terrace, where he could take in the full panorama of the splendid scenery.

Henrich got along with all the nurses; they all gossiped about him, how handsome and interesting he was. These were intelligent, hard-working women, taught never to show favoritism to one patient over another, yet with him they all went the distance to ensure he received the best of care. Being a priest somehow created a certain mystique about him, as the younger nurses mildly flirted with him, and the older ones mothered him and gladly endured his good-natured teasing. Henrich loved the attention showered on him, especially coming from Gabi, a young woman with the most cheerful, ready-to-help attitude. She was his favorite, and it was always a good day for him when she was on duty, fussing over him, showing special care. She would gladly sit with him in the open air, chatting about trivial things to keep his mind at ease, or read from the poetry of Goethe and Schiller, if that would calm his nerves.

During their talks Henrich found out that she was from Fiume, a busy harbor city on the northern shores of the Adriatic Sea, and that she was in her late twenties, unattached and totally dedicated to her work. She laughed it off when Henrich playfully asked if she ever had time for romance in her busy life, saying that she was a failure in that department, and that she was long resigned to be an old maid. She was happy and contented in her role as a caregiver.

Henrich did not reveal much about himself, only that because of his illness he would soon be released from the Church. As for his future, he hoped to fit into civilian life as a teacher, but had misgivings about getting hired without experience. Hearing this, Gabi casually mentioned that her father was the principal of a gimnazium in Fiume, and if he did not mind moving, she was sure he could help him to get a job there. Their talks were lighthearted, sprinkled with easy laughter, as between friends comfortable in each other's company. With Gabi around he forgot his troubles and felt free to let his imagination rise above the humdrum of the present and reach a height where he could see the future, as he perceived it to be.

But when he was alone at night the awful nagging feeling of being trapped returned, keeping him awake, his mind searching for an explanation of why he felt this way. What had changed since the last time he saw Angela? He was the same man who loved her through the long years of separation, utterly dedicated to her, never wondering how would it feel to be with another woman. What made him see her in a different light now?

Was it because apart from adolescent schoolboy crushes, he never had an intimate relationship until she came into his life? Before Angela he never held the naked body of a woman in his arms, never made love; was it any wonder that he fell in love with her? She made him happy, how could he ask for more? Of course, being a priest, he never had the opportunity to compare her to others. The thought that someone else might thrill him just as much never entered his mind. Only now, surrounded by all these nurses, did his curiosity begin to stir. He couldn't help but see the differences between them and Angela.

Take Gabi, for instance, an educated woman exuding self-confidence, always smiling, happy in her chosen career. And there was poor little Angela. Granted, she was physically more attractive, but with only eight years of schooling and with all the unfortunate family problems, she never had the chance to grow intellectually. The burden of caring for her siblings and running that large household took all her energy; it was no wonder that she was often discouraged and gloomy. True, she built up a little dressmaking business, but it was just sewing; every woman could do that. And if he thought of her family situation, he could only pity her. Losing her mother so early and living with an uncaring, selfish father who would turn out his own daughter, she couldn't help but becoming needy, so desperately clinging. Especially now that she was alone and pregnant. Her whole world seemed to revolve around him and the baby. All her letters were full of emotional sentimentalities. In the latest she wanted him to pick a name for a boy, but asked if she could choose Helen if they had a daughter. She carried on how she always loved that name, perhaps for no other reason that her very first doll was named Lensie, a diminutive for Helen. And would he mind if she added Theresia as a middle name after both her mother and her sister Rezie, whom she asked to be the baby's godmother? She hoped he had no objection to it, and that his sister Katie wouldn't feel slighted; she would definitely ask her to be the godmother to their next child.

These were the kinds of letters she sent him regularly, each a dismal reminder of his obligations that left him depressed. They brought into focus that the bright future he envisioned for himself was merely wishful thinking, and instead of spreading his wings and savoring new discoveries, he had but a dull life to look forward to. Marrying Angela meant exchanging one confinement for another. It would make him miserable for the rest of his days, forever wondering what could have been if he were allowed to follow his dreams. And what would this do to their marriage? Feeling bitterly disappointed and haunted by regrets, how could he make Angela happy? Would this be fair to her?

The more he thought, the more he convinced himself that staying together would be a mistake; it was best if they went their separate ways. Their expectations were so different that in the long run, neither of them would be happy. Some people would consider his logic a poor excuse, nothing but cowardly reasoning to get rid of her, but to him it was justifiable. He must break his commitment; it was only a question of how to go about it. Would he be strong enough to withstand the crying and pitiful pleading if he told her face-to-face that he was leaving? Even his own family would side with her. Perhaps it would be easier, less dramatic, if he let her down slowly by writing less, giving little hints that he was not the same man anymore. Or better yet, make her believe that it was not worthwhile waiting for him by exaggerating his illness, saying that his relapse caused serious complications, and the doctor could not predict when he would be well again, only that it would take much longer than originally thought.

If he hoped that this would discourage Angela, he was wrong. She wrote back that if she had waited this long, another year or even longer would not make any difference; her only concern was his full recovery. Her letter put him back to square one. He would have to find some other way to escape, but how? When after several nights of tossing and turning he couldn't come up with a new approach, he almost gave up the whole idea. Then from the murky depths of desperation a thought began to emerge: he could make a clean break if he just disappeared. He would walk out of her life, leave everything behind, and let things fall as they might. It was the best and only way! And as the idea took root, he began to make his plan. He would stall her as long as he was at the clinic, but once he got on his feet, he would be gone. Even his parents would have to be kept in the dark, at least for a while, to prevent them from tracking him down.

He knew perfectly well how much his treachery would hurt Angela and he was sorry for that. He felt remorseful about keeping her waiting for all these years, and that as an unwed mother she would be left alone to live under the shadow of disgrace. His desertion would be devastating, but he must have his freedom. She was a strong woman, she would get over the heartache, and who knows, even with a child some man might still marry her. She was young and attractive looking enough; maybe with a little luck she could catch a husband and live a happy life.

He thought he knew Angela well. But if he believed that after such a betrayal she could ever trust a man again, he did not know her at all.

By the end of April Vienna was in full bloom. Flower stands displaying spring flowers in riotous colors sprang up on every street corner, and the already blossoming chestnut trees in the park where Angela took her daily walks provided enough shade to protect her against the unusually strong sun. She always took along a handful of crumbs to feed the birds and loved to watch the young sparrows hopping around her feet picking up the morsels.

By now her girth expanded all around her and she jokingly wrote to Henrich that no matter how much she wished him to be at her side, it might be a good thing that he was away and did not get to see her in her present condition. She told him not to worry about her; Rezie was coming to stay with her for a few weeks to help with the baby. On her final checkup the doctor set the delivery date no later than May 10th, and so she reminded him that he forgot to pick a name for a boy and asked him to hurry, in case the baby came a little earlier.

Rezie arrived on the first day of May, as Angela entered the final days of her pregnancy. By then the baby's constant kicking and shifting kept her awake most of the night, reaching the point where it was hard enough to find a comfortable position, let alone sleep. Rezie took good care of her, massaging her aching back and taking her for her afternoon walks in the park, endlessly talking about the pending birth. As the mother of a two-year-old boy, she considered herself an authority on childbirth and to prepare her sister for the coming event, she thought it her duty to describe in vivid details what to expect.

"If you are trying to scare me, Rezie, you might as well give up," Angela laughed. "Your horror stories won't frighten me. I know it won't be easy, but I am ready and I know I am in good hands. With your help and Frau Muller's I will get through, and I promise, I will live to hold my baby!"

Everything was ready to welcome her child. The bassinet with all its frilly trimmings stood near her bed, tiny shirts were neatly stacked in the drawer, and a goose down bunting waited to keep the little newcomer warm and cozy. Angela stopped working a month before and there was nothing more for her to do but wait in blissful anticipation.

There was only one cloud on her rose-colored horizon: for weeks now she received no word from Henrich. Day after day she waited for the mailman, only to be left empty-handed. Finally, on May 4th a large envelope arrived, but as she tore it open, instead of a letter from him she found several others bundled together, all unopened and addressed to him by his mother. A note from her said that they were actually Angela's letters written to Henrich during the past three weeks, which she had forwarded to the clinic. Strangely, they were now returned along with her own letters to him, and without any explanation why they were refused. It didn't make any sense, she wrote; the only thing the family could think of was that Henrich must have left the hospital without telling where he went, and when he failed to return, they decided not to hold his incoming mail any longer. About what happened to him, the Pollingers could only speculate. Perhaps he wanted to surprise Angela and be there for the birth of the baby, but didn't dare to tell the doctors. Was it possible that he could be in Vienna already? Would Angela contact the family as soon as possible?

Angela was baffled. Could this be true? Could he be standing at the door the next time she opened it? But of course, that must be it! He is planning to surprise her! And it was so typical of him! He always liked pulling pranks. He is probably setting her up! Oh, only if it were true! To have him here and watch his face when Frau Muller put his newborn child in his arms!

Excitedly, she ran to Rezie to tell her the possibility, but her sister's reaction was skeptical. "You say he left the hospital three weeks ago? Don't you think that's enough time to get here? Well, where is he? I don't see any sign of him! I am sorry to disappoint you, Angela, but he should be here by now. There must be another reason, but whatever it is, this whole thing is very strange, just disappearing like that!"

Angela had to agree. Rezie was right, but then where was he? What had happened to Henrich? She must find a logical answer or she would go crazy! Was he in trouble? Did he get hurt or fall ill somewhere on the way? No, it couldn't be; knowing him he would have found a way to write or send word by now. It must be something else; maybe he went back to the Church to finalize his release papers and something went wrong. If they retained him for some reason, he couldn't contact her from there. But that couldn't be true either, because she remembered that in his last letter he wrote that his dispensation was official, and he was now a free man. He even printed the words in capital letters and underlined it for emphasis: A FREE MAN! How excited she was when she first read it, and even now, just thinking about it filled her with new hope. Against all odds, he still could be knocking on her door any minute, they still could get married right away now that he was finally free.

Then something struck her. Where was that letter? She ran to the bedroom and pulled out the drawer of her nightstand where she kept all his letters. There it was, lying on top of the pile, and as she smoothed out the page and read the lines again, her heart sank. Yes, the words were there that he was a free man, but nothing else, no mention of being free to come for her, that he was free to marry her! Was she wrong to assume that that's what he meant? How could it be anything else? To her the emphasis and the punctuations were all clear signs of his excitement, his jubilation over winning the battle. Their long wait was over and soon they would be together! That he didn't gush about his feelings was because by nature men were like that; even when face-to-face, they seemed to have a hard time finding the right words to express how they felt, let alone on paper, scribbling about sentimentalities. It was simple as that. She never nagged him about not writing her love letters, or lately for not taking more time to answer hers. She found excuses for him; perhaps he didn't want her to worry about the relapse, or that lying in bed, sick as he was, there was not much he could say. And yet, she couldn't deny that it bothered her. She remembered that not so long ago he did use sweet, endearing words when he wrote. When did that stop?

She glanced back at the letter and tears sprang to her eyes. She could no longer explain away why there was no expression of love for her, not a word that he missed her, nothing about the baby or their future together. And as she stood there staring at his handwriting, slowly, painfully it dawned on her what Henrich really meant when he wrote that he was a free man. He was free to live his life that no longer included her!

As the letter slipped from her fingers and floated to the floor, Rezie bent to retrieve it but froze halfway when she glanced at her sister's face drained of all color.

"What's wrong, Angela? You look like you've seen a ghost! Come on, sit down, you shouldn't let stupid me upset you! You know that I did not mean what I said about Henrich. Of course there's got to be a good explanation why he would disappear without telling anyone—"

Uh-oh, she stopped in mid-sentence. *I shouldn't talk about disappearance if it upsets Angela this much,* she chided herself silently, even though she didn't understand why Angela took her remark so seriously. Everyone knew how she always talked before thinking!

But Angela did not hear what Rezie said. She was in a dark and desolate place where no words could reach her, alone and deserted, betrayed by the man she loved with her entire being. He had abandoned her and their unborn child without a word, not even a goodbye, letting his returned letters tell the story. She thought her father was cruel and coldhearted, but at least he did not run from his responsibilities! Compared to him Henrich was worse, much worse. He had no heart at all.

She loved this man unconditionally, trusted him, waited for him, and believed him when he said he loved her. But it was all a lie, he never loved her; he did not care if she lived or died, didn't want to know if she had given him a son or a daughter. He left her, just as he left the Church, and she knew she would never see him again.

She could bear it no longer. Her heart broken, she had no strength left to fight her way out of the darkness. Let it take her, she'd gladly surrender, was her last thought before her knees gave out and her body sank to the floor.

Thank God, Rezie was there and the moment she saw her sister collapse she took control. Since Angela was too heavy to lift, she left her where she was, then ran to get the smelling salt and a wet towel for her forehead. She put a pillow under her head and gently patted her cheeks.

"Angela, wake up, do you hear me? Wake up sweetie, everything is going to be all right," she talked to her firmly until finally Angela's eyes fluttered and slowly focused on Rezie's face.

"Why am I on the floor? Is something wrong? Is it the baby?" she asked, alarmed, her voice awash with fear.

"No, don't worry, nothing is wrong with the baby, it's you Angela, you fainted—scared me to death! We have to get you off the floor. How do you feel? Can you get up? But take it easy, here, let me help you."

Carefully, together they made it to the bed, but Rezie was truly concerned. Being so close to giving birth, a collapse like this could cause complications. It must have been something in that letter that put Angela in such a state, not her stupid babbling about Henrich vanishing in thin air, she thought while gently smoothing her sister's hair and fluffing her pillow.

"Now isn't that better? Do you want me to bring you anything? No? OK, just lie back; take a deep breath and blow it out slowly, it will help you relax. Is there enough air in here? The windows are open but I could open the door, too. It's important to fill your lungs with fresh air. And try to rest, sleep if you can."

She kept on chattering, but Angela wished she'd stop. She knew what Rezie was trying to do, keep her calm by diverting her mind, but right now she just wanted to be left alone with her thoughts, go back to the moment before she lost all sense of the world and sank into the blissful state of oblivion. Drained to exhaustion, she closed her eyes and waited until slowly it all came back to her—the letter, and the realization that Henrich left her. And with it came a flood of agonizing questions. Why did he abandon her, what made him do it, could she be blamed for it? The thought tormented her. Did she do something so awful in his eyes that left him with no choice but turn his back on her? Pain tore at her heart. If she did, she didn't know what it was, and now, with him gone, she would never find out! Lying on her pillow, she rolled her head from side to side as if in denial and began to weep, giving way to her grief with a deep, mournful sound.

"Angela, please don't cry; maybe we assume the worst! There must be something we can do to find out what happened," Rezie tried to comfort her. "These returned letters mean nothing; the hospital might have lost track of him, but the Church should know more. We have to contact them; I am surprised that the Pollingers did not think of it. I'd go there right now, but I am afraid to leave you alone! We'll get some answers, so please stop worrying. You can't let yourself go like this! The baby will be here any day! You have to get your strength back; if nothing else, you must do it for the baby!"

Rezie had to find a way to bring Angela back and she was glad when she finally opened her eyes and accepted the glass of water she urged on her. But then she almost started to cry herself when she heard the utter resignation in Angela's voice saying, "You are right, Rezie, I can't let my baby down. I have to be strong, doubly strong, now that he has no father to welcome him."

"Don't talk like that, Angie, we don't know it for sure."

"But I do, Rezie, I know it in my heart that he left me, and that I am on my own now." With profound sadness she glanced at the cradle. "But it's not important; all that matters is the baby, and I'll see to it that he arrives healthy and strong."

"So, it's a boy now? You talk like you know for sure!" Rezie eagerly changed the subject to keep Angela's mind off Henrich.

"It's just wishful thinking. Life without a father is difficult for any child, but boys can handle it better; they are stronger, less vulnerable than little girls."

"Nonsense Angie, whether it's a boy or a girl, it will have you as a mother, and I know you! Anyone who'd try to hurt that child better be ready to deal with you," Rezie laughed goodheartedly and babbled on. "Though I have to admit, I was glad when mine turned out to be a boy; they carry on the family name, and if the next should be a girl, it's nice for her to have a big brother."

The minute she said it her hand flew to her mouth, but it was too late to take it back. She did it again! Talking about family name and the next baby! "Oh, I am sorry Angela," she started to apologize, "it was stupid of me. I didn't mean it for you."

"I know, Rezie, I know, you always manage to put your foot in your mouth. But you are right; it's nice for girls to grow up with an older brother. That's why I hope it's not a girl, because she will never have a brother. Or a sister, not even grandparents—you know about father, and the Pollingers can never reveal who they are. That leaves only me, and that's why I must stay strong. If I give up, my baby will be left all alone in this world."

"How can you say that, Angela? Your baby will never be alone! That child will always have us—aunts and uncles and cousins—we'll take care of him or her, if you should die!" That was Rezie again, speaking before thinking! "Well, I don't mean that as it sounds; I am just saying it because you seem to forget that you do have a family. You should know we would always look after your child if something happened to you." She was quite indignant that Angela could even think they would not take care of her child, especially her, as godmother to the baby.

"Of course, Rezie, I know you will do the right thing if it should come to that. Let's just hope that nothing goes wrong with the birth, and I survive to bring up my son or daughter as well as I can under the circumstances, without a real family."

"I wish you wouldn't talk like that Angie, like it's the end of the world!" Rezie was getting impatient. "You will meet somebody and will get married! I can think of several eligible men right now who would be interested in marrying you and adopting the baby! It's really up to you if you want to give this child a chance to grow up in a real family, as you put it. At least you should think about it."

"No Rezie, I will not go down that path, I can't. You are happily married; you couldn't possibly understand what I am going through and what this has done to me. You don't know how humiliating it is to feel unwanted, rejected, left alone with a child on the way, knowing that the man you loved stopped loving you. I can't let that happen to me ever again. I wouldn't be able to survive another betrayal. My trust in man is dead; it died today."

"I hate to hear you talking like this. I am sure that when you feel better, you will change your mind. Time is a great healer, Angie. Besides, how can you be so sure that he left you? We really don't know what's going on. Like I said before, we'll have to check with the Benedictines."

"Rezie, it's no use. He is gone for good. Even if we found out where he is, what could we do? We can't force him to come back. He took great care to cover his tracks, leaving even his parents without a clue. That reminds me, we must write to his mother and let her know that he is not here. I'll do that a little later so you can take it to the post office first thing tomorrow morning."

A few days later Mrs. Pollinger wrote back a disheartening letter that they still had no word from Henrich and that they were doing everything possible to look into his disappearance. As bereaved as she was about the uncertainty surrounding her son's whereabouts, she tried to console Angela and promised to write her immediately if she had any news.

Angela and Lensie

JUST BEFORE DAWN on May 8, 1906, Angela was jolted out of her light sleep by a sharp cramp in her belly. It was not a kick; she knew the difference. She lay still. Would this be her big day? When a little while later she felt it again, then again, each time a little stronger, she knew her time was at hand.

It was still dark outside; the streets were empty in this early hour, with only an occasional horse-drawn carriage heading for the marketplace. Angela kept counting the time between contractions but as the first rays of sun began to filter through the drapes, she decided to alert her sister. Sitting on the edge of the bed it took a moment to push her bulging body upright, then after gaining a foothold she padded across the room where Rezie slept on a folding cot.

"Rezie, wake up, I think it's time to call Frau Muller," she said, poking her gently. Half asleep and rubbing her eyes, Rezie sat up. "I'll be right up," she murmured and sank right back on her pillow.

"I don't think you heard me," Angela shook her a little harder. "I am getting cramps pretty regularly now. You have to get up and get Frau Muller, unless you want to play midwife yourself," she teased Rezie, pulling back the cover.

That was enough to get her out of bed. Once she realized what was about to happen she dressed in a hurry and went to fetch the midwife. After a few questions about the timing of the contractions, Frau Muller came promptly founding Angela curled up in bed and panting as the first truly intense pain gripped her body. It took her breath away. She knew that childbirth meant great pain, but nothing had prepared her for this.

"Well, how are we doing, Frau Bohaczek?" she greeted Angela, and after a quick examination declared there was still time before the real labor began.

"Real labor? What do you mean, real labor? I am racked with pain already; you mean there is more to come?"

Frau Muller was a professional midwife but lacked diplomatic skills. Her words did little to put Angela at ease, and seeing the pathetic pleading in her eyes, she softened her tone. "Now don't you worry, Frau Bohaczek, I will be here to help you through it, and I guarantee, the minute I put your baby in your arms you will forget all about the pain. I've seen it a thousand times."

Time passed slowly, stretching Angela's labor to seemingly endless hours. Frau Muller prepared everything for the delivery while Rezie comforted her sister as much as it was possible. Towards the final stages the midwife offered Angela a rubber stick to bite down on, but she refused. She kept breathing through her clamped teeth, intermittently breaking into a high-pitched wail, but did not scream until the very end. Then it was over. Her baby slipped out of her body and into the midwife's hands at 7:48 PM.

Half dazed she heard Frau Muller announce, "Congratulation! You have a beautiful, perfectly formed daughter."

So, it is a girl! Disappointment mixed with pity was all Angela could feel at the moment of her daughter's birth. At the sound of the baby's first cry, she burrowed her face into her pillow. She could only think of all the pain and hurt her daughter would have to endure in her life. *Go ahead, and cry little girl; you better get used to crying,* she talked to her in bitter silence. *You don't know it yet, but life will not be kind to you. No matter how innocent you are, others will mock you, call you names, make you feel ashamed, and I am powerless to protect you. You might blame me and learn to hate me for all the humiliation coming your way, and you would have all the right. I was too gullible, too trust-*

ing, and now you must suffer for it. But I swear to you now, I will make sure that what happened to me will never happen to you!

She heard the door open as Frau Muller brought in the infant, all cleaned up and snugly tied into her bunting. Rezie, walking beside them, was cooing to the baby and talking to Angela at the same time. "Aren't you like a little angel? And look at that hair, where did you get all that hair? Wait till you see her, Angela, you could almost tie a ribbon in it. And she has a nose just like yours, her mouth, too!"

Angela turned her head and, seeing her daughter's beautiful face for the first time, all her anguished thoughts flew out the window. In a gesture of fierce demand she reached out for her, fingers wiggling, her eyes blazing with impatience, until the midwife put Lensie in her arms. She cradled the baby against her breast and in that moment of supreme surrender, she felt all the disappointment, all the resentment and self-pity she harbored since Henrich's desertion suddenly dissolve, vanish without a trace. Gone was the immense hopelessness, replaced by an overwhelming love, and something else: a flicker of forgiveness toward the man who broke her heart and violated her trust, but gave her this small miracle now nestling next to her heart.

Rezie stood rolling her eyes and tapping her toes as Frau Muller was giving exact instructions on how to care for the child until she'd come back the next day. As if she didn't know all that already! With a condescending smile she informed the midwife that she had a little boy herself, she knew well enough what to do.

"Well and good, I just want to make sure that Frau Bohaczek and the baby are properly cared for. I'll be back in the morning to see how she is doing and to fill out the papers to record the birth." With that, she cast a final proud look at the new mother and child and marched out in utter satisfaction. To bring babies into the world always left her with a feeling of a job well done.

As promised, she was back early the next morning. The baby was in her crib, sleeping after her morning feed. Angela had plenty of milk and had fed little Lensie several times already. So far she was a good baby, eating, crying a little, but sleeping most of the time. Frau Muller praised Angela about how well she held up during the delivery and heaped compliments on the baby.

"She is a real beauty, Frau Bohaczek, a little living doll. She has such a rosy complexion, and such a pretty little mouth. She seems to be healthy, too, but you make sure to have the doctor check her out when you take her in for a look. You and your husband can be very proud of her."

Rezie was coming into the room with a tray, bringing warm milk and some toast with butter and jam for Angela and coffee and a sweet roll for Frau Muller. The midwife made herself comfortable and, after finishing her coffee, pulled out a blank birth certificate.

"Well, let's see. The address, the last name, and date of birth I know. What I need from you is the child's given name and the personal information about yourself, the father, and grandparents on both sides. That includes everyone's name, birthpalce, occupation, and religion. So let's just go down the line. What are you going to call her?"

"Officially it's Helen Theresia, but I call her Lensie, and we are all Roman Catholics, including my parents and grandparents."

"Very well, I am Catholic myself, but then there are very few Protestants in Austria. So next, I need the father's name."

"You have to leave that blank, Frau Muller," Angela said without hedging. "She does not have a father. He deserted us."

"Oooh? Tsk, tsk," Frau Muller clucked her tongue and shook her head. "I see. Now that's too bad; that poor little creature deserves better. You had to hitch your wagon to one of them rats! That's what they are, rats, in my opinion, running away at the first sign of trouble. But you are not the only one dear, if it's any consolation to you. I've seen it plenty of times in my practice, some girls from real good families, too. These rats, if you ask me, should all be hanged by the tail for ruining innocent lives." She gave an indignant little huff, then continued, "But of course it's none of my business; I just do my job here. So let's see, what's the next line? Oh yes, it's your maiden name. I suppose it is Bohaczek."

Once she collected all the information, Frau Muller stood up to leave and said she would stop by again in a day or two. On the way to the door she cast one more glance at the crib, shook her head with obvious pity, then left.

With Rezie hovering nearby, Angela dozed off but was immediately awake when she heard the baby making noises, not quite a cry but leading to it.

"Ah-ha, it's time for your lunch, little Lensie," Rezie cooed as she lifted her out of the bassinette. She handed her to Angela then went to the kitchen to prepare their meal.

Angela alone with her daughter looked down on that sweet face as the baby hungrily took her breast. She loved her unconditionally. The intensity of her emotion, the overwhelming tenderness she felt in that moment was utterly new to her. Yes, she took care of Mitzie almost from birth, nurturing, and loving her as her own, but it couldn't compare to the depth of her passion for Lensie.

And as the baby nestled in her arms she swore that she'd never be deprived of love and affection. She prayed that God would give her strength to protect her child against the social stigma of her birth, and also plant compassion in her heart so she wouldn't turn against her for having to grow up without a father. She would try her best to fill the void in her young life by giving her all the love she had in her heart. And when the day came, as it must, that Lensie would ask about her father, she made a promise never to speak ill of him.

As for herself, she absolved Henrich the day Lensie was born from all the wrong he did to her. But betraying Lensie, his own flesh and blood, and not giving a damn to know if she lived or died—she would never be able to forgive.

By the next week Angela felt strong enough to care for her daughter without help, and so Rezie left, offering to come back if Angela should need her again. With her experience in raising her brothers and sisters, Angela easily slipped into her role as a young mother. Thank God, the baby was healthy, eating well, and growing fast. She was alert from the start, her light green eyes—inherited from Henrich—focusing on everything that came into her vision. She came to recognize her mother's face early on, and it melted Angela's heart whenever she smiled at her, gurgling happily and punching the air with her little fists. She was a good baby, quiet most of the time, but if she lost her grip on a favorite toy she could throw a tantrum, wailing until it was back in her hands. She looked prettier by the day, drawing compliments even from strangers when Angela took her out in her pram.

Henrich's family came to see them often; they were simply enchanted with Lensie. She never shied away when her grandmother took her in her arms, covering her chubby cheeks with kisses and looking into those green eyes, exactly like her son's. Katie already talked about the time when Lensie would be old enough to come and spend time with them in Kismarton.

Of course, their talk always turned to Henrich's disappearance. The Pollingers continued their frantic search for him but it led to nowhere. The police checked if perhaps he was involved in an accident or was a victim of foul play while traveling, but everything turned out negative. The Benedictines had no idea either; his sudden disappearance was a mystery to them, too.

What little the family knew came from the sanatorium. They learned that Henrich was making good progress but was not ready to be released. Occasionally, the doctors allowed him to walk down to the village and browse in the little shops there, always in the company of a nurse. On the day he disappeared, nurse Gabi was with him, but she didn't return either. Questioning the shopkeepers if they had seen them turned up nothing. The two simply vanished, presumably together, and without a trace. It left no doubt in Angela's mind that Henrich left her for this woman, they planned their disappearance, and that they didn't want to be found. The pain their selfish and inconsiderate act inflicted on the families apparently meant nothing to them.

Regardless, the Pollingers kept hoping that someone somewhere might recognize Henrich and send word to the family. It was only a slight chance, but they couldn't give up on finding him one day. They also clung to a desperate belief that the baby would lure their son back, that he wouldn't be able to stay away from his child forever. Angela knew better, but she didn't have the heart to discourage them. As far as she was concerned, Henrich was gone, and the search was over.

Angela loved spending her days with her daughter, but she knew that sooner or later she would need to replenish her funds. She called on the fashion salons to let them know that she was ready to take up sewing again, and they were glad to have her back. Work poured in, and for a while she managed to handle the load and also take care of the baby, but when Lensie began to crawl and needed constant attention she put out word that she was looking for help. She wanted a babysitter who could also chip in with the sewing, if needed.

Angela picked seventeen-year-old Sofie, who lived in the same apartment building and whom she met a few times before while coming in and out of the building. Sofie would hold the door open for her when she was struggling with the baby carriage, cooing to Lensie with genuine affection. The attraction must have been mutual, because the baby responded to the girl's obvious fondness by smiling back and excitedly flailing her little hands.

In the beginning, during Lensie's naptime Sofie helped Angela with simple finishing work, but when she showed interest in learning more, Angela started to train her on the sewing machine. She proved to be quite capable and soon was handling more demanding tasks, which in turn allowed Angela to take in more work. Within a year she was able to phase out the salons and work exclusively for herself.

With her business expanding and the baby growing, Angela decided to look for a bigger place. She found a large three-room apartment, one room to serve as part living room, part reception room for clients, another to do her sewing, and a large bedroom for herself and Lensie. This time she rented it unfurnished; she wanted the apartment to reflect her own taste, to be inviting and comfortable as well. By then Vienna was undergoing major modernization, plumbing and electricity were being installed, lines were put down on streets for electric streetcars, and since her flat was situated in a better part of the city, it offered all these latest conveniences that made life so much easier.

All and all, she was contended with the life she created for herself and Lensie. Working hard and raising her daughter kept her busy and left little time to brood over her great loss. Although she missed her brothers and her friends in Sopron, she didn't feel lonely. It helped that her sisters visited her regularly; Rezie came with her little boy and Lizzie, while Gertie always brought Mitzie with her. It was pure joy for Angela to watch her youngest sister, only six years older than Lensie, playing with the baby.

Then in the early summer of 1908 Mrs. Pollinger and Katie came with exciting news. A woman they hardly knew stopped by their house a day before and told them that she met Henrich while attending her nephew's graduation in Ljubljana, a medium size city in Slovenia. During the ceremony she noticed Henrich sitting among the teachers and she thought it neighborly to go and say hello to him. He didn't much remember her, but regardless, he was friendly, and had only nice things to say about her nephew. After some small talk she told him that she was returning to Kismarton the next day and would be glad to take a letter or message to his family, but he politely declined. Raising an eyebrow the woman then proceeded to tell Mrs. Pollinger that she was surprised seeing Henrich, a priest, wearing civilian clothes, and asked outright, did he leave the Church?

Mrs. Pollinger was more than annoyed by the impertinence of this woman to ask such a personal question. They had only met once or twice and had nothing in common, but because she desperately needed to extract more information from her, she ushered her in, and putting on a friendly facade acknowledged that yes, the Church released Henrich because of health problems. She was thinking fast how to make the woman reveal the school's name without arousing suspicion as to why she did not know where her son was working. She had to stall for time.

"What a coincidence that you ran into our Henrich," Mrs. Pollinger gushed, "and how kind of you to take the time talking to him. The rascal should have taken up your offer to bring a message! I haven't heard from him for weeks, but you know how young people are these days. I am so glad that you came to see me! Please tell me how is he? Did you think he looked well? I can't help but worry that he neglects to take care of himself, especially when he is still recovering from his long illness. I wanted him to come home for the summer so I could look after him, but he said he was staying to conduct classes for students who failed their exams. I have a good mind to write to that school, if I could only find their address, that they should let their teachers take a little time off to visit with family!"

"Mrs. Pollinger, you have no cause to worry, your son looks wonderful, as handsome as ever. He is very well respected too, my nephew was telling me. By the way, you don't need a street address, everyone knows the State Gimnazium for Boys; it's one of city's best preparatory schools. My nephew wants to be a doctor and he is transferring to . . ."

Mrs. Pollinger let her rattle on a little longer without listening. Once she got the information she no longer needed her, and after a few minutes she thanked her again and promptly excused herself.

"Well, what do you make of this, Angela?" Katie asked. "At least we can rest assured that he is alive and well. You know, we even thought that he could have suffered a memory loss, that he didn't come home simply because he couldn't remember anything, not his home nor the sanatorium. But now we know it isn't the case."

"Did this woman mention whether he is married or not?" Angela asked.

"No, she didn't, and of course, we couldn't ask. It would have seemed strange that we didn't know about that. But listen, Angela, I think we should go to Ljubljana right away, you and I and Lensie, and confront him before he can skip town again. Writing is useless. If you are too busy, Mother and I will go, but if he is still there, it would make a much bigger impact if he sees you and the baby."

Angela was ready to go at once. If the trip should take longer than a few days, she might lose some of her customers, but so be it. This was a chance she couldn't pass up, even if in her heart she was almost sure he'd make his getaway before they could catch him.

In two days Angela, Katie and Lensie were on the train to Ljubljana. They checked into a hotel in the center of the city, and Katie wasted no time in making inquiries about the school; it was not in the immediate vicinity, but still in walking distance, and she decided to check it out while it was still daylight. The janitor was just closing up when she got there and told her that the principal was usually in his office at eight in the morning, and that he remembered seeing Mr. Pollinger a day or so before.

Returning to the hotel Katie bounded through the door with the news that Henrich was still there. They would see him tomorrow! Seeing her joy, Angela was happy for her. Yes, for Katie and her family the search will be over. Whether he was married or not made no difference to them; they would have him back, but what could she expect? Her instincts told her that he was lost to her even if he was not married; he had obviously stopped loving her. Only through Lensie, and only if he cared enough for his daughter, was there a chance that they could perhaps still become a family.

Yet the thought that she might see him in the morning kept her awake most of the night. With the first daylight she got out of bed and, locking the bathroom door, stared into the mirror, scrutinizing her face. She was now in her late twenties, but aside from a few fine lines around her eyes and mouth, she retained her youthful look. Her forehead was smooth, her skin taut and firm, no sagging around the jawline or neck. There was no sign of gray in her thick honey-blond hair, either; it was still soft and shiny as ever. Her figure was slightly fuller now, but she hadn't lost her shape; her curves were intact. Any man would be proud to have a wife like her, except Henrich. She had lost her appeal to him and she was powerless to change that. She once believed that his feelings for her went deeper than the surface, that he saw her inner strength, her perseverance, the goodness of her heart, but these things apparently did not matter to him. And this is what hurt her most.

It was still early but she got dressed and went down to the corner store to buy some crescent rolls, milk for the baby, and coffee for Katie. She herself couldn't eat anything; she was too nervous, too anxious to leave, until finally at eight o'clock they walked into the principal's office.

"Well, well, isn't it too early for this young lady to start school yet?" the principal greeted them with a smile at seeing Lensie in Angela's arms.

"It will be soon enough," Angela laughed as she sat down with Lensie in her lap. Katie chimed in that her little niece was just trying to crash the school's coeducational barrier. She then apologized for the early call and told the principal that she was Henrich's sister, and Angela his cousin, and why they came to see him.

"You see, we haven't seen my brother for quite some time; he never even met little Lensie here, so we concocted a silly plan to surprise him with our visit. He doesn't know that we are here. What we want to do is wait for him at the entrance, Angela and I would hide behind the gate and let Lensie run up to him and greet him as Uncle Henrich. He wouldn't have any idea who the child was, and that's when we would step out and surprise him. It would be great fun, but we need to know his schedule, when he is expected to arrive."

"It is a delightful plan, and it would have been my pleasure to help you carry it out, but I am afraid that's impossible. You see, Mr. Pollinger is no longer with us. He turned in his resignation a little over a week ago, just after the commencement ceremony. When he came to see me he said he was suffering from a recurrence of his earlier tuberculosis, which he believed to be cured. He had the same symptoms and wanted to return to the hospital for further treatment. I am truly sorry to disappoint you and spoil your surprise, but the day before yesterday was his last day. If I can help you in any other way, please say the word."

After hearing "he is no longer with us," Angela no longer listened. She did not care what story Henrich gave to the principal. It no longer mattered to her. As she guessed all along, he skipped before they could confront him. She vaguely heard Katie asking the principal whether he knew if his wife went with him to the clinic?

"That I don't know. But since she is a nurse, it would make good sense if she wanted to accompany him. If you don't find her at home, check with the hospital where she works; it is only two blocks from here and they should know more."

Katie thanked him and gently guided the dazed Angela out of the building and into the street.

"I know you are disappointed, Angela, and so am I, but this is what we half expected. At least now we know that he is married and doesn't want to be found, but please, don't let it get to you, he is not worth it. Take a deep breath; you'll feel better. Here, let me take Lensie." She reached for the child, but Angela jerked her shoulder in defiance and, holding the girl in a tight grip, rushed ahead as if fleeing from someone or something. All she could think of was how she had squandered her years on a coward and a sneak. This was his chance to come forward and at least try to explain what happened; there might have been a reason, a circumstance to justify what he did. He had the opportunity to come clean, to ask for forgiveness; instead he chose to run.

With lips pressed together and oblivious to where she was going, she refused to listen to Katie's pleas to slow down until she caught her heel on a crack in the pavement and almost dropped Lensie. As it was, the child slipped to the ground, scraping her knees, wailing pitifully, until her cries finally cut through Angela's trance-like state. She knelt beside her little girl, comforting her, blowing on her boo-boo to lessen the sting. Her daughter needed her and she would never again allow herself to forget that.

The year Lensie turned four, Angela enrolled her in kindergarten at a nearby convent. At first she was concerned about how she would get along with other children since she was always among adults, but she had no cause to worry. Lensie turned out to be an outgoing child, quick to make friends, liked by both her peers and teachers. She remained the same when she entered school and learning her ABCs replaced playing Ring Around the Rosie. She was always mindful in class, did her homework and attended church with deep devotion. The nuns soon noticed that she seemed to have a natural talent for play-acting and often chose her for the leading role in their school plays. She also liked playing theater at home, bringing her friends over to act out her favorite fairytales, although they soon lost interest when no one else got to play the princess but her.

During the summer Angela let Lensie spend weeks with the Pollingers on the condition never to reveal that they were her grandparents. They must remain aunt and uncle to her to protect Henrich's identity, which Angela swore to hide from the public forever and from Lensie as long as possible. Katie spoiled her niece, taking her on small trips around Burgenland. She remembered how excited Lensie was when they took her to Ljubljana, how she boasted to everyone about her train ride, a real one, not like the one in the Prater, Vienna's amusement park. They went boating and swimming at Lake Ferto, the second largest body of water in Hungary, and on the weekends visited neighboring village fairs, where Lensie would ride the children's carousel and visit the petting zoo. But she loved best when they went on a religious pilgrimage to Mariacell to see the famous painting of the Virgin Mary, believed to have shed tears once a long time ago.

Angela also made sure that Lensie spent equal time with her aunts, Rezie and Gertie. Rezie's little boy became her "big" brother, and although Gertie and her husband had no children, they had Mitzie living with them, a perfect playmate to Lensie. Both families welcomed her every time she came for a visit and readily agreed that anyone would be hard put not to love this outgoing, friendly little girl.

Whenever Lensie was away, Angela put Sofie to work fulltime as a seamstress, and after seeing how well she performed she decided to keep her on the job permanently. Her business was thriving and eventually reached the point where Angela had to make a choice, either cut back or expand. She chose the latter, and to meet the demand she purchased additional machines and hired several more seamstresses. Lensie was now attending school and didn't need a fulltime babysitter, only someone to look after her in the afternoons.

Angela couldn't have been happier with her life as 1912 rolled around. She was the owner of a well-run business and her daughter gave her nothing but joy. Everything was perfect, except for one thing: she found herself more and more longing to be back in Sopron. It didn't happen overnight. From the day she was banished from home she always missed having her family around, but knowing that she had no choice, she accepted her forced separation. Only when she sneaked back from time to time and saw the many changes taking place in her brothers' lives without her being a part of it, did she began to feel left out, a real outsider. By now the young boys she left behind were all grown men, except Miska. Henrich, the oldest, was married, though still living at home, trying to save money to open a shoe repair shop. His wife ran the household and took care of Miska, who at sixteen was already working as the youngest clerk at the post office. Jozsef joined the Army on the day he turned eighteen in 1911, and was now stationed in Koszeg, another small town south of Sopron. And Franz was about to marry a girl from Modling, a village in Burgenland, where her family ran a general store; he would be moving there after the wedding, planned for January 1913. Of course, Angela could never bring Lensie to see them; her uncles only knew her from photographs, and it upset her greatly that her daughter was deprived of their love and affection, robbed of the warmth a big family could give her.

Yes, Vienna was good to her, but it was not home, she didn't belong there. Deep down she was just a small-town girl at heart, homesick for the place where she was born and raised, and she knew that one day she would leave Vienna and go back.

That day came in June 1913 when she received a telegram that her father had passed away. She was aware that he was not in the best of health, he had heart problems, so it didn't come as a total surprise to learn that one evening, while having his supper, he slumped over the table and was gone. He was sixty years old. Standing at his grave Angela shed no tears but sent a silent prayer to let him know that she had forgiven him. He was stubborn and judgmental and especially cruel to her, but still, he was her father.

After the funeral there was a brief reception for friends and co-workers, and when everyone left, the family sat down to discuss the will and what should be done with the house. Angela immediately told them that she wanted to move back with Lensie and intended to live in the house, with Mitzie and Lizzie also brought home. She would take care of them and Miska, too, just as she did before she was forced to leave. As for Henrich and his wife Maria, she suggested they find a place of their own. Then later, when the nest is finally empty, they would sell the house and split the money in equal shares.

Everyone accepted her proposal without argument. The only protest came from Gertie, and it was about losing Mitzie. When the girl left the room for a moment she confronted Angela.

"She has lived with us for seven years, and now you want to uproot her and bring her back? Why, she spent more time with us than with you, Angela! To take her away is not fair to us, and more importantly, not fair to Mitzie. She is going to school there and has many friends; she should not be yanked out just because you want her here. Let's ask her what she wants to do."

"It is true that you took great care of Mitzie, and we—all of us here—are forever grateful for that," Angela calmly told her. "Your resentment is only natural, and believe me, I know how you feel. You have no idea how much I suffered when I had to leave. We both love her and want the best for her, and that's exactly why I insist on bringing her home. She belongs here where she was born, where most of her family lives, where her parents are buried. I promise, she can spend her summer vacations with you and naturally, you are always welcome to visit her and stay as long as you like."

When Gertie still objected that Mitzie was just a little girl and she should have a say in whether she wanted to come back or not, Angela's voice took on a sharper tone. "Look Gertie, I know you love her, but there is one thing I can't and will not do. I am not going to ask Mitzie where she wants to live and put her in the position where she must choose between us. She is still a child and this kind of decision must be made for her. I hope you will see it my way and accept my judgment in this." Then, softening her voice, she added, "Mitzie is thirteen, and who knows, in a few years she might fall in love and decide to get married, then we both have to let her go."

Grudgingly, Gertie made a face and pulled a shoulder, but she knew the argument was over. She grumbled on for a while about possibly moving back to Sopron to be closer to "her" little girl, but in the end they all agreed that Angela was right. It was not because she was the oldest, but because for Angela the welfare of the family always came first. They trusted her insights and respected her decisions. In all her life she only made one big mistake; she fell in love with a man who was not worthy of her. And they all suffered for it.

Return home

WHEN ANGELA RETURNED to Vienna she began preparing to close her business. After finishing the work in progress, she let all her girls go except Sofie. She wanted to come along, and Angela was more than glad to take her. She became an excellent seamstress, and although Angela would have to start from scratch again to build up her business in Sopron, eventually she would need help.

Next she gave notice to her landlord and made a deal with him to buy her furniture. By the end of August she was packed, her sewing machines crated and shipped, a chapter of her life closed. She was ready to say goodbye to Vienna.

As always, Lensie was excited at the prospect of going on a trip, but Angela explained to her that this was not just another vacation; they were leaving Vienna for good. Just the same, she started counting the days until they would be moving to this new city, a place she had never been before. Changes never fazed her; they only aroused her curiosity about what she would find, what new friends she would make. She had a barrage of questions about her uncles, whether her new school would be as nice as in Vienna, and if Angela knew any of the girls who would be her classmates. She dismissed it when her mother cautioned her that perhaps she expected too much. Moving to a new place might sound exciting, but it also meant lots of changes in their life, even disappointments.

Angela knew what to expect when they arrive in Sopron. She had no illusions about the small town prejudice awaiting them, and she was trying to prepare Lensie for it. Pretending to be Frau Bohaczek worked in Vienna because nobody knew her there, but she would be returning to Sopron as a disgraced woman, an unwed mother with an illegitimate child. Somehow she would deal with the scandal, but Lensie was too young to understand rejection and cruelty. So far she only knew that one day her father disappeared without a trace, and no one knew what happened to him. He was never found and was assumed dead, but that was no reason for people suddenly treating her with scorn, calling her names, and taunting her that she had no father.

Angela would have to find the right words to explain to her seven-year-old daughter that while in Vienna everyone loved her, people might treat her differently in Sopron. For the time being the best she could do was to tell her that she would be a stranger there, and people tended to be aloof, even unfriendly when meeting someone they didn't know. She would have to be patient and give them time to get to know her. Her heart ached when she heard her outgoing, trusting little girl promise that she would not force anybody to be her friend; she'd always have Sofie, and Mitzie would be there too, so she was not worried at all. How could Lensie know about the narrow-minded intolerance awaiting her, the snobbish prejudice that would bring an end to her world of innocence?

The day they arrived in Sopron all her local relatives and close friends were at the station to welcome them and to meet the little girl they had heard so much about. She charmed everyone with her obvious confusion at meeting so many new people, her green eyes darting from one face to the other, as one by one they scooped her up and showered her with kisses. Sofie finally took her by the hand and together they followed Angela and her noisy relatives as they headed for home. Along the way they ran into some of Angela's old clients and acquaintances, all greeting her with warm smiles, but while wondering about her long absence, they mercifully refrained from stopping her with questions in the midst of her joyous family reunion.

For the first few days Angela was busy unpacking and rearranging the rooms. Mitzie and Lizzie would share a room with Sofie, Miska got a room all to himself, and she took the large bedroom for herself and Lensie. After settling in she hung back her Mode a la Vienna sign on the gate to announce that she was open for business, then sat back, waiting to see how many of her old customers would show up. It didn't take long before they were at her door, more from curiosity than to bring work. They all wanted to know why she left town so abruptly over seven years ago and what happened to her since. Angela first told them that she had better opportunities in Vienna, but she missed Sopron too much to stay away any longer. Her answer, however, was met with skepticism; it didn't satisfy the ladies. They remembered the hushed rumors back then that she was forced out of her home, and they knew there must be more to her story. Some of the ladies politely kept fishing for a better explanation; others came right out without beating around the bush—was it true that her father kicked her out?

Angela hesitated, but only for a moment. She knew the truth must come out sooner or later, and that stalling for time would not stop the questions; it would only create new ones and encourage speculation. She decided it was best if she told them now what had happened, and be done with it. She kept the story short, acknowledging that she left Sopron to be with a man she loved and they were planning to be married, but he disappeared shortly before the wedding. By then she was pregnant. What happened to him was an unsolved mystery; no one ever heard from him again, not her, not his family, not the police. He could still be alive, but after so many years he was considered dead.

Ears immediately perked up. Man she loved? Not married? Pregnant? They were prepared to hear a spicy story but this was scandalous! This was not the Angela they used to know and admire! If it's true, then the little girl they all thought belonged to that new woman in the house must be Angela's daughter! Had she no shame, to come back here acting like nothing had changed?

The news spread fast, raising eyebrows, as Angela knew it would. She only hoped the gossiping would die down as soon as something else ignited the imagination of the good people of Sopron. With time, they'd get used to her situation and accept her as if she were a young widow bringing up a child without a father.

Not everyone condemned her; there were those who felt sorry for her and openly said so. She deserved better! She was too young, too innocent when it happened; she never had the chance to get to know men during those years when she was struggling to care for her family. Besides, what happened to her was an old story. Like many others, she probably fell victim to some self-indulgent brute without a conscience, a rat who took advantage of her innocence, seduced her, then when she got into trouble, treacherously skipped town, leaving her to cope alone with the shame and rejection.

Of the two factions, those who regarded Angela's misfortune as a forgivable moral stumble tended to be younger and more open-minded, while the older women saw her as a fallen woman who could blame no one but herself. For them, once disgraced, her previous good conduct and excellent reputation lost its merit.

Angela remained calm, trying to weather the storm that blew around her. In her usual way, she was polite and friendly to everyone; still, it hurt when people snubbed her greeting, or crossed to the other side to avoid her on the street. If at church or at some other social gathering she overheard a derogatory remark directed at her, she pretended not to hear. For the sake of her daughter she even endured an occasional direct slight without a word of protest. So far Lensie was spared from humiliation; she was safe at home, but Angela knew that come September when she would begin school, the shield that now protected her would be too fragile to withstand the cruel blows.

The day Angela went to enroll Lensie at the Sisters of Mercy, a nearby parochial school, she asked to speak to the Mother Superior. The nun remembered her from the time when she was a student herself and listened sympathetically as she described Lensie's situation, assuring Angela that Lensie would be treated like any of the other children; their school did not discriminate.

"Oh, I know that, the sisters were always kind and fair to all of us in school," Angela said. "What I am concerned about is her classmates, and whether you can prevent the mocking and teasing that I am afraid will start once the children find out about her. It's always great fun for children to pick on someone who is different for whatever reason. They just don't know better; they don't realize how much their behavior can hurt. And my daughter is such a spirited and outgoing little girl. I need your help to keep that spirit intact and save her from heartache."

"Angela, you know that we teach our children from the start that they are equal in all respects. But you must not forget that Lensie will be new in the class, so naturally the others will be curious about her—who she is, where she came from, and yes, because it is the habit of youngsters to brag about their fathers, the question of who her father is very likely to come up. I understand your concern, and I'll see to it that when her teacher introduces her to the class she will not refer to her family background. What the children will say or do when not under strict supervision I cannot say, but if we notice any kind of teasing or confrontation, we'll certainly stop it. And that's about all I can promise. Look, in a little while she will blend in and as soon as a new boy or girl comes aboard, her classmates will lose interest in her and switch their attention to the newcomer."

There was nothing much left for Angela to do but wait and see. On the first day of school she could hardly wait for Lensie to come home and find out what, if anything, happened.

"Well Lensie, how did you like your new school?" she asked, trying to sound casual.

"It was fine Mama, the sisters are very nice; I like Sister Adele the most. Look, she gave me this welcoming gift, a picture of the Virgin Mary holding the baby Jesus. Isn't it beautiful? She said to keep it next to my bed and ask her to remember me when I say my evening prayer. And she said if I do that, she will protect me and I'll never be abandoned."

"Sister Adele is right about that. We'll get a nice little frame for it and put it on your nightstand. But tell me, what else did you do in school. Did you meet all the other girls?"

"Yes, everyone, we all had to stand up and say our names. And there are boys in the class too, but only three: Tibor, Janos and Zoltan. It's funny, because in Vienna we only had girls."

"Each school has its own rules, but I think having boys there is a good idea. You know how they like to tease girls, to make fun of them, but if they go to school together, they will learn to get along better. I hope they were nice to you. I mean all your classmates. Remember what I told you, that they might not be very friendly at first."

"I know what you told me, and it's true, they did not say much to me, and kept pretty much to themselves. There is one other girl who is also new and we stayed together. This was only during breaks when we were let outside to play; back inside Dori, that's the new girl, and I had to sit at different desks."

Angela felt relieved. Perhaps she really had no reason to worry so much about how Lensie was received. She should just leave it up to the nuns to see that the children got along. After all, that was their job, part of their training. And as the weeks passed without an incident, she became more confident about the smooth integration of her daughter.

Lensie loved going to school, and just like in Vienna, here, too, the nuns quickly grew very fond of her. They also discovered, again like in Vienna, that she had artistic talents; she could act and also had a lovely voice. It was no surprise that as Christmas approached and the sisters began planning their traditional holiday festivities, they picked Lensie to portray the Holy Mother in the reenactment of the Nativity scene. Traditionally, the children would recite their lines, but this year they decided to introduce something quite new: to make use of Lensie's voice they wrote a lullaby that she would sing to the baby Jesus.

Lensie was thrilled, and so was Angela. To her this was another encouraging sign of acceptance. Still, when mothers and nannies gathered to watch their little darlings at rehearsals, she stayed away and sent Sofie instead. Unfortunately, it didn't make any difference. Some of the women knew about Lensie's circumstances and when they saw her cast in the part, they raised objections to an illegitimate child portraying the Virgin Mary. As their voices got louder and Sister Adele learned of their complaint, she stopped the rehearsal and dismissed the children for the day, except Lensie. She waited until everyone left, then told Sofie she needed to see Angela first thing in the morning.

Unaware of the uproar she caused, Lensie was still on cloud nine for being singled out to portray the Blessed Mother. She was convinced that because she prayed to her every day it was due to her influence that she was given the role. She talked of nothing else, and when Angela took her to school the next day instead of Sofie, she assumed it was to check on her performance.

"Mama, if you are coming to see me rehearse, it's too early, you know," she said. "You will have to wait until classes are over."

"No darling, I am coming because Sister Adele sent for me."

"Why?"

"I don't know; we'll find out when we get there."

It was only half the truth. Angela knew from Sofie about the problem with Lensie's role, but not the extent of it. Sitting in the nun's office with Lensie tucked in the corner out of earshot, she was most anxious to find out more.

"What is it Sister, what happened yesterday? Is it something Lensie did?"

"No, nothing of the sort; she is a very sweet child, talented too, and we are happy to have her. Regardless, I am sorry to tell you that we have to take her out of the Nativity scene."

"But why? Please, Sister Adele, don't do that to her. It'll break her heart! She was so thrilled when you chose her for the part of the Blessed Mother. She is so devoted to her, praying to her every night."

"I am truly sorry, Angela, but some of the mothers are complaining about our choice, a child born out-of-wedlock given the role of the Virgin Mary. We had quite an argument about it, but they are adamant that being illegitimate, she is not fit to portray the Holy Mother. Please understand, sometimes we must compromise. It's unfortunate that some people think this way but they can stir up sentiments, and before you know it, the whole thing is blown out of proportion. In a sense, by removing Lensie we are protecting her. This kind of scandalous gossip can easily get out of hand to the point when we can no longer control it, and we surely don't want that to happen, do we? I know Lensie will be disappointed; perhaps she can play something else—one of the angels, if that would make her feel better?"

"Sister Adele, she has her heart set on playing the Holy Mother, and you yourself said she has the talent to do it! Isn't there some way you can reason with these people that she is just a child, that the play is not about her, but about celebrating the birth of our Savior?"

"Angela, don't you think I tried that? I pleaded with them that if for no other reason, consider the spirit of Christmas, but it was to no avail. They are wrong, of course, and it's not fair that Lensie will have to suffer for their blind prejudice, but I am afraid, she must be told the truth. I will try my best not to hurt her when I explain why we have to take her out of the scene."

Angela's heart sank as she glanced at her daughter waiting in the far corner, so innocent, so trusting. She felt her eyes smarting with tears. So this was when pain would make its first mark on her young life. The rejection would be hurtful enough, but learning the real reason for it would be devastating! No, she wouldn't let that happen!

"Please Sister, you can't tell her the truth! She is too young to understand what born out-of-wedlock means! She never heard the word illegitimate! All she knows that her father disappeared before she was born and is assumed dead. Please, there must be some other way to explain why she is removed, there just got to be another way . . ."

The nun looked at the unsuspecting little girl. She felt pity for her, but what could she do? It would do more harm in the end if she made up a story, only to have the truth come out later. And Angela should not forget that she was a nun; she made a vow never to lie!

As if seeking help from above, she lifted her eyes and remained staring at the ceiling for what seemed to Angela the longest time, but when she finally looked at her again, her eyes were softer. "Well, maybe there is something we can do," the nun said tapping her mouth with her index finger. "We could tell her that she is needed in the choir, since a strong chorus is more important for the entire presentation than one little lullaby Mary sings to her son. And because we couldn't find anyone to replace her, someone who could sing as well as she does, we decided to do away with her solo altogether and present the Nativity scene as we always did, the traditional way, using dialogue only. What do you think, Angela? We would be stretching the truth a little, but I am sure we'll be forgiven."

It was a perfect solution. Lensie wouldn't feel slighted that her role went to someone else, and the explanation would also satisfy the other children's curiosity about the change. Angela couldn't thank the Sister enough for finding a clever way to avoid hurting her little girl. But the nun raised her hand in caution.

"Let's hope it will work, Angela. It will put a stop to the complaining, but what the parents say about it at home is another matter. If they discuss the incident within the family, it's likely that the children will pick up on it, and if that happens, the truth will trickle down into the schoolroom, and no matter how we try to prevent it, the teasing will start about Lensie's predicament. Have you ever thought of what to say to her then, how to tell her that the real problem is that you and her father were never married?"

"A thousand times, but I still don't know what to do when the time comes. I hoped you might help me how to answer Lensie when she starts asking questions about her birth. In your experience, you must have had similar situations. How should I handle it? What did others do?"

The nun promised to talk to another sister who was more qualified to give her some advice, then closed the discussion. Children started to arrive, and so Angela kissed her daughter goodbye and left. She spent the rest of the morning worrying about how Lensie would react to losing her role, and waited impatiently until she returned from school. She searched her face for signs of disappointment, but there was none. She acted as nothing happened, telling all about what they learned that day, mentioning almost as an afterthought that the nuns transferred her to the choir, because she was needed there more. She even sounded proud that they couldn't do without her.

It seemed that all went well; there was no reason for Angela to fret. But it was just the calm before the storm. It did not take long before Sister Adele sent for her again, this time to alert her that as she predicted, some of the children were caught whispering about Lensie. It was just a matter of time before they would openly confront her. Certainly not when the nuns were around, but children will find a way. She also told her that the sisters had discussed her situation and thought it best if Lensie learned the truth. She would understand better why her classmates singled her out if she knew the facts about her birth. And if Angela wished Sister Adele be present, she would gladly give support; it might lessen the impact if the child saw that the sisters did not condemn her.

Angela replied that she wanted to think it over before deciding what would be the best way to handle it. Time, however, ran out for her; the inevitable happened before she could make up her mind. Picking up Lensie from school a few days after the warning, Sofie found her in a sullen mood. Instead of her usual chatty way, she walked without talking and would only say there was nothing wrong when Sofie probed further.

Arriving home, the minute Angela saw her daughter's gloomy face she knew that what she feared most came true. And when Lensie wouldn't touch her food during lunch, she took her by the hand and led her into a room where they could be alone.

"Sweetheart, I know something is troubling you," Angela said, lifting her little girl's chin, "and I think I know what it is, but first let me ask you if what makes you sad has anything to do with your father?"

Her eyes downcast, Lensie nodded without a word.

"I see. You heard some of your classmates saying bad things about him, right?"

Another nod.

"Did you hear them say that you don't have a father, is that it Lensie?"

This time she looked at Angela and there was fierce defiance in her eyes. "Yes, that's what they told me and they laughed at me, but I told them that I did have a father; it's just that he died. But they didn't believe me and kept laughing, and I don't know why. There was nothing funny about what I said. Then I told them, well, what about Marika, she does not have a father, either, but they never laugh at her! This is another girl in school, you know. And they said yes, but her father is buried in the cemetery and mine isn't, and that's because I never had one at all. Then they started singing, 'Lensie has no Papa, only a bad Mama' until one of the sisters came and forbade them. They stopped but when she walked away, they still kept humming it in my ear. Did you do anything bad, Mama? Why are they saying such things?"

"It's because they don't know any better, Lensie. They tease you because our circumstances are different from theirs—I will explain that in a minute—and you know how children are; they love to pick on anyone who is different. Now tell me, what else did they say? I want to know everything that happened."

"Well, they called me a name." She lowered her eyes again and would not go on until Angela coaxed her, that she must tell so she could do something about it.

"They called me a bastard," she blurted out and when she raised her head to look at Angela, her eyes were brimming with tears. "What does it mean, Mama? Why are they calling me that name? I did not do anything bad, but I think that word makes me bad."

"Lensie, I will answer you, but first tell me, where were you when this happened?"

It was exactly as Sister Adele predicted, outside during a break. Angela knew that it was hard to control children at play but she must talk to the sisters and ask for increased supervision. Then she pulled her daughter into her arms, stroking her hair.

"Lensie, of course you didn't do anything wrong, you are a wonderful little girl; people who know you all love you, and I want you to remember that. But you are right in one thing. That word is not nice, and I am sure the children who used it don't know what it means. They just heard it from their parents, and they know it has something to do with not having a father, so they repeat it to your face. I will try to explain the meaning of it, and that stupid little rhyme as well, but it's very hard, because children at your age are too young to understand such things. You see, the parents of your classmates are married to each other, which means that they made a vow in Church in front of a priest that they would love each other until they die. That ceremony makes a man and a woman in the eye of the law husband and wife, and when God sends them children, they raise them together.

"It is in this sense that our situation is different, Lensie, and perhaps you will understand why when I tell you what happened with us. When I met your father, we loved each other just as much as any other couple, and we were making plans to be married in the Church. And when God saw how happy we were, how much we loved each other, he decided to send you to us to become our little girl. Then suddenly, without warning, your father disappeared before we had a chance to be married. You were on your way when that happened, and I was sick with worry that God would take you back. But because I wanted you more than anything else in this world, God let me keep you. And this is why people say that you have no father, not because you didn't have one, but because we lost him before we could get married. Some people—not all, but some—think that only married couples should have children and so they came up with that bad word to mark those born to mothers who were not married. It does not mean that the woman or her child is bad; it only means that the people who invented that world have bad judgment. They can't stand it if somebody is different from them. You are a smart girl, Lensie; you know that all people can't possibly be the same. We can only hope that one day these people will realize how wrong they are, but until that time they will continue to be hurtful and teach their children to think and behave the same mean way.

"So you see, you can't really blame your schoolmates for repeating what they hear at home; they don't really know what they are saying. You must forgive them and try to accept that you can't change them. The more you fight them and the more they see that they can upset you, the more they will keep at it. I know, it will not be easy, but if you just ignore them, eventually they will get tired of the teasing and stop. Some might even take the time to get to know you, and when they see what's in your heart, they might even become your friends. Until then you will have to be patient and be nice to everyone, but just keep to the girls who are friendly to you. Do you think you can do that, or at least try?"

Lensie listened to every word Angela said, but just stood there, as if sorting out what she heard.

"What are you thinking, Lensie? I know it's hard to understand everything I told you, and if you want me to explain some part of it again, don't be afraid to ask."

"No Mama, I think I understood most of what you said," Lensie looked at Angela tilting her head slightly. "We are different because you and Papa were not married when I was born. This is really why they say that I have no father, not because he disappeared or died." She paused for a moment, then her serious little face brightened. "But Mama, that can be changed! All we have to do is find a new father, you and he will be married in the Church, and then they can't call me bad names anymore!"

Surprised at her young daughter's logic Angela smiled to herself. *My clever little girl! Let her come up with an answer!* And although she knew that it would never happen, she tried not to dampen her hopes by outright denial.

"Yes, if I was lucky enough to find a man I could love as much as I loved your father, we could get married," she pretended to go along with Lensie. "It would be wonderful to have someone, and he, too, would be very lucky to have you as a daughter! The only problem is that I am not so young anymore, Lensie.

If I did not meet such a man in all the years we lived in Vienna, what chance do I have now that I am getting old and more set in my ways?"

"But Mama, you are not old! Aunt Pollinger is old, but not you! And I will help you to look for a husband! You know that I love you, Mama, but I'd love so much to have a father too."

"I know, sweetheart, I know. We will try to look." Angela was almost in tears when she saw the yearning in Lensie's eyes. "But until we find him, promise me you will do as I asked, be nice to all the children in school, and just ignore those who tease you. Will you promise me that?"

Lensie gave her solemn promise, and from that day on she pretended not to hear the insults. *Let them call me names while they can,* she gritted her teeth. *It will not be for long! I will find a new father, and when I do, I'll make sure he and Mama get married so no one can ever laugh at me again!*

A few days later Angela confronted the sisters about the incident and was told they had already called together the parents whose children were bullying Lensie and told them such behavior would not be tolerated. They reminded them that everyone was equal in God's eyes and berated them that they ought to set a better example for their children than teach them bigotry. They also emphasized not to discuss adult matters at home when the children could hear them.

More than that they couldn't do. Their stern criticism, however, seemed to produce results, or perhaps the children simply got bored with their cruel games, since the insults slowly diminished and eventually stopped. And as weeks turned into months the hurtful gossiping about Angela eased, too. Some righteous diehards still ostracized her, but most folks looked at her with empathy as an unfortunate woman who had suffered enough, and a hardworking mother trying to raise a child the best she could under the circumstances.

It took a year of adjustment but slowly, by the summer of 1914, Angela's little family settled into a pleasant, enjoyable everyday life. Lensie had just finished second grade, while Mitzie at fifteen, after graduating from *polgari*—a middle school from grades five to eight—left for a long stay with Gertie. Lizzie was helping a great deal around the house, but Angela made sure that upon turning sixteen she put in her first appearance on the social scene. She was the prettiest, if not the smartest, of all the Bohaczek sisters with her honey blond hair, sparkling blue eyes, and curvy figure. She was vivacious, always cheerful with an infectious laugh and a genuine desire to please. No one could stay in a sour mood for long in her company. With her looks and shapely ankles peeking from under the shorter skirts that had come into fashion recently, she had no problem attracting young men, and soon she was high on the list for invitations to balls and parties.

Angela suspected that she would lose her soon to some young man, but to her surprise, Lizzie turned out to be quite choosy. She didn't like this one, could not stand the other, and would not marry the third if he were the only man left on earth. She had endless excuses, until one day during early summer Angela took her and Lensie to an outing in Vienna. As usual, they wound up in the Prater, the popular amusement park, where the girls immediately headed for the giant Ferris wheel. It always drew the biggest crowd with a long wait to get on, which didn't bother them. Angela, however, was not about to stand in line when she had taken the ride many times before. She'd sit it out this time.

The buckets had three seats and when it was finally the girls' turn to board, a young man hopped in next to Lizzie. His name was Guido Guerini and in the twenty minutes it took to reach the top, Lizzie knew she had found her perfect man. Within a year she changed her name to Frau Guerini and moved to join her husband and his family in Vienna. Originally, Guido and his parents—his Italian father and Viennese mother—lived in Tuscany, the lovely northern part of Italy, but made the move to Vienna when she inherited some amusement stands in the Prater. One was a ball-throwing stall, another a shooting gallery with rows of moving ducks, and a third, a miniature train ride for small children. Lizzie happily took over the ball-throwing booth from her mother-in-law; it was a perfect outlet for her outgoing nature. She was in her element calling out to customers, encouraging others to buy another round of balls, or chasing away children trying to use their own balls. A year later, after the birth of their son, Guido, Jr., she stayed home to raise the child, but when the boy was older she readily went back to the Prater.

The only time Lizzie's joyful spirit deserted her was when a few years later she suffered a miscarriage and was told she could not risk having another child. After growing up with eight brothers and sisters it was especially hard for her to accept that there would be no more babies in her Guerini family.

CHAPTER TWO

1914 - 1934

Jeno

AS SOPRON WAS a border town between Hungary and Austria, in the northern region lying near the Slovak border was another small town, Selmec. Nestled in the lower slopes of Hungary's majestic mountain range, the High Tatras, it was famous for its University of Mining, Smelting, and Forestry, established in 1770 by Maria Theresia, the Empress of Austria and Queen of Hungary.

The core of this fully accredited university was a small academy called the School of Mining funded in 1735 by Charles III of Austria (later renamed Holy Roman Emperor Charles VI). It was one of the first schools in Europe to provide better-educated managers for the developing mining industry. To head the school, the emperor appointed Samuel Mikoviny, a well-known Hungarian mathematician, geologist, engineer, and cartographer.

Mikoviny, the son of an evangelist cleric born in 1700 in Abelfalva, Hungary, was educated at various European universities, spending most of his time at the University of Nuremberg in Bavaria, Germany. Returning home, he set to work, first surveying and mapping the mining fields of Hungary and making the first topographic map of the entire country, then building canals to divert water from the oozing wetlands around the royal seat of Buda. When the swamps dried up, the area yielded one of the richest coal mines in Hungary. By the age of twenty-seven he was married and settled in Pozsony, the then-capital of Hungary (now Bratislava of Slovakia), and it was there in 1735 that he received his appointment to head the mining school in Selmec.

Three generations later, in 1792, his great-granddaughter Eva married Ignacz Zachar, one of the graduates of the University, and from there on, according to family lore, the Zachar name was ever-present in the student registry. And no wonder: Adam Zachar, the great-great grandson of Samuel Mikoviny, sired sixteen children by two wives, and out of this brood ten of his sons were graduates of the university. Not all were mining engineers, though. Seduced by the lush forestry and variegated fauna around Selmec, some of the boys abandoned the family tradition of studying mining or metallurgy and chose forest engineering instead, a new faculty added in 1808. One of the "renegades" was Gyula, the sixth child of Adam, born in 1854, who after graduating took a position in nearby Besztercebanya to manage a large estate owned by the Crown.

The place around Selmec was postcard perfect, with towering mountains and bottomless crystal clear pools formed after the ice age. Farther down, where the slopes flattened into green meadows, shade-giving trees invited picnickers to spread out a blanket and enjoy the tranquil scenery. It was at such a picnic in the late summer days of 1884 that Gyula Zachar met his future wife, pretty Maria Plech. Her family lived near Pozsony, but that fall she and her two sisters, Anna and Nella, were sent to spend a few months with their aunt in Selmec to enjoy the bustling social activities the college town offered and perhaps to find suitable husbands for the girls. Characteristic of small towns with all-male universities, Selmec was a magnet for young ladies of marriageable age; there were endless invitations to parties and picnics before the new semester began, followed by the first ball of the season, the traditional "Balek Ball," held every year to welcome the new crop of freshmen, the so-called baleks. These activities gave mothers and daughters a chance to observe all the available bachelors, while the boys were equally busy checking out the young ladies on parade. The Plech girls were particularly popular; they were attractive, but it also helped that their uncle happened to be an esteemed member of the faculty.

Among the three girls Nella, at sixteen, was the youngest and prettiest and the most sought-after. Anna was twenty-two already, but with her youthful looks and peachy complexion, nobody guessed her true age. Between them stood eighteen-year-old Maria, a willowy girl with a heart-shaped face, light brown hair, and blue eyes beaming with intelligence. She was pretty with an attractive figure, although not in the way the heroines were portrayed in the currently popular novels. Fashion in the 1880s favored women with slightly plump bodies and ample bosoms, both of which she lacked, but with hoop skirts and padded corsets, her slight shortcomings were easily camouflaged. She was the one who caught the eye of thirty-year-old Gyula Zachar.

They were married after a short courtship and immediately set out to raise a family. Their firstborn was Gyula, Jr. in 1886; then came a little girl, Etelka; a son, Jozsef; another boy named Jeno, born on November 11, 1895; and last, a baby girl, Sárika, in 1900. The older daughter died when she was only twelve, but the rest survived the various childhood illnesses long before the lifesaving immunization vaccines were developed.

Gyula, Sr. often took his sons on his surveys, pointing out the various trees and plants by their Latin names to give the boys a head start for the time they would be entering the university to represent the Zachar family's next generation of forest engineers. Although four-year-old Jeno had a long way before sitting in lecture halls, he loved to tag along with his father, always on the lookout for juicy berries to pick. On one such occasion he noticed a large bush full of ripe blackberries, a temptation he found too hard to resist. Only after his father's repeated calling did he leave the bush and run to catch up with him.

"Where were you and what kept you so long?" his father scolded him. "I told you a hundred times not to wander away! You are too young to be alone out here!"

"I was just picking some blackberries, and I was not alone. There was a big black man picking berries on the other side of the bush," little Jeno said defensively.

"A black man—what black man are you talking about?" his father asked, somewhat alarmed; then, grabbing his son's hand, he headed back without waiting for an answer. "Let's see if he is still there!"

When they reached the spot near the bush he readied his gun and motioned to the boy to keep quiet. The next second, hearing the sound of heavy stumping and twigs snapping, a noise typical of a large animal running, he froze. Pushing his son behind him, he raised his shotgun just as he saw a brown bear disappearing between the trees. He picked up little Jeno and hurried from the scene as fast as he could, not taking any chance that the bear would return for a second helping.

Once on safe grounds he put the boy down and, crouching to his level, spoke in a calm but firm voice. "This is your lucky day, son; it was not a man you saw there but a big bear that could have killed you with one flap of his paw." He let it sink in before continuing in a sterner tone, "I know your mother reads you stories about lovable teddy bears, but that kind of bear lives only in your picture books. Here in the forest they are for real, they are dangerous and we must be on the lookout for them at all time. So from now on, unless you promise to stay by my side, I won't take you along anymore. Do you understand?"

Frightened by what his father said, he mumbled a weak promise, but in his heart he knew it would take a long time before he would come near the forest again. He'd rather stay home and play in their backyard. Then, remembering his mother's blackberry bushes, he felt his heart jump. "There are no bears in our garden, are there?" he asked in a small voice. Although his father assured him that bears and other wild animals stay in the forest and he had nothing to fear at home, it took a while before he ventured near the bushes. At first he circled around cautiously, making threatening noises, and only after thrusting his toy shotgun through the branches a few times, dared to get close enough to pick the berries. His older brothers teased him relentlessly, calling him a scaredy cat and a sissy, but he did not care. Let the bear eat the big bullies, he thought, and continued to keep to the security of their home. Perhaps it was because of the fright over the bear encounter that later, when entering the university, he refused to follow in his father's footsteps, and unlike his two brothers, chose to study metallurgy instead of forestry.

He was an average student who loved sports and wanted nothing more than to join the soccer team. When he was rejected because of his slight built, he took up fencing and became very good at it, winning competition after competition. But where he really excelled was on the tennis court. There he found his niche. He was quick on his feet and could hit the ball with surprising strength and accuracy. It made him a sought-after tennis partner, especially in mixed doubles, where his handsome looks, dark wavy hair and deep blue eyes gave him extra leverage with the ladies. He enjoyed the game, but still, it was not soccer! Ironically, it was tennis that finally got him onto the soccer team. Watching him playing a set, his good coordination and fast reaction to the ball caught the eye of the soccer coach. His team recently lost its goalie, and when he invited Jeno for a try out, he made the cut easily.

Jeno was also an enthusiastic supporter of the strong patriotic movement that existed in Hungary's northern region bordering Slovakia. Its aim was to nurture and promote the spirit of Hungary and protect all that was Hungarian against Slavic influences. Clashes with the Slovak minorities were not uncommon, and when conflicts flared, even minor disagreements could escalate into dangerous confrontations. To reduce the threat, whenever rumors started that a group of Slovaks planned to raise a ruckus, the Hungarian community rallied to stop it before it could get out of hand.

The Zachar boys were avid participants in these activities. Although their family name, Zachar, was not Hungarian—it thought to have derived from the Czech word for sugar, "sacharin"—and the maiden name of their mother, Plech, was pure Slavic, for generations the Zachar family ardently considered itself one hundred percent Hungarian, and the children were all brought up to be proud of their Hungarian nationality.

This ethnic feud was nothing new. Its roots went back to the year 896 when the Magyars, a group of seven nomadic tribes made up of fast-riding warrior horsemen and led by their chief, grand prince Arpad, arrived at the Carpathian Mountains and rode into present-day Hungary. They found the land sparsely populated, various ethnic people living in far-apart settlements, all peacefully plowing their fields and tending their flocks. None were a match for these fierce, rampaging raiders from the East, and so, rather than risking bloodshed, the locals willingly paid homage to them. Words quickly spread about the ferocious war tactics of the Magyars and their cruelty to all who resisted, prompting priests everywhere to recite a special prayer besieging God to save the people from the arrows of the Hungarians.

Their easy victories carried the conquerors across the Carpathian Basin until they reached Moravia, a country occupied mostly by Slovaks. There the Hungarians found themselves facing a well-organized nation ruled by a king who could easily assemble an army to challenge them on the battlefield. According to legend, rather than risk fighting, the chieftains decided to dupe the Slovaks into submission. They invited the king to a peaceful meeting held in an open field where they presented him with a magnificent stallion harnessed with gold and precious stones and a saddle made of the finest leather.

Taking it as a sign of goodwill, the king accepted the gift, and wishing to reciprocate, invited Arpad to choose something equivalent in return. To his surprise the chief only asked for a handful of earth and some water from the nearby river. The king found it a strange request, but then these were strange people, and he willingly obliged. He scooped up a clump of earth and to show his generosity, used a gold goblet when dipping into the water. Handing them to Arpad the chief praised him lavishly for saving his land from plunder and the people from slaughter by accepting the exchange.

"Exchange? What exchange?" asked the confused king. When he finally understood the meaning of what had taken place, that in the mind of the Hungarians he had sold his country for the horse, it was too late to back out. He was surrounded by Arpad's soldiers and was powerless to do anything, but from that day forward the Slovaks never forgot or forgave the Hungarians for steeling their land with such a dastardly and treacherous act.

The long-festering ethnic hatred against Hungary deepened further when in 1867 the country was granted full partnership with Austria and given more authority than any of the other nations that made up the newly created Austro-Hungarian Empire. Leading up to the birth of this so-called Dual Monarchy were the turbulent nationalistic uprisings that sprang up nearly twenty years earlier, threatening Imperial Austria with disintegration. As the oppressed states rose one by one against their common Habsburg ruler, Hungary, too, joined the fight for independence. It started on March 15, 1848 when a revolt broke out in Budapest sparked by a young and prolific poet named Sandor Petofi. He has written a fiercely patriotic poem, urging all Hungarians to rise up, the time was now or never to throw off their shackles. His powerful call to freedom, recited from a platform at an anti-Habsburg demonstration, inflamed the crowd, sending thousands into the streets, demanding independence from Austria.

The popular struggle for freedom was fought with high idealism and heroic courage, but without adequate military backing it was doomed to failure, especially when Tsar Nicolas I intervened at the request of his ally, Emperor Franz Joseph. Squeezed between the superior forces of Austria and Russia, the revolution had no chance to succeed. The twenty-six-year-old Petofi was among the casualties, struck down by a Russian sword, and even though his body was never found, his fame didn't die with him; it lives on to the present as the nation's greatest poet. His famous patriotic poem of 1848 proved to be equally inflammatory when it was recited on the eve of another revolution in 1956, this time against the ruthless domination of Stalinist Russia.

The defeated Hungarian army, to show their hatred for the Habsburgs, refused to surrender to the Austrians and instead, on August 13, 1849, laid down their arms at Világos to the Russians. Their leader, Lajos Kossuth, escaped into exile, but thirteen of his generals were hanged on October 6, 1849 at the city of Arad. Sixteen years of brutal oppression followed, until a compromise was finally reached on May 29, 1867. According to its terms, the country was re-established as the Kingdom of Hungary, a separate sovereign nation with its own Parliament and Prime Minister, but still united with Austria under their common ruler, Emperor Franz Joseph of Austria, known in Hungary as King Jozsef I after he and his wife, the beautiful Queen Elisabeth, were crowned in Budapest on June 8, 1867.

This pacified the rebellious Hungarians, but their elevated status drew the ire of the other minority nations. They deeply resented that Hungary now had more freedom and authority in conducting its internal affairs than they did. The festering ethnic hatred directed against Hungary was perhaps the only common ground between these ever-bickering neighboring countries. Although the Dual Monarchy ceased to exist after World War I, the nationalistic envy toward Hungary still exists today, especially on the parts of Slovakia and Romania.

The Great War

WHILE THE ETHNIC conflicts between students and the Slovak minorities in Selmec continued, the occasional head butting never got out of hand and didn't interfere with life at the university. College boys, including Jeno, sat listening in lecture halls, competed in sports, and flirted with girls, not necessarily in that order. Then came June 28, 1914, a day that changed their lives and brought disaster to Hungary.

The shot fired on that day by a Serbian assassin in Sarajevo, the capital of Bosnia-Herzegovina, killed Archduke Francis Ferdinand, the heir apparent to the throne of Austria-Hungary, and ignited the fire that set Europe ablaze and eventually engulfed the entire world. The West tried to solve the crisis through diplomacy, but to no avail. On July 28 Austria declared war on Serbia, an act that changed the course of history.

The outbreak of the war was greeted with enthusiastic hurrahs by Hungary's youth. In a burst of nationalistic sentiment, flags were unfurled and proudly displayed, and everywhere the sound of patriotic songs filled the air. Young men talked of nothing but the war and volunteered in droves long before the army stepped up its recruiting campaign.

Seventeen-year-old Miska Bohaczek's reaction was no different. He couldn't wait to quit his job at the post office and join the military. He parroted slogans that screamed from every billboard, calling all men to the defense of the Motherland, and when Angela tried to dissuade him, he argued back that he wanted to be like his brother Jozsef, already serving the country. It was the right thing to do for every able-bodied man in time of war!

"Miska, Miska, you are just too naive!" Angela pleaded with him. "Love for one's country is fine, but what about love for one's family? Doesn't that mean anything to you? This house is full of women and children—we need you here! It's enough if one of you will be fighting! Please try to see it my way; at least don't volunteer. The army will find you soon enough if the war is not over in a short time."

Her reasoning was sound, but not convincing enough to change the foolish boy's mind. Her only hope was that by the time Miska was through with training the war might be over. The Serbs would be taught a hard lesson for their crime against the Empire, and the boys would be home by Christmas, if not sooner. Who would have believed that it would take four bloody years for them to come back, if they were lucky at all to have survived?

The confrontation between Austria and Serbia soon exploded into a world holocaust that crushed all hope for a speedy conclusion. By May 15, 1915 much of Europe was at war: Russia, France, Great Britain, and Italy against Austria, Hungary, and Germany. At first it seemed that the German army was unstoppable, winning a crucial victory in August 1914 at Tannenberg in East Prussia (today's Poland), but soon they suffered a great defeat by the French at the Ardennes on the Western Front. From there on, the war was fought from hundreds of miles of dugout trenches with deadly attacks and counterattacks, causing tremendous casualties on both sides. One of the bloodiest onslaughts took place in the spring of 1916 at Verdun, where losses amounted to nearly 375,000 on the French side and 340,000 for the Germans, with a high percentage of fatalities.

As if conducting war on two fronts was not enough, the British also challenged the Germans on the high seas. They began a naval blockade to cut off enemy supply lines, to which Germany replied by launching its famous U-boats. One of their first victims was the *Lusitania*, the great British luxury passenger liner with 1,959 aboard, torpedoed on May 7, 1915 on its way from New York to Liverpool. It sank within eighteen minutes, killing 1,198 people, many of them American citizens.

Other new weapons were also introduced. The Germans began using poison gas and flamethrowers, plus carried out air attacks not only against military targets, but also on major cities, inflicting extensive damage on civilian populations. On the other side the British rolled out their first tanks with devastating effects. Crushing over the German dugouts, they created such panic that if the West had even a relatively small fleet, they could have ended the war right then and there.

With every passing year, hope for victory was fading and uncertainty grew. People thought that the death of Franz Joseph on November 21, 1916 would hasten the end of the war, but it only passed the baton to his grandnephew, who became Emperor Karl I of Austria and King Karoly IV of Hungary, although a king in name only. Due to his deep anti-Hungarian sympathies, he never submitted to the traditional crowning with Hungary's Holy Crown, and without that, no king was ever truly recognized by the Hungarians. This crown, a most revered and sacred relic, was given by Pope Sylvester II to the country's first king, Istvan I—later canonized as Saint Istvan—in recognition for establishing Hungary as a Christian nation in the year 1000.

By the end of 1916, the Austro-Hungarian Army had suffered substantial losses and to reinforce the troops a great number of men between the ages of 18 to 35 were mobilized, amongst them Angela's two married brothers Franz and Henrich. The fact that all four Bohaczek men were now fighting on the various fronts left her frantic, especially when on April 6, 1917 the United States entered the war and U.S. troops began to arrive in France.

That same year Russia was near exhaustion and heading toward collapse. The Tsar was forced to abdicate in March, but it was too little too late. The general discontent erupted in a revolt on November 7, 1917 and the newly formed Bolshevik Socialist-dominated Soviet government put him under house arrest. The new leader, Vladimir Ilyich Lenin (formerly Ulyanov) agreed to a separate peace with Germany, and regardless of the harsh and arrogant German-dictated terms, he signed it on March 2, 1918 at Brest-Litovsk. With that, the fighting on the Eastern front ceased, but the war was far from over.

With so many men fighting, the reduced workforce at home couldn't keep up with production, and soon industrial and agricultural shortages began to appear. Rationing was introduced, not only for meat, bread, and dairy products, but also for soap, leather goods, coal, and other vital provisions. Long lines formed in front of stores where Angela, Mitzie, Sofie, and even Lensie took turns waiting, often in vain, going home empty-handed if there was nothing left by the time they got to the door.

The quality of the products declined, too. Milk was diluted, bad-tasting margarine was substituted for butter, and bread was dense and gummy from mixing cornmeal into flour. Sticky molasses took the place of sugar, and instead of lard there was only low grade cooking oil available. Thanks to the strip of land Angela owned in the Loevers and leased out to a farmer, as part of the contract she received a share of the produce that provided them with fresh vegetables and fruits. Some of it she even used for bartering, which became widespread as the value of money steadily declined and inflation set in.

On a personal level, the war actually helped Angela's situation, as it diverted people's preoccupation from the scandal that brewed about her. People simply lost interest in the triviality of personal affairs. The growing number of widows experiencing difficulties in bringing up children without a husband probably played a role in it, too. In turn, as she gained sympathy, even respect, for raising a daughter alone, her business picked up, and one by one her old customers returned, bringing others as new clients. To handle the growing workload she soon needed help and hired three additional seamstresses.

She gained further social recognition when she opened her purse to contribute generously as collections sprang up to help support families that lost breadwinners to the war. Ladies began extending invitations to her for social and charitable events and included Lensie in their children's birthday parties, picnics, and other activities. It pleased Angela greatly to see Lensie becoming popular, which increased the girl's growing self-confidence. As a sure sign of feeling more secure, she finally gave up the idea of finding a new husband for her mother. She was doing fine in school, although her interest in reading, writing and arithmetic was lagging. She probably could have done better if she had tried, but as long as her grades were passable, Angela didn't pressure her. In her opinion it was more important for a young lady to have good manners and social skills than to be a genius.

Lensie's devotion to the Church and her love of music endeared her to the nuns. At their recommendations, Angela paid for private voice and piano lessons, although she often wondered where her daughter got the talent. It must be a gift from her father, she decided, since everyone on her side of the family was born with a tin ear. She had to admit that Lensie had a lovely soprano voice and her piano recitals earned nothing but accolades, and so when her music teacher suggested that Lensie had real potential for a musical career if developed professionally, she took her to the Vienna Music Conservatory for evaluation. It made Lensie jump for joy when she was accepted, although it meant a lot more practicing. She could do her voice exercises at home, even though it drove everyone to distraction, but because Angela didn't have a piano she had to stay after classes to practice at school. Seeing her commitment, Angela promised herself to surprise her with a piano either for Christmas or for her birthday.

This perseverance was part of Lensie's nature; if she set a goal, she threw herself whole-heartedly into achieving it. On one hand Angela admired her determination, but she also worried that if things didn't turn out exactly as expected, she would be hurt and disappointed. Yes, she had certain talents, but was it enough to make her outstanding? What if her ambition led to nowhere? Angela was a realist. She would wait a few years before asking Lensie's teachers for an honest opinion, and if they were discouraging, well, she would have to find a way to steer her interest in some other direction. She knew that Lensie also liked to act; she was always in school plays, which was fine, as long as she didn't start thinking of the stage as a profession. She wouldn't let her go that route. Actresses had such questionable reputations; working in the theater was not suitable for nice girls—not for her daughter, anyway.

The promise Angela made to buy a piano for Lensie unfortunately came to nothing. As the war continued and the economy plummeted, her income also declined. She had enough work, but it consisted mostly of alterations as women tried to create new looks by updating their existing wardrobes instead of buying new outfits. That, of course, didn't bring nearly as much money as she used to get for designing and making suits, dresses and gowns, and by the and of 1917 she was forced to cut back, letting two of her seamstresses go. Still, she put up a Christmas tree and had a small gift under it for everyone. It was a sad celebration with all her brothers away at the front, huddling in some miserable dugout hundreds of miles away, longing to be home, and thinking of bygone holidays that might never come again.

Her only consolation was that in spite of mounting losses, none of them were killed or injured. Sporadic letters came, describing the dreadful conditions at the front, the inadequate supplies, shoes with cardboard soles that dissolved in the muddy trenches, and thin uniforms that lacked the warmth to keep them from freezing in the bitter cold. They also complained about the food, and how dysentery was taking its toll among the troops. It was difficult to read these letters, especially the closing lines full of yearning to be home, to embrace a wife, to hold a child.

The raucous noisemaking that usually greeted every New Year was absent in war-torn Europe that year. Instead, churches everywhere offered a special service in hope that God would listen to their prayers, grant victory, and put an end to all the suffering. Unfortunately, nothing could save Germany and its allies from sliding toward defeat. In a supreme effort, they mounted a huge offensive on the Western front that lasted from May 27 through June 6, 1918. As the fighting heated up Hungarian soldiers, under the command of Austrian and Czech officers, who cared little for Hungarians, were thrown in as fodder into the middle of the worst battles. Casualties were tremendous. Sadly, one of the fallen heroes who would never come home was Jozsef Bohaczek.

When Angela got the news of her brother's death, she felt more anger than grief, anger at powers that could compel young men to put on a uniform, pick up a rifle and in the name of God and country march into war to kill and be killed. And for what? Vengeance? Glory? Expansion? Would it ever stop? This lust for bloodshed must be an integral part of human nature, or Cain would never have slaughtered his brother Abel. Ever since that day the killings continued, even to the end of time, as long as two men with different ideals and goals were left on Earth to face each other. There will always be warlords to start the carnage, men insensitive to the suffering and devastation they unleash.

Angela's anger and her condemnation of war stemmed from the personal tragedy of losing a beloved brother and from fear that she could lose the other three, too, if the war continued much longer. It had little to do with politics, although the longer the war dragged on, the closer her beliefs came to echo some of the preaching of the pacifist demagogues and Bolshevik agitators who sprang up and were hard at work at home as well as behind the front lines.

Angela was still struggling to cope with the loss of her brother when in June she was struck with a life-threatening illness. It started with an insistent dull pain in her right wrist, which she tried to ignore at first. Only when it became difficult to perform simple tasks did she go to her doctor. After an initial examination, he referred her to a bone specialist for further tests. She didn't think it was necessary, and pooh-poohed the doctor's concern. Didn't they always frighten the patients with the worst scenario? What bone disease was he talking about? She had probably pricked her finger with a needle, causing some infection that spread to her wrist and could be cleared up in no time. Or perhaps it was the early onset of rheumatism, no more than that.

Unfortunately, when at the doctor's insistence she saw the specialist, tests confirmed the impossible. She was diagnosed with advanced tuberculosis of her wrist bone and was told that unless it was amputated immediately, it would spread through her entire arm and eventually could cost her life. The news struck Angela with a force that made her lose her usual stoic calm. This could not happen to her! Her right hand was her livelihood! How was she going to survive, to provide for her family?

The first wave of panic hit her with the harsh reality of her desperate situation. The ground gave away and she found herself sliding toward a black void from where there was no escape. It took a minute before the doctor brought her back, all the while talking to her in a soothing yet firm voice.

"Now Angela, it is not the end of the world. I have patients who lost arms and legs, yet carried on courageously, just as you will with time and patience. You know how lucky you are that we caught it early? You could have easily died if not treated. Yes, you will lose your hand, but we will fit you with an artificial one, and with therapy and training to use your left hand more efficiently, you will be able to do almost everything."

Seeing the desperation and hopelessness in her eyes he kept on talking, as if to a bewildered child who was lost and couldn't find a way to safety. "I know you are a strong woman, Angela, so don't lose faith now. You were saddled with some tough problems in your life but you always handled them admirably, so what makes you think you can't tackle this one? Think of all the severe injuries the war inflicted on our soldiers; they are coming home maimed, blind, disfigured, but do they give up? No, they learn to live without limbs, or if sightless, adjust living in darkness. They survive and go on. Take courage from their example. Compare yourself to their sufferings and perhaps you might find it a little easier to accept your situation."

She heard the words, but they failed to comfort her. She could bear the disfigurement, the personal discomfort, but what would she do when robbed of her capabilities? Without her right hand she wouldn't be able to draw the intricate patterns that were her forte and set her above other dressmakers. And the custom fittings, pinning the needles—how was she going to do that with stiff wooden fingers? Customers would lose confidence in her ability to provide the usual service and would rather go somewhere else. And who could blame them? She would lose her business and with it the income needed to provide for her daughter and Mitzie. Her sister was almost nineteen, and bound to marry soon; how was she going to provide her with a dowry, the same as all the others received?

Pitifully clinging to a hopeless hope, she asked the doctor if there was absolutely no other way to avoid amputating her hand. If they could wait a little longer, perhaps her condition would improve. Of course, she knew the answer before she heard it. No, the doctor stood firmly, the operation must be done right away; there was no time to lose. It would have to be performed in Vienna since the hospital in Sopron lacked some of the needed facilities. He would schedule the surgery as soon as she made the arrangements to stay in Vienna and have someone to care for her during the postoperative weeks, until her wrist healed sufficiently to be fitted with the prosthetic.

Angela left the doctor's office still dazed from the dreadful news that struck her so unexpectedly. How could a little pain suddenly become life threatening? She had never even heard of tuberculosis in the bone. In lungs, yes, like with

Henrich, so how could this be happening to her? Why was she cursed with so much bad luck? In all her life she was always trying to do the right thing, yet she is being punished again and again. Wasn't it enough that she spent her young years burdened with monumental responsibilities, that the man she loved betrayed and abandoned her, leaving her pregnant to battle rejection and bigotry? And now, when she was finally gaining acceptance, her very livelihood was being snatched away from her! What was next? What else could they do to her? Take her daughter from her? But that she would not survive! If anything happened to Lensie, she would not want to live. She would refuse the operation and let the sickness consume her body; her soul would be dead long before that.

As bitter and scared as Angela first felt about the future, she slowly drew strength from her love for Lensie. It was the only reason she was willing to go under the knife. She would find a way to go on. Lensie would not be left without a mother, as she was when she was eighteen. Life might have shortchanged her, but her child would not suffer because of her mother's misfortunes.

In time she even found the courage to joke when she warned everyone at home they'd better behave after her operation, because with her prosthetic hand she'd deal with them more heavy-handedly. But no one had the heart to laugh. On hearing the news Lensie and Mitzie reacted the same way as Angela had, with utter disbelief. This couldn't be true! Sofie and the other seamstress were just as shocked, as well as afraid of losing their jobs, until Angela told them that she had no plans to close the business. They were to carry on as usual while she was away, hopefully not longer than a month.

A day before her operation she took the train to Vienna, left her suitcase with friends where she'd be staying during her recovery, then in the afternoon checked into the hospital. The surgery took place in the morning and went without complications; it was a total success, but Angela was traumatized when told that they had to amputate her hand almost three inches above her wrist. Seeing the bandaged stump, Lensie, too, burst into tears when she and Gertie visited her later in the day. Leaving the room, her aunt warned her that if she couldn't control herself, it was better if she stayed away. Tears and pity were not what Angela needed now.

Gertie stayed with Angela for a few weeks after she was released from the hospital and took care of her until Lensie could learn to step in and take over the task. She was barely twelve years old, too young to assume such responsibility, but she had no choice. Seeing how despondent her mother was about the future she learned to hide her fear, even smile a little to show confidence, though many times she felt like crying.

Angela was finally allowed to go home, but she found it extremely hard to adjust to living with her handicap. It was a trying time for her and everyone around her. Regardless of all the therapy she went through learning to use her artificial hand, she knew she would never be the same. How could she, with a prosthetic strapped to her arm? It was made of wood, with a tube-like leather extension that fastened over the stump, and while the fingers were adjustable at the joints, the whole thing was heavy and cumbersome to wear.

For a long time it was an ordeal to perform even small everyday tasks, and feeling helpless made her irritable. If she reached for something and it slipped from her hand, the futility brought angry tears to her eyes. It annoyed her having to rely on others, when until now she was the one who helped everyone else. She didn't know how to accept help graciously or express gratitude; instead, she became bitterly resentful. When she didn't improve as fast as she expected, she took out her frustration on others, snapping at the seamstresses if they did not do exactly as she would have. She was losing her temper even with Lensie; the poor girl couldn't do anything right. If she offered help, Angela would yell that she was not an invalid and was capable of doing things herself; the next day she complained that Lensie was not fast enough to lend her a hand. She was cross and intolerant, and the tension made everyone in the house nervous and edgy. The worst of it was that deep down Angela knew that her flare-ups were uncalled for, and it made her feel guilty, yet she was helpless to control it.

Lensie was still attending school, and while she was in class, Angela kept Mitzie by her side to do her bidding. She was even harder on her than on Lensie, criticizing her for every little thing. The worst came on the day when Mitzie broke the news that she wanted to marry a young man, Janos Moser, a soldier she had met a year ago. They saw each other during his occasional leaves from the front, but when he suffered a shoulder injury a few weeks ago and came home for treatment, they decided to tie the knot before he was sent back.

Angela knew who the young man was but had no idea of Mitzie's involvement with him, and took it personally that she had said nothing until now.

"How dare you to keep this a secret!" she exploded. "You never said a word about him before, but now that I have problems and sometimes things get a little tense around here, suddenly you want to get married! You are not fooling me, Mitzie. I know exactly what you are doing. You are marrying this man to get away from me. Is this what I deserve after all I did for you? Using marriage to escape? You ought to be ashamed of yourself is all I can say!"

Mitzie was equally indignant about Angela's accusations. "How can you think so low of me? I am not trying to get away from you, as you put it. I know what you did for me and for all of us when Mother died, and we are all grateful, but can I help it if I fell in love? Janos is a good man, and he is from here. I won't be moving away like Rezie, Gertie, and Lizzie when they got married. I'll be right here whenever you need me."

When Angela still carried on about "desertion," Mitzie no longer argued. She had her own life to live. Actually, in her opinion Angela should be happy that she was marrying Janos, and she told her so. His parents owned a small restaurant and got their food supplies directly from the farmers. With the wartime shortages, Angela could benefit from such family connections; it would save all of them hours of standing in line at stores, especially now with the cold weather approaching.

Angela knew she could not stop her sister from leaving, and she had to admit that what Mitzie said about the restaurant was true. It would help the family. The way things looked, the war could go on for some time to come, making life more and more miserable. And so, after another day of sulking, all hard feelings were forgotten. Angela only regretted that she could not afford to provide a dowry for Mitzie, but it didn't matter. Janos's parents were not rich but financially well situated, and all they cared about was having their only son home safely, seeing him happily married, and then waiting for the arrival of grandchildren. They were getting up in age and were looking forward to handing over the running of the restaurant to the young couple. They liked their future daughter-in-law, especially her cheerful and sunny disposition, which would come handy in dealing with the sometime fussy patrons.

After a small family wedding and no honeymoon, Janos went back to the front, but because of his injury they kept him out of the trenches; he would not be thrown into combat. His parents and Mitzie were worried nonetheless, praying every day for his safety. This war could not last forever! He would be coming home soon! And they were right. By the fall of 1918 the Hungarian government lost all hope for victory and ordered the troops to return home. Soon war-exhausted soldiers started arriving, among them Janos and the three Bohaczek brothers. Franz and Miska came back fatigued but unharmed, but Henrich was not as lucky. During the last days of fighting he got hit by shrapnel in his right knee and thigh and suffered a permanent injury that left him with a limp for the rest of his life. He walked with a cane, but he was alive and home and that was all that mattered to his family.

The war was fast drawing to a conclusion, bringing Hungary closer to the disaster waiting in the wings at the Trianon peace conference in France. On November 11, 1918 Germany capitulated and one of the bloodiest wars in history came to an end. Five days later, on November 16, Hungary cut its ties with Austria and proclaimed itself a People's Republic.

Along with the rest of Europe, the new government eagerly awaited the arrival of Woodrow Wilson, the President of the United States, bringing his fourteen-point peace proposal that was to end all wars. He was greeted with great enthusiasm, but while the idealistic internationalism he planned for Europe might have been well intended, it did not bring peace to Hungary. The fighting continued within her borders as national tensions flared between the former member states of the now dissolved Austro-Hungarian Empire. The always hostile Czechs and Romanians demanded large chunks of the country for themselves, and when they began to march into Hungary, the Czechs from the north and the Romanians from the south, the barely four-month-old government, unable to halt the invaders, was forced to resign.

On the same day, March 21, 1919, Bela Kun (born Bela Kohn), the head of the newly organized Communist Party, took power into his hands. He proclaimed Hungary a Soviet Republic and immediately started to build up a new army by recalling the already discharged soldiers. They beat back the Czechs but could not stop the Romanians, who reached Budapest by November. His failure to repel them was only one cause of his subsequent downfall. He couldn't find a broad popular support for his Soviet style dictates that brought on bloody persecutions against the upper classes, the landowners, the intelligentsia, and the Catholic Church. He patterned his reign, quickly named Red Terror, after the Bolshevik takeover in Russia, not recognizing that Communism was alien to the majority of the Hungarian people, and neither the peasants nor the middle classes were willing to accept a proletarian dictatorship.

On July 31, 1919, after a mere 133 days, Bela Kun and his Communist regime were ousted, and although he escaped to Russia, fate caught up with him when in 1937 he fell victim to the infamous Stalinist purges. Many others of his party cadre also wound up in Russia, among them Matyas Rakosi, who would return decades later, thoroughly steeped in Marxist theories, to unleash another era of blind terror.

A period of political chaos, the so-called White Terror, followed, with severe reprisals and gruesome acts of personal vendettas against the Communists. Marked by on-the-spot killings with bodies hanging from lampposts, it matched the cruelty of its predecessor. Miska Bohaczek was almost caught in the turmoil. When he was yanked back into Kun's army, he was assigned to guard a high-ranking government official, and because of it, he found himself accused of being a Communist after the regime fell. He was herded with a group of similarly charged people toward Sopron-Kohida, a huge cavernous stone cave near the city where political prisoners were held before execution. Fortunately someone in charge of the prisoners, a former commanding officer of Miska's unit during the war, recognized him and vouched for his innocence. It was a narrow escape and the incident shook Miska to the core. He was never afraid of dying on the battlefield, but being stood against the wall and executed by his own countrymen for nothing more than obeying orders was beyond his bravery.

During Kun's final weeks in power a counter-revolutionary government was forming under the leadership of Miklos Horthy, a Rear Admiral in the former Imperial Navy and a long time aide-de-camp to Franz Joseph. With help from Austria, Horthy defeated the Romanians, and on November 16, 1919 entered Budapest at the head of his troops, riding a white stallion and wearing his full admiral regalia. He set out to bring back some normalcy to this much-suffering country and within a few months had restored Hungary to its previous form of kingdom, albeit in name only, as the throne was left without a king. The deposed Habsburg Karoly IV tried to reclaim his realm but without success, thus becoming the last king to rule Hungary.

On March 1, 1920 the National Assembly elected Horthy as Regent with prerogatives similar to those of a king, among them his official title, His Serene Highness the Regent of the Kingdom of Hungary. The form of the government was a Parliamentary Republic with a Prime Minister at the head, but with the Regent retaining the power to convene and dissolve Parliament, appoint and dismiss Prime Ministers and command the armed forces. Horthy, like Franz

Joseph, whom he faithfully served and greatly admired for his strict adherence to duty and discipline, was a somewhat rigid but dedicated leader with little tolerance for insubordination. Although lacking exceptional talents, he loved his country and always served its interests to the best of his ability. People longing to return to their peaceful pre-war existence trusted him to bring back stability and looked forward to a just conclusion of the ongoing peace negotiations. They believed that under his leadership and with God's help, a new independent Hungary would finally be recognized as a sovereign nation, equal among others in the Western world.

But as so many times in this poor country's history, God looked the other way. What Regent Horthy was able to prevent in 1919, namely the carving up of Hungary by the Czechs and the Romanians, a year later the Peace Treaty of Trianon managed to accomplish with a stroke of the pen. Overnight she was deprived of roughly two-thirds (72%) of her former territory, reduced from 125,526 square miles to 35,936, and lost 64% of her population—31% of it pure ethnic Hungarians—dropping the number from 18.2 to 7.6 million. It condemned millions of Hungarians to live under vengeful foreign governments and become mistreated minorities of the so-called Successor States of Romania, Czechoslovakia, and Serbia. With the lost territories these states now possessed most of Hungary's best natural resources and raw materials, so essential to survive as a modern industrial nation. The Czechs and Romanians even saw to it that the newly drawn borders included the railroads on their side.

Trianon stunned the people. Under protest, Hungary signed this shameful and terribly unjust treaty on June 14, 1920, a date that became one of the saddest days in its thousand-year history. This proud nation, steeped in western culture and nestled within the natural border of the great Carpathian Mountains, was now cut down to nothing more than a flat agricultural plane crossed by two major rivers, condemned to eke out an existence by plowing the land and raising cattle. It is no wonder that from that day forward Hungary never gave up seeking recovery of her territorial losses and used every available avenue to reverse the Treaty of Trianon. In the decades that followed, governments came and went, but the goal remained the same: the restoration of Greater Hungary.

From Selmec to Sopron

THE WAR AND its senseless cruelty left its mark on almost everyone, including Jeno's family. At first, when hostilities broke out in 1914, it had little effect on their lives. The three boys were all university students, and as such, exempt from military duty. Jeno was a metallurgic freshman, while his brothers Jozsef, a sophomore, and Gyula, in his senior year, were both studying forestry. They did suffer a great personal loss when their father died suddenly in the fall of 1916, just before his 60th birthday. Walking in the woods he caught a chill during a downpour that turned into pneumonia, and while the family mourned him deeply, his passing did not create financial difficulties. Mrs. Zachar received a generous pension and, for a minimal rent, the use of the house as long as she wished to stay.

But as the war continued, everything changed for the brothers. By the middle of 1915 Gyula was in the army, drafted right after graduation, followed by the other two in January 1917, when most military exemptions were suspended to make up for the heavy casualties the army had suffered. All three were sent to the Russian front, serving in separate units, but all of them had their share of heavy fighting. Gyula, the oldest was killed; the other two survived, although not unscathed. Jozsef spent weeks in a hospital with pneumonia he caught in the icy dugouts, and then in November 1917, after the Russians pulled out of the war, was sent to France on the Western front. At the same time Jeno's decimated unit was transferred to Italy, arriving there just before Christmas. He and his army buddies spent Christmas Eve in a northern Italian forest, gathered around a pine tree flecked by snow and hung with tin cans for decoration. He served as a courier, running dispatches behind the lines, a somewhat safer assignment compared to combat duty on the Eastern front. So far he had escaped injuries, but his luck ran out in the summer of 1918. He was caught in a heavy fire exchange, and while he survived in a dugout, he lost his hearing and suffered from shell shock that caused considerable damage to his nervous system. It brought on fits of shaking he couldn't control, not even after weeks of treatment in a military hospital in Budapest. Although his hearing was restored, he was declared unfit for duty and sent home with an honorable discharge.

His brother Jozsef also came back at the end of hostilities, ragged, hungry and disillusioned, but alive. They both needed time to regain their strength and learn to adjust to civilian life, but eventually they were able to return to Selmec and resume their studies.

Then in June 1920 came the shocking news of Trianon, the treaty that handed the northern part of the country where they lived to Czechoslovakia. The transfer also included Selmec with their beloved university, a city where patriotism always ran high, but now forced to change its name to Banska Stiavnica. The annexation meant taking down the red, white, and green flag of Hungary and learn to live as undesired minorities, forbidden even to speak their ancient language. According to the terms of the treaty, Hungary was to turn over all property within the annexed area to Slovakia, including governmental establishments, fully equipped factories, all institutions, schools, and churches—everything intact and without compensation. Any attempt to sabotage the transfer would be subject to severe punishment.

The thought that their old university would fall into the hands of the Slovaks struck at the heart of the students. How could any red-blooded Hungarian stand by and let this happen? They swore, foremost among them Jeno, whose ancestor Samuel Mikoviny became the first dean of the fledgling academy in the year 1735, that they would rather put a torch to their school and watch it burn to the ground than live to see the day when classes would be taught to them in Slovakian. Obviously, they could do nothing to change the outcome of Trianon; the territorial transfer was only a matter of time, but they decided that even though the entire city couldn't be saved, their university would never be surrendered to the Slovaks. They would organize its rescue, and no amount of scare tactics would deter them. There was still time to act, and act they did. In alternate shifts they worked day and night to dismantle the university, carting off everything inside: all the furniture, lamps, the lab, and the entire library. Even blackboards, maps, and pictures were removed from the walls, and fixtures bolted to the floor pulled up, until nothing was left but the bare walls. After storing all in containers at a warehouse behind the train station they waited until a decision could be made about where to relocate.

The Hungarian Ministry of Education suggested three cities to consider for the transfer: Pecs on the southern border, Veszprem near Lake Balaton, and Sopron near the Austrian border. Inquiries revealed that Pecs already had two universities; they couldn't handle a third one. Veszprem had room for the school but needed more time to find living quarters for the students and professors. Sopron, however, was eager to welcome the newcomers with open arms. In compliance with the mandatory disarmament as dictated by the peace treaty, the city's former military academy had closed its doors and now stood empty, ready for immediate occupancy. There was only a small problem with the use of the dormitory across from the university: Hungarian refugees pouring in from Czechoslovakia were temporarily lodged in it. The city was working to remedy the situation in the shortest possible time, but until the misplaced people could be moved, the students and faculty would have to be housed in a recently evacuated military casern.

One of the professors in Selmec was familiar with Sopron and the surrounding areas and talked about the similarities between the two cities. Because both were situated at the foot of a mountain range, Selmec at the lower Tatras and Sopron at the end of the Alps, the vegetation, including extensive forestry, was comparable, and the regional climate was almost the same. He also recalled the existence of an abandoned coal mine a short distance from the city that could be put to good use for students studying mining engineering, provided a permit could be obtained. The city not only granted their request, but also offered the use of a large fenced-in park-like area adjacent to the academy that could be converted to a botanical garden for the forestry students.

The move was thus settled in favor of Sopron, and the students began making final preparations for the journey. They loaded the wagons and said farewell to families, sweethearts and friends, then boarded the train that would take them across the country to a new home and a new beginning. Hundreds of people came to see them off, waving white handkerchiefs and little Hungarian flags, saying goodbye perhaps for a very long time. Students crowded the windows waving back and shouting promises to return, no more than empty words thrown to the wind. They remained standing there long after the train began to move, straining their necks to catch the last glimpse of those left behind until the last of Selmec faded into the distance. Many of the boys, overcome by emotion, eyes brimming, found good use of the tiny cinder particles blown from the engine to explain away the tears they could no longer contain.

Although Selmec was now lost to them, and its name would be missing from the newly drawn map of Hungary, they swore that this much-loved city would never be forgotten. Through their defiant action they would keep its essence intact, its time-honored traditions alive. A chapter of their lives that held so many memories was closed now, but as the train sped toward Sopron, the spirit of Selmec rode with them guarded and protected, confident, and unafraid of what the future would bring.

Throughout the summer the possibility of an all-male university coming to their city kept the young ladies of Sopron talking in animated whispers. There were five gimnaziums for boys in Sopron, but not one university after the recent closing of the military academy. It meant that college-bound young men now left town to complete their education in other places, creating a void in social activities for girls in their late teens and little older. For them, adopting the university was a most welcome prospect; the students' presence would enliven the city and bring back the fun the girls sorely missed.

Mothers, however, didn't share their daughters' enthusiasm. Who needed a gang of wild college boys running around, causing nothing but trouble? Everyone had heard stories about their rowdy conduct and arrogant disrespect for authority, the kind of behavior that no law-abiding citizen should be forced to put up with. Not only that, but most of these men were war veterans! They would be looking for fun to make up for the years they lost while fighting the war; the reputations of innocent girls could be in danger! Whose bright idea was it to invite them, anyway? They must be stopped; let them go somewhere else.

They grumbled and protested, but it accomplished nothing. These boys were coming, and they would be here to stay. The city fathers would not be pressured into reversing their decision to adopt the university. They argued that it would lend prestige to the city, create jobs, and bring vitality to the community. And who knows, it might even prove to be a windfall to families with marriageable girls. Once the dust settled, mothers might start viewing these students not as a threat to their daughters but as potential husbands to them. They ought to remember that eligible young men were in short supply after the war decimated their ranks.

In response, the doomsayers banded together. If the city refused to hear their pleas, they would make sure that the intruders knew that they were not welcome. They would be shunned and their greetings ignored, making them as uncomfortable and unwanted as possible. All their social and sporting events, balls, outings—anything planned by the university—would be boycotted to prevent any interaction between the girls and the students, and if every mother adhered to these simple rules, in the face of such hostility the university might just reconsider to pack up again and leave before putting down roots.

To be effective, daughters must also be warned against the dangers these scoundrels presented. They must be told why it was necessary to lower their eyes and avoid eye contact when passing them on the street, or to turn up their noses should one, no matter how handsome, dare to approach them with some foolish excuse, such as asking for directions, a well-known tactic used by these types of rascals to strike up a conversation.

It might not be easy to make the girls understand that this is being done for their own good; they might resist, but parents must not give in. Not this time. Young women nowadays got away with too much freedom already. It was not enough that they could do pretty much as they pleased, go shopping and visit friends alone, or take tea in public without a chaperone. That was bad enough, but they seemed to want more! And it was all because of the war. Since then their heads became full of strange ideas, like working in fields other than teaching or nursing, so different from what was acceptable. Some of them went so far as to demand the right to vote! What was this world coming to? Well, they would lose some of that freedom now; they wouldn't be allowed to walk about town without their mothers. Most likely they'd balk at the new rules, but obey they must!

Angela, being a mother of a vulnerable fourteen-year-old already showing signs of beauty and grace, was sympathetic and supportive of their agenda but felt that the issue did not concern her; Lensie was still too young to worry about her getting involved with the opposite sex. Angela had other problems, serious difficulties to overcome. As she predicted when she lost her hand, her business suffered and she was losing her customers. When they first learned about her operation they remained loyal. They were patient and were willing to wait while she was recovering, but once she was back they expected her to run the salon as before, providing excellent workmanship and treating them with the cheerful enthusiasm and pleasing attentiveness that had attracted so many of her clients. To their disappointment she remained depressed, always in a somber mood, and although they felt sorry for her, they were not prepared to listen to her unending complaints about her misfortunes. It made them feel uncomfortable to see her standing on the side during fittings, erect, her hands folded with the left covering the artificial one, her face full of resentment as she watched the seamstresses do the job that used to be exclusively hers. She acted bossy and domineering with the help, and it reached the point where customers were reluctant to tell the fitters if they were not satisfied with a tuck here or a hemline there, because Angela would angrily scold the girls in front of everyone. Her whole personality changed and when it became clear that Angela was not and perhaps never would be the same again, her customers started to abandon her. Gradually, one by one they left, taking their business elsewhere.

With work dwindling practically to nothing, not enough to keep her two remaining seamstresses busy, she had to let them go. Her faithful Sofie was the last one to leave, and when Angela closed the door behind her she tore down her Mode a la Vienna sign and tossed it in the garbage. She wouldn't need it anymore; that part of her life was over. Disfigured and feeling deserted, she had no drive, no ambition, and no interest in what would happen. She would sit and stare at nothing, hardly saying a word when Lensie tried to talk to her. Yes, Lensie was still with her, but she knew that soon, just like everyone else, she would also want to leave, and then she would be left all alone. When Lensie was in school there were days when Angela hardly got out of bed, letting herself slip further into a despondent, dreary state. It was a far cry from her former cheery, pleasant self to the world-weary, sullen woman she became.

Mitzie came by every day, bringing them meals from the restaurant, and with her no-nonsense, simple ways tried to shake Angela out of her present gloom. “So you lost a hand, and the business went to the dogs; it’s no excuse to behave as if the whole world came to an end! Can’t you think of something better to do than wallow in self-pity all day? Because that’s all you are doing, feeling sorry for yourself and let everything else go to pot.”

She knew it sounded harsh, but she had more to say. “Don’t you see or care what you are doing to poor Lensie? She is only a child, for heaven’s sake, but because you decided to give up, she has to do everything around this house besides going to school and doing her homework. She should be going out a bit to have fun, not cooped up here, doing what you’re supposed to do! She is scared to death to leave you alone ever since you almost burned down the place. It just isn’t right! I am going to hire a woman to help her, if I can find someone who could stand being around you, that is. It’s really a shame that you let your spirits sink this low. And I am telling you, Angela, you better snap out of it, or keep it up and wake up one day to find everyone gone. Then you will really have a reason to feel sorry for yourself.”

Her every word was true; Lensie was afraid to leave her mother alone since that scary incident with the matches. At home Angela hardly ever attached her artificial hand; it was too heavy to wear for long periods, and she would try to do small tasks without it. One day she wanted to heat up some water and tried to light a match with her left hand while holding the matchbox between her chest and the stump of her arm. The match ignited the entire box, burning her arm and scorching her blouse. Luckily, Lensie was home, but still, a fire can spread so quickly that they could have been easily trapped. Since then, fear had become constant in Lensie’s life. What if this happened when Angela was alone? It was impossible to watch her every minute of the day!

Slowly, painfully, Angela began to realize that Mitzie was right. She was making her daughter’s life miserable and if she wanted to see her happy, she must change. She must “snap out of it,” as her sister put it bluntly. That was Mitzie all right, never one to beat around the bush. It was perhaps the first time since Angela’s operation that a tiny inward smile bubbled up from the depths of defeat. She had to admit that Mitzie had hit the nail on the head; she couldn’t go on giving up like this! But Mitzie also said something else that helped to cut through the murk that seemed to have taken over Angela’s mind: wasn’t she always the strongest in the family, never to let bad luck beat her down? Why, if it were not for her courage, no telling where would they be today. Faced with difficulties—and there were plenty—Angela always knew what to do, and she must never forget that!

. . . .

Between Mitzie's well-meaning scolding and morale-building encouragement, Angela found a way to sit up and size up her situation. She would have to make an effort to overcome this latest setback! She did it before; she could do it again. Once she reached the mental stage where she regained some resemblance of will and stability, she was able to take a good look at her life and make some hard decisions for the future. Hand or no hand, she would find a job, something she would be able to do by using her left hand. Then she could hire someone to take care of the house and free Lensie from doing all the work.

Then suddenly she remembered the family agreement to eventually sell the house. With her business folded and all her siblings married and living elsewhere, this was a good time to do it. Who needed this big old house anyway? Why not sell it now, divide the proceeds, and move into one of the newer apartments in the heart of the city? These new flats were equipped with all the latest conveniences: electricity, plumbing, water closets, and even bathrooms with showers! They would be closer to stores, churches, the market, and Lensie's school would be nearer, too. No more climbing the steep street where their house stood, especially when returning from shopping loaded with groceries.

And wouldn't it be grand to ride the new streetcars the city had installed recently with lines running in all directions from the downtown area. That's where she would look for an apartment to take advantage of all these things designed to make life easier. Some of the buildings were said to have a caretaker as well; they handled small repairs, swept the courtyard, shoveled the snow in the winter, plus they kept the entrance locked after eleven in the evening so they could keep track of strangers entering and leaving at such late hours.

When Angela called for a family meeting and made her proposal to sell the house, it was accepted with great enthusiasm. Everyone needed money, especially her brothers, struggling to start over after the war. They all lost years of regular income while in the service and catching up financially was difficult, although no one had the heart to tell Angela about it when she was going through such a difficult time in her life. With the money from the sale of the house they could all get back on their feet.

The prospect of moving revived Angela's spirits, and with her newfound energy, she threw herself wholeheartedly into putting her life back together. She first focused on finding a place to live. She knew she wanted to be close to downtown, and when a three-room apartment on Szena Square in the heart of the city became available in the fall, she immediately took it. The four-story building was fairly new with two shops on ground level and three stories above it, each floor with four flats. Her apartment was on the second level over the shops, bright and airy, with a balcony overlooking the plaza, a busy place where five streets converged from different parts of the city. One of them was the main boulevard called Varkerulet, lined with the best shops and restaurants, and a popular place for promenading after Sunday Mass.

Lensie loved their new place, especially the balcony, where she would spend hours watching the flow of people below. She resumed her weekly trips to Vienna for her voice and music lessons—she only stopped during Angela's illness—and because her school was much closer now, she could stay longer after classes to practice her piano. Angela's favorite church, the beautiful Baroque St. George Church, was also much closer.

Most families living in Angela's building welcomed them when they moved in. A widow, Mrs. Szep, and her two daughters, Hilda and Irene, both a little older than Lensie, lived above them, and the girls soon became fast friends. They shared much the same interests, especially the love of outdoors and hiking in the Loevers. This lovely green belt, dotted with gardens that gave way to ozone producing forests as elevation increased, encircled the city on the south and had an allure that brought people out regardless of the season. In early spring with patches of snow still on the ground, it offered the first of the tiny white snowdrops just poking their heads through the earth. The warmer weather carpeted the meadows with an abundance of wildflowers, and by July the search was on for the hard-to-find star-shaped Alpine Edelweiss. There were berries to pick, and colorful edible mushrooms to collect from the lush undergrowth. The onset of fall meant gathering everyone's favorite flower, the miniature wild cyclamen, so unique to the forests of Sopron. These delicate purple flowers, easily betrayed by their dizzying scent, defied visitors' attempts to transplant them elsewhere, refusing to take root in any other part of the country. Their image became identified with Sopron, widely featured on postcards, souvenirs, and local art objects. People flocked to harvest the precious flowers, so much so, that in later years the city had to put restrictions on picking them to ensure their survival.

During their outings, Lensie and her newfound friends were getting quite familiar with the trails criss-crossing the forests. One would take them to the Deak Fountain, a natural spring, and a popular spot for hikers to quench their thirst before climbing the steeper pathways. They'd follow the gradually ascending trail to the Karoly Kilato, a three level lookout tower with a panoramic view of the city and its surrounding area, from the forests around the tower that extended into Austria, to the gentle rolling hills bordering Sopron on the opposite side. Since the loss of Hungary's northern region with its immense woodlands to Czechoslovakia, these forests around the city were credited with producing the best quality air in the entire country, drawing patients with respiratory problems from near and far.

Unfortunately, it was for this reason that Angela also began taking walks in the woods. She was diagnosed with asthma when a nasty recurring cough that made her gasp for air sent her to the doctor. He gave her some medication, but also recommended to get out in the fresh air as often as she could. It helped stabilizing her condition, and as she started feeling stronger both physically and mentally, she decided it was time to look for a job. It was not for need of money; she had a sizeable bank account after selling the house, but without a large household to run and her business closed, she felt useless sitting idly at home. Friends rallied to help her with suggestions as to what kind of work would suit her best, which firms were hiring, and whom to contact for an interview. And when she heard that the post office was expanding and was looking for people, she put in an application and was hired on a temporary basis for sorting the mail. It helped that the man in charge was the husband of one of her former clients, and he took her under his wing. Thanks to her lengthy rehabilitation, by then she was quite skillful in using her left hand, and when her trial period was over her status became permanent. She spent her earnings on little extra luxuries: season tickets to the theater for herself and Lensie, and taking small trips. On her first paid vacation she took Lensie to Lake Balaton, the country's favorite recreational spot. It was the first time in Angela's life that she had the time to do so. They stayed in a modest hotel, went to the beach, and took boat trips to other places around the fifty-mile-long lake.

Spending time together, Lensie saw the progress her mother had made in handling herself and felt confident enough to leave her when Angela insisted that she visit her aunts and the Pollingers, just as she did before the operation. There was no reason Lensie shouldn't go. With all her setbacks and bitter disappointments behind her, Angela was on her way to a new and contented life. At work she got along well with her co-workers, many of them young women who spoke of nothing else but the prospect of the new university coming to town. They couldn't comprehend why their mothers would fear the students and resented the silly rules and restrictions they would be forced to follow once the boys arrived. Listening to their complaints Angela could sympathize with them, but she also understood the mothers' concern. She could see validity in the steps they were prepared to take to protect their daughters. Aware that Angela worked, some of the ladies in her neighborhood went so far as to offer to take Lensie into their homes until she could pick her up; it would save her from unwanted approaches. She thanked them but politely declined. Her daughter was but a child, not likely to draw the attention of adult males. Perhaps in a few years, when Lensie was older, she would gladly accept their kind gesture.

Angela was pleasantly surprised, though. These women were not close friends; they usually kept their distance, most likely because of her tainted reputation. Yet now, her past seemingly forgotten, they had no reservations opening their doors to her daughter. Of course, Lensie was known never to cause any trouble. She was a good-natured and outgoing, friendly girl who loved to be around people and felt equally comfortable with adults and children. People liked her; they could sense her basic honesty.

No, Angela was not overly concerned about her daughter's activities when left alone. She knew that when Lensie was not in school, doing her homework or practicing her piano, she was with her friends, either walking the Loevers if the weather was good, or if indoors, gossiping about the last slumber party or about the latest trend in fashion and hairstyles. They were beyond playing with dolls, but only a few in her circle of friends had reached the stage when they would start talking much about boys.

Angela still had a year or two before Lensie's interest would turn toward the opposite sex. She thought about her own experience, how she trusted a man who misled her, and swore she'd prevent the same ever happening to her daughter. She did not have her mother to guide her, but Lensie did! And thank God, they had a wonderful mother-daughter relationship, trusting, and confiding, although not the "best friends" kind. Angela tried to find a good balance between nurturing and disciplining by maintaining a certain aura of authority, a rule usually fathers played when it came to settling an issue, or meeting out punishment. Still, Lensie knew she could always come to her mother with all her questions or problems and she would always be there to help.

It made Angela happy that Lensie welcomed her advice, accepted her guidance, and followed her rules without much resentment. She only hoped that the foundation their mutual trust and respect rested on was strong enough to last, and wouldn't change with the coming of the more difficult and often rebellious teenage years. Lensie might be a perfect daughter now, but she might rail against her mother for watching over her like a hawk when boys began to appear on her horizon.

The day finally arrived when the train from Selmec pulled into the station. A delegation consisting of the mayor, the police chief and other dignitaries, with a selected few from the academic field, came to welcome the professors as they stepped onto the platform. Speeches were exchanged and afterwards the newcomers were escorted to their temporary living quarters in the vacated military casern. The mayor proudly pointed out that in their honor the street running along one side of the complex was renamed Selmec Street. At the special dinner that evening toasts were kept mercifully short to let the newcomers enjoy a good night's rest after their long trip across the country.

Early next morning the mayor was back to lead them to their new alma mater, but instead of going there directly, he decided they should get to know the city first. He took them on an impromptu city tour with stops at various historical buildings along the way, proudly pointing out statues of statesmen and other memorials. Here and there he would gather students and faculty in front of some centuries-old house, explaining what famous people, perhaps a king, slept there and when, as confirmed by the plaque fixed to the wall. At first the students, impatient to get to their new university, resented listening to the long-running narratives, but soon they were caught up in the spirit of the city, its culture and rich history, going back to Roman times.

With every street they passed, every corner they turned, the students expected to see their new school, but when finally it came into view they stood in awe of its size and beauty. They'd seen pictures, of course, but what they now saw couldn't compare to the black and white photographs. Entering the campus through a beautifully sculpted wrought iron gate, a group of three-story red brick buildings greeted them covered with ivy and set in park-like surroundings. A wide path led to the main building, a structure with a covered portico supported by high columns. There the mayor mounted the steps, delivered his well-prepared speech, then with a dramatic flair befitting the occasion, threw open the doors and ushered in the new occupants.

With wild enthusiasm the boys bounded through the entrance, eager to discover the inside of their new home. They ran from building to building, checking every room, inspecting the lecture halls, the grand auditorium, the lab, and library. There was a gym with a basketball court, and behind the buildings a good size athletic field. Excitement ran high as they all felt the importance of the moment; this was the start of a new beginning that strangely also seemed like homecoming. They immediately felt drawn to the place where in time new traditions would be born and passed down along with cherished old ones to the next generation of students and to those who would come after them.

There was still a month before the start of the semester, and with time on their hands the boys set out to further explore the city and its surrounding areas. As the warm, sunny days continued into September, the lush landscape of the Loevers, with the leaves just turning colors, was at its most spectacular, and quickly became the students' favorite, second only to the gently rolling hills of the Becsi Domb that ran north of the city. It proved to be a worthy rival with its fruit orchards and vineyards, and most importantly, the fine wine cellars that dotted the hills. For swimming and fishing there was Lake Tomalom, a popular small lake about four miles from the city, or for those interested in sailing, a few miles farther to the west the much larger Lake Ferto. This salt-water lake was the remnant of an old inland sea, the third largest in Central Europe, and the nesting ground of a number of rare water birds.

Discovering the countryside was undoubtedly an important aspect of getting to know their adopted city, but it was not the only reason. The boys flocked to these popular places hoping to meet some of the locals, especially the young ladies of Sopron. The girls were around, some quite beautiful even by the students' strict standards, but they were beyond approach. Guarded by stern looking chaperones, any friendly attempt to open a dialog was promptly rebuffed, sometimes downright rudely, as if the approach was a criminal act.

Endless speculations followed. Why such uncalled-for animosity? What were people afraid of? None of these young men caused any trouble, on the contrary, they were grateful to have found a new home and they had shown nothing but appreciation and respect for the city. Pulling the usual pranks typical of college kids was long behind them; the war had sobered them from the arrogance of youth. But how could they remedy the situation and prove themselves if not given a chance?

One of the students suggested that perhaps if they held one of their popular torchlight processions, it might dispel the prevailing misgivings; it was always a crowd-pleaser in old Selmec. Traditionally, it was to honor members of the graduating class, the so-called "Veterans," a solemn march that required precision and discipline, accompanied by singing age-old university songs. It was beautiful to watch, and the boys hoped that it might change the unjust perception people seemingly held against them.

They obtained a license from the police for the following Saturday evening, which left enough time to make the necessary preparations and freshen up the packed-away college uniforms. Their outfit consisted of black slacks and a high-buttoned single-breasted jacket resembling a military coat with brass buttons and a stand-up collar. To distinguish the three faculties, the jackets varied in color: all black meant a miner, black with red velvet collar identified a metallurgist, and forestry students wore brown coats with green collars.

On the appointed evening, just after sundown the boys began to assemble at the beginning of Varkerulet Boulevard, lining up according to faculties, first the miners, next the forestry students, with the metallurgists bringing up the rear. Not knowing what to make of the gathering, people stopped on the street, and windows opened to see what the students were up to. They did not have to wonder for long. As soon as darkness fell, the boys were ready to start the march. They lit the torches and at a signal began to move, walking in single file down the middle of the boulevard, singing their traditional songs. The student at the head of the column led them at a forty-five degree angle toward the right side of the street, then, reaching the curb, turned and proceeded the same way, diagonally in the opposite direction. Swinging from side to side as if following in the trail of a giant salamander, they continued their way, while more and more people filled the sidewalks to watch with open curiosity. Reaching the end of the boulevard at Szena Square, the students stopped the singing and with torches still burning marched quietly into the plaza.

Windows and balconies overlooking the square were crowded with people, among them Angela and Lensie, all wondering what was happening below, as they watched the students closing ranks according to faculties. When they were all in place, they waited patiently for the general noise to die down and then, as silence fell, their voices rang out once more. First they sang the hauntingly beautiful Miners Hymn, its lyrics prayer-like, how the miners' fate was in God's hand every time they descended into the deep. Next came the spirited Forester Hymn about the glory of nature, and the harmony between man and creatures of the forest, as God intended it. They ended their singing in praise of the foundry workers, an upbeat anthem full of rhythmic sounds imitating a hammer striking red-hot iron.

As the voices faded away and the boys put out the torches, the crowd erupted in wild applause, cheering with enthusiasm. Most ladies remained on the sidewalks, but the men came to shake hands, mingling with the boys and patting them on the shoulders. They wanted to know about the tradition behind the march and the reason for staging the procession. The students simply told the truth: it was their way as newcomers to introduce themselves as members of the university, hoping it would bring them closer to the people of Sopron. They wanted nothing more than to be accepted, to be part of the community, to have a place in the city that so generously invited them.

It seemed they achieved what they aimed for. Although the warm reception they received was only the first step on a long road toward full acceptance, it was a start. The ice was broken.

After settling into their new surroundings, Jeno finally found time to sit down and write home that they had arrived safely and their rescue operation was successful. The letter ended with the typical postscript routinely tacked on by students studying away from home: urgently needing money! He knew it would take much longer to receive a reply from the annexed territories, and indeed, it took six weeks before a letter finally arrived. It brought good and bad news. On the positive side, with the ongoing population exchange forced by the Czechs to oust Hungarians and replace them with Slovaks living in Hungary, their family was not kicked out. His brother Jozsef was allowed to work—he was managing a Church estate near their mother's place—and to Jeno's relief, he also wrote that help was on the way; they were sending him money, and if the post office was right, he should have it within two weeks.

As for the bad news, the Slovak authorities kept their promise to punish those who participated in destruction or removal of property before the annexation. They compiled a list of these "criminals" and tried them in absentia, slamming them with a twenty-year jail sentence. Jeno's name was on that list, and so he was not only *persona non grata* now, but also a fugitive subject to immediate arrest should he try to return. Relatives remaining in Slovakia were also barred from visiting family members in Hungary; they simply couldn't get an exit visa for any reason, be it special occasion, emergency situation, or business. Sadly, this meant they wouldn't see each other for a very long time to come.

Jeno was stunned. Twenty years? No Slovak minority living in Hungary before Trianon was ever sentenced so severely, unless for high crimes. His mother was in good health now, but unless there was an amnesty, he might never see her again. The only other hope for torn apart families was the renegotiation of the Treaty of Trianon.

The government was actively pursuing a review of the justification of all territorial grants to the Successor Nations, but especially that of the annexation of Burgenland to Austria, which included Sopron and eight or nine surrounding villages. Austria's claim to Burgenland was a bitter pill to swallow and was vehemently contested, since the two countries were allies in the war, fighting side by side, with Hungary remaining faithful to the end. Their demand was a desperate attempt to compensate for the loss of their own southern region, South Tyrol, to Italy. To justify their right to Burgenland the Austrians pointed out that the overwhelming majority of the population there was German-speaking, which was true, but so was the fact that since the year 1043, according to a peace treaty between the Holy Roman Emperor Otto III of Germany and Samuel Aba, King of Hungary, the country's western border was defined to include Burgenland. It was also true that in 1440 the area was occupied by Austria, and between 1483 and 1647 Burgenland was mortgaged twice to Germany, but in 1647 Kaiser Ferdinand II returned the territory to Hungary.

At a vigorous protest from Hungary, the Allied powers agreed to look into the situation. Hopes ran high that the annexation would be repelled, but when Austria refused to give up its claim, Hungary was obliged to transfer the territory within a specified time after the ratification of the peace treaty.

By the summer of 1921 the government began preparations to evacuate the region. The university students in Sopron, however, were determined to put up a fight. They did not rescue their college from the Slovaks to hand it over to the Austrians! They would stand their ground and defend their new home even if it meant armed resistance. Secretly they began to organize against the threat of takeover.

On August 21, 1921 Austrian occupational forces crossed the border at Agfalva, a small village some three miles from Sopron. The troops were told that the mission was a routine undertaking protected by the peace treaty, and opposition was not expected. They were thoroughly taken by surprise when they ran into fiery resistance by forces made up mostly of the students. In the ensuing battle the Hungarians had the advantage, fighting from behind barricades, and after a rapid exchange of gunfire the Austrians retreated. The fight was over with relatively few casualties, including one killed on each side.

The students marched back to Sopron to a mixed reception. Those lining the streets cheering, welcomed them as heroes, while others staying behind closed doors called them traitors. But personal opinions did not matter much. What counted was that the Entente Powers finally ran out of patience about the endless squabble over this issue and ordered the two countries to find a way to resolve the deadlock.

To settle the dispute Hungary demanded that the people be allowed to decide their own fate by voting. Italy, many times in history sympathetic to Hungary's plight, came to their aid by putting pressure on Austria. The situation between Italy and Austria was the reverse of the Burgenland matter, with Italy demanding the annexation of South Tyrol and Austria rejecting it as utterly unacceptable and demanding a plebiscite. Using tactics that were tantamount to blackmail, Italy announced that they would allow the voting but only if Austria granted the same right to the Hungarians. Austria finally relented, mostly because they believed that the election outcome in both areas would be in their favor. The agreement was signed in Venice on October 13, 1921 and the voting in Sopron was scheduled to take place on December 14, 1921.

The students again swung into action. To ensure a pro-Hungarian victory they conducted open meetings presenting solid arguments why Burgenland belonged to Hungary. They relentlessly rallied the people, reminding them that their entire future depended on this election and appealed to national sentiments that it was everyone's patriotic duty to get out and vote. They carried the same message to the surrounding villages, except speaking in German, since the population there hardly spoke Hungarian. The turnout in these places was always small, the reception bordering on hostile, but it didn't deter the students. If they could persuade some of these ponzickters to cast their vote for Hungary, it could make a difference on Election Day.

Lensie and Jeno

ON A MILD AND sunny October afternoon, Jeno and a few of his buddies were returning from one of their voting rallies in Agfalva when he decided it was too early to go back to the dreary dormitory. Instead he headed for the Lo-evers, where the fall colors were still on a dazzling display. He was approaching one of the narrow trails leading into the forest when a young girl stepped out from the woods, stood for a moment, then looked back as if waiting for someone. The vision of the girl, her figure bathed in the warm glow of the late afternoon sun edged against the darkening forest behind her, stopped Jeno in his tracks. She took his breath away.

A slight breeze ruffled her light chestnut hair, blowing loose strands across her face, and as she smoothed them back Jeno noticed they were entwined with tiny flowers. They were wild cyclamens, the same flowers tied in a bunch she held in her hand. As she stood there waiting, she buried her nose in the small bouquet and peering over its edge scanned the street up and down until her glance fell on Jeno. With their eyes locked, he stood there as if struck by thunder, unable to take his eyes off her face; he only knew that he must meet this girl before she'd disappear. He began to move toward her, his mind feverishly searching for something clever to say, but try as he might, he could only think of trifle banalities.

"Please forgive me, your flowers, they look like cyclamens, but I've never seen one so tiny."

"Then you must be new in Sopron," Lensie looked at him quizzically, "otherwise you would know that they are wild miniatures that won't grow anywhere else but here."

"That solves the mystery, thank you. And you are right. I am new here."

"Well then, you can have these if you like," she said plucking a few from her posy and holding them out to Jeno. "They smell wonderful too!"

Stepping closer, he was reaching for the flowers when out of nowhere two young girls pounced on Lensie, surrounding her protectively. "Just what do you think you are doing, Lensie?" one of them asked snatching the flowers from her fingers.

"Who is this man? Is he bothering you?" the other demanded to know, then without waiting for an answer scolded Lensie. "You know you are not supposed to talk to strangers. What got into you?"

Lensie opened her mouth to say something in her defense but the girl cut her off. "Let's just hope this does not get back to your mother. If she finds out, she'll never let you come with us again."

With that she grabbed Lensie's arm and pulled her away. "Come on, we are going home, it's getting late anyway," she said with an indignant glance in Jeno's direction.

Turning to go, Lensie glanced back over her shoulder and shrugged with a helpless gesture but kept in stride with her two friends.

Jeno stood there staring until he lost sight of them. There was nothing he could do for the moment but go home, taking with him the image of that lovely face, the smile, and captivating green eyes, knowing only her name and that she loved flowers. He also knew that somehow, somewhere they would meet again.

Day after day Jeno waited for the money his brother promised but it never came. It was understandable that mix-ups could occur during the territorial transition; the currency exchange might have caused delays too, but in any case, he should have received it by now. He wrote back to see if they could put a trace on the missing money order.

His keep at the dorm was cheap, but the cost of tuition and books was not, and his reserves were getting low. He was not the only one; students whose families remained in Slovakia had the same problem. They were all running out of money. Other fellows with parents living in Hungary got regular help and could afford to move out of the barracks, but they ran into another kind of difficulty: there was not a single room available for rent in the entire city. Not for students, that is. Undeniably, people's attitudes had softened since the torch-light ceremony; they were friendlier now, greetings were returned and some men even stopped for small talk, but to allow them to live within one's home was an entirely different matter. The poor rejected fellows were forced to continue sharing the casern's skimpy accommodations with the have-nots. They could only improve their lot by refusing the mess hall food and taking their meals elsewhere. The dorm served three meals a day, but the quality was almost as poor as what the boys ate in the trenches during the war.

With the fall semester well under way, in better times the students would be busy organizing their traditional Balek Ball, honoring the freshmen. This year, however, there were no freshmen, and somehow no one was in the mood for gaieties anyway. It just didn't feel right. The war and Trianon had left its mark on all of them. The recent border skirmish with the Austrians also had a sobering effect on the students. The possibility that they might be uprooted again weighed heavily on their minds; it all depended on the outcome of the upcoming plebiscite.

In early November Jeno received another letter from home with the good news that the replacement money was in the mail. He was by now in dire need of warm clothing; he was still wearing his summer garb that put him at risk of catching pneumonia. Slovak restrictions made it impossible to get his winter clothes from home, yet the weather was turning cold. Unless the money was in his hands soon, he'd be in real trouble when the nasty winds started sweeping down from the lower Alps bringing snow and freezing temperature.

He was counting the days, but in the meanwhile there were classes to attend and voting rallies to conduct. The day came when he was forced to borrow a jacket from others, no matter how embarrassed he felt about it. Help came not only by gesture of camaraderie, but also because he could speak German fluently and was needed to deliver speeches to solicit the ponzickter votes. It was a thankless task, for these people stubbornly clung to their Austrian roots and refused to assimilate or learn to speak Hungarian. Jeno did his best, even if only a few people would show up at meetings, and not so much to listen, but to heckle. To the ponzickters these rallies were nothing but bullying, and they did not hide their animosity. They shouted down the speakers as outsiders who didn't know the history of Burgenland; they had no right to tell how to vote when people were perfectly capable of making up their own minds about the issue. Some even demanded to send the bunch of them back to where they came from and leave the locals alone.

To get a clearer picture of how strong the opposition was, the students began checking public records to compile a list of people who declared German as their mother tongue. Assuming that these votes would go against Hungary, the boys soon came to realize that if nothing was done, by their sheer numbers the ponzickters could tip the scale of the plebiscite in favor of Austria. But that would never be allowed! They must find a way to prevent such disaster, even if it meant taking dubious measures.

In closed meetings they started drawing up plans to counteract the "enemy." They set out to learn more about the character of the ponzickters—what was their nature, what did they value? In the end they found them to be honest, hardworking farmers with very little education, who cared little about politics. They had lived in Burgenland for a very long time, and although they got along with their Hungarian counterparts, they kept pretty much to their own kind. With a few exceptions they were law-abiding people and had great respect, if not fear, for the authorities, especially when dealing with people wearing a uniform. Their main concern about the voting was that if they were to remain in Hungary, nationalistic sentiments would turn against them; they would be subjected to restrictions and forced to take up that hard-to-learn and alien sounding Hungarian language.

The better understanding of these people made it clear to the students that no amount of patriotic speeches would convince them to cast their vote for Hungary, and to win the election they must figure out ways to gain the upper hand. Chewing over the possibilities, they came up with several ideas they could use at least within the city: create false IDs and extra voting vouchers, enough to offset the ponzickter votes; volunteer at the polling places to help pass those with fake IDs without scrutiny; and use whatever means necessary to keep the ponzickters from going to the polls.

Getting the IDs was easy; with a few clandestine visits to the cemetery they collected the names for the extra voting slips. Printing the vouchers was no problem, either, since the university had a printing press, and when they offered to man the polls on Election Day, the city, always short of volunteers, accepted it gladly. As for intimidating the ponzickters, there would be some robust-looking students patrolling the two German neighborhoods dressed in their uniforms and carrying half-hidden batons.

The voting went without a hitch, and after counting the votes all night and most of the next day, the results were in: Sopron voted 72.8% for Hungary, and even though the votes from the surrounding villages were decidedly pro-

Austrian, the overall result was still 65% in favor of Hungary, against 35% for Austria. Jubilation broke out everywhere, except in the ponzickter districts and the villages. The voting earned Sopron the title of *Civitas Fidelissima*, the Most Loyal City, awarded by the Hungarian government on January 1, 1922.

As history would have it, a few decades later the good people of Sopron wished they had voted the other way around. As the result of the Yalta Conference in February 1945, when Roosevelt and Churchill gave into Stalin's demands for booty, Sopron found itself on the wrong side of the Iron Curtain, forced to live for forty-five miserable years under Soviet domination.

A month had gone by since Jeno was assured of the replacement money from home, but by now he was giving up on ever receiving it. He knew it was useless to blame the post office; they were not the culprits. Failure to deliver the money twice in a row could not be chalked up to coincidence. Some clever thief must have found a way to steal his money. He finally wrote to his family not to try again; somehow he'd find a way to get by. In reality, he didn't know how to hold out much longer. By next semester his pockets would be empty. He put in an application for financial aid at the university and was confident that due to his circumstances, cut off from his family, it would be granted, but if not, he would be in a truly dismal financial state.

With winter at the door and without a warm coat to keep out the cold, he spent his evenings and weekends cooped up in the dorm, reading, holding discussions with his buddies, and playing cards. Their favorite games were tarok, a sophisticated game developed in Italy in the 14th century, and gin rummy, played for a penny a point. Unable to come up even with the small change needed to play, Jeno just sat and kibitzed, and got to play only if his tips paid off and the winner was generous enough to share some of his winnings. He quickly became known as a sharp gin rummy player and got invited to kibitz some of the financially better-off fellows for a small percentage of their take. These boys played at the Hungaria Coffeehouse on Szena Square, where the points were higher, and the atmosphere definitely more pleasant than at the casern. It gave him a chance to make a little money, enjoy a good card game in agreeable company, and have his coffee, his cigarettes, and an occasional glass of wine free.

Jeno was kibitzing on a Saturday afternoon when during a break, stepping out to stretch his legs and clear the smoke from his eyes, he saw Lensie and a lady, presumably her mother, coming out of a building opposite the coffeehouse. As they began walking down the street, his first reaction was to dash after them, but he caught himself. What was he thinking? Lensie didn't even know his name; he would just embarrass her in front of her mother. He returned to the card game, but from then on, whenever he was in the coffeehouse he sat near a window so he could keep an eye on the building across. If she lived there, he was bound to catch her again, hopefully alone the next time. He only saw her for a second but she was as lovely as he remembered.

A few days later Jeno received a letter from his brother that explained the mystery of the missing money. Thieves were not at play. Without publicizing it, the Slovak government withheld monies sent to blacklisted individuals in Hungary, keeping it as compensation for loss of property the government failed to hand over during the territorial transfer. The letter also mentioned that an acquaintance of the family traveling to Hungary would soon contact him. He guessed it right away what the message meant: his family was sending him money via a third party. The news put him in such a good mood that he decided to dip into his reserves and buy a winter coat to ward against the freezing weather. It was approaching Christmas, and now that he was able to move about without the risk of catching a cold, he joined his fellow students in planning to resurrect another old university tradition, the lighting of an outdoor Christmas tree erected on college grounds. They cut a tall tree in the Loevers and placed it on the circular clearing in front of the main building entrance. Next, they posted notices throughout the city inviting the community to join the lighting ceremony on the evening of the 23rd; they only asked to bring an ornament or candle to help decorating the tree. There would be caroling and later refreshments served inside.

To everyone's surprise, the response was tremendous. By late afternoon people started to arrive, bringing not only the requested decorations but also all kinds of homemade cookies, finger sandwiches, and fruits and nuts. An hour or so later, with the last ornament hung and all the candles lit, the tree stood in its glittering glory, casting a glow over the festive crowd gathered around it. In the sudden quiet several students stepped to the front and with their violins raised began to play one of the most beloved Christmas carols of Hungary, "The Shepherds of Bethlehem." The air was cold but nobody noticed as voices one after the other joined in, filling the night air with joyous singing. Goodwill warmed every heart in the spirit of this first community Christmas celebration that brought the local people another step closer to acknowledging that these boys were good and decent young men, deserving of acceptance.

Then came the most touching moment of the evening as the violins quietly sounded the first notes of *Stille Nacht* ("Silent Night"), that magically universal Christmas song heard for the first time in an Austrian village church in the year 1818. In its timeless simplicity this song has the power to evoke nostalgic memories in anyone who once as a child stood enthralled in front of a Christmas tree. The locals were deeply moved, more so by knowing that so many of these young men were left without a home, separated from their families. Seeing them standing in the midst of the crowd, yet seemingly so alone, some visibly struggling to keep emotions at bay, the people poignantly waited in silence at the end of the singing to give them time to regain composure. A minute later the celebratory mood returned with everyone cheering and wishing Merry Christmas to friends and strangers alike.

When it was time to move inside for snacks and hot coffee or cider, the poor students fell on the table set with trays of food, delicious pastries, and cookies. The sight of these hungry boys, stuffing their mouths as well as their pockets with treats, drew pitying glances from a number of ladies. Soon they were huddled together, whispering about how they could make Christmas a little brighter for them. It was not a difficult decision to make: they would open their homes and invite them on Christmas Day to share a home-cooked meal and a hearty cheer on this most celebrated of holidays.

Of course, not everyone received an invitation; many were left behind to eat the less desirable mess hall food. To make up for it, those leaving solemnly promised to bring back as much leftovers as decency would allow. Most of the hosting families turned out to be elderly couples whose children had flown the nest, or worst, who had lost sons or grandsons during the war. Only a few among the students were fortunate enough to be invited to homes where a young lady was also present. True, none of these girls would win beauty contests, but how many of the boys had any resemblance to Adonis? And when some of these first contacts with the opposite sex blossomed into romance, it resurrected another old Selmec tradition: the pinning of a red velvet heart embroidered with the young lady's name to the left breast area of the student's uniform jacket. It announced that the wearer was "taken," and the young lady named on the patch was no longer fair game to others. Being "pinned" was a step away from a formal engagement.

As more and more students walked the streets sporting a red heart on their uniforms, mothers began to take notice. Their initial fear of the students and the determination to shield their girls from them were already mitigated to a certain degree by the way the boys had proven themselves so far, but now with all these embroidered hearts popping up all over the city, it was time to reconsider in earnest. Perhaps they were wrong in their thinking, a bit hasty in passing judgment without first giving the boys a chance. It seemed that they were turning out to be reliable, well-mannered, respectful young men with honest intentions, many of them apparently serious enough to commit to lasting relationships. With a diploma in hand they would be making a fair living, enough to support a wife and family. By all estimation they would make good husbands and providers, and what more could a mother hope for a daughter?

More invitations followed for dinners on New Year's Day, but regrettably, none was extended to Jeno. He spent the evening in the dormitory playing cards and drinking some of the good local wine. At the stroke of midnight the boys said goodbye to an eventful year and raised their glasses to usher in 1922. General expectations for the coming year ran high; everyone believed that somehow Trianon would be rectified, and the country would be made whole again.

For Jeno, however, the future looked rather dim. No one contacted him about the money he was supposed to receive by Christmas. Not a word from the individual his family trusted, mistakenly it seems, with the delivery. This last failure made it clear that he could no longer count on financial help from home, and without that he must find some way to keep afloat. He urgently needed a part-time job, or he would be forced to quit his studies. Instead of going to the coffeehouse, he began making his rounds, calling on offices, shops, and restaurants, all without success, until someone suggested he should try tutoring.

His mood lightened at once. He was always good in mathematics, grammar, and history; he could easily give lessons in these subjects. He posted notices in every school and on street kiosks offering private tutoring, and at the same time asked his buddies with newly formed connections to families to spread the word.

Responds to his ads started to trickle in, first only a few, but soon tutoring took up all his free time. After buying some sorely needed clothing and treating himself to an occasional better meal, he put aside all the money he earned. As his only recreation, he still went down to the old coffeehouse to play cards on Sunday afternoons, but now he had enough change to play, instead of just kibitzing to others. It all seemed that his luck began to turn. Not only was he winning more than losing at cards, but he also learned that his request for financial aid was granted.

With his life getting back on track, this was the first time since they left Selmec that Jeno began to look to the future with real confidence.

By the middle of March some students came up with the idea that giving a grand ball would further advance their social acceptance. There was just one small problem: they did not have the money to finance the enterprise. To attract attention the ball must be held at the great room of the city's cultural center, the prestigious Kaszino building, but how to pay the rent and utilities with empty pockets? After discussing possible solutions, they decided to approach the mayor and ask the city to subsidize the event. It was an unspoken understanding that Sopron owed a lot to these students, for without their efforts they would be part of Austria now. To even the score the city fathers agreed to foot the bill, and with that accomplished the boys sat down to compile a list of the available young ladies to invite. When the invitations were mailed out, one bore the address of Miss Lensie Bohaczek.

Soon the upcoming ball became the subject of all conversation. In the streets, at the marketplace or at social gatherings one heard nothing but mothers debating whether they should allow their girls to attend the ball. In Mrs. Szep's opinion there was no reason why her daughters shouldn't go; after all, they would be well chaperoned.

Her friend, Mrs. Verecky, disagreed. "It is true what you are saying," she countered, "but you can't be on their heels all the time. With the music playing, the romantic atmosphere, and the dim lights, you'll see how fast couples disappear into dark corners where it's impossible to see them. And the way they dance these days! It's a far cry from our time when we waltzed around keeping at a decent arm's length. No, I think I'll keep my daughter home!"

But if judged by how seamstresses were suddenly inundated with orders for new ball gowns, it seemed the "pro" voices were winning. Sofie, who worked for Angela before she lost her hand and now had her own dressmaking shop, was running a brisk business, too. She expected Angela and Lensie to come in any day to work on a design for Lensie's dress.

When the invitation first arrived, Lensie's thoughts immediately turned to the young man she met in the Loevers. Would he be at the ball? Her mother knew nothing about the encounter; apparently no one noticed them since no word got back to her. Lensie never mentioned it either; her mother would only press for details, asking who he was, how they met, and if she'd found out the truth, it would only lead to a lecture on proper behavior.

Greatly excited, she could hardly wait for her mother to come home and show her the invitation, but Angela's reaction was not what Lensie expected.

"You just put that ball out of your head, Lensie, you are too young to go," was her answer. "You are not even sixteen; there will be plenty of other balls later on."

"But Mama, Hilda and Irene are going, and they are only a little older than me! If they can go, why can't I?"

"If Mrs. Szep is taking her daughters, that's her business. I think she is wrong, but it's up to her. It does not mean we have to do the same."

"It's not just them! Many of my friends are going, too. I can give you their names if you want to talk to their mothers. I would like so much to go, please, Mama."

"I am sorry Lensie, perhaps next year," she said and, raising a firm hand, put a stop to further arguments.

She had her reasons for being so unrelenting. These men were much too old for Lensie, not the usual boys of eighteen to twenty-two who normally filled the university lecture halls. They had served years in the military, had seen battle and were hardened by war. She would have no objection next year when the first crop of the new freshmen arrived, students just out of high school who were only a year or two older than Lensie, their age better suited for socializing with teenage girls.

Lensie pleaded and fought, but Angela stuck to her guns. She did not feel she had to explain her true motives, and only repeated that Lensie was too young and would have to wait a year. But Lensie wouldn't give up, either. She came up with one argument after another, crying and begging, but what finally wore down her mother's resistance was when she reminded Angela how her own mother's death deprived her of all the rightful enjoyment of youth. Wasn't she only a few years older than Lensie when her mother died? What if something similar should happen to Angela? God forbid, but the tuberculosis that took her hand could reappear, and although Lensie might be old enough then to go dancing, she could never do it with her mother stricken with the dreadful disease. Let alone the possibility that the illness should claim her life, leaving Lensie alone, mourning for the rest of her life!

At that point Angela threw in the towel. There was truth in what her daughter said. What would happen to her in case she died suddenly? She thought how different her life would have been if her mother had lived, if she had been there to steer her in the right direction. She would have known better than to throw herself into the arms of the first man who showed her kindness and compassion.

No, she wouldn't let that happen to her daughter. Better if she let her meet these men while she was still here and could watch over her.

Lensie almost jumped to the ceiling from sheer joy when Angela told her that she had changed her mind. Grabbing her, she danced around the room one minute; in the next she pushed her mother into a chair and brought out a pad and pencil and drew some sketches for the gown she would wear. Then she ran next door to tell Hilda the news, only to rush back to say that what she designed was all wrong because her friend's dress would be too similar. She must have something completely different. She went to great lengths trying to prove to Angela that she was not too young to attend the ball. Didn't she take good care of her during her illness? All she wanted was to have some fun, to dance a little and see what a big formal ball was all about. They would have so much to talk about after it was over.

Angela chose a soft cream color taffeta for Lensie's gown, to complement her chestnut hair and peachy complexion, and with sketches in hand they went to see Sofie. Together they picked a pattern that showed off Lensie's slender figure, with a modest décolletage trimmed with lace. As for her hair, she would wear it loose around her face with a simple pearl clip on one side. She was too young for elaborate updos, not to mention the new "bob" that was becoming the latest in hairstyle.

On the night of the ball Angela and Lensie rode in a hired carriage to the Kaszino, where students wearing their formal uniforms lined up to escort the guests to the second floor ballroom. Once seated, mothers and chaperones kept up a lively chat waiting for the opening, while their daughters were just as busy, surveying the boys from behind fluttering little fans. The students standing around the bandstand were not idle, either; they were conducting a survey of their own, deciding which girl to ask once the dancing began.

Promptly at eight o'clock the professors walked into the room led by the dean. He greeted the guests, welcoming everyone to this first ball that would set the precedent for others to follow. He talked about the tradition behind the two dances the students held every year, the "Balek Ball" in the fall to welcome the freshmen, or baleks, and this one in the spring called the "Valeta Ball," honoring the graduating seniors. He announced that a midnight buffet would be served on the first floor, with more dancing to follow until the two o'clock closing. He then wished everyone a grand time, signaled to the orchestra to start the music, and taking his wife's hand, led her to the dance floor, thus officially opening the ball.

Now the students made their move. The floor was soon crowded with couples waltzing to the tune of the beautiful "Blue Danube." Lensie, too, was dancing with a handsome young man, but her eyes were scanning the room in search of the stranger she met at the edge of the forest. Disappointed for not finding him, she almost gave up when suddenly she saw him shouldering his way toward her. He tapped Lensie's partner on the shoulder, then leaving the disappointed fellow standing, took her in his arms and waltzed away. Not that

Jeno could hold on to her more than a few turns. She was too much in demand. Being an excellent dancer, light on her feet, leaning easily into the turns that waltzing required, Lensie danced without stop, changing partners often, taking a moment here and there to see if her mother needed anything. She didn't have to worry; Angela was far from being bored. Chairs pulled together, the ladies formed their own party, gossiping about who danced with whom, and how often, discussing the men, and criticizing the dresses the girls wore.

Early on Jeno asked if Lensie and her mother would do the honor of being his guests at the midnight supper, and of course Lensie gladly agreed, pending her mother's approval. Introductions followed and when Angela accepted the invitation, Jeno escorted them to the dining room. They were the first to sit down at a table set for eight, and while Jeno left to bring refreshments, Angela quickly turned to her daughter.

"I saw you were dancing a lot with this young man. He seems to be nice and shows good manners but you just met him; why spend so much time with him? There are so many others here; give yourself a chance to get acquainted with more than just this Mr. Zachar."

Lensie hardly had time to whisper back, "Oh Mama, come on, I danced with everyone, it's just that Jeno is the best dancer," before he was back with a pitcher of lemonade. Others joined the table and soon they were all talking about the ball, praising the food, the music, and the overall good time everyone seemed to be enjoying. Jeno was attentive in his own quiet way, seeing to it that glasses were never left empty, and while he took part in the conversation, he preferred listening to what others had to say. By nature he was even-tempered and poised, never too loud or presumptuous when expressing an opinion. He was known back in the dormitory as impossible to provoke into an argument; he simply refused to get involved in a confrontation. Blessed with a dry sense of humor he often used it effectively to defuse a potentially tense situation. Feeling comfortable in his own skin and acting with a natural ease, people responded to him likewise.

When the music started up again, couples returned to the dance floor for another hour before the lights dimmed, signaling that it was time to leave. As people were lining up for carriages, instead of waiting, Angela decided to walk the short ten minutes it took to reach Szena Square. With her permission Jeno accompanied them, hoping that by the time they got to the house he'd gain her confidence to let him visit Lensie. On their way he expected some personal questions from Angela, but she kept the talk centered on the university's transfer to Sopron and about his studies.

Reaching home, she turned to Jeno. "It was a pleasure to meet you, Mr. Zachar, and thank you for entertaining my daughter and seeing us home safely." Then, without allowing him time to respond, she addressed Lensie. "We better get upstairs, Lensie, it's getting late, so say goodnight to Mr. Zachar while I ring the concierge." With that she turned toward the door but Jeno's voice made her stop.

"The pleasure is all mine, Mrs. Bohaczek. You have an enchanting daughter, and I can hardly find words to tell how much I enjoyed spending time with her. I'd very much like to get to know her better, so please forgive my boldness, but may I have your permission to call on her in the future?"

Angela looked down, then to the side before settling her eyes on Jeno. "Mr. Zachar, your compliments are most flattering, thank you, but please understand that I must say no to you. Lensie is too young to start dating; she is not yet sixteen, and in my opinion even this ball was too early for her to attend. She wanted to go, so I gave in, but that's where I draw the line. She is not ready to carry on a social life, so for the time being, I must ask you not to pursue her in any way or manner. I hope you will respect my wishes. Now say goodbye, Lensie, we really must be going."

Disappointed and visibly embarrassed, Lensie thanked Jeno for the beautiful evening then, managing a smile, she said she would be in a hurry to grow up if he'd promise to be patient. Jeno, smiling back, whispered not to worry; it was only a matter of time. Then he assured Angela that he understood and accepted her decision, and only hoped that perhaps the next time he asked, her answer would be more favorable.

On his way home Jeno thought about his promise to Angela not to pursue Lensie. But what did she really mean by "pursue"? Exchanging a few words if they met on the street surely would not count as pursuing. No rational person could object to that. What would she have him do, cross the street to the other side if he saw her coming? That would be simply ridiculous. He wouldn't break his promise if they ran into each other by accident and talked a bit. And if he did a little pre-arranging for such a "chance" meeting, it was only for him to know.

And so, whenever Jeno had time between attending lectures, studying, and tutoring, he was at the coffeehouse with an eye on the entrance to Lensie's building. He even stopped playing cards and just kibitzed so he could leave if Lensie should appear. During the month following the ball he caught sight of her only a few times, but never by herself. On the afternoon when he finally saw her leaving alone, he sprang to his feet and ran out without an excuse. He didn't dash after her, though; instead, he kept running on a parallel street to gain some distance ahead of her. Reaching the end of the block he crossed over to her street, then catching his breath and trying to look casual, strolled down toward her.

"Why, hello little Lensie! It must be my lucky day, running into you. What have you been doing since the ball?"

The late sun was in her eyes and she raised a hand to shield against the blinding glare. "Oh, it's you," she said, peering into his face. "I am doing fine, Mr. Zachar, and you?"

"Can't complain, but I would feel a lot better if you'd call me Jeno, just like you did at the ball—or did you forget already?"

"Of course I didn't forget, a girl never forgets her first ball; it was such a lovely affair."

"I hope you remember more than just the ball, perhaps some of us poor fellows you danced with."

"Oh, you are just teasing me, Jeno, but seriously, I hope everything is going well for you."

"Yes, I manage, thank you. But my God, it's good to see you. Where are you going? Could I walk with you so we can talk a little? I don't see any harm in that, do you?"

"Well, I suppose mother wouldn't mind if we just walked together. I am on my way to the bookstore. I need to buy some sheet music for my next piano lesson." They fell into step as they started down the street.

"So you are studying piano? You see, how little I know about you, what you do, what you like. I don't even know your exact name. Lensie is short for what?"

"It's Helen, but nobody calls me that. It's too formal."

"Helen is a German name; it would be Ilona in Hungarian. So far we only spoke German; do you speak Hungarian at all?"

"Yes, I learned it when we moved to Sopron from Vienna nine years ago. It's harder for my mother; she still struggles with the language, and so do a lot of other people around here. I guess all that will have to change now that Hungarian is so emphasized in everything."

"And it is about time too, Lensie. This poor country is now one third of what it used to be; it needs every bit of help to keep it alive, don't you think?"

"Oh, I don't know much about politics, but I guess you are right."

"I wish we could sit down and talk a little. Look, the Roth ice cream parlor is right there on the corner. Let's have a soda or tea, just for a little while?"

"I would like that very much, but you heard what my mother said. I am sure she wouldn't approve. Besides, I don't really have time. I have to get back to prepare dinner before my mother gets home from work."

"Your mother works?"

"Yes, she works at the post office. Well, here we are, this is the shop. We better say goodbye now."

He wanted to wait for her, but she said no. It was not a good idea. If her mother should hear of their meeting, she could explain a chance encounter, but letting him wait might lead to a quarrel. Perhaps they'd run into each other again, she said with a mischievous smile.

Jeno was smitten with Lensie. She was so natural, so honest, without any pretensions, and so pretty with those green eyes and beautiful smile. He wanted to find out more about her, although he agreed with her mother that Lensie was a bit too young to get involved with dating. But still, what harm would it be if she'd just let him come to visit under her supervision? He must find a way to gain her approval, to earn her trust—not an easy task when denied the opportunity to prove he meant no harm. Well, until she softened her stance, he had no choice but continue to hover around the coffeehouse and wait for another "chance meeting" to present itself.

Sweet Sixteen and beyond

SPRING CAME EARLY to Sopron in 1922, filling the air with the promise of a new beginning. April showers gave way to clear blue skies, and naked trees, soaking up the sun, began sprouting their first tender buds. The whole city came to life as people shed their dreary winter coats and joined others in strolling up and down the promenade, greeting each other with renewed smiles.

The joy that spring brought, however, was nothing compared to the excitement Lensie felt as her birthday approached. On May 8 she would turn sixteen, a day she hoped would bring so many changes in her life. To celebrate it, Angela made plans for a luncheon, inviting the whole family and all of Lensie's girlfriends, but asking everyone to keep it a secret. It was to be held at Lensie's old school, with some of her former teachers also coming. Although Lensie had finished her mandatory schooling, she still sang in the choir and practiced piano at the Sisters'.

Angela took the afternoon off from work and suggested to Lensie they stop at the church and ask God's blessing before taking her to lunch. As prearranged, the nuns kept them from entering the church on some pretext and directed them to wait in the reception hall, where a chorus of "Happy Birthday, Lensie" greeted her. She was thrilled by the surprise, to be the center of the celebration, showered with kisses and surrounded by people she loved.

When the sisters brought in her birthday cake, she took a deep breath, squeezed her eyes shut and made the only wish she had in her heart, to be allowed to see Jeno with her mother's approval. Then she opened her eyes and blew out all the sixteen candles in one take.

The cheers and celebration continued, with the girls sitting at one table, giggling and sharing little secrets, and the adults at another. With all the Bohaczek sisters and brothers and their families together, Lensie's birthday party turned into a true family reunion. When it finally broke up late in the afternoon, Lensie couldn't thank her mother enough for giving her such a wonderful party. At home she tried on Angela's present, a beautiful new outfit, saying repeatedly that she felt *real* grown-up wearing it. Angela just smiled; she knew full well what her smart little girl was hinting at. Lensie could feel grown up as much as she liked, she still wasn't mature enough to start dating.

It was not long after her birthday that Lensie and Angela ran into Jeno, this time truly by chance, and stopped for a few minutes, just enough to say hello and exchange a few polite words. When he said he was doing fine, it was far from the truth. Schools were closing their doors soon, which meant losing his income from tutoring. He would be left without funds to carry him through the summer unless he found some other way to make money. The question was how? Jobs were still scarce, especially for students; employers were reluctant to hire them, knowing well enough that they would be heading back to college in the fall. As he racked his brain trying to figure out how he was going to keep his head above the water, a thought began to form in his mind. Tutoring worked so well for him, why not find something else to teach? How about tennis? He was a good player and giving lessons could be fun! He could easily do it if he could line up enough people interested in learning the game. He'd start by putting out the word among the students he tutored, advertise a little with "Tennis anyone?" postings, then see what the reaction would be.

The city maintained a fenced-in area with two tennis courts—that also served as a skating rink in the winter—but besides a few college students and some high school kids, hardly anyone played there. Most of the time youngsters were using it to roller-skate, causing considerable damage to the cement and the nets. Still, regardless of the neglect and misuse, with some repairs it could serve Jeno's purpose.

When the response to his advertising was encouraging, he obtained a license for teaching tennis, and persuaded the city to issue an ordinance barring children from treating the court as a playground. By the time the cracks in the cement were filled and the holes in the nets fixed, he was ready to launch his business as a tennis instructor. The job needed a lot of patience and an upbeat personality to keep the fledgling players interested enough to continue their lessons, but he was well suited for that. Only if people would show up! It didn't take long. After waiting with fingers crossed, it surprised him how many signed up, and not just boys, but quite a few girls and young ladies, too. In no time he had a full schedule that kept him busy and solvent, at least for the time being.

As word spread and Lensie got wind that Jeno was giving lessons, she started to come around with her girlfriends to watch from outside the fence. The main attraction for her was seeing Jeno, but it was also great fun to watch the beginners fumbling with their rackets, hitting the air while the balls zapped by their ears. Even parents found their children's first clumsy attempts at the game amusing, but given time, it became quite rewarding to see them develop skills to the point where spectators would burst into enthusiastic applause at a scoring shot. Soon it was fashionable to be on the tennis court, as young people made it their new place to meet, make friends, and socialize. Inevitably, another instructor appeared on the scene, but by then Jeno was fully booked, so the competition didn't hurt him.

Lensie immediately saw her chance to spend time with Jeno if she could only talk her mother into letting her take lessons. She spent the whole day thinking of ways to convince her why it was so urgently important that her hitherto un-athletic daughter should learn to play tennis. And so, when Angela got home from work expecting the usual greeting, she was met with a bewildering barrage of words Lensie unleashed on her.

"Oh Mama, I wish you could have been with us when we went by the tennis courts today with Hilda and some other girls. You know how it was a playground for kids and nobody much played tennis there, but you should see it now! It's all fixed up, there is no more roller-skating allowed, they only let tennis players in, and everyone is signing up for lessons. And that's not just boys, but girls, too. We watched for a while, and it was so exciting! I guess you don't know much about tennis, but it's really a fun game. Either two or four people can play; they face each other on opposite sides of a net, hitting a small ball back and forth with a racket. I don't exactly know the method of scoring, but it's being called out as they play. Sometimes it's a number, or words like love, or ad-in and ad-out—anyway, it's a fast game. And a friendly one, too, with everyone shaking hands at the end, the losers congratulating the winners. We are going again on Sunday and you must come with us so you can see it for yourself. It's such an elegant sport, Mama, the players are all dressed in white. But not only that, it's also an excellent exercise; it involves just about every part of the body. You swing your arm when you hit the ball, and stretch upward when you serve—that means tossing the ball—and they are constantly running around the court. Watching them play made me realize that since I quit school I am not getting any exercise at all, and it would be a great way to keep in shape if I got to learn this game. All the girls want to take lessons, and it does not cost very much. Could I please sign up for it, too? Please say yes, Mama!"

Angela tried several times to put in a word, but it was no use. It was true, she didn't know much about the game, but she had heard about tennis gaining popularity among women as a social game, and she saw no reason to deny Lensie the lessons.

"Lensie, sweetie, I haven't seen you so excited since you received that ball invitation. I don't know why this sudden interest in tennis that you girls can't live without chasing a fist size ball around a court, but all right, if it's such a good exercise, I will go with you Sunday after Mass and see what it's all about, then we can talk some more."

"I am sure there will be a game, but I will find out for sure. Oh Mama, you'll like it; I know you will. And isn't it wonderful to live in such modern times when girls can do just like the boys? And it's about time! Why should they have it better than us? It's only fair, don't you think, Mama?"

"Well, boys are just different, Lensie; God intended them to be so. Life prepares them to be stronger, to be able to provide for their families, and while you think women are pushed into the background, their role is just as important. They are the caregivers, giving the love and emotional support children need. This is what marriage is all about, a wonderfully balanced partnership that worked for thousands of years, and still does."

Although Lensie didn't say a word, Angela could see the condescending little smile on her face. "I know from your look that you think I am old-fashioned but believe me, most young girls today still have the same dream as my generation had, to fall in love, to have a good husband and raise a family. You might not see it that way with your aspiration for a career in music, but how many girls have special talents like yours, and have the ambition and determination to develop that talent? Just look around your friends, listen to them talk about what they want in life, and you'll find that I am right. You and I were born in a different century, and it's true, a great deal has changed since I was young, but those 19th century sentiments I grew up with are deep-rooted and are still valid today."

"Mama, you got me all wrong! I want to get married and have a family! What I meant about boys is that I wish we could do things they do all the time, and not be judged for being unladylike."

"What do you mean, what things are you talking about?"

"Well, it's nothing big, just to have more freedom to do things like going to places without constantly being chaperoned. A boy can go on a date without his mother tagging along, so why can't we do the same? All we hear that it's not nice, but why? What's so bad about sitting down in an ice cream shop and having a soda with a boy? What harm could be in that? And another thing, why am I always expected to order tea or cocoa when I'd rather have an espresso? What's wrong with drinking espresso, or smoking a cigarette, for that matter? I might not even like it, but at least I'd like to try."

But then Lensie suddenly caught herself and stopped. This was not a good time to bring these things up, just when she wanted her mother's approval for tennis lessons. To get back on track she quickly changed the subject. "Oh, this is so silly," she said with a flick of her wrist, "I don't know what got into me talking like this when I don't really mean any of it."

"My sweet girl, of course you mean it," Angela patted Lensie's face "You are at an age when you want to try new things, and it's only natural. Wanting changes is part of growing up. But don't be in a hurry, Lensie. I know you are tired of hearing this, but I have to say it again: you have all the time in the world. It will be soon enough when you'll be able to do as you please. Give yourself time to enjoy your few remaining carefree years. You don't realize it yet, but you have a kind of freedom now that you might never have again, freedom from responsibilities and freedom from problems and worries. These years go by so fast; take full pleasure in them. It is not easy being sixteen when you think you know all the answers and want to spread your wings. I know how that feels; it has not been that long since I went through the same thing. Like you, I couldn't wait to join the adult world. Unfortunately, I got my wish when my mother died so young. I had to grow up real fast and the independence I wanted so much turned out to be quite different from what I imagined it would be. And this is exactly why I am telling you to wait; I know the difference. Have patience, Lensie, use your time to learn from the changes that each year brings, so when the time comes to be on your own you will be able to say, 'I am ready for the next phase of my life.' And with more maturity you'll be so much better prepared to experience all the new things that are waiting for you in the future. You'll be so glad that you did. Will you at least try?"

"You are right, Mama; please forget the stupid things I said. It's just when I am together with my friends, we talk and complain about this and that, but I should never bother you with it. I am sorry that I brought it up and it won't happen again, I promise. Am I forgiven? Can I still sign up for tennis lessons?"

"There is no need to apologize, Lensie, I am glad we had this little talk and that you felt you can tell me things that are on your mind. We might not agree on everything, but even if I say or do something that you resent, remember, it's because I want the best for you, always." Angela opened her arms to Lensie and she hugged her back. Yes, she loved her mother with all her heart; she only wished she'd see that girls today were growing up faster than in the old days!

"Now about those tennis lessons," Angela said when she finally released her. "You take me to see the game on Sunday, and if it is as wonderful as you say, we can sign you up right there and then."

Angela meant to keep her promise, even though her instincts told her there was more to Lensie's sudden overwhelming enthusiasm about tennis. Her suspicion proved to be right when they arrived at the court and she saw Jeno in the middle of a game. *Ah-ha, so that's what this is all about,* Angela thought, but watching him play she had to admit, the game was all as Lensie described: graceful, wholesome, an overall good sport. She made up her mind, that regardless of Jeno, she'd let Lensie take the lessons. In spite of their recent talk, Angela knew that times were changing, and she must accept the fact that young people today had a different outlook on life. They were bolder, more demanding, and they did everything with such urgency, as if afraid to miss out on life.

Perhaps the war helped to bring this about. She was just grateful that they lived in a small city where it took longer for new ideas to take root and trends to catch on. Last summer when she was visiting Lizzie in Vienna, she could hardly believe how young girls looked and behaved there. They wore revealing sleeveless, low-cut dresses that did not even cover their knees, and cut their hair short, letting it fall loose. And the makeup! Cheeks colored with rouge, lips painted bright red, nails lacquered in the same color! They were smoking cigarettes held in long holders, their hands without gloves. They even walked differently; those high heel sandals made their hips move with a rhythmic sway. She also heard, although she never saw it, that they engaged in wild dances, kicking their legs high, shaking their whole body to a music called Jazz. If someone asked her opinion, she would like to see all of it outlawed. By all means, let Lensie take tennis lessons, no harm in that as long as she followed the rules she was about to impose.

"Well, Lensie, you are right, this is a nice sport," Angela said turning to her daughter. "I like it and I can see why you want to learn it. I also see that Mr. Zachar is quite involved in the game. Any chance that he is the one giving the lessons?"

"Yes Mama, but you see how well he plays; he is simply the best! There is another instructor but Jeno is much better and everyone wants to sign up with him. I hope he can squeeze me in, because I know he is fully booked."

"I don't think you have to worry about that. I am sure he'll find a way, even if he has to kick somebody out. We'll go and see him after he is finished playing, but you must promise me one thing. You take your lessons, but when you are through you leave the court, and you leave alone and head straight for home. In other words, your activity should revolve around tennis and not Mr.

Zachar. You come here for one thing, and one thing only, to learn to play tennis. Is this understood?"

"Yes Mama, I understand," she nodded vigorously and would have promised anything Angela asked. She could hardly keep from jumping from joy. She was afraid her mother would object after seeing Jeno; it was almost too good to believe that she still agreed, and so easily. Of course, she would also try to learn the game, but if she could not master it, she could care less.

Jeno's temporary work as a tennis instructor helped to get him through the summer, but the money he made was not enough to continue his studies when the fall semester started. That would depend on whether he'd be granted financial aid again, a rather dubious likelihood since his grades had slipped on account of his tutoring work. What he would do if they turned him down, he didn't know. For the first time, he had serious misgivings about his decision to leave Selmec. Perhaps his brother did the right thing by staying. The Slovaks let him work, and according to his latest letter, he was about to get married. And here he was, cut off from his family, facing an uncertain future, and struggling to maintain the barest existence. Perhaps he made a mistake, but if he did, it was too late for regrets.

The first bright moment in his gloomy state of mind came the day when Lensie signed up for tennis lessons. During the past weeks he saw her several times coming around the courts to watch from behind the fences, but she was always with her friends, never staying long enough so he could catch a moment with her. It was the last thing he expected when he saw Lensie walking right into his court with her mother at her side. If her sudden appearance caught him off-guard, it was nothing compared to the surprise over the change in Angela's attitude. She was gracious and friendly, complimenting Jeno for winning the game and even poking fun at him for virtually single-handedly making tennis such a popular game, especially among young ladies. She remained in good humor during their discussion about the fees and the number of lessons Lensie should take, and only turned serious when she made it clear that the games should be played strictly on the court.

As Lensie began her lessons, it soon became plain that she'd never play at Wimbledon, but she looked very pretty dressed in all white, swinging her racket, bouncing happily around the court. She had no feeling for the game and found it extremely difficult to follow one of the principal rules, to keep her eyes focused on the ball, when all she saw was Jeno. But none of this mattered, not when she could spend time with him and do it with her mother's blessing. If she had to suffer through the silly lessons and run around with the sun beating down on her to be near Jeno, she'd do it a thousand times.

Jeno saw her struggling with the racket, and with infinite patience hit the balls where she could easily reach them, then praised her to heaven when she managed to return one. She knew he treated her preferentially and felt flattered by his attention. Eventually, through sheer willpower, she learned to play a fair game, if for no other reason but to prove to her mother what a great instructor Jeno was. Most of the time she kept her promise and left after her lessons, staying only to watch Jeno if he had a chance to take a break and play a game. She sat on the sidelines, and whenever he scored a point she'd shout enthusiastically, "good shot," or "nice return," showing off her newly acquired tennis lingo.

To her, he was the most handsome man with his deep blue eyes, dark unruly hair, and golden tan against the all-white tennis attire. But it was not just his good looks Lensie found so irresistible. She also admired his self-confidence, the easy manner with which he interacted with people, and his good judgment in handling different situations. He could be stern if a pupil would slack off, not paying attention, but also encouraging if someone was truly struggling, ready to give up. The way he'd play down unwanted attention from girls who carried the game a step further and tried to flirt also impressed her. Of course, he'd carry on a harmless little flirtation with Lensie, but beyond that his conduct was totally proper; only once or twice did he put his hand to the small of her back as he escorted her off the court, a gesture without the slightest hint of intimacy.

When scheduling her lessons, Lensie always booked one for Sunday noon in case her mother wanted to stop by after church to watch her play. As the weeks went by, Angela could see the progress Lensie made, and when she announced that on the morning of the last Sunday of August she'd be playing for the first time in a mixed double with Jeno as her partner, Angela promised to be there. She arrived a little after nine o'clock and finding the game already in progress, remained behind the fence to wait until the players switched ends. Marching down to the courts in the middle of a game was against the rules of tennis etiquette; it would distract the players. As she watched her daughter expertly hitting the balls and moving around the court quickly yet with grace, she had to admit that Lensie was no longer the awkward teenager of yesterday, but a confident young lady. Sadly, she realized that time was fast approaching when she would come into her own and she would have no choice but to let her go.

But not just yet. Lensie might look and feel grown-up, but she still lacked the experience to make the right decisions for herself. Take, for example, her obvious infatuation with Jeno. No doubt, they made a wonderful looking couple, but they were not right for each other. Since Lensie started her tennis lessons, Angela made it her business to find out a little more about Jeno, and from what she heard she knew he was much older than Lensie, and had seen too much of life's dark side already. Fighting the war, being torn from his family, and struggling financially was enough to make any man bitter and disillusioned. He might overcome his difficulties, but the memories would remain, and how could Lensie, an idealistic sixteen-year-old girl, relate to them when they were not shared memories? Such gaps would create difficulties in any relationship. No, he was simply the wrong man for Lensie, and Angela was determined to keep him out of her daughter's life. She needed someone close to her age, a younger man who saw the world in similar hues, a true partner for life as they built memories together without the shadow of a separate past.

When the game ended, Angela walked inside the court and watched the rest of the set from the benches. After winning the match, Lensie and Jeno shook hands with the other couple and as they turned around, flushed with excitement, it hit her again how beautiful they looked together. A minute later they were standing in front of her.

"It's nice to see you again, Mrs. Bohaczek," Jeno greeted her. "Your daughter is becoming quite a tennis champ. It's much to her credit that we beat our opponents."

Angela accepted the compliment with a nod, "If you say so, Mr. Zachar; I am not an expert in tennis but I could see she played well. She just loves the game; if I'd let her, she would live on these courts."

"Tennis can do that to people; it's highly competitive, and she has the drive to win. I told her that she has picked up as much as I can teach her, so there is no point to continue with her lessons, but she must keep practicing to stay at the level she attained."

"I know, I know, practice makes perfect," Lensie laughed, mimicking Jeno then turned to her mother. "Well Mama, what do you think? Since today is kind of a graduation day for me, should we reward Jeno for turning me into such a great tennis player, as he says I am, and treat him to some ice cream?"

"The reward should be yours Lensie," Jeno protested. "An instructor can do just so much, it's up to the student to take it from there. It's you who deserve a special treat, so please, Mrs. Bohaczek, may I invite you for a soda or ice cream? There is a parlor just two short blocks from here."

"Thank you, Mr. Zachar, it's very kind of you to ask us, but I am afraid we must leave. I promised to take my nephew to church since his mother is under the weather and unable to take him. We are running late as it is, so Lensie, get your things, we must hurry if we want to catch the twelve o'clock Mass. You still have to change and we have to pick up Franz." Then she turned back to Jeno. "I am sorry for the rush, but it can't be helped. I hope you understand the situation and give us a rain check, Mr. Zachar."

She didn't fool Jeno. This was an obvious excuse to soften the rejection, making it clear that regardless of his earlier impression, he had made no headway in gaining Angela's approval.

"Perhaps another time then, when it will be more convenient," Jeno smiled as he bowed his head to Angela, just as Lensie was coming back with her tennis bag. He saw the disappointment on her face, but with Angela standing there all he could say that he hoped she would continue practicing and that he'd always be happy to play a set with her.

On their way out Lensie, following behind her mother, looked back at Jeno and pulled a shoulder with a helpless expression and upturned palms, but once they were on the street she turned on Angela.

"What was that all about, Mother? I just saw Aunt Mitzie yesterday at the market, and there was nothing wrong with her. You made up this whole story and I want to know why. Even if it is true about taking Franz to church, there is another Mass later we could have gone to. And don't think a minute that Jeno didn't see through this silly excuse. Please tell me, why do you hate him so much? What did he ever do to be treated like this?"

"We'll talk about it when we get home, Lensie."

"Fine, but talk we will, Mama, and I want a straight answer as to what you have against Jeno!"

They continued walking in silence, but as soon as the door closed Lensie confronted her mother. "Well, we are home now, so let's have it out!"

"Sit down, Lensie, and get off your high horse. You wanted a straight answer so I will give it to you. I don't want you to get involved any deeper with that man. It's as simple as that."

"His name is Jeno, Mother; please don't refer to him as 'that man.' He deserves better."

"So, you think you are such an expert judge of character that you know him inside and out after meeting him a few times? It takes a lot more to get to know a person than a spin around the dance floor and a couple of tennis lessons. You are smitten with him, Lensie, and invest him with qualities you wish him to possess, but that doesn't mean he has them."

"And how am I supposed to know him better if you don't let me spend enough time with him, huh, Mama?"

"Lensie, it would take a long time to find out if he is really as trustworthy as you think, and I don't want you to waste your time on it. Even if he turned out to be without a single fault, you must trust me on this; he is not the right man for you. He is a complex individual, not like some eighteen-year-old with nothing but school years behind him. Jeno has a past that you don't know anything about. The age gap between the two of you is too great; he is too old for you, Lensie."

"He is only eleven years older than me. You make him out like an old man, Mama!"

"Only eleven years? That makes him twenty-seven to your sixteen! Ah, Lensie, you are so naïve; you have no idea what such an age difference means. You two live in different worlds. He is a mature man, experienced in life, while you are a sweet, innocent young girl full of idealism and romantic expectations. You are just beginning your life while he has already lived half of his. What will be new to you is just an old story for him. Those eleven years he has on you are his alone; you can never be part of it, and that creates a distance that will always be there between the two of you. Give him up Lensie, believe me, he would be happier with someone older, who had a similarly realistic outlook on life. I know it's not going to be easy; he is the first man who touched your heart. But there will be others, closer to your age, if you just give it a chance. You know that I am not against you going out with younger boys. I want you to have fun, to enjoy yourself. I know I am repeating myself but it's true; these are the best years of your life. Appreciate them! An involvement that is not right for you would only complicate things, it would bring you heartache, and that's why I am so against you and Jeno."

Lensie did not interrupt her mother and when she stopped talking, she did not start arguing back. She sat for a moment, staring at Angela as if mulling over what she just heard, but when she opened her mouth again, the defiance was still there.

"You know what I think, Mama? I think because you had a bad experience in your life with my father, you assume that the same thing will happen to me. You never really talked about him or told me more about his disappearance. Was he much older than you? Is that it? That's why you hate Jeno?"

"I told you, I don't hate Jeno—how could I? I don't know him. I only hate to think of you falling in love with an older man. But you are right, Lensie; perhaps it is time I tell you about your father. His name was Henrich Pollinger, he was a teacher, and he was seven years older than me. I was eighteen when we got involved, right after my mother's death, a very trying time for me, and he was there helping me to cope. We fell in love because of the circumstances; it only happened because I lost my mother. For a reason he had to leave and we did not see each other for a long time, but we made a promise to wait for each other. We planned to get married, but until then we managed to steal away occasionally so we could be together. It was a secretive, passionately intimate relationship, until two things happened that changed everything. Your father became ill and was sent to a sanatorium in Tyrol, and I found myself pregnant with you. Before he left for the clinic he took me to meet his family in Kismarton, and told them—"

"The Pollingers and Aunt Katie, where I spent vacations?" Lensie's eyes flew wide open in total surprise.

"Yes, they are your grandparents and Aunt Katie is your father's sister. They were wonderful to me, and they loved you from the very moment they learned that we were expecting you. Because of your father's illness we had to postpone the wedding until he was well again, but then one day he disappeared without a trace, and we never found out what happened to him. Years later someone saw him in Yugoslavia, but he was gone again before we could contact him. It was useless. Up to this day no one knows where he is and what became of him—not his family, not me, not anyone else. He might be dead, but we can't be sure."

Angela paused for a moment; the memories still cut deep. With a sigh she looked at her daughter. "Now you know everything, Lensie, how your father deserted us. And yes, his betrayal left a mark on me. It made me determined that nothing like this would ever happen to you. And it won't, I promise. I did not have a mother to look out for me, but you do! I am here and I won't let you get hurt."

"Oh Mama, how could he have done this to you?" Lensie held her hands against her face. "And all along you kept telling me what a wonderful man he was. No wonder you hate men! Oh, I hate him, too, for hurting you, for abandoning you!"

"You must not talk like this, Lensie! He was your father, and we really don't have any idea what made him walk away from everything. Who knows, perhaps he was more seriously ill than we thought, and when people are not well, they sometimes act irrationally. We will never know the reason, that's why you must not condemn him for what he did. I don't hate him. I forgave him a long time ago, but I did not forget the lesson I learned: that even though you might think you know a man, you can never be sure. That's why I want you to understand how important it is not to give your heart away to someone with a past. It's so much easier to get to know a younger man. They are more like an open book, with the pages still being written. You only have to read the lines to see if the young man is honest and kind, worthy of trust, and capable of love. A girl is safer with them against heartaches. Is this so hard to understand?"

Lensie looked at her mother with profound compassion. Being half in love with Jeno, she could imagine how she would feel if he disappeared tomorrow without saying a word. Multiplying that a thousand times could not compare to what her mother must have gone through, and all this time she never complained, she kept it all bottled up inside! She got up and tenderly put her arms around Angela.

"I am so sorry, Mama; I had no idea! You must have suffered so much! I am still in shock from what you just told me. My mind is in such turmoil right now. I need to find a quiet place to think. Maybe I'll go to church; praying might help. Would you want to come with me?"

Angela nodded. She, too, wanted to be alone with her thoughts. For a long time they knelt side by side in the cool quiet of the church, their heads bent in silent prayer, and while each had their own unique way of praying, the meaning of their prayers was the same: asking God to grant them better understanding of one another and give them strength and tolerance to overcome their growing differences.

As hard as Lensie wanted to abide by her mother's wishes, she could not give up seeing Jeno and kept showing up on the tennis court to be near him. What could be so wrong with that when there were always people around? She remembered, though, what Angela said about certain qualities that are important in a man, and she began steering their conversations in ways she hoped would reveal more about Jeno's character. Little by little, she learned about his interests and convictions, his strong attachment to his family, how the war affected him and what his expectations were in life. In the end she was convinced that in almost every way Jeno would meet all of Angela's strict standards, except the age difference, and that couldn't be helped. To find out if he was trustworthy and honest would take longer, but how could she do that when their time together was limited to a few minutes spent on the court, a busy public place?

And even that was coming to an end. It was almost September; in a few weeks Jeno would be starting his fall semester, and what would they do then? So far she had kept her word not to see Jeno outside the courts, but when summer was over, she would have to break that promise. It was clear by now that nothing would soften her mother's heart against her dating Jeno, and she would have to sneak around to see him.

Well, it wouldn't be exactly dating if she just let him accompany her on the street, and if it got back to her mother, she could always say they ran into each other. She would only be guilty of setting up the time and place to meet, but she could live with that. For starters, Jeno could wait for her on Tuesday mornings when she took the train to Vienna for her music lessons. How could a harmless stroll to the train station possibly be interpreted as pursuing? To her, it was an innocent arrangement, but she was wrong, and she would pay a price for the assumption.

Trouble started when the train was late on the morning of their third rendezvous. While it allowed them a few extra minutes, others also had more time to observe people on the platform and notice the young couple saying goodbye. Oblivious of the stares, they stood facing each other, eyes locked, seemingly indifferent to the world around them. They didn't talk, didn't even hold hands; only their fingertips touched caressingly. When a sharp whistle and a call to board brought them back to earth, Jeno brushed his lips slightly against Lensie's forehead, then waited until the train began to move, with Lensie waving and blowing a kiss from the window.

That evening coming home from work, Angela's face did not light up as usual when Lensie greeted her. "Did you have a hard day, Mama?" she asked without much concern, but when her mother ignored the question and kept glaring at her as she took off her hat and gloves, she became alarmed. "Are you all right? Is anything wrong?" she asked.

"I should think you know very well what's wrong," Angela snapped at her, her voice full of sarcasm. "I heard you made a spectacle of yourself today at the train station. I guess all the talk we had was for nothing; your promise to keep away from Jeno is all but forgotten. Aren't you ashamed to compromise yourself in public by clinging to him like a lovesick puppy?"

"Mother, you are exaggerating. I don't know who told you what, but you can be sure there was no spectacle! We met on the street by chance and since he was going in the same direction I let him walk with me. He waited with me until the train arrived, and that was all. You can't object to that. We kept our promise not to meet outside the tennis courts, but you couldn't possibly mean that I can't talk to him or walk with him if we should run into each other. What would you have me do? Order him to the other side of the street?"

"No, you wouldn't have to order him, just ask him politely to leave you alone, and if he is any kind of a gentleman, you should not have to ask twice. I thought I made it clear to you why I want you to stop seeing him, but apparently it was not clear enough. It's no use to repeat myself, so I am just going to ask you for the last time that you respect my wishes and keep your distance from Jeno. You are a minor, and whether you like it or not, as a parent I must make certain decisions for you, and this is one of them. Do you understand?"

"What I understand, Mother, is that you are against Jeno because you have this theory that he could not be good for me, and you have to protect me against him. But you know what? I think the real reason behind this is that you are afraid you might lose me to him. You want me to date these younger boys because it would take years before they are ready to commit, and there is no threat for a while that you will be left alone."

"You have said enough, young lady! Think what you will, but the fact remains that until you are eighteen you are my responsibility and will do as I say. This subject is closed. Thanks to you, I have a giant headache and have lost my appetite; you can eat your supper by yourself."

It always upset Angela when they argued, but today was the worst. How could Lensie accuse her of keeping her away from Jeno for a selfish reason? It was absurd! She was not afraid of being left alone! The only reason for opposing the relationship was the age difference and the problems it would create.

Yet she had to admit that ever since she lost her hand she had relied more on Lensie than she liked, and that her health, although she never complained about it, was not the best lately. All the stress over Lensie started to take a toll on her, sending her blood pressure soaring. Could it be that subconsciously she had developed a fear of losing her daughter? And now that the possibility of that was becoming real, her fierce prejudice against Jeno was just a manifestation of that fear? As Angela kept questioning her motives for opposing Jeno she suddenly stopped, as another thought emerged from the back of her mind. Could Lensie's attraction to an older man be the result of growing up without a father? Could Angela be partly blamed for that? Perhaps if she had remarried, things would be different now. There were men interested in marrying her after they returned to Sopron, but that was something she could never force herself to do. Henrich destroyed her trust in men forever.

The thought of Henrich brought back long-forgotten memories, and remembering how much she once loved him made her wonder, what if Lensie and Jeno truly loved each other? Did she have the right to stand between them?

She battled question after question long into the night, seeking answers but finding none. Her head throbbed, and though she felt exhausted, she couldn't relax. It was going to be one of those long, sleepless nights. Finally, after midnight she got up and took a pill that mercifully lulled her into a dreamless sleep.

Lensie spent an equally distressing night after their heated argument. She had no idea how those accusations about her mother's fear had crept into her head, and she was sorry the moment the words slipped out of her mouth. She didn't mean to say it; she was just too angry to think. It was because of that ultimatum to stop seeing Jeno! It just wasn't fair! *Well, I can't do that, and I won't! Whether she likes it or not, I will see Jeno!* Lensie fumed as she lay in bed. She blamed it on her mother that she had to sneak behind her back. Why must she be so old-fashioned? They were not doing anything bad. *There is one thing for sure,* she said half-aloud, *I will never force stupid outdated rules on my daughter! I will remember what my mother put me through.*

Her last thoughts before closing her eyes were about finding some new ways to meet Jeno where her mother's spies wouldn't see them. She drifted in and out of sleep, dreaming of secret trysts and endless labyrinths without an exit.

Even after getting up in the morning she continued inventing scenarios how to keep seeing Jeno risk free, and when she finally came up with a plan she stopped at the courts and asked Jeno to meet her on Friday before the 8 AM Mass at the Church of the Holy Trinity. She had something important to tell, but it wouldn't take long, he would be back for his nine o'clock lesson.

Lensie chose that church because it was away from her neighborhood, and as far as she knew, no one among her mother's friends lived in the area. Still, she was glad when she woke up Friday morning and it was raining; the umbrella meant extra protection from prying eyes as she hurried along. They wouldn't have to worry about Jeno's schedule, either; the lessons would be cancelled.

The church was empty when she got there except a few old women kneeling in front of the main altar. She looked around for a safe place to talk and settled on a dark side-altar. She was sitting there in the last row when Jeno walked in.

"Sorry to ask you to come," Lensie whispered to him, "but somebody saw us at the station and it got back to my mother. She got very upset and absolutely forbade me to see you. But I can't do that, Jeno! I don't care what she says; I want to see you! I tried to reason with her, but she won't budge. She said it's the last time she'd warn me to stay away from you, but don't worry, I figured out how we can get around her."

"Lensie, I want nothing more in this world than to see you as much as possible, but to go against your mother's will would destroy any trust we might gain by accepting her wishes. I never thought it would upset her this much if I walked with you on the street occasionally, but apparently it did. Look, perhaps she'll change her mind when she sees that you do as she asks. Hard as it will be, I think we should give it a chance and wait. I don't want to come between you and your mother. After all, you two have to live together and get along with each other, otherwise what would your life be?"

"So you are taking my mother's side? You don't want to see me, is that it?"

"Now Lensie, that is a childish thing to say. You know that I'd love to see you, I just believe that if we bide our time, we'll be better off in the end. Perhaps this is some kind of test; she wants to see if we would drift apart, and when she finds out that this 'out of sight, out of mind' theory won't work with us—at least it won't for me—perhaps she'll come around. Don't you think it's worth the wait?"

"You don't know my mother, Jeno! She is stubborn and won't ever stop harping about our age difference. We are wrong for each other, and that's it, period. She is convinced of it and won't let us prove her wrong."

"Lensie, sweetheart, I can understand your resentment, but don't fight her," Jeno took her hand into his. "We have time; we can wait until she learns to trust us. Trust is so important and we have to earn it. Try to see the situation from that angle and you won't misinterpret what I am saying."

"I wish my mother could hear you talking; you almost sound like her when she tells me 'have patience Lensie, you have all the time, Lensie'," she made a face mimicking Angela, but when a couple of ladies came in and sat down in the first pew, she lowered her voice before continuing. "All right, I give up; I can't fight both of you. But don't you want to know what I was going to tell you when I asked you here?" she whispered leaning closer to Jeno. "I thought we could meet in Vienna on Tuesdays. We would take different trains, of course, but after my lessons we could spend almost a whole day together. Wouldn't that be fun?"

"My clever scheming little Kitten!" Jeno stifled an impulse to laugh. "Well thought out, but it had one drawback. I could not afford what you planned. I wouldn't have the money to go to Vienna and take you around, not even once a month, let alone every week. Cut off from my family I have to save every penny just to keep my head above the water, and I need financial aid to complete my studies. As it is, I am holding my breath to find out if it would be granted. If not, well, I don't even want to think about what will happen then."

But then he stopped, realizing that he shouldn't burden this young girl with his problems. He quickly checked himself and apologized. "If I sounded complaining, I am sorry, I didn't mean to. This is not your concern. But just the same, think how lucky you are to have a loving mother who looks after you, and asks very little in return. Appreciate it, Lensie, and go along with her decision. It's the right thing to do."

"Well, all right, I will, I promise, but I still see no harm if we run into each other on the street. *Accidentally,* of course." She shot a sly glance at Jeno and when he pulled back and raised an eyebrow in mock surprise, Lensie had to keep from giggling. "Did you really think you could fool me with that trick, running around the block to come out ahead of me? Of course I saw you darting out of the coffeehouse when I stepped into the street. Who is calling whom a schemer now?"

Jeno dropped his head, admitting his guilt, but when people began turning around with disapproving glances, Lensie turned serious again. "What I mean is that if I tell you my routine stops during the week, you could be there and we could just talk a little, then we'd go on our separate ways. It's better than nothing. My mother just has to understand that I can't turn my back on you on the street. Any realistic person would agree with that, am I right?"

"Of course you are right, no one could find fault in that, but promise me, on those days you will tell your mother that we met and had a little chat, before she hears it from someone else. And let's hope she will be reasonable about it!"

"I'll tell her, but it wouldn't surprise me if she locked me up after hearing it. So if you don't see me for a while, you'll know the reason."

She stopped talking when she realized that their little sanctuary was filling up with worshipers. It was time to leave. Holding hands for a minute longer, Lensie mouthed silently, "Wednesday morning at the market," then stood up and walked out of the church. She felt good about their talk, and she made a mental note to add honesty and trustworthiness to Jeno's growing list of virtues.

Out in the street she looked around cautiously, but saw no one familiar. She was reading a book when her mother came home from work that afternoon, and when she asked Lensie about her day, she said she never left home because of the pouring rain.

By next morning the weather cleared and after making her usual rounds to the various stores and spending a couple of hours at the nuns practicing her piano, Lensie hurried home to prepare their mid-day meal. It was Saturday, and with offices closing at noon for the weekend, her mother would be home any minute. In no time she heard the door open, but instead of greeting her in the hallway as usual, she yelled out that she was stuck in the kitchen. A few minutes later Angela walked in, and ignoring Lensie's welcoming smile, marched up to her, raised her left hand and with an open palm slapped her across the face, then swung back, hitting her on the other side with the back of her hand.

It was so sudden and so unexpected that Lensie had no time to shield herself against the smarting blows. Her head jerked back and her ears started to ring as she vaguely heard her mother's voice, "This one is for lying to me and this one for sneaking around with that no-good Jeno. If I can't reason with you with words, maybe this will teach you to heed."

She was still shouting but Lensie no longer listened. Holding her hands against her burning cheeks she ran to her room, slamming the door behind her, then threw herself on the bed, sobbing hysterically. This couldn't happen to her! A beating, just when she was ready to submit to her mother's bidding? She did not deserve this, no matter what!

Feeling herself a victim of a great injustice her sobs grew louder, the pitch higher, until she heard the door flung open. In a second Angela was standing over her.

"I asked you over and over again to stay away from him, but you just wouldn't listen. You don't know how many sleepless nights I spent thinking about the two of you, trying to see things from your perspective, but each time I ended up with one question: what would a man his age want with a sixteen-year-old girl? You might not know the answer, but I do, and it's one thing, and one thing only. It's only a matter of time before he'd come around to it, and I won't stand by and allow it to happen. I know you hate me now, but I guess you will have to be my age before you realize that all I want is to protect you. I hoped to make you understand that what I am doing is for your own good, but I see you are deaf when it comes to Jeno.

"So this is what I am going to do. Since he won't respect my wishes to stop chasing you and you are obviously incapable of resisting his advances, I have no choice but to remove you from further temptation. You are going to your Aunt Gertie. I am sending her a telegram right now and as soon as she wires back that it's all right, you are leaving. I am tired of arguing, tired of extracting promises that you won't keep, and I have had enough of your lies. I always thought if there was one thing I could be sure of, it was to trust you to be honest with me. Well, I was wrong, but then, I've been wrong before. I survived bigger disappointments in my life. But if you think you can outsmart me, think twice; you have a long way to go, missy, before you find me blind to your shenanigans."

Lensie sprang upright on her bed and the flood of tears stopped instantly when she heard what her mother planned to do. But that was impossible, she couldn't do that to her!

"Mother, you can't send me away! What about you? You are working, who will take care of the house, do the shopping, and cooking? You need me here, please! I don't want to leave you. Let me stay, and I promise you, really honestly, that I will not see Jeno! I do everything you say, just don't send me to Aunt Gertie!"

"No Lensie! You might believe that you can stay away from him, but I know better by now; sooner or later you'll give in and we will be back to where we are now. Sending you away might bring you to your senses. And you don't have to worry about me; I can handle the household well enough." Angela turned toward the door. "I am going now to send the wire to your aunt, I am sure she'd love to have you."

Hearing the finality in her mother's voice, Lensie knew that no amount of arguing would save her. "How long am I to be exiled? Can you tell me that much?" was all she could say.

"That remains to be seen. It's really up to you, Lensie, and you know why."

As soon as Angela was out the door, the tears started to flow again. Only now did she truly realize just how serious her mother was about stopping her relationship with Jeno. And now she would have to leave, and if she wanted to come back anytime soon, she would have to be on her best behavior at her aunt's. She liked her Aunt Gertie; she didn't mind spending a few weeks there once in a while, but to live with them in that little town? What on earth would she do? She'd die of boredom there!

This was an awful blow to Lensie. She felt utterly helpless, completely at the mercy of her mother. Angrily, she made a face mouthing Angela's words: *These are the best years of your life, Lensie! Appreciate them, Lensie! Well, I don't! Being sixteen is terrible! I wish I were fifty; at least I could do as I please.* She carried on ranting against her mother one minute, then moping and feeling sorry for herself the next, until her thoughts turned back to Jeno. Just thinking that she wouldn't be able to see him, not even from a distance, brought on the tears again, her inconsolable sobs echoing through the house.

By Monday she had no more tears to shed. Emotionally exhausted and without hope to change her mother's mind, she resigned to her fate. Angela felt sorry for her; she knew the heartache her willful daughter was going through. Perhaps she was to blame for letting her have her way in just about everything until now. Wanting to compensate Lensie for the many setbacks she suffered on account of their circumstances, she gave into her every whim, but it only made her overly confident, headstrong, and defiant. Spending time with Gertie would be good for her; they always got along well and she might listen to her aunt more than to her. She packed her daughter's suitcase and sent another telegram to Gertie to let her know the time when Lensie would be arriving the next day.

Angela wished she could stay home and take Lensie to the station in the afternoon, but she couldn't afford to miss time from work. Instead she asked her neighbor, Mrs. Szep, to keep an eye on her daughter's comings and goings before she was to leave, and just hoped that Lensie would not try to sneak out and see Jeno one more time. She made it clear to her that doing so would double the time at her aunt's.

Lensie did not care anymore. She had to find a way to see him and tell him what happened; otherwise he'd be waiting for her on Wednesday at the market place, and she would never show up! But how to reach him, where could she find him? The only place she could think of was the tennis court; he might be there, even though he hardly had lessons anymore. Not daring to go herself she asked Hilda, and she was willing to do it. Luckily, she found him playing a set, and quickly gave him the message to be at the train station at 2 PM. She didn't say why, only that it was important.

Jeno was standing in front of the station, and when he saw Lensie coming down the street carrying a suitcase he rushed to her side with a cheerful "Hello Kitten." Taking the bag out of her hand he was surprised at its weight and quipped with a smile, "You must be hauling all your sheet music in here!" But then he saw the look on her face and dropped the humor; he knew she was in no mood for his teasing.

"Jeno, you have no idea what I've been through since Friday! I am so miserable! We can't see each other anymore; my mother found out about the church and she beat me up, and now she is sending me away to my aunt," she blurted out all in one breath, her eyes brimming with tears.

Jeno stopped and put down the suitcase. He looked at Lensie, incredulous at what she just said. "What do you mean, she beat you up?"

"She hit me in the face, boxed my ears—that's what she did! And the awful things she told me, just when I was ready to obey her. You are my witness that I was going to do as she wished. It's so unfair, I could just cry! I won't be able to see you, not even for a few minutes as we planned. I tried everything I could to change her mind but no matter how much I begged, she wouldn't let me stay. I even promised not to see you again, and I would have kept it too, because she apparently has a way to find out anyway; she must have a whole bunch of spies who have nothing better to do but report on when and where we met. Oh Jeno, I feel so helpless; she gave me no choice." She was swallowing hard to keep the tears down.

"Lensie, sweetheart, calm down. Let's go into the station; we can talk better there." Not waiting for an answer, he picked up the suitcase and holding Lensie by the arm, steered her toward the entrance. They sat down in the back, away from people, hoping no one would notice them. Jeno was still shaking his head, still unsure that he heard her right. "It's hard to believe that your mother would hit you. Did she put her hands on you before?"

"Never, she never even spanked me when I was little, and that's why I can't understand what possessed her. How could she be so mean? But anyway, what's done is done. I have to leave." Feeling utterly miserable she stared at the ceiling, blinking her eyes to keep the tears in check. Then her anger flared. "I can't stand to be banished like this! Not to be able to see you, to talk to you! I don't even dare to write you, because she threatened to let me rot in that place if I keep in touch with you!"

"How long will you be away?"

"I have no idea! I guess she'll keep me away as long as it takes for me to get over you! That's what she is aiming at! She said she would see how things are before she let me come back. And believe me, she is serious about it. If I want to come home I just have to pretend that I've forgotten you, which will never happen in a million years! Isn't this awful?"

"My little Kitten, do you know how adorable you are carrying on as if the world was coming to an end? True, it will be hard not be able to see each other for a while, but it won't be for long, you'll see. She'll come around and bring you home when she starts missing you. And I will be here, just the same as I am sitting now next to you."

"Is that a promise? Will you wait for me? How will I know what is happening with you when we can't even write to each other? My aunt is sure to tell my mother if you wrote. The only way I can see to keep in touch is through Hilda. I know she won't mind and she can be trusted. But isn't this ridiculous, using her as a go-between, go through all this, because my mother thinks she can break us up?" She shook her head slowly and sighed. "I don't know how am I going to stand this awful separation. I haven't even left, and I miss you already."

"I'll miss you too, sweetheart, and you must remember it if you shouldn't hear from me at times. I will let Hilda know when something important comes up, but otherwise I think it's best not to break the rules too often. I want you back as soon as possible, so why chance it that your mother finds out that we are in contact? I only hope you won't forget me, even though she is sending you away exactly for that purpose!"

"Never, never! How could you even . . ." was all Jeno heard as the rest of her words were lost in the blaring announcement calling everyone to board. Her eyes welled up, and in that moment nothing in the world could stop her from clinging to the man she knew she'd never stop loving.

Separation and reunion

WHEN JENO SAID he'd miss Lensie, he meant it in all sincerity. This pretty, vivacious, excitable girl was the only bright spot in his life. When she left, she took away the magic only she could conjure up to make his troubles disappear. Without her the days were the same, Sundays as drab as Mondays.

He left the station feeling depressed. He skipped going back to the tennis courts; he had no more lessons scheduled anyway. Summer was drawing to a close, yet he had not heard from the tuition board, and he truly did not know what he would do if they turned him down. Administration offered him a part-time job in their office when the fall semester started, but without major financial help this was not enough to sustain him.

It was a frustrating, idle time, not knowing what to expect. While waiting, he and his buddies spent the last days of summer hiking to the lake for a swim, kicking up some dust on the soccer field, or just passing the time discussing current issues, the inflation, the dim outlook of the economy, and the shrinking job market. Letters from home arrived regularly; his brother got married and his sister Sárika was engaged to a man named Gusztav Gero, an art teacher at the gimnazium in Losonc—or Lucenec, by its new Slovak name. His mother was also well, still trying to figure out ways to help him, but regardless of their best intentions, Jeno knew he was on his own.

When September finally rolled around and the new freshmen started to arrive, Jeno could not get into the mood to participate in the fun that the traditional greeting of these green "baleks" involved. Just like back in Selmec, it was a great source of merriment and laughter for the city folks to watch the older students putting the newcomers through some good-natured public humiliations. It was part of their initiation, never vulgar or done with malice, only with limitless ingenuity. Typically, after enduring some long and flowery welcoming speeches at the station, the tired and thirsty boys were lined up in the middle of the street and led on an extensive "city tour" to acquaint them with their new surroundings. Along the way the old returning students stood on the sidewalks drinking ice-cold beers, smacking their lips and raising their frosty mugs in a salute to the new crop of boys, but offering them none. Others pelted them with insulting remarks, making fun of how they looked, the clothes they wore, and the towns they came from. Nothing was sacred. When the poor baleks finally arrived at the main square, they saw a temporary platform built with no steps, only a slide fastened to the front. One by one the unfortunate creatures were prompted to climb to the top any way they could, introduce themselves, then were given a choice either to recite a poem, act out a part of a famous play, or sing a song, with the sole purpose of putting them to ridicule. The crowd, of course, found it hilarious, especially when there was no other way to descend but to slide down the chute, landing on their behinds.

Jeno was at the end of his wits when finally word came that his tuition was approved. It was somewhat reduced because of the part-time job offer, but he would manage. His life was finally shaping up; he could go to sleep at night without worrying what the next day would bring.

And then a letter arrived from his brother:

Dear Jeno,

We were happy to hear that you are able to continue your studies, but what I am about to tell you might change your mind. I wrote you before that Mother never gave up trying to help you, and it seems that she finally found a way.

As you know, with the dissolution of the Monarchy the previously common ministries of Home Defense, Finance, and Foreign Affairs were dissolved, and now Hungary must re-establish these departments. We recently had a visitor, you'll remember him, Karoly Kahn, a one-time assistant to father, who never forgot how he helped him to secure a job he wanted in the Ministry of Internal Affairs in Budapest. He is still working there, by now as the head of the recently formed Department of Customs and Tariff, and when he mentioned that they were in the process of setting up customs offices along the borders, Mother's eyes lit up at once. She told him about your situation, that you are in Sopron, and asked if a position could be arranged for you there. He promised to look into it and thought that the chances for it were good, since they just started recruiting people. We gave him your address and you should hear from him soon.

Jeno, it is of course up to you to accept or decline the offer, but considering the bleak state of the economy, when young engineers wind up sweeping the streets, we think this would be a very good opportunity for you. You would be stepping into a government job with a fair salary and good possibility for steady advancement, especially when you have a friend in the ministry looking after your interests. Another point I might bring up in favor of taking this job is that you are now twenty-eight years old, and if you are thinking of getting married and starting a family, a secure position like this could make a difference.

Mother would be so happy to know that your problems are over and you are on your way to a brighter future. So think about it hard, weigh all the pros and cons, and let us know what you decided.

Wishing you the best, always, your loving brother, Jozsef.

The letter with its unexpected proposal put Jeno in a spin. What should he do when Mr. Kahn contacted him with the offer? He must be ready with an answer, or vacillate too long, and the job would go to someone else. With the postwar depression still rampant, the job market at an all-time low, and inflation out-of-control, an opportunity like this did not come along too often. Cancellation of war contracts brought about the closing of factories and widespread unemployment, while those lucky enough to still hold a job were forced to accept pay cuts. As a sure sign of hopelessness, many of the poorest segment of the population, the peasants and unemployed manual workers who had nothing to lose, began to pull up roots and leave the country. Huddled in overcrowded steerage decks of immigration boats, they sailed for the United States, where Madam Liberty beckoned, offering a chance for a better life. Arriving in New York, thousands of Hungarian immigrants shuffled through the long lines at Ellis Island, then went on to settle in the East side of the city, or Cleveland, Chicago and Pittsburgh, never to return to the homeland they left behind.

The outlook was indeed dismal in 1922, and even though the League of Nations, through a network of commercial treaties, offered some financial assistance, there was not much hope for a sudden economic recovery. Heavy industry was virtually non-existent after Trianon robbed the country of its rich natural resources, and without that the prospect for a young metallurgical engineer to find work was very limited. He should have studied forestry like his brother, Jeno thought bitterly; at least one could still find trees in the country! It was anyone's guess when and how the government would bring about stability.

He spent sleepless nights over the decision he would have to make, knowing that it would affect his future, perhaps his entire life. If the letter had come during the uncertain days of summer, he would not have hesitated for one moment, but now, with his tuition secured and only one more year to go before getting his diploma, it was a hard choice to make. He was nervous and edgy, and under the constant stress his wartime peptic ulcer that was in remission in the past few years flared up again. Finally, he decided to stop worrying. All his mother's previous attempts to help him had failed so far, so why should this be different? And as a few weeks passed without a word from Mr. Kahn, Jeno was sure that his mother had once again trusted the wrong man.

He almost forgot about the whole thing when one afternoon, returning to the dorm, he found a message waiting. It was from a gentleman claiming to represent Mr. Kahn, asking Jeno to meet him the next day at a certain restaurant. The news put Jeno back to tossing and turning all night; should he stick to his studies or take the chance with a job he knew very little about? Talking to a recent graduate nudged him toward the latter, when the man said he couldn't find a job in five months, and that in Jeno's place he would take the offer without a second thought.

Jeno was at the restaurant at the appointed time, still anxious, still undecided, and to keep a clear head he ate his meal without a sip of wine. Sober and attentive, he listened to the man describing the job and telling that it was definitely held open for him. He was in town for three days on official business and would need an answer before he left.

He did not have to wait that long. After posing some questions and receiving encouraging answers, Jeno knew there was no other option for him but to accept. So rather than spending another torturous night, he decided to say yes right on the spot. He was told to report for an interview and a written test scheduled for the first week of October in the city of Gyor—about one hour by train from Sopron—and that if he passed, he would be required to attend a year-long educational course there. Once he finished his training the job would be waiting for him, because Sopron, being a busy port, was given priority to start operations.

The minute he made up his mind, the pressure was off. He felt elated as he walked out of the restaurant, confident that he had made the right decision. He turned into the corner tavern to celebrate his good fortune with a glass of wine, but back at the dorm he kept the news to himself; he would continue attending lectures until his acceptance was confirmed. Only after he passed the tests in

Gyor did he quit his studies and said goodbye to his alma mater, as well as to his buddies at the dorm. Next he sought out Hilda and asked her to write Lensie about the change in his situation, and also to find some way to let Angela know that he was gone, so Lensie could come home.

With that he collected his belongings and boarded the train for Gyor, his new home for the next year.

Lensie received Jeno's message with mixed emotions. She was free to go home but Jeno wouldn't be there! And without him, it really did not matter where she lived. She blamed everything on Angela. If she hadn't banished her, she knew in her heart that Jeno would not have left, and to show her resentment she refused to return to Sopron. Childless, Gertie and her husband spoiled her to no end as they did with Mitzie back in 1906 when she was put into their care. They took her to Vienna on shopping trips, to attend concerts, and on one occasion to see *Il Trovatore,* her favorite opera, at the famous Viennese opera house. It was also a lot easier to get to the music conservatorium for her lessons; she only had to travel twenty minutes instead of almost an hour. And what she liked most was that her aunt had a piano so she could practice at home. With her outgoing nature she also made new friends, and as much as she hated the idea in the beginning to live in such a small place, she now truly enjoyed its warm and welcoming atmosphere. Why should she want to go home, to cook, do errands, and listen to her mother's sermons?

Angela, too, managed well without Lensie. She took her meals in Mitzie's restaurant and had a cleaning woman once a week, but she missed her greatly and wanted her back. When Lensie resisted, she took the train and brought her reluctant daughter home. She hoped that with Jeno gone they could start rebuilding their relationship, but Lensie held out, and the atmosphere remained strained between them. The arguments continued, Lensie claiming that Angela never gave Jeno a chance, while Angela stuck to her belief that he was wrong for her, and the decision to send her away was the right one.

Angela tried to extend the olive branch by giving Lensie a homecoming party, inviting her friends and their dates, and asking them to bring a few extra young men, but it did not work. Lensie was gloomy and sulking, acted as if bored, and with that attitude the party broke up before it started. Word spread quickly that she was pining over a man who left her.

Her closest friends rallied around her to help get over her heartache, but after a while Lensie herself realized that nothing is accomplished by acting resentful and reclusive. Jeno was gone and there was nothing she could do about it. They couldn't even keep in touch through Hilda anymore. Her mother caught the letter he sent from Gyor with his new address and threw it away. All she knew was that he was coming back in about a year, but would he? Lots of things could happen in a year! With the social season in full swing and plenty of young men around to escort her, she accepted invitations to parties and found that she enjoyed her newfound popularity. Angela, eager to prove that she had nothing against younger suitors, welcomed them to call on Lensie and encouraged her daughter to go out and have fun. Suddenly, it was all right to sit with friends in a café sipping a demitasse, or go to a party without Angela tagging along. Lensie savored these small freedoms and found the male attention flattering. She was friendly with everyone, even flirting with some of her beaus, but she kept romance out of the relationships. Her heart still belonged to Jeno, even though she heard nothing from him.

It was during the university's Christmas tree-lighting celebration when, standing around the tree with her girlfriends, Lensie felt two hands covering her eyes from behind and heard a familiar voice whispering in her ear, "Merry Christmas Kitten." As she spun around and saw Jeno smiling down at her, she jumped into his neck, caring little if anyone witnessed her unseemly behavior. She only knew that he was standing there, next to her, the best Christmas present she could wish for. Holding hands, they joined the carolers until the outdoor festivities came to an end, and everyone headed inside for a hot drink and some snacks. Hilda and other friends surrounded them, teasing Jeno if he had come back to check on Lensie, but once inside they mercifully left them alone to enjoy their reunion.

After bringing a cup of hot chocolate for Lensie, and grabbing some apple cider for himself, Jeno took her aside. "Kitten, we have so much to talk about. Could we go for a little walk? It's not that cold tonight. I want to be alone with you, unless you'd rather stay."

Stay when she could be alone with Jeno? Of course Lensie was ready to go, she only told Hilda not to leave without her, they'd be back in a short while, then taking Jeno's hand, the two of them disappeared between the towering pine trees. They walked in silence, the crunching of snow under their feet the only sound. The night air was crisp and clear, not a cloud in the star-studded sky. When they came to a small clearing Jeno stopped and turned to Lensie. Her upturned face, brightly lit by the moon, was as lovely as in his dreams.

"You don't know how I missed you, Lensie, how many times I imagined a moment like this, alone with you, yet wondering if it would ever happen, if you'd still be waiting. That's why I had to come back, to be sure that you haven't forgotten me, that you are still my little Kitten. Please say that it is so."

"Yes, yes, a thousand times yes, you should never—" her unfinished sentence melted into their first kiss as Jeno's mouth hungrily covered her still moving lips. Her arms reached up and curled around his neck while she tilted her head in response to his deepening kiss. If she was smitten before by his good looks, impressed by his style, or found him irresistible on the tennis court, in that moment she fell hopelessly in love. Her heart began to race and she felt herself floating, carried to the verge of swooning. She held on to Jeno, and when he pulled away she opened her eyes and looked at him in child-like amazement.

"Am I in heaven?" she breathed, her voice hardly audible, as if wondering how a kiss could be the source of such thrill. Looking down at her, his own heart beating fast, Jeno felt the magic, too. That first kiss filled him with awe. Her innocence, her vulnerability touched something deep in his soul, a keen awareness that this kiss carried responsibilities. The girl in his arms was no longer the same as a few minutes ago. With that kiss she had given herself into his care; it was now up to him never to betray that trust.

Slowly he released her and, reaching into his coat pocket, took out a small gift-wrapped box. "Merry Christmas, my sweet Kitten," he said softly, holding it out for her. "It's just a small token, and you probably can't even wear it because of the problems with you mother, but perhaps it will remind you that I exist."

"Do you think I need a reminder? Especially after today?" she protested as she tore off the wrapping and opened the box. Inside, pinned to the dark blue velvet lining was a delicate gold chain with a heart-shaped pendant.

"Oh, it's beautiful, Jeno! Thank you, I love it!" she beamed at him. "Will you put it on for me? I feel like never taking it off! But you are right, my mother would want to know how I got it, and I could never tarnish it with lies. I'll keep it together with my prayer book. I only wish I could give you something in return, but I had no idea that I would be seeing you."

"But you have, Kitten; you gave me your heart today, the greatest gift I could hope for! Now I can put my head down at night thinking of you and know, not just hope, that I am in your thoughts, too. We have to be satisfied with dreams only until I return. I still have a way before I finish my training, but when I am back, we'll just have to get through to your mother and convince her that I am not here to hurt you or compromise you in any way."

Lensie made a grimace at the mention of her mother's stubbornness, but Jeno put a finger across her lips. "Shhh, I know, it will not be easy to make her accept me. I will have to work on that. But for the time being, I think it would be better if she doesn't know about our meeting tonight. She might pack you up again and send you to Timbuktu this time. Did you notice any of her friends here?"

"I don't think so, but don't worry. After all, we are at a public celebration! Oh, I wish we could be in the open and not sneak around like this."

"Me, too, but we must be patient. The time will come, I know," he said, his fingers stroking her face. But then he glanced at his wristwatch. "Speaking of time, I think we should head back, Kitty. Perhaps it's better if you go ahead and I stay here to avoid attention. I am going back to Gyor tomorrow, but here is my address, write me if you can, if it's safe. I am so glad I found you here today, because from now on even if I don't hear from you, I will know that you'll be waiting for me. You will wait for me, Kitten?" He wanted to hear it again.

"You know I will, and that's forever! Still, I wish you didn't have to go away." She pouted, then drew herself up on her toes, and whispered to Jeno, "It was real, wasn't it? Tell me that I didn't dream the whole thing?"

"No, you didn't my darling Lensie. It is real, you and I are real." And to prove it, he kissed her again lightly, but just as deliciously.

Seeing Lensie in a dreamy state of mind when she returned home that evening Angela assumed that the festive tree lighting had put her daughter in such a wistful mood. As usual, they spent Christmas Eve quietly at home exchanging gifts and attending Midnight Mass; then on Christmas day after church all the relatives gathered at Mitzie's for dinner. It was a chance to catch up with all the changes since last time they were together, see the children, and talk about plans for the coming year.

Lensie was unusually quiet; she sat by the Christmas tree, gazing at the flickering candles, the smell of the pine taking her back to the night before. She was still under the spell of the magic of their first kiss, still wrapped in the glow of the sensation it brought. Her aunts and uncles, looking at her, asked Angela what had gotten into her daughter, sitting there like she was in a trance. Angela downplayed the sarcasm, reminding them that Lensie was at an awkward age when she didn't fit in with the adults and was too old to play with the kiddies. But secretly she thought Lensie must have met someone new; that would explain the sighs and the mellow mood she had displayed all day. She was delighted, though; there was nothing better to cure the pining over lost love than finding a new one.

On the way home she casually asked about the ceremony last night, but when Lensie ignored the probing, she did not press further. All in good time! If someone had cast a spell on her daughter, she'd find out sooner or later. They were going to a big New Year's Eve dance, and Angela was certain the new boy would be there.

At the dance she kept a close watch on Lensie. Did she flirt with anyone special? It did not take long to notice a nice young man paying a lot of attention to her. He frequently cut in when Lensie was dancing with others, and when they walked out to the open terrace for a breath of fresh air, she saw him putting an arm around her. As she found out, his name was Gabor Szilagyi, a student studying medicine in Gyor, and he was in Sopron to spend the holidays with his cousin's family. *Hmm, a doctor in the making; no wonder Lensie is attracted to him,* Angela thought. She admitted that he was not nearly as handsome as Jeno, but Lensie must have come to her senses and realized that looks were not everything. And when at the end of the evening he escorted them home, Angela invited him to visit before going back to Gyor.

Later that night when talking about the ball, she heaped praises on Gabor. "Now there is a nice young man, and he is obviously taken with you, Lensie! I know his cousin's family, not well, but enough to tell you that they are good people. I was so glad to see you dancing with him, having fun. He'll make you forget Jeno. You are such a beautiful girl, I hated to see you just sit and sulk, waiting for him to come back. And did he? No, and good riddance. Better he stays wherever he is. It's wonderful to see you happy again, laughing and having a good time." She pulled Lensie in her arms and, looking into her eyes, asked with a hint of uncertainty, "You are happy, sweetheart, aren't you?"

"Yes Mama, I am happy, I am very happy," she said and pleading exhaustion kissed her mother good night. *Yes Mother, I've never been happier, but not the way you think,* she smiled to herself slipping into bed. There was absolutely no romance between her and Gabor, at least not on Lensie's part. When they met at the dance she found out that he was originally from Selmec and knew Jeno well; their families were old friends. He, too, was cut off from his parents; that's why he was in Sopron spending Christmas with relatives. He didn't know that Jeno was also in Gyor until Lensie told him, and when she asked to take a letter for him, he gladly agreed. She slipped it to him when he came to see her before returning to Gyor, whispering that her mother need not know about the role he was playing. It was their secret.

That night, as every night before turning off the light, Lensie took out the necklace from Jeno and kissed it reverently, then put it away again. Ready to go to sleep she closed her eyes, but the excitement over finding a way to hear from Jeno more often through her newfound friend kept her awake. Then her imagination took over. Maybe there was a way she could even go and see him! It was obvious that her mother liked Gabor, and that she had no idea that Jeno was in Gyor; perhaps she could take advantage of this situation. Her friends, Hilda and Irene, had an aunt in Gyor and the girls occasionally went to visit her. Maybe her mother would let her go with them? Angela was so bent on erasing the last traces of Jeno from Lensie's mind that she might agree to it, thinking she wanted to meet Gabor there.

Although nothing came of her plot to go to Gyor, thanks to Gabor, she now had a solid link to Jeno. The young man was in Sopron almost every other weekend, delivering letters back and forth, while Angela stood by, naively encouraging what she assumed to be a budding romance. This could have continued indefinitely if not for a young lady Gabor met in the spring. Their courtship was turning serious and eventually jealousy reared its ugly head about his friendship with Lensie. When the girl heard Angela bragging all over town about her daughter and Gabor, she made it clear that he must choose between Lensie and her. It was an easy choice since Gabor was smitten with her, and playing the postman was becoming burdensome, anyway. He didn't mind it in the beginning, but lately he was looking for a way out. He felt uncomfortable that everyone, including his relatives, thought he was romancing both girls, and he wanted to put a stop to the rumors.

When Gabor handed Lensie's next letter to Jeno he told him it was for the last time; he was ending his dubious involvement. Jeno half-expected it, but pleaded with him to do one more favor. "Look Gabor, Lensie's seventeenth birthday is coming up in May, and I want to surprise her, but I can't do it without your help."

Gabor started to protest, but Jeno insisted. "Please, just hear me out; this is nothing complicated. I know you told me that your girlfriend is jealous, so you tell her that this is the last time you will see Lensie and only to break up your friendship with her. She'll have no objection, I am sure. As for the surprise, you take Lensie out to celebrate her birthday without telling her about me coming, and a little later I walk in. There is a good restaurant in the Loevers, the Hunter's Inn; it has partitioned booths that would give us more privacy. Of course, I would cover all expenses, and would be forever grateful to you. So what do you say? If for nothing else, please do it in the name of love!"

How could he say no to that? Good natured as he was, Gabor gave in and agreed to play the part. All went exactly as planned. Lensie was thrilled to see Jeno, and double thrilled when he presented her with a gold brooch in the shape of a rose. Pinning it on her dress she flirtatiously asked for a rain check to thank him under more private circumstances.

Angela was truly happy seeing Lensie so gay when Gabor brought her home. He excused himself shortly after, and it was the last time Angela saw him. At first she assumed the couple had a quarrel, and in no time he'd be back, but after a few weeks curiosity got the better of her and she asked Lensie what happened to Gabor.

"I don't really know, Mama, we did not have a fight; everything was just fine until my birthday. I guess he got tired of me or found someone else. It only proves one thing, Mother, that age really does not matter when it comes to trust. It seems that the younger men you favor so much can't be trusted, either. They can leave you in the cold just the same as older ones." The sarcasm in her voice was unmistakable and intentional, and it hit its mark. Angela knew exactly what her daughter was referring to. But she was not in the mood for another confrontation and let the remark slide.

"I must say I am just as disappointed as you are," she said, "but don't let it bother you; chalk it up to experience. He is only one fish in the ocean. A girl as pretty and popular as you won't have any problem finding someone new. Summer is around the corner with picnics and garden parties, you'll be too busy to think of him." She hugged and kissed her daughter, but Lensie knew she had scored a point that day.

Jeno spent the summer in Gyor studying the prescribed courses and idling away the weekends watching soccer games or playing tennis with newfound friends. He rented a small room and saved most of his paycheck to get an apartment when he returned to Sopron. He did not like Gyor; it was flat, no place to go hiking, even the air was stagnant as pollution from the slowly developing industry in the area settled over the city. He missed the fresh alpine air of Sopron, the surrounding forests and lakes, the Loevers with its fragrant fruit orchards, but most of all he missed Lensie.

What he felt for her was not infatuation; at his age he was long past that kind of juvenile romanticism. He wouldn't deny the enchantment he felt seeing Lensie for the first time, the vision of a girl with wildflowers in her hair, as she stood at the edge of the forest. He would never forget that moment, but that was far from calling it love. It took watching her realistically in the snippets of time they spent together, and resisting to build an aura around her during their long separation. But as the real Lensie emerged, he saw a very young, trusting and impressionable girl, unsophisticated and vivacious, who loved to laugh, did not mind a little teasing, but drew the line if someone tried to make a fool of her. What he liked most in her was her simplicity, her natural wit and intelligence, and her precious innocence. It was that first virginal kiss that took his breath away and opened his heart to welcome love.

He was counting the days to be back in Sopron to start his new job, get his own place, and hopefully win Angela's trust and approval. This was important to him and he made a decision not to sneak behind her back to meet Lensie. He'd bide his time and hope that her staunch resistance against their relationship softened by next spring. If not, Lensie would be turning eighteen then, and Angela would have to understand that her daughter would be free to make her own decisions.

As for Lensie, time seemed to drag on forever that summer. Occasionally she played tennis with Hilda or some other friends, but her enthusiasm for the game was gone. Yes, she could hit a ball, but she freely admitted, her coordination was never good, and instead of running around on a cement court sweating under the hot sun, she would rather go hiking in the cool forests of the Loevers. It was during one of these outings with the Szep girls that they discovered a new swimming pool being built at the edge of the woods. Every time they passed the construction site they'd peek through the fence, making guesses as to when would it be finished.

The prospect of a new pool created great excitement among the younger generation, but women like Angela and Mrs. Szep criticized it as an unnecessary and frivolous expenditure on part of the city. Why spend all that money on another swimming pool when they already had one, and when only boys used it, anyway? Young ladies of good reputation would never think of parading half naked around a public pool. They always went to Lake Tomalom for a boat ride and an occasional dip in the water; no one objected to that, but that's where the line for decency was drawn.

It was not easy to convince them that there was nothing wrong with young people of the opposite sex sharing some fun at the pool. Angela was working on the opening day, but the Szep girls succeeded dragging their mother to the ribbon-cutting ceremony, hoping they could wheedle her into buying them a summer pass. Watching people splashing in the crystal clear water, the city's first chlorinated pool, and seeing that bathing suits were modest and all activities were kept under control, Mrs. Szep halfway agreed, but still held back. Only when Hilda and her sister pulled out their trump card, that the pool with a lifeguard was a much safer place to swim than the lake where every year several drowning accidents occurred, did she finally gave in.

After hearing from Mrs. Szep that she found the pool indeed a proper place for young ladies, Angela was still skeptical. The next weekend she went to see it for herself, but when she came home, Lensie, too, got her pass, and from that day on, the pool became a second home for the girls.

The arrival of fall weather put a stop to their outings, ending the summer, but not the fun, as college students returning for the new semester, along with a new crop of freshmen, brought new excitement to the city. Lensie did her part in partying with the young crowd, although she was secretly overjoyed when she got word from Jeno that he would be coming back soon. He suggested they meet at the Balek Ball, and Angela, unaware of the planned reunion, gladly ordered a new gown for Lensie, a little more sophisticated than the last one she wore, showing a hint more of her lovely curves. She looked picture perfect with her hair swept up and her arms in long white over-the-elbow gloves.

Jeno arrived a little after the music started, but as soon as he spotted Lensie, he went straight to her side. The dance floor was crowded and Angela didn't notice them; she had no idea that he was back. Her ears perked up, however, when she overheard a couple of ladies talking near her.

"Well, well, look who is here, that handsome tennis instructor, Mr. Zachar," one of them said.

"I thought he left Sopron for good," said the other. "He made quite an impression on my daughter when she was taking lessons from him. She sounded almost smitten, singing his praises about the gentlemanly way he conducted himself, but of course he couldn't be considered an acceptable suitor, not for my daughter anyway, when he is forced to give instructions to make ends meet."

"Oh, but that was a year ago! I hear he is now an officer in the new customs department. It's a steady government job with a very good salary. He must have connections to get that position in these hard times. I wish he'd taken an interest in my daughter instead of Lensie Bohaczek, but he seems to be quite taken with her. He hardly let her dance with anyone else."

Angela's heart sank at hearing the news. So, Jeno was here. Her eyes found them dancing with abandon. How long had it been since Lensie met him? It was here, two years ago, and in spite of all her opposition, they still glowed with obvious happiness. Was she wrong to stand in their way? Attraction this strong couldn't be a fleeting romance or a lighthearted flirtation. She recalled her own years of waiting for the man she loved, and how her feelings only grew stronger with separation. Maybe it was time she gave Jeno a chance. If after all this time Lensie still couldn't forget him, perhaps it was best if she stopped interfering. As much as she wanted to protect her from possible hurt, it was time to give in. She wouldn't fight them anymore. She was still convinced that their age difference was too great, but she would make an effort to know him better. And if he was anything close to what Lensie and these other women say about him, he just might make a good husband. With the steady job she heard Jeno now had, he would be able to support Lensie, a point to consider in view of the dismal state of the current economic situation.

There was another reason that Angela threw in the towel. She was not well. Her asthma attacks had grown more severe lately and they were more frequent, leaving her gasping and exhausted. She knew the illness was incurable; the medication only brought temporary relief, and she began to fear that she might die before Lensie could look after herself. Yes, she decided, it was time to stop her animosity. She would find out what Jeno's intentions were, how serious he was about Lensie, and if he wanted to marry her, she would give them her blessing.

It came as a total surprise to Lensie and Jeno that during the break Angela acted friendly and welcoming toward him, congratulating him on his new job, even telling him how much Lensie had missed him during his absence. And when the ball ended and she invited him to come and visit them soon, Lensie could hardly believe her ears. Behind Angela's back she made a little grimace to Jeno, eyes wide open, eyebrows raised, a look that said, *what is happening?*

The next morning she asked her mother the same question, what made her change her attitude, and when she heard the answer, she jumped onto her neck, hugging and kissing her.

"I knew one day you would understand how much we love each other! And when you get to know him you will like him, too, Mama, I know you will; he is such a gentle man, I mean literally. He is a good man, Mama, and I know he will be good to me."

"Well, I hope so, Lensie; I hope so. To tell you the truth, I didn't think that your feelings for him were this strong. I thought you wanted a career in music; you have taken these lessons for years and years now; what happened to your aspiration?"

"I am glad you brought it up, because I have wanted to talk to you about this for some time now. In the last six months or so, I came to realize that I am not improving anymore. I have reached my peak both in singing and playing the piano, and my teachers have told me the same. I am realistic enough to see the difference between me and some other girls with real talent. I have limitations; I know I could never be a concert pianist or a first class soprano. I'll always be grateful for your support Mama, but it's time to stop taking lessons and save the money. Not that all these years of studying were for nothing! I could teach piano if it ever became necessary, and I will continue to sing in the church choir."

"It is entirely up to you Lensie. If this is how you feel, I agree, there is no reason to continue. It's foolish to throw good money away. And what you said about learning is also true; knowledge is never wasted."

That night Lensie climbed into bed with a great sense of relief. She and Jeno were now free to see each other, no need to lie or cover up anymore. It took a long time but she won her battle. She hugged her pillow and closed her eyes dreaming of the happily ever after that was now within her reach.

The light was still on when Angela passed her room, and finding Lensie sound asleep, she tiptoed in to turn it off. Standing at the bedside she looked down at her daughter's lovely face, so peaceful and innocent, lost somewhere in dreamland. She bent to kiss her forehead and sent a silent prayer for her dreams to come true. She knew too well that some never do.

The postwar austerity lingered on well into 1924. The steadily growing budget deficit, coupled with inflation, was crippling the country. The money Jeno had saved during his training in Gyor lost almost half of its value, and instead of an apartment, he could only afford a rented room. It was a great comfort to him that with Angela's change of heart he was now allowed to visit Lensie. At first Angela was always present, but when she saw his commitment deepening and became convinced that Lensie was not wasting her time with a long relationship that led to nowhere, she was more willing to let them have more privacy. It was not only a question of trust; she also realized that times were changing, the present was a far cry from her own days, even from what it was five years ago. The war was forgotten, and everyone seemed to be in a hurry to make up for what they missed during the long, lean years.

This rush to enjoy life was further accelerated when in 1925 the government finally took decisive steps to shore up the sagging economy. They did it by introducing a new currency, the Pengo, made possible by negotiating and successfully obtaining considerable amount of foreign loans. It jumpstarted the climb toward recovery, and when the economy began to show signs of steady, sustainable growth, it invited additional foreign capital. Invested in light industry, production was rising, foreign trade flourished and tourists from the West started to arrive, rediscovering Budapest. The city was once again alive with glitter and gaiety, catching up fast to the developed nations of Western Europe.

Entertainment also reflected the changing times. People were no longer satisfied listening to soulful gypsy music, or waltzing to the once-popular Strauss tunes. They clamored to hear the newest sound coming from America, called Jazz, and as nightclubs sprang up, pulsating with the new rhythm, elegant couples crowded the dance floors doing the Charleston, the latest dance craze, also from America. Young women bound their breasts to prevent unflattering bouncing while they shimmied and bobbed, arms flailing and legs kicking. It was a sight to see, if one could see at all through the thick smoke swirling in the air and smarting the eye. Everyone smoked; it was no longer shocking to see women light up, puffing away on cigarettes, or even on cigars, and why not? It was the 20th century! Life must be enjoyed as they smoked and danced with abandon.

The horse-drawn carriages were also gone from the streets of Budapest. When the clubs closed and the patrons were leaving, shiny new automobiles lined the curbs waiting to take them home. With the automobiles came noise and pollution, but nobody cared; the novelty of driving a car or even riding in one was too exciting to pay attention to such trivialities.

Fashion also underwent dramatic changes. The sight of young ladies showing knees and more no longer raised eyebrows, nor did the garish makeup they wore. Those not following the new trends or frowning upon it were immediately labeled old-fashioned, backward fuddy-duddies. Women everywhere were on the march to break old traditions, challenge taboos, and stretch boundaries. For them it was a time of exhilarating liberation, shedding inhibitions, and tasting freedom for the first time.

These changes slowly trickled down from Budapest to provincial towns, including Sopron. Ladies, even from the best families, thought nothing of painting their lips bright red, smudging their eyelids, or loosen their hair into free-swinging bobs. They wanted the latest style in everything, vying to be the first to parade in some daring new fashion creation. Angela shook her head at this exuberant striving for change, and while some mothers put up a fight, trying to turn back time, she wisely accepted it as inevitable. She was once part of the fashion world and knew well enough that women always wanted something more than the norm to stand out and be noticed. Back then a brighter color, an extra frill around the neck, or an inch deviation in the length of a skirt was enough to make a difference, but these days a dress had to be the flashiest, the barest, and shortest.

Lensie, of course, was not about to be left behind. The next time Angela ordered a few dresses for her she wanted them to be more revealing, all to please Jeno. She expected some opposition from her mother, but to her surprise, she let her do as she wished. A bigger surprise was in store for her when Jeno didn't react with the expected enthusiasm to the trendy little party dress she wore for their next date. Feeling especially daring, she pirouetted in front of him when he came to pick her up, finishing with striking a voguish pose for total effect. She held the pose waiting for an appreciative whistle or applause, but instead Jeno slowly looked to the side, then back to Lensie, an indulgent smile on his face.

"What?" she asked, somewhat deflated. "Why are you smiling like that? Don't you like my new dress?"

"Kitten, it's not the dress, it's you!" Still smiling, he reached for her but she held him off.

"What's that supposed to mean? That you don't like me?"

"That's right, I don't like you. I adore you! You are so darling, trying to look so sophisticated."

"Well, it's because I feel sophisticated. In case you don't know, this is the latest style!"

"I know, sweetheart, I know, but do you really need to follow every trend that comes along? You would look just as beautiful in that elegant little dress you wore the last few times we went out."

"Oh that one, I wore that to death! What would my friends think, that I have nothing else to wear? You men just don't understand it! But how could you, you have no clue about fashion."

"But you are wrong, I do appreciate it when people dress fashionably; it's only that there is a difference between fashionable and trendy. You girls go for the latest to make you look different, but wind up looking exactly the same. I don't know how to put it so you won't take it the wrong way, but I think if you didn't do exactly as everybody else, *that* would make you unique. To me, what makes a woman stand out is choosing a style that reflects her personal taste. Does this make any sense to you?"

Lensie spread her arms and looked down on her dress with rows of fringes down to the above-the-knee hemline. "What do you mean, personal taste? This is my personal taste and I don't see anything wrong with it! Just what is it you have against my dress? I thought you'd like it, but I can go and change, if that's what you want me to do," she said with a trace of defiance in her voice.

"No, that's not the point I wanted to make, Kitten. Maybe I am just not used to the new look; or maybe I am too old-fashioned; it really does not matter. It's not important. To me you are lovely no matter what you wear. If you like the dress, if it pleases you, wear it, by all means, just don't do it for my sake. Now, let's just go and have a good time. The garden party should be fun. It already started; I heard the music when I passed the place on my way here."

Lensie's face lit up at the mention of the garden party. She could hardly wait to show off her new dress to all her friends. It was perfect for the occasion. *What does Jeno know about dresses anyway?* she was sulking silently. She wouldn't be caught dead wearing that old-fashioned dress he called "elegant." Like it or not, Jeno just has to get used to her new look! And with that she tossed her hair and, turning on her heel, marched out the door.

Bliss at last

AS CHRISTMAS 1925 approached, Jeno visited the local jewelry store to purchase an engagement ring for Lensie. It was now close to four years since they first met but time had not changed his feelings for her. The initial attraction was as strong as ever, and as he watched her grow through the years he fell deeper in love with her exuberant spirit, her giving nature and sense of fairness. He also knew that she could be stubborn at times, insisting that her way was the right way, and although she could charm him into agreeing with her in almost anything, if their differences sharpened and headed toward an argument, she usually gave in. She didn't sulk or carry a chip on her shoulder; her sunny disposition had no room for playing the victim. Life was there to enjoy rather than to spoil it with needless squabbling.

They had many talks about their future together. He laid it on the table how much he earned, what they could spend and how much they should save. Hearing it, Angela suggested that since her apartment was spacious enough, and to save money, Jeno should move in after they were married. It was a good and workable idea. Once Angela put aside her initial hostilities against him, they got along well; she actually came to appreciate his realistic, cool-headed nature, which she hoped would have a calming effect on her excitable daughter.

Lensie was thrilled with her engagement ring, a small but clear diamond set in platinum. They left the wedding date open, hoping that Jeno's relatives might be able to obtain a visa and come, but his mother warned not to expect much since the treatment of Hungarian minorities in Slovakia was still vindictive. As hated minorities they were slowly, painfully learning to live with the restrictions forced upon them, and accept the idea that their situation was permanent. The family managed to adjust the best they could; at least they had jobs and a decent enough existence. Jeno's brother Jozsef and his wife were parents of a little girl, Judit, and were expecting their second child. His sister Sári, married since 1922 to her long time beau Gusztav, also had a two-year-old boy, Lorand. Her mother came to live with them in Losonc after the baby's birth, although it was not an easy decision for her to make, leaving behind the graves of her husband and two of her children, and say goodbye to the place where she first came as a young bride.

After the holidays, Jeno was bound for Budapest to attend another three-month study course required for officers considered for promotion. The Customs building on the Pest side, overlooking the Danube, offered accommodations, although he spent most of his weekends at his uncle Istvan's place. This younger brother of Jeno's father was his closest relative in Hungary, a warm-hearted man with a loving family, who made him feel at home from the first day he knocked on their door. Soon he was there on several weekday evenings as well, enjoying not only Aunt Mariska's home-cooked meals, but also the camaraderie that sprang up between Jeno and his cousin Sandor. Six years younger than Jeno, he was attending the elite Ludovika Academy, the prestigious military school similar to West Point, preparing young men for a military carrier.

Lensie had never been in Budapest and was greatly excited when Jeno asked her to come for a visit. A formal invitation from his aunt and uncle soon followed, sending her on a shopping spree, buying new luggage and several gifts for her hosts, her future relatives. Jeno and Sandor's sister Margit, only two years older than Lensie, greeted her at the station, Jeno with obvious joy, and Margit with genuine affection. The girls quickly became friends, and it didn't take long either before Lensie, with her cheerful, natural ways, charmed the rest of the family. They couldn't do enough to make her feel welcome. Day after day, while Jeno was busy studying, they took her sightseeing around Budapest, the city that was fast becoming known as the Paris of Central Europe. She didn't know that Buda and Pest used to be two separate cities—old historic Buda on the left bank of the Danube and across it the newer urban Pest—until they were united in 1873, barely fifty years ago.

There were trips to museums and visits to historical sites, some on the Buda side going back to Roman times. They took her for lunch at the elegant new Gellert Hotel, already attracting the rich and famous of Europe with its spa that claimed to have curative powers. Another day they dined at the Grand Hotel on Margit Island, a tiny mile-long strip of land embraced by the river. She was thrilled to ride the Metro that ran from downtown Pest to Heroes' Square, the second oldest underground in Europe built in 1896. Before heading home via crossing the famous Chain Bridge, one of eight bridges connecting the two sides, they usually ended the day in downtown Pest, where exclusive shops and fashion boutiques coexisted with quaint cafés and intimate little espresso bars, always crowded with people sipping strong black coffee and sampling delicious pastries smothered with whipped cream.

Lensie was overwhelmed by the discoveries of the city. Although patches of snow still covered the ground and for a day or two a wintry mist hung in the air, the images were forever imprinted on her impressionable mind. Jeno's aunt and uncle invited them to come back in the summer when the beauty of the city could truly be appreciated. It was a different world with the flowers in full bloom and the sun smiling down.

Their evenings were spent in quiet conversation or playing cards. For entertainment the best the family could offer was their season tickets to the opera, with *Aida* playing the night before Lensie's departure. When she declined, pleading that her train was leaving at eight in the morning and there was much packing to do, her hosts exchanged knowing glances over the seemingly valid excuse. Of course, the young couple would prefer to spend time alone before saying goodbye!

With everyone away, it was perhaps the first time since they had met that Jeno and Lensie found themselves free to spend a cozy evening together, undisturbed and completely alone. Sitting on the sofa and feeling melancholy, she rested her head on his shoulder.

"I'll miss you, Kitten," Jeno whispered, with his arms around her. "It was so good to have you here, even though I could not be with you all the time. My relatives love you, you know, as would my mother and my family if only I could take you to meet them."

"Maybe someday soon," she said snuggling closer. "I am really grateful to your aunt and uncle for inviting me; they were so wonderful to me, the way they took me around, showing everything. I had the best time of my life. But the best part was being with you every evening; it made me feel like we were married already. I just wish it did not end so soon! Now I have to go home again and sit and wait for you. How long is it before you can come back?"

"Only a couple of weeks, but I'll be very busy preparing for my exams. I won't have much time to think about you unless you give me something to remember you by," Jeno said softly, lifting Lensie's chin and looking into her eyes. With the lights turned down to a faint glow and in the safety of the warm and secluded surroundings, his hand slowly slid to her breast and down along the curve of her body. It was not a totally unfamiliar journey; there were few stolen moments here and there during the year before, just enough for hurried explorations, but never beyond that. Now, as his hand roamed further and deeper, touching her more intimately than ever before, they both felt the old safeguards slipping away.

"Kitten, I don't know if I can stop! I want you, I want you so much, you have to make me stop," his words came between gasps, as if in pain.

"I want you too, my darling, and I am not going to stop you. We have waited for so long; I don't want to wait any longer." Lensie whispered back, and when Jeno asked if she had any doubts, her answer was firm. "No, I want to make love as much as you do, but you'll have to help me because I don't know what I am supposed to do."

"My sweet, innocent darling, my little wife to be," Jeno said with an almost unbearable tenderness. "I'll be gentle, I promise, just try to relax. Think of it as our wedding night. What we are doing is beautiful; it will bind us together for the rest of our lives," he continued soothingly as he slowly began to undress her, marveling at the lustrous glow of her skin as layer after layer of clothing fell away. She stood in front of him, waiting, while his eyes hungrily took in every inch of her nakedness. With tremendous control he took his time to help her recline on the sofa, then looking down on her beautiful body in total amazement that all this loveliness was his to possess, he reached out and turned off the light.

. . . .

The brief moment of passion that Lensie so willingly submitted to had lifelong consequences. By April she was sure that she was pregnant. At first she complained of stomach flu or food poisoning, but when the symptoms persisted, a few probing questions from Angela that Lensie reluctantly answered solved the mystery of her "illness." She was going to have a baby! The news brought a quiet joy to all three of them. Nothing could make Lensie happier than to have Jeno's baby; perhaps it happened a little earlier than planned but regardless, her joy was boundless. Angela, too, was thrilled. The thought of holding her grandchild in her arms filled her with blissful anticipation. She had always loved children, and although she was grateful to have Lensie, there were times when she felt cheated for being denied having more. Fate was not kind to her, but now she would forgive it all to see her grandchildren grow. And for Jeno, it didn't matter if they were a little ahead of schedule. He was not getting any younger; at past thirty he was ready for fatherhood. During their courtship, whenever they talked about having a family, Lensie made it clear that since she always missed having a brother or sister, she couldn't imagine going through life without children. She wanted babies, at least three and not too far apart, which was fine with Jeno. His position was secure; he could support a family of five.

Of course, with a baby on the way, the wedding could not be postponed a minute longer, and it wouldn't be the grand affair Angela had in mind for her only child. No white wedding gown, no marching down the aisle, although any of her uncles would have been proud to give her away. There was no sign yet of Lensie's condition, but regardless, Angela felt it was safer to have a quiet private ceremony; later they could always repeat their vows in a church somewhere else, perhaps in Budapest with Jeno's relatives. This way the wedding date could be fudged better when people started counting the months backwards after the birth of the child. She knew too well that some still remembered Lensie's illegitimate birth and would gleefully say, "Like mother, like daughter."

And so, on May 10, 1926, two days after her 20th birthday, Lensie and Jeno were married in a quick civil ceremony with only the immediate family present. Lensie looked lovely in a mauve dress and matching hat worn over her fashionable short bob. Aside from a necklace, Jeno's first gift to her, and her ring, she wore no other jewelry and carried only a small bouquet of pink roses. Mitzie served a sumptuous luncheon at her restaurant, and then at four o'clock the couple left for a short honeymoon in Austria.

As Angela suggested, Jeno moved into her apartment, an arrangement that caused very little change in her routine. If anything, his presence, and seeing Lensie so happy brought a new tranquility into her life. Old arguments were forgotten; all they talked about now was the baby, if it would be a boy or a girl. They didn't bother picking names, since Lensie insisted on naming the children after Jeno's brothers and sisters, Gyula and Jozsef for boys and Eta and Sári for girls. If they had only girls, the third daughter would be named Juliana—Gyula in Latin is Julius, and Juliana its female version—and the fourth Jozefina, but

Jeno put a stop to the naming game right there. After four daughters and no sons, reproduction would be halted.

Living with his mother-in-law caused no problems for Jeno, either. He was used to smoke outside on the balcony as not to irritate Angela's asthma. In the evenings they played cards, read, or just talked, although Jeno quickly realized that his low-keyed humor didn't always hit its mark with his no-nonsense mother-in-law. His only passion was soccer, and during the season he would be out watching a game on Sunday afternoons. Occasionally, he still played cards in his old hangout, the Hungaria Coffeehouse, without any objection from Lensie or her mother.

On the morning of November 27 Jeno had already left for work and Angela was about to leave, too, when Lensie felt the first mild contraction. Angela immediately went to get the midwife, Mrs. Polgar, stopping only at work to tell that she was not coming in and why. By the time she was back with the midwife, the contractions were stronger, but Lensie held up heroically. After a brief examination, Mrs. Polgar assured everyone that all seemed fine, and with Lensie's round hips, she should have an easy birth. In the meantime, Angela sent word to Jeno that he was about to become a father but not to rush home just yet. Have lunch, stock up on cigars, then about four o'clock or so, head home to meet the new arrival.

Typical of first-time fathers, Jeno was nervous. He stayed at the office but was on edge all afternoon, taking some good-natured teasing from his colleagues. Promptly at four, he was on his way home, stopping only at the florist to pick up the flowers he had ordered earlier.

"Congratulations, you have a daughter," Angela greeted him at the door. It put a happy grin on his face; he had a little girl he could spoil! When Angela cautioned him that Lensie was asleep. he put down the flowers and quietly followed her into the room, heading straight for the crib. They didn't realize that Lensie was only resting, totally exhausted and eyes closed, but awake. Hearing the footsteps, she raised her eyelids just enough to see Jeno leaning over the bassinet. Picturing his face at that tender moment—the doting father meeting his infant daughter for the first time—brought a faint smile to her tired lips. She was about to call out to him when Jeno drew himself up, murmuring, "My God, is she an ugly baby!"

"What did you say???" Lensie's voice rang out with a startling pitch. "How could you say such a thing? She is bruised and blotched a little from going through a horrific, painful passage, but she is not ugly! Haven't you ever seen a newborn baby?" she wailed pitifully.

"I am sorry, darling, I didn't mean it. But it's true, I've never seen a baby minutes after birth. All the babies I've seen were round-faced cherubs with rosy cheeks. I had no idea they could look like this. Is this normal? Is she otherwise fine?"

"There is nothing wrong with her!" Lensie managed to say between sobs.

"Please sweetheart, it was just a stupid reaction; you must know that I didn't mean what I said," he pleaded in earnest.

"But you did, I know you did, and it hurts! It was such a cruel thing to say! Thank God her tiny ears couldn't hear you!" She had no more strength left; worn out and deeply wounded she turned her head away, crying into her pillow.

Taking her hands and covering them with kisses, Jeno apologized over and over that the thoughtless remark just slipped out of his mouth.

"Could you ever forgive me? I love you so much, and the baby, too; I just really did not know what to expect. It was stupid, and I would do anything to take it back. I know she will be as beautiful as you, and I will tell her so every day of my life. Please say you forgive me."

"Of course he did not mean it, Lensie," Angela chimed in soothingly, feeling sorry for Jeno by now. She could sympathize with him because to tell the truth, the poor little creature looked battered and bruised indeed. Contrary to the midwife's prediction, it was not an easy birth.

But Lensie was not so forgiving. This supposed to be one of the happiest days of her life, the birth of her baby, and he ruined it with his hateful words! *He says he is sorry, but what if it was just to make me feel better? What if he really hates the baby?* she sobbed as new tears welled up behind her tightly squeezed eyelids. In her mind she kept replaying the scene she just witnessed: Jeno standing at the crib, but instead of taking his poor little daughter in his arms, saying how ugly she was. Meant it or not, those words came out of his mouth spontaneously, that's how he felt, and she would never forgive him for that!

Silently cursing himself for the unintentional slip Jeno kept on apologizing, but she waved him away without opening her eyes. She wanted to be alone. There was nothing he could do for now. He would try to make up for it again tomorrow, and the day after, and again, as long as it took her to forgive his blunder.

The baby's baptism was set for the second week in December with Mitzie and her husband Janos standing in as godparents. Half an hour before the ceremony the priest also sanctioned Lensie and Jeno's marriage, which made them officially man and wife in the eyes of the Church. By then Jeno's unfortunate remark was all but forgotten, although the pair of diamond earrings in Lensie's ears might have played a small role in that. The little girl was adorable, tiny as a doll, and with her bruises gone her skin turned to a healthy glow. She had a shock of silky dark hair and her mother's green eyes and upturned nose. Her name was Etelka, but they called her Eta for short.

Angela doted on her granddaughter, spending every minute with her during the two weeks she took off from work to leave Lensie time to recover. Every day someone from her big, warmhearted family would come by to ooh and aah over the baby, inundating her with soft little teddy bears and a dozen other equally lovable stuffed toys. With her daughter's crib already overflowing with gifts, finding something new to give her for Christmas won't be easy for Lensie.

This year was the first time they were celebrating the holidays together as husband and wife, and as they stood in the front of the candlelit tree with little Eta in her arm and Jeno beside her, Lensie truly felt blessed. They were the picture of a happy young couple looking forward to a bright future with confidence and hope.

The outlook for 1927 was promising indeed. The country's economy was humming; the new currency kept inflation at bay and the job market was improving at a steady pace. Modernization was getting a foothold in every city, and Sopron was no exception. Extensive renovation of older buildings got underway, upgrading them to meet recently established city codes. New apartment houses sprang up beyond the inner city and a beautiful three-story hotel was being built in the Loevers. It even had an elevator!

There was no such convenience in Angela's building though, and Lensie found it increasingly difficult to handle the baby carriage, dragging it up and down the steep flights to their apartment. The obvious solution was moving to a ground floor flat, and she began to look for one. She was all excited when she came across a new two-story apartment building on Eszterhazy Street in the final stages of construction, offering one- and two-bedroom units with the latest conveniences. True, it would take a little longer for Angela and Jeno to walk to work, but there was a church and a good school nearby. She heard the place was renting fast, and if they didn't want to lose out, they would have to make a decision soon.

After checking it out Jeno agreed, the place was ideal. The extra fifteen-minute walk to his office didn't bother him; it was good exercise. Angela, however, made it clear that she was not moving. With her asthma getting worse, she was out of breath going to work as it was; she simply couldn't handle the extra distance. When Lensie argued that they could not possibly leave her alone she became quite indignant. How could they think she was not capable of taking care of herself? She would be fine; they would see each other often; after all, they were not moving to the other side of the globe! Seeing her determination, it occurred to Lensie that maybe Angela had enough of living together under the same roof, especially now with the baby on board. It was understandable if she wanted more calm and quiet in her life.

Without Angela they only needed a one-bedroom apartment, and they took one on ground level facing the tree-lined street. It had a spacious and bright living room, a large bedroom with plenty of room for the crib, a nice kitchen, a bathroom, and in the back of the building a playground, with a swing and sandlot for the children. The day they moved in was cause for celebration: they were finally setting up their very own household. For Lensie it meant cutting the umbilical cord that tied her to Angela, and for Jeno it was finding a place he could call home. After the long journey from Selmec that took him through uncertainty, hardship, and loneliness, he felt for the first time that he truly arrived home.

The move kept Lensie busy, but once they settled in she realized how much she missed her mother's presence. She also worried about her living alone, beset with growing health problems. Angela was now forty-four years old, a little heavier, a little grayer, her movements slower, battling asthma and never free of the angst that her old tuberculosis would reappear in some other part of her body. In time it led her to think of making a will, and to start she asked Lensie and Jeno what would they do with the parcel of land she had in the Loevers after she died.

"Don't talk about death and dying and making a will, Mama, I don't want to hear about it!" Lensie protested at first, but when Angela pressed, she calmed down. "Well, if you must know, I wouldn't bother with the subletting; I'd rather sell it and use the money for our new apartment. We bought some basic furnishings; you saw what we have, but it's a long way from the perfect home I want for us."

Jeno had little say on the subject since the property would be Lensie's inheritance and she would have all the right to decide what to do with it, but he made a remark that the Loever was expanding, the tourists who came here year after year for the exceptionally good air quality were building small summer cottages in the area, and if the trend continued, the property values would increase.

Angela was nodding her head in agreement but Lensie thought otherwise.

"You might be right, but that would take years and years, and there are always problems and disputes with that farmer who rents the parcel. I know how many times Mama had to run after him to collect the dues, and with you working and me running the household and taking care of the children, who will have time for that? It's a headache I could do without."

"Well, in that case, Lensie, why wait until I am gone?" Angela said. "Why not sell it now so you can use the proceeds right away?" And so she did. Even though deep down she felt Jeno was right, she would do whatever pleased her daughter.

Another thing Angela wanted to do was to visit the Pollingers in Eisenstadt, the former Kismarton that was now part of Austria. She had kept in touch with the family and when Katie, Henrich's sister, wrote that her parents were not in the best of health, she decided to go and see them before it was too late. In her letter Katie blamed Henrich for the mental suffering her parents had endured over his desertion; it never ceased to haunt them and it greatly contributed to their physical decline. Angela took Lensie and Eta for a bittersweet weekend visit, knowing that this was probably the last time they would see the dear old couple.

As the young family began to settle into their new place they received good news from Jeno's family. The Slovak government finally eased travel restrictions for the Hungarian minorities, granting exit visas for one visit every ten years. His mother was still barred from leaving, but his sister Sári, her husband Gusztav and their son Lorand were coming for a two-week stay in August. It was a joyous reunion, and after years of forced separation it took days to catch up with all the changes in their lives. They were thrilled to meet Lensie and to watch the two little cousins together for the first time. Since Angela had the extra bedroom, they stayed with her, and she took time off from work to be on hand to watch the children when needed.

During their visit talks inevitably turned to politics. Sadly, for the Hungarian minorities in Slovakia there was very little improvement since the annexation; the oppression of everything Hungarian continued. In the Hungarian communities, teachers were forbidden to teach in their native language, as were priests preaching in Hungarian churches. Forming any kind of social clubs for the purpose of nurturing Hungarian culture was outlawed; even charity events to help needy Hungarian families were banned, claiming they only served to disguise anti-Slovak activities. Better jobs and promotions only went to Slovak nationals, even if lesser qualified than their Hungarian colleagues. Hungarian women were forced to tag the hated "ova" after their family names, as Mrs. Zachar now became Zacharova. Treaties guaranteeing certain minimum rights for minorities living under the Successor States were simply ignored by the Slovak government, especially when the League of Nations, put in charge to oversee the execution of these provisions, showed very little interest in monitoring the situation.

When they did not discuss politics, Jeno and Lensie introduced the visitors to Sopron and its surroundings. They were impressed with the beauty as well as the historical background of the city that reached back to 2500 BC, as evidenced by rare findings on display in the Museum of Antiquity. There were artifacts left by Stone Age people, as well as from the Bronze Age from circa 2000 to 800 BC: a beautiful urn, a carved moon-idol, and several other items unearthed from burial grounds. The city itself was first established by the Roman Empire between 27 BC and 37 AD during the reign of Emperor Augustus and later Tiberius, and bore the name of Scarabantia. According to Pliny the Elder, the famous Roman writer and scientist, around 67-79 AD the city, being near to an important crossroad of Roman military transports, became a bustling place, as evidenced by excavations in the center of Sopron, that included a perfectly intact portion of the main street called "cardo," the hub of any Roman city.

Many other items from the Roman era were discovered and preserved: statues of the gods Jupiter, Juno and Minerva; numerous burial sarcophagi with clearly visible inscriptions; a Roman bath; and in the Becsi Domb area, the remains of a 410' by 280' amphitheater. The city went into decline in the 5th century, when the Roman Empire crumbled under the Great Migration from the East, but still survived the wave of invaders, the Huns, Ostrogoths and Avars on their push to the West. Thanks to its geographical location the city escaped the horrific Turkish occupation that lasted from 1526 to 1699.

There were plenty of other things to do besides visiting museums. They attended a concert at the Kaszino building where in 1820 the young Hungarian-born composer Franz Liszt gave his first public piano recitation at the ripe old age of nine. Another one was held outdoors at the Versailles-like palace of Prince Eszterhazy, the highest-ranking Hungarian aristocrat, where Franz Joseph Haydn, the family's court musician for thirty years, gave one of his first concerts in 1775 and later wrote many of his compositions.

While exploring the city and its surroundings the conversation was always in Hungarian, but Jeno's sister found it strange that in Anglea's presence they only spoke German. It brought into glaring contrast that while Hungarians in Slovakia couldn't use their beloved mother tongue in public, here in a Hungarian city so many people preferred speaking German. Jeno explained that the older generation from the days of the Austro-Hungarian Empire never bothered to learn Hungarian well enough to follow a lively conversation, but his sister's remark remained with him long after they left. It made him notice something that had escaped his attention until now, that little Eta often answered him in German when he asked her something in Hungarian. Was Lensie talking German to her even when Angela was not around? They would have to talk about this. He could excuse his mother-in-law, but he would make sure that in his own home his wife and daughter would speak Hungarian!

Another thing that bothered him was Lensie's name, a nickname for Helen. He wouldn't say anything about it now, but after Angela was gone, he would ask her to start using her Hungarian name, Ilona, or Ilonka, if she preferred, although at home he still called her Kitten, a nickname that fit her kittenish charm and feisty personality.

The year Eta turned two, Lensie began talking about having another baby. Jeno knew she wanted the children to be close in age, but after discussing it she agreed to wait a little longer. Her mother's health showed serious signs of decline and visiting her as often as she did would be more difficult with two babies in tow. There was no denying that Angela's asthma attacks were becoming more severe, leaving her exhausted, and there were days when she was unable to make it to work. Lensie tried to convince her to retire and move in with them, but she would not hear of it. She insisted that she was getting better; she had switched to a new medication that she said helped, but she was only fooling herself. There was no cure for her illness. Finally, in the spring of 1929 she was forced to quit her job, as the relentless coughing kept her awake at night and left her too weak to get up in the morning.

It pained Lensie to see her mother suffer and not be able to help. Each morning after Jeno left, she took Eta to spend the day with Angela, sometimes coaxing her into taking a walk in the Loever as the doctor suggested. On Sundays Jeno would also come over, but after a short stay Lensie insisted he join his friends to watch a soccer game; it wasn't fair to spend his only day off sitting with her sick mother. She also sensed that Angela might never get well and just wanted to spend time with her alone.

Family members stopped by frequently. Lizzie, Rezie, and Gertie came from Austria to see if Angela would like to visit them, but she would not leave her home. She loved her sisters, but at times she found their noisy chatter exhausting. Her wheezing got progressively louder and because the constant coughing made her voice hoarse, it was difficult for her to speak. There were moments during some especially prolonged spasms, when her eyes bulged, and her neck muscles strained from gasping, that Lensie truly thought it would be the end. It made her eyes clouded with tears to see her mother's face drenched with sweat from the exertion, and just watch, unable to do anything.

She now spent the nights, too, with Angela, sitting at her bedside, mopping her forehead, and keeping her comfortable as much as possible. Then one day the wheezing suddenly stopped and her breathing seemed easier. She lay quietly, feeling more restful than any time in the past weeks; the only strange thing Lensie noticed was a bluish tint that appeared around her mother's lips. She wanted to call the doctor, but Angela said no, not now, when she could finally breathe without exertion. It proved to be a fatal error. The calmness was a sign that air could not escape through her inflamed bronchial tubes and the discoloration was from lack of oxygen.

In her rundown condition she also developed kidney problems that led to a complete kidney failure. The end came on July 29, 1929, when Angela's heart gave out and freed her soul to find peace and perhaps the answer to the tragic mystery of Henrich's disappearance that so unjustly altered her life.

The loss of her mother and witnessing her suffering during the final days took a toll on Lensie. She deeply mourned Angela. Her passing created a vast void in her life that became emotionally difficult to overcome. The loss of a parent is always hard, but the unique bond between Lensie and Angela, the long years of exclusive dependence on one another, made it so much more painful. Living outside the boundaries of a traditional family, Angela without a husband and Lensie growing up without a father and siblings, these two women relied solely on each other for support, love, and affection that didn't change when Jeno came into their lives. She burst into tears every time little Eta asked when were they going to visit her grandmother again. Engulfed in her solitary grief, she made a silent promise that when her time came to leave this earth, her daughter would have brothers and sisters to share their sorrow and lessen their anguish by consoling each other.

Jeno missed Angela too; they had become good friends once she let go of her initial mistrust. He comforted Lensie as much as she allowed him to, and eventually, with the healing power of time, Lensie began to accept her mother's death. Jeno never put demands on her; he was waiting patiently until she was ready to join him, but when she did, it was with the fierce determination to have another baby. She put down her foot when he tried to convince her that they should wait a little while longer.

"Wait for what, and for how long? Eta is three years old already; by the time we have another baby she'll be four, and I don't want them to be so far apart in years. Older children lose interest fast in their younger siblings. Besides, we are not getting any younger. You will be thirty-five by the time we would be parents again a year from now, and forty-five when he is ten years old."

"He? So you know already that it's a boy!" Jeno laughed, teasing her good-naturedly.

"What else? We have a girl, of course it's a boy next time," Lensie jumped into Jeno's lap. But he turned serious again.

"Kitty, I think we should wait and see what the next year will bring. I hear some pretty scary things are happening in the world. The stock market crashed in America, and it's bound to have drastic effects on Europe, too. You remember how bad the situation was after the war—the inflation, the shortages, how hard it was to find work, and how long the recovery took. It could all come back if the economy collapses. What if I lose my job? Think of it, Kitten; we would have a hard time with just the three of us, let alone caring for another baby. So let's wait and see what 1930 brings."

"But you can't lose your job, Jeno, you practically run the customs here; they can't do without you! And we have some money Mother left us. We should not be worrying about what happens in the world!"

"The money from your mother belongs to you, Kitty. I know you mean well when you say it's ours. And sure, I can see using it in an emergency. But we are not there yet, and hopefully that day will never come. What I earn gives us a comfortable living. All I want is to wait another year, and if it turns out that I was worrying about nothing, we'll have our little boy."

"I think you are seeing monsters when there are none, Jeno. It's true about the crash in America; I heard about it too, but for God's sake, there is an ocean between us! And Europe is not America; they have always been greedier, taken a lot more risks, and when you push things too far you get hit harder. That's how I see things, if you ask me. But then you know more about these things." Lensie always acknowledged that she was not on Jeno's level of thinking and she respected his opinion. In the end she gave in.

"I suppose you could be right," she said, "we could wait another year, but then I want to have twins, you hear?"

For a while it seemed that Lensie was right. At first, Europe only felt a slight repercussion from the problems in American, a minor slowdown that caused no more than a ripple. Hardly anyone noticed, and life hummed along with indifference to what was happening in the United States. By the end of 1930 there was still no sign of an economic meltdown in Hungary, and to ring in the New Year Mitzie organized a big party at their restaurant. All the Bohaczeks came, including those from Austria, and even though they missed Angela, they didn't let it ruin their celebration. With good food, and wine and beer flowing, everyone was in high spirits, ready to join the countdown as midnight approached. Cheering wildly, they literally rang in the New Year by clanking an Austrian cowbell that Lizzie brought with her. After the children were put down to sleep, the reveling stretched into the early morning hours, with plans to continue the next day.

Walking home, still in a jolly mood, Jeno and Lensie had a hard time keeping their voices down as not to wake their sleeping daughter. There was no denying they both were a little tipsy, but they had a good excuse: New Year's Eve only came around once a year! Laughing, they teased each other about their New Year's resolutions, Lensie to loose the few extra pounds sneaking up around her hips, and Jeno to shave his head. He began toying with the idea ever since he noticed that after each combing there was more hair left in his comb than he liked. Shaving was rumored to strengthen the hair follicles and prevent further loss. It was worth a try, but the mere thought of seeing Jeno baldheaded made Lensie giggle the rest of the way.

Once at home she put little Eta down, but they were still not ready to call it a day. Feeling merry and a bit lightheaded, they fell in bed and closing the door continued celebrating New Year's with great abandon.

As confident as they were about the coming year, Jeno's fears concerning the stability of the economy were not unfounded after all. The Atlantic, as it turned out, was not strong enough of a barrier to hold the American depression in isolation. The collapse of Wall Street on October 24, 1929, was only the beginning. U.S. investments in Germany and Austria ceased immediately, and as Wall Street became more desperate, they started calling back their loans. It started an avalanche of bank failures. The first to close its doors was the Austrian Credit Anstalt in May 1931, followed two months later by the Darmstadt Bank of Germany. The collapse of these major financial institutions placed the weight of the Western World's economy wholly on the shoulders of the Bank of England, but left entirely alone and without the help of any foreign aid, it too was doomed to fail. With England forced to abandon the Gold Standard, the Pound fell to a fifth of its worth, causing devastating effects on all countries conducting trade with London. Soon the old financial and trade arrangements of the world were in ruins, and as a consequence governments tumbled in country after country, blaming all ills on outside circumstances.

Jeno followed the unfolding world events with increasing alarm. He recognized the first signs of the coming depression that would soon crush the country's hitherto exuberant expectations for continued prosperity. Rumor had it that the prime minister, unable to find a solution to the mounting economic problems, was about to resign. It made Jeno jittery to think what it would mean for the future of the country.

On a cool spring evening he was reading the newspaper when Ilonka, as she was now called, came into the room, sat beside Jeno, and crossing her legs, peered into the paper.

"Anything new in the world today?" she asked, swinging her leg and twirling a strand of hair around her finger. She was not really interested; the question was just an opening line to talk. "Personally, I don't see any earth-shattering changes around here. Everyone is still working, stores are stacked with goods, we even have a movie house now; I hear they play some American movies. We should go and see some."

Jeno put down the paper. "I heard about it, too. We could go on Sunday. I'll stop by tomorrow on my way to work and check what's playing. I hope their movies are better than their economy. Wall Street is wiped out and the same thing is happening in Europe. Remember when I told you that we might be heading toward hard times? I am afraid I was right; it's going to hit us soon.

Aren't you glad that you listened to me about having another baby? Whatever is coming, it will be easier to manage with just the three of us."

"Hmm, well sweetheart, I am afraid it's too late for that," Ilonka cast a sidelong glance at Jeno. "Somewhere along the way we forgot all about the collapsing economy. Depression or no depression, you are going to be a papa again."

Seeing Jeno's reaction of utter disbelief, she laughed out loud. "You should see your face! If I had said that the Martians had landed, you couldn't have a more dubious expression. But yes, we are going to have a baby!"

"But how? I thought we were pretty careful!"

"Apparently not careful enough! Oh, come on darling, what problem could a tiny little baby create? What are you worried about? He gets his food from me, so you just take care of mama here, as you always do, and everything will be fine, you'll see."

By then she was snuggling against Jeno's neck, purring into his ear, kissing his face, and how could he ever resist such an enchantingly artful plea? And there was not much he could do about it, anyway. He broke into a smile, joking that one night during the holidays they must have been pretty naughty indeed.

After the initial shock wore off, he was just as excited about having another child as Ilonka was. They would manage no matter what, and wouldn't it be grand to have a son to take to the soccer games? Within a few days the entire neighborhood had heard the news that in the fall the stork will be making a delivery, all wrapped in blue, to the Zachar's doorsteps.

Everyone was happy for them, especially Grety and Jozsef Varosy, a couple living in the next apartment building. Ilonka first met Mrs.Varosy on moving day when she came over offering help, and from there, friendship grew. Her husband worked in a government office and she stayed home raising their son Kurt, a few years older than Eta. They frequently got together for dinners, the two men talking politics and sports, while the topics for Ilonka and Grety were mostly the children, cooking and general gossiping. They enjoyed each other's company, playing gin rummy on regular basis, a passion both couples shared. When they learned that Ilonka was expecting, Grety immediately declared their candidacy to become the baby's godparents. Ilonka originally thought to ask her aunt Gertie and her husband; they never had children and she remembered how well they treated her when Angela banished her there, but the fact that the Varosys had become such close friends and that they lived next door made them better suited to be active participants in the life of her child.

With the country wallowing in the throes of economic crisis and unemployment steadily climbing, both Jeno and Jozsef Varosy were relatively safe in their government jobs. Ilonka took special pleasure in telling Jeno that she knew it all along that his job was secured, they wouldn't let him go, and that he just worried too much about everything—his job, the country, the whole world—and for what? Worrying did not help any; things would fall into place, as they always did.

To her, the future looked bright. She had a happy life with only one concern for the moment: would she have a boy or a girl? Family and friends all predicted that it would be a boy; they could tell from the different way she carried Eta. Even the midwife agreed. One of her aunts claimed to have a surefire test, to hold a ring tied on a string over Ilonka's belly, and the direction it swung would tell the sex of the baby. This, however, was never put to test, for Jeno vetoed the use of such superstitious nonsense.

When Jeno's mother received the news that she would become a grandmother again around the middle of September, she put in an application for an exit visa, asking for a three-week stay starting on September 15th. The Slovak government was slow to respond, but finally she was granted the leave, but only for two weeks.

It had been over ten long years since Jeno last saw his mother, now sixty-five, still a willowy figure and in excellent health. The day she arrived and stepped off the train Jeno caught her up in his arms, overwhelmed by emotion and not ashamed to show it. Ilonka, standing back with Eta, waited discreetly until finally Jeno broke away and reached out for her to come and meet his mother. Still holding Eta by the hand she started to go but the little girl jerked her hand away and wouldn't move. "Come on sweetie," Ilonka coaxed her, "your grandmother is waiting to meet you," but Eta shook her head, and pointing to Mrs. Zachar announced, "This is not my grandmother!" It took a few days and some toys and candy before she warmed up to her and accepted that she had this second grandmother who loved her just as much as Angela did.

Jeno took time off from work and made elaborate plans to entertain his mother. Ilonka was too heavy to tag along; the most she could do was to join them for dinner when they decided to eat out. But Jeno soon discovered that regardless of his well-intended efforts, his mother was not all that interested in sightseeing. She would rather stay home and spend time with the family, getting to know her little granddaughter.

Eta, two months shy of her fifth birthday, was a quiet child, even a bit reserved, with adult-like mannerisms and vocabulary. Ilonka was concerned about how would she interact with other children when she enrolled her in kindergarten, but according to the nuns, she had no problem adjusting. She was attentive, learned quickly, and participated in the children's play, except she would stay out of their more raucous activities. The nuns assured Ilonka that her behavior was typical of a single child and she would soon outgrow it. At home too, she preferred playing with her dolls and toys rather than going out to the backyard where children were noisily tossing balls, jumping rope or riding the seesaw. Her grandmother saw a great resemblance between Eta's nature and her own, for she, too, was and always has been rather reticent.

Noticing this trait in her mother-in-law, that she didn't like to be the center of attention, Ilonka held back fussing over her, asking a bit too often if she needed anything. She also tried to keep quiet and just listen whenever Jeno and his mother talked, instead of adding her two cents worth to the conversation. It was in the kitchen where the two women found common ground. Exchanging recipes, Mrs. Zachar introduced Ilonka to a few dishes Jeno loved, like *strapacska*, a pasta dish not known around Sopron, and in turn Ilonka showed her how to make Angela's rich deserts from their days in Vienna.

Almost every day one or another of Ilonka's relatives would stop by, partly to meet her mother-in-law, but more than that, expecting to see the baby. When she missed her due date, the midwife, Mrs. Polgar assured everyone that a few days' delay was common; there was no need to worry, but Ilonka was not so easily convinced. Where was her son? There was no sign that he was getting ready to make his grand entrance.

Jeno's mother was nervous, too. Her time was running out, and if the baby did not arrive in the next three days, her visa would expire, leaving her with two choices: either return home without seeing her grandchild, or stay and face stiff penalties.

"What can they do to you if you overstay your visa?" Jeno asked. "Slap you with a fine, I am sure, but they are not going to put you in jail!"

"No, of course not, and the fine doesn't even bother me. What I am afraid of is that they might never allow me to leave the country again." Deeply concerned, Mrs. Zachar was silent for a long moment but then lifted her head in defiance. "But you know, Jeno, I don't care. I am staying until this baby is born!" She nodded several times as if to confirm her decision. "I am not going back until I see my grandson. I have three granddaughters, and of course Lorand, Sári's boy, but he is a Gero; only this one is going to carry the family name." She then turned to Ilonka, pointing to her stomach. "I am staying, but could you ask him to hurry up a little as a favor to his grandmother? I am going to break the law because he is too lazy to come out."

The tension eased, with everyone laughing, including Jeno. "He does seem to enjoy where he is right now, doesn't he?" he said, still chuckling. "And don't worry, Mother, we'll think of something to keep you out of jail! I talk to our doctor and get you a statement to verify that you are too ill to travel. We'll go and see him tomorrow."

A few more days went by, until finally, on the morning of September 30 Ilonka felt the first contractions. By noon they sent for the midwife and Jeno took Eta next door to stay with the Varosys. It was unusual for her to resist, but this time she did not want to go, so Jeno promised that a great big surprise would be waiting for her when she returned.

Around seven o'clock in the evening the baby slipped into the world and, defying all predictions, it was a girl, a second daughter. Ilonka, too exhausted to care, was just glad that her ordeal was over. As the midwife promised, the delivery was smoother than the first, and this time there were no stressful bruises on the baby. She was a healthy little creature, and after recovering from the letdown about her gender, everyone fell in love with her.

When Jeno went to fetch Eta, she immediately asked about the promised surprise. Was it ready? What was it, a toy, maybe a new doll? "Well, yes," Jeno smiled, "it is kind of a doll, you'll see in a minute. But be quiet, Mama might be sleeping and we don't want to disturb her." Taking her by the hand he led her to the bassinet where the baby was lying.

"Look Eta, this is your new sister; the stork brought her this afternoon. Isn't she beautiful?" he whispered to her.

The little girl stood there speechless, eyes wide open, then, finding her voice and forgetting all about keeping quiet, she exclaimed, "Now this *is* a surprise! I was not counting on this!" Reaching into the cradle, she touched the baby to make sure it was real, and once satisfied, she ran to her grandmother boasting that she now had a little sister. Next she asked about her name and was told she would be named Sárika.

No one could guess on that day that in years to come her name would change to Charlotte, then Cherie, and finally Shari, as life took her from her small provincial birthplace to the far corner of the globe thousands of miles away.

Jeno's mother, after obtaining a doctor's statement declaring her too "ill" to travel, spent a few more precious days in Sopron, dreading the time when she must say goodbye. Jozsef Varosy, a serious amateur photographer with his own darkroom, took dozens of pictures of the new baby that she could take home and show to the rest of her family. On the day Jeno put his mother on the train back to Losonc, Ilonka was still too weak to accompany them to the station, but she promised that next time she would present her mother-in-law with a grandson, and hopefully by then politics would have changed, allowing her to stay as long as she wished.

Although it would be another eight years before they'd see each other again, Ilonka kept her promise, and on July 24, 1933 delivered a healthy baby boy. His proud father was handing out cigars at work, and at home champagne corks popped to welcome little Gyula, or Gyuszi, as he was immediately nicknamed.

Happily married and raising a family, life couldn't have been better for the young couple. At work Jeno was steadily advancing, Ilonka had her three beautiful children, and they had close friends to enjoy an active social life. With their growing family, however, and friends and relatives regularly coming for visits, the apartment that seemed so spacious when they first moved in with only Eta, now felt small and confining. They needed a larger place and decided to look for a house to rent. They wanted to stay close to their quiet neighborhood where most people knew each other and where Eta was already attending school, and when they found one in the summer of 1934, only two blocks from where they lived, they immediately signed a ten-year lease and moved in.

The single story house stood on the corner of Flandorffer and Kolcsei Streets, directly across from the army compound where Jeno once lived during his college days. Originally the building was used as an office that sat on top of a large wine cellar built in the later part of the 19th century by a prominent wine merchant named Ignac Flandorffer. It was rumored that the Emperor Franz Joseph once honored the owner during a hunting trip by bringing a party there for wine tasting, the plaque attesting to the royal visit, however, was no longer found. In 1915 the merchant closed his business and sold the property, and the new owner decided to convert the place into two separate apartments: a large house in the front, and a small two-room flat in the back.

The two were structurally different because of the layout and the construction of the wine cellar below. It only extended beneath the house that Jeno rented, and due to raising the cellar ceiling some two feet above street level to provide good ventilation through several small openings, the house above it was also elevated to a higher level with the windows placed about seven or eight feet from the ground. And indeed, when entering the house from the street, one had to climb ten steps to reach a terrace that led to the entrance of the living quarters. From the terrace then another set of stairs descended to the backyard, where the lower structured small flat occupied by the Gruber family stood.

Inside Jeno's place, a seven-foot wide hallway ran through the length of the entire house, ending with a kitchen toward the street, and a large storage room and a water closet at the other end. Doors on the left side of the corridor led to three rooms, all with parquet floors and tall ceramic wood-burning fireplaces. The largest was up front with two windows looking to the main street and two to the side. Ilonka planned to divide this spacious rectangular room into two parts: a parlor, and a formal dining room. From there, a double door with delicately etched matching glass panels led to what she called a family room, which in turn was separated by another set of double doors from a large bedroom. The adjoining bathroom had both tub and shower with a wood-burning water tank, needed since the house had excellent plumbing but only cold running water.

To furnish the front room Ilonka used the money she inherited from her Pollinger grandparents. They had passed away shortly after she and Angela visited them in 1927, and they remembered her in their will. She bought a beautiful dining room set with a server and hutch, and a large Persian rug to go under the table. Then, to make up for all the years she had to practice her piano at school, she indulged in buying a Bosendorfer grand piano for the parlor. It was not only her childhood dream-come-true, but also an incentive for the children to begin taking piano lessons. Finally, she splurged on a full-length fur coat for herself—well deserved, as everyone agreed.

Settled into their new home, Ilonka and Jeno had every reason to be grateful as 1934 drew to a close. Preparing for the holidays they put up a towering eight-foot tree, and as the family and their close friends, the Varosys, gathered around it on Christmas Eve—the day of gift exchange in the European tradition—in the warm glow of the flickering candlelight Ilonka sat at her new piano and accompanied the singing of their beloved Christmas carols. How perfect life was, surrounded by the husband she loved with all her being, the children she cherished and adored, and friends she held dear. Her heart full of joy and pride, yet humbled with gratitude, she silently gave thanks for all the blessings they had received during the years that led to this wonderfully joyous day of complete fulfillment.

CHAPTER THREE

1935 – 1945

Tranquility before the storm

DURING THE YEARS while Jeno's family grew to five, events hardly noticed by the world were slowly unfolding in Germany. Adolf Hitler, a former Army corporal who served time in prison for an ill-conceived attempt to seize power in 1923, reappeared on the political scene and found a large number of sympathizers. Sharing his ideas they eagerly flocked to join his National Social Party that advocated nationalism, anti-Semitism, and the glorious future of a united Germany Hitler promised to create.

At first, sober-minded people did not take him seriously, but when he came in second in the 1932 presidential elections, he could no longer be ignored. His prestige grew further when in January 1933 Hindenburg, the eighty-five-year-old President, teetering on senility, named him Imperial Chancellor. His phenomenal rise to power, however, didn't raise alarm in the West, even though he made no secret of his plans for world domination, not even when they saw his Nazi followers carrying out organized attacks against the Jews. They looked the other way when on February 27, 1933 the Nazis set fire to the Reichstag, the seat of the German Parliament, and then blamed it on a Communist conspiracy to squeeze out the left-wing members of the government. Less than two years later, at the death of Hindenburg in August 1934, Hitler became the undisputed leader, the Fuhrer of Germany.

These events didn't go unnoticed in Hungary, as demonstrated by the spreading of pro-German ideology, greatly promoted by the new prime minister, Gyula Gombos. As a great admirer of Hitler and Mussolini, his far-right policies soon allied Hungary with the Rome-Berlin "Axis," a word he himself invented. Although the Regent Horthy, an honest man with conservative views but without outstanding abilities, did his best to restrain him, yet he kept him in office. It was perhaps due to Gombos' part in easing the country's economic crisis by securing favorable trade agreements with Germany, which drew Hungary out of its deepening depression. As a result, the government was able to improve the standard of living by introducing national health insurance, a forty-eight-hour workweek, and holidays with pay, while keeping unemployment under control. Housing conditions were good, arts and sports flourished, the music of Bartok and Kodaly became world-known, and writers were free to express ideas; even those leaning to the left were tolerated. There was no Secret Police, and although the Communist Party was outlawed, other political parties were left undisturbed with the understanding that the prime minister's party must hold the majority. Generally, the government upheld the law without resorting to totalitarian methods.

Paying little attention to politics, Ilonka felt on top of the world, contented with the life they had established. As the mistress of a nice home well furnished by middle-class standards, they could even afford to hire a live-in maid to help with the household and look after the children. This was her world, why worry about what the prime minister did or did not, when ordinary folks couldn't do anything about it anyway? Let politics take care of itself. She was a true believer in "live and let live."

When word got around that Ilonka was looking for domestic help, several girls from the surrounding villages rang her doorbell. She hired Rozie, a small but wiry girl about twenty-five, with good references, especially in handling children.

Gyuszi was never a problem, but the two girls proved to be a handful, often getting into fights. The squabbling usually started with Sárika wanting something that belonged to her sister. Whenever Eta was in school and Sárika became bored playing with her own dolls, she saw nothing wrong in raiding her sister's toy box. After repeated warnings to leave those toys alone she made an effort, but the temptation became too much when at Christmas Eta got a pretty Japanese doll that Sárika dearly loved and desperately wanted. At first, using a fair approach, she offered two of her dolls for an exchange, but Eta refused. Well, that left her with no choice but to do the forbidden, take her sister's doll and play with it while she was gone. Sárika was usually careful to put it back before Eta came home, until one day she got caught, and the fight was on. Somehow during the tug-of-war, they shattered one of the finely edged glass door-panels, which brought Ilonka running to see if they were all right. She found them unharmed, but breaking the glass plate called for retribution! With one side of the matched set in shards, the other was useless, and although the girls tried to blame one another, in the end it was Eta who stood in the corner, because she was old enough to know better than fight over a silly doll. There was no spanking, and considering the cost to put in new matched set of panels, the punishment was mild.

The two sisters were not the best of friends. It was not so much for the five-year age difference, but because they had different personalities. Eta was calm unless provoked, while Sárika was the opposite—excitable, demanding, head-strong, and a little spoiled by her father. Cute and vivacious, she was Daddy's little girl. She, too, was drawn more to her father, perhaps because her mother was always around, whereas Jeno was away a lot working long hours to provide the modest little luxuries that made Ilonka happy. It was always a special treat for the children to spend time with their father. One day when he came home for lunch and found Sárika in bed with some minor illness, he put on an act to cheer her up by pretending he had lost his way home. He wandered around the room, opening wardrobe doors and mimicking disappointment that it was not the door to the house, while she clapped her hands, laughing in utter delight. When she later told Eta about it, she accused her of dreaming up the story, because their father would never make such a fool of himself.

While the marriage was solid and Ilonka enjoyed having the extra money, at times she resented her husband's absence from the home. She understood that he worked hard, but expected him to spend at least Sundays with them, to accompany her to church and take the children for an afternoon promenade. She took great pride in showing off the children and wanted her husband by her side to share the compliments. Instead, he would sleep late, and when the weather was good, preferred spending the afternoon watching a soccer game. This was a sore point with Ilonka, something to argue about. When he said he deserved to spend half a day at his leisure after working six days, she retorted that sleeping late and skipping church accounted for that! She would never object to that, if he'd spend the other half with her and the children. They grumbled back and forth, but when Jeno drew her close, saying that he would make it up to her other ways, she could not help but forgive him.

Aside from complaining once in a while, Ilonka's life circled around her husband, the children, and friends, occasionally interrupted by out-of-town visitors, mostly from Jeno's side of the family. One of them was his mother's unmarried sister, Aunt Anna, a teacher and a staunch patriot who moved to Hungary in 1920 rather than submitting to Slovak domination. Throughout the years she came to see them a few times, and always talked about retiring in Sopron, a city she grew to love. It surprised no one when one day in 1936, the year she retired, she reappeared, ready to fulfill her promise to spend her golden years in her favorite city. When she rang Ilonka's doorbell, she only meant to stay with them until she found an apartment, but when Ilonka invited her to live with them, she gladly accepted. Both Jeno and Ilonka were genuinely fond of this jovial and easygoing woman and happily welcomed her into their home. It took some rearranging, but she had her own room, ate with the family, and in no time became a substitute grandmother for the children. She loved all three, but having been a schoolmarm to young girls all her adult life, it was only natural that Gyuszika became the apple of her eye.

And the feeling was mutual. The little boy responded to the affection of this warmhearted elderly lady, spending hours in her ample lap while listening to the fairytales she read from his favorite storybooks. The girls were not as lucky. Whenever their squabbling called for disciplinary action, the tongue-lashing now came mostly from Aunt Anna, not from their mother. On one such occasion, as their aunt delivered a highly animated chastisement for something Eta did, her upper denture popped out of her mouth. She caught it quickly and pushed it back in place, but the act totally astonished little Gyuszi standing quietly in the background. When Eta was dismissed, he came forward, still awed, timidly asking his aunt to please, do it again. He couldn't have enough of this magic trick and bragged to his friends how his aunt's teeth could miraculously fly in and out of her mouth.

Another time it was Sárika who needed lecturing. It happened just before Easter 1937 and it involved the maid Rozie. She didn't have a separate room but slept on a folding cot in the kitchen and kept her belongings in a wardrobe closet in the hallway. Passing it one day with its door open a few inches, something shiny caught Sárika's eyes. It was a coin—about fifty cents worth—lying on a lower shelf, and while Sárika knew that it was money, she had no idea about its value. Looking around cautiously she took it and ran up the street where store windows were full of chocolate Easter bunnies and egg-shaped candies. She surrendered the coin and walked home with a bag full of sweets she planned to give as Easter presents to her family. Hiding it, she spent the day trying to decide who would get what. The large chocolate bunny she would definitely keep for herself, the smaller one she'd give to her parents, and the marzipan Easter egg will go to Aunt Anna. The rest of the candy was for everybody else, except Eta would get the smallest portion.

The next day Rozie reported the missing money, whereupon Ilonka and Aunt Anna lined up the children, asking each if they knew what happened to the coin. When Eta and Gyuszi answered with a firm no, all eyes fell on Sárika. Fidgeting a little, she admitted taking the money, but whined that now her Easter surprise was ruined. It was obvious that she had good intentions, but still, to teach her right from wrong, Aunt Anna delivered a long lecture on "Thou shall not steal."

Later that summer Ilonka welcomed another visitor, Jeno's cousin from Budapest, Sandor Zachar, now an officer in the rank of major. She remembered him fondly from the week she spent with his family back in 1926. Jeno, of course, was greatly interested in his opinion, what he thought of the political developments in Germany and Italy. They talked about Mussolini's invasion of Ethiopia and Hitler taking the Rhineland, and what all this aggression was leading to. No one could deny the vast increase of Germany's power position, and that the successful expansionist policies of these two fascist leaders had strengthened the pro-Nazi sentiments in Hungary. Determined to put a stop to it, the Regent Horthy finally changed prime ministers, dissolved the Arrow Cross Party (*Nyilas Párt*), the country's leading fascist party, and put its leader, Major Ferenc Szalasi, in jail.

Regardless of these developments, for Ilonka world affairs remained of minor interest. She thought it foolish for Jeno and Sandor to talk about things that couldn't be changed. Hitler and Mussolini were dictators, not likely to take orders from outsiders. Here in Hungary, in Sopron, life was good, Jeno made her happy, the children thrived, and there was not one cloud in her sky.

And as the year was winding down and the holidays approached, she threw herself wholeheartedly into preparing for Christmas. Last year Sárika was unhappy with her gift, a cute lifelike baby doll that could cry and had its own little stroller. She wanted the gorgeous French porcelain doll in billowing gown and wide-brimmed hat that Eta got, so this year Ilonka decided to take them window-shopping to get an idea what to get for them. As they stood in front of the toy store Ilonka asked Eta first what she'd like to find under the Christmas tree. Always shy and unassuming, she shifted her weight and raised her shoulders, saying she didn't know. In the meanwhile Sárika could hardly wait for her turn, pulling her mother's hand and fixing her eyes on her face, as if afraid to miss her chance. Ilonka had to scold her to be patient; her time would come. When finally she was allowed to speak her eyes lit up and pointing her finger at several items, she rattled on, "That and that and that and that!" Before she could name everything in sight, Ilonka doused her enthusiasm by telling her she could only have one wish. It was only fair to leave some of the toys for other children. With a grimace and a sigh, she surveyed the window more carefully and settled on a toy violin, a strange wish for a six-year-old. Ilonka could see if she had picked a toy piano, but a violin? What on earth made her choose that instrument?

With shopping done, everyone waited for the arrival of Christmas Eve. There are varying ways to celebrate Christmas in the world, but in many European countries, including Hungary, children believe that their Christmas tree and the presents are brought by the Baby Jesus and his angels on the evening of the 24th, and have no inkling of their parents' involvement in it. To keep it a secret—and to gain time to put up the tree—youngsters are usually sent to relatives for the afternoon or taken to see *Heidi*, the movie traditionally shown that day. By the time they would return home the tree was decorated but kept behind closed doors, making the children wait until they heard the sound of a silver bell, a signal that the angels have finished their work and the celebration could begin. The door is then opened to reveal the glittering tree in all its glory, standing in the dimly lit room with only the candles flickering on its richly decorated branches.

It was always a thrill for Ilonka to see the children's faces all aglow, their eyes wide with wonder, as they walked into the pine-scented room and saw the tree and the gifts under it. It was not easy for them to resist the temptation to rush and retrieve their presents, but first there were prayers to recite and carols to sing. It was no different that year, except for a small surprise Sárika had up her sleeve. Finished with the caroling, Ilonka got up from the piano to join the others, when suddenly she felt her younger daughter tugging at her dress and whispering there was more to come. With everyone wondering what she was trying to do, she stepped forward, made a curtsy, and recited a little Christmas poem she learned in kindergarten:

The long awaited Eve is here
The sky sparkles with stars,
Angels alight on silent wings
To light our world of dark:

Christ was born to us this day,
The Lord's promise fulfilled,
He sent his son to show the way
How mankind will be saved.

Our tree would soon be gone,
But not you, Sweet Lord, we pray,
Please stay with our family
And protect us night and day.

As she finished she looked up to her mother seeking approval, but instead found her dabbing at her eyes.

"Why are you crying? You did not like my poem?" she asked anxiously, but Ilonka just gathered her up in her arms, saying she was moved because it was so beautiful. Even Eta acknowledged that her recital was not bad.

Then it was finally time to claim the presents. The girls were on their knees collecting their toys from underneath the tree, but three-year-old Gyuszi just stood frozen, staring at the beautiful rocking horse Ilonka got for him.

"What's the matter, Gyuszika? Don't you like your horsie? His name is Raro," Ilonka knelt beside him, touching the horse to show there was nothing to fear. "Why not take a ride on its back? Come, I'll help you get on it."

"No, no, no, Raro back! Back!" he cried, scared of the horse. He backed away and no amount of coaxing could make him go near it. Even later, when the Varosys came over for a Christmas cheer and Jozsef Varosy lined up the children for picture taking with their new toys, he would not look into the camera until Ilonka moved the horse away. It was just not in him to grow up to be a cowboy.

Sárika received the toy violin she wished for—totally on impulse and soon to be ignored—but what caught her interest more was another present lying next to it: a shiny pair of ice skates. She always envied Eta for going skating, and now it was her turn to conquer the ice. She had to wait though, since the weather was too mild and the ice-skating rink remained closed. When it finally opened in mid-January and Eta grabbing her skates headed for the door, Ilonka stopped her and asked to take Sárika along and teach her to skate.

She was not thrilled; she could do without her sister hanging on to her, but she had no choice. Arriving at the rink Rozie helped fastening the skates to their shoes, then Eta put Sárika next to the railing and told her to just watch what she was doing. Skating was really easy, she'd learn it in no time, and with that glided away. Left alone to learn the hard way, Sárika started out with ankles turned inward and arms flailing, and promptly found herself sprawled on the ice. Someone took pity on her and after lifting her up gave her some tips: keep her ankles straight and hold onto the bar while practicing. By the time Eta reappeared she had managed to let go of the handrail and could remain on her feet while pushing forward. It was not exactly skating, but she was not falling on her behind either.

"You see, I told you it was easy," Eta said and then skated away again with her friends. When returning home Ilonka asked about their ice-skating, only Eta answered. "It was a lot of fun," she said, "though Sonja Henie has nothing to fear from Sárika."

Ilonka didn't know how to skate, but she never missed a movie showing the famous triple Olympic winner sliding gracefully across the silver screen. Ever since the first movie house opened in Sopron, she had been a devoted movie fan. Unfortunately, Jeno had very little interest in sitting in a dark room and looking at images on a screen, but thank God, Aunt Anna shared her enthusiasm. Ilonka accepted that her husband didn't care for the glittering Ziegfield productions or schmaltzy romantic films she loved, but she was convinced that he would want to see the movie *King Kong* she saw a few days ago.

"Jeno, you must see this movie!" she told him, all excited. "Not only because it's a fantastic story, but to see what Hollywood is capable of doing these days! There is this giant ape that climbs up the Empire State Building, and they can't catch him so they attack him with airplanes. It's really something to see! I wouldn't mind going again if you'd come with me."

"A giant ape? Loose in New York? Attacked by airplanes? I don't think so, Kitten. You know I am not crazy about movies."

"You never do anything I want to!" Frustrated and feeling rejected, Ilonka turned on Jeno. "You never go to church with me, or come for a walk with the children! When was the last time you spent any time with them? You did not even come to Eta's piano recital. But God forbid you miss a soccer game!" She worked herself to a pitch, giving vent to other grievances as well. "We never do anything together! You'd rather play cards with your buddies, and don't tell me that's because you work all the time and need some relaxation. That is just a sorry excuse because if you really wanted to, you would make time for your family. Look at your colleague, Mr. Jakab! He is always with his wife and daughters. Of course, he never misses Sunday Mass either, if you can see the connection there!"

Just to stop the nagging Jeno reluctantly gave in, but they were not in the best mood when they went to see the movie the next day. Aunt Anna also left the house to visit friends, and with the cats away, Sárika turned into a naughty little mouse, and decided to try tap dancing on top of the piano. She invited her siblings to participate in the fun, but only Gyuszi joined her. Eta knew better and warned them they'd be sorry, but they paid no attention. They kept bouncing happily up and down, scratching the polished surface badly, until Rozie finally succeeded pulling them down.

When Ilonka and Jeno came home there was an apparent tension between them, and although the maid noticed it, she had no choice but to tell immediately about the piano; if she did not, she could later be blamed for the scratches. Hearing what happened was just what Ilonka needed in her agitated state of mind. Infuriated, she stormed into the room, ready to grab the culprits for a good spanking but by then, guessing what was in store, they had started to run. She went after them, screaming that no matter where they tried to hide, they wouldn't escape punishment. She caught Gyuszi first, just as he threw himself belly down on the nearest couch. The soft cushion took the edge off the spanking, but Sárika did not fare so well. She ran into the bathroom and crouched down under the pedestal sink, wrapping her legs around the stand, but it was not enough to save her from her mother's fury. Her side remained open, and when Ilonka couldn't pull her out, that's where she began to kick her.

Her daughter's screams brought her to her senses. She stopped, panting heavily and gasping for air, then walked out and sat down covering her face with both hands. How could she lose control like that? She felt drained and ashamed. It was the first time she had lashed out so viciously at her children, and she swore it would be the last.

She kept that promise, and to erase the incident from her mind she never ever talked about it. Well, there was one time, when many years later Sári remembered the episode, laughing that the punishment they got was well deserved.

War at the door

IN THE SPRING of 1938, to her surprise Ilonka found that after five years she was pregnant again. She was almost thirty-two, and with Eta, now twelve, attending second year in the gimnazium, Sárika at seven and soon to start elementary school, and five-year-old Gyuszi in kindergarten, she felt her children were growing up too fast. The thought of holding a child once again to her breast filled her heart with utmost joy. Nothing made her happier than nurturing her babies and seeing that precious smile when they first recognized her face, and now she would have the chance to experience it again.

To Jeno the news came as a surprise, but he was happy about it. Their financial situation was solid and it would be good to have another boy, a little brother to Gyuszi, who was completely surrounded by women. Aunt Anna was also thrilled by the coming birth, especially when asked to be the baby's godmother. Following the tradition to name their children after Jeno's brothers and sisters, a boy would be called Jozsef, or if a girl, Jozefina.

They made an exception however, when they learned about the commemorative celebration planned that year for the 900th anniversary of the death of Hungary's first king, St. Istvan. He is forever credited for choosing the Roman Catholic religion for his country instead of the Eastern Byzantine Rite, thus setting the course of Hungary from the year 1000 onward to join the Western world. He ruled as a Christian king and was canonized when decades after his death in 1038 his right hand and wrist were discovered miraculously intact, somewhat shrunken, and darker in color, but without decay. It became a venerable relic, the so-called "Holy Right" (*Szent Jobb*) that has been encased in a shrine and held as a national treasure ever since.

St. Istvan's name later was added to the Calendar of Saints, with August 20 proclaimed as his feast day. The day became a national holiday celebrated through the centuries with special Masses and fireworks, much like the 4th of July in the United States. To add importance to the commemorative festivities, the Vatican announced that papal Secretary of State, Cardinal Eugenio Pacelli (later Pope Pius XII), would preside over a Eucharistic Congress to be held in Hungary in August and would celebrate High Mass on the 20th. During the same period the Holy Right of St. Istvan would be taken on a nationwide exhibit, placed in a transparent shrine and displayed inside a golden train with large glass panels on both sides that would give a once-in-a-lifetime opportunity for thousands to see it and pay respect to it.

And so, as a humble gesture in honor of St. Istvan, Jeno and Ilonka decided to name their son Istvan, or, if it was a girl, Stefania—the female version of Stefan, which in turn is the derivative of the Latin Stephanus for Istvan. The 4th of November solved which would it be, as during the night Ilonka gave birth to a healthy blue-eyed, darling little boy. He was so fair that Mrs. Polgar, the midwife who had delivered all four of Ilonka's children, declared that her babies were getting prettier by each birth.

The newest addition to the family was not the only reason for a joyful celebration. It coincided with the national jubilation over the partial return of the northern borderland territory taken by Slovakia in 1920. It was the culmination of events that started with the unification of Austria and Germany on March 12, 1938. Disregarding the Versailles Treaty that specifically prohibited the union between these two countries, Nazi troops crossed into Austria that day as the first step in Hitler's grand design to unite all German-speaking people. It was a bloodless takeover, and no shots were fired; in fact, people lined the streets cheering the troops, and a hurriedly organized plebiscite ended with 99.73% in favor of the Nazis.

With this so-called *Anschluss* Germany became Hungary's immediate neighbor, hopelessly tightening the strings that held the country bound to Germany. From there onward anti-Jewish slogans got louder and pro-Nazi propaganda more aggressive, and although Regent Horthy changed prime ministers again and again, it didn't stop the trend. Under mounting German pressure new directives were imposed, including the first anti-Jewish laws passed by Parliament on May 29, 1938, excluding Jews from the professions.

Hitler also increased his demands for military assistance to support his planned action against Czechoslovakia, but Horthy found a way out. Pointing to the peace treaty that left Hungary practically without an army—limited to 35,000 troops—he used the excuse that rearmament would require a minimum of two years. Hitler was skeptical and remarked with unmasked sarcasm, ". . . he who wanted to sit at the table must at least help in the kitchen."[1*] The incident was the first sign of a rift in German-Hungarian relations that helped to develop Hitler's later distrust and deep-seated antipathy toward Hungary. He began to view Horthy as a weak leader and never forgave him for his refusal, even though Hungary's cooperation was not all that important to him. Hitler easily managed to get his way single-handedly.

Counting on the current appease-minded mentality of the West, he first accused the Czechs of intolerable mistreatment of German minorities living in Sudetenland near the German border, then, to remedy the situation, demanded the annexation of the area. He solemnly denied any further territorial aspirations, and taking his word at face value, Great Britain, France, and Italy agreed to put pressure on Czechoslovakia to give into Hitler. The result was the Munich Agreement, signed on September 29, 1938 without the presence of a Czech representative. A few days later the British negotiator Prime Minister Chamberlain flew back to London, announcing, "I believe this is peace for our time."

Seeing how easily the world yielded to Hitler and let aggression go unpunished, the Hungarians also stepped up their never-ending demands to return territories they lost to Slovakia after the war. With a nod from Hitler, they began diplomatic negotiations with Czechoslovakia, and with Germany and Italy acting as arbitrators, a decision was handed down on November 2, 1938 in Hungary's favor. This so-called First Vienna Award restored the northern Highland territory to Hungary, an area that consisted of roughly 4,680 square miles based mainly on ethnographic factors. Of the slightly over one million regained inhabitants, about 84%, or 800,000, were Hungarians; the rest were Slovaks and Ruthenians. This news in Hungary was received with overwhelming enthusiasm, but it ended any possibility for the country to remain neutral.

The Vienna Award became a reality when during the first week of November 1938, Hungarian soldiers peacefully marched into Slovakia to retake the designated cities and villages, among them Losonc. It opened the door to Jeno's mother to come for the baby's baptism. She arrived before Christmas for a three-week stay, and this time when she left there was no trace of the sadness that had engulfed them during her last visit in 1931.

Her sister, the children's beloved Aunt Anna, was leaving with her; with the border rolled back she decided to move to Losonc to be with her family. It didn't mean goodbye, she said, they could visit each other anytime now that the restrictions no longer existed. In fact, she and Jeno's mother both insisted to have Gyuszi and Sárika come and spend next summer with them.

With all the effort Ilonka put into making her mother-in-law's stay pleasant, and so soon after the baby's birth, it took her longer than usual to recover her strength. She felt weak and got tired fast, suffered from headaches, and experienced irregular heartbeats. Jeno insisted that she go and see Dr. Visnyei, a heart specialist, who prescribed some medication and ordered her to rest. He

---

1 [*] William Shirer: *The Rise and Fall of the Third Reich*, page 377

ran a private practice from his home and while there Ilonka met his wife, Sári Visnyei, a vivacious women much younger than her husband. It was rumored that the marriage was not a happy one; he was possessive and jealous of every person who came in contact with his wife, including women offering friendship. He denied her the joy of having children for the same reason, and barely tolerated the little white dog she kept. Although they lived in a large and elegant house with servants, they had no social life, and if Mrs. Visnyei left the house for any reason, she had to account for every minute of her whereabouts. Ilonka saw her occasionally at ladies' luncheons or at church, and gradually their casual acquaintance grew into a warm friendship. If she had the chance to stop by, Mrs. Visnyei always came with a box of candy for the children, sometimes even bringing her dog, much to their delight. She took a special liking to Sárika, perhaps for no other reason than they shared the same name.

As impartial as Ilonka was about her girls, she couldn't deny that it was easier to like her younger daughter. She was outgoing, chatty, and eager to please. She was now in first grade, although a year older than most of her schoolmates. She was held back from registering the year before because the system required that children must be six years old by September 1 to start school, and her birthday was on September 30. She missed it by one month, and it was not easy to make her understand why she must stay in kindergarten while her friends were entering school.

Once enrolled, however, she took learning rather seriously. Ilonka never had to prompt her to do her homework; it was her first priority after coming home from school. The sisters had nothing but praise for her, until she fell out of grace one day, and that had nothing to do with her schoolwork. As parochial schools required students to attend church every morning before classes started, Sárika never missed a day until winter set in. The church was cold and damp, and when she caught cold after cold for kneeling on the bare stones, her parents protested against the practice. They worried about her health and for good reason. During the summer of 1935, at age not quite four, she came down with a strange illness that three doctors couldn't diagnose. She had no specific symptoms, only a constant low fever that kept her in bed for three months. When she was finally allowed to get up, her legs gave out; they were completely atrophied and she had to learn to walk all over again. She recovered and the illness never returned, but the fright over the possibility of losing her made her parents especially protective. Their concern grew even more when about the time she entered school three children in the neighborhood came down with crippling polio.

They decided to keep Sárika from attending morning mass, but when told by the nuns that only the Bishop of Gyor could grant such exemption, Jeno submitted a request and got the permission. One little girl missing from early service didn't make much difference at first, but when other parents soon followed suit, the sisters took their resentment out on her. They couldn't find fault with her homework, so they complained that she did not pay enough attention in class, or her crocheting was not as precise as it should be, and even criticized her popularity, because it led to pride, and pride was a sin, as every good Catholic should know.

The subtle harassment continued and came to a head when on a spring day in 1939 Sister Rosalia informed the children that instead of regular classes, the Mother Superior would be holding a special hearing on a very delicate matter, and instructed them to sit quietly until they were called. The "delicate" matter was about how babies were born, and that the girls were heard whispering about it. To find the culprit who started the talk and to learn how much the children actually knew about the subject, the nuns decided to question each girl individually. When Sárika's turn came she answered that she knew plenty about babies; she had a brand new baby brother, but how they were born she had no idea, except that the storks delivered them. When the nuns pressed her if she had talked about this with the other girls in her class she said no, why should she, when everybody knew about the storks. At the end of the day all the children were dismissed except nine girls, among them Sárika. They were lined up in front of the "interrogators" and labeled as "sinful ringleaders" because regardless of how much they denied it, others singled them out as having spread details about this disgusting subject. They were told that they had committed a grave sin and were ordered to stay home and send in their parents the next day.

Sárika did not know what to make of the whole thing. She never even thought about birth and such, yet she felt guilty. She told her mother that the sisters wanted to see her, but not the details. In the morning when Ilonka started to get her ready for school she claimed to be sick and stayed in bed, waiting anxiously for her mother's return. Ever since her mysterious illness a few years back she learned she could get away with pretending to feel poorly, and used this whenever it was to her advantage. But as soon as Ilonka was back and walked into her room, she was out of bed, her health suddenly restored.

"I didn't do anything wrong, Mother! Honest, I don't know what they told you, but it's not true!"

"I believe you, and I told the sisters that they must be mistaken," Ilonka said sitting down on the bed. "Apparently, Lenke Palfalvi made the accusation of hearing it from you that babies come out of the mother from down there, like when she pees."

"She is lying," Sárika shrieked. "I never told her such a thing. It was Lenke who asked me if I knew anything about it, but it was weeks ago, and I forgot about it. But now I remember, she talked about this peeing stuff. She stopped only when I told her I didn't believe it." Highly indignant for being falsely accused, the words were tumbling out of her mouth.

"I know that Lenke was lying, and I'll tell you why," Ilonka said. "The nuns told me that during her interview she was very convincing, covering her ears with her hands to show how she tried to block out what she didn't want to hear. I told them that only a child who feels guilty and desperately wants to avert suspicion would go to such length as to prove her innocence with theatricals."

"So you are not angry with me?" Sárika threw her arms around her mother's neck. "I knew you'd believe me. But just wait until I see that lying sneak Lenke! I'll kick her in the shin for what she did!"

"You do no such thing, Sárika. Fighting won't accomplish anything. She knows that she was lying when she accused you to the nuns, and it will be on her conscience whenever she sees you. There are other ways you can let her know that she is no longer your friend; the next time she wants to walk with you, just tell her you'd rather not, and walk away. You don't have to explain. If she asks you why, just tell her that she should know the reason. She will know in her heart that you found out about her lies." With that Ilonka rose, kissed the top of her daughter's head and patted her face. "Now you can get dressed; you don't have to play sick anymore."

"What about school? What did the sisters say? Can I go back?" Sárika asked before her mother reached the door.

"Of course you are going back. This matter is closed; they will not bring it up again."

Seemingly calm, she walked out of the room but inside she was seething about the nuns' stupidity to make such a mountain out of a molehill. Children are naturally curious; they might speculate about such things, but they usually lose interest and forget about pursuing it. Dragging seven-year-olds in front of an inquisition-like panel for questioning would not only traumatize them, but also would keep their attention focused on the very subject the nuns wished them to avoid. They were educators, for heaven's sake! Didn't they know any better? The whole procedure was ridiculous, telling these poor children that they were sinners. They hadn't even been taught the Ten Commandments; how were they to know about mortal sins? The whole thing should be dropped immediately, Ilonka thought angrily and if she heard one more word about the incident, she would write a letter to the Bishop of Gyor herself, a letter he would not be pleased to read.

It did not come to that. The subject was indeed closed, but Sárika never forgot the injustice done to her by the Church.

The hopes of the Western powers that Hitler would keep his promise for peace were shattered when on March 16, 1939 he invaded Moravia and Bohemia, proclaiming the whole of Czechoslovakia as a protectorate of Germany. At the same time, he expanded the Vienna Award, granting Hungary another territorial restitution, that of Carpatho-Ruthenia, or Kárpátalja in Hungarian. This area along the Eastern Carpathian Mountains was for nine centuries an integral part of Hungary until 1920, when the Trianon Peace Treaty transferred it to Czechoslovakia. (Hungary lost it again in 1946 to the Ukraine). With this "goodwill" gesture Hitler hoped to gain Hungary's support in his next plan of action, the invasion of Poland, but Horthy again flatly refused to participate. It evoked such furor in Germany that, fearing a "friendly occupation," a euphemism for invasion, the Regent personally met Mussolini to propose an alliance with Italy against Hitler. It was a wasted effort. The Duce remained diplomatically reserved, committing to nothing, and without him Horthy had no choice but to remain on Germany's side. He could only hope that through a delicate balancing act he would be able to maintain the country's neutrality and independence in the dangerous days on the eve of the Second World War.

When a month after the takeover of Czechoslovakia Hitler cancelled his non-aggression pact with Poland, the West could no longer look the other way. Realizing that conciliatory attitude did not work, they started looking in the direction of Russia as the only possible ally of any strength. They sent a mission to Moscow to negotiate, but it proved to be too late; the Germans had beaten them to it.

Preparing for war, Hitler clearly saw the danger facing him if the West joined forces with Russia. It would put him in the position of fighting on two fronts, the Soviets in the east and France and Britain on the west, and to safeguard against it he approached Stalin with an offer of alliance. With Germany and the Allied Powers both vying for his favor, Stalin decided that dealing with the Nazis would be more advantageous for Russia, and on August 23, 1939 signed the Russo-German Non-Aggression Pact. A week later, on September 1, Hitler ordered the attack on Poland.

As Polish refugees began to pour over the border into Hungary, many of them Jews, and Horthy refused to shut the door to them, Hitler threatened him again. These quarrels, however, were unknown to the Russians; they only knew that Hungary and Germany were allies, and proceeded to renew diplomatic relations with Hungary. As a reconciliatory gesture they returned the banners the Russian Army took during Hungary's 1848 fight for independence from Austria, and in exchange Hungary released to the Russians Matyas Rakosi, a Hungarian Communist leader jailed since the failure of the Communist regime in 1919. Once safely in the Soviet Union, Rakosi became a Soviet citizen and in less than ten years would return to carry out Stalin's bidding to keep Hungary under Russia's thumb.

Jeno followed the current events with nervous apprehension. He believed that Germany represented a great menace to Hungary, and watched in alarm as Nazi ideals slowly but steadily began to advance in the country. To offset the spreading of rightwing politics, on February 16, 1939 Horthy appointed a new prime minister, Count Pal Teleki, a man of utmost moral integrity and a staunch supporter of the Regent's every decision. Unfortunately, it was too late to undo the damage done by Teleki's pro-Nazi predecessors, as evidenced by the general election held in May 1939. An increased number of delegates sympathetic to Germany were voted in, replacing the middle-of-the-road and left-leaning members, and drastically shifting the balance in Parliament to the right.

That anyone with any intelligence and rational thinking could fall for Nazi ideas was baffling to Jeno. Even some of his colleagues expressed admiration for Hitler, especially as Germany achieved victory after victory without any opposition. As a customs officer he had daily contact with Austrian and German travelers and if he witnessed their pro-Nazi enthusiasm, he shrugged it off; they were Germans, but how any Hungarian could be impressed by such nonsense was beyond his understanding. He only hoped that as these foreign and un-Hungarian ideas were taking hold in the country he would learn to live with the changes, and do it without compromising his integrity.

The world outside might be changing, but within his home all was right and life went on as before. Ilonka only complained that the children were growing up too fast. Eta was already entering her teenage years, and while it was expected, she never turned rebellious, but remained submissive, faithfully keeping to the rules both at home and at school. Unlike many of her schoolmates, she had little interest in fashion and could care less when Ilonka enrolled her in a dance school; she only went because her mother insisted. She seemed indifferent, taking in stride whatever came her way without making much fuss about anything. On one occasion, while learning to use the sewing machine, the needle accidentally stuck halfway through her index finger, but instead of crying and carrying on, she calmly let her mother free the finger, then after cleaning and bandaging it, continued her sewing without further ado.

Had that happened to Sárika, her screams would have been heard in Timbuktu. Excitable, high-spirited, easy to laugh or cry, she was the opposite of her sister. She fussed about her clothes: the hem was too long, or the color was not to her liking, and there was always a fight when it came to wearing lace-up shoes instead of her patent leather Mary Janes. She constantly complained about her hair, why was it mousy and straight, braided in awful pigtails? She wanted Shirley Temple curls, and to stop the whining Ilonka promised to bring out the curling iron on her birthdays and at Christmas. The girls also differed in their attitudes toward school. Unlike Eta, who had difficulty to keep up with Latin and mathematics even with private tutoring, Sárika was a very good student, eager to learn, with homework always put before playing. She only lacked enthusiasm about her piano lessons and the lengthy practicing they required.

While Eta was quiet and reserved, Sárika possessed boundless energy, bursting into the room if she had some news, her voice echoing through the whole house. She was also showing signs of independence. Instead of accepting her mother's help with homework or crocheting, she would rather do it herself, even if she had to struggle with the task. This tendency to do everything herself was evident even earlier. She must have been no more than four when she wet the bed one night, but instead of calling for her mother or scooting to a dry spot, she got up, pulled off the sheet, and in complete darkness tiptoed toward the bathroom to wash out the stain. Ilonka, of course, caught her, and after telling her that it was all right, accidents happen, put her back in the freshly made bed.

By nature, Eta was more like her father, while Sárika resembled her mother, each mirroring the distinctly opposite personalities of their parents. Considering the contrast that existed between Ilonka and Jeno due partly to their different social background, dissimilar interests and, of course, the age gap, it is remarkable that disagreements between them were relatively minor and were kept under control. Most arguments still centered on Ilonka's complaints that Jeno didn't devote enough time to the family and rarely accompanied her and the children to church. He had little interest in religion, perhaps because his parents were of different creeds: his father was Greek Catholic, his mother Protestant, and neither placed particular importance on the religious upbringing of the children. Ilonka also resented that he'd rather watch a soccer game, or play cards at the coffeehouse, even though she knew he didn't gamble. He played at moderate stakes and on the average won more times than lost. It helped a little to quiet Ilonka's grumbling that whenever he won, he handed her his winnings.

Another peeve of hers was about vacations. She felt they could manage an occasional holiday, but Jeno wouldn't go. His excuse was always the same: trips were expensive, especially with their large family, and in order to have the extra money, he had to forfeit his own vacation by substituting for colleagues on leave or wanting time off. Ilonka could have gone with the children, but handling four kids alone was not what she'd call a vacation. After a while she gave up on the subject and resigned that she would have to wait until the children were grown before she would see the Balaton again, the beautiful lake where Angela took her once as a child.

Yet in spite of their differences their marriage of thirteen years was solid, their commitment to one another strong, and their dedication to the family unshakable. In time they both came to understand that neither of them would change, and gradually learned that by tolerating each other's seemingly annoying, sometimes irritating habits, they could avoid potentially unpleasant scenes. To do so was easier for Jeno, since he had more patience and had a way to disarm Ilonka. She could be stubborn and provoking, but Jeno simply refused to be drawn into an argument, a tactic that worked most of the time. If something upset her and she started to quarrel, he would offer a brief explanation of what he did and for what reason, then wait until she ran out of words. He'd keep out of her way until she calmed down, seeing that it was useless to pick a fight with someone who refused to fight back.

With the passing years Ilonka realized how trivial her grievances really were. Jeno never did anything drastically wrong; he did not drink, hardly looked at other women, and was a good father and a gentle and loving husband with infinite patience toward her. He worked hard to support the growing needs of their four children and provide a comfortable lifestyle, so compared to problems some couples faced in their marriage, what did she have to complain about? Nagging her husband without real reason accomplished nothing.

In the summer of 1940, keeping the promise to his mother, Jeno took Sárika and Gyuszi to Losonc, stopping for a day in Budapest to visit his relatives and also to take the children to the zoo. This would be their first trip, their first train ride, and while Gyuszi slept through the night before their departure, excitement and anticipation kept Sárika awake.

At the station she listened halfheartedly to her mother's last minute reminders not to forget her manners and to watch over her little brother, nodding absentmindedly while keeping her eyes on the train to make sure it didn't leave without her. When the moment arrived to say goodbye, she could hardly wait to get on the train, while Gyuszika was on the verge of tears, clinging to his mother until Jeno finally pried him away. Once on board he ran to the window, waving his little hand to Ilonka, unlike his rambunctious sister, who was already exploring the train. She only stopped when the train began to move, pressing her face to the window to watch the never-before-seen sight of roofs and treetops drifting by.

After some fun scurrying up and down the aisle and changing seats left and right on the sparsely occupied benches, the children got tired and settled down in their compartment, only to jump up again whenever the train made a stop. "Are we there? How long before we get there? Will the zoo still be open?" they badgered Jeno on and on until finally in mid-afternoon they pulled into Budapest's great glass-domed Eastern Train Station. Jeno took a taxi—another first for the kids to ride in an automobile—and checked into the guest room at the Customs Office building, the place he always stayed during seminars. Later he took the children to meet their Zachar uncles and aunts, but the highlight came next day with the trip to the zoo. Sopron didn't have one, and although they knew about the animals from their children's books, seeing them in real life left them spellbound. A short summer storm trapped them inside the lion exhibit, where the ferocious beasts were lined up in back-to-back cages, pacing nervously from one end to the other in their confined spaces. For twenty minutes, Sárika and Gyuszi listen to them roar, as if trying to compete with the crashing sound of thunder outside. Only Jeno wished a quick end to the rain. He'd had enough of the noise, the odor of acid animal scent mixed with the smell of the steaming wet cement, and the annoying piped in music continuously playing the most popular song of the day, "Hungary the beautiful, the glorious."

Finally the storm was over, and when the sun came out hot and bright, they were on their way to see the rest of the zoo. Passing an ice cream parlor Jeno stopped to treat them to their favorite ice cream, double scoop vanilla studded with juicy raisins on top of a crispy wafer cone. Leaving the place, Jeno offered a hand to help them down a short flight of stairs leading to the street, but asserting her independence, Sárika refused. Bouncing happily from one step to the next she was almost at the bottom when she lost her footing and found herself spread-eagled on the pavement, the ice cream flying out of her hand and landing in front of her face. Jeno lifted his wailing daughter to check if she was all right.

"Are you hurt, Sárika? Let me see your knees," he dabbed at her scrapes with his handkerchief. "Now, now, don't cry baby, it will only hurt a little while," he tried to comfort her.

"My knees don't hurt, but look at my ice cream!" She was bawling louder by the minute as she watched her ice cream melt on the cement.

"Oh, don't worry about the ice cream; we'll get another, even bigger than that. Why don't we go back to the shop, order a dish and eat it there at the table?"

Her tears stopped immediately. “You really mean it? I could get another one?” But she didn’t wait for confirmation. She knew her father’s word was good as gold and was already running up the steps.

The next morning they arrived in Losonc, the children exhausted but excited at the same time to be reunited with their grandmother and Aunt Anna. Jeno stayed for a couple of days before returning home to a suddenly quiet house. He brought with him news of his cousin, Laszlo Riedl, whom he hadn’t seen since 1915. Laszlo and his mother, Jeno’s aunt born Zanda Zachar, were passing through Losonc and stopped by to visit the family while Jeno was still there, giving the two men a chance to reconnect and fill in the gaps the past twenty-five years left in their lives. As Jeno found out, the Riedls—wife Erzsebet, daughter Liza, and two sons Laszlo, Jr., and Erno—lived in Esztergom near Budapest, where Laszlo managed the vast estate of Hungary’s only papal delegate, Cardinal Justinius Seredi. During their talk he mentioned that the older boy Laszlo, Jr., nicknamed Lasko, would be coming to Sopron in a few years to study forest engineering, and asked if Jeno and Ilonka would look after him when the time came.

At the closing days of summer Jeno returned to Losonc to pick up the children, both a little taller and a little chubbier than when he left them. As he said goodbye, he promised to bring the other two children the following summer, and when his sister insisted that Ilonka should come too, he promised at least to think about agreeing to such a long separation.

Deeper in war

WHILE MOST OF Hitler’s army was fighting in Poland, a smaller German force stood guard along the French boarder, poised to move at the Fuhrer’s command. It took seven months, until April 1940, before Hitler was ready to launch his attack against France, first invading Denmark and Norway, and then pushing south through Holland and Belgium. On June 14 his troops marched into Paris and three days later the French surrendered.

These stunning victories made a deep impression on Hungary. They also saw Soviet aggression, first against Finland in the Baltic, then their partial takeover of oil-rich Romanian territories, all acting as kindle to reignite Hungary’s hope to reclaim Transylvania. This region, called Erdély in Hungary, was integral part of the country from its very existence until losing it to Romania in 1920. Maintaining a non-belligerent attitude, they pressed the issue with Romania, but having just lost territories to Russia and Bulgaria, they refused to negotiate. They insisted that Transylvania was always rightfully theirs, until the Hungarians took it from them almost a thousand years ago.

Akin to the handling of the northern territorial demands against the Slovaks, the case was again submitted to arbitration. As the Western Powers began to hear arguments, a joke circulated in Hungary to support their demand: The Hungarian delegate stood up and voiced a complaint that the Romanians stole the horses from the Hungarian tribes as they crossed into Hungary over the Verecke Pass in 896. He was asked if he wished to put the statement on record, but he declined, saying it was not necessary. In response the Romanians protested, vehemently denying the allegation. The next day Hungary repeated the same grievance, declined to have it recorded, and Romania protested again. On the third day when the Hungarian delegate started with the same story, the Romanian representative had enough of the foolish accusation and, jumping up, shouted, "These Hungarians don't know what they are talking about! Romanians were not even around in 896." The moment he said it the Hungarian was on his feet, demanding loudly, "*THAT,* gentlemen, we wish to put on record!"

At the end of the mediation, headed by Italy and Germany, the northern part of Transylvania was restored to Hungary. According to this Second Vienna Award signed on August 30, 1940, Hungary regained approximately 17,000 square miles, with a population of 2.5 million. The solution remedied the injustice of Trianon only to some degree, because Hitler left the best part of Transylvania with all the important mineral oil and natural gas resources in Romanian hands. It appeased the Romanians and at the same time assured Hitler a smooth access to the much-needed oil supplies of the area. It was simply easier for him to deal with Romania than with the always resistant, knucklehead Hungarians.

Expecting gratitude, Hitler now asked and received permission from Horthy to allow German troops free passage through Hungary to Romania. He claimed it was necessary to maintain a line of communication between Germany and Romania, but in fact he wanted to safeguard the Romanian oil transports. And for that purpose he also demanded to have German military personnel man the railroad stations along the way. This request, however, was restricted to only a few important stations leading into Germany, among them Sopron. There, from the winter of 1940 onward, to the dismay of Jeno and most of his colleagues, customs was forced to allow high-ranking German military staff members and their trains to pass back and forth without being subjected to inspection.

As the war deepened, in the spring of 1941 Hitler again applied pressure on Hungary to participate in his next plan of action, the attack on Yugoslavia. Not risking another refusal from Horthy, he decided to bypass the government and deal directly with Hungary's more compliant General Staff. Ironically, this happened while Prime Minister Count Pal Teleki was in the midst of completing a pact of eternal friendship with Yugoslavia. When the duplicity came to light, it was too late for the government to alter the course of events, and on April 3, 1941, after learning that German troops entered Hungary on their way to Yugoslavia, Teleki committed suicide. Winston Churchill noted in his memoirs, "His suicide was a sacrifice to absolve himself and his people from guilt in the German attack upon Yugoslavia. It clears his name before history."[2*]

With Teleki out of the way, nothing could save the country from escalation toward war and subsequent disaster. The new prime minister came to believe that to rescue Hungary from total submission to Hitler, a limited cooperation

---

2 * *The Grand Alliance*, Chapter 9, page 168

was necessary. Consequently, a week after the Germans attacked Yugoslavia, the Hungarian troops followed, occupying those territories taken from Hungary at the end of World War I.

Horthy, however, drew the line at blindly giving into Hitler when on June 22, 1941, the day Germany put into effect their secretly planned Operation Barbarossa, the invasion of the Soviet Union, he firmly declared his intention to stay out of the war. Regretfully, four days later he was forced to break his pledge in response to the bombing of Kassa, a northeastern city, by three allegedly Soviet airplanes. Disputes exist that the airplanes used in the attack were in fact German with fake Soviet insignia to provoke Hungary into entering the war, but it has never been proven.

Left with no choice, the next day, on June 27, the government declared war on Russia, but Horthy still defied Hitler's demand to send troops to the Russian front. The Regent's refusal, stating that complying would leave the country's borders defenseless, further infuriated the Fuhrer. He angrily pointed to the Slovaks, Czechs, Croats, and Romanians as being more cooperative in helping Germany, and threatened that Hungary's stubborn attitude might have unpleasant consequences. Yielding to the relentless pressure, by the end of summer one-third of Hungary's military forces were committed to Hitler's Eastern front with the understanding that no Hungarian forces would be thrown into fighting.

At the onset of the German blitzkrieg the Russian frontier quickly collapsed, rolling back the utterly surprised and bewildered Soviet army. Their retreat left the civilian population at the mercy of the rapidly advancing enemy troops. The Ukraine, with Kiev, fell; the Don Basin was soon occupied; then came the Crimea; and by October 9 the Germans were within twenty miles of Moscow.

The rapidly developing political events of 1941 came and went without much negative effect on the life of the ordinary Hungarian citizens. Everyone worried, of course, but life continued in a fairly normal way. In the spring Sárika underwent the rite of confirmation with her namesake, Sári Visnyei, standing in as her spiritual sponsor. Dr. Visnyei had died the year before and his wife, freed from his tyrannical control, began living the life she was deprived of during their marriage. She sold their large home in the suburbs and moved into the inner city, a short walking distance from shops, restaurants, the theater, and movies. She took a spacious flat on the second floor of a newly renovated and modernized three-story apartment building and opened her doors to receive her long-denied friends. Her confirmation gift to Sárika was a gold necklace with a delicately crafted gold cross.

Eta finished her fourth year at the gimnazium but with rather poor grades in Latin and mathematics. In view that these college preparatory courses would be even more demanding during the next four years, her teachers recommended switching her to another school with less emphasis on the academics. Around that time Ilonka heard of a new curriculum being introduced that fall by the Sisters of St. Orsolya, a four-year high school where Latin and higher mathematics were replaced by agricultural courses. This seemed to be a better choice than a simple secretarial school to complete Eta's education. As fate would have it, there came a time when what she learned about planting vegetables and raising animals spared her and her children from going hungry.

To Ilonka's disappointment, none of the children inherited her love of piano. Eta, always agreeable and obedient, kept taking lessons for six long years before dropping out. She was not musically inclined and loathed practicing, blaming it for her failure to get better grades in school. As for Sárika, the ordeal lasted for three years and ended when Ilonka found out that her darling daughter was regularly skipping lessons. Her defense was that she had learned enough to play the piano socially, but since she did not aspire to become a concert pianist, to continue with the lessons was a waste of time and money. Ilonka tried it with Gyuszi, too, but after a couple of years it became clear that the little boy had neither interest nor talent, and so Ilonka sadly gave up. She was not going to force her children; besides, these private lessons were not cheap, and she could use the money for better things than throwing it down the drain. She gave her ungrateful children a long lecture on how one day they would all regret passing up an opportunity for which, if given the chance, half the children in the world would gladly give up everything. They stood listening with downcast eyes, their faces reflecting just enough contrition, but when it was over, behind her back they breathed in unison a great sigh of relief.

If not in playing the piano, Sárika did show artistic talent in other areas. She loved to stage little shows with self-made finger puppets. Ilonka bought her the little papier-mâché heads and with her help Sárika dressed them up to create the various figures she wanted for her plays. Her friends were the audience, but occasionally Ilonka and Mrs. Varosy also watched, amused how well she could maneuver the dolls and use different voices. She was also very good in sketching and drawing. She could make freehand copies of her favorite storybook characters, such as Dorothy and Glinda the Good Witch from the Wizard of Oz, though she cared nothing for the ugly Wicked Witch of the West.

In the fall Jeno's cousin Sandor, recently promoted to Brigadier General, and by now a member of the General Staff, paid another short visit, bringing Jeno a personally dedicated copy of the book he had written recently for the Army, a military manual called "Soldiers' Pocket Lexicon." Naturally, talk again turned to politics. He described the general mood of the military as optimistic, firmly believing that the war would be a short one. With Hitler's rapid advancement on the eastern front, he'd be finished with the Russians in no time. Sad as it was that sisterly Poland had to fall, it nevertheless demonstrated Germany's awesome power. If Hitler could destroy a civilized country in three weeks' time, what chance did backward Russia have to stop him? Yet, there were pessimistic whispers that Hitler could not possibly fight on two fronts and win. When Jeno asked how Sandor saw the situation personally, he said that although he disliked the Germans, he had to give them credit for their military achievements. As for Hungary, he felt the country had no chance to pull out safely from the present conflict. He himself would probably be in Russia by the spring. He heard that orders were pending to send him to Kiev to direct the Hungarian occupational forces stationed in the Ukraine.

Then, on December 7, 1941, came Pearl Harbor, the Japanese bombing of the U.S. Pacific fleet in Hawaii that drew America into the war. President Roosevelt signed the declaration of war against Japan on December 8 and against Germany on December 11. Germany immediately responded by declaring war on the United States, but Hungary didn't follow suit. The country only severed diplomatic relationships, which again further increased Hitler's hatred for Hungary.

According to a contemporary story, when the Hungarian ambassador closed his office in Washington, President Roosevelt asked his staff just what kind of country Hungary was. They replied it was one of the Balkan countries. "Which part of the Balkans?" the president wanted to know. This Balkan country actually was not located on the Balkans, he was told. "OK, well then, what is the government of Hungary?" he asked. "It's a kingdom," the experts replied. "Ah," Roosevelt said, "then it must have a king!" "No, it does not," came the answer. "Hungary's kingdom is the kind that has no king; instead it is ruled by an Admiral." "I see," said the president, "then the country must have an ocean." "Not exactly; in fact, it is not even close to any ocean." "Surely, it must have some ships?" "Ships? No, the Admiral only has a white horse (note: Horthy entered Budapest riding a white stallion when he took over the leadership in 1919)." Roosevelt then switched his interest to Hungary's involvement in the war. Learning that they were fighting the Russians, he asked what was their purpose? Territorial gains? "No, not against the Soviet Union, only against the Slovaks and Romanians, who stole large portions of Hungary in 1920." "That's a legitimate cause," agreed the president. "It's understandable if they go to war against those two countries." "Sorry Mr. President," the aides informed him, "Slovakia and Romania are actually Hungary's allies!"

On a more serious note, pressured by Germany and Italy, on December 11, 1941 Hungary was forced to dispatch a declaration of war to the U.S. Government. It was considered as having been made under duress and contrary to the will of the majority of the people, as expressed by President Roosevelt in his message to Congress on June 2, 1942. Regardless, three days later on June 5, Congress declared war on Hungary.

When school vacations began in June 1942, Ilonka started packing for her trip to Losonc, taking Eta and Istvan with her. Jeno accompanied them but returned home a few days later with lengthy instructions from Ilonka on what to do and how to do it while she was away. Earlier that year their faithful maid Rozie had left and Ilonka hired another younger village girl named Panni. On her first day she took the girl to the kitchen window facing the military compound and told her that for her own good she was to keep away from that window as much as possible. Catching the soldiers' attention would only create problems, often with undesirable consequences. Beyond warning, there was not much Ilonka could do to safeguard the morals of the girl in her charge, but she told Jeno to keep a close eye on her.

The weeks spent in Losonc were unforgettable. She got along well with her mother-in-law, having a better understanding by now of her reserved nature. Her relationship with her sister-in-law Sári went much deeper. The affection between them was heartfelt and genuine ever since they first met in 1928, a feeling that only grew stronger during her stay, and was to last for the rest of their lives.

To make herself useful, Ilonka wanted to help out in the kitchen but when they wouldn't let her, she thought that removed from the scene of temptation to nibble, it would be a good time trying to lose some of the hard-to-shed extra pounds she had gained lately around her waist and hips. She blamed it on having four children, or on her habit to finish the food left on the children's plate. She just didn't have the heart to throw out good food, not after experiencing the severe food shortages during the First World War. To start, she began eating more fruits and vegetables picked from their own garden and even instituted "apple days" when she ate nothing but apples, hoping to see faster results when stepping on the scale.

To her disappointment, the scale tipped the other way. What was worse, the new diet didn't seem to agree with her stomach, it made her queasy, almost the same way as she always felt during the early weeks of her pregnancies. But that would be impossible, and she quickly discarded the idea. At thirty-six she was too old, practically on the brink of menopause. When a few weeks went by and the symptoms still plagued her, she went to the doctor and was stunned to hear it confirmed that she was indeed going to have a baby. At first she was incredulous, but when the shock wore off and she had time to consider what to do about it, she knew with absolute certainty that acceptance was her only choice; she would keep the baby. In a few years Eta would be all grown up, probably married, Sárika would be the next to go, and soon her boys would start resenting her mothering, but with this baby she would still have a little one to nurture and cuddle.

She wrote to Jeno, telling him how proud he should be to become a father again at age forty-seven. The news was a great surprise to him, but he took it calmly. They would manage, and a new baby would make Ilonka glow. Spending more time with Sárika and Gyuszi while Ilonka was away made him more aware of just how fast the children were growing. He made sure to spend time with them, taking them to the lake on weekends or to the public pool, but in time he realized that they would just as soon entertain themselves. All the neighborhood kids congregated in the small park where Jeno's side street ended, splashing in a shallow fountain there, and playing their favorite games. The latest and most popular one was a charade-like play-act called "I come from America and my profession is . . ." at which point the player had to mimic a particular line of work for the others to guess at. It was great fun as they tried to outdo each other by creating more exotic, less familiar occupations.

. . . .

Later that summer Sandor stopped by again creating a great excitement for the children when he arrived with a chauffeur-driven automobile. Unfortunately, a few days earlier Sárika developed a temperature, and no amount of begging or crying would change her father's mind to let her get out of bed. She had to stay behind while Uncle Sandor took Gyuszi and Jeno for a nice ride and treated them to a sumptuous lunch.

During their talks Sandor confided to Jeno just how difficult and precarious Hungary's present situation was. So far, through political maneuvering and showing limited cooperation with Hitler's military and economic demands, the government kept him from overrunning the country, but this relative safety made Hungary a haven for foreign refugees. So far about 140,000 had crossed over from Poland, roughly half of them Jews, while from the West a steady trickling of Dutch, Belgian and French political refugees and even some Russian, British, and American war prisoners escaping from German camps found their way into the country. Most of them found shelter in churches, but there were also brave individuals who provided a hiding place at a great risk to themselves. Among the Jewish refugees, many would be able to reach Palestine with the help of Hungarian and other outside organizations.

Hungarian Jews in 1942 still felt reasonably safe. Under constant German pressure, the government, hoping to take some of the wind out of the Nazi sails, enacted several anti-Jewish laws, but these did not menace their physical existence and did not apply any of the inhuman measures practiced by Germany and other satellite states. Surrounded by countries that carried out the systematic annihilation of Jews, Hitler called Hungary the "Jewish Island of Central Europe."

Until recently Jews in Hungary were completely integrated into society; they never lived in isolated ghetto-like communities as in Poland, and differed from other Hungarians only by religion, and even in that, very few followed the Orthodox teachings. Between the two World Wars, they made up roughly 5% of the population with opportunities wide open to them in commerce, banking, the arts, and professions. In fact Jews owned 91% of the banks, they controlled 50% of all industry and roughly 88% of the major corporations, while in the professions 60% of doctors were Jewish, 50% lawyers, 39% engineers, 34% journalists and writers, and in universities one quarter of the students were Jewish. The first anti-Jewish law, already in existence since May 29, 1938, was enacted to reduce these high participatory numbers to a maximum of 20%, bringing it more in line with the percentage of the Jewish population. The second anti-Jewish law, passed on May 5, 1939, extended their restriction to 5%, and also defined Jews racially by the standards of the Nuremberg Laws of Germany. The third and last anti-Jewish law passed on August 8, 1941, prohibited interracial marriage between Jews and Christians, but still, there were no ghettos, no yellow stars, and no deportations. Very few believed that it was only a matter of time before Hitler had enough of Hungary's harboring the Jews. He never liked the Hungarians but their attempts to protect the Jews made him despise them even more.

Hitler was critical of Hungary for other reasons, as well. He blamed them for not making the maximum effort in helping Germany's war efforts, as did Romania and Bulgaria, by converting the country's industry to war production. His angry outbursts included threats of occupation, since Germany could extract more from the occupied territories. Goebbels noted in his diary, "The Hungarians still dare to commit acts of effrontery toward us that go far beyond what we can stand. I suppose, however, we must keep quiet for the moment. We are dependent upon them. But every one of us is yearning for the moment *when we can really talk turkey to the Hungarians.*"[3*]

The Germans were also well aware that regardless of some pro-Nazi elements in the government and within the armed forces, conservative and anti-Nazi sentiments were prevalent and hard at work to keep Hungarian politics from complete Nazification. Sandor, by now a major general of the General Staff and appointed as second-in-command of the Hungarian military forces in Kiev, told Jeno during a short leave from the front that he was criticized by the Germans for putting too much restraint on his troops. The implication was that by not allowing looting and mistreating of civilians, he was creating a behavioral distinction between the Hungarian and German soldiers. His voice was full of sarcasm when uttering the word "mistreatment"; it was a mere euphemism for a wide range of German atrocities he had personally witnessed. During the Western Campaign German soldiers behaved in a fairly civilized manner, but in Russia they had no reason for restraint.

Soon after his return to Kiev came the disturbing news of the accidental death of the regent's eldest son, Istvan Horthy. In March 1942 he was made Deputy Regent, but since he was well known for his anti-German views, the possibility of replacing his seventy-four-year-old father was strongly opposed by both the Nazis and the rightwing Hungarian politicians. As a trained pilot he was stationed at an airfield around Kiev and was flying missions over Russian territories when on August 25, 1942 his wife, a volunteer nurse in the Red Cross, came to visit him. The couple was photographed at the airport, happy and smiling, with several officers, among them Sandor, welcoming Mrs. Horthy. A few days later Horthy's plane mysteriously went down behind the Hungarian lines, killing him instantly. According to never-proven rumors, it was a staged accident to get rid of him. He received a state funeral with military honors and was buried with a delegation of high-ranking German officials in attendance. His death broke the Regent's heart, but it made him more determined not to give into Hitler.

At the end of August Jeno took the train to Losonc to bring home Ilonka and the two children. He could only stay for a couple of days, but before they left they agreed that next year it would be his mother's turn again to visit and meet her new grandchild. Their plans, however, remained plans only. Although

---

3 * "*. . . wenn wir einmal Fraktur reden können . . .*"—The Goebbels Diaries 1942-1943, entry on March 5, 1942, translated by Louis P. Lochner

she lived twelve more years, and in excellent health, mother and son would never see each other again.

After being away for two months, Ilonka was happy to be home, reunited with the family. Gyuszi was overjoyed to see his mother again, and even Sárika complained loudly for leaving them alone for too long. There, however, was another reason she was so anxious to have her mother back. Last June, when she graduated from elementary school, the nuns highly recommended that she continue her studies in the gimnazium, but Ilonka thought otherwise. They expected Eta to do well when they enrolled her there, and look what happened: she was unable to cope with the high demands and had to change schools after four years. It was true that she did not have the drive to study as her younger sister did, but still, having good grades in elementary school was no guarantee that Sárika could keep up with the pressures of a gimnazium. Besides, studying Latin and calculus for eight years was unnecessary for girls in Ilonka's opinion, unless they wanted to be in the professions, but Eta and Sárika were not going that route. They had two brothers, and they were the ones in need of higher education. They were going to be breadwinners one day; the girls would marry, and for that, they didn't need a university diploma.

Jeno agreed only half-heartedly. Sárika was so bright, and so eager to learn, she deserved at least the chance to try. Still, Ilonka stuck to her guns that she should go to the less demanding polgari—only four years of studying and no Latin or higher mathematics—and then go on to secretarial school to learn typing and shorthand. These were useful skills; she could always get a job and support herself as a secretary, if for some reason she did not get married. Ilonka had to smile at the thought. Looking at her daughter getting prettier by the day, she doubted that she was destined to remain a spinster.

But Sárika did not agree with her mother's limited view about education. She wanted a future, more than just being a wife and mother or working as someone's secretary. There was prestige in graduating from college. People with a diploma were treated with more deference. She had nothing against marriage, but for her, education must come first.

At first she couldn't understand her mother's objection to the gimnazium when her teachers recommended it and all her best friends in school—and most of them not as smart as she—were heading there. The denial, however, didn't dampen her determination. It was only June; her mother might change her mind by September, and so, she stopped arguing and waited until she returned from Losonc. Unfortunately, when she brought up the subject again, Ilonka still insisted to enroll her at the polgari.

Knowing that she'd never settle for that—polgari was for dummies—Sárika at that point decided to take matters into her own hands: she'd just enroll herself in the gimnazium. To do so, schools required a signed parental consent, a minor obstacle for her, easy to overcome. All she had to do was sit down and practice her father's signature, which she did to near perfection. When she was ready, she filled out the enrollment form, signed her father's name to it, then took her school record and went to register at the State Gimnazium for Girls.

As the deadline for registration at the polgari approached and Ilonka asked her daughter to get the necessary papers ready, she was baffled by Sárika's answer that she was already enrolled in the gimnazium. When the truth came out after posing a few questions about when and how, she got a severe scolding for forging Jeno's signature and was grounded until school started, but secretly Ilonka could not help but smile. Her headstrong little girl! She had a mind of her own, and once she wanted something badly enough, it was no use, she would get her way one way or another.

When Jeno heard about it, he also gave Sárika a long lecture on how wrong it is to falsify someone's signature and warned her never to do it again. Then, out of curiosity, he made her sign his name and had to admit that it was almost a perfect likeness. *Imagine the gumption of this child*, he mused. He had no doubt that she would succeed in school, but about her promise not to forge his signature again, he was less sure.

By the summer of 1942 the government had reached the point that it could no longer resist Hitler's demand for more Hungarian troops without risking German occupation. The call-up for military duty was widened, and soon trains loaded with some 200,000 soldiers began to move eastward with Hitler's renewed promise that they would be kept out of combat and serve only behind battle lines as auxiliary units or part of the occupational forces. Hitler also promised to supply weapons, ammunition, and other material that the Hungarian army lacked.

Sopron was the collection center for recruits from several surrounding villages, and the city swarmed with men in uniforms. Whenever a military train was scheduled to leave for Russia, schoolchildren were at the station distributing little gift packages with cigarettes and cookies, handing out flowers, and giving their addresses to the soldiers to write back about the victorious conquests they would make. A military band played patriotic songs, while the platform was crowded with relatives saying goodbye to husbands, brothers, and sons heading into harm's way.

Moved by the tearful scenes, Ilonka hit upon a fresh idea. She took her new camera, a birthday present from Jeno, and snapped pictures of the soldiers, jotting down their names and home addresses with the promise to forward the photos to their families. It soon became so popular that the boys were lining up for picture taking, while she was clicking away to the very last minute before boarding. As the train began to move, these young men—officers in passenger cars, the ordinary troops in boxcars—were cheering wildly, waving small flags and shouting pledges for a speedy return, while new recruits still in training lined the platform at stiff attention in honor of their front-bound comrades.

As transports were leaving on a regular basis, the same scene played out over and over again, keeping Ilonka busy with taking the pictures then faithfully forwarding them to the families. She used Jozsef Varosy's darkroom to develop the photos and paid from her own pocket to mail them out. In response, letters and thank-you notes poured in, giving her a feeling of satisfaction that in a small way she made people happy.

Then, as winter set in, terrible news started to filter back from the front. In January 1943 Hitler, forgetting his promise to keep the Hungarian troops out of direct fighting, ordered the 2nd Hungarian Army Division into the battle of Voronezh, a strategically important city about two hundred and eighty miles south of Moscow, where they were to dig in and hold the line along the Don River. Due to another German "oversight," crucial supplies of winter uniforms did not arrive in time, and as a result thousands of men huddling in open trenches, still in their summer uniforms, froze to death in the heights of the Russian winter with temperature hovering between 22 to 31 below zero Fahrenheit. So many lives lost unnecessarily, and the fighting was still to come! The guns and heavy artillery support Hitler also promised earlier were never delivered, either, and without them these poorly equipped soldiers, their numbers already decimated, did not have a chance when the Russians launched into an offensive, crossing the river with enormous force, heavy tanks and other superior military armor. They fought back but in the end, over half the remaining troops were either killed or taken prisoner.

The horrendous loss was a tragedy for the entire nation, but for Ilonka it also brought personal heartache. Her spirit was crushed as pitiful letters started to arrive from families she had sent photographs to, all telling the same story: the loss of a soldier killed or lying frozen somewhere in the bitter Russian snow. The letters begged for copies of her pictures, as each became a last memento of a fallen hero. In gratitude they offered her money, a chicken or goose, or whatever she'd want, but of course Ilonka refused to accept anything. She sent them the requested photos, but she cried and cried looking at the pictures, mourning each boy she met, if only for a few minutes, now dead, their faces staring at her as so many ghosts. She hardly ate and slept badly, as recurring nightmares haunted her night after night. She became lethargic and was overwhelmed by sadness that caused concern about her well-being; her pregnancy could be in danger. The doctor prescribed some pills and sternly told her that if she wanted to have a healthy baby she must stop reading and answering the heart-wrenching letters.

She did stop, but the pictures were still mailed out, thanks to Jozsef Varosy, who stepped in and took over the task. It was never far from his thoughts that his own son Kurt, a graduate of the Ludovika Military Academy and currently promoted to Army Captain, could someday be among the casualties, even though for the moment he was safely tucked away at the Ministry of Defense in Budapest.

Gradually Ilonka regained her strength and emotional balance, and could concentrate on the pending birth of her baby. The due date was set for the middle of February, only a few weeks away, and although all indicated a smooth delivery, the doctor recommended checking into a hospital instead of giving birth at home as before. His concern was not so much that Ilonka was close to thirty-seven, an age when complications could set in, but because of the war. What if she went into labor at night and electricity was disrupted, as had happened a few times already? She would be safer in the hospital, where they had their own generator. Chances were remote, but why take the risk? Arrangements were made, but when Ilonka told the midwife about it, she huffed and puffed indignantly, telling her she should be ashamed to have the baby in a hospital at her old age!

In spite of her "old age," Ilonka delivered a healthy little boy on February 16, 1943. He was named Jeno, Jr. after his father, but immediately nicknamed Ochie, meaning "little brother." Although the birth went without a problem, it left Ilonka extremely weak. After spending five days in the hospital she was still exhausted when she brought her infant son home, laying him in the same wicker bassinet that had cradled all her children. To help her caring for the baby while recovering, the girls quickly learned how to give him a bath or change his diapers.

It took weeks before Ilonka regained her strength, much longer than when Istvan was born. Perhaps the midwife was right, she thought, she was getting too old to bring children into the world. Little Ochie would be her last baby, but she hoped that by the time he started to resent his mother's open affection, there would be grandchildren to pamper and spoil. She couldn't imagine her life without having children around; they made her feel complete and brought her a joy beyond compare.

As tragic as the destruction of the 2nd Army with staggering 84% casualties was to Hungary, the Germans also began to suffer serious setbacks on the Russian front. Despite the six months of fierce fighting, Stalingrad did not fall, and for the first time since the outbreak of the war, Hitler saw an entire German army captured by the Russians. The effectiveness of Soviet military was greatly enhanced by the introduction of the American Lend-Lease program, created in 1941 to extend financial help to U.S. allies fighting the Axis powers, mostly Russia and Britain, by supplying them with war material on which the war was fought and won. With the better equipment, the Soviets launched an offensive to establish a stronghold in the southern part of Russia, a line they firmly held in the face of repeated German counterattacks.

In view of the recent losses Horthy feared that Hitler would turn to him again with further demands for military support and sought contact with England and the United States to express the country's willingness to turn against the Germans and accept the Casablanca formula of unconditional surrender. He acted on the assumption that the Allied forces, advancing from Italy and the Balkans, would reach Hungary's southern border by the beginning of 1944, or possibly even sooner. The answer came through diplomatic channels that although the invasion through the Balkans was one of the options, it might never be put into use, and that they could only offer suggestions how Hungary might improve her position when the war was over. Their long list of conditions included, among others, the gradual reduction of military and economic cooperation with Germany and eventually turning against Hitler; ridding the Army Staff of Nazi sympathizers to ensure that such attack would be carried out; and allowing passage of Allied airplanes to attack German bases.

Since Hungary was hemmed in and controlled by the Germans, it was not easy to live up to these conditions, but the government made a serious attempt to comply. It immediately ceased to fire upon Allied planes flying over Hungarian airfields and rejected Hitler's plans to establish several German flying bases in the western part of the country. In recognition, the Allies refrained from bombing Hungary; there were no air attacks until April 4, 1944, two weeks after German troops occupied the country. The Regent also asked Hitler to release the Hungarian troops from the Russian front, reasoning that with the line of battle steadily approaching, they were needed at home to defend the country's borders. Compliance with the condition to reshuffle the Army Staff was more difficult and needed further negotiations. By then fascist ideas were widely rooted in the military, a direct result of introducing politics into the army. Nazi ideologies injected into patriotism confused the minds of many officers, especially those from the lower or middle classes.

As the talks continued, the Americans began suggesting that since Russia was their ally and territorially closer to Hungary, it would perhaps be better if Hungary started negotiations with Moscow. The Hungarian delegate strongly objected, saying that they had a taste of Communism in 1919, and a Soviet occupation would be worse than the Germans. He could hardly believe the naïve perception the Americans had about the Soviet Union and Stalin. They considered him to be reasonable and took his word at face value when he promised that Russian occupation of Hungary would only be temporary. Naturally, Hungary would need to make changes when the war ended, the Hungarian delegate was told. They'd have to form a new government led by coalition parties that included the Communist Party to make it acceptable to the Soviets, and put through a long overdue land reform.

Listening to them talk about the Russians, it seemed that these western negotiators truly believed that after the conclusion of the peace treaty the Soviets would stay in Hungary and in other occupied countries only until they had a chance to create their independent political existence. In their simplistic idealism, they pictured the coming world as a peaceful coexistence between the capitalist West and communist Russia, two diametrically opposed political systems, with the Soviet Union gradually adapting to the ways of the western democracies. They viewed some recent positive changes in Russia as a sure sign of this possibility, pointing to the dissolution of the Comintern (Communist International) in May 1943, the formal reestablishment of the Orthodox Church, and the acceptance of the Four Freedoms in the Atlantic Charter: freedom of speech and expression, freedom of worship, freedom from want, and freedom from fear.

The Hungarians walked away from the negotiations, steadfastly refusing to deal with Moscow and clinging to their wishful thinking that in the end they could surrender to the Western Allies. To them it was incomprehensible that the

Western Powers would hand over Central and Eastern Europe to the Soviets, thus allowing for the creation of an exclusive Russian zone. And so, Hungary eagerly pursued preparations for an Anglo-American occupation, while the British and the Americans gradually lost interest in further discussions. They never considered Hungary's geographical situation that made an all-out attack against Germany suicidal, and even hinted that when the war ended they would hold the country responsible for failure to turn against Hitler when they were given a chance.

During the summer of 1943 fighting on the Russian front was dragging to-and-fro, the Russians advancing and being pushed back and the Germans doing the same. The list of war casualties grew longer by the day, yet the Nazi propaganda never ceased to boast about glorious victories for the Wehrmacht, Germany's military might. People of course knew the truth; they saw the hospitals crowded with wounded soldiers, but somehow this didn't have a demoralizing effect on civilian life in Hungary. With the exception of shortages, the situation was relatively stable and life continued without much hardship. War production was in full swing, work opportunities were plenty, children attended school as usual, and ladies went about running their households and caring for their families.

Sopron was no different. Eta in her new school was learning to tend vegetable gardens, milk cows and raise chickens, and when classes were over, stayed a couple of afternoons to help rolling bandages for military hospitals. The nuns took the girls to visit wounded soldiers and hand them flowers and prayer books, but there were also school dances and parties to attend, although Eta found most of them boring. She looked down on her silly girlfriends who could talk of nothing but who they met at what dance, which boys they liked and which they loathed, like it was something important! She went to these parties only because Ilonka insisted; with her seventeenth birthday around the corner, it was time for her to circulate. It also gave Ilonka a chance to survey some of the available young men and pick up some background information on them. After all, one could very well become her son-in-law.

Every time Eta reluctantly put on her party dress for a dance, Sárika was itching to go along—not to dance of course, only to "keep her mother company"—and just as many times she was told to be patient, she was too young, her turn will come. Oh, those hateful words, thrown at her every time she wanted to do something on her own. She longed to cut her hair and get rid of those awful pigtails, but no, perhaps a few years from now. God forbid wanting to see a movie alone with her girlfriends! Not until she was older! And what was wrong with experimenting a little with makeup? The one time she tried that, her mother scrubbed her face until it stung, and to top it off, she had to listen to her speeches about vanity and frivolity! All because she was too young! Why couldn't she be Eta's age? She would not have to be pushed to go dancing like her!

It was during that summer that Ilonka and Jeno went on a weekend trip and were not expected back until Monday. This was Sárika's chance to put on her mother's lipstick, let her hair fall free, and watch people's reaction to her new look. Not that she would dare to leave the house in such a state; she'd just stay by the window so people could take notice. She picked six o'clock Sunday evening to do it when many of their neighbors would be passing by the house coming from evening devotions.

The maid warned her that for a girl not yet twelve, such display was not befitting, but as usual, she just ignored her. She was at the kitchen window, elbows on the windowsill, convinced that she was the epitome of sophistication, when suddenly she saw her parents rounding the corner. Surprised by their unexpected return and too happy to see them, she forgot all about the makeup and bolted out the kitchen, racing down the long hallway to the entrance. Too much in a hurry to greet them, she was pushing the door open when her hand slipped from the handle and crashed through the glass panel, slicing her right wrist to the bone.

Ilonka and Jeno, still on the street, heard her ear-shattering scream and rushed inside, unprepared for the sight of their daughter holding out her hand with blood spurting high, spraying the walls, even the ceiling. Ilonka flew up the stairs, took one look at the open wound, and knew instantly that wrapping her handkerchief around it would not stop the flow. She sent Eta running for Dr. Graser, their family doctor, while she tied a tourniquet around Sárika's upper arm and kept the arm extended above her head until the doctor arrived. By the time he walked in the bleeding had stopped, and seeing only a small bandage Dr. Graser thought they had dragged him here for nothing. He quickly changed his mind when he removed the wrapping and saw a gaping wound with torn pinkish tendons, a severed artery, and the bone clearly visible. He put on a new bandage, praising Ilonka for having the good sense to use a tourniquet, then told them that the injury was serious and Sárika must be taken to the hospital without delay.

There was no public telephone nearby to call for emergency, and Dr. Graser suggested they should just hurry to the hospital on foot; it would be faster than waiting until he got home and called the ambulance, which, being Sunday night, would probably take some time to show up. He put the injured hand in a makeshift sling then rushed home to call the hospital and alert the doctor and his staff to be ready for surgery. The nurses, already retired for the evening when the call came in, were not pleased to go back on duty, and they didn't hide their resentment against unruly children who always picked the night to get into trouble.

Dr. Zimmerman, the surgeon on call, immediately put Sárika on the operating table and asked if she could make a fist then squeeze and open it a few times. She was able to do it, and while looking at the wound she saw the cut tendons jerking back and forth, a good sign, according to the doctor, that they didn't shrink back further into her arm. By eleven o'clock he was finished, the wound was closed, and the patient transferred to the ward.

After assurances from the doctor that he did everything that could possibly be done, Ilonka and Jeno thanked him and left. Reaching the house Ilonka managed to walk up the steps, but once she closed the door her legs gave out and she collapsed in a heap without saying a word. During the ordeal she had held up admirably; she remained composed and acted quickly to treat the wound, but the shock finally caught up with her. She could only take so much. It was her daughter's right hand that was at stake! She could be crippled! She remembered all the suffering her mother endured when she lost her right hand. *Please God, don't let that happen again,* she managed to send a silent prayer before losing consciousness.

Sárika stayed in the hospital for a few days, with the doctor regularly checking on her healing progress. He was satisfied with the results: the fingers were stiff but they moved, and he said that aside from a lifelong scar, she could expect a complete recovery. For therapy she was told to lie on her back and hooking the fingers under the bedrail above her head gently stretch the injured hand. She was also learning to use her left hand, although for bathing, plaiting her hair and tying her shoelaces Sárika had to rely on her mother's help.

She still wore a sling when school started in September, but eventually her hand was declared good as new, which meant no more exemption from gym classes. It worried Ilonka to no end. What if she reinjured her hand? She never ceased to warn her somewhat reckless daughter to be extra careful, slow down, walk rather then run, and always look where she was going.

Not that she listened. It went in one ear and out the other. Always in a hurry, she almost made her mother's fear come true when one afternoon leaving the classroom she tripped on the doorway, stumbling headlong, her books flying in all directions. With arms flailing, she tried to regain her balance but would have hit the floor if one of her classmates, Wanda, had not caught her in time. It gave her a good scare, but she quickly pulled herself together, and soon they were both laughing their heads off at Wanda's remark that it was not the most graceful imitation of Tinker Bell flying off to a mission.

They had known each other since elementary school, but only as casual classmates. The mishap changed all that. Within a short time they became best friends, almost inseparable. Their families lived only a few blocks apart, and so they started walking home from school together, talking incessantly about the day's events, criticizing their schoolmates and teachers, which ones they liked or couldn't stand. Blessed with a sharp wit and a sense of humor and having a knack for mimicking and making fun of people, it was great fun to be around Wanda. They both loved the movies and were avid fans of movie stars, had similar tastes in clothing and style, and ice cream was their most favorite food. Like Sárika, Wanda, too, had an older sister and they spent endless hours complaining about their mean ways.

They were alike in all respects, except in their attitude toward school and studying. Wanda did not care to spend her time doing homework while she could do other things. She was very bright, but solving math problems and memorizing Latin were not her favorites. She relied solely on her ability to retain what she learned in the classroom, just enough to maintain passing grades. But now that they became friends, Wanda could look to Sárika to improve her standing. She would come over to her house and copy her writing assignments, although to avoid detection she altered a phrase here and there, changed the sentence structure, or even inserted minor errors on purpose. She would do the same with math homework, and would sit and listen while Sárika was conjugating Latin verbs, hoping that some of it would also stick to her mind.

When Ilonka saw what was going on, she confronted Sárika that letting Wanda copy her work was nothing but cheating. The girl was using her and she did not need friends like that. From that day on Wanda fell from Ilonka's graces. She wanted the friendship stopped, but of course she couldn't. The girls would just switch to Wanda's house, but there the situation got just as bad. At Sárika's place, with Ilonka always hovering around, Wanda at least kept her nose to the books, but on her home turf she quickly got bored with studying, and often interrupted the work with childish pranks. A playful poke or a funny grimace was sometimes enough to provoke both girls into shrieks of laughter. Wanda's mother soon had enough of this immature behavior; it was now her turn to admonish Sárika, accusing her—never her daughter, she could do no wrong—of distracting Wanda from her studies. She told her that if she couldn't behave herself, she should stay away.

In time the two mothers realized that opposing the girls' friendship only made it stronger, and slowly, albeit reluctantly, accepted their daughters' inseparable togetherness.

Shortly after the start of the new fall semester in 1943 the doorbell rang at the Zachar residence, and when Sárika answered it she saw a tall, very handsome young man standing on the threshold. He introduced himself as Laszlo Riedl, Jr. and asked to see her parents. Ilonka was at the door in a second, welcoming him with open arms. They were expecting him after his father, Jeno's cousin, wrote that Lasko was on his way to Sopron to start college as a forest engineering student. They had never met him before, but they instantly accepted this polite, well-mannered young man as a member of the family, embracing him with warmth and affection. They invited him to visit as often as he liked, with Ilonka already envisioning him bringing some of his equally courteous and well-brought-up friends to introduce to Eta. These were the kind of young men she wished for her seventeen-year-old daughter to meet.

Around the same time one of Jeno's co-workers asked if he would be interested in buying a home in a new housing development under construction near the South Train Station. They were building twenty-five single-family homes there, reasonably priced, and if he liked, he could put him in contact with the real estate agent for the project, who happened to be his brother. Jeno and Ilonka had already discussed buying a home when their ten-year lease expired next year; this would be a perfect opportunity to move into a brand new house where nothing leaked and everything functioned perfectly. There was only one drawback: with the front drawing closer by the day, Hungary might become a battlefield, and Jeno was hesitant to invest all their money in a piece of property that could be destroyed in the fighting. It would leave them virtually penniless. The time just did not seem right to take such a risk and he decided against the purchase. He was lucky that he followed his instincts. The first American air attack to hit Sopron a year later destroyed the entire area near the station, leveling the new homes to the ground.

But that was still hanging in the future. For the present, even though people became more aware of the war due to increasing shortages and the introduction of rationing, civilian life went on as usual. The Varosys, Ilonka and Jeno's closest friends, were regulars on Saturday nights, when after dinner they would stay up late into the night playing cards. Soon the room was filled with cigarette smoke with everyone smoking. Ilonka had picked up the habit from Aunt Anna when she lived with them, but she would only light up during their card games or on special occasions.

With the arrival of December, the children began counting the days, first to December 6th, the feast day of Saint Nicholas, then to Christmas. In most of Europe Santa Clause, or Mikulás in Hungarian, has a different role than in America, where he slides down the chimney on the night before Christmas dressed in a red suit, bringing presents. Here he puts in an appearance on the evening of his feast day and not as jolly old St. Nick, but as a stately bishop wearing a tall mitre and carrying a crosier, his pastoral staff. The only similarity to the American Santa is his ample white beard to help disguise the identity of the pretender imitating him. While visiting families he is accompanied by a hideous creature, the devilish Krampusz, rattling a chain and carrying a big sack, a frightful sight that always made children tremble. The bishop then asks each child if they behaved well during the past year, a silly question, since the answer was always a firm "Yes." But they couldn't fool St. Nicholas; he seems to know all about their naughty deeds, and while he enumerates them—with a little input from the parents—the Krampusz opens his sack, ready to grab the culprits and drag them away. They are saved, however, as the kindly bishop gives them another chance to repent and promise never to misbehave again. Before leaving he bestows his blessings and distributes little gifts, small toys and some sweets and fruits.

Ilonka's friend who usually played Santa bowed out that year, and Sárika immediately volunteered to step into his role. The robe and accessories fit her with a little adjustment, making her a splendid-looking bishop. As soon as darkness fell she was ready to ring the doorbell, her evil companion at her side. The adults stood in the background to watch her performance, and she did not disappoint them. Five-year-old Istvan, believing in St. Nicolas with all his heart, and Gyuszi, doubtful but still not sure if Santa was real or not, were both awed by the sight of the magnificent bishop and terrified at the same time by his chain-rattling servant. When Sárika addressed them with a deep booming voice, little Istvan inched toward his mother, ready to hide behind her skirt in case the red creature made a move for him. After delivering a stern lecture on how the boys should behave in the coming year, Sárika handed them some oranges, figs and chocolates, patted them on the head, and after bestowing a blessing, it should have been the end of the ritual. But not for Sárika! Instead of a quiet and dignified exit, she pulled herself to her full height, called the boys to approach her, and bidding them to kneel, made them kiss her gloved hand. It was hard for her parents and the Varosys to keep a straight face and stifle their laughter.

The evening was a total success and for years the memory of it brought smiles to everyone who witnessed the scene. Sárika offered a repeat performance for next year, never knowing that St. Nicolas Day in 1944 would be tragically different.

War turns to hell

THE SEEMINGLY TRANQUIL atmosphere began to change as 1944 brought a drastic turn in the war. The Russians staged an all-out attack along the entire front line, taking back Leningrad, Nikopol, and Odessa, and soon the Soviet forces were back to their 1938 border. As German losses mounted, Hitler began to lose patience with Hungary's refusal to contribute more to his war efforts and also to settle the Jewish question. Other German satellites, to gain favor from Hitler, willingly adopted and carried out the anti-Jewish Nuremberg measures; only Regent Horthy refused to accede. Ignoring Hitler's threats, he went a step further in provoking the Fuhrer when on February 9 he formally requested the withdrawal of all Hungarian troops from the Russian front. In response Hitler invited him to Klessheim, Germany, to discuss the issue, and suggested that since the subject matter concerned the military, he should also bring the Minister of Defense and the Chief of Staff.

The three men left on March 17 in spite of receiving reliable reports of unusually heavy German troop concentration along Hungary's western border, a sure indication of Hitler's intention to occupy the country. When Horthy confronted Hitler about it the Fuhrer, in a violent outburst, admitted that unless Hungary changed its tune, German military occupation of Hungary was inevitable. Horthy retorted that in that case he would resign, and with that left the room to immediately return to Hungary.

Using various delaying tactics, the Germans prevented him from leaving, and while stranded, members of his delegation tried to convince him to change his mind in order to save the country from the Nazi takeover. Yielding to pressure, Horthy went to see Hitler again, but by then it was too late; the trains with German troops were already rolling toward Hungary and couldn't be stopped. Hitler could only promise that if Horthy remained as Regent, the occupation would be temporary, until a more acceptable government could be appointed.

And so on the morning of March 19, 1944 German army units crossed into Hungary and by noon Budapest, with all its strategically important places, was in German hands. Armed resistance was impossible with the Regent, the Minister of Defense, and the top military leader still being retained in Germany. That tragic day was a turning point in Hungarian history that brought about radical changes. The Allieds no longer spared Hungary from bombing; the Gestapo—the German security police—swung into action, arresting members of Parliament and rounding up military personnel known for anti-Nazi sentiments; and with the help of a newly-instituted puppet government, the mass deportation of the Jews was set into motion.

Adolf Eichmann, the head of the Gestapo, personally went to Hungary to deal with the country's Jewish population, approximately 800,000 to 825,000 in number including those living in the recently regained territories. With astounding speed, by the end of March the Jews were forced to wear the infamous yellow star; the following month they were moved into ghettos and in May the deportation began to various concentration camps, but mostly to Auschwitz, Poland, one of the most notorious death camps. He ordered that by the end of June Budapest must be cleared of all Jews, approximately 227,000 at the time. This, however, was not carried out, as the Regent would not permit it. Horthy put the military on alert and threatened to use force to prevent the deportations from Budapest, and at the same time called his plight to the attention of the International Red Cross, the Pope, the King of Sweden, and other neutral states. As a result an organized rescue mission began to take shape, an effort to save as many Jews as possibly by issuing safe-conduct passes and letters of protection. Raoul Wallenberg, the first secretary of the Swedish Legation, alone saved the lives of several thousand Jews. Eventually, with outside intervention, an international ghetto was established in Budapest and under the protection of neutral powers about 95,000 Jews in that ghetto survived. At the end of the war others coming out of hiding and those retuning from concentration camps and forced labor brigades thrown into battlefields on the Russian front, raised the number of the Budapest survivors to 150,000.

Unfortunately, the provincial Jewish population could not be helped. The deportation proceeded according to zones from Ruthenia in the eastern region, down to Transylvania, followed by the northern district, then the southern sector, and lastly western Hungary. Upon arrival at Auschwitz children up to age twelve or fourteen, older people, the sick, and those with criminal records arriving in separate transports were taken immediately to the gas chambers and killed. As for the rest, an SS doctor by mere glance selected who was fit for work and who was not. Those rejected also went to the gas chambers, while the others were assigned to slave work. According to German records, by July 437,402[4*] Hungarian Jews were deported to Auschwitz alone, most of them to perish either in the camp or during a forced death march to Austria near the end of the war, driven to dig trenches in the defense of Vienna.

The Jews in Sopron, being part of the last zone scheduled for deportation, were still confident at the beginning that by some miracle they would escape what the Nazis called the resettlement to the east. Although forced to wear

---

4 * The estimated total number of victims is 565,000, with 260,000 survivors

the yellow Star of David, they were allowed to remain in their homes. When orders came requiring everyone to prove non-Jewish origin by producing birth certificates, including those of all four grandparents, the Jews appealed to the Catholic clergy for help. Many sought instant conversion in exchange for verification of Aryan ancestry, while those who were originally Christians but had converted to Judaism were eager to reverse the conversion. Jews by birth who became Catholics were trying to demonstrate their religious fervor by attending daily Masses and taking the sacraments. Unfortunately, none of this helped. Even if a false birth certificate could be obtained, Sopron was small enough for people to know the truth, and there were many Nazi sympathizers who would gladly expose them to the authorities.

A segment of German-speaking folks, those who had felt wronged ever since Sopron voted to remain Hungarian in 1921, now came out of the shadows, professing their sentiments for Germany. They felt liberated and became avid supporters of the Nazis, boasting loudly about their German allegiance, eager to be part of the *Volksbund*, a National Association of peoples of German ethnicity. Their time had finally arrived! To vent the vengeance they had harbored over twenty years, these Volksbundists singled out the Jews, following them around, taunting the pitiable victims, shouting mean-spirited insults; even children would mock them, yelling degrading anti-Jewish rhymes. Disgusting posters, some of them depicting Jews as giant leaches with Semitic faces sucking the blood of Gentiles, appeared overnight, plastered on every public wall space and advertising kiosks. Cruel jokes laced with Jew-baiting slogans could be heard at anti-Jewish rallies, or even at playgrounds, where children mouthed them, some without understanding of their meaning, others with full knowledge. Ordinary civilians, fearing the Volksbundists, stayed out of their way, avoiding confrontation whenever possible.

The Jews, still living at home and free to come and go, endured the humiliation without a word, hoping that this was as bad as it would get. That hope, however, was shattered when on June 1, 1944 they were ordered into a ghetto set up in the heart of the city. Some went into hiding, and there were instances when people chose death rather than give up their homes, but most of them peacefully complied.

Overnight the city became like an anthill as the Jews, young and old, scurried toward the designated housing area, carrying only small bundles of belongings. Inside the ghetto, people were jammed together into rooms without any privacy, while on the outside heavy chain links blocked the street. Sentries were on guard day and night to ensure that no one left, allowing only a chosen few to go out and bring back food. If some of them were lucky enough to escape, they immediately headed for the "Sanctuary Ghetto" in Budapest.

Less than a month later, in the early morning hours of June 29 the blaring sound of loudspeakers woke the Jews with new orders to evacuate the ghetto. They were to be transferred to a large storage building near the train station, for what purpose, they didn't say, but everyone knew this could only mean deportation! Although everyone had heard rumors about the camps, people desperately wanted to believe the Nazis that the deportations were nothing more than repatriation to the eastern territories, and that all allegation about "mistreatments" was malicious outside propaganda. Perhaps it would be better there than living under the miserable conditions of the ghetto.

These Jews, some 1,885 people, herded through the streets under armed guards, yielded one of the most pitiful sights Sopron had ever seen up to that day. It was enough to break the heart of anyone with an ounce of compassion to see small children holding on to their mother's hand, eyes darting fearfully, shuffling their little feet as fast as they could to keep up with the adults. Arriving at the storage building, they were all thrown into large empty rooms to wait for a final inspection before deportation. In separate groups men and women were stripped naked and thoroughly searched for hidden money and jewelry, a process that took six days without civilized accommodations. People slept on straw thrown on the floor and ate what they brought with them. Their condition was worse than the Jews held back in the city for forced labor service; they, too, were kept in miserable conditions and were often kicked around and beaten for no reason at all, but at least they had a cot to sleep on and a warm meal to eat.

July 5 marked the day when the "death trains," mere cattle cars jammed with the ill-fated victims, started to roll out of the train station in the direction of Auschwitz. With hands pushed through narrow openings people waved their final good-byes to the place where they were born and raised, to the city they loved and served, and to the people they had known all their lives, no different from themselves except for their creed.

As if to remind the good citizens of Sopron that times were changing, Nazi flags were on display all over the city. They flew on every governmental and public building and hung at the entrance of each military compound, even at museums and the theater. Although not mandatory, all higher-ranking city officials were encouraged to wear the despised red armbands with the swastika emblem, and adopt the "Heil Hitler" raised-arm salute to express their solidarity with the Nazis. Most people ignored both, and Jeno declared at home that he'd rather have his arm cut off than submit to using the loathsome greeting. And he never did.

The change was noticeable in schools too. Old history books were re-written to glorify German heroism and the victories and achievements of the Germanic people. Emphasis was placed on the fellowship between Hungary and Germany, and how their development and fate had intertwined throughout the centuries. Reference to British, French, and American history was minimized or completely altered. Karl Marx, a German philosopher-economist, and Friedrich Engels, a German socialist theorist, who collaborated in writing the Communist Manifesto in 1848, became despicable Jewish revolutionaries, if mentioned at all. Russia, with its Bolshevik system, was the ultimate evil, bent on forcing the world to accept and live under the dictates of Communist ideology. The teaching of English or French as a second language ceased. In literature, previously mandatory readings from the work of the literary giants of Russia,

England, and America were no longer required, and as for music, Mendelssohn, Offenbach, and Chopin, along with all Russian composers, were banned from play lists.

With the occupation, all efforts on the part of the former government to negotiate with the West came to a halt, and the Allied air attacks began in earnest. So far Sopron was spared, but as American bombers on missions from Italian bases to target important German junctions, military installations, or industrial facilities involved in war production regularly flew over Sopron's airfield, they often dropped leaflets written in Hungarian. Their message was clear: by tolerating the German occupation, Hungary's leaders were condemning the country to the same fate as awaited Germany. They warned that the longer they continued to support them, the more severe their punishment would be.

In early summer the city's civilian population received instructions on what to do in case of air raids. Drills were conducted with mandatory attendance for men, blackout was instituted and strictly enforced by local vigilantes, and alarm squads were organized to ensure that when the sirens sounded everyone caught on the street reached a designated public bomb shelter. Hundreds of volunteers were trained to give first aid, and other detachments formed for rescue operations, some to clear away debris at bombed-out sites, others to handle the injured and dead.

All was in state of readiness but when the bombs did not fall on Sopron, adherence to air raid regulations slackened and people went about their business ignoring the alarms. Whenever the Viennese radio, which had better reception in Sopron than Budapest, interrupted its regular program with the familiar *Achtung, Achtung, Eine Luftlage Meldung* airfield alert, an announcement that was soon followed by the shrieking sound of sirens, instead of rushing to shelters people just stood looking up at the sky, counting the planes. Judging by the size of the fleet they would guess whether the mission was going to be a serious one or just a minor harassment, and later on, by listening to the sound of explosions, they could even tell where the bombing was taking place: if it was loud, the Americans were hitting nearby Winerneustadt; if it was a distant murmur, the bombs were falling on Vienna. A sense of false security took hold of Sopron, that regardless of the threatening leaflets, the city was safe from destruction and somehow would escape the horrors of air raids.

Then on July 20th came the news of Hitler's attempted assassination. The confusion among German authorities that followed gave Horthy the chance to quickly dismiss the German-installed prime minister and call for a secret meeting with top-level cabinet members to discuss the possibility of a separate armistice. Disagreement and indecision about whom to approach prevailed until finally, on September 22, 1944 the Regent decided to seek out the Allies in Italy and present his proposed peace agreement to them. The West, however, turned him down again, insisting that Hungary must deal with Moscow. Left with no other choice but to turn to the Soviets, a hurriedly chosen armistice delegation was secreted out of the country to deliver Horthy's letter to Marshal Stalin. It was presented to him on October 1, and on the 11th a preliminary armistice agreement was signed.

Four days later, on October 15 at 1 PM the Regent went on the radio and addressing the nation declared his intention to withdraw from the Axis:

> . . . Today it is obvious to any sober-minded person that the German Reich has lost the war. . . . I decided to safeguard Hungary's honour even against her former ally, . . . [who] instead of supplying the promised military help, meant in the end to rob the Hungarian nation of its greatest treasure, its freedom and independence. I informed a representative of the German Reich that we are about to conclude a military armistice with our former enemies and to cease all hostilities against them. . . . [5*]

The announcement did not come as a surprise to Hitler; the German intelligence had discovered the Regent's plan to surrender even before the peace delegation was dispatched to Moscow and immediately advised the Fuhrer. Without delay he began preparations to replace Horthy with Ferenc Szalasi, the leader of the extremist Hungarian Arrow Cross Party, who was living at German headquarters ever since Horthy ordered his arrest in August 1944. Kept under their protection he had been groomed to take over the government at the appropriate time, which was now at hand. To ensure a relatively smooth transition, the Nazis had a plan. On the same day of the broadcast they set a trap to kidnap Horthy's younger son, Miklos Horthy, Jr., and use him as a bargaining chip to force the Regent to abdicate. During the attack the young Horthy was wounded and several of his guards were killed, but they succeeded in capturing him. When the Regent learned that his son was in German hands and kept in the Mauthausen concentration camp near the city of Linz in Austria, he knew he had no choice. With his son's life in the balance, he signed the resignation and surrendered control to the Nazi puppet Szalasi. According to the official statement, Horthy "voluntarily" placed himself under German "protection," when in fact he was kept under house arrest in Bavaria until the end of the war.

When Horthy ended his broadcast the Nazis immediately took possession of the radio station and refuted his proclamation. Szalasi was quickly installed, calling himself The Leader of the Nation (*Nemzetvezetö*), and with him now in power, his Arrow Cross gang immediately unleashed a new wave of political persecutions. The pro-Horthy military commanders, including Sandor Zachar, were taken into custody and kept in a hotel under house arrest for several weeks. The Bishop of Veszprem, Jozsef Mindszenty, was also arrested for speaking out against the legitimacy of Szalasi's leadership, and when a former opposition leader, Endre Bajcsy-Zsilinkszky, and several others plotted to overthrow the Szalasi regime, they were caught and later executed at Sopron-Kohida.

Extreme right-wing mobs roamed the streets of Budapest, targeting Jews, even those living in the hitherto safe, internationally protected ghettos. During the next four months, until the end of the Siege of Budapest on February 13,

---

5 * Admiral Nicholas Horthy: *Memoirs,* Appendice 1, page 321

1945, they dragged between 10,000 to 15,000 Jews to the bank of the Danube and shot them into the icy water. Another 30,000 were herded toward Vienna, forced to march some 135 miles on foot in the dead of winter. Most of them died either on the road or later in death camps.

Meanwhile, the Red Army broke across Hungary's eastern Carpathian border, advancing steadily toward Budapest. For lack of weapons and without the promised German support of air cover and heavy artillery, especially anti-tank guns, resistance by the Hungarian forces was easily crushed, and by December the Russians were closing in on the capital. Evacuation of a million civilians was impossible, but Szalasi and his Arrow Cross government managed to flee to Sopron, the last bastion that still offered relative safety.

On the heels of the government came a large number of German troops and armored units, an indication that the Nazis meant to hold the city before the Russians could cross the border and carry the war into German soil. They took up position in the Loever, where the entire area was cleared of civilians; even former residents were barred from entering under the threat of death. Fear quickly spread that such military buildup would expose Sopron to heavy defensive fighting and possibly Allied bombings, evaporating hopes that the city would escape the war unscathed.

The presence of the Nazi puppet government backed by German army units brought rapid changes to civilian life in Sopron. As first priority, all higher-ranking officials were replaced with trusted Szalasi followers and everyone working for the government was required to take a mandatory oath of allegiance. There was no question in anybody's mind what would happen to those who refused. Left with no choice, Jeno, as so many of his colleagues, had to compromise by mouthing the required words while silently cursing Szalasi and the Nazis. Even after the swearing-in, only those who were known to be ardent supporters of the Arrow Cross government were trusted enough to work in the city. Others, including Jeno, were transferred to isolated border villages and were given insignificant assignments to type up reports, make inventories of confiscated goods, and the like. Every working day in the dead of winter Jeno walked the three-mile stretch to his cubbyhole of an office in Agfalva, the same place where back in 1921 he had fought in an armed skirmish to beat back the Austrians from taking possession of Sopron.

Quality of life also fell to a new low. Shortages became rampant, not only of food but of other necessities, as well. Even lead pencils were hard to come by. With the Germans taking everything first, it was simply impossible to satisfy the needs of civilians, especially with the tremendous influx of refugees. Thousands of tattered and exhausted, fearful people, carrying but a few belongings, streamed into Sopron, swelling the city's population from its normal 38-40,000 inhabitants to 130,000. To accommodate close to 90,000 homeless people the city first used the vacated Jewish homes and now empty ghetto to cram several families into each apartment, but when that was not enough, they forced the local residents to take in refugees, which created nothing but friction and discontent.

Although schools opened in September, by November students were sent home on a "coal vacation" of undetermined length. Lack of coal, however, was not the only reason. It was increasingly difficult to hold the children's attention when they were coming to school already tired and sleepy from huddling in the cellar during nighttime air-raid alarms. Conducting classes became unsafe when they were frequently interrupted by the sound of sirens signaling possible air attack. Each time students had to be herded down into shelters, a task not easily accomplished in an orderly fashion when classrooms designed for twenty grew double in size with the newly arrived refugees. These uprooted children caused further problems by creating panic during the alarm; they were greatly afraid, having lived through air attacks already before fleeing their homes.

Schools closing their doors, however, did not stay empty. Most were converted to makeshift hospitals to treat slightly wounded soldiers, although with the front drawing closer by the day, soon they were forced to accept even the mortally wounded.

It always fell to Ilonka to keep track of all the birthdays and name days of relatives and friends, and so at the beginning of December she reminded Sárika not to forget Mrs. Visnyei's birthday coming up on Wednesday the 6th; she would be fifty-seven, and being her confirmation sponsor, it was only proper to congratulate her with a bouquet of flowers. For that day, however, Sárika had other plans, and offered to visit Mrs. Visnyei on the Sunday before; she would attend Mass at the church near her place, then go and see her. She had too much to do on Wednesday: first, she must prepare for a home-study session she'd hold for several of her schoolmates coming over to the house in the afternoon, then later in the evening, being St. Nicholas Day, she'd repeat her last year's performance as the much awaited bishop.

Mrs. Visnyei was fond of Sárika and was happy to see her on Sunday. She was always kind to her, buying her little presents, but this time she brought out her jewelry box and, after selecting a gorgeous emerald and diamond ring, put it on Sárika's finger. It was an early Christmas present, she said, since she might not be here by then. Conditions were getting so bad in the city that she was making arrangements to stay with friends in the country until things would improve.

Wednesday, December 6, 1944, started out as a crisp clear day without a cloud in the sky. Ilonka was busy in the kitchen preparing their mid-day meal, while Eta was carrying a stack of plates to set the table. The two younger boys, six-year-old Istvan and little Ochie, not quite two, were chasing each other in and out of the room, almost knocking her over. They only stopped when she yelled at them to behave, or the Krampusz—the hellish servant of St. Nicholas—would get them tonight.

As the weather was exceptionally beautiful, the backyard of the three-story apartment building next to Ilonka's was full of people chatting and enjoying the sun. Sárika, too, went outside, and was standing on a wooden structure they used for beating carpets, talking over the fence with the neighbor girls, when her father arrived home for the noon break and saw her.

"I told you not to climb on that rickety stand, Sárika, it's not safe!" he chided her with a stern voice. "If you must talk to your friends, go over there. Ask your mother; perhaps there is still time before lunch."

She got Ilonka's permission, but she was told to take the baby with her. She had too much to do and the toddler was giving her a hard time. Eta must have scared him with the devil, because he was crying and clinging to Ilonka, his little arms reaching up, begging to be picked up. He stopped his whining only when Sárika held out his coat, promising to take him out to play.

They were in the neighbors' court when the sirens began to scream. Ignoring it, she and her friends continued gossiping with an occasional glance at the children playing near them. No one paid the slightest attention to the alert, not even when the planes appeared above. They were used to seeing them passing overhead on their way to hammer Vienna or some other place over the border. A few men looked up after noticing that the sound from the airplanes was markedly louder than usual and had a much deeper resonance, but the rest remained indifferent. All conversation stopped, however, when the droning increased and became a roar, drawing all eyes to see the planes flying above in perfect V formation with long silvery contrails trailing behind. Still, no one sensed danger, not even when the planes changed course, and instead of continuing toward Austria, made a sweeping turn. Only when they suddenly swooped down with a deafening noise did alarm set it. At the sound of the first ear-shattering explosion people finally woke up and began running in utter confusion. Grabbing children and pushing and shoving, they squeezed through the door leading down to the basement, crushing anyone who stumbled on the stairs. In a futile attempt to create some sort of order someone tried to stop the panic but was swept down the steps with the rest.

Sárika, with little Ochie in her arms, was caught in the middle of the hysterical stampede, making it impossible to cut loose and run home. Jammed between adults she hardly knew, and without anyone looking out for them, they were dragged and shoved down to the cellar until she finally was able to get a foothold and steady herself. They stood in total darkness as the lights flickered and gave out. Scared, yet finding courage to comfort the crying baby, she pressed his head into her neck, all the while soothing him that everything would be fine; the lights would come back and they would be going home. It would soon be over.

Except it was not. The attack continued, with planes coming wave after wave, dropping bombs weighing 500 pounds in seemingly systematic order. In sheer terror, they listened to the sound of explosions coming ever closer, shaking the building to its core, stirring up dust and raining down broken plaster, and then, just as the detonations began to fade into the distance, bringing relief that the danger had passed, the cycle would start over again. Choking and coughing from breathing the dirty air, their heads and shoulders covered with loose debris, people huddled in the dark, holding onto loved ones, some crying, most of them praying.

Sárika, too, was praying silently, asking God to keep the bombs from falling on them or on her family next door. When the explosions got terrifyingly loud, and the rolling and shaking of the building was at its worst, the thought that her home might be in ruins and her family could be dying, buried alive in that very moment, was almost too much for her to bear. With eyes squeezed shut, she forced the dreadful image out of her mind. It couldn't, it must not, happen to her family, her beautiful mother, her beloved father, and yes, she loved her sister, too! She started praying again. *God, please, if you would just direct your eyes toward them, look at them, see them, I know they would be safe!*

Then suddenly, blissfully, they heard the high-pitched release sound of the sirens, signaling the end of the attack. In that instant people began to push again, groping in the dark toward the exit, not knowing what they would find once out in the open. Would they still have a roof over their head? When Sárika emerged from the cellar, her first anxious glance over the fence told her that her family was safe. The house stood, although the windows were blown out and there were holes in the roof. By the time she reached the street her father was already running toward them, his arms wide open, his face a mixture of extreme worry and immense relief. The next minute he swept them up, cuddling his little son in one arm, the other protectively around Sárika's shoulder. And in the security of that embrace she buried her head deep in his coat to mute the great sobs that broke from her throat. Her ordeal was over. She was safe. She was home.

No word could describe what awaited people once they crawled out from their hiding places. Most of the inner city was in complete ruin. The hour-long carpet-bombing did not spare the residential area that included churches, schools, and historical buildings; they were hit with equal force as the railroads and supply depots. Fires were raging out of control at several areas, as firefighters were unable to get through the streets covered with debris or torn up by gaping craters where bombs missed their targets. Where the water main broke, water gushed high as geysers, flooding the streets and causing further delay in the rescue operation. Everywhere electric lines dangled dangerously loose or hung tangled up in tree branches. Here and there dead horses could be seen still hitched to overturned carts, and worse, dead people, some with torn limbs, as they lay on the spot where death caught up with them. A heavy layer of dust, mixed with the acrid smell of smoke, hung over the entire city.

The destruction was overwhelming. Both railroad stations were reduced to rubble, rails ripped up and twisted, boxcars burning, some with the charred bodies of wounded soldiers trapped inside. The row of houses near the South Station where Jeno had considered buying a home was razed to the ground. Part of the Customs building at the Western Railroad Station had collapsed and was burning. The 14th Century St. George Church was still standing but was heavily damaged, its tower blown to pieces and the beautiful stained glass windows all but shards. In the next street Eta's school and the church adjacent to it also suffered considerable structural damage. Along Varkerulet Boulevard, every other shop or apartment was a pile of rubbish or near collapse. At one section an old frontier bastion hidden for centuries behind the back wall of the fallen building came into view.

Away from the inner city the damage was somewhat less severe, although the roof of the hospital caved in and the museum's sidewall was torn open, exposing empty rooms. The director had the good sense to store their priceless treasures in underground vaults. The back of Sárika's school was hit, too, but from the street the building seemed in good standing.

The devastation, almost an apocalyptic sight, stunned the grief-stricken citizenry. Some people just stood around, bewildered, others rolled up their sleeves ready to help those who lost everything and were frantically rummaging through the wreckage, pulling out pots and pans, bits and pieces of clothing, anything that could be salvaged. Families separated when the bombing began were running from place to place, frantically searching for missing loved ones, not knowing if they would find them dead or alive.

Faced with the enormity of the disaster, the various organized brigades swung into action. The first priority, of course, was saving lives, and within the hour after the relief sounded, groups of men trained in rescue operations were on the scene. They were furiously shoveling the waist-high debris to reach those trapped in cellars below, while others were busy setting up makeshift first-aid stations to treat the injured as they were pulled from the shelters. Another group had the sad task of carrying the dead to designated places, where still others began identifying the victims. Relatives were carrying their dead to the cemetery, but the bodies that no one picked up by the next morning were buried in shallow, quickly dug community graves at various burial sites throughout the city, each location marked and officially recorded with the names or other identifiable signs of the individuals buried there. The dead soldiers brought to St. Mihaly cemetery were also put in a common grave. Altogether, an estimated 310 people died that day, not counting the 140 who died later of injuries.

Most locals rendered homeless by the bombing could look to relatives to take them in, but for the refugees, shelters had to be found. Churches and charitable organizations that escaped serious damage opened their doors and took in as many people as they could. The St. Benedictine Church, the largest parish in Sopron, was relatively unharmed, and they had rooms in their school dormitory, but only a few became available for victims. The rest were taken over by members of the puppet government, whose headquarters were destroyed during the attack. The rag-tag number of desperate refugees shared accommodations with luminaries such as the Ministers of Finance, Transportation, and Internal Affairs, two former Prime Ministers, and other dignitaries. But these bigwigs didn't stay for long. They did not feel safe remaining in the inner city and hurriedly set up government operations in the surrounding Loevers, occupying the Hotel Loever and taking possession of private villas around it.

The option to move to a safer place, however, was not open to the ordinary citizens. Those lucky enough to have a roof over their head scurried to find material to replace missing shingles, stuff up holes in the ceilings and cover blown-out windows. Anything would do—bits of wood, blankets, or glued together cardboards—to keep the cold draft out until they could be boarded up. Fortunately, Jeno's house was in fairly good condition, considering that the military compound across the street received two hits and a historical building next to the little park behind their home was also bombed out. The windows, of course, were gone, and several large cobblestones flew through their roof, but all in all they felt lucky to have survived the bombing with such minor damage.

Inside the house, dust and plaster covered everything. Ilonka had no time to cover the food when the bombs started to explode, and their dinner was ruined. The dishes Eta set on the dinner table lay scattered on the floor in broken pieces. Many of Ilonka's treasured lead-crystal vases, bon-boniers, and Herendi figurines displayed throughout the house were also broken or damaged. With profound sadness she went from room to room, picking up the pieces, hoping that some could be glued back together, when her glance fell on a framed photo lying on the floor, its glass cracked. Through the jagged edges Sárika's face smiled up at her, disguised by a white beard and wearing a tall mitre. It was taken exactly a year ago when she played St. Nicolas. Tears sprang to her eyes as she lifted it up. There would be no St. Nicolas calling on the children tonight. Then suddenly a chill ran down her back. St. Nicolas wouldn't be coming, but his devil companion had surely been here today.

Stunned as they were, they found strength to clean up the debris and patch up the windows before Jeno ran to check on their friends, the Varosys. Thank God, he found them shaken but fine, their place in relatively good shape. While there, he learned about the devastation in the inner city and his thoughts immediately turned to Sári Visnyei who lived next to the St. George Church and whose birthday was today. Returning home, he took Eta with him and rushed to the site. What greeted them was utter chaos and despair. A heavy bomb hit her apartment building, piling debris from the collapsed three-story structure on top of the cellar and igniting a raging fire that left everyone trapped under the burning rubble with little hope for survival. The blazing fire made it impossible for the rescue team to start digging, forcing them to stand by and wait until the firemen could come and put out the flames.

Relatives and friends arriving at the scene had to be restrained from charging into the fire. Hearing a warning shot stopped them momentarily, until they realized it was not someone trying to hold them back; the sound came from the shelter below! Mayhem followed. The image of the trapped victims signaling that they were alive was too much to bear. In desperation, people ran up to the edge of the smoldering pile of rubble, pulling away broken bits of bricks and stones with their bare hands. They were angrily shouting at the men still waiting for the fire truck, demanding to do something, anything, when another shot was heard. It sent a hysterical woman rushing at the rescuers, screaming that people down there were killing each other!

With daylight growing dim and the fire still burning out of control, all hope of finding a way to save the unfortunate victims began to fade. There were no more shots or any other signals from below. In the quiet only a priest's vice could be heard, praying for a miracle that never came. By the time the firefighters put out the flames it was too late; everyone in the cellar was dead, suffocated. No autopsy was needed to see from their distorted faces that the cause of death was lack of oxygen. After identification, Jeno claimed Mrs. Visnyei's body and arranged for her burial.

When finally night fell and the children were put to bed, Jeno and Ilonka, dead tired and emotionally drained, sat by the kerosene lamp, stunned at what happened to their city. Listening to him as he described the ordeal of seeing the body of their friend pulled from the cellar, Ilonka thought about fate, and how strangely it affected two lives so close to her heart: saving one and condemning the other. Sári Visnyei was making plans to leave the city, but her time ran out and now she was dead, while Sárika's life, by deciding to visit her on Sunday instead of today, has been spared.

During the afternoon, while rescue operations at Mrs.Visnyei's place stalled, Jeno and Eta left the site for a short time to check on the apartment building where Eta's boyfriend, Laszlo Kontra, or Latzi as he was called, rented a room. They met during the last days of summer, and it was on account of Sárika. She left home to enter a swimming competition, but when the weather suddenly turned cool, Ilonka sent Eta with some towels and a cover-up to keep her sister warm. Latzi was one of the judges and was handing out the second prize to Sárika when Eta arrived, exactly the same moment when Cupid was raising his bow in search of victims. If Eta was taken at first sight with the handsome, athletic young man, it was no surprise that, caught up in the unstoppable power of first love, she soon fell head over heels in love with him. As they began to see each other regularly, she learned that he was from Budapest, and was in his senior year studying forest engineering in Sopron.

On the day of the bombing Latzi was out of town for a few days, and Eta wanted to see how his place had fared during the attack. The building, being close to the heavily bombed Western Train Station, was bound to have suffered damages, and sure enough, they found half the facade crumbling. His rented room on the second floor was wide open, exposing furniture, bedding, and most enticingly, his new bicycle. Knowing that it wouldn't be there tomorrow, Jeno and Eta managed to climb the stairs, gathered up his personal belongings, and carried them over to the customs buildings where Jeno could lock them up in one of the storage rooms.

When Latzi got back the next day and came to see Eta, he was relieved to find her and her family safe, but was thoroughly disheartened that looters broke into his place and cleared out everything, taking even his toiletries. Without saying a word, Eta left the room briefly and came back holding his toothbrush. At least his possessions were safe, but he was still homeless. He didn't know that Jeno and Ilonka had already decided to offer him a spot in their home, a folding cot in the front room, which he eagerly accepted. It was a bit drafty and cold, but so was their own bedroom with the blown-out windows poorly patched and not enough coal to heat every room. Besides the kitchen only the family room was kept warm, and when it came time to retire, everyone took turns holding up pillows and comforters against the porcelain-tile stove, then ran to slip into the waiting ice-cold sheets.

Erzsi, the new maid Ilonka had hired only six months earlier, was so badly shaken by the bombing that she immediately packed her things and declared that six oxen could not keep her from returning to her village. She was not the only one to run. When the railroads were repaired enough for the trains to start rolling, an exodus began. The stations were jammed day and night, people sleeping on the platform, afraid to leave the spot for fear of missing the first available ride. The trains were packed like sardines, including the steps, where people hung eight to ten deep, grabbing onto handrails.

After most of the major emergency work was done, people turned to speculation. What purpose did the ruinous destruction of the inner city serve? What possible interest could the Allies have in old residential apartments, churches, and museums? These were not military targets! There could be only one explanation: the Nazis used the center district for secret operations, perhaps directing movements on the approaching front, or transmitting important information to Germany. The theory proved correct. When the government left the city and set up headquarters in the Loevers, the American bombers returned, this time targeting nothing but the Loevers. The accuracy of their mission gave strong evidence that an effective anti-German underground was at work, giving exact intelligence to the Allies regarding the movements of the hated Nazis and their puppet government. Unfortunately, forty civilians lost their lives during this second air raid on December 18.

The Germans, of course, were not blind either; they knew what brought on the attacks. In retaliation they arrested the chief of police and a score of others suspected of working for the underground. They rounded up educators, students, and workers, even priests, foremost among them the Bishop Jozsef Mindszenty, already targeted earlier for criticizing the leadership of Szalasi and vehemently opposing the deportations. Some, like Mindszenty, were kept at headquarters, but most were marched off to the stone caverns of Sopron-Kohida and dragged in front of a hastily formed military court on various charges, ranging from spying and treason to spreading Communist propaganda. On-the-spot executions followed, with the bodies dumped in shallow dugouts near the site.

Since the Loevers were declared off limits to civilians, obtaining a Christmas tree was quite difficult, but Jeno managed to bring one home from Agfalva, where he now worked. Ilonka and the girls decorated it with ornaments, tinsel and angel hair, even with some traditional foil-wrapped candy she bought on the black market, and when they finished, the tree looked as beautiful as any in happier times. Standing around it on that Christmas Eve, their prayers carried a passionate plea asking the Lord to bless and protect them in the increasingly dangerous days ahead, bring the horrors of war to an end and stop the bleeding of their beloved country.

In spite of the shortages and difficulties in finding gifts for the children, they were not left wanting. During the praying and caroling Sárika's attention was immediately drawn to a gorgeous burgundy coat with a dark beaver collar and matching cuffs draped over a chair near the tree. Burning with impatience to find out if it was meant for her or Eta, she caught her mother's eye at the piano, and raising an eyebrow rolled her eyes toward the coat. When Ilonka nodded slightly, she knew it was hers and ran to try it on as soon as they were done with the singing. She thanked her parents profusely, saying it was the best ever gift she received in her entire life, her very first grown-up piece of clothing. She was thoroughly enamored by her beautiful coat, touching the silky fur and imagining the impression she'd make parading in it in front of her friends. She would go to Mass twice tomorrow to make sure that all of them had the chance to notice her elegant new coat.

The day after Christmas Ilonka was opening the kitchen window to let in some fresh air when a truck pulled in front of the house and to her amazement, she saw the entire Riedl family piling out of the vehicle. They had left their home in Esztergom near Budapest that morning and came to seek refuge with Jeno's family. Laszlo, wearing an officer's uniform, apologized for descending on them so unexpectedly, but their decision to leave was made in such a hurry that left no time to write. They believed until the last minute that the decisive battle sealing Hungary's fate would take place around the city of Debrecen to the east, and that a Russian victory there would convince the Germans to give up Hungary and leave. It would have allowed them and thousands of other people to remain in their homes and would have spared heavily bombed Budapest from further destruction and unnecessary bloodshed. It was not to be. Hitler insisted on making a stand at Budapest, declaring it a fortress city, to be defended to the last man. He made it clear that withdrawal was not an option.

The siege began on December 25, with the Russians closing in on the capital and cutting off all German supply lines. Entering the city from the suburbs around Pest, they advanced steadily, halting only at the Danube, where the Germans blew up all eight bridges. The Russians were stranded on the Pest side, while the Germans remained entrenched in Buda. Facing each other, they prepared for an ultimate showdown. In the ensuing battles the outcome hung in the air, one side gaining one day, only to be beaten back the next. By February the Red Army was able to cross the river and, seeing the futility in prolonging the fight, a group of Hungarian officers attempted to surrender. The plot, however, was discovered, its leaders executed, and the fighting continued with tremendous loss of life, both military and civilian. People were living in damp, freezing cellars, daring to leave only to scavenge for food and bring back some water. Sickness and starvation set in that lasted throughout the siege, a dreadful two months before the jaws of the Russian vise finally clamped closed on February 13.

One reason the Riedls wound up in Sopron was that Laszlo, a reservist recently called to active duty, was sent there to wait for further orders. He would be quartered in the casern across the street from Jeno's house, so they only needed a place for his wife and two younger children. His son Lasko, studying in Sopron, had only a small rented room, not big enough to take them in, and Jeno and Ilonka, of course, opened their home to them without the slightest hesitation; it was only a question of where to put them. The best solution seemed to have Latzi, Eta's boyfriend, sleep in the kitchen—he didn't mind, since it was the warmest place in the house—and move the Riedls into the front room. Conditions were crowded, but it kept away the authorities scouting the city for extra room to house the homeless. It was infinitely better to live with relatives than with total strangers.

Besides personal belongings the newcomers brought with them some non-perishable food, sacks of coal, and several bolts of homespun textiles from Mrs. Riedl's home-run business that proved to be an excellent item for bartering. It took a few days to settle in and get used to each other's company, but after that life in the household continued without much friction between the two families. They shared the main meals by pooling together their rationed allowances and using the food each family had. Ilonka supplied potatoes, carrots, and onions stored in the cellar and some of the milk she received for the baby and Istvan, while the Riedls had flour, and a little sugar and lard. Occasionally Ilonka's former maid Erzsi knocked on the door, bringing a few eggs, a crock of real butter, and just before the holidays a goose for their Christmas dinner, a rare treat for most city folks celebrating that festive day in 1944.

Knowing that a peaceful coexistence required patience and tolerance, everyone tried to keep tempers from flaring, especially when the children got too boisterous, or the budding romance between Eta and Latzi got a little too schmaltzy. The only one who seemed to be thoroughly unhappy with the prevailing circumstances was the younger Riedl boy, Erno. The beautiful, athletic teenager, not yet sixteen, was annoyed with being cooped up in a house full of women and children, unable to make friends with other boys of his age. Bursting with boundless energy and no outlet to release it, he became withdrawn and would sit by the radio all day, listening to announcements of glorious victories and the boastings of an incredible new wonder weapon that was just a step away from being unleashed to annihilate the enemy. There were no defeats, only temporary withdrawals necessary to regroup and redirect the fighting forces. Total victory was near. These broadcasts aimed to whip up patriotic sentiments in naïve and easily influenced youngsters, urging them to come to the defense of their country against the barbaric Russian forces. They played on their conscience using never-ending propaganda that it was up to them to save their mothers and sisters from being ravaged by brutal Asiatic hordes. There was no let-up in trying to convince them that it was their duty to take up arms and join the brave men already in uniform in their heroic effort to achieve final victory.

These messages had a profound effect on the boy. Every able man should be in uniform! He even confronted his brother, how come he was sitting at home instead of fighting the war? It was simple, Lasko explained. All university students were exempted from military duty on the ground that they represented the future brainpower of the nation. They would be sorely needed when the war was over to help rebuild the ruined country. They could volunteer as reservists in the National Guards (*Nemzetörség*), an armed paramilitary unit created to safeguard public safety and help to maintain civilian order in emergencies, but they would never be sent to the front to die on the battlefield.

Then on New Year's Eve, as the two families sat down to their meager holiday meal, everyone noticed that Erno was only pushing the food around his plate, hardly taking a bite. He was nervous and had no appetite, and for good reason. He knew he could not stall any longer confessing that he had enlisted in the army and would be leaving almost immediately.

His parents scolded him not to joke about such things; they had enough problems as it was. He was not yet sixteen, the minimum age to sign up—except in some paramilitary youth brigades where boys as young as thirteen were accepted. But when he pulled out papers to prove that he was telling the truth, all hell broke loose.

"This cannot be! They can't take you, you are underage!" his father was out of his seat, shouting, "unless you . . ." His half-finished sentence was left hanging in the air as Erno, lowering his head and not daring to look him in the eye, admitted that he had forged his birth certificate.

Everyone sat in stunned silence, staring at the boy. Was he crazy? How could he be so foolish? Then his mother was on her feet, wagging a finger in front of his face. "Oh no, you are not going anywhere! Your father will tell them that you lied and falsified your papers. Once we prove it, they have to excuse you and that will be the end of it." She then turned to her husband, expecting confirmation. "You are in the military, you can do something for this stupid boy—anything to get him out of this mess—can't you?"

But he couldn't; it was too late. He checked the order twice, there was no doubt; the boy was to report for duty in two days. Still refusing to believe it, Erzsebet snatched the paper out of his hand, but after glancing at the January 2 date, she collapsed in her seat, sobbing uncontrollably. There was not enough time to intervene.

The helpless father now turned on his son, venting his anger and frustration.

"How could you do this to us, to your mother? It's because you are listening to that stupid radio all the time! How could you believe that idiotic propaganda about victories? Victories, hah! Nothing but lies! And you, you believe them, when even a blind man could see that the war is lost! Do you realize what you have done, what you are getting into? You were safe here, together with your family, had a roof over your head and food to eat; all you had to do was wait a little longer! But no, you had to throw it all away and play the big hero, and for what? For nothing! You'll be nothing but fodder for the Nazis! Remember that when you are staring at a Russian with his machine gun pointed at your head, and you left without a reliable weapon to shoot him first! I know what kind of equipment the soldiers are given today. Nothing but junk, guns that jam before they have a chance to pull the trigger. Oh, you silly, ignorant boy! I should kill you now, at least we'd know where you are buried."

Suddenly he stopped shouting; it was useless, it wouldn't accomplish anything. The sad fact remained that they most likely would lose their son. He sank back into his chair, gripping the armrest until his knuckles turned white. Resting his head on the back of the chair he squeezed his eyes shut to arrest the angry tears building behind his lids.

Erno sat motionless, looking down to avoid the stares. His brother Lasko quietly asked him if there was a chance to change his mind. He could go into hiding, as so many others deserting the army were doing. It was only a matter of weeks before the war would be over. Even those still in uniform talked among family and friends that to continue the fight was sheer lunacy, all was lost, and no magical secret weapon could turn things around. Lasko pleaded with him to stay, if for no other reason but for the sake of their mother. He did not have to go; they'd find a hiding place for him.

Erno admitted that he might have made a mistake by enlisting, but it was too late now, he would have to go. It was the honorable thing to do. He was not a coward like those who were running away. And when he said that deserters should be shot or hanged, his brother threw up his hands. The gullible young fool was mindlessly mouthing the garbage he heard on the radio.

Ilonka and the girls immediately brought out the knitting basket and feverishly began to knit woolen socks, gloves, and scarves, hoping they would help to keep him warm at the front. A day later when he left, he carried the ardent prayers of all who loved him, but the Zachars would never see him again.

As the war became more desperate the Szalasi regime changed the official salutation, thinking it would bolster the sagging spirit of the population. The stiffly raised arm gesture of the Nazi salute remained the same, but instead of "Heil Hitler," they shouted "*Kitartás*" (Perseverance)! It was meant to encourage the citizenry to stand firm and keep faith until victory was achieved, but instead, people interpreted it to hold out until the Germans would be defeated.

The word, however, held most meaning for the Jews held back from the summer deportation and used for hard labor. If they could only keep going for a few more weeks, they would be safe! When first selected for work these men were in good physical condition, strong enough to dig ditches and clear the roads, but by now they were down to skin and bones, their eyes sunken, faces vacant, dragging themselves clad in threadbare jackets that could not keep out the icy wind. Those who had shoes, however torn, were the lucky ones compared to the poor devils whose feet were wrapped in rags fastened with a string, constantly shuffling to keep from freezing, while the guards shouted at them, howling with laughter, "You must be enjoying this fresh air after the stinking ghetto!"

Still, as long as they could stand they were ordered to haul dirt to fill the open craters, shovel snow after a storm, remove debris and pick up and bury the dead after an air attack. If someone lagged behind, the young Volksbund and Arrow Cross gangsters immediately struck them with clubs or poked them in the ribs with their gun barrels, taunting them, “Take this, Mr. Jew Banker!” and kept them moving with similar mean-spirited sarcastic remarks.

Some bystanders watching the scene joined in, egging on the thugs, but most just stood in silence, pity in their hearts, but afraid to speak out against the brutality. Stripped of all human dignity and terrified to say a word under the threat of beating, perseverance was indeed these Jews’ only hope.

There were yet some other Jews still in the city who were exempt from deportations and forced labor, at least so far. They were treated with more tolerance because they were either of mixed blood or being married to Christian spouses, and were placed in specially created categories patterned after the Nuremberg Laws. These laws defined anyone having three or four Jewish grandparents as racially 100 percent Jewish, or “full Jew,” as were individuals without a drop of Jewish blood, a pure Aryan for example, but who had converted to Judaism, thus declaring themselves to be Jewish. These were all gone, deported during the summer. Those with only two Jewish grandparents, classified as “half Jews” or “first degree Jews,” and people with only one Jewish grandparent, called “quarter Jews” or “second degree Jews,” were given somewhat more lenient consideration.

Later, when the law was extended to prohibit marriage between Christians and Jews to protect racial purity, another set of categories was established for Jews already in mixed marriages. Accordingly, Jewish spouses were divided into two groups, one labeled “privileged,” where the wife was Jewish, and the other “non-privileged,” which applied to Jewish husbands. This division seemed to reverse the Jewish concept that the maternal linage determines who is a Jew, while according to Nazi theories it was the paternal side that defined it.

Most of the privileged Jews, the mixed-blood quarter Jews, and even the half Jews, were not forced to wear the yellow star and were not ordered into ghettos until toward the very end of the war, perhaps because the authorities didn’t want to alienate their Aryan spouses and relatives. The lesser tolerated non-privileged Jews, however, were moved into the ghetto after Szalasi came to power in October, although family members were allowed to visit them and bring them food and other necessities. There they lingered, waiting for an unknown fate that hung on laws, forever shifting, revoked and reinstated, until someone could decide what to do with them. In the end they shared the fate of those taken to Auschwitz a few months earlier.

Sárika’s gym teacher, an Aryan woman who refused to divorce her husband, a Jewish lawyer labeled non-privileged, became one of these victims. The couple had been married for eight years before she gave birth to a son, who was raised in his father’s religion. The boy was about four years old when the persecution against them tightened, and because the mother refused to leave her husband and give up her child, they were all deported. Tragically, she and her son suffered the fate that awaited mothers with young children at arrival in Auschwitz, only her husband survived.

Wanda's mother, a converted Jew married to a Christian, thus a member of the privileged group, fared better. These people were allowed to remain in their homes until March 1945, but then were ordered to report to a building across from the university, originally a mess hall for students. It has been damaged by the bombings, but there was no other lodging available, not after the refugees pouring into Sopron took over the old ghetto. They found the conditions deplorable with the kitchen dismantled, the plumbing out of order, and no heating, either. Only bare walls, boarded up windows, and cement floors greeted the internees, creating a panic from fear of immediate transportation. What would happen to them? Nerves calmed down only when they were told that improvements were under way and that relatives were allowed to bring in bedding, food, clothing, and other limited personal items of hygienic nature to make the people more comfortable.

Armed Arrow Cross guards were on duty day and night, with the Gestapo periodically checking on the detainees. Although only immediate family members were allowed to visit, exceptions were granted for a few priests and clergymen when they appealed for permission to hold religious services for them. After all, many among these people were converted Christians, devout members of parishes and congregations. The poor priests, however, were constantly harassed, taunted and mocked by the guards as Jew lovers, Communists, or even traitors. Why comfort the Jews, when the hospitals were full of wounded soldiers, and so many people were left homeless? Weren't they more deserving to receive spiritual care and kind words from the clergy than these people, who were only pretending to be Christian to save their necks?

A few days before the Russians reached Sopron an order came to empty the ghetto and send these last remaining special Jews to various Austrian and German concentration camps, but this was never carried out. What saved them from certain death was that every train was needed by the Germans themselves to evacuate their troops and war machinery. Although someone issued a new order to put the Jews on the road and march them to the West, in the rush to get all the Germans and members of the Szalasi government out of the country, nobody bothered to follow through. Without directives and the Arrow Cross gangs and the Gestapo in flight, local policemen were put in charge to guard the building and wait for further orders. Many of them were sympathetic from the start to the plight of the victims and looked the other way when relatives sneaked inside under cover of darkness and whisked them to safety.

It seemed that those final weeks brought out the worst in people, especially in those without moral sensibility and lacking tolerance or empathy for their fellow humans. Unfortunately, these were the kind of people who now filled the important positions. Puffed up with arrogance, they wallowed in self-importance for being able to exercise power, something they could never do before. Until now many could only hold low positions, harboring deep resentment against anybody a step above them on the social ladder. Now it was their time to flex their muscles. They were quick to learn that using threats was an easy way to keep people in line. A favorite tactic was to hint that they knew something about them that the authorities would appreciate hearing. Even if people had no idea what that "something" might be, it was enough to keep them intimidated.

Ilonka found herself in such a situation. She was always outspoken and opinionated, and when she saw the drastic changes taking place in the city, she did not make it a secret how she felt about it. And she did it rather loudly. Jeno told her repeatedly to stop making open remarks against the regime and try to keep her voice down even at home; these were dangerous times, someone might overhear what she said and could report her to the authorities, which could put the entire family in danger. With a flip of her wrist and a toss of her head, Ilonka disregarded such nonsense as typical of Jeno, always overcautious, ever expecting the worst. True, she had heard of people turning others in for mouthing off against the Germans, but not here, not in their neighborhood! And so she kept on talking. After her young nephew Erno left, she was telling Mrs. Varga next door that it was all because of Nazi propaganda, how the radio filled the boy's head with stupid ideas, nothing but a deceitful scheme to entice young boys, practically children, to fight and be killed for a hopeless cause. It was a shame he could not wait a little longer! The Russkies were almost at the door and as much as she hated them, she was counting the days until they'd tear down that obnoxious Nazi flag across the street.

Mrs. Varga did not report her, but Ilonka received a stern letter from Erwin Gruber, an activist in the Arrow Cross, living in the apartment at the back of their courtyard. It was addressed to her:

> *Madame,*
>
> *Your anti-Nazi sentiments are well known to me and as much as I am offended by your derogatory comments against our policies and our German friends, in consideration of your five children, and for that reason only, I refrain this time from reporting you. However, I must warn you, if you do not change your attitude and I hear one more of your hateful remarks, I am obliged to go to the authorities. You should concentrate on raising your children to be better citizens than yourself, if you care at all about what their future will be in the new world after we won the war.*
>
> *Erwin Gruber*

The letter was a wake-up call for Ilonka, accomplishing what Jeno could not. It brought home to her that nobody was safe, that a few reckless words reaching the wrong ears could jeopardize survival not just for the individual, but also for the whole family. It was a lesson well learned; it kept her silent for the remaining days of the war, and also in later years, living under the shadow of the Red Star.

As the Russian front drew closer and the war intensified, the wail of sirens became almost constant, interrupting not only daily activities but the nights as well. By the end of February 1945 Jeno and Ilonka had dragged several mattresses and bedding to the cellar, and when the night alarm came they just picked up the sleepy children and carried them down to continue their sleep there. The cellar was cold and damp and miserable, but Ilonka kept from complaining in front of the Grubers, even if Erwin happened to be away. She had nothing against the parents, a quiet couple of solid German background, who kept pretty much to themselves. Although they were already living there when Ilonka and Jeno moved in more than ten years ago, their families didn't mix for lack of common interest. The couple's three sons, between nine and fourteen at the time, were too old to play with Ilonka's small children, and the fact that the Grubers were ardently pro-German and greeted Jeno with "*Guten Tag*" and "*Wie geht es Ihnen*" instead of "Good Day" and "How are you" was enough for him to keep his distance.

By the time the bombing started, only Erwin, their youngest son, was living at home and only because he was ill with tuberculosis. As far as Ilonka knew, the two older boys were married, living elsewhere. She only learned it now, sitting together in the cellar, that the Grubers lost their eldest son fighting on the Russian front, one of the thousands frozen to death at the Don River in the winter of 1942-43. The middle son, who joined the German army in 1943, was serving somewhere on the Western front, but they had not heard from him for months now. That Erwin had to stay home to undergo treatment was regrettable, but they were proud that he could still be an active member of the Arrow Cross Party.

As the three families, the Zachars, Riedls and Grubers, were spending more and more time together in the cavernous cellar, each tried to create a little privacy by taking up a separate corner. Conditions were poor, with hard-packed dirt floor, limited ventilation, and electrical wires strung below the ceiling, but then who thought people would be living there one day when Mr. Flandorffer built his wine cellar? There was one room—Ilonka used it as the laundry room—that had cement floor, running water and good drainage, making the place far better than the overcrowded cellars people shared under three or four-story apartment buildings, not to mention the public shelters.

On February 21 everyone was down in the cellars when, after a short pause between bombings, another air attack hit Sopron. Casualties were lighter this time, but when Jeno read in the paper that only fifteen people were killed, he just stood, shaking his head, wondering how could people become so lethargic about death as to say *only* fifteen people died. In peacetime such death, so many people killed by one occurrence, would have made major headlines, but now, with the dead from the previous bombings hardly buried, news of fifteen more victims did not amount to much.

During this latest attack the German air defense shot down an American plane and captured five of its crewmen. They were all injured, mostly with broken limbs, and were taken to a military hospital but placed in different rooms to prevent any contact with each other. No one among the authorities or at the hospital spoke English, so they brought in a priest, Father Alajos Nemeth, with some limited knowledge of the language, and had him interrogate the prisoners. Of course, they only gave their name, rank, and serial number. Sensing the priest's kindness, one of the airmen named John DeSoto, a Catholic with serious injuries, asked if he would hear his confession. Father Alajos needed permission, and it was granted, but only with the condition that he'd press for more military information. Not trusting him though, a German armed guard was also ordered to stand at the bedside during the confession, not that he knew English, but since English and German were members of the same language family, they hoped he might be able to catch a few familiar sounding words in case the prisoner talked about their mission. The priest kept visiting the boys, giving them cigarettes, even an English book he dug up in the church library, but he got into trouble for that. They accused him of coding secret messages in the book, and he was ordered to stop giving comfort to the enemy. One day he found the Americans gone, taken away, their fate unknown.

Whenever an air raid alert sounded all the wounded soldiers were taken down to the basement either on stretchers, or if they could walk, with the help of nurses. Wearing nothing but a hospital gown and underwear, they were left squatting bare-footed on the cement floor, shivering for hours until the release sounded. As a result, in their rundown condition many of them wound up with severe colds that often turned into pneumonia. Prospect for recovery was dismal with the medicine supply completely exhausted, yet with every passing day more and more injured arriving from the approaching frontline. Doctors and nurses manning the overcrowded makeshift hospitals could offer very little help and began to show apathy, throwing up their hands in utter frustration.

And there was worse to come.

On Sunday morning, March 4, Ilonka had an unexpected visitor, Dr. Kontra, the father of Eta's boyfriend Latzi. He was extremely relieved to see his father at the door, since they had lost contact after the Russians cut off Budapest. Dr. Kontra was a medical doctor currently working in the Ministry of Health and Education, and was now en route to Germany with other members of the Ministry to rescue medical equipment and precious medicine from the grasp of the Soviets. Their group, which included family members, Mrs. Kontra among them, got stranded at the railroad station in Gyor after the Germans took away their locomotive, leaving the rest of the train sidetracked until further transportation could be secured. It gave him enough time to hitch a quick ride to see his son in Sopron, but he would be going back later in the day.

Dr. Kontra had never been in Sopron and it was the first time he had met Eta and her family. Ilonka insisted that he stay for lunch, but since it was still early and the weather was exceptionally beautiful, the young couple and Jeno took him to see a little bit of the city. They were gone only about an hour when the sirens began to wail.

Not again, not now! Ilonka protested. She could not afford to sit in the cellar while the food she was cooking needed constant tending. She asked the Riedls to take the children to the shelter but she remained in the kitchen and continued with her chores. The sound of the first ear shattering explosions, however, quickly changed her mind. Dropping everything, she ran for the door but then, remembering how all the food was ruined during the December 6 bombing, she rushed back and was pulling the pots and pans from the stove when Laszlo Riedl grabbed her by the arm and dragged her down to the cellar. "Are you out of your mind, Ilonka? From the sound of the explosions I doubt if anyone will have an appetite to eat today!"

By the time the heavy metal door to the basement clanked closed behind them, the house was shaking so hard that Ilonka slipped on the steep wooden steps and could have been hurt, if Laszlo had not caught her. He was steadying her when suddenly her body slackened again.

"Oh my God! Jeno and the others!" was all she could say before her knees gave out and she sank against Laszlo's chest.

"Come on, Ilonka get hold of yourself! It's no time to panic!" he told her in a stern voice. "I am sure they are safe; there are shelters everywhere. Don't worry about them. It's the children here who need you!" He then pushed her into a chair, picked up the crying baby from the mattress, and put him into her lap. Feeling the frightened child's little arms clutching at her, she found her strength, and, focusing all her attention on comforting him, remained composed while the attack raged all around them.

All hope that it would be a short mission like the last one in February vanished as the bombing continued, with planes coming in wave after wave. Every time the ear shattering explosions got closer the dirt floor shook under their feet, whipping up dust that filled their noses and choked their lungs. It truly felt like the end was at hand. The Riedls stood together in a quiet embrace, while the Grubers huddled somewhere in the back of the cellar. Gyuszi was sitting on top of an old chest, his head bent, fingers clasped, seemingly calm and serene. Little Istvan, trying to act brave in the beginning, ran scared to his mother at the first nearby explosion, burrowing his head in her lap.

Only Sárika was nowhere to be seen. They knew she had made it down because her voice could be heard between detonations. She was there all right, crouching under the wooden staircase, Jeno's old fencing helmet on her head, and reciting every prayer she ever learned. During a short interval all heads turned in that direction as they clearly heard her say, "Bless me Father for I have sinned. My last confession was . . ." but before she could go further, Uncle Laszlo's voice boomed out of the darkness, "Just keep to the venial sins, Sárika! No one here cares to hear any of your mortal sins!" Even Ilonka could not help but smile at the humor that broke the fearful tension, if only for a moment.

The bombing lasted about fifty minutes, but in spite of several nearby hits, the house stood without much additional damage. When the release sounded, Ilonka was out on the street ready to look for Jeno, but Laszlo held her back. Where would she go? Thank God, half an hour later Latzi bounded through the door, dirty and out of breath, but relieved to find everyone unharmed. Seeing him coming alone left Ilonka frozen with fear, but he quickly assured her that the others were safe, too; he just ran ahead to say that it might take some time for Jeno and Eta to get home. The bombing caused tremendous damage, fires were burning everywhere, streets were blocked with debris, and the rescue brigades were asking people to either give a hand or stay out of the way. His father was hard at work at a first aid station in front of Eta's school, where almost every building was in complete ruin. When Ilonka asked what happened to them during the attack, all he would say that it caught them on top of the City Tower, then ran to rejoin his father.

Anxious as Ilonka was to know more, she had to wait until late afternoon when tired and exhausted Jeno and Eta finally arrived and told the details. After they left the house to take Dr. Kontra sightseeing, they first took him to Sopron's famous landmark in the heart of downtown, the picturesque 190-foot high City Tower with a circular viewing platform on top that offered a panoramic view of the entire city and its surroundings. Climbing the narrow, tube-like spiral stairway, Dr. Kontra had to rest a few times to catch his breath, but he admitted it was well worth the effort to see the lovely scenery unfold before him.

Being Sunday and a beautiful clear day, the platform was crowded with spectators, until the start of wailing sirens sent everyone running for the exit. The stairway was immediately jammed with people stampeding to get down, making it impossible to evacuate the tower in an orderly fashion. Stranded and with nowhere to escape, people grabbed onto the railings as the first bombs exploded somewhere near and the structure began to sway. Luckily, the hit was two blocks away posing no danger of collapse, and when the relief sounded everyone got down safely.

Once out of the tower, however, the small company of Jeno got caught in another jam as hundreds of people emerging from the neighboring shelters spilled into the narrow streets. In the midst of the pushing and shoving, sometimes separated, then together again, they were swept along in the direction of St. Orsolya Square. Trying to hold on to each other, they were about halfway there when the onrush suddenly came to a halt. People up front, reaching the square, found their way blocked by burning debris, with nowhere to go but back. They turned around, pressing against those still coming, trampling over anyone too slow to give way in the ensuing chaos. To escape, Latzi fought his way to the side of the street, pulling Eta with him and shouting over the noise for his father and Jeno to follow. There they huddled under a doorway, waiting for the crowd to pass, talking about what to do next. That's when they decided that Latzi should run ahead and check on the family, with Eta and Jeno following whichever way they could.

Dr. Kontra decided to go back to the square and offer help to treat the wounded. By the time he reached the end of the street rescue brigades were already at work. The chaotic scene of devastation that greeted him was straight out of Dante's *Inferno*. The small square had received two direct hits, causing further damage to the surrounding buildings, already wobbly from the December bombing. Eta's three-story school building, now a military hospital, stood torn open as if a giant saw had sliced off its facade. Beds closest to the edge were dangling in the air, some with patients still stranded in them, pleading for help. The attack came so suddenly that the nurses ran out of time to carry everyone to the shelter. As fate would have it, the people left behind were the lucky ones; those in the cellar had a lesser chance to be saved. The rubble covering the small square was blocking access to the underground, making rescue next to impossible. Time was crucial in reaching the people trapped below; even an hour delay could jeopardize their survival.

Sadly, when a passage was finally opened, mostly dead bodies were dragged from the ruins. Sixty-eight people, men, women and children, lost their lives in one cellar alone. Twenty-nine victims were dug up from another shelter. The bodies were lined up on the ground until horse-drawn carts could be brought in to take them to the cemetery. Father Alajos and several other priests from nearby parishes were busy comforting the wounded and assisting the dying. Heightening the apocalyptic sense of the hellish scene was the grief-stricken lamentation of relatives and friends as they arrived only to find the dead bodies of loved ones.

Dr. Kontra, reaching the square, was immediately put to work. They sent him to the emergency station, and while picking his way around the soldiers digging and shoveling feverishly, he noticed small, bloody body parts scattered among the dislodged debris. To his horror he saw men, their pickaxe raised high, whacking at the rubbish indiscriminately, sending bricks and stones mixed with flesh flying through the air. They were ordered to clear the site as fast as possible, but in their rush they were also hitting bodies, people who might still be alive under the pile. He quickly alerted the officer in charge to have them slow down and use more caution.

Typical of scenes of tragedy, the curious gawkers soon began to show up, hindering the rescue workers. These people never missed an opportunity to come and stare, nor did they have the decency to leave when asked. They had to be chased away with shovels and axes, and to keep them from coming back soldiers were posted to stand guard.

By nightfall a light snow began to fall, coating the dead bodies lying in one corner of the square. It seemed nature's way of showing respect to the victims by spreading a soft blanket of snow over their mangled remains. This time the handling of the dead was better organized than at previous bombings. Carts and trucks pulled up to take the bodies to St. Mihaly Catholic cemetery, where after unloading, bloodstained and grimy, they turned around to pick up the next load. The cemetery staff worked through the night identifying the corpses so relatives could claim them. As before, those unclaimed or unidentifiable would be buried in the morning in common graves.

The number of civilian victims totaled 239, with military losses, both Hungarian and German, much higher. And as cart after cart carrying the dead continued making the tracks to St. Mihaly's, it soon became clear that the cemetery couldn't handle all of them. By a quick decision, bodies of soldiers were kept there, but newly arrived carts with civilian victims were redirected to other non-Catholic cemeteries. In death, on that sad night, there was no distinction between Catholics and Protestants, or Hungarians and Germans.

. . . .

It was well after ten o'clock when Latzi and his father finally returned, cold and wet from the snow and covered with dirt. They knew that both railroad stations were hit hard, and even though repair work began immediately and continued after dark, it was impossible for Dr. Kontra to return to Gyor. Yet he couldn't just sit and wait until the trains would start rolling again! Hearing the news of the bombing his wife must be worried sick, wondering if he was dead or alive, not to mention what would happen if the train with her aboard should pull out before he got back! He simply couldn't take that chance; he must find his way to Gyor tonight, even if he had to walk. Luckily, Laszlo Riedl was able to get him on a military convoy heading for the front; they would drop him off at Gyor. When Dr. Kontra and his son said goodbye, they did not know if they would ever see each other again.

The next day it was the Riedls' turn to say goodbye to Laszlo, as he received orders to report for duty. Before he left, the two families debated what to do in the troubled days ahead, and he strongly suggested that rather than join the exodus that had already begun toward the West, they remain in Sopron. Fearing further bombings and the approaching Russians, people were clogging the road to Vienna, their possessions piled high on horse-drawn carts, if they were lucky enough to have a horse. The less fortunate harnessed themselves in front of their cart, with other family members pushing from behind. The refugees, however, who had come to Sopron only a few months earlier, were fleeing on foot, carrying even less than the pitiful bundles they had when they arrived.

The noise, the shouting and yelling, horses neighing under the sting of a lash, and insults hurled back and forth if someone did not move fast enough, mingled with the drone of low-flying Russian airplanes buzzing and strafing the pitiful refugees. As soon as the rumble of airplanes was heard, the caravan came to a halt, and people scattered in all directions, throwing themselves into the slush that filled the roadside ditches. When the danger passed they were on the move again, taking the injured but leaving the dead behind. There was no time for burials. The bodies were left on the roadside until a Jewish work brigade would come to collect them.

Handling the dead was becoming critical in the mild spring weather, especially in the city where more and more bodies, already swollen and starting to decompose, surfaced after the debris was cleared away. Several people coming in contact with the corpses came down with typhoid fever, creating a great fear for the spread of the dreaded disease. The already frightened and nervous people demanded to know what was being done in case of an outbreak, when there was no medicine to be had anywhere at any price? Doctors could only recommend frequent hand washing and cleansing open wounds with alcohol, excellent suggestions but easier said than done with soap and alcohol scarcely obtainable.

When sores began to appear on the backside of Sárika's leg, Ilonka cleansed it with some cologne she still had, but it didn't seem to help. After a week she sent for Dr. Graser, who calmed her that the open sores had nothing to do with typhoid; instead it was a sign of malnutrition. A healthy diet would easily cure the condition and he suggested sending her to the country for a while. He also said that drinking a small amount of red wine would help to strengthen her immune system.

Ilonka wouldn't hear of letting Sárika out of her sight, but that day she watered down the baby's milk and gave her a small glass to drink. Then she thought of the bar down the street owned by their neighbors, the Jeagers, and sent Jeno knocking on their door to ask if they would sell them a bottle of wine. Everyone knew that Mr. Jeager had a large, well-stocked wine cellar, and even though he claimed that the Germans drained all his barrels and took every single bottle, leaving him with not a drop to sell, nobody believed the story.

His wife, a very pretty woman in her thirties with a ripe peach complexion and violet eyes, opened the door to Jeno and listened politely as he explained the situation with Sárika. She was sympathetic, the more so because she also had two young daughters, but she said they just didn't have any wine left. If they did, they would gladly give him some free. With that she was ready to close the door, but Jeno continued to plead with her.

"Mrs. Jeager, your daughter and Sárika play together; you know she is not a strong girl. Perhaps if you search your pantry you might find a few bottles saved for your own use. It would be a great help if you would let me have a cup or two, please!"

Mrs. Jaeger was quite indignant at first, taking Jeno's remark as a veiled insinuation that she was not telling the truth, but then she stopped and lowered her eyes. When she looked up her expression had changed to deep sadness.

"Mr. Zachar, you are right, we do have some wine, but as much as I'd like to help you, I am sorry, we just can't. You see, if we make one exception word would get around and in no time others would be at our door demanding the same."

"You need not worry about that, Mrs. Jeager, I can assure you, we will not say a word, if you just could—"

But she didn't let him finish. "I am sorry, we just can't risk it. People have a way to find things out. Please try to understand; refusing is nothing personal, but we must think of our own safety first. These are desperate times, and who could tell what people would do in desperation?"

When Jeno told Ilonka what happened, he expected an outburst of a bitter tirade against the Jaegers, and rightfully so. But to his surprise, instead of anger, she was only disappointed. It's not them, it's the war that was changing otherwise decent people, she said. Under normal circumstances the Jeagers wouldn't have hesitated to help; in their place perhaps she would act the same way. Ilonka accepted the refusal but she would not rest. She knew that the restaurant Mitzie's in-laws owned went out of business a while ago when supplies dried up, but they surely had some wine tucked away. She ran over and came home with a bottle hidden under her coat.

It solved one thing, but she could do nothing about changing the children's diet. The food shortages had gone from bad to worse since the bombings started. The ration cards were tossed away, expired, because they could not be redeemed. There was simply no supply coming in from the villages. The military confiscated everything, emptying every storage place and taking the livestock to feed the soldiers. Bread, if it could be called that, made of bran and corn, the staple of pigs in peacetime, was black, dense, and sticky, but was more available. People waited in long queues in front of stores and butcher shops, even though the only meat they offered was horsemeat. People got their first taste of horsemeat after the last air attack. Bombs did not discriminate; they killed horses, too, and women soon began carving out chunks from their shanks right where they lay dead on the street. After that the butchers began killing horses to sell the meat.

It was not beneath Ilonka to line up for horsemeat. Actually, it did not taste all that bad. Adding potatoes and onions, a little of which she still had in the cellar, and seasoning it with paprika, it made a hearty stew, a tasty Sunday meal. But most days all she could cook was *stertz*, a lumpy mush made of flour fried in half-rancid cooking oil. No wonder that eating so poorly even she lost weight, while the children looked emaciated, and Jeno, naturally slim, became downright skeletal. Because of the constant stress and bad food his ulcer grew worse, and while he ate most of what Ilonka could put on the table, he just couldn't bring himself to eat horsemeat, even if he had to starve.

Besides food, shortages of other essentials were just as bad. When clothing needed repair, there wasn't even thread to patch things up, and shoes were resoled over and over again, not with leather, only with rubber. A permanent look of dingy poverty took over households everywhere.

The only thing that kept spirits alive was the hope that the end was near; it couldn't be much longer before the Russians would reach the city. People feared them greatly and believed the horror stories preceding them about the raping and looting, the shooting of civilians, and the roundups, men randomly taken never to be seen again. But that could not last forever. Sooner or later order would be restored; Hungary would be free again, ready to start rebuilding the war-torn country.

Although the Nazi propaganda fueled the fear of the citizenry by plastering every wall with posters depicting the atrocities committed by the Russians, any mention of them ever reaching the city was forbidden under the threat of death. One such poster showed a viciously grinning giant black bear thrusting his hairy paw with enormous claws into a birdcage that held a horror-stricken blond girl. It was to stir the consciousness of men about what would happen to wives, mothers, and daughters if the Soviet beasts were allowed to advance. The implication was clear. Unless they joined the fight to beat back the Russians, women would be subjected to unimaginable horrors.

For many it was this fear, not some political reason that led them to flee the country. The question whether to stay or leave kept Jeno awake many a night, as newly formed worry lines testified to his struggle to find the right answer. Should he expose his wife and five children to the hazards the refugees faced on the open road, not knowing if they would have shelter for the night and food to eat, or stay home and take the risk to ride out the Russian onslaught? He leaned toward Laszlo Riedl's opinion that it was better to remain in Sopron until the storm blew over, but still, it was up to him alone to make the final decision, a responsibility he found overwhelming.

When taking her husband's advice Erzsebet Riedl decided to stay, Ilonka sided with her. She would, of course, leave it up to Jeno to decide, but reasoned with him that whatever their fate, it would be easier to endure under their own roof, among friends and people they knew. What would they gain by leaving? With the Russians only a step behind, it would be only a matter of time before they would be captured and there was no telling what would happen to them then.

Jeno was tormented by indecision. Were those stories about Russian brutalities really true, or just exaggerated Nazi propaganda to frighten the people? How he wished he could talk to Sandor about it! He must have witnessed the Red Army's treatment of enemy civilians in the wake of the German retreats! Laszlo was only a reservist, should he rely on his opinion?

Night after sleepless night he would stare into the darkness, weighing Laszlo's every word as they echoed through his mind about what to expect of the Russians and how to react to them: "Pray that the Germans don't make a stand, which would mean house-to-house fighting. If there is no armed resistance, make sure you display a white flag on the door and that you have no guns in the house when the first wave of Russian troops arrive. These soldiers make up the fighting force and usually present lesser danger, especially to women; their job is to take the city and immediately move on to the next one. Of course, there is no guarantee that they won't behave any better than the occupational forces coming on their heels. These are given a free hand for three days to let loose and take revenge on the enemy. During the onslaught the city will become a no-man's land, and you should find a place to hide Ilonka and the girls. Little children are generally safe; even these uncivilized soldiers, many of them from Asia, like kids and won't harm them. And Jeno, don't keep any alcohol in the house; they can be more dangerous if drunk, and they do get drunk every chance they get. Stay out of their way the best you can. If they order you to do something, do it; don't try to resist. Give them whatever they demand, be it your watch, money, jewelry, the shirt off your back. No heroic actions! You must do anything, bear any hardship, and endure all humiliation in order to survive. The time will pass, and life *will* begin again!"

In the end, Jeno felt he had to trust Laszlo, and the family stayed. Once he made up his mind, the next step was to find a hiding place where hopefully Ilonka and the children would be safe. In times of trouble churches always offered the best protection, except by now most of them were already filled to capacity and forced to turn away hundreds of women and children looking for shelter. The only one that remained a possibility was the Benedictines where Gyuszi went to school, and although they were also crowded, Ilonka thought she had a good chance to get in. First, the principal, Dr. Palos, was fond of their family, dropping by occasionally to chat with Jeno and share a glass of wine with him, and second, the Riedls carried an impressive "To whom it may concern" letter of recommendation from Laszlo's employer, Jusztinian Seredi, the country's only Cardinal. He wrote it before they left, hoping it might carry a little extra weight with churches when seeking protection during their escape.

As it turned out, they didn't need the small leverage. When Ilonka presented it, Dr. Palos waved it aside, saying that as long as they had room, all women and small children would be welcomed. He would have a place for them, but beyond that all was in God's hands.

Chaos and the Red Army

AS THE RUSSIAN front drew closer to Sopron, the American bombing stopped to let the Soviets take over carrying out future air attacks. The Russian planes appeared a lot more frequently, and by mid March they flew in and out without interference; no one fired at them since the German anti-aircraft defense by then was non-existent. Although the bombings went on regularly, people did not fear them as much as they did the Americans; they caused fewer casualties since the Russian bombs were considerably lighter and exploded before penetrating into underground shelters. On the other hand, they were incendiary bombs, igniting fires on contact that quickly spread, burning down whole neighborhoods.

To the great relief of the city's civilian population, German and Hungarian troops were seen packing, preparing to pull out; it meant they would not put up resistance. The streets were jammed with trucks, tanks, cannons on horse-drawn carts, motorbikes, some with sidecars, the rag-tag remnants of the once glorious German Wehrmacht. Bringing up the rear came the Hungarian units, mostly truckloads of soldiers with far less heavy equipment compared to the Germans. The tooting, shouting, the ear-shattering rumble of these military convoys went on day and night, adding to the noise of the unrestricted air traffic above.

Straggling behind the military came another column herded on foot by gun-toting Arrow Cross guards. These were the Jews kept back from the deportations and harnessed for slave labor, but now ordered to march toward Germany. The thugs kept them at a steady pace with shouts and beatings, themselves in a hurry to leave for fear of reprisals if caught by the Russians. They left only a few dozen Jews behind to collect the mounting number of dead for burial. With their tormentors gone, however, there was no one left to guard them, and without an alternative, the police chief ordered Father Alajos and a few other clergymen to take over the task and see that they don't escape. This, however, the priests flatly refused, arguing that if the Russians suddenly overran the city and found them overlording the Jews, they could be killed, or at best, held accountable as servants of the Arrow Cross regime. After haggling back and forth, they only agreed to go to the cemetery and say prayers over the bodies as they were brought in.

Taking advantage of the chaotic situation, some soldiers shed their uniforms, put on civilian clothes, and went into hiding, risking a summary execution as traitors if they should be caught while fleeing. Instant shootings and hangings were carried out on the spot; there was no time to drag the deserters to be court-martialed at the Sopron-Kohida military prison. Two former Russian soldiers who earlier in the war came over to the German side were unceremoniously executed in front of people for trying to run away. When they first switched allegiance they were welcomed and well rewarded for giving valuable information, but as the Russian front closed in they turned coat again, thinking they would be better off to rejoin their former Red Army comrades.

Then on March 25 the first German soldiers in full combat gear staggered into the city. Coming straight from the front, they were bloodied, dirty, and weak; some could hardly walk, but instead of seeking medical treatment, they just dragged themselves towards the road to Austria. People ran up to them asking about the front, only to be told that it was but a few miles from Sopron. They seemed to have given up hope, saying that all was lost, Germany was beaten, the war was practically over, and to fight any further was insane. Some of them were even heard murmuring a few uncomplimentary words about the Fuhrer.

With the military leaving, civilian life in the city came to a standstill. The sirens no longer sounded alerts; they had outlived their purpose with Russian aircrafts flying in-and-out virtually unhindered, and people already living in cellars and bomb shelters. Men within the same block formed vigilante groups to check the latest situation during a lull in the bombing, and also to keep an eye over the abandoned apartments.

Hospitals and makeshift emergency facilities also moved the wounded into basements—dark, airless, and unheated shelters—where lying on dirty, bloody cots, they moaned and cried out for help, all in vain, since not even aspirin was available. Providing treatment was next to impossible; the most doctors, nurses, and nuns could do was give them water and say a comforting word. Those who did not survive the night were hastily wrapped in sheets and buried in the backyard. Nobody dared to leave the shelters more than a few minutes; to haul the dead to the cemetery was too risky.

Office buildings and government offices that withstood the bombings were all but abandoned. Doors left ajar, confidential files lying open on desktops, and sheets of papers strewn all over the floor testified that no one cared anymore what was left behind. City officials had only one concern, leave the place as fast as possible. But even in their great hurry, before scurrying away, they managed to get rid of the framed pictures of Hitler and Szalasi hanging on the walls, tossing them out to the street.

Jeno also stopped going to his office in Agfalva. His duty now was to be with his family and protect them if it was possible at all. To escape the continuous bombing some people began to desert the city, thinking it safer to hide out in the surrounding forests. At first Jeno was hesitant to leave the house, but later changed his mind. They'd be safer in the hills. The Riedls, including Lasko, who came to stay with his mother and sister during the crucial days, did not join the flight when on the morning of March 29 Jeno set out with the family and Eta's boyfriend Latzi to find a spot in the woods and dig a bunker big enough for all of them. Bundled in warm clothes and carrying shovels, a pickax, and meager provisions, they hurried along, occasionally ducking in doorways when airplanes passing overhead droned dangerously low.

They were close to the Loevers, passing one of the large garden villas there, when a couple of blankets fluttering on a clothesline caught Ilonka's eye. Without a second thought, she dropped her bundle and darted toward the gate. She was halfway across the street before Jeno saw her and dashed after her. He knew his wife. She would think nothing of taking those blankets to keep the children warm during the cold nights in the open. He caught up with her just as she was about to open the gate.

"Ilonka, leave those blankets where they are. I know you mean well, but we are not thieves. They belong to people who live here." His stern voice stopped her but only for a second before turning on him defiantly.

"I am taking those blankets, Jeno, whether you like it or not! We'll need them at night. These people probably left already and if we don't take them, somebody else will!"

But she did not take them. When Jeno took her by the arm and pulled her away, reminding her that they had much to do, she grudgingly followed him, grumbling to herself as they crossed the street. "It's chaos everywhere, but he can't bend the rules for a minute, not even for the sake of his children," she said loud enough to hear what she thought of her overly righteous husband. "If taking those wretched blankets makes me a thief, what would he be, if the children should catch pneumonia and die?"

Once they reached the forest Latzi suggested staying near the Deak Kut, a natural spring, where they would be near drinking water. A sloping hill behind it seemed to be a good place to start digging, Jeno and Latzi first, then Ilonka and Eta taking their turn, while Sárika looked after the children. By late afternoon the bunker was big enough to sleep in; the earth, however, as they found out, was not ideal. Much of it consisted of slippery yellow clay, with beads of water dripping from the ceiling. After spending a sleepless night in the damp, smelly, freezing bunker, Jeno knew it was a mistake to leave home. Early the next morning, on Good Friday, they scurried back through the deserted city, taking one block at a time to avoid drawing the attention of the low-flying planes. Their droning, the sound of a broken coffee grinder, was by now mixed with the distant booming of heavy artillery.

As soon as they got home Ilonka took the children down to the cellar and put them to bed. Sárika, exhausted from the sleepless night, collapsed fully dressed on her mattress and immediately fell into a deep sleep. Eta stayed up to help bringing down some additional items—important papers, family photo albums and what jewelry they had—before she, too, lay down to rest. As tired as she was, Ilonka remained on her feet to prepare lunch, some baked potatoes and a pot of lentils with onions. It was not by choice that the family abstained from eating meat on this Good Friday.

Down in the cellar they noticed that the Grubers were missing. Jeno rang the bell to their apartment but there was no answer. Knowing of their pro-Nazi sentiments, he was sure they had decided to flee. His suspicion was confirmed when Latzi pried open the door and found the place empty. Ilonka couldn't help remarking that although she had nothing against the elder Grubers, should they have stayed, it would be her turn in a day or two to report their son, that no-good Nazi bum! It would serve him right for the threat he made to her.

The Riedls took good advantage of the Grubers' disappearance and moved into their apartment. Erzsebet packed up personal items the family left behind, clothes, photos, and knickknacks, and stored them in the attic, except the large framed picture of the Fuhrer that hung on the wall. It was put to torch in the backyard, along with Erwin's Nazi books. With great regret Jeno also burned his cousin Sandor's military lexicon he had inscribed for him. Was it necessary to destroy a book that had sentimental value to him? Probably not, but he did it anyway. These were days when possessing a military manual issued by the enemy could put them in danger, and he couldn't take the risk.

After the military and the masses of fleeing refugees left the city, people huddling in shelters and cellars knew that the end was near. By Good Friday the blackout was no longer in effect; it was pointless when rockets kept the night sky bright as daylight. The sound of the Russian Katyushas—a multiple rocket launcher the Germans nicknamed "Stalin Organ" for its high-pitched screech—mixed with the continuous roar of other heavy artillery that was a distant rumble only a few days ago, now boomed menacingly close. Adding to the noise was the sound of explosions as the last remaining Germans were blowing up the railroad tracks they had repaired only a few weeks earlier.

Then suddenly, on Saturday morning, like the still before the storm, a strange lull descended over Sopron. The Russian guns ceased firing, and no airplane flew over the city. At first only a few men dared to leave the shelters, but when word got around that it seemed to be safe, others followed. Like testing the waters, they branched out to see if the calm was real and not some kind of trap. And as more and more people emerged, it took only a few furtive suggestions, some carelessly dropped words about hidden supplies behind the boarded up storefronts, before a full-scale looting began. Hordes bent on taking whatever the Germans left behind attacked the abandoned stores and warehouses, breaking down doors without the slightest hint of shame. In the spreading chaos, huge mobs began roaming the streets, tossing all safety aside, shouting and cursing, fighting and bloodying each other to get their hands on the find. They grabbed anything in sight, carrying the goods by hand, on their backs, or in pull-carts, hauling their loot in the greatest of hurry to come back for more.

Compared to the inner city, where most of the shops and restaurants were, Jeno's neighborhood remained relatively calm until one of the vigilantes making his rounds noticed a sudden activity at the Sanbergers' house. It was the last home on Jeno's side street next to the little park, a large property owned by the Sanberger family who operated a meatpacking plant across town. As the man watched through the wrought-iron gate, the hurried comings and goings inside the courtyard told him that the family was preparing to flee. They were busy emptying a small storage building built behind the home, two men hauling large wooden cases to a waiting truck, while Mrs. Sanberger and her two teenage daughters carried smaller boxes.

Noticing the vigilante, Mr. Sanberger enlisted him to help with the heavier crates, and admitted that they were indeed leaving. He said they waited this long, until the last of the military left, fearing that if the Germans saw them packing, they would discover that he still had some food supply. These items were from his meat plant, saved by hiding them behind a fake wall he put up to make the storage shed look empty. The Nazis would not only have confiscated everything, but worse, they could have charged him with sabotage, since he convinced them that his stocks were depleted. He also managed to save his truck from being taken by camouflaging it and reporting it stolen.

When they finished loading, a considerable amount of goods still remained, crates of lard, rods of hard winter salami, and shelves of canned meat; they just couldn't take it all with them. Mr. Sanberger thanked the man for helping and, as he started the engine, told him to take whatever he could before the crowd discovered the place. That didn't take long. The news spread through the neighborhood like wildfire and in no time the rush was on. Amongst the first to arrive were Latzi and Lasko, with Jeno and Gyuszi close behind, pulling a small cart. They loaded it up with two cases of lard, each weighing about twenty pounds, and bags filled with canned meat and salami.

Turning to leave, they had to push against people, both neighbors and strangers, storming to get to the storage before the shelves would be empty. After unloading everything, Latzi and Lasko elbowed their way back, each returning with additional cans of meat, some marked goulash, others filled with plain chunks of cooked beef. Ilonka put a few in her pantry but everything else was immediately buried in the cellar. It would save them from going hungry, and although the Sanberger family never returned, she remembered them in her prayers for years to come.

The boys were on their second round when Ilonka, standing behind the boarded-up kitchen window, peered through a slot and saw the scary scene unfolding in front of the house. The crowd had turned into a mob, masses of people pushing and shoving, trying to make headway in one direction while others pressed against them. Fights broke out when some people tried to grab the merchandise out of the hands of others, a futile attempt when there was no room to run. Staring at the unbelievable sight, Ilonka noticed that some people nearest to the padlocked entrance to the casern climbed over the wrought iron gate and, jumping down on the other side, disappeared into the guardhouse.

They soon reappeared, brandishing rifles and pistols the soldiers had apparently left behind. One of them shot out the lock on the gate, letting the people pour into the courtyard.

As Ilonka watched them running in all directions, attacking every building, she heard her own voice, *I should have thought of this! We should have gone in there earlier!*

"What are you talking about?" Jeno called out, just coming through the door. "You shouldn't be up here Ilonka, this commotion could turn real ugly!"

Without a backward glance, Ilonka was flipping her hand for Jeno to come. "Come here quick, look what these people are doing! They are looting the casern! We should have known better and gone in after the soldiers left! But it's still not too late! I want you to go over there before more people discover that the gate is open. Right now most of them are still at the Sanbergers, but once they run out of the stuff there, this is where they'll be heading. Hurry up and see if you can find something we could use!"

Indignantly Jeno started to protest but she silenced him with a look that could kill.

"Not this time, Jeno, don't start again with that 'we are not thieves'! Just look at all the people hauling things away; most of them are our own neighbors!" She pressed Jeno against the peephole. "Can you see? Even Father Alajos is there. I am sure he is taking it for the people at his shelter, but if he thinks it is all right, then it can't be wrong for us, either, can it now?"

Before she could continue, Latzi and Lasko were back and immediately volunteered to go over to the casern. "Bring back whatever you can find except guns," she yelled after them as they were running out the door, then with a mixed feeling of shame and frustration, she turned to face Jeno. How could she make this always correct, honor-bound husband of hers see that the way she acted lately was out of sheer desperation? It was anarchy out there and in a world turned upside-down, a different set of codes applied! When everything was collapsing and there was no guarantee that they would live to see the next day, she would not sit back for righteousness' sake! They had the right to do everything within reason to make it through this hell.

"I know you don't approve some of my doings, but these are terrible times, Jeno, and there is no room for gallantry," she said, trying to justify her actions. "Right or wrong, we must do everything to help us survive; that's my motivation. If you could only think in terms that all is for our children's sake?" She held out a hand in a plea for understanding, then dropped it, murmuring, "Oh, what's the use . . ." her voice trailing off.

No longer expecting any sympathy, she turned away, when she felt his arms encircling her shoulders.

"I know, Ilonka, I know. I wish I could do more; but I tell you what I will do. I'll go to the office and see what's happening at the customs warehouse. I might be able to salvage something there."

The compassion in his voice was unmistakable, and it touched Ilonka deeply. Knowing how hard it would be for him to do this, she became overwhelmed with emotion and clung to him in silent gratitude.

Always cautious, keeping close to the wall and occasionally stepping behind a door if the street seemed unsafe, Jeno made it to the custom building, but what he saw on the way shocked him to the bone. With only a few Jews remaining to do the dirty work, dead bodies were left where they fell. People just passed them by; there was no time to bury the dead when their only concern was to keep alive. Horses, too, lay with legs stiff and bellies already bloating. And there was the looting, still in full swing with the mob milling around, breaking into stores, even in abandoned homes.

The customs warehouse, as expected, was also under siege, but Jeno was not about to fight the crowd there. Opening a locked door he went down to the basement, where they kept some confiscated items until a decision could be made what to do with them. In the first compartment he found a sack half full of small packets of saccharin. He was about to check the next locker, hoping to find something more useful, but by then people had discovered where he went and were stampeding down the stairway. In a few minutes there was hardly any room to move, and giving up, Jeno just grabbed the sack and fought his way out to the street.

As he crossed the empty Szinhaz Square, where they once lived with Angela, he encountered several Hungarian soldiers loitering on the corner. Jeno quickly looked for a doorway to hide, but it was too late, they saw him. To his relief they didn't want his bundle; they only asked for directions to the border, claiming to be separated from their unit during their march toward Austria. Jeno put them on the right course and wished them much-needed good luck. They were obvious deserters, and he wondered why they risked being caught and shot. It was easier to change into civilian clothes; the gutters were full of discarded uniforms.

When he reached home he found Ilonka on edge, anxiously waiting for him. The latest word was that the Russians could be in Sopron by the morning, and it was time to leave for the Benedictines. She hardly looked at the sack Jeno carried back, just wanted to know what was in it. Saccharin? She did not think much of it. Why, there must have been coffee in that warehouse—the real thing, not the junk called *ersatz coffee*! Everybody wanted good coffee; it was good as gold in bartering on the black market. Well, she had no time to dwell on it now. At least Latzi and Lasko had found something useful in the casern. If nothing else, they brought an armful of sleeveless sheepskin vests the soldiers were supposed to wear on the snowy Russian steppe when the front was still there. Now that it was at their doorsteps, the useless vests were dumped in the basement, but they would come handy for Ilonka to keep the children warm in the cold, damp shelter. She handed one to each child, already bundled up and ready to go, except Sárika. She vacillated about putting on her beautiful new coat when her mother held it out for her. Should she put it on? What if it got dirty in the dusty shelter? No, she wouldn't wear it; her old winter coat would do until they returned home.

Then it was time to say goodbye. Would they see each other again? Ilonka put on a brave face but almost lost her composure when she hugged her eleven-year-old son, Gyuszi. The priests considered him too old to bring to the shelter where only women, girls, and small children were allowed, and so, no matter how heartbreaking it was, she had to leave him behind.

Out on the streets she found the atmosphere calmer compared to the earlier madness, either because there was nothing more to take, or people had enough and crawled back in their underground holes. Hurrying along, they reached the parish shelter without incident and were led down to the cellar, a large room already crowded with women and children sitting on cots with hardly any space between them. The light was dim—the priests had removed a few light bulbs on purpose—but after her eyes adjusted to the semi-darkness, Ilonka spotted Erzsebet Riedl and her daughter waving their hands. They had arrived earlier and were holding several cots for them. The mood was somber, many praying silently, counting rosary beads, fearful about the uncertain future and the fate of loved ones left at home. Yet there was no hysterics, no loud lamentations. Occasionally a suppressed sob would break the silence, but generally the women remained remarkably composed.

At seven o'clock one of the priests, Father Lanyi, came in to say evening prayers and announced that a confessional booth has been set up behind the stairway. The next day was Easter Sunday, and with God's help there would be an Easter Service, not in the church above, but down in the cellar. He praised the women for their courage in facing the unknown alone, separated from husbands and other family members. His only regret was that the parish could not take in everyone. He said a white flag would be pegged on the Church door as soon as the Russians entered the city, and assured the women that everything possible would be done to protect them and the children. They will have food twice a day, in the morning and mid-afternoon, even a cup of wine was available to quiet the nerves. Last, he talked about the importance of keeping calm, then with a final blessing bid them good night and withdrew to spend the night on his knees, begging God not to turn away from his children, but to watch over them in this dark hour of need.

As Father Lanyi and countless others in the city prayed during the night, the last remaining German troops were driving toward the west, only a few hours before the first Russian tanks rolled into Sopron. With the first light of dawn came the sound of sporadic machine gun fire mixed with the rumbling of the cautiously advancing Soviet war machine. Anyone unfortunate enough to be caught in the peripheral vision of the Russians, whether civilian or a German or Hungarian soldier lagging behind, was shot on the spot. For lack of resistance the Russians easily reached the main square and immediately took over the city hall as their command center. In clear view across the square they spotted the fluttering white flag—a piece of torn sheet tied to a pole—stuck to the door of the St. Benedictine Church. Within a few minutes several Russian soldiers were dispatched to check out the place and ensure that there was no threat to the security of the newly established Soviet Commando.

When the priests saw the first Russian tank pulling into the square, Father Lanyi hurried to alert the women. Mindful that it might create panic, he used the calmest voice he could summon to say that the Russians arrived and were setting up headquarters next door, and at the same time urged everyone to trust in God, who sent his only son to die for the salvation of mankind, and whom he did not abandon but resurrected from the dead on this very day almost 2000 years ago. Since the unfolding events made it impossible to hold Mass now, he implored them to remember in their prayers the significance of that miraculous long-ago Eastern morning, and God would surely listen.

Made aware that Russians were in their vicinity, the younger women smeared dirt on their faces and covered their heads with black kerchiefs to make them appear old and unattractive. Mothers clutching their children, older sisters cradling their younger siblings, huddled together, praying in silence, preparing to endure whatever the coming hours would bring. These were times that could easily damn man's soul to hopeless desperation, were it not for prayers and the trust in the Divine. It had been proven time and again, that fear of real danger could turn the eyes even of the unbeliever toward heaven to seek help and compassion from above.

Suddenly loud voices and the sound of approaching heavy footsteps broke the deadly silence. Holding their breath, the women watched as the door swung open and several Russian soldiers pushed their way into the room. With machine guns held at the ready they ordered Father Lanyi and the other priests to stand aside, then cautiously proceeded to check the room. Satisfied that there was no danger to them, they lowered their guns and turned their attention to the fear-stricken woman. One of the soldiers, smiling reassuringly, addressed them in broken German that they had no reason to be scared; the Russians had no intention of hurting anybody. Still smiling, he then pointed toward a child and wiggled his fingers in a friendly gesture. It broke the tension, and the mother of the little boy lifted his hand and made him wave back.

Their task finished and content that the place was secure, the Russians turned to leave. On their way out, however, the same soldier who spoke pulled Father Lanyi aside and told him it's better to keep their wives and children inside—apparently they had no clue about clerical celibacy of the Catholic Church—or some unruly soldiers might get ideas and try to cause trouble. If that should happen, just come to the commando across the square; they would take care of the problem.

As the door closed behind them, the subdued and fearful atmosphere suddenly gave way to a noisy jubilation, women talking, all at the same time, how their fears were indeed unfounded. These Russians were not as bad as people were led to believe! They weren't savage beasts! It was all German propaganda! Once they felt secure they acted quite civil, even friendly. Tremendously relieved, everyone breathed easier, knowing that those at home were in no danger.

How wrong they were! About the same time Jeno, Gyuszi, Latzi, and Lasko were sitting in the cellar, talking quietly, recalling what Lasko's father said about cooperating with the Russians. Their more valuable items were already buried in the dirt floor, but knowing the Russians' fondness for wristwatches, they kept some cheaper ones, along with fountain pens and cigarette lighters, to hand over if demanded. They had heard stories about angry soldiers shooting people if they had nothing to surrender.

Then suddenly, all talk stopped as the sound of heavy rumble filtered down to the cellar: armored vehicles pulling into their street. Curious if the Russians were taking over the military compound across the house, Jeno decided to go upstairs and see. Through the cracks in the boarded up kitchen window, he watched as a long convoy loaded with troops was indeed rolling into the casern, the soldiers jumping off the trucks even before coming to a stop. There was a lot of shouting, and since he spoke Slovakian, one of the Slavic languages similar to Russian, he could understand enough to know that the soldiers were ordered to search house to house for possible armed resistance.

Holding their guns ready to shoot they spread out in groups, running toward the homes and apartment buildings across the street. When he saw three of them coming his way, instead of going back to the cellar, he stayed upstairs, thinking that perhaps the soldiers would appreciate talking to someone in a language close to theirs. He was hurrying outside to meet them on the open terrace when he heard a crash as they kicked down the street entrance, even though it was unlocked and had a white handkerchief tied to the handle. Taking the stairs two at the time, they rushed at Jeno who, standing with his hands raised, told them in a calm, steady voice that there were no *Nemetzkies*—Germans in Russian—in the house. Hearing the familiar words seemed to slow the Russians for a moment, but it did not change their hostile attitude. Pushing him aside and shouting they would see it for themselves, they charged into the house. Finding it empty, they demanded to know where the rest of the family was, and when he said his three sons were down in the cellar but no one else, they gave him a good shove to show the way, cursing foully, *Yob tvoju maty*, he better be telling the truth.

The cussing got louder as they tore open the cellar door and saw the steep rickety wooden steps leading down into semi-darkness. Half stumbling, half sliding, they got down, and while one herded Jeno and the boys into the laundry room, the other two disappeared to check the rest of the cavernous place. Finding it empty, the soldier obviously in charge swung his gun menacingly at Jeno and demanded to know where the women were. Remaining calm, Jeno said his wife and younger children were staying with her parents in a nearby village, a safer place against air attacks. Releasing another string of curses, they pushed Gyuszi aside and told the others to empty their pockets. They took two watches and some money, but when there was nothing else, they left with stern warnings not to leave the cellar.

This time Jeno stayed put, but they could hear running and yelling, some occasional shooting, as the nightmarish hell broke loose over the neighborhood. Catching a few words from the ruckus outside he sadly realized that what he feared the most came true: the Jeagers' wine cellar was not empty, and the Russians discovered it. He remembered Mrs. Jeager turning him away when he asked for a cupful of wine to treat Sárika's infection, and now drunken soldiers massed in their cellar, soaking up the wine, outdrinking each other.

And drink they did! When the place became too crammed, they filled their flasks, jugs, even pails, anything that would hold the wine, and spilling out to the street continued drinking in the open. Staggering around in drunken stupor two soldiers staged a mock holdup, one mimicking a frightened local, while the other pretended to take his watch, both roaring with laughter. Another one had several watches strapped to his wrists, boasting loudly and showing them off, but when his comrade tried to snatch one away a fight broke out, both throwing punches and knocking each other to the ground. Many of them became belligerent, waving guns just for the fun of it, until they decided they had enough wine and now wanted women. Emboldened by the alcohol and snickering over the "fun" they would have, they started toward the nearest apartment building and began banging on the doors.

The shelter underneath the apartment building adjacent to Jeno's house was crowded with people, amongst them the Jaeger family. When the marauding, drunken Russians knocked down the door, the women frozen with fear began to wail. Sadly, nothing could save them from violation; no amount of begging, pleading, crying, or supplication would halt the brutal assault. They were dragged off indiscriminately, the young and the old, the pretty and ugly. There was no escaping. A mother gesturing to offer herself in a desperate attempt to save her young daughter was cruelly taunted by the soldiers, pretending to go along with the *Matuska* (Russian diminutive for mother), then dragging both of them away.

To stop the hysterical shouting and crying, one of the Russian brutes pointed his gun at the terrified people and, rattling rat-tat-tat-tat, swung it around at head level to the drunken laughter of his comrades. A group of soldiers began pushing and shoving the terrorized women out the door, while others herded the men into a corner, warning them with a sardonic sneer to stay put.

And so the brutal raping began. Left with no choice, the horror-stricken husbands and fathers stood by in helpless anger, some cursing, some hitting the wall with both fists, others just wringing their hands in frustrated resignation. Powerless to do anything, they turned on Jaeger, blaming him for their misfortune. It was all because of him! He should have flooded the gutters with his wine before the Russians arrived, but no! He was too greedy, couldn't even part with one cup of his precious wine when people were practically begging him! If heaping vile insults on him was not enough, some stooped so low as to say it served him right that his wife was now being ravaged by Mongol hordes upstairs!

One woman, a middle-aged wife who escaped the roundup by putting on her husband clothes, cutting her hair and gluing on a fake mustache, tried in vain to put an end to the bitter accusations by shaming the men for losing their sense of human decency. Wasn't it enough that Jaeger's innocent wife was suffering the same fate as all the others? At first she was shouted down that safe and snug in a disguise it was easy to be righteous, but eventually her remarks cut through the rage, and slowly, one by one they turned away in silent embarrassment.

The savage rampage and the unchecked cruelty continued throughout the day. As terribly as people suffered though, it was nothing new. They were the conquered, and according to the unwritten rule of war, from time eternal conquerors had the right to vent their vengeance and claim the spoils of war. But when darkness fell and the soldiers finally withdrew into the casern, the deeply remorseful Mr. Jaeger led the men through a connecting underground corridor to his wine cellar and together they smashed all the barrels. When they finished, wine stood knee deep over the hard-packed dirt floor and the air reeked with the fumes of alcohol, strong enough for a match to blow up the whole place.

The sight of the vandalized barrels and the cellar flooded with the precious wine almost caused a riot in the morning when the soldiers returned to continue their drinking orgy. Their angry cursing could be heard blocks away, the sound penetrating down into the shelters where people trembled in fear over what would come next. Jeno listened intently, trying to learn what caused such a furious uproar; was it something drastic that could bring on life-threatening retaliations? He did not have to wait too long to find out. Banging and kicking their cellar door open, several soldiers rushed down the steps and, brandishing their guns, ordered all of them, including Gyuszi, up into the courtyard. From there they marched them at gunpoint out to the street and into the neighbors' yard already crowded with men. An officer, a wiry little man, was barking at his soldiers to line up everyone with backs against the wall. He watched with a menacing scowl as his underlings pushed and shoved the poor frightened souls until they all stood facing him. Not knowing if they would live or die in the next minute, Jeno pushed his young son protectively behind him. Standing next to them, Lasko saw the desperate move and whispered from the side of his mouth, "Don't worry Uncle Jeno, if they meant to shoot us, we would be facing the wall!" There was a hint of a smile in Jeno's eyes as he shot a quick glance at Lasko. Intended or not, the remark had a humorous undertone that Jeno could appreciate even in their perilous predicament.

Their exchange didn't go unnoticed by the officer. In an instant he jumped in front of Lasko and, shouting at him, swung his arm, aiming to slap him across the mouth. When he came up short, barely scratching his jaw, he became angrier, and gearing up to do better, tried again. As Lasko snapped to attention with chin up and his six-foot-plus frame drawn to its full height, he missed the second time, but didn't give up. If not for the seriousness of the situation, the scene would have been almost comical, with the Russian standing on toes, repeatedly trying to smack the young man, but only swatting the air. Once he realized that with Lasko towering over him he couldn't punch him in the face, he began losing control and was reaching for his pistol just as another officer entered the court, ordering him to stop. He was obviously of higher rank, because after exchanging some loud words and gesticulating angrily, the little man turned on his heel and left with a last menacing glare at Lasko.

The other officer then took a headcount and addressed the men in limited German, sending them to fetch as many pails as they could find. They were to start bailing the wine from the cellar floor and carry every precious drop across the street to fill the large containers lined up inside the casern. He warned that armed guards would be watching their every move, and those foolish enough to try running away would be shot.

The men did as told. Returning with buckets and pails, even watering cans, they began scurrying back and forth between the wine cellar and the casern, their shoes and trousers soon thoroughly soaked in wine. If they spilled a drop, or stopped even for a second to change a grip, the guards were on their backs, shouting and threatening. When one soldier down the line, angered by something, fired a round in the air, it soon became a favorite practice, as the Russians howled with laughter at seeing the poor, frightened men ducking and trying to balance the pails at the same time.

Lasko was cursing under his breath for being forced to do the miserable chore, but Jeno told him he should be grateful; it actually saved his life! That little officer would have shot him if the other one hadn't talked him out of it. Jeno clearly heard him saying that they needed every man to rescue the wine; it was more important than settling a score with some idiot. "Do it later when the job is finished," were his exact words. The little Russian might still come after him, so Lasko should do everything to stay out of his way and hope and pray that by the time they were finished, the man would be too drunk to remember the incident.

While carrying the wine, they looked on helplessly as the Russians began looting the neighborhood. Singly or in groups, they went from house to house, coming out with armloads of clothing, radios, comforters, and boxes full of booty. They emptied wardrobes and drawer chests, picking out what they wanted, then left everything else strewn on the floor until the next bunch came to pick over what was still there. The female soldiers, the so-called *baryshnya*s, were especially fond of furs, while the men's main interest was finding alcohol. Anything would do. They poured cologne and aftershave lotions down their throat, coughing and spitting madly, but finishing to the last drop.

Sometimes a fight broke out between two soldiers over an item they both wanted. Again, it was almost comical to see them pulling and tugging, shouting profanities, and while they kicked and punched one another, a third one stole the loot. Two young soldiers came out of a house carrying bicycles and they decided to stage a race. They acted like children, laughing, until they collided and one fell off his bike, hitting his head on the pavement. The race ended with the two bloodying each other.

In the midst of it, suddenly a truck with several armed Russians drove into the street and stopped at the first apartment building. They ran inside, rounding up the women and pushing them onto the open truck. This time the men didn't care. They dropped their buckets and, waving their arms and shouting, raced toward the truck to prevent it from leaving. It was no use. The driver pulled away, while the soldiers on the street stood around poking each other, sniggering at the frustrated men left milling in angry confusion. To bring back order, one of the guards told them in broken German not to worry; the women were most likely needed for kitchen duty to peel potatoes and would be back later. When this didn't pacify them and the men kept protesting, the Russians fired a round over their heads and chased them back to work.

A woman who managed to hide during the roundup sent her young son running to their parish and alert the priest. These women needed help; he must do something! Braving the streets, the priest hurried to the commando and after a short wait was led in front of several officers. They greeted him cordially pulling a chair for him, but he declined, saying that he only came to report a problem: the behavior of drunken soldiers and their mistreatment of women. The officers listened, but offered no help. They didn't deny the fact that misconducts occurred here and there, and acknowledged that the transgressions were reprehensible, but then, raising a shoulder, they added that such is the nature of war. There were good and bad soldiers amongst the Russians, the same as in the German and Hungarian Armies. They referred to the atrocities committed by the Nazis and their allies in Russia, and so, who could blame them if some of these soldiers now felt that it was their turn to get even, especially if they, or someone in their family, had suffered the savagery of the German occupiers.

The Father could not dispute the officers' allegations about German atrocities against civilians in Russia and Poland. SS soldiers themselves used to brag about the cruelties they inflicted upon the inferior Slavs, whom they considered only a notch above the subhuman Jews. It was pointless to bring up the difference between the Germans and Hungarians. He hung his head in silence and only asked in a low voice how long before some sort of order would return? This chaos couldn't go on forever. When could the city expect an end to the lawlessness? The chief officer, patting him on the shoulder, suggested patience and cooperation during these difficult days; they were working hard to improve the situation.

There was nothing the priest could do but return to the parish with the sad news that there would be no help from the Russian Commando. They let the marauding soldiers do as they pleased, and there was very little hope that normalcy would be re-established anytime soon.

When the wine cellar was finally empty, the men were let go. Jeno and the boys could hardly wait to wash up and put on some clean clothes, but when they entered the house they could not believe their eyes. After watching all day from the street the comings and goings of the Russians, they expected to find some of their belongings missing, but they were unprepared for what greeted them. The scene was beyond comprehension. Everything was in shambles. Closets stood empty with doors ajar, drawers pulled out, clothes—what little were left—lay in piles on the floor, trampled by boots. Pieces of furniture were thrown across the room, broken; the mirror on Ilonka's dresser smashed, her cosmetics spilled out; chairs kicked over. All of the crystal pieces and porcelain figurines left intact by the bombings were swept out of the étagère and lay shattered; the bookcase was turned over, books strewn on the floor. They found drunken soldiers passed out on every bed and sofa, with two sprawled on the kitchen floor snoring, shards of plates and glassware all around them. The air was foul, reeking of vomit and worse. Jeno wished he could hose off the filth, but the most they could do was to pick up some clothing, go down to the cellar, wash up in the laundry room and collapse on the mattresses.

None of them could sleep, though. They saw what alcohol would do to the Russians, turning them into wild animals, and they were sick with worry, thinking of the women at the Benedictines. What if the soldiers discovered the extensive wine collection there? The thought kept them awake for long hours, until finally exhaustion set in. But before Jeno closed his eyes he decided to risk sending Gyuszi to check the situation at the Benedictine's shelter. It was the only way to find out if Ilonka and the girls were safe.

The next morning Gyuszi left the house, anxious but not afraid. The Russians seemed to leave children alone, and with his baby face and thin body he looked younger than his eleven years. He reached the parish without a problem and found his mother and everyone else well and in good spirits. The spring weather was warm and sunny and the women spent most of their time outside in the garden, quietly talking, reading, and watching the children at play. They were all safe, thanks to the immediate proximity to the Russian Commando. The officers there were highly disciplined and supportive, they even posted a Russian notice on the church door, baring soldiers from entering. It worked, since there were no intrusions.

Ilonka was overwhelmed with joy when she saw Gyuszi and was eagerly listening to the news from the "home front." He, of course, didn't know anything about the raping; he could only report on the wine-carrying incident and the condition of their home, the drunken soldiers in the house, and that despite of everything, no harm had come to them so far.

After spending a few hours together, Gyuszi returned home and found the Russians gone from the house, but so were his father and Latzi and Lasko. He went down to the cellar to wait for them, passing the time reading and napping, but when by nightfall there was still no sign of them, the scared little boy, sitting alone in the dark, started to cry. He didn't dare to move, not even when around eleven o'clock he heard noises above. Only when the cellar door opened and Jeno called out his name did he run up and into his arms.

Jeno and the boys were tired and covered with dirt but otherwise safe. They were taken in the morning along with other men from the neighborhood to work at the railroad clearing away debris. They were given an armband and some Russian papers that declared them members of the railroad repair brigade, which also gave them safe conduct during curfew hours. With the exception of a short break at noon, when food was doled out, they worked all day and well into night under the glaring lights charged by generators. After nine o'clock they were finally let go with orders to report back to work at 6 AM the next day. They should have been home earlier but soldiers grabbed them on the way home to help put out a fire in a burning building. They were passing buckets until now.

Tired as they were, the good news about the women in the shelter lifted their spirits. Thank God, from now on they didn't have to worry about them. After washing up, the three men made a quick trip upstairs to check on the house. As Gyuszi said, the soldiers were gone, but the place was still a horrendous mess, and being too exhausted to start cleaning and dragging the bedding up to the bedroom, they returned to spend another night in the cellar.

The work at the railroad was hard, but having been assigned to it turned out to be a blessing in disguise. Several other work brigades had far worse tasks to perform, such as collecting the dead bodies of fallen Russian soldiers or digging graves in the cemetery for their burial. Laundry work was a little easier but just as odious, washing bloody and soiled bed linen in hospitals. Women, too, were randomly picked up and put to work in kitchens, peeling potatoes and washing dirty dishes.

By the third or fourth day into the Russian occupation, more people worked up the courage to dare voicing their complaints about the abuses. Not that going to the commando solved anything. Upon receiving a report, the officers made a note of the incident, but then demanded to identify the culprit so he could be apprehended and punished. Of course that was the end of the case. Eventually they got tired of listening to the mounting grievances and summoned the former police chief, ordering him to start exercising his power and bring the situation under control. What power, the poor man asked, when policemen were forbidden to carry arms, not even a baton, leaving them utterly helpless to confront soldiers caught during misconduct. Left to the mercy of these often drunken Russians, his men would only risk their lives and accomplish nothing. To do their job, that is to enforce the law, safeguard the public, and secure the streets, under such circumstances was simply impossible.

Yet by the end of the week there were signs of improvement, and the women at the Benedictine sanctuary felt that it was reasonably safe to return home. They were anxious to rejoin their families and began leaving in small groups and in timely intervals to avoid an exodus. Ilonka and the children left in the morning and arrived home without incident. It was only when they stepped inside the house that the shock set in. Coming from a safe place, they were unprepared for what greeted them: the horrific filth and disorder, the empty closets, broken furniture, all the beds stripped bare. There was not even a blanket left. They could consider themselves lucky that the Russians did not check the cellar when they were looking for additional bedding for their hospitals; at least they still had what was down there.

As they started to clean up the place, picking through the pile of cloth on the floor, Sárika was frantically looking for her beloved new coat. Of course it was gone, and when she realized it, she first broke into tears, then began cursing the person whoever stole it in such language that it shocked Ilonka. She had to remind her how fortunate they were to have escaped all the violence and abuse so many others were made to suffer.

Slowly, they were making some progress, and by the evening the house was in a presentable shape. Ilonka was preparing supper, canned meat and some baked potatoes, when Jeno and the others arrived home from the railroad. What a joy it was to see each other after the week's ordeal, to have the family together, unharmed, and once again under the same roof! The tearful hugging and kissing had no end. The worst was over! They had seen the gates of hell opened and skirted its horrors, but they escaped. They had survived!

If Ilonka thought they were safe at home, she soon learned that they were not out of danger. The sudden appearance of women in the house quickly drew the attention of the Russian soldiers in the casern, and the next morning after the men left for work, one of them came knocking on the door. It was an officer, and when no one came to let him in, he began banging and shouting. Ilonka needed the few minutes it took for Eta and Sárika to climb out the bathroom window at the back of the house and run to the neighbors next door. Once they were safe, she was ready to face the Russian. On her way to the entrance she picked up the baby, grabbed little Istvan's hand and with Gyuszi at her side opened the door to the angry, wildly gesticulating officer.

Remaining calm and acting contrite she apologized in Russian—*Izvinitye, nye ponimayo po Russki*—for not understanding the language, words that every Hungarian had learned by then and used often when accused of lacking cooperation. Then thinking fast, she switched to German and made an excuse for her delay, hoping he'd understand it, as quite a few soldiers knew at least a few words in that language. He answered back with surprising fluency, and pushing his way in announced that he was looking for living quarters and wanted to inspect the house. He went from room to room, with Ilonka following him every step of the way, as he scrutinized every corner, opened closet doors and even peeked under the beds. Then he stopped abruptly and without further pretense, demanded to know where the young girls were and warned Ilonka not to lie, because they were seen. Her heart pounding but forcing a smile, she explained that those were only visitors, there were no girls living in the house. Cussing angrily, the Russian accused her of being a Nazi liar and said he would find out the truth, because he was moving in later in that afternoon.

When he left, Ilonka quickly wrote a note to the neighbors asking them to keep the girls for now, packed some food for them and sent it over with little Istvan. Worried and tense, she waited all afternoon for the Russian to return, but when the doorbell rang, instead of him, a female officer with a flat round face and slanted black eyes stood at the door. She only spoke Russian, her loud and arrogant voice ringing through the hallway as she marched in and headed straight to the front room that faced the military compound. Without checking the rest of the house, she gestured that she was taking the room, then pulled out an official-looking sign, scribbled something on it, and after posting it on the street entrance, marched back to the casern.

A little later the German-speaking Russian showed up again. He tore down the sign and waving it in front of Ilonka's nose began to yell and scream belligerently, how dare she let in someone else. Unsteady on his feet and his breath reeking of alcohol, he ignored Ilonka's pleading that she had little control over the other officer, and in his growing rage began to threaten her. He pulled out his pistol and was brandishing it when out of nowhere, the female officer stormed into the room and in a flash grabbed his wrist, twisting the gun out of his hand. It landed on the floor, with Ilonka cowering in the corner, watching as they yelled and cursed at each other. The confrontation escalated into pushing and shoving, until finally the woman drew her gun and pointed at his head. That seemed to sober him up, unfortunately, not entirely. He took off running but apparently couldn't remember which way to the door, and wound up in the kitchen. With the baryshnya chasing after him, he had no choice but to jump out the window, landing on the street a good seven feet below. They could hear the loud thump as his body hit the pavement, followed by his screams, but the patron saint of drunks must have protected him because he got up and limped away to the raucous laughter of the sentry at the casern. After that the female officer posted a new sign, ordered the street entrance door locked and retired to her hard-won quarters.

That evening, when Jeno learned what happened, they decided to bring the girls home but hide them in the bathroom until things calmed down. Ilonka made up a bed in the bathtub for Sárika and put a small mattress on the floor for Eta. The girls would be safe there with the door locked and a heavy wardrobe closet placed in front of it. In an extreme emergency they could always escape through the small window looking toward the park and unseen from the casern, then wait at the neighbors until the danger passed. Being cooped up didn't bother them; they had books to read and played chess or cards all day, safe not only from any intruding Russian but also from doing chores to help their mother.

As the days passed, it became evident that the female officer represented no threat; in fact her presence rendered the house safer. The posted sign protected them from other rowdy Russians who were barging in and out of the neighborhood homes to find accommodations close to the casern. She was gone most of the time, and even when home, she kept to her room. She used the kitchen only to wash up there, never asking where to bathe. This was not entirely strange, since many of these soldiers, including her as judged by her Asiatic features, came from remote places in the Soviet Union, such as Uzbekistan, Kyrgyzstan or Mongolia, where plumbing was unheard of. At least she knew what to make of the toilet, because many didn't. They used the bowl to wash their shirts and underwear in it, and when they pulled the chain from sheer curiosity and saw the water flushing down their garments, they angrily accused the residents of using dirty Nazi tricks to rob them of their possessions.

All in all, the co-habitation with their "resident" officer worked out well for the family, and so after a few days Jeno and Ilonka brought the girls out of their hiding place. It was another step toward normalcy, or so they thought. The relative tranquility ended when after two weeks the baryshnya took her sign off the entrance and left without saying a word. It put them back to square one, wondering who would be knocking on their door next. Would there be another fight over who got to set up quarters in their home? And how would Ilonka handle that kind of trouble alone, Jeno worried, when he and the boys were still working at the railroad? She tried to play down his fear by saying she was strong enough to face any intruder; besides, things were calmer now and the beastly behavior of the soldiers was getting more under control. God had watched over the family so far; what made Jeno think that he would desert them now?

Either God, hearing her, rewarded Ilonka for her faith, or simply by luck, the next morning a soft-spoken higher-ranking Russian officer and his aide-de-camp walked into the house to take up one of the rooms. He did not speak German, only a few words, but the young soldier was fluent, and through him he politely asked to inspect the house. When he finished, instead of the large front room, he chose the master bedroom with the bathroom next to it. Ilonka immediately sensed a certain civility in the officer and gladly obliged to make the room ready for them. Rearranging the furniture was a small inconvenience in exchange for having the protection of this seemingly decent man. As Jeno and Ilonka got to know him better, her instinct about his character proved to be correct. He was a cultivated man with good manners, who treated everyone in the house with kindness and respect. He was fond of the children and often brought them a piece of fruit or occasionally a loaf of freshly baked bread. He had a social ease about him, listened to classical music on a phonograph he brought with him, and with Ilonka's permission, even played the piano, and surprisingly well, proving that not all Russians were uneducated brutes.

His servant, a nineteen-year-old boy named Vasil, was not a soldier, as they learned, even though he was wearing a uniform. During the German advance into Russia he was captured and taken to Germany to work in one of their slave-labor factories. He learned the language there and when the Red Army liberated him, they put him to work translating for officers. He was a good-natured and friendly young man, always with a grin on his broad Slavic face, happy to do his superior's bidding. His main job was to run errands for his boss, keep his room clean and neat, and cook his meals. One day shortly after they moved in, he brought a huge slab of beef, almost half a carcass, to the house and, after placing it in the bathtub, announced that it was for the entire family to enjoy. Ilonka gladly took him up on the offer; armed with a sharp knife she began cutting away pieces of meat, one day for a delicious roast, next for a pot of goulash or hearty soup, until the meat began to spoil. There was no ice available anywhere, not even for the Russians, and even if there were, it would have quickly melted away in the warm spring weather. To prevent flies feasting on the beef, Vasil filled the tub with cold water and kept changing it but it was of no use; nothing could save the meat from going bad. Only when maggots started to squirm in the flesh and the stench became overwhelming did the boy finally chop up the stinking remains, dumping it far from the house. It took Ilonka days to get rid of the smell.

The family was now eating better. With the canned meat and lard from the Sanberger warehouse and some potatoes and onions still in the cool cellar, Ilonka could cook more nutritious meals. Stores, of course, were closed; there was nothing to sell, not without supplies coming from the villages, where the Russians took everything the Germans left behind. From time to time trucks pulled into the casern unloading cases of goods, and knowing that the Russians didn't harm children, Ilonka sent six-year-old Istvan across to just stand near the gates, perhaps the soldiers would give him something. Most of the time the little beggar returned with scraps of vegetables, an apple or a couple of eggs, but when others in the neighborhood saw what was going on, and more and more children lined up for handouts, the Russians stopped the giveaways.

To introduce a little variety to their meals, Ilonka decided to bring up a rod of salami, still buried in the cellar. When she started digging she saw that some rats had beaten her to it; they gnawed through the sturdy wrapping, and started nibbling on the meat. *Well,* she thought, *from the looks of it, we are not the only ones hungry these days!* Lifting out the whole package, she saw with relief that they only chewed on one rod, and even that was not wasted; what harm was in it if a few bites were missing? After cutting away the bitten parts and giving a thorough cleansing, she fried the rest and served it with potatoes. Still, she let a few years go by before telling Jeno the story of how the rats sampled their salami first.

By the end of April all three men were released from the work brigade. The railroad tracks were functional enough for the trains to start rolling, if they could be called trains at all. The Germans had already taken all the engines and passenger trains that had escaped major damage from the bombings, and now it was the Russians' turn to pick over and take the best of the remaining lot. What was left for the locals was practically junkyard material, pitiful skeletal frames with torn roofs, but no matter, it would have to do as long as the wheels could turn. They were all packed with returning refugees who had fled to the West only a few weeks before, and war-weary soldiers coming back from liberated areas, all longing to go home. Freed prisoners of war from the various nations, men and women taken by the Germans for forced labor, and Jews from concentration camps strong enough to stand were also squeezed into these dilapidated trains, anxiously trying to find their way home. Thousands and thousands of these emaciated people clad in dirty rags, their faces unshaven, hair matted and crawling with lice, rode these trains in desperate hope of reaching their homeland, not knowing if they still had a home and family waiting for them.

When these returning trains crossed into Sopron, everyone in uniform was ordered off and put through a registration process by a hastily composed military forum. Their guns were taken, and after grouping them according to nationalities, the foreigners were given papers to continue their travel. The Hungarian soldiers, however, were marched to a casern, where they had to surrender all Army-issued items down to their socks, go through disinfections, and change into an unsanitary looking set of cotton tunic and pants. Their stay there was only temporary, they were told, until their military ranks could be verified. At the same time orders were plastered on every street corner calling for soldiers still on the loose, including those who had deserted in the last days of the war, to come forward and report to the military registry office. They'd be given a discharge certificate and would also be officially counted as survivors of the war. With so many troops killed and missing, this information would help the government to establish an accurate list of war casualties.

The smart ones still at large, guessing a trap, ignored the order. Others who dutifully showed up paid dearly, as they were not let go. With the rest of the detained soldiers they were loaded into covered military trucks and driven to nearby Sopron-Kohida, the notorious former Nazi military prison camp, already cramped with captured German soldiers. Together they were all labeled prisoners of war and hauled off to Russia, some 35,000 troops from this location alone, sent to the Siberian gulags to work as slaves under horrid conditions at various postwar reconstruction projects.

Next came the arrest of civilian leaders suspected of membership in the former Nazi or Arrow Cross parties. They were interrogated and kept at police headquarters, barred from any contact with relatives and friends. When the police ran out of prison cells they turned to the Russians for directives. Who would provide for all these prisoners? The pitiful daily slop that passed for soup could barely sustain them. The Russians responded with a pat on the back and some reassuring words that they had full confidence in the police to find a solution to the problem. In the end no one took responsibility. The entire country was at a standstill, void of administration or any kind of authority. All was in Soviet hands, and their only concern was to take care of their own. As for the Allied powers, they were still fighting the war and had little interest in following events unfolding in liberated countries to the east.

With so much uncertainty about tomorrow, everyone was tense when on the evening of May 8 fear gripped the people again at the sound of rockets bursting and Russian soldiers shooting their guns. Were the Germans coming back? To find out what was happening Jeno turned on the radio and heard the news: Germany had surrendered and the war was over! Like everyone else, they rushed outside to see the night sky ablaze with fireworks, strangers hugging each other, the Russians singing and dancing, and if they were drinking, it was all right, too, on that historic day.

Most people, however, still afraid of Russian excesses, dared not stay outside for long. Back in the house, Ilonka opened a bottle of wine she brought home from the Benedictines—it was free for the taking—and kept hidden for just this occasion. They had double cause for celebration; it was her birthday and the war was over, the greatest gift she could wish for. No more living on the razor's edge, they can start walking on solid ground again.

With tears in their eyes, tears of relief that they had pulled through such terrible times, they raised their glasses to a new beginning for the family and for their beloved country. Stepping out of the darkness, the nation could now concentrate on building a new, stronger Hungary, free of the Nazi terror and hopefully, soon without the Soviets.

It took five weeks after the Red Army rolled into Sopron before people finally began to notice a gradual change in the attitude of the Russian Commando. At least they made a halfhearted attempt to reign in those soldiers still brawling and marauding. If caught, they were reprimanded, sometimes even in front of the injured parties, although no harsh punishment followed. Still, it was a start. They also put pressure on the civilian authorities to step up efforts and bring back a degree of normalcy. They were ordered to hurry up with the political screening that was taking place, so people could return to work and start putting their affairs in order. Jeno passed the review and was back in his old position at the main customs office.

By middle of May schools opened their doors, and to make up for time lost during the past six months, they remained open for the summer. Many of them ran a second shift, holding afternoon sessions to accommodate students whose schools were bombed out. Eta and Sárika fell into this group. Only the university, which took several hits, remained closed, partly due to the structural damage, but also because most students were from different parts of the country and were still absent. Factories missed a number of workers too, but they were organizing to start operation, mainly for fear that if they stayed idle too long, the Russians would dismantle and confiscate their machinery and equipment.

Even a few restaurants, more like family eateries serving meager home-cooked meals, opened for a few hours during daytime. The restaurant Mitzie and her husband used to own, however, was not among them. It did not survive the war, and they lacked the means to start over again. Forced to find another way to make a living, they applied for work at the textile factory that was getting ready to open, and when they were both hired, Mitzie came by asking Ilonka if she, too, would be interested in working there.

"They are still looking for people to replace workers who escaped to the West, and I am sure you could get a job there, Ilonka. Work is in two rotating shifts, morning and afternoon, and the pay is not bad."

"I don't have any experience, Mitzie, why should they hire me?"

"Because they need to start production! We don't have experience either, but management is willing to train people. It's a good place to work; you should think about it. But don't wait too long; there are plenty of people lined up for the job."

"Could I work only in the morning?"

"Well no, you have to take turns, just like everyone else."

"Then it's not for me. Eta and Sárika are at home until noon to look after Ochie and Istvan, but I can't leave the boys alone in the afternoons; they are still too young. I tell you what, though. I'll ask Latzi and the Riedls, I am sure they would be glad to start working. It was good of you to come and tell me about it."

They were all hired, even Eta, when she, too, applied for the job. She was still attending school in the afternoons, but management agreed to put her solely on the morning shift until she graduated in the fall. She could keep half of what she earned, while the rest went to pay household bills. The extra money made quite a difference, and Ilonka began to have second thoughts about staying home. If she worked, they could start making repairs to the house.

Nothing came of it, however, when Jeno wouldn't let her take the job. It was not worth it, he argued, if they had to pay for a baby-sitter whenever she worked in the afternoons. Besides, how could she think of walking home alone after a late shift, or even with Latzi, if they happened to be on the same schedule? The Russians might behave better during the day now that security was improving, but at night they still prowled the streets, usually drunk and in groups, accosting people and robbing them. They had even invented a new trick to avoid being caught. They were stripping their victims naked and taking their clothes, a useful tactic to delay them from running to the Commando for help. What's more, this practice proved to be so effective that some unscrupulous civilians dressed up as Russians were doing it, too.

And so, Ilonka remained at home, but it was not entirely safe there either; she got a good scare one afternoon when a Russian tried to drag her out of the house. A few days before the incident she had badly scraped her leg when going down to the cellar one of the rickety steps broke and trapped her. By the next day the leg was swollen, she was in pain and burning up with fever. She sent for Dr. Graser who, after examining it, found no broken bones, but an acute inflammation of the skin and the underlying tissues. He gave her some aspirin and told her to stay off her feet and keep it wrapped in a cold, wet towel. Ice of course was nonexistent.

Following the doctor's orders, she was lying on a sofa, fully dressed, her legs covered with a blanket, when she heard the doorbell ringing and someone rattling the door and shouting in Russian. Unable to get up, she kept Ochie and Istvan at her side, praying that he'd go away, but instead the man broke down the door panel and managed to force his way in. She listened helplessly as the Russian proceeded down the hallway, opening and slamming every door, until he was in her room, standing over her. Talking rapidly and gesturing wildly, he ordered her to get up, while at the same time Ilonka was frantically trying to say both in Hungarian and in German that she was too ill to move. The Russian finally had enough and, grabbing her arm, tried to yank her off the couch. He only let her go when in the struggle the blanket and the wet towel slipped off and he saw the red and badly swollen leg. Cursing loudly, he stormed out of the house in search of someone else to snatch.

She found out later that the Russians were rounding up people in the neighborhood to obtain blood urgently needed for transfusion. A dormant bomb buried under rubble exploded, severely injuring a number of soldiers, but when they were rushed into the makeshift hospital at the Sisters of Mercy on Ilonka's street, they found the blood supply completely exhausted. The roundup was necessary since no one would donate blood voluntarily to help a Russian.

Ilonka's leg improved slowly, but until she was well enough to walk, Jeno kept Gyuszi home from school. Almost twelve, he was an intelligent boy, affectionate and loving, always ready to help. There was never a problem with him; his teachers at the Benedictines could only praise him and not only for being a good student, but also for his devotion and deep inner faith. He regularly served as an altar boy, and it was not to gain favors with his teachers either, but because of his strong beliefs.

Ilonka often told the story that as a baby Gyuszi did not talk until he was past two, but when he finally opened his mouth, his first words were "Jesus." *Now there is a boy born to be a priest*, Ilonka laughed out loud when she heard him. Jeno laughed too, but with a different view: perhaps his son had heard somebody in the house taking Christ's name in vain a bit too often.

Ilonka secretly admitted that she wouldn't oppose it if her eldest son should decide to become a priest. She herself never missed church on Sundays and Holy days. Her faith in the Church was unshakable but she also loved the mysticism of the Catholic rituals. The chanting liturgy, the wafting clouds of incense, and the angelic voices drifting down from the choir always soothed her soul. Someday, she thought, when the children were older, she'd join the choir; at least all those singing lessons she took in Vienna wouldn't have been wasted. Her religious fervor grew even stronger during her stay at the Benedictines. She felt greatly indebted to God and the Church for the sanctuary that saved her and her daughters from the cruelty so many women in their neighborhood were forced to endure. To have her son enter into God's service would be a small gesture of gratitude; after all, she had two other boys to carry on the family name.

Her girls, however, had no interest whatsoever donning a nun's habit. Although they had the same religious upbringing, Sárika would happily skip Sunday Mass if Ilonka did not make her attend. Eta was never ardently devoted either; she went to Sunday services because it was required by her parochial school. It was only lately, since her relationship with Latzi, a Protestant, began to turn serious, that Ilonka noticed the two of them spending hours discussing religion. She encouraged it, thinking that by analyzing the differences between the two beliefs, Latzi could be converted to the Catholic faith. Little did she know that the chance for that was next to zero! Aside from being the nephew of the head of the Reformed Church in Hungary, he was not only a staunch Protestant, but true to the famous characteristic of the founder of his religion, he was as obstinate as Calvin ever was.

With Bible in hand, Eta and Latzi would sit together, arguing about doctrines and about whose religion adhered more to God's designs for mankind. In the end Latzi won, not entirely by convincing Eta that he was right, but simply because she was in love, and he mattered to her more than religious dogmas. Later when they became engaged, she did not convert, only agreed to get married in his Church. Jeno had no objection, after all, his own parents were of mixed religion, but Ilonka was deeply disappointed. Her only consolation was that anyone who went to sleep reading the Bible every night and would go to such lengths as to crusade for his beliefs could not be all bad.

She couldn't have guessed that in less than a year the Bible would disappear from Latzi's nightstand and the writings of Marx and Engel would take its place.

CHAPTER FOUR

1945 - 1950

A rough beginning

ON JANUARY 20, 1945, weeks before the war ended and while Budapest was still under siege, a hastily formed Provisional National Government signed an armistice agreement in Moscow with all three of the major Allies. The harsh terms reflected that the victors did not forgive Hungary for not turning against the Germans. Italy, Bulgaria, and Romania were all given credit for deserting the Nazis and surrendering to the Allied forces, but no one considered that Hungary made similar efforts, first toward the Western Allies, which were rejected due to their indifference, then later to the Russians. These were serious attempts to break with Hitler that brought on the kidnapping of the Regent by the Germans and the installation of their puppet government. They completely ignored the country's isolated geographical placement, virtually in the claws of the Nazi giant that made it simply impossible for the tiny country to break away as others did. The negotiators also overlooked that after decades of passionate but futile appeals to the world to remedy the tragic territorial losses Hungary suffered after World War I, Germany was the only country that offered help. It was through Hitler that the First and Second Vienna Awards corrected the injustice of Trianon by returning not all, but large areas of what Slovakia, Romania, and Yugoslavia took from her.

All provisions of the armistice—political, military, economic, and financial—aimed to punish the country. She was reduced to her pre-war frontiers by simply declaring the two Vienna Awards null and void, and was slammed with heavy reparations payments to the Allied Control Commission, or ACC for short. Composed of Russia, the United States, and Great Britain, the ACC was created to deal with the urgent problems of devastated post-war Europe, with Klementy Voroshilov, a trusted member of the Soviet politburo, chosen as its Chairman. It was an unfortunate choice, since it put the ACC under Russian control, with the United States and Britain exerting only nominal influence. As a result, Hungary was compelled to accept the terms of the armistice agreement according to Russian interpretation, which only served Soviet interests.

While these negotiations were taking place, a group of Hungarian émigrés living in Moscow left the Soviet Union to follow the Red Army as it advanced through the eastern region of Hungary, and began organizing a new government in the liberated city of Debrecen. Many of these so-called Muscovites were former members of the short-lived 1919 Communist takeover who fled to Russia, became Soviet citizens, and were totally indoctrinated in Stalinist ideology. Showing absolute obedience to the Kremlin and familiar with the process of world revolutionary conquest as explained in the works of Lenin and Stalin, they were handpicked to apply these principles to politically disintegrated and economically ruined Hungary. The fact that they were born in Hungary, spoke Hungarian, and knew the country well was only secondary in their selection; their loyalty was only to Russia.

Most prominent of the returning Muscovites were Matyas Rakosi (born Mihaly Rosenfeld), Erno Gero (born Erno Singer), and Mihaly Farkas (born Mihaly Loewy), all Moscow-trained Communists, and all of them Jewish, their names Hungarianised. Their close association earned them the name "troika," the old-fashion Russian carriage pulled by a team of three horses abreast. These Muscovites were greatly different from their Hungarian comrades who remained in the country after the Communist Party was dissolved during the Horthy era and continued their work underground. They were considered by the Moscow-based émigrés as old time "nationalistic" Communists, not to be trusted to support the new Stalinist political aims. For the time being they were to play a transitory role to gain confidence in the Communist Party, since the Muscovites were well aware that due to the recent atrocities by the Red Army, their Russian backed party lacked popular support. They would have to bide their time, but once they won over the majority of the toiling masses, the old timers would be eliminated.

As its first legislative act, on March 15, 1945, even before the war came to an end for the country on April 4th, the provisional government carried out a sweeping land reform. Until then most land belonged to the aristocracy and the Church, or in some cases to rich farmers, while nearly three million peasants, one third of the population, held a few acres, or worked as landless laborers. The agrarian redistribution was long overdue in part for social reasons, but also because it was a strong incentive to jumpstart the vitally needed agricultural production.

Under the decree, wealthy landowners with over 1,420 acres were deprived of all their holdings and had no recourse whatsoever, while the small landowners were allowed to retain up to 142 acres, and 642,342 landless peasants received small allotments. The reform was hailed as a great achievement, an economic progress that turned working peasants into independent and prosperous farmers with their property rights respected and protected. None of the new "landowners" were aware that granting small parcels was in fact the first step toward collectivization. It was to prove later that small, privately owned farms were incapable of operating successfully in modern agriculture, but anyone even hinting at it in 1945 was promptly denounced as a reactionary agitator and an enemy of the people.

With the land reform accomplished, the new provisional government's next move was to organize the various ministries. Unlike in other Russian-occupied countries, where Soviet-style proletarian dictatorship was quickly established, the Muscovites had Stalin's approval to take time, perhaps ten or more years if necessary, to achieve the same goal. Accordingly, from the very start the Communists advocated the forming of a coalition government where all democratic parties shared in the leadership. They promised adherence to democratic principles, even cooperation with the clergy, and to prove their sincerity they took active part in helping to rebuild destroyed churches. They loudly professed patriotic sentiments and emphasized that the Russians were here only to weed out the reactionary Fascists and Nazi collaborators, not to interfere with Hungary's internal politics. To help the Russians and at the same time strengthen their own power, the Communists created a special political police, where no other than members of the Communist Party could obtain a position of importance. They claimed that only they possessed the expert knowledge to rid the nation of former Nazi-oriented elements, but promised that once it was accomplished, non-party members would have equal share in higher-level control. That, of course, remained just that—a promise.

During this first postwar period the Communists acted with such extreme caution that only a few people saw what was to come in later years. In the general euphoria created by false promises for a new and more just Hungary, no one seemed to notice the subtle changes already taking place. While preaching freedom of speech, no one was allowed to question the good faith of the Party in carrying out those promises, and although other parties were given equal voice, the Communists extended certain favors to the Social Democrats in order to create a bond between their two parties. Together they would represent the leftist majority needed for control.

Next on their agenda, the Communists descended on every city, town, and village to organize "national committees," created to handle all public affairs on the municipal level. They were entrusted with electing officials who formed the Provisional National Assembly, the center of authority of the Hungarian State that operated through a cabinet. For its members suitable persons were recruited from all parties but with a careful eye on maintaining a healthy balance in their own favor by insisting to place at least one member of the Communist Party in key positions. Through them the Communists could exert influence in every decision, including how Hungary's preliminary peace proposal should be prepared, what its aim should be and to whom to address it.

The primary task of the proposal was to outline the country's economic difficulties, due largely to the war, but also—and not in a small way—to the systematic looting by the Russians. The Red Army dismantled whole factories and removed them to Russia, including the so-called "German foreign assets" that consisted of investments the Nazis made in Hungary during the occupation. They sacked every financial institution, braking into vaults, confiscating money and banknotes, and emptying safe deposit boxes, regardless whether their contents were private, public, or belonging to neutral legations. When the Foreign Ministry, in charge of writing the peace proposal, produced a draft on August 14, 1945 that included a request for the return of all assets taken by the Soviets, or at least be counted as part of the reparation payments instead of war booty, the Communists objected so vehemently that the entire project was abandoned.

By the end of summer the continued Soviet abuses committed against the devastated country began to endanger the physical survival of the people, a breach according to international law that holds an occupying power responsible for the population living in territories under its control. Unfortunately, with the ACC controlled by the Russians, Hungary had very little voice to protest against these violations, and even if the two western members of the ACC heard it, their reaction was mild. Only once, in July 1945, did they express an interest to visit Hungary and review the alleged mistreatments, but their request, carefully worded as not to offend the Soviets for the sake of a small country formerly allied with Germany, was flatly refused. To stop further accusations and demonstrate Moscow's concern, the Soviets then extended a loan to the famine-threatened people, an act hailed by the Hungarian Communists as the greatest gesture of Russian generosity. In fact, the money involved was what the Red Army stole from Hungarian banks during the first days of the occupation.

With the backing of the powerful Soviet Union, the Communists were steadily gaining power while the non-Communist politicians couldn't expect any help from the West. Once they realized that the country's recovery depended entirely on Russian goodwill, they had no choice but to accept the leading role of the Communist Party to help maintain a reasonably good relationship with the occupying Soviet authorities. It took some time before they woke up and saw that the Party did nothing of the sort; they only carried out orders from Moscow. And by then it was also too late for the West to stop the Russians from completely dominating Hungary and other states under their influence.

These satellite countries had to pay dearly for the mistakes the Allies made, first at Yalta in February 1945 by naively trusting Stalin's word that he won't interfere with the shaping of the future of these nations, and then by handing over the control of the ACC to the Soviets. Although Churchill had some doubts about the sincerity of the Russians—it was he who coined the phrase "The Iron Curtain" long before it descended, trapping millions of people—he signed the shameful Yalta Agreement, regardless. The sole voice speaking out against the abuses was that of British Foreign Secretary Ernest Bevin in a speech delivered on August 20, 1945 in the House of Commons, stating that ". . . the impression we get from recent developments is that one kind of totalitarianism is being replaced by another."

Although by the middle of 1945 civilian life slowly began to resume a degree of normalcy, the random roundups of people typical of the early days of the Russian occupation still continued. Those caught could never be sure if they were needed for some temporary work, or if they were to be dragged to a Soviet labor camp. Many simply disappeared, never to be seen again, so it was no wonder that everyone picked up on the streets by the Russians was on the lookout for a chance to escape.

One day Latzi was on his way to work when Russian soldiers stopped him, and even though he showed his working papers, they ordered, or rather, shoved him into a large group of men lined up in the middle of the street. Once they started to march in the direction of the railroad station, his instinct told him he must get away, they were not herded there for *malinko robot*, some light work, such as cleaning the cattle cars after the animals were removed. The menacing attitude of the Russians, their rude prodding, and forbidding the men to talk, all indicated that this was not an ordinary work roundup.

He nervously scanned the area, weighing his chances to flee, when suddenly out of the corner of his eye he saw a young woman with a baby carriage coming down the sidewalk toward them. He elbowed his way nearest to the curb and when the woman was about to pass him, he darted out and quickly stepped next to her. Without a word, he grabbed the pram and turned into the next side street. It was sheer luck that at the same time a truck on the other side of the column was trying to pass, and the honking and yelling distracted the Russians for a moment. They were too busy trying to prevent anyone jumping on the truck to escape.

His heart pounding wildly and his breath coming in short bursts, he apologized to the woman for his scary behavior and thanked her for not screaming or making a scene, which would have ruined his dash to freedom. She patted his hand, saying that she knew exactly what he was doing, and praised his quick presence of mind. It was a close call, but after regaining his composure, Latzi still went to work. He felt relieved but at the same time strangely guilty. He knew that the Russians would find someone else to replace him, and that his successful getaway meant there would be a mother or wife tonight waiting in vain for the return of a loved one whom they might never see again.

Latzi escaped the roundup, but a few weeks later got involved in another unpleasant incident. By then Ilonka was running low on the canned meat; even the potatoes were but gone, yet the stores were still empty. Peasants were unwilling to sell needed supplies to shop owners at wholesale prices when they could get more money on the black market. Then, as money started losing its value, they switched to bartering, accepting items in exchange for something they lacked or wanted. The practice was illegal, and soon the police stepped in and began fining the farmers and confiscating their goods. It didn't stop the bartering though, only turned it around, with city folks bringing items to the surrounding villages in exchange for food. And so Latzi found himself on Sunday mornings pedaling his bicycle to nearby places with pieces of jewelry, some silver, a crystal vase, or Herendy porcelain—anything Ilonka could spare. During one of his excursions two armed Russians confronted him on his way home and "liberated" his bike, as well as the food he had obtained, then left him stranded some ten miles outside the city. He made it back on foot and reported the robbery, but of course the Hungarian police could do nothing. They told him to try his luck with the Commando, which he did, although carefully avoiding a direct accusation when asked to describe the culprits. He only said that no doubt, they were criminals disguised in Russian uniforms. They made a note of the complaint, but he never saw his bike again.

As bartering spread, stories soon emerged about what items were most popular to trade, and also what would make a fair exchange. One item that proved to be in extremely short supply was sugar and hearing about it, Ilonka's ears perked up. If sugar was hard to come by, she had the next best thing: the saccharin Jeno dragged home from the customs warehouse during the last chaotic days of the war. At the time Ilonka didn't think much of the small packets, but now she realized what excellent value they had in bartering. She didn't even have to peddle it; as people heard that she had saccharin, they came knocking on her door. So did the baker across the street, offering Ilonka a deal. He would give her flour for the sweetener and would also put aside bread for her, so she would not have to stand in line. Ilonka had to admit to Jeno that after all, bringing home that sack was a blessing in disguise. They were eating better again, at least while the saccharin lasted.

But what about clothing and other necessities? The children were outgrowing their shoes and there were none available in shops. The earlier practice of wearing hand-me-downs no longer worked, since the older kids, having only one pair instead of several, wore out their shoes to the last. Gyuszi only had a pair of open sandals left, which carried him through the summer, but what was he going to do when the weather turned cold and rainy? Eta could share Ilonka's shoes, but Sárika was not so lucky. At the awkward age of thirteen she was going through visible changes, just recently growing several inches taller, her feet a full size larger, yet she could not just go around barefooted. The only solution was to stuff newspaper in an extra pair of loafers Jeno was fortunate to have. His feet were rather small for a man, so Sárika did not look like a clown wearing his shoes. Still, she was embarrassed putting them on, but what choice did she have? She couldn't even complain; she knew better than to grumble about her lot. But one day she would make up for the humiliation! She would have shoes for every occasion, a different pair to fit her fancy! The day would come when she would have everything!

She hated the poverty all around them; her only consolation was that it would be worse if she were at Eta's age. For once she was glad to be only thirteen. She remembered how she always wanted to be older like her sister, always in a hurry to grow up, but not anymore! She didn't envy her now, working all morning and going to school in the afternoon, all the enjoyment taken away by these awful times. Thank God, by the time she would turn eighteen, these wretched days would be all forgotten, and she would be on her way to living the kind of life she secretly imagined for herself.

By the summer a large number of refugees who fled to the West in the last days of the war were returning to Hungary, and when the Varosy's son Kurt did not, it crushed his parents' hope of ever seeing him again. They always thought he was only waiting until order was restored before coming back, but now they learned that he and his wife decided to immigrate to Argentina where she had relatives. Sitting in Ilonka's kitchen, Grety Varosy was lamenting tearfully that it was all their daughter-in-law's fault; otherwise, she knew it in her heart, Kurt would be home by now.

Just then they heard the doorbell, and fearing that it might be another Russian, Ilonka was cautious to approach the door. Peeking out, however, she only saw an old man, his face unshaven and deeply lined, a threadbare jacket hanging on his shrunken frame. It took a minute before she recognized that the broken man standing there was their old neighbor, Mr. Gruber. Overtaken by pity, she quickly opened the door and ushered him toward the kitchen. He shuffled along the long hallway and with obvious gratitude accepted some hot soup and a slice of bread Ilonka put in front of him. With eyes haunted and his head wobbling slightly, he told her that he was the sole survivor of his family, there was no one left.

Ilonka already knew before the Grubers left that the oldest boy died fighting the Russians, and another son was serving on the Western front, but not that he, too, was killed. Now she learned that they also lost their youngest boy Erwin to tuberculosis during their flight to the West, and that the same illness took Mrs. Gruber's life a few weeks later. The old man got as far as Germany by the time the war ended and lived in a refugee camp until he was strong enough to make the journey back. He knew he would die soon, but he wanted to die at home. He didn't come to reclaim their old apartment now used by the Riedls, only asked if they would allow him to stay in the attic above for his remaining days. All he needed was a spot to sleep and a little food and water.

Ilonka agreed without hesitation. She set up a folding cot in the loft next to a window and told him to use the bathroom downstairs, the Riedls wouldn't mind. But when she saw that he could hardly climb the steep stairs, stopping after each rung to steady himself, she knew he would not be able to come down again. For the obvious short time he had left on this earth, Ilonka tried to make his life a little more bearable; she placed a pail of water, a sliver of soap with a washcloth and towel next to his cot, and brought up a chamber pot, which she emptied every day. Of the food Ilonka brought him, he would eat very little; he just lay there, reduced to a living skeleton, waiting to die. He lasted a few more days, dying alone, but not completely abandoned as so many others in a roadside ditch, buried in some unmarked grave.

Hardly a week had passed when Laszlo Riedl, Sr., wearing civilian clothes, walked in the door, considerably thinner, but in good spirits. He didn't stay long, though. After a joyous family reunion, he took one of the rundown trains back to Esztergom to see if their house still stood, and if there was any news about their younger son Erno.

Lasko went with him and was back within a week with the good news that they found everything in relatively acceptable order at home, and the best of it, Erno was alive, or at least he was when he wrote them a letter. Finally they knew what happened to him after he left: his unit was taken to the fighting front in the northern part of Hungary, where he suffered a leg wound, was captured by the Russians, and put on a train to a labor camp in the Soviet Union. A man who managed to escape during the transport forwarded the letter but did not give his name and address. He could not risk revealing his identity for fear that he could be traced and sent back to Russia. It was a happy day for the Riedl family; they could finally return home, and with the information about Erno in hand, they could begin the search for their missing son. They knew important people at the Red Cross, or perhaps Laszlo's employer, Cardinal Seredi, would know where to turn for help.

Unfortunately, there was also sad news: Jeno's cousin, Sandor, was also taken prisoner and sent to Russia, his whereabouts unknown. Lasko's father heard it when he went to see him during a trip to Budapest, but only found his mother and sister at home. So far he only knew that after Horthy attempted to surrender to the Russians last October, the Gestapo kept Sandor and other officers under house arrest at the Metropol Hotel, and that they were released at the beginning of the siege of Budapest when the Germans needed every able man. Now he learned what happened next. Sandor fought defending the city to the very end, until the Red Army closed in on all sides and new orders came to fight their way out at all cost. They were to join the German army for a final victorious assault against the Bolshevik hordes, but seeing the insanity in fighting a war that was lost, instead of following orders, he went underground. Later, when the Russians were firmly in control, he went home to look after his mother and sister. By then the fighting was over, but because the situation was far from safe with the Russians randomly picking up people to feed their hungry gulags, most people still lived in shelters, venturing out only in search of food and water to survive. And so one day, when Sandor went looking to find something to eat and didn't come back, it left no doubt in his mother's mind that he, too, was taken.

This threat of abduction was constant. The Russians needed slave workers to rebuild their country, and if the captured troops didn't fill the quota, they simply took civilians—men and women alike—packed them into cattle cars, and shipped them to the dreaded Siberian labor camps. The reason for taking so many ordinary people, tens of thousands from cities and in some cases entire villages, was due perhaps to the relatively small number of soldiers the Russians captured in Hungary. The Soviet High Command overestimated the strength of the military forces remaining in Hungary, and taking civilians was the only way to make up for the shortage. If someone managed to escape during the transport, the guards would encircle the next railroad station and pick up the necessary number of persons to replace those missing. It happened on occasions that trains with Jews returning from Nazi concentration camps were intercepted and rerouted to Russia. It was entirely a matter of sheer luck whether or not one was taken and turned into a war prisoner. And there was no authority capable of protecting the victims against these large-scale, indiscriminate civilian deportations. Even though the government made some lame efforts to intervene, especially in known cases when a person worked in the resistance during the war helping the Allied cause, or specifically the Russians, the appeals were simply ignored. It clearly proved that the liberty and dignity of the individual, the cornerstone of Western civilization, was non-existent in the Soviet mind.

That Sandor fell victim to such civilian roundup was tragic enough, but his true misfortune came during the time they were waiting for transport to Russia. Until wagons could be secured, which sometimes took days, prisoners were kept in corral-like enclosures, given minimal food and water and were left without hygienic facilities or medical attention. It was there that someone in the crowd recognized Sandor as a high-ranking former military officer, and perhaps hoping to gain some privilege, if not freedom, went to the guards and reported his discovery.

The Russians were particularly bent on catching former officers, especially those in the higher ranks. According to the Peace Treaties, the Hungarian Government was compelled to help apprehend and punish persons perceived to have committed war crimes—in the Soviet view just about anyone who served on the Russian front—and the Soviets were greatly dissatisfied with the "lax" attitude the Hungarians displayed in this matter. Whenever they caught an officer, they were quickly indicted, put on trial without defense, and summarily convicted. As it came to light later, this was exactly what happened to Sandor. Having been second in command of the Hungarian occupational forces in Kiev during 1942, he drew a twenty-five-year sentence in the Russian gulags. Fortunate for him that he was not appointed as chief commander! It saved him from ending his life hanging from the gallows, the fate of his superior officer, Szilard Bakay. As it was, he simply disappeared in Russia without anyone knowing which of the labor camps swallowed him.

Communist Party tactics

AS ORDER BEGAN to take shape and people went back to work, they were subjected to a more thorough screening than in the earlier days to ferret out Nazi sympathizers. This time they meant to catch the politically "tainted" elements. Anyone known for Horthy-era sympathies, suspected of anti-socialist sentiments, or had any contact with the West, was dismissed. The practice led to widespread abuses, granting important positions to unqualified relatives and friends, or venting vengeance for some personal slights.

People who passed and were allowed to keep their jobs were unaware at first that during the interview the committee compiled a virtual profile of their background, political affiliation, and attitude toward the ongoing changes. Patterned after the Soviet system, these confidential personal files, called *kader records*, were kept in strict confidence, without ever allowing employees to view the contents and learn what had been written about them. A mild unfavorable joke uttered about a Communist leader, for example, could put the breaks on advancement, not to mention a more serious offense against the Party, or God forbid the Russians, that could affect an entire career, if not worse. People had no chance to correct a false statement, or give an explanation, or challenge the impartiality of the opinions as written. They could be demoted, transferred, or dismissed without ever knowing the true reason. They would only know that there was something detrimental in their record, but what it was, they'd never find out. It was a permanent file that followed the individual from job to job, with further comments and observations added by subsequent employers.

Different from this secret file was the *munkakönyv*, or work booklet, introduced to keep track of the jobs people held. It was not a confidential paper; employers kept it, but when workers quit, changed jobs or were let go, they walked off with the booklet in hand. It recorded each employer's name, date of hire, date of termination and reason for leaving, which could be a transfer to another job, voluntary resignation, unsatisfactory performance, or in the worst case, judged politically undesirable. The last two would make it very difficult to find another job, and while good connections and slipping a stuffed envelope into the right hand sometimes helped changing the dismissal from unsatisfactory performance to voluntary resignation, nothing could help those marked with a political stigma. It would condemn the individual to the lowest kind of manual work, such as sweeping streets or cleaning public toilets.

Yet another document, a personal ID called *személyi igazolvány*, was issued with pertinent information, including primary residency. It was to be carried on the person at all times and presented if stopped, with or without any reason, by the police or other authorized personnel. Being caught without this ID, or neglect to keep it current, meant trouble. A delay to report a change of address to the police within 24 hours drew a hefty fine.

The introduction of all these bureaucratic papers and regulations was a sure sign that the rusty wheels of public administration had begun to turn. With it came an intensified competition within the coalition government to gain a better footing and seize the lead by the time general election rolled around in November. Parties held political rallies, with the Communists fervently trying to convince people of their sincerity and prove that they represented the best interests of the workers. They visited factories and picked out people who were not necessarily party members but excelled in production, then they organized public gatherings to put them on the podium, praising them loudly as heroes and pioneers of the new social order. They were given medals and monetary rewards for their dedicated work and held up as role models to follow. These meetings were sprinkled with slogans glorifying the infinite wisdom of Comrade Stalin, who embraced and guided the Hungarian people with fatherly love. They always ended with proclaiming profound gratitude toward the heroic Red Army, liberators of the country, for making it possible for the people of Hungary to live in freedom, which was then followed by seemingly endless rhythmic hand clapping and shouting of "Long live Stalin."

When Ilonka and Jeno learned that people had seen Latzi attending these rallies, they confronted him.

"Why on earth are you wasting your time listening to such nonsense?" Jeno asked him.

"I don't think it is a waste of time wanting to be well informed," Latzi retorted. "I am just getting ideas about the different parties and their programs so I can make up my mind for whom to vote."

"Frankly, I am surprised that with your strong religious beliefs you don't know that the only party worth considering is the Christian Socialist Party. How could you think otherwise?"

"Well, that's a very conservative view, Jeno, but knowing you, I understand why you feel this way. As for myself, I am keeping a more open mind. I want to learn about each party and compare their programs. And listening to these speeches is the only way I can distinguish between the different political agendas and see what direction each party plans to take the country. Let's face it, Jeno: the old world is gone, and the enormous mistakes the Horthy regime made must be corrected; it's time to build a better future, a free and democratic system where all social classes would be treated with equal fairness. And when I find out which party is best equipped to achieve this goal, I will support that party."

Jeno could not argue against Latzi's reasoning, but something about the way he talked made him feel uneasy. He sounded almost like one of the Communist council members in his office. But he let it pass, hoping that when he found his ideal party, it would be any one but the Communists.

Regardless of how hard the Communist Party worked, and in spite of all the advantages of having the support of the occupying forces, the media, and other propaganda facilities not available to non-Communist parties, people didn't flock to join up. Losing the industrialized territories at Trianon made Hungary a mainly agricultural country where the peasants never warmed up to Communist ideology, and just as it happened in 1919, the spread of Communism again met with stubborn rural resistance. Instead, they sided with the Smallholder Party, which, in view of the recent radical land distribution, was a shocking disappointment to the Communists.

When the Communist Party, under the dictates of Marshal Voroshilov, the Chairman of the ACC, set the agrarian reform into motion, it had three major goals: (1) liquidation of the old landowning class, (2) winning support of the former landless peasantry, and (3) gaining gradual control of the whole agrarian population by collectivization. Now that the land was taken from the rich landowners, the first phase was successfully completed. It was time for phases two and three. That, however, proved to be quite a different story. Land distribution didn't buy the support and loyalty of the peasants as the Party expected. For one reason, the Communists failed to anticipate that giving land to formerly poor, land-hungry field laborers, no matter how small the parcel, it made them proud landowners and staunch supporters of private ownership. They did not trust the Communists, and stayed away from joining their party.

The Communist Party found better support among factory workers, not so much because they were more open to Communist ideals, but because as soon as the war ended the Party was able to seize control of the trade unions. The old moderate union leaders were labeled rightist deviationists and traitors to the unity of the workers, and quickly replaced with left-wing socialists. The unions were quickly expanded to include every branch of the state administration until practically everyone, factory or office worker, belonged to one union or another. Under Party control, strikes were forbidden and the right to organize for the protection of the workers' interests was entirely suppressed on the principle that since the state belonged to the workers, strikes could only harm their own cause. The whole system, following Soviet philosophy, was designed to have a small Communist elite rule in the name of the proletariat.

As the day of the general election approached the Communists, who were in control of the radio and newspapers, did their best to spread their propaganda, yet on Election Day, November 4, 1945, they only pulled 17% of the total votes. The Smallholder Party held an overwhelming 57% majority, a high number that included not only the peasants, but also most of the anti-Communist elements of the population. Their victory represented a national unity against Communist domination.

The West, loudly praising the results, took it as important evidence that elections could truly be free while under the control of the Red Army. Further proof was Voroshilov's statement to the Smallholder leaders wishing them success and expressing his desire to continue a friendly relationship with them. This apparent passive Soviet attitude at the election results encouraged everyone to expect a new era of constructive Hungarian-Soviet cooperation.

In the Zachar family only Jeno and Ilonka were eligible to vote, since Eta was not yet twenty, the official voting age. It was no secret which party they voted for, and even though the Christian Socialists had no chance to win, Jeno was pleased with the outcome and opened a bottle of wine to celebrate. While filling the glasses he looked quizzically at Latzi, and more from curiosity than sarcasm remarked that he was not sure if he wished to join the toast to victory. Latzi knew exactly what Jeno aimed at, and good-naturedly laughed it off, holding up his glass and saying that even if not for Jeno's party, he voted for the Smallholders.

The Communists were astonished by the election results. The party leader, Rakosi, was summoned to Moscow to give an explanation and face a severe dressing down. Hadn't he learned anything from the mistakes of the short-lived radical communist takeover of 1919? The Hungarians were of a different breed! The Party must slow down and find a better way to turn the people around. They sent him back with new directives. The Party had to change tactics to adapt to the prevailing general mood of the country and become more respectful, its members more gentlemanly in their attitude toward the victorious coalition parties. And so they toned down the political rhetoric and the glorification of the Soviet Union, and instead focused attention on the great common task of rebuilding the devastated country. This they undertook with seemingly great dedication, fervor, and energy, but beneath the deception, their only aim and driving force remained the burning determination to gain total control. In relation to this ambition, economic and social reforms played a secondary role. They saw that to achieve their goals they must fudge the differences between the parties and have patience before moving full speed ahead.

The shocking voting result was a setback for the Communists, but politically it didn't really harm them. Without their great lands the aristocracy and the Church stood paralyzed, the middle class lived in constant fear and insecurity that they'd be the next victims of communist purges, and workers were held in check through the unions and factory committees. Everywhere the Party held supervisory power. The police was in their hands, and fifth columns were carefully planted in all parties. And above all, they worked under the protective shield of the Red Army, estimated to be one million strong. Their presence precluded any serious attempt to halt the advancement of the Communist Party.

Ten days after the election a new coalition government was formed, with Zoltan Tildy, the leader of the Smallholder Party, as Premier. Then on January 31, 1946 the National Assembly declared Hungary a Republic with Tildy as President. A newly created constitution guaranteed all the rights incorporated in western democracies, including right to due process of the law. All pointed to a bright political future, were it not for another law, which in March 1946 decreed that, to protect the democratic order, any attack, verbal or otherwise, perceived as threatening or harmful to the Republic was considered a criminal act. It meant that anyone criticizing the activities of the government could be hauled into court and punished, regardless of the validity of the accusation. The crime was always subject to the interpretation of the Party and it drew specifically prescribed punishment, with the courts applying the law and handing down the sentence accordingly.

This law became a powerful tool against free speech and was based on Lenin's "No more opposition" directive that was unanimously adopted in 1921 by the 10th Party Congress. It reflected his view that to fight effectively against dissidents, an absolute party unity must be maintained, and it was acceptable to use the harshest measures against anyone, including the most trusted comrades, if they presented a danger to this unity.

The Communists immediately set out to use the new law in their party politics. They cleverly attacked the Smallholder Party by accusing some eighty deputies of slandering the Republic. Mass meetings and demonstrations were organized, demanding the expulsions of these so-called "fascists" and "reactionaries." These rallies were not spontaneous; other than the opportunists, most participants were pressured by various fear tactics to attend, yet the sight of such crowds succeeded in giving the impression of righteous indignation. As a result twenty-one of the deputies were expelled, their removal carried out as the "will of the people."

And so, even though in the beginning of 1946 the Communists were a minority in the parliament, with the backing of Moscow they held the means necessary for control. Had the western powers asserted more influence, the development of democracy in Hungary would have had a better chance to stay on track and keep the multi-party system alive, which was the only way to save the country from a total Communist takeover.

Still laying low in this transitional period, the Communist Party willingly let the coalition parties do the hard work for realistic social, economic, and cultural solutions. In the meanwhile, faithful to the blueprint of the Russian revolutionary conquest, they began to train a well-indoctrinated Marxist elite to be ready to replace them at an appropriate time. Eventually, the Party would start looking for mistakes on part of the government, and blaming the non-Communist experts for failure to carry out their duties, would proceed to oust them as reactionary fascists, class enemies, or simply "undemocratic" elements.

In preparation for this step-by-step takeover, the Communists looked for bright and enthusiastic individuals leaning toward leftist ideas, or at least those with an open mind, and showing potential for leadership, and in Latzi Kontra, they found an ideal candidate. The factory committee watched him attending rallies, listening to speeches, and discussing politics with other workers. They heard him comparing the different party platforms and saw how convincing he could be when expressing an opinion in favor of one over another. They recognized his ability to persuade people, to argue with stubborn insistence until his opponent accepted his views. Even though his background was solid middle class, they flagged him as a good candidate to be developed into a useful tool to toe the party line.

As a first step, the factory committee suggested that he join the trade union. During his interview they pointed out the advantages the union membership would bring, the chance for advancement, even leadership if he proved himself capable. He accepted the offer and proudly showed his new union card to Eta and his in-laws. He talked enthusiastically about his newfound solidarity with the laboring masses and how only now, working side by side with the workers and hearing firsthand about the various means of oppression and exploitation they had suffered under the previous regime, did he realize the social injustice done to the proletariat by the old upper classes. He went on about how he came to realize that the future was in the hands of the working class, that it was the factory worker who would rebuild the country, not the people sitting in offices, nor the peasants bickering amongst themselves about who received a few acres more or had one more cow. He suddenly had the clear vision that in order to regain a solid economic foothold, the country needed to develop its industry, and who but the workers, united in their common goal, were equipped to do the job? As a union member he would do everything he could to help them on the difficult road ahead.

Eta said nothing, but Jeno raised one question.

"Your dedication to this newfound cause is admirable, Latzi, but what happened to your studies? You only need one more semester to get your diploma. I can understand that you want to work while the school is shut down; you couldn't just sit around doing nothing, but I hope you don't plan to give up going back and finishing your courses. So why get so involved with this union business? Don't you think there are plenty of nation-building tasks waiting for engineers, too?"

Latzi nodded in half-agreement. "Of course, I would go back to get my diploma when the doors are open again, perhaps not right away, but definitely later. First I want to earn more money to save up for—"

"Saving money shouldn't be your concern right now, Latzi," Ilonka cut in. "You have free room and board here and the money you earn by the time classes begin should be enough to pay for your expenses during that final six months! Start saving after you got your diploma."

"Well, I feel it's not right to live off your back; you've done enough for me already. I want to save money to rent a place so Eta and I can get married, and even until then I think I should start contributing something to the household."

"You keep your money, Latzi, but what is this about getting married?" Jeno said raising an eyebrow. "If I heard you right that you intend to marry our daughter, aren't you overlooking something? Or are we too old-fashioned to expect that you ask us first for her hand?"

Latzi apologized, saying that he thought his intentions were obvious, and Ilonka quickly came to his defense.

"Ah Jeno, we are living in difficult times, it's easy to forget formalities. This is between Eta and Latzi, and if she agrees to marry him, just be happy for them. In any case, you have my blessing!" she said and, turning to Latzi, opened her arms to welcome him into the family. Jeno also congratulated the young couple and dropped the subject of finishing college; he was satisfied with his promise to do so. There was not much that could be done right now anyway. The university was not likely to reopen anytime soon; the structural damage was extensive and the repair work was slow. They would also need to recruit several new professors to replace those who left the country and didn't return, or were deemed politically unfit and barred from teaching.

That night going to bed Ilonka brought up the subject of Latzi again.

"I am glad for Eta; they seem to really love each other and Latzi is a good man. I just hope the big ideas those union people are putting in his head won't stick," she said. "He already sounds like he is mouthing the standard party line about exploitation of the proletariat, the social injustices of the past, struggle of the working classes and all that bunch of nonsense. The sooner he gets away from that place, the better. It's not just him, you know, Eta's future also depends on what he is doing. I am going to see Mitzie and her husband and find out what is really going on in that factory. I know they are not Communists;

they will tell me the truth. And if he is turning to be a real Commie sympathizer, it's not too late to talk to Eta. She is a pretty girl, easy-going, she can do ten times better than marrying a Communist."

"Let's just see what happens," Jeno commented. "If she is truly in love with Latzi, as she seems to be, no amount of talk will change her mind. She is almost twenty; we should let her use her own judgment. They work at the same place; she must know what's going on. I would only talk to her and warn her if we see a drastic change in him, going the wrong direction, but the final decision should still be hers."

And so Eta and Latzi were married on June 28, 1946, and when eventually things did go wrong with Latzi, Eta staunchly stood by him. Only after he was gone and buried did she admit that marrying him was the biggest mistake of her life.

For ordinary people it was not easy to adjust to life with all the changes, but rising inflation, coupled with a thriving black-market, made it so much more difficult. The government could do nothing to improve conditions, it simply had no funds to pay for its operations, cover the cost of keeping the Red Army, and fulfill reparations obligations all at the same time. The only solution was to print money in sufficient quantity, which brought on a hyperinflation unparalleled in history. The value of one dollar on the black market went from 250 pengos on April 1, 1945 to a staggering 460,000 quadrillion pengos by July 31, 1946 (46 followed by 28 zeros, or 4.6 x 10 to the 29th power in the traditional European system). It was the highest printed single bank note ever issued in the world and as such it found its way to the Smithsonian Institution in New York.

Bartering continued to be the way of life, and since Ilonka's saccharine supply was exhausted and most other tradable items already exchanged for food, she had to dip deeper into their remaining jewelry to provide for Eta's wedding. One ring went to Sofie, Angela's faithful seamstress, for a white chiffon wedding dress, while a bracelet put food on the table for the small reception that followed the church ceremony. As for their honeymoon, the newlyweds spent two days in the local Pannonia Hotel, then returned home to continue life as before. Ilonka let them have the master bedroom, and she and Jeno moved into the front room, sleeping on daybeds, with little Ochie's bed tucked in one corner.

With so many bombed out apartment buildings and repair work going at a snail's pace, there was such an acute shortage in living quarters that even if Latzi had the money, it was impossible for them to find a flat. That they were forced to live at home turned out to be a blessing for Ilonka though, when to ease the severe housing problem, the government introduced shared housing. They set up new guidelines allowing 220 square feet per capita living space—excluding the kitchen, hallway, and bathroom—for every adult, less for children. A new bureau was created to survey every house and apartment, and then, based on the number of permanent residents, they determined whether the place was in line with the established standards. If they found surplus space, it would be assigned to others, complete strangers in most cases, with the kitchen and bathroom shared by all. According to the authorities, these were only temporary measures until new housing construction could begin, but when that would be was anybody's guess. With a quick calculation Jeno knew that without Eta and Latzi living there, the threat of losing part of their large home to strangers would be real.

Another way to find additional housing opened up when in December 1945 the government ordered the deportation of ethnic Germans from Hungary to ascertain that German spirit would never be able to dominate the country again. The drastic decision was based on Article XIII of the Potsdam Agreement, signed in August 1945, which sanctioned the orderly and humane transfer of the German population of Poland, Czechoslovakia, and Hungary to Germany.

Even before Potsdam, as early as May 1945, the idea of expelling all citizens of German origin was proposed by Hungary's provisional government, but the Foreign Ministry argued that to punish people solely on account of ethnic origin or speaking German was wrong and should be rejected. It was tantamount to applying the principle of collective responsibility to an entire group of Hungarian citizens, instead of to individuals judged as war criminals and traitors. They emphasized that in the 1941 census taken in the heyday of German victories, a large segment of the population with German ethnic background demonstrated their opposition to Nazi ideas and policies by declaring themselves Hungarian nationals. Some even participated in the resistance movement during the depths of German oppression. Instead, the Foreign Ministry proposed setting up investigating committees to screen out those individuals who played part in some Hitlerite organization during the war, or who voluntarily joined the SS or the Volksbund, and only they should be expelled to Germany.

According to that same census, over 477,000 German-speaking Hungarian citizens lived in the country with about two-thirds declaring German nationality. Regardless of widespread demonstrations against the expulsion, in the end all, except those married to Hungarians were deported. The first trains carrying people stripped of citizenship and deprived of their properties left on January 19, 1946 heading for the American zone of Germany, but after June 1, 1946 the destination was changed and subsequent deportees were sent to the Soviet-occupied part of Germany. The expulsion ended on June 15, 1948 with about 200,000 of those with German background remaining in Hungary, although at the 1949 census only 22,500 people indicated German origin.

One of the hardest-hit cities, with its large German-speaking population, was Sopron. To see these unfortunate people carrying only a few belongings as they marched toward the train station reminded everyone of the Jewish deportations only a short time ago. It seemed that such cruelty to fellow humans would never stop. Most of these were ordinary folks, well-known families, administrators, shop owners, tradesmen, intellectuals, clerks, factory workers, and of course, the agrarian pontzickters. They left behind relatives, including those buried in the cemetery, friends, homes, land, and livestock. Interestingly, there were some exemptions, known former German sympathizers, loudmouth

Volksbundists, who truly deserved to be expelled but were clever enough to turn coat and join the Communist Party as soon the war was over.

Ilonka's uncle Henrich, now a widower with a twenty-one-year-old daughter and fifteen-year-old son were amongst the deportees. It did not matter that he fought under the Hungarian flag during the First World War and carried shrapnel fragments imbedded in his thigh that left him with a permanent limp. Middle-aged, handicapped, and faced with an unknown future, he was forced out of his home and country, because on a piece of paper in 1941 he marked in all sincerity German as his mother tongue. His only consolation was that his wife, dead for the past five years, did not live to see this day of shame and injustice.

All the relatives came to say goodbye, encouraging him that with his trade as a shoemaker he would be able to make a good living anywhere. They made him promise to write as soon as he had an address so they could help him any way they could. As the train began to roll, not one of them could guess that it would be Uncle Henrich, settled in beautiful Heidelberg in West Germany, who in the not-so-distant future would be sending care packages to help his poor relatives left in Sopron.

And poor they were! Even though Jeno, Eta, and Latzi worked, their earnings were worthless due to the horrific inflation, and Ilonka, as so many others, was forced to ask for public help. In spite of opposition from the Soviets, help from the West had slowly begun to filter in through the International Red Cross and the United Nations Relief and Rehabilitation Administration, or UNRRA. After close evaluation to validate their need, Ilonka periodically received packages marked "A gift from the American People." It made her wonder, where were the relief packages from Russia, when one heard nothing on the radio but endless gratitude for the gifts the Soviets granted to the Hungarian people. What a joke! Everyone knew, although dared not say, that all the Russkies ever did was to take! And here were these gift packages from the West, mostly from the United States and Canada, whom the Communists labeled heartless imperialists and exploiters of the working classes, sending much-needed supplies to a country halfway across the world. Where was the official gratitude to them? There was not a word of appreciation from the government. Ilonka was not fooled by the Communist propaganda unleashed against these generous nations, but remembering the incident with the Gruber boy about her anti-Nazi outbursts, this time she kept from voicing her opinion.

These UNRRA packages were filled with non-perishable goods like powdered milk, cocoa, canned meat, cigarettes, and most enviable of all, genuine coffee. There was chewing gum for the children, and sticks of Juicy Fruit quickly became the most sought-after commodity for youngsters eight to eighteen. While parents traded jewelry for food, their children bartered with gum. One stick could buy half an hour's ride on a friend's bike, or for a packet of five, a girl could negotiate to borrow a pretty dress for an important occasion. They acquired the art of chewing from watching American movies that local theaters began to show again for the first time since the start of the war. The actors and actresses, all beautiful and set in glamorous surroundings, were seen constantly lighting up cigarettes or chewing gum, which made a great impression on this young post-war generation accustomed to deprivation, hardship and struggle for minimal existence.

Sárika and her friends at school gossiped endlessly about these American movies, especially those with contemporary stories. They quickly learned the names of their favorite movie stars—foremost among them Robert Taylor, Clark Gable, Katherine Hepburn, and Bette Davis—and spent their pocket money buying their glossy photos. Through the movies they could see the current styles in America, not just the fashions, makeup and hairstyles, but also the bright and airy homes people lived in, the rooms beautifully furnished, every kitchen with a refrigerator. And the cars, those big beautiful automobiles driven on the streets of New York, Chicago, and Los Angeles! The girls argued where would they rather live, in a towering skyscraper in New York—they pronounced it Neveeyork—or along the wide sunny beaches of Los Angeles.

Ilonka, ever a fan, also loved the movies. She was especially fond of the highly entertaining, lighthearted musicals America had produced more than a decade earlier but reaching Hungary only now. They were full of wonderfully choreographed dance numbers and catchy tunes, and since she couldn't drag Jeno to the movies, let alone make him sit through films like *The Great Ziegfeld, The Gay Divorcee,* or *Broadway Melodies,* she always took Sárika with her. After seeing for the first time Fred Astaire and Ginger Roger gliding around the mirror-like dance floor, Sárika was beset with the idea of becoming a dancer. She could do it; she felt it in her bones! On their way home she talked of nothing but signing up for lessons at the Kosztola dance studio. Originally the studio only held rhythmic gymnastic classes for girls, but lately they had added modern dancing, including tap-dancing.

Ilonka smiled at this latest ambition of her excitable daughter. She remembered her own teenage years, how she wanted to be a singer and a concert pianist until she came to realize that her talent was mediocre. She didn't want to dampen Sárika's sudden enthusiasm, so she told her that although right now they didn't have the means to pay for private dancing lessons, she was not opposed to the idea.

Sárika couldn't wait to get home. She would have the "means" for the lessons! She would ask her mother to sell the ring Mrs. Visnyei gave her before she was killed in the bombing. It was too large for her to wear anyway; she'd rather have the money and use it to pay for the lessons.

Once at home, she hurried to open the little compartment at the bottom of a cabinet where she kept her various memorabilia, including the little velvet box that contained her few pieces of jewelry. Kneeling on the floor she reached for the box and gasped. It was empty! Her first thought was that the Russians took them, but then she remembered that the jewelry was buried in the cellar until her mother brought them upstairs shortly before Eta's wedding. She clearly recalled wearing her gold necklace on that day. With one sweep of her arm, she swept everything out, sending papers and photos flying, and sure enough, she saw something glittering in the back of the compartment. She found the ring! With a great sigh of relief, she threw her head back and, squeezing her eyes shut, whispered a quick prayer of gratitude. Her peace of mind, however, lasted only for a moment, until she realized that the pair of earrings and her beautiful necklace with a delicately etched gold cross, a gift for her confirmation, were still missing. Piece by piece she lifted up and shook the scattered papers, checked every envelope, and soon found the two earrings but not the necklace.

She tried to remember if there was any other occasion when she might have worn it, or if she had put it back at all in the box after the wedding. Perhaps she left it in her purse after taking it off. But it wasn't there. She had no luck with turning every coat pocket inside out either; she still came up empty-handed. But this couldn't be! She couldn't just lose a necklace! It must be here somewhere! She went through everything again, checking more carefully the second time, but finally gave up on finding it. She must have lost it, but where or how, she had no idea.

At least she had the ring, and she got up to tell her mother what she intended to do with it, but then she stopped cold. The ring might remind Ilonka to ask about the necklace, and then she must confess that she lost it. Better if she stayed off the subject of jewelry for now. Besides, it still could turn up someday, miracles do happen. Putting the ring back, she was upset and angry for being so careless as to lose her favorite piece of jewelry, but what brought on the bitter tears was giving up her chance for an early enrollment at the dance studio.

In May 1946, as time to settle the Hungarian peace agreement in Paris approached, Prime Minister Ferenc Nagy traveled to Washington, DC and London to ask for support and to express the government's wish to maintain a close relationship with the West. Although sympathy and understanding of the Western powers were increasing, Hungary was still viewed as a former partner of the Axis that didn't merit special consideration. That Hungary was the last among the Axis satellites to conclude an armistice treaty with the three major Allies was one sign of the unfriendly, if not hostile, attitude the victorious states exhibited toward the country.

As one positive gesture, the United States proposed to reduce the amount of reparations Hungary was ordered to pay over the next six years from $300 million to $200 million. The original sum was established in 1945 as a reasonable 19% to 22% of the country's estimated national income, which, however, never came close to that level. The slow recovery was due to two factors unforeseen to Western Allies in 1945: first, that the country would be burdened for an undetermined length of time with the cost of maintaining the occupational Red Army, and second, that according to a separate agreement, Hungary was to pay an additional $30 million to the Russians. The overall combined obligations would represent a devastating 31% of Hungary's national income, which meant that with the population of Hungary being 8,943,533, a share of $33.54 for reparations plus $3.35 for the repayment of additional Soviet-related debt would fall on every citizen, men, woman, and child, when the average *monthly* salary topped at $3.00 at the then existing exchange rate.

The Russians, however, these supposedly great friends of Hungary, rejected every proposal on the agenda, including granting a moratorium on reparations payments for two or three years until a degree of stabilization could be achieved. Instead, they agreed to extend the repayment period from six to eight years. Thus Hungary was compelled to make payments of $200 million to Russia (on top of the $30 million), $70 million to Yugoslavia and $30 million to Czechoslovakia in the form of commodities, specifically in industrial products. This was a tremendous hardship in this crucial postwar period, when most of what the almost destroyed and slowly reviving Hungarian industry produced went to fulfill reparations demands, instead of paying for reconstruction.

As a last resort to extend help, the United States then proposed a tripartite aid program to lend assistance in the country's economic restoration, but this, too, was rejected by the Soviets. What they did not object to was the approval by the Paris Conference to dissolve the Allied Control Commission, thus ending its nominal Western influence. It left Hungary—a country whose ideals from the very beginning were tied to the West—entirely defenseless against forced bolshevization, compelling its government to carry out instructions issued exclusively by the Soviet High Command with the aim of the country's total absorption into the Soviet Empire.

At the end of the Peace Conference, with the Soviet Union vetoing every proposition the Western powers put forth, the United States saw one last opportunity to save the Hungarian economy from total disintegration and help stabilize the devastated country. The American authorities decided to return the gold reserves of the Hungarian National Bank, which came into their hands after bank officials took the money to Germany in the last days of the war, thus saving it before the Red Army could seize it as war booty. With the reserve back in the treasury, on August 1, 1946 the government introduced the Forint as the new monetary unit, with one forint being equivalent to 400,000 quadrillion of the outgoing pengo (4 followed by 29 zeros).

The stabilization was one step in the right direction, but mainstream life was still far from normal. As students started the new school year in September 1946, many, including Sárika, were still attending afternoon sessions, and still had to do without books. According to the dictates of the Armistice, all Fascism-related literature had to be eliminated, and that included most schoolbooks issued during the war. Judging the content of books was trusted to Communist dominated committees, some members with only a fourth grade education, clearly not qualified for the task. Due to ignorance or zealous dedication, there were regrettable overreactions during the selection of "fascist" books, where some valuable books published centuries ago were senselessly destroyed because a word was misinterpreted. Only two libraries, both closed to the public, were kept intact.

Until new regime-approved books could be printed, Sárika took copious notes during classes, then the next morning her more ambitious classmates would come over to her house and use them in doing their homework. Wanda was there regularly, although she could care less about studying; she just wanted to get away from home. She was only interested in one subject, learning English. The Ministry of Education had introduced it as a second language to replace German. Their first preference was Russian, but for the time being this had to be postponed for lack of qualified teachers and unavailability of books printed in the Cyrillic alphabet. German language teachers were quickly trained to conduct English classes on the basis that both German and English belonged to the Germanic language group. Studying English proved to be vastly popular among the students, and both Wanda and Sárika eagerly signed up. They wanted to learn it so they could understand the American movies without reading the stupid subtitles that sometimes made them miss the best scenes on the screen.

There was one movie, called *Sun Valley Serenade* that the two girls could not stay away from seeing again and again. It introduced the great Glenn Miller tunes "In the Mood" and "Chattanooga Choo-Choo," and another song that became Sárika's absolute favorite, called "I know why." This movie with Sonja Henie dancing on ice also perked up her interest in skating. As the cold weather set in and the ice-skating rink opened, she went searching for her skates. Using a cranking key she was about to fasten them to the sole of her new lace-up ankle shoes, when her mother yanked them out of her hand.

"Not with your new shoes you don't," she cried out. "This is the only pair of winter shoes you have; don't you realize that the skates could squeeze the sole out of shape and ruin them? There is a pair of boots down in the cellar. I don't really know whose it is, maybe the Riedls left them or the Grubers—anyway, see what you can do with them, or you can forget about skating." Well, they did not exactly fit Sárika, but again, with the help of a little stuffed cotton they would do well enough. Her long wool slacks covered most of the ugly boots, and with her pretty hand-knit sweater and matching cap and gloves, who would notice them, anyway?

She and Wanda became regulars at the rink, always on weekends, and sometimes even in the evenings, going after classes with the understanding that they had to be home no later than eight. But skating gracefully to the sound of the "Skater's Waltz" or practicing figure eights and threes was not the only reason the two girls suddenly became so fond of ice-skating. It was there that they discovered boys, or perhaps the other way around, the boys discovered them. Schools in Hungary from grades five to twelve were not co-educational, and interaction between girls and boys was strictly limited to supervised social activities. School authorities deemed it inappropriate for young ladies to be seen in public alone with a male escort, and if caught, suitable punishment was doled out.

The rule, however, didn't apply in the crowded ice-skating rink, where girls were considered safe from dubious advances by the opposite sex. So when the first boy slid to Sárika's side asking her to skate, she happily took his hand, leaving Wanda standing on the sidelines. They both knew the young man; he was Andor Varszi, or Andy by his nickname, a handsome eighteen-year-old senior in the State Gimnazium, and a brother of one of their schoolmates, Maria Varszi. Although they were refugees from Erdély—also called Transylvania, the beloved part of the country that was lost to Romania in 1920, and regained only briefly from 1940 to 1945—the family decided to settle in Sopron, rather than return to live with the same cruel persecutions and discriminations the Hungarian minorities suffered there between the two World Wars.

Andy and Sárika skated around the rink a few times, but noticing a resentful expression on Wanda's face and an angry glare every time they passed her, Andy suggested that perhaps he should also ask her for a round. Sárika thought it was a nice gesture and was surprised when Wanda turned her nose up with a firm refusal, then grabbed Sárika and skated away.

"That was rude of you to leave me standing there alone," she chastised her with obvious annoyance.

"What do you mean, I was rude? We are not glued together. I would not mind one bit if you left me for a few minutes to skate with somebody. I don't understand; why are you so upset about this? Are you jealous or what?"

"It's simply not right, that's what! I won't stand you picking up boys in front of all these people when we are together! It reflects on me, you know!"

"Picking up boys?? I did not even notice him until he was in front of my nose and asked me to skate! You are a fine one to accuse me of picking up boys! Weren't you the one who pretended the other day that the chain on your bike came loose, conveniently, when that guy you have such a crush on just happened to walk by? You told me yourself what a brilliant move that was to catch his attention, and that he had already asked you for a date. If that's not picking up boys, I don't know what is!"

"Well, that was different. Nobody was around to see us and I really like the guy a lot. I had to do something to make him notice me. But you never told me that you were interested in Andy! Anyway, let's not talk about this anymore. I hate arguing with you. If you are so crazy about this guy, go ahead and skate all you want with him. I've had enough for today anyway; I am going home."

"You can't leave alone, Wanda, it's not safe and you know it! I'll go with you. And you are all wrong about Andy; I have no interest in him other than he is a nice boy. Nothing like Rudy Somogyi! You know the guy on the Zrinyi Gimnazium's soccer team? He is a dream! I wish he'd take up skating! It would be so easy to meet him here, staging a fall near him so he'd have to pick me up, or I could 'accidentally' crash into him."

"Not a good idea, my friend, you run him over and you'd never see him again!"

"I am just kidding. But you know what, I might use your trick with the bike! It worked for you, didn't it?" By then both girls were giggling and laughing again, the little spat all but forgotten. What neither of them realized was that by asking Sárika to skate first, instead of Wanda, Andy sparked a rivalry for attention in Wanda that only grew stronger with each passing year.

With the conclusion of the post-war realignment of Hungary's borders to those of the Trianon-dictated boundaries, Jeno was again cut off from his family in Slovakia. Before the territorial settlement was finalized, the leaders of Hungary, fearing recurring persecutions of the Hungarian minorities, sought to establish a neighborly relationship with Czechoslovakia by proposing a plebiscite to define the border according to nationalities. Prague's answer was stepped-up organized mistreatment of the Hungarians. In Nazi-like methods they deported some 30,000 Hungarians to concentration camps in the Sudeten area; others were subjected to sanctioned terrorized gang activities. Hungarians were placed outside the law, stripped of citizenship, and dismissed from public service. Their schools and cultural clubs were closed, media publications shut down, and the use of Hungarian language in public forbidden by law.[1*]

In view of the humanitarian abuses, Hungary formally appealed to the Allied Control Commission to halt the discriminatory and anti-Hungarian measures in Slovakia, or at least provide some form of international supervision to ensure fair treatment of the minorities. When the request was ignored by all three major powers, Hungary began to submit specific cases of abuse, some 184 notes by July 1946.

In response the Slovaks, in their boundless racial hatred, threatened to expel the entire Hungarian population and confiscate all their possessions. After lengthy negotiations and with pressure on Hungary from the ACC to abide, a population exchange agreement was reached, which contained many unilateral benefits to Czechoslovakia. Accordingly, on a supposedly voluntary basis, an equal number of Hungarians were exchanged for Slovaks living in Hungary, but when not enough Slovaks crossed the border to resettle in their homeland, many more Hungarians were pushed out with nothing but the shirts on their backs.

Jeno's mother and his sister's family escaped the deportation and remained in Losonc. Leaving voluntarily was out of the question; where would they go, what would they do? They'd be losing their home, all their belongings, and Mrs. Zachar, now close to eighty, would be left without her pension. Going to Sopron and expect Jeno to take them in was not an option when he had enough problem to feed his own family. They stayed in Slovakia and tried to adjust living in the prevailing hostile environment. At least Jeno's brother-in-law Gusztav still had a job working as a teacher, although in reduced capacity, teaching part time only. Steady jobs went exclusively to Slovaks. He was also allowed to work in an art gallery where he could sell his own paintings, mostly still lifes and landscapes in oil. They knew that chances to see Jeno anytime soon were slim, but they kept faith that when all the dust settled, circumstances

1 * Such discriminatory practice was re-enacted on September 1, 2009, affecting more than half a million Hungarians (about 10% of the population) living in Slovakia. Violation against this so-called Slovak Language Law first drew a fine up to 5,000. Euros ($6,900), but was reduced to half on February 2, 2011 by Parliament's approval over a presidential veto.

would change for the better, and eventually they would be able to visit each other again.

The only one who voluntarily left Slovakia was Jeno's sister-in-law, the widow of his brother Jozsef. He died of cancer before the war, and now she took her two teenage daughters, Judit and Vera, and crossed the border to Hungary, but not to relocate there. When she showed up on Jeno's doorstep one day, it was to say goodbye. She had enough of the endless wrangling between the two countries, never knowing from one day to the next if they were going to wake up in Hungary or Slovakia. She was leaving for Brazil to join her brother in Sao Paulo, where he had immigrated during the Depression.

The country was still reeling from the bloodletting of the war and staggering under the weight of the Red Army, and yet, as the final days of 1946 approached, life began to sprout with the promise of renewal. A sure sign that people had hope for the future was the increasing number of young mothers seen around town pushing baby carriages. Following the trend, the stork also put Eta on notice that a delivery should be expected by next summer. She waited until Christmas to share the news with the family, when she picked up her not yet three-year-old little bother Ochie and told him to gear up to be a role model for his future baby nephew. Everyone rushed to congratulate her when, in the joyous clamor, Sárika's voice rang out.

"Nephew? Why a nephew? We have enough boys around here! If we must have another baby, it should be a little girl! Or maybe you think I am not a good enough role model?" With hands on her hips and chin up, she stared defiantly at her sister.

Ignoring the challenge, Eta just smiled. "Don't hold your breath, but you might get your wish! It's not up to me to choose, you know. It would be nice if we could place an order, and it wouldn't surprise me if you'd pull it off when your turn comes. But until then we'll just have to wait and see if I have a boy or a girl. The most important thing is that I have a healthy baby with ten fingers and as many toes."

"And so it will be," Ilonka hugged her daughter affectionately. At twenty, Eta was exactly her age when she was carrying her. Secretly, she was also rooting for a granddaughter; after three boys wouldn't it be wonderful to have a little girl to spoil?

Girl or boy, it made no difference to Latzi; he couldn't have been happier when he heard the news. He was still working at the factory, still spending long hours with the committee after he finished his shift, discussing working conditions, ways to improve safety at the plant, and how to increase production and refine the quality of the products. The committee welcomed his suggestions, impressed by his concern for the welfare of his fellow workers; they became convinced that he sincerely took up the cause of the labor movement, and suggested he submit his candidacy for undersecretary of the trade union in the upcoming election.

Eta, also still working, was proud of him for getting involved with these issues. Unlike her parents, she never objected to his late hours, and found excuses when Jeno and Ilonka wanted to know why he was not home on time, and if he was getting paid for helping the committee.

"Well, you know Latzi," she told them, "he is an idealistic man and he wants to help people; that's why he joined the union in the first place. It takes time and a lot of work to get results, and no, he does not get paid for it."

"What, work free for the union?" Ilonka was adamant. "And you let him? Neither of you realize that these people are just using him? They are an uneducated bunch, men who never amounted to anything before, and he lets them pick his brain? How naive can he be? I can see working longer hours to earn extra money, heaven knows, you can use it especially now with the baby on the way! Latzi should ask to be paid for the work he puts in, or just leave it to them and see how far they would get with their union. I just don't understand! He knows he is there only temporarily until he could finish his studies. There is no sense getting himself so involved with these committee people!"

Eta did not argue with her. How would her mother know about these things when she never worked outside the home? She held her tongue and only said that the union was helping them to get an apartment; they had the power to cut through the red tape.

"Well, we'll see what comes of that," Ilonka said with a hint of sarcasm. "You hear a lot of promises these days, but only those with a party membership seem to benefit from it. For ordinary folks to get an apartment I should think would take more than a few hours of volunteer work."

"Perhaps Latzi already joined the party," Jeno interjected, then turning to Eta, asked, "Well, did he? And which one, the Socialists or Communists?"

"No, he didn't. I know he talks a lot about politics, but that's just the way he is. He gets excited about ideals, and gets carried away."

"You can say that again," Ilonka said with a smirk. "First it was religion, then he was all for the cause of the poor landless peasants, and now he is the shining knight, championing the workers' plight. What is next? Can't he just pick something in the middle of the road and stick to it?"

"Just leave him alone, Mother. Like you said, he goes through phases, no harm in that. It's better than if he stayed out drinking or chasing girls. We are happy, and that's what counts."

They dropped the subject, but a vaguely unsettled feeling hung in the air. The way Latzi talked, constantly using the newly invented political slogans, began to irritate Jeno. It was getting to the point when they couldn't talk to him without having to listen to his political lectures. Jeno finally had enough and told Latzi to stop it; he was not going to enlist any of them to his causes.

Not that it made any difference; in fact, he was getting worse. A recent damning remark about his father revealed just how far to the left he drifted, when one evening Jeno asked him how his parents were doing since their return from the West.

"They are all right, I guess. Father worked for a while in a hospital, but when his part in transferring valuable assets out of the country toward the end of the war came to light, he was stripped of his license to practice medicine for ten years, and he is now working in some kind of clerical job."

Both Ilonka and Jeno were shocked at the news. "That's terrible and we are truly sorry to hear it. Your father is such a wonderful man, how can they do this to him? Taking his license away when there are not enough doctors!" They meant every word with utmost sincerity. Even though they had only met Dr. Kontra once, they saw him as a deeply caring man and a loving father.

"You must feel awful, Latzi!" Ilonka cast a soft, sympathetic glance at her son-in-law. "It's a shame that such things could happen to good people these days."

What Latzi said next left them speechless.

"It serves him right!" he said, his voice full of contempt. "These people deserve what they got for robbing the country."

At first they could not believe that they heard him right. What did he mean by "these people"? He couldn't refer to his father! But he did, and with full conviction.

"You don't understand what damage my father and the likes of him caused when they took precious equipment and supplies out of the country! It was a cowardly and treacherous act, and we are all suffering for it. It will take years to recover from the setback they caused in building our new social democracy. It's no excuse that they just followed orders. He could have refused, but he didn't, did he?"

This was too much even for Eta, who loved her in-laws.

"Robbing the country??" She turned on him, totally disgusted that he could say such cruel things. "What do you think the Russians are doing now?"

"And saying no to the Germans?? Like he had a choice!" Jeno was shouting at him, hardly able to contain his indignation. "He was ordered, and disobeying meant a bullet in the head! You should be thoroughly ashamed!"

"Ashamed? It's not enough," Ilonka was just as angry. "To take the side of this Communist-infiltrated government against your own father is not only shameful, but simply inexcusable!"

They ignored Latzi for a while, but then they gave him an ultimatum. If he wanted to stay in their home, he better stop talking about the struggle of the proletariat, the achievements of the international workers' movement, and the people's determination to build a socialist system that was superior to any other in history. They had it with being fed such poppycock when everyone knew that the Soviet workers' paradise he held in such high regard was nothing more than a prison for every free-minded individual.

"Frankly, we are surprised that you, a well brought up, educated and intelligent man, could be fooled by such Communist doubletalk," Jeno put it on the line. "Of course, it's your business, except when you try to make it ours too, and that's got to stop. And if you won't, as much as we love Eta, we would have to ask you to find another place to live."

Eta also put her foot down and told Latzi to apologize to her parents and leave politics behind when he came home, or else. This he promised, and there was no more talk about the grand things to come that would lift Hungary out of her fascist past and set her on the path toward a free and glorious socialist future.

Sári

WHEN THE WAR ended it left most European countries in ruins, their economies exhausted, their resources extended beyond limits. Incapable of renewal without outside help, the spread of Communism became a real threat as Stalin saw the opportunity to expand his control over the entire continent. What prevented it was the "Marshall Plan," named after General George Marshall of the United States, a reconstruction program on a tremendous scale implemented in 1947. Just as during the war America came to the aid of its Allies with its generous Lend-Lease program, now again it stepped in with a far-reaching proposal, officially called the European Recovery Plan, to assist in rebuilding the countries devastated by the war. In its first year $4.9 billion was paid out in Western Europe, with a total of $12.7 billion by the time the plan ended in 1953.

The Soviet-dominated nations were forbidden to accept the aid, claiming that it was an American imperialist plot to enslave the war-weakened countries of Europe. Yet, in spite of being left on its own to face horrendous challenges, the economy in Hungary slowly started to improve. The harvest of 1946 was good and although rationing was still in place, a sufficient amount of produce found its way to stores. The long lines disappeared as shops began to fill their shelves with Hungarian-made consumer goods, their quality third rate and the quantity limited, but it was a beginning. With the stable Forint holding its value, bartering gradually became a thing of the past, and Ilonka was able to use cash to get new outfits for the children and replace worn-out shoes with new ones. To reward Sárika for bringing home a straight-A report card at the closing of the school year, her godmother surprised her with a much in fashion slingback platform sandal, even though it only had a slotted wooden sole. Once again birthdays were celebrated with candle-lit cakes and small gifts. Even the children were able to pool together enough money to buy the recently translated American novel *Gone with the Wind* for Ilonka's name's day.

As fashion magazines appeared on newsstands, their pages full of the latest styles of Paris and New York, Sárika and her friends pored over them, lamenting about the mid-calf or longer skirts the models were wearing. Their own skirts and dresses ended at the knee, and of course, very few among them could afford to buy new ones just to follow the trend. But Sárika would not rest; she was determined to find a way to have the latest look. And eventually she did. She pestered her mother to let her buy a strip of yardage in contrasting color to her favorite skirt, then cut a few inches off from the bottom of the skirt and ran to Sofie to have the strip inserted. When it was finished, Sárika was thrilled; the skirt looked exactly what she had in mind.

But when she put it on and pirouetted in front of Ilonka to show off her new look, her mother was aghast. "Now look what you've done! You ruined a perfectly good skirt that should have lasted for years. The way it is, it will be out of style by next season. We can't afford to follow such foolish trends, Sárika. The last time Sofie was making you a dress you were fussing to keep the hem above the knee, anything longer would make you look like an old maid. Now you want it down to your ankle? You stick with classic pieces; they never go out of style. You can always update them with accessories to give them a fresh look. I am warning you, don't you dare to cut up your other skirts."

"But I don't like classic pieces; they look nice on you but they are just too old-fashioned. No one in school wears anything like that anymore! And if I can't convert my skirts, you might as well give them away because I won't wear them!"

"Oh yes you will, or you'll go naked, you hear? What your friends wear is their business; you don't have to be like everyone else. You have to learn that we don't have the money to get you a new wardrobe every time you look at a new fashion magazine. You are old enough to understand the difficult times we live in, that there are far more important things at the present than the length of your skirt. So let this be the end of it."

But the argument didn't end there. Sárika pleaded, pouted, reasoned endlessly, and by the time she produced a few crocodile tears, her mother was worn down. *Where does this girl get her stubborn streak*? Ilonka wondered, her own battles with her mother long forgotten. *And how is it that once she sets her mind on something, she usually gets it in the end?*

While fashion magazines were plentiful, movie magazines were still a rarity in Sopron. The girls had heard of *Photoplay*, the famous American tabloid, but never had a chance to see one. Glossy photographs of the Hollywood movie stars, however, were abundantly available, and Sárika had a good collection of them. Her favorite of the day was Vivien Leigh after seeing *Gone with the Wind*, while Wanda liked Rita Hayward the best. She studied her picture and announced that they had similar features; their eyes and mouth were exactly the same! She immediately started to grow her bobbed hair so it would resemble the star's long flowing mane.

Sárika still wore her hair in pigtails, but Ilonka noticed that they were getting shorter by the day. When she asked about it, her daughter was ready with excuses: the ends were too brittle, or her hair would only grow if she cut it back. It did not fool Ilonka. One day she calmly sat Sárika down in front of the mirror, brushed her hair out, and casually remarked that in her opinion girls at fourteen outgrew pigtails. Resting her chin on top of her hurry-to-grow-up girl and looking at her in the mirror, she said "I take it you won't fight me on this and insist that we keep braiding your hair?" Jumping onto Ilonka's neck and showering her with kisses, Sárika bolted out of the chair, running to the corner hair salon.

Ilonka's eyes followed her younger daughter, admitting with a sigh that she was indeed growing up. She marveled how different her two girls were; Eta in her quiet, unassertive way always accepted whatever happened in her life, while Sárika, exuberant and headstrong, seemed to challenge life to make it happen her way. They were widely apart in their attitudes, interests, needs, talents and temperaments, and it made her wonder if there was any purpose why God created them this way.

Well, Eta was married now with a baby on the way, Ilonka reflected; it was time to focus on Sárika. She was only a couple of years younger than when Eta met her husband; it wouldn't be long before boys would be coming around again, this time in pursuit of her less compliant daughter. She'd better be prepared, because without a doubt, this girl would be popular, and double no doubt, she wouldn't be easy to handle.

And so, as customary for young girls of Sárika's age, in the fall Ilonka enrolled her in a social dance school held at the Kosztola studio. The lessons were from 7 to 9 PM, with music provided by Lasko Riedl on the piano. He was in his final year at college and made a little extra money playing at various gigs. During the lessons partners were assigned and rotated, except the last half hour, which was reserved for free choice, fifteen minutes for the girls, then for the boys, with cut-ins highly encouraged. This was not a popularity contest, the instructor emphasized, everyone should be on the dance floor. Regardless, it soon became clear which of the girls or boys were the most popular. Sárika and Wanda could hardly take a few steps before someone would cut in, but interestingly, when it came to ladies' choice, Wanda always asked the best-looking young men, while Sárika preferred those who could dance well. With a good partner, others often stopped dancing to watch them, which annoyed Wanda to no end.

Sárika's time to take the back seat to her friend came whenever they went to the public swimming pool in the Loevers. Bikinis had just come into fashion that summer of 1946, and it seemed no one could fill them better than Wanda. Although she was barely five feet two inches tall, her figure was fully developed, boasting a gorgeous bust line and slender, boyish hips. It was natural that she would be among the first in Sopron to show up at the pool sporting a two-piece bathing suit. On the other hand, while Sárika was four inches taller, and just as slender with long legs, she had hardly a bud to show for breasts. Still, she was pining for a bikini, only to run up against Ilonka's veto again. There was nothing wrong with the swimsuit she inherited from Eta! Besides, bikinis won't last, she said. Just because some designer decided to push the limit of decency, it doesn't mean that the idea of exposing belly buttons would catch on. Well, that's what her mother thought, until the day she saw a wet bikini drying on the clothesline. Somehow the navy blue color and the fabric looked familiar, and when she took a closer look she couldn't help but laugh. Leave it to her daughter! She got hold of Jeno's old swimsuit—a tank suit worn off one shoulder—cut it in two and with a few stitches, fashioned it into a cute little bikini.

At the pool Wanda, modeling her yellow bikini, would dip a toe in the water then stretch out on a lounge chair or walk around, showing off her perfectly proportioned assets. She knew exactly what effect she had on the opposite sex, especially when she made a show of rinsing off under the poolside shower. She would pull up her hair, a move that lifted her chest high, then, turning on the water, twisted her torso this way and that, making sure the spray covered every inch of her body.

There was no way Sárika could compete with that, none whatsoever.

Instead, she was in the pool most of the time, swimming lap after lap, coming out of the water to dry up a bit before diving back in. But on the days when Andor Varszi was there, he would not leave her side. Jumping in the pool, they raced to see who could beat the other in backstroke or crawl, or could stay longer underwater when diving from the board. It was all fun and games. She would dunk him and he would pull her under, both coming up gasping for air and spewing water, laughing from the sheer joy of the sport. Here Wanda never resented Andy's presence, not as long as she could hold court, surrounded by a number of young admirers.

When it was time to go home there was never a shortage of boys waiting at the exit, offering to carry the girls' tote bags, or giving them a ride on their bikes. Wanda could hardly wait until July when her parents promised to get her a bicycle for her birthday. Sárika could not count on such a magnificent present. Her family could afford only one bicycle, and it was for her brother Gyuszi, who had to walk twice the distance to school. Oh well, she thought, she could always borrow it from him, even though that rod across made it awkward to get on and off. No matter, it would have to do for now, but there would come a time when she had her own bike with a colorful net over the upper half of the back wheel. It was only a matter of time!

That fun-filled summer was perhaps the most carefree time in Sárika's life since becoming a teenager. The dark days of the war were fading fast, and it was too early to catch a glimpse of the hard times waiting around the corner. Only the present existed for her.

After finishing her chores at home, she spent her days at the swimming pool, went to the movies, or taking Gyuszi's bike pedaled out to Lake Tomalom, always with Wanda. But wherever the two girls went, the boys followed. These were high school kids, boys they knew from dance classes, from church or various interschool activities. When Ilonka asked Sári—the shorter, more grown-up-sounding name she now preferred—what they did all afternoon, the answer was always the same: oh, nothing much, just the usual thing. They liked to hang out playing games typical of young teenagers, teasing each other, perhaps flirting a little, but that was all. If she paid a little more attention to the boy Mishu, it was only because he was Rudy Somogyi's roommate, the boy she had a huge crush on.

Spending so much time outdoors, Sári got into a habit of running her tongue over her lips to keep them moist. She was out of the house one day when a letter arrived, the very first addressed to her, and of course, Ilonka promptly opened it. Holding it up she was ready to confront her daughter when she walked through the door.

"Just who is this Mishu and what does he mean by—well, let me just read it to you: '. . . you don't know how cute you are when you lick your lips like you do. I only wish I'd be the one licking those luscious lips . . .' Luscious lips? Luscious lips??" Ilonka's voice escalated with each syllable. "I'd give him a smack right across the face, so he has something to lick—his own bloody mouth!" Outward Ilonka seemed quite outraged but inside she was thoroughly amused by this boy's clumsy, unromantic approach at wooing her daughter.

"I hardly know this guy, Mother, he is just a stupid boy, and I will tell him off the next time I see him. But how come you opened my letter? Let me see that envelope. It is addressed to me! How could you? It's not your business! Please don't do this again."

"Well, I don't think you are mature enough to start receiving private correspondence. And just so you know, everything that concerns you *is* my business! And that includes reading your letters. It shows me how others look at you, what they think of you, and judging from this one, it seems to me this fellow is not very respectful to you. He is not the kind of boy I—"

"Oh, stop it Mom! You are making too much out of this," Sári wailed. "I don't care if I ever see this boy again! And if he writes me again, you can just throw it away without opening it. I am not interested in what he has to say. And you shouldn't be, either. Did you open Eta's letters, too, when she was my age? I bet you didn't; you always treated her differently!"

"Now you are trying to change the subject, but yes, for your information I used to read her letters, but I gave it up since none of them ever mentioned licking her luscious lips, or similar vulgarities!"

In the end Ilonka agreed that in the future, if Sári received a letter she could open it, then read it aloud in her presence. It settled the issue, but this little incident proved again how different the two sisters were. Eta never protested when Ilonka opened her letters. They simply had no problems with her in anything. She had a few romantic dates, all proper and innocent, before she met Latzi, and after that it was a given that one day they would be married.

And look at her now, in a few days she would have her baby. It was too bad that her husband was not there to share the excitement they all felt about the impending birth. Ilonka deeply resented his absence so near the crucial day. She'd never understand what was so urgent about attending some stupid political seminar in Gyor for eight weeks during the last phase of his wife's pregnancy, and miss the moment of the birth of his firstborn. Even though Eta shrugged it off, to Ilonka it was just not the right thing to do.

He was still away on August 2, when in the early morning hours Eta felt the first contraction. She decided to have the baby at home, and so by nine o'clock Ilonka sent for Mrs. Polgar, the midwife who brought four of her children, including Eta, into this world. When she arrived, Sári was told to take the younger children to the Varosys and wait there, but she balked, arguing convincingly that she should stay around just in case something went wrong and they needed to send for Dr. Graser. Her real reason, however, was that she hoped to finally find out exactly how babies were born. When Ilonka allowed her to remain—not in the bedroom, of course—she glued her ear to the door, listening to every sound that filtered through. So far all she knew that giving birth was painful, and she expected to hear cries and screams but disappointingly, she heard nothing. With superhuman control Eta gave birth to a beautiful healthy baby boy with nothing more than a prolonged, muffled, high-pitched squeal that escaped through her clenched teeth toward the very end of her ordeal.

When at last Sári heard the first cry of the baby and eventually was let into the room, she saw her sister resting on her pillow, her eyes closed, clearly exhausted, while her mother was holding the baby on her lap, gazing at him with pure love and enormous pride. The image belonged to an artist's canvas, portraying the silent welcoming of this tiny creature, the first of a new generation, into the family. Sárika tiptoed across the room and, leaning close to her little nephew, announced that he looked exactly like his father.

"There is not one iota of Zachar in this boy, but I have to admit he is very cute for a newborn." Still bending over him she turned her head, looking up at her mother. "I hope you are not getting ideas, Mother!"

"What ideas? What are you talking about?" Ilonka asked.

"You know what I mean," Sárika stood up, rolling her eyes. "We have enough children in this house as it is."

Ilonka, amused by the hint, gave a chuckle. "You don't have to worry; I am too old for that!" Then, lifting the sleeping child, she asked if Sári would like to hold him.

"Sure, I'll hold him," she said, taking the baby. "He seems to be a good little boy, sleeping like an angel. I hope he stays like this during the night!"

"Well, babies do cry, that's how they let us know if they are hungry or hurting," Ilonka said, then added, "You sure had your share of crying when you were born. You cried so much in the first few months that I used to say you cried enough to last a lifetime."

"I know, I know, you've said it a hundred times, how I got blisters all over my body, and that some even had to be lanced. I still have the scars to prove it. Did the doctor ever find out what caused it?"

"No, he never did. He only said that it was some unusual skin condition that would clear up in time."

"And a good thing it did. I must have looked awful, though. But you little guy, you are as cute as can be," she was cooing to the baby, rocking him gently.

Eta woke up just then and asked for her son. Soon the other children were brought home to meet their little nephew, while Ilonka sent word to Jeno to come. He arrived shortly, bringing flowers for the new mother, his eyes shining with pride as he held his first grandson. In the clamor and excitement nobody thought of Latzi, until Eta asked if anyone had sent him a telegram.

. . . .

He first saw his newborn son when he returned home in the middle of August, a spitting image of himself as compared to his own baby pictures. Besotted with him and enormously proud to be a father, he wished he could spend more time with him, but that was impossible for the moment. He was needed in preparation for the upcoming general election, scheduled for August 31, 1947.

The Party was confident of the outcome, but to ensure victory they held political rallies in every city, provincial town, and village, courting the people with endless speeches and renewed promises in an effort to sway public sentiment toward their socialism-building platform. On election day local cells were organized to use all means, including incentives—or threats, if needed—to deliver votes in favor of the Party. The disaster of the last election would not be repeated! Squadrons of the political police were on display everywhere, their mere presence intimidating enough to send people to the polls; they had all heard stories about being labeled a fascist or saboteur if they dared to stay away. In the villages, however, the Communists used a different method; well aware that because of the peasants' strong resistance to forced collectivization they couldn't count on their votes, they barred them from voting. People were ordered out to the fields to work on the harvest, then to cover the shortage, truckloads of outside party members with special ballot cards were bussed in to cast leftist votes.

Regardless of these fraudulent tactics, the final result was still only 22.3% for the Communists and 61% combined for all other parties, including the Social Democrats. It was a bitter pill to swallow, prompting the Party leadership to rethink their methods in capturing the majority. They would not suffer another setback!

As it proved later, for the next four decades the 1947 election became Hungary's last multi-party election.

Seeing Latzi's obvious disappointment, Jeno tried not to rub his nose in the humiliating defeat. As Jeno and Ilonka feared, their son-in-law returned from the seminar in Gyor as a full-fledged Bolshevik, totally immersed in Communist ideology. They were simply baffled by his quick transformation from a deeply religious young man to a left-standing politico. They knew him as an intelligent man, albeit somewhat innocent and gullible, always searching for the ideal, and in their eyes that was the reason for the drastic change in him. Exposed to relentless political re-education and constantly bombarded with slogans about democracy, freedom, socialism, world peace and such, he eagerly took them at their face value, not realizing that in the Party's recruiting effort these words were only used as part of the orthodox Communist jargon to confuse impressionable minds. This could be the only explanation for how he came to believe that the ideal form of society was built on the basic principle of Communism: work according to ability and receive according to need. It was certainly a noble idea, but it was also an idea that will never work as long as human beings could manipulate those abilities and needs. Such an honor system was pure utopia, and to convince people otherwise, the Party needed these endless political seminars, always pointing to the example of the Soviet Union to prove that the ideal could be achieved.

Interestingly, regardless of the ever-increasing brainwashing, the number of people who had doubts about the coming glory days of Communism grew larger by the day. They put more trust in the way people lived in the West, and leaving everything behind—jobs, possessions, sometimes families—more and more came to Sopron from all parts of the country with only a backpack and a map to find their way to Austria. The city suddenly became a very popular destination for these "tourists" wanting to enjoy the Loevers and explore the many trails in its forests, although oddly enough, always in the middle of the night. They knew exactly the risk involved in the attempt to get across the border, but they didn't care, they tried anyway. They willingly faced barbed wire fences and heavily armed border patrols with guard dogs, fully aware that if caught, some lame excuse such as being lost in the woods would not save them from punishment. Many never made it across; instead, they were herded through the city toward the notorious prison camp of Sopron-Kohida, always during daylight to show everyone what happens to those trying to leave the country.

Extracting confessions from these defectors was assigned to the AVO,[2*] a newly organized Soviet-style Hungarian secret police with headquarters at Andrassy Avenue 60 in Budapest and a web of local centers throughout the country. It was created in October 1946 by the Ministry of Interior Affairs and was under the direct authority of its minister, Laszlo Rajk. The day-to-day operation was left to his appointee, Gabor Peter (born Benjamin Eisenberger, a former Jewish tailor). The AVO, a greatly feared "state within the state" organization, consisted of several departments, including an army of uniformed men, a trusted core of plainclothes investigative detectives, a wide network of informers, a well-developed wiretapping unit, a cell to conduct interrogations, and another group of individuals who carried out coercive measures, including beatings and other forms of physical torture. There was no official manual or set of rules as to what was acceptable and what was not regarding interrogations. Each department conducted its own affairs in utmost secrecy, creating a fierce rivalry, where vying for favors from higher-ups was rampant and gave way to excesses to prove one's capabilities over another.

Among those caught while attempting to escape, younger boys claiming to be driven by the spirit of adventure might get away with a few slaps across the face and a warning not to try it again, but adults were not as lucky. They were interrogated, charged with one or another ridiculous crime against the state, then quickly convicted as traitors, deserters, saboteurs, fascist rats, or the worst, imperialist spies. Based on the number of spy convictions, Hungary seemed to crawl with CIA agents. These charges were the choice labels the Communists pinned on everyone they accused of being the "enemy of the people," those

---

2 [*] AVO is short for *Allamvedelmi Osztály,* or State Protection Unit, a name that was later changed to AVH, short for *Államvédelmi Hatóság,* or State Protection Authority, but for simplicity AVO was used throughout the book.

who committed crimes for which the "people's voice" cried out for harsh punishment. If someone refused to sign a confession, the AVO used "persuasive" methods, anything from beatings to threats to harm family members. Their order was to break resistance at all cost, and in most cases they succeeded; in the end, confessions were signed.

There were no hangings for trying to escape, but the guilty ones were not returned to the comfort of their homes, either. They became "residents" of the newly created labor camps, the Hungarian gulags, populated not only by political convicts but other "undesirable" elements of the new order as well. These were the ex-capitalists, ex-landowners, hostile members of the clergy, former high-ranking officials and well-to-do people of the past regime, all dragged into these camps to become slave workers to provide the free labor on which the new socialist Hungary would be built, a system based on lies, threats, fear and oppression in the image of the great Soviet Workers' Paradise. The material produced by the sweat and blood of these "offenders" was used to rebuild bridges and factories, even to construct an entire new city south of Budapest named Stalin Város, the Hungarian Stalingrad, that was to represent the center of Hungary's new heavy industry.

Although the threat of the work camps was real, when it didn't seem to stop the ever-increasing political exodus, the government decided to seal the border to Austria more efficiently. In addition to the existing wire fences, they planted a wide strip of land along the entire western border with explosives, and erected watchtowers mounted with machine gun-toting guards. Together with the armed guards and trained attack dogs patrolling the area, the Iron Curtain now seemed foolproof, and from there on, desperate people still attempting to reach freedom on the other side were in real danger of losing their lives.

As summer was coming to an end, word came that repairs on Sári's school building were completed and in the fall the girls would be back in their old alma mater. The good news, however, was offset by the announcement that their old principal, mild-mannered and well-liked Mr. Csabai, had been removed as politically undesirable, and was replaced by Mr. Augusztin, known to be a strong disciplinarian. If that was not enough, on the first day of school Sári's class learned that this much-feared principal was also to be their new Latin teacher. For most of them it meant that the days of copying home assignments from Sári or other high achievers were over. Nobody could fool Mr. Augusztin; he could smell a cheat from a mile.

Other changes were put into effect, as well. Religious classes were suspended and attendance to Sunday Mass was no longer organized by schools. In spite of its popularity, English as a second language was dropped, and German was reinstated. Textbooks were now available, but when students thumbed through the pages they discovered that in literature the works of many hitherto famous writers and poets had disappeared, and what they had learned before about history was no longer valid. The role of Western civilization was downplayed and greatly distorted, with kings and queens and the Church portrayed as evildoers, their power corrupt. They could forget about the earlier teachings of philosophy and social development, too, and learn that capitalism was the scourge of the working classes and all western art was decadent and without purpose other than self-aggrandizement. On the opposite side stood the shining example of the glorious Soviet Union, the inventor of everything good and worthwhile, builder of the most advanced, pure, just, and honorable social system on earth, where freedom and equality existed in its truest form. Led by the proletariat and guided by the ideals established by Lenin and perfected by his faithful follower Comrade Stalin, it stood unchallengeable in achievements and unbeatable in war. Indeed, all must be learned anew.

But not all was doom and gloom in the students' lives; they managed to squeeze some fun into their dreary existence. The unusually long Indian summer kept the athletic fields alive with fierce competition, basketball courts echoed with the shouts of cheering fans, and there were soccer games, loved by the young and old alike. Going to a match on Sunday afternoons was still Jeno's favorite pastime, and he was a little disappointed when Gyuszi did not show much interest in joining him. He would have loved to share the excitement of watching a good game together, but he never expected it when one Sunday, leaving for a high school championship playoff, Sári asked him if she could come along. Jeno gladly took her but, knowing that his daughter had no idea about the game, suspected there was something behind her sudden interest.

He soon found out the reason, when he noticed how she focused all her attention on one player in the Zrinyi team, a young man named Rudy Somogyi, never taking her eyes off the boy, cheering him loudly whenever he made a good pass and jumping from her seat if he scored a goal.

"Isn't he the best player Father? Wasn't that a great kick? Did you see how he butted that ball?"

Her enthusiastic commentaries would not stop until Jeno quietly, without looking at her, said, "I take it you like that fellow quite a lot. Do you know him?"

"I wish I did, but he does not seem to be interested in meeting me. I know his roommate, and I found out from him that he is from Cenk and he has a girlfriend there."

"Sárika, this young man is a very good soccer player; he has a good chance to be drafted in the national league when he is finished with school here. He'll be moving to Budapest and I doubt if his girlfriend in Cenk will see much of him after that. You'll save yourself some heartache if you stop pining after him. You are so young and pretty, soon you will have many Rudies running after you, so just watch the game and enjoy it, but it's best if you put him out of your mind." Putting his arm around his daughter's shoulder he pulled her close and she snuggled against him, sighing that it won't be easy, but she'd try.

Try as she might, she could not resist the chance of meeting the boy when Ilonka asked her which of the upcoming school dances she would like to attend; without hesitation she picked Rudy's, hoping he would be there. And he was. Entering the large auditorium, decorated with balloons and banners, and the band already playing, she spotted him immediately on the crowded dance floor. He was tall and athletic, a very handsome young man with dense blond hair and classic features reminiscent of Michelangelo's *David*. Sári wasn't the only girl who found him irresistible.

The minute Ilonka found a chair and sat down Sári was gone, waltzing with a boy from the dance school, then on the arm of another as the band switched to a slow foxtrot. But when the musicians plunged into a fast-paced number several people, Sári among them, stopped dancing and formed a circle around the parquet floor to watch the few remaining couples doing the newest dance called jitterbug. It was more like a performance with fast twirls and kicks, thrusting of the hips and some acrobatic maneuverings, definitely not taught at the dance school! When the spectators cheered and clapped with the rhythm, the mothers rose to check what caused the sudden racket. Seeing the vulgar movements, some yanked their girls off the dance floor, others demanded to put a stop to this kind of music, but most of them, including Ilonka, just booked the exaggerated gyration as part of "progress."

Another new dance, although not as wild, was the so-called swing. Most kids knew this one and as soon as the band sounded the popular "In the Mood," they all started bobbing up and down and pounding their feet to the beat. It seemed simple enough, but Sári didn't know the exact steps and decided to take a break and get a sip of water. She started to walk away when she felt a slight tap on her shoulder.

"May I have this dance?" she heard someone ask.

Her throat went totally dry as, turning around, she saw Rudy smiling down at her, holding out his hand. She felt her heart jump, racing with excitement that he finally found her, but at the same time she was burning with anger that she would have to turn him down.

"I'd love to, but I am sorry, I don't know this new dance," she said blushing from embarrassment.

"Nonsense, I'll teach you; there is nothing to it," Rudy said refusing to take no for an answer, and taking her hand led her back to the dance floor. Keeping her eyes on his feet, she watched as he tapped out a few easy steps, but then he stopped and drew her close.

"Just follow the music. I know you can dance because I watched you before! You see, you are doing it already," he winked at her encouragingly as they began bouncing to the rhythm. She picked up the move quite easily and flashed him a radiant smile, while her mind searched for something clever to say. She took his complimentary remarks as sort of invitation to flirt, and was desperately trying to come up with a witty, sophisticated way to respond, but her mind simply went blank. If she just had a little more time! But even that worked against her. When the band finished the number they put down their instruments and left for a break, taking with them her chance to hold on to Rudy. After a few seconds he thanked her for the dance, led her where her mother sat, and with a polite bow walked away.

That was her first encounter with the boy of her dreams, which also turned out to be the last. For the rest of the evening she hoped he would ask her again, but he never did. He only danced with other girls and her subtle attempts to get his attention were ignored, if noticed at all. She cursed herself for being so awkward with him; no wonder he lost interest. Why is it that she never ran out of words when she was around Andy, but froze like a stupid country bumpkin with Rudy? Now that it was too late, she could think of all kinds of smart things she should have said, but it was no use, he was never going to ask her again. *And I don't blame him! I was so clumsy!* she fumed silently. *I had a chance and I blew it! Just the same, it's not fair, it just isn't fair,* she kept repeating to herself.

On the way home when Ilonka asked if she had a good time, all she got for an answer was a shrug and a grumpy "It was OK." Ilonka did not probe further, but she was sure the reason for her daughter's gloomy frame of mind was that Andor Varszi was not there. She and Jeno both liked the young man; they knew he could be trusted when he took Sári out on a date. Inwardly she smiled, thinking that although Sári always denied having any romantic interest in Andy, the way she obviously missed him tonight proved that she did have feelings for him. Of course nothing serious, they were both too young, but if Ilonka had a choice to pick a suitor for her daughter, it would be him.

She couldn't have been more wrong. Andy never entered Sári's mind; all she could think about was the handsome blond Adonis, the choice of her heart, and how she missed her one and only chance with him.

With school now in full swing, Sári did not have much time to brood. Her first priority was to study. Every day as soon as she got home from school, she sat down to do her homework, and she would not stop until she was finished. It was unthinkable for her to go to class unprepared, so she spent hours memorizing Latin words, solving math problems, and writing her essays. In addition, as a member of the literary club, she had special assignments, preparing for a presentation, or learning a poem by heart she was asked to recite, all of which took extra time. When the weather turned wintry and there was still not enough coal to heat the whole house, she studied in a cold room to avoid interruption from the children. At times, when Jeno looked in on her or brought her a cup of hot tea, he truly felt sorry for her, sitting there bundled up in a blanket, a knit cap pulled over her head, her nose in her books.

"Sárika, you don't have to do this. It's not that important that you get the best grades," he would tell her. "You'll only catch a cold sitting in this freezing room. You are smart enough to get by on what you learn in class. Put away your books and come, stay with us where it's warm."

But she would not budge. "I will as soon as I am done, Father, but you see, I have to do this because I am not as smart as you think. I have no problem comprehending what they teach us in class, but by the time I get home I forget half of it. I don't seem to have a good memory. If I want to do well, I have to go over my assignments more than once to make it stick. Take this math problem here; when Miss Szende demonstrated the solution I understood it perfectly, but now I don't know how she did it. It's very frustrating, because I can't rest until I find the right answer."

She recognized her shortcomings, but her drive to excel made up for it. She was willing to put in time and effort to be the best she knew she could be, and nothing could deter her from reaching that goal. Not many knew about this stubborn determination and relentless endeavor. Her classmates all assumed that she was naturally gifted, when in truth, it was her resolve and stamina that carried her to the top of her class. To them, she could answer any challenge, whether running through lengthy equations if called to the blackboard when everyone else tried to look invisible, or explain what dialectical materialism meant, when no one had a clue. Her essays were always among the best, and her Latin conjugations seemed effortless.

Her art projects, mostly watercolors and charcoal sketches, also earned high marks, but again, while she could draw anything, including portraits with good facial likeness, the spark of originality was missing from her work. She was at a loss when it came to creating something out of sheer imagination. Her talent was there, just bubbling below the surface, but somehow she didn't have the key to unlock it and let it burst to life. She knew this, and it bothered her, but she would never underestimate herself. Overall, she was above most of her classmates, those willing to settle for the average. Mediocrity could never satisfy her, and if her lot was to work hard to reach the top, so be it; she would do the necessary to stand among the best.

This striving for perfection and to overcome limitations was part of her nature, not only in the academic field, but in the physical sense, as well. For this reason it came as a sour disappointment that no matter how much she wished to have frontal curves like Wanda's, they never materialized. By now she had to give up the idea that she was a late bloomer and the missing breasts would develop soon. She had to settle for what she had—a fresh lean look that many of her girlfriends would gladly exchange for their own limitations. Looking in the mirror, she was satisfied with her heart-shaped face, high cheekbones, and small nose, and no one denied that her teeth were beautiful and she had a lovely smile. She was somewhat critical of her mouth—it ought to be a bit fuller—and her chin was a little weak, but what she disliked most was the undetermined color of her eyes: a smudge of brown around the pupils, blending into green and bordered by a darker green circle. Her mother had beautiful green eyes, as did Eta and Ochie, and her father's were blue, the color her two other brothers inherited; why did hers have to be different? She would even settle for plain brown, although given the choice, she'd definitely prefer green.

As for the rest of her body, her 5'6" frame was slender, almost coltish, with long legs that she judged to be her best feature. She had no complaints about her backside curves and the shape of her calves tapering to narrow ankles, but felt ashamed wearing size nine shoes. There was no way she could ever fit into Cinderella's slipper, if a prince ever came around offering her a chance to try.

That others were blind to her perceived "imperfections" became apparent when she received an invitation to the upcoming ball, the traditional Balek Ball given in October 1947 by the newest crop of university freshmen. As always, it was a big event for girls in their upper teens no longer interested in geeky adolescent high school boys, but to be invited at sixteen was unusual. No one in Sári's class dreamed of getting invited for at least another year, so the invitation came as a total surprise to her. It was from Andy Varszi, a boy her parents liked and trusted, but still, she expected a resounding "you are too young" objection from them. She could hardly believe her ears when, instead, her mother asked if she'd like to go. Would she ever! Of course she'd love to go, she was dying to go! She would have to get special permission from school but with her parents requesting it, no doubt it would be granted. Oh, what a buzz this would create among her friends!

Her only disappointment came when Ilonka told her they couldn't afford to buy her a new gown when they needed every penny for repairs on the house. The initial patchwork to cover up the war damages was no longer holding up, and since rental regulations held the tenants responsible for maintaining the building in good condition, they would have to hire a contractor at a considerable expense. It simply couldn't be postponed anymore. Eta's beautiful chiffon wedding dress with a little alteration, cutting the sleeves short and such, would have to do, or she could just forget about going. Well, what about matching shoes? She couldn't wear Eta's; they were too small for her. Unfortunately, she got a thumb down for that, too. Buying a pair of white heels with winter around the corner was sheer luxury, especially when she might outgrow them before the summer.

Wearing her navy pumps and a hand-me-down dress was not what Sári had in mind for her very first ball, but there was nothing she could do about it if she wanted to go. Feeling shortchanged and momentarily gripped by resentment, the thought that her parents would be able to pay for a gown and new shoes if she did not have so many brothers entered her mind, but she immediately felt ashamed and guilty for being so selfish. Dismissing it quickly she turned her attention back to focusing on all the fun she was going to have. The only thing that still dampened her excitement was the fear that her mother might ask her to wear her gold necklace, and she would have to tell her that she had lost it. Well, so far she had gotten away with it; perhaps her luck would hold a little longer. And it did, the question she dreaded did not come up.

She had her hair done in soft curls, and Ilonka applied a touch of color to her lips and some blush to her cheeks, so when Andy arrived to escort them, he could hardly take his eyes off her. On the way to the ball they picked up her godmother, Mrs. Varosy, who had generously offered to sit with Ilonka and keep her company at the dance, when in truth she loved to go; it gave her a chance to get out of the house, watch people, and engage in her favorite pastime, gossiping.

This time Sári did not need instructions to do the swing or the latest dance craze called the "pony," where couples skipped and hopped circling the floor. When the band switched to a slow number it was the first time that she ever danced cheek-to-cheek, but as Andy held her close, still in love with her, all she could think of was how she wished it were Rudy's arms around her. He was gone from Sopron by then, and she would never see him again, but his image, imprinted on her adolescent mind as a handsome, blond, blue eyed young man, remained with her forever as her perfect, irresistible ideal.

After the birth of her son, Eta did not return to work in the factory. Having completed the political seminar in Gyor not only solidified Latzi's position in the union, but also got him a promotion. In recognition for his rapid transition to leftist ideology, the Committee lifted him from the factory floor and set him up in the personnel office with a salary enough to support his wife and son. Part of his new job was to maintain a close watch over each worker's performance, conduct periodic interviews to evaluate their attitude toward the ongoing changes, and decide who among them was politically conscious enough to be trusted, and who was not. He also made motivational speeches about increasing productivity modeled after proven Soviet methods, and constantly reminded the workers how lucky they all were to have the shining example of the Soviet Union to follow in the arduous task of building the new and free socialist Hungary.

But however vocal Latzi was on the job, at home he adhered to the house rules to keep the political rhetoric to himself. The two families maintained a quiet harmony, focusing on the new baby, who was a joy to everyone. Ilonka and Jeno had to admit that Latzi was a very good father, spending as much time as he could spare with his little son. Eta was breastfeeding the baby, but changed to formula when she felt she was coming down with the flu. The symptoms were there—sore throat, fever, and muscle ache—but it turned out to be much worse: scarlet fever, a highly contagious bacterial disease. Dr. Graser immediately rushed her to the hospital, and as heartbreaking as it was to be separated from her baby, she had to spend the next six weeks in isolation. She did not have to worry about little Latzi; Ilonka took care of him as one of her own, although it took the little fellow some time to get used to the bottle. Latzi visited Eta often, occasionally even taking the baby so she could see him through a glass window. She was released to a big welcome the day before Christmas to celebrate the holidays at home that could possibly be the last one they'd spend in this house, since the apartment the committee promised to Latzi was expected to be ready soon.

On New Year's Eve Sári was going to Wanda's house for a party, the first one where boys were also invited. Andy was her escort again, with a promise to Ilonka and Jeno that he'd bring her home by one o'clock. At the party Wanda gathered all the young men around her new record player, a Christmas present from her parents, along with a stack of the latest hit records, and gave them careful instructions on how to crank up the machine and change the records without scratching them. They were to take turns providing continuous music for the evening.

She planned her party as a sophisticated affair with the lights dimmed low and soft music playing. They danced, nibbled on finger sandwiches, and when it was time to ring in the New Year, she handed out champagne glasses, although they toasted only with apple juice. In those first few seconds of 1948, Sári received her first real kiss, as Andy gently drew her close and bent to kiss her on the lips. At first it was just a slight touch, but when she didn't pull away, he probed deeper. With eyes closed, she completely gave into that sweet, dizzying sensation only a first romantic kiss could bring. It kept her lightheaded and dreamy for days to come, a reaction that surprised her since Andy was just a good friend to her, nothing more. They had fun together, they kidded each other endlessly, but that was it. Why, at the Balek Ball she even asked him not to cut in if she was dancing with a certain young man she liked, and he humored her without any sign of hurt feelings.

When she finally opened her eyes and looked into Andy's face, expecting to see him in some sort of magically different light, she almost felt cheated because nothing of the sort happened. Sparks failed to ignite and music didn't rise to a crescendo; she still felt the same way about him. He was her pal. Yet she loved the kiss! The warmth of his mouth, the softness of his tongue, and the way it left her breathless.

Her head swam in confusion and she was glad when Wanda grabbed her hand and pulled her into the kitchen where everyone stood around a pot of ice-cold water and some molten lead, waiting to perform a customary New Year's ritual. Wanda would pour a thimble-sized amount of lead into the water, and as the wildly churning and hissing mass began to take shape, one of the girls would claim it for her New Year's omen. The form was supposed to hint at something significant waiting to happen in the coming year, but the fun of the entire process was to guess what the form meant to foretell. Wanda's omen suggested a form of a boot, and the teasing went on about which of the boys would be booted out from her circle of friends.

For Sári it was clearly a shape of a leaf. Needless to say, it immediately brought to mind Adam and Eve, but no one thought for a moment that, if not a leaf, something to do with forests would soon add significant meaning to her life.

Communists in control

BY THE END OF 1947, a few months shy of three years into peace, the horrors of war began to fade giving way to renewal. Once again the young could dance and laugh and the old had time to remember the happy youth of their own. But as the promise of a better tomorrow shimmered on the horizon, disturbing events began to stir the barely settled dust. More and more, it became apparent that the Communist faction of the government was taking steps to solidify their position. The banks were already in their hands since May 1947, but that was not enough. Now they set out to reorganize property ownership, first nationalizing all factories with more than one hundred workers, a job finished on March 25, 1948, then taking over any enterprise employing over ten people, and all factories owned by foreigners.

Next on their agenda was the elimination of the clergy. On June 11, 1948 parochial schools were seized, and all their property, including real estate, furniture, and school equipment, was confiscated. In spite of massive demonstrations against it, priests, monks, nuns, and clerics, including those in the teaching profession, were thrown out on the streets to fend for themselves. Arresting the protesters and sending them to the dreaded labor camps quickly silenced anyone who dared to utter a word in their defense. Churches were still left open, supported by donations from the parishioners, but that, too, stopped eventually through intimidation directed at the churchgoers; the Communists suggested that if they had money to give to the church, perhaps their salary was too high and should be reduced.

To survive, the discharged priests and nuns changed into civilian clothes, hoping to find work, but it didn't help; jobs were closed to them even on the lowest manual level. They were forced either to turn to relatives or seek refuge in Austria. Crossing the border was always at great risk, but even if they succeeded, they were not out of danger. Austria was divided into four zones, American, British, French and Russian, and if caught in the Soviet-occupied zone, they were rerouted back to Hungary and put on the road straight to Recsk, the most notorious of the country's gulags.

The next victim in the struggle for overall Communist domination was the peasantry. It included the so-called kulaks—a word imported from the Soviets—who owned some land before the 1945 agrarian reform and worked the fields themselves with occasional hired help, as well as those formerly landless field workers who were recently granted a few acres of land but refused to give it up to join the newly created state-operated farm cooperatives. The resistance to the co-ops—or kolkhoz, another name borrowed from the Russians—was fierce, since as members, the peasants worked merely as employees, and what they produced was sold to the government at fixed prices. They were allowed to keep a small amount for their own use, but it had to be raised by working after-hours. No wonder the pressure on them to join was relentless, and to entice them, whenever a new co-operative opened, the Party celebrated it with a big fanfare and high praises for those who, seeing the "advantage" in signing up, "voluntarily" offered up their land.

Farmers were not the only ones forced into cooperatives. Various trade co-ops were also created for small businesses and tradesmen—tailors, shoemakers, barbers, repairmen, and the like—and if they refused to join, the owners were taxed out of business.

There were protests within the coalition government against some of these measures, which soon sharpened into finger-pointing accusations. To stifle the voice of the opposition parties, the Communists and Social Democrats held a two-day unification congress in June, forming an alliance and merging under a new name, the Hungarian Workers Party, or MDP, short for *Magyar Dolgozók Pártja*. To secure Communist control within the new party, the MDP's first order of the day was to elect the Muscovite Matyas Rakosi, the country's Deputy Prime Minister, as the party's General Secretary. Now they were in position where they could press the leftist members of the former Social Democratic Party to start squeezing out their right-leaning leaders by using an assortment of charges. They would be denounced as being incompetent, accused of deliberately sabotaging the country's development, thus conspiring against the republic, or condemned as reactionaries, nationalists, or spies.

This mania about spying for the West stemmed from Stalinist Russia and became characteristic of all the satellite countries. Anyone who had ever lived in the West, was educated there, or kept contact with Western representatives, was suspected of treacherous behavior. Because of exposure to western contamination and dangerous bourgeois ideas, even those returning from German concentration camps or people who had risked their lives working in a foreign underground during the war fell into this category. Instead of welcoming them home, they were subjected to interrogations and carted off to detention camps.

On June 28, 1948 a new field of spy hunting opened up when the Yugoslav leader, Marshall Tito, suddenly fell from Stalin's graces. It yielded a flock of victims dispatched to the bottomless work camps as "Titoist collaborators," quickly forgetting the treaty of friendship and mutual assistance Hungary signed with Yugoslavia only six months earlier. Tito's downfall came about as Moscow realized that Marshall Tito was developing a self-styled Communist dictatorship patterned more after the Marxist-Leninist form of socialism than as dictated by Stalin. To openly disagree with the wise Father of the International Communist Movement and prefer to build a social order according to Tito was tantamount to rebellion.

The reason he was able to defy Stalin and reject the absolute loyalty expected of all eastern bloc countries was the absence of the Red Army. It was a big mistake on Stalin's part to yield to Tito's demand at the end of the war to remove all external forces, including the Soviet military. He apparently trusted Tito as one of his Moscow-trained followers to fall blindly into the prescribed orbit around the USSR and do his bidding without the Red Army looking over his shoulder. By the time Stalin recognized that Tito aimed to create a strong, independent national economy, there was nothing he could do but declare him a hated traitor who sold out to the imperialists, never to be trusted and forever condemned.

To remove the threat of Titoism infecting the satellite countries, an immediate "housecleaning" was set into motion. Dropping all pretensions of adhering to democratic principles, the Party now turned up the heat to expel the moderate members of the coalition government. With unrestrained power, they picked no less than Zoltan Tildy, the President of Hungary, as their next victim. Of course, it was done in the name of the people, who demanded Tildy's resignation. He was removed from his post on July 30, 1948 and arrested shortly after that on the trumped-up allegations that he had collaborated with his son-in-law, the ambassador to Egypt, who was recalled, charged with spying for the CIA and quickly executed for his "crimes." Tildy's phone and house were bugged, but because nothing turned up that could put him in jail, he was kept under house arrest until the spring of 1956.

Then suddenly, people noticed signs of a beginning power struggle within the Party itself. The attacks were subtler and less vicious than against the coalition opposition, but just as serious and were led by the highest-ranking Stalin-bred Muscovites against the leaders of the old national Communist movement. They were accused of pretending to be faithful Communists while stealthily plotting to bring back the old fascist regime, or worse, of being Titoist conspirators in cahoots with the West. In truth, their only "crime" was refusing to follow the Stalinist dictates.

It was the start of the prefabricated trials that mirrored the Stalinist purges of 1938. To build a case against the chosen victims, Rakosi used the AVO to carry out his orders with the clear directive that if the enemy resists and won't give up, it must be eliminated. They presented the trumped-up charges, made the arrests, conducted interrogations that included threats and torture to wring out a confession from the falsely accused victims, and carried out the punishment, all according to Rakosi's designs. Some idealistic members of the AVO perhaps truly believed that they were fighting a war to bring about social changes, and wars were never without bloody sacrifices. It was the price paid for victory. But the majority was fully aware that the struggle was not about ideals but to solidify the dictatorship of the Party, and for that they were richly rewarded.

When people saw formerly trusted Party members, one after the other, put on trial for betraying the Party from within, a doubting question rose to mind: how was it possible to discover these treacheries in such a short time, when in the Soviet Union it took Comrade Stalin twenty years to unveil the traitors hiding among the faithful party cadre? It was a question no one dared to ask openly.

At the beginning of 1948, to indicate that the government was firmly in power, Rakosi announced that the Soviets had agreed to leave the country. Only a small number of units would remain, and only temporarily, to ensure the smooth withdrawal of the Red Army. In fact, this "withdrawal" only meant their removal from the cities, where their sight was a great source of irritation to the people, and the "small number of units" and their "temporary" stationing translated to the permanent presence of about one half to one million Russian soldiers and their families for the next four decades. The government merely transferred the Russian military bases to remote out-of-sight areas, their maintenance a great burden to Hungary. They had stores stocked with products not available to Hungarians, schools for their children and movies for entertainment.

When the Russians pulled out from the casern across Ilonka's house, she hoped to say goodbye to the hated roof-to-ground red flag hanging on the building. It was an eyesore to look at day in and day out, and she couldn't wait for that repulsive banner with the sickle and hammer symbol to come down, just like the other one with the swastika did. To her great agitation, not only did the flag remain when Hungarian soldiers took over the compound, but they hung a same size Hungarian red, white, and green flag on the other side of the entrance, except with the old royal coat of arms removed from the middle. Causing further indignation not only to Ilonka but also to the majority of people was the newly designed military uniform, which made Hungarian soldiers hardly distinguishable from their Red Army counterparts. At least they were shouting commands in Hungarian, but how long would that last, Ilonka wondered.

She noticed that when soldiers marched out for field exercise, only a few mothers in the neighborhood would bring their children to watch them, and unlike in the past, no one cheered them anymore. Once in a while she spotted their neighbor Mrs. Yeager and her three-year-old daughter among the spectators, a little girl with markedly Asiatic features, slanted eyes, yellowish skin, and straight black hair, so much in contrast to the peachy complexion and sparkling blue eyes of her beautiful mother. There were other similar-looking children, their birth the result of rape committed by soldiers from the Central Asian regions of the Soviet Union, but there was never a shame or embarrassment attached to them, only a deep-felt empathy for the mothers for what they must have endured.

Seeing them always made Ilonka feel indebted to the Church for taking her and the children into what she came to regard as sanctuary, thus saving them from the fate other women had suffered at the hands of the Russian "liberators." Perhaps this played a role in her turning more and more toward religion in spite of government pressure to abandon church practices. She was always a devout Catholic and never missed Sunday Mass, but now she also went to evening devotions, sometimes several times a week. The abuses against the priests and nuns affected her profoundly and she had tears in her eyes when Father Palos, the priest who took them into his church during the Russian onslaught, came to say goodbye. He was leaving for Pannonhalma, the ancient seat of the Benedictines in Hungary that was under the protection of the Vatican.

Knowing Ilonka's need to attend church, Jeno couldn't find the heart to stop her and never mentioned that her behavior reflected negatively on him at the office. To the work committee it meant that even though he himself didn't go to Mass, he had neglected to convince his wife of the danger in listening to anti-state agitations ceaselessly emitted from the pulpits. Another reason for not discussing politics with Ilonka was the fear that she wouldn't hold her tongue. He remembered how she almost got into trouble during the Nazi occupation for that same reason. He knew how fast the political atmosphere was changing in the country and that it was no longer safe to talk freely even behind closed doors. In fact, to talk against the regime in front of the younger children was more risky now that they were no longer toddlers and could pick up bits of the conversation, then innocently repeat it in school or other public places. He even started to have doubts about saying anything damning in front of his son-in-law. How could he be trusted when he condemned his own father for what the poor man was forced to do? What is the world coming to when a man couldn't speak his mind in his own home?

He kept everything bottled up, never complaining about the constant political pressures at work, or how he worried about the future. What if they found some label to pin on him and let him go? What would happen then? This feeling of uncertainty never seemed to leave him, and the stress started to take a toll on his health. His stomach ulcer that bothered him on and off since WWI now flared up again, and the old nervous jitters, remnants from nerve damage he suffered during that same war were returning as well. He managed to control them even in the recent war years, but now the attacks started to plague him again. He'd feel faint at first, then a mild seizure would set in lasting several minutes. They could strike him anytime and anywhere, in the office, while on inspection, or walking on the street, causing him great embarrassment. The medication the doctor prescribed didn't help much; the best he could do when the tremors started was to stop whatever he was doing and wait until calm returned. He only hoped that in time he'd overcome the annoying condition, as he had before.

Although living with constant worry left its mark on Jeno, it helped that the confrontations with Latzi ceased and they no longer butted heads. That changed, however, the day he found out that his son-in-law was a member of the Communist Party. They heard it from Mitzie when she came to complain about him, how everyone at work resented him now that he had become a card-carrying big shot. It all began when he started going around the floor, clocking everyone's performance and came up with a daily quota for each worker as a production goal to achieve based not on the average performance, which would be fair, but using the highest possible output. The method was first introduced in the Soviet Union when an overachiever named Stakhanov out-produced every co-worker, and his output was held up as the standard to follow. Needless to say, people were not happy about it, but without a forum to raise objections, they had no choice but work harder to meet the Stakhanovist quotas. And when production increased and the factory received recognition, he became the golden boy of the union bosses and the Party committee.

Jeno could not let the news pass without confronting Latzi. When asked, he not only admitted that he joined the Party but practically glowed with pride. Breaking his own rules not to talk politics with him, Jeno decided to confront him and seek an answer to what bothered him ever since his son-in-law had started displaying leftist tendencies.

"Latzi, we know you are a man of high ideals, that's why we never opposed you marrying Eta. But please explain, how could you leave your religion and embrace such totally opposite ideals as Communism? What made you change? It's hard to understand that someone like you, with a solid middle-class background, brought up with strong Christian values, whose uncle is a bishop, the leader of Hungary's Reformed Church, yourself an educated man, could turn 180 degrees in a matter of a few years."

"It's very simple, Jeno. You see, it's exactly my upbringing that prevented me from seeing beyond the bourgeois world. I was so sheltered that I'd never seen neglect, never knew what poverty was and what it did to people. I went to private schools; I played with similarly privileged boys; I learned the proper etiquette and social graces of my middle class; and were it not for the war, I would have carried on with my life without ever knowing the difference. But when the world turned upside down, it opened my eyes to see how the other side lived, and from that moment on, all I wanted was to help these people, try to make up for what they suffered, to ask forgiveness. I joined the Communist Party because it is the only one that wants the same thing, to erase social injustice and create a better world, a world without prejudice and with equality not just for some because they happened to be born privileged, but for everyone. I listened to what the other parties offered and became convinced that only the Communist Party is strong enough to create such a world. They were the ones who recognized that it's not the remnants of the decadent aristocracy, nor the self-centered bourgeois, nor the lazy peasantry, but the workers, the previous have-nots, who possess the vitality, the life force that will lead us there. All we are doing is opening opportunities for them, educating them, and teaching them the know-how. Now is that so wrong, Jeno?"

"But at what expense? Look at what they are doing to decent people, ordinary people who did not get rich by taking money from others, or the clergy, whose mission was to help the poor, to practice charity. You tell me, what did they do wrong to be treated so unfairly? What you are talking about, Latzi, is but a visionary world. It is impossible to create perfect equality because of human nature, the greed for power. It will never happen! Let's take your father, a doctor. Would you have him treat patients for free? How would he feed you, educate you, provide for his family? And when he finds himself penniless, how many of his former patients do you think would come to take care of him and you?"

"Ah, but that's exactly why the Party is needed! You are right; today individuals are not ready yet to share equally; it will only happen when we reach Communism. We are just taking the firsts steps in that direction, and the road ahead is not easy. It is strewn with obstacles, which we must overcome. It will take time; people must be taught, starting with the young. And that's when the Party steps in to take the lead, give guidance, oversee the progress, and guard against those who try to stop it and bring back the old world. Like the clergy; that's why they must go, Jeno. They are reactionaries. Yes, they were preaching charity, but look what wealth they accumulated in the process. The huge estates, the income from their private schools, their elevated social standing—why, one way for any poor young man to climb out of poverty was to become a priest! Let's not even talk about their teaching, that the poor must suffer in silence, bear their lot with patience, their reward would come in the afterlife, when heaven will compensate them. We can't possibly allow them to continue filling young minds with such utterly harmful nonsense. Besides, in our new system poverty will be wiped out. Everyone will be working, fair wages will be established, there will be free education, free healthcare—but first we must cut off those elements that fight tooth and nail to block our way."

"My God, you truly believe what you are saying! They have succeeded in brainwashing you! I know people who join the Party because it seems to be the only way to get ahead these days, but they are doing it for personal reasons; they pretend, but never really believe any of that Communist propaganda." Jeno wanted to tell Latzi how few people agreed with his thinking, how everyone lived in fear because of the Party, but he saw it as hopeless and just shook his head and walked out of the room.

Latzi, too, walked away feeling equally disappointed in Jeno. He liked his father-in-law; he was a man of high principles, an honest man. It was too bad that he clung to the old ideals, unable to change, refusing all reasoning, exactly like those the Party called class enemy. It was unfortunate, because the day was coming when he would no longer be tolerated and by then there was nothing he, or anyone else would be able to do for him.

Come to think of it, Latzi thought, it might reflect on him badly to live with his reactionary in-laws. The Party promised him an apartment in the future, but who could tell when that would be. He didn't want to wait much longer and decided to talk to Eta about finding another place. The sooner they moved, the better.

The expulsion of priests from nationalized parochial schools created a shortage in teachers, and until the empty positions could be filled, teachers from other schools were enlisted to substitute. When Gyuszi and his classmates learned that Mr. Augustin, the principal of the State Gimnazium for Girls, would be their temporary Latin teacher, they were not thrilled. They all heard that he would not accept poetic interpretations of the ancient Roman texts, but insisted on exact translations and could split hairs over the use of one word he found better than another. Gyuszi was a good student, and a studious one, but this was too much even for him. To help him live up to Mr. Augusztin's demands, Ilonka was considering getting him private tutoring, when an idea hit him. Didn't he also teach Latin in Sári's class? It sent Gyuszi searching for his sister's Latin homework from the previous year. These notebooks were clearly marked with corrections and notations by the teachers and were very much in demand as hand-me-downs at the end of each school year. Some enterprising students even made a little money by selling them, so Gyuszi was happy to find that Sári still had hers. From that time on, to the amazement of the class his translations were perfect, except some minor errors he slipped in intentionally. This worked for quite a while, until one day after commenting on his excellent translation from Cicero, Mr. Augusztin looked up from his desk and, with a puzzled expression on his face, asked Gyuszi if by any chance he had a sister or cousin named Sári Zachar? And if so, was she a student at the girl's gimnazium? There was no use denying it, and Gyuszi regretfully had to hand over Sári's notebook. On top of losing his source, he had to do his homework in school for a whole month under the watchful eye of Mr. Augusztin.

That same year a new program was introduced in high schools everywhere with the purpose of increasing the students' political awareness. The practice already existed in the workplace, where employees gathered thirty minutes before starting time to discuss the daily newspaper articles and talk about the current topics. Most people hated it, especially the part when the committee representative presiding over the reading session asked for personal opinions from the participants. To respond was like pulling teeth; it meant talking in glorious terms about issues most of them hated.

Now it was the same with the students. Already resentful for getting up half an hour earlier, they thoroughly detested sitting through such a stupefying exercise. Teachers were busy with their own collective readings, so the political leader of the class took over picking the articles for discussion, posing the questions, and asking for opinions. Everyone knew that the answers must be laced with rapturous praises for the Soviet Union and felt embarrassed in front of the others for making such obviously fake commentaries. Doing less, or God forbid, refusing to participate, would draw a scrutinized background check on the girl's family to dig up a reason for the reluctance.

In Sári's class it was Dora who conducted the meetings, while the rest of the girls just sank into their chairs with blank stares, wishing to be somewhere else. Relishing her role, she would pick someone to analyze the subject in question, and if the girl neglected mentioning the Soviet's role in the country's accomplishments, or even if she did, but without proper enthusiasm, it would elicit a castigating remark from her. She would sarcastically suggest that they all should be more appreciative of the Russians, because without them they would be sitting here speaking German. Interestingly, her mother was one of the first to have joined the Communist Party in 1945, after changing her allegiance from the former Arrow Cross Party the minute the Russians arrived.

Dora also made mental notes about the attitudes of the participants and periodically reported to the school's political committee who demonstrated a higher level of political consciousness and who lacked interest. These were filed away in the hated kader records the school maintained for each student. At first the girls were not aware of the importance of these records, that they could be the key to admittance to a university for someone with passing grades, while shutting the door in the face of a straight-A student, strictly for political reasons. Sári only realized it when Wanda's sister Tessa applied to two universities and both turned her down. She graduated with high marks that fully qualified her to enter college, and her parents wanted answers. They soon found out that several others at Tessa's achievement level, even the top graduate, received rejections, while girls with questionable marks and dubious potential to succeed in the demanding field of higher education were accepted.

Further checking revealed that those turned down all came from the "wrong" social classes or had low marks in political awareness—the apparent justification for automatic denial—while most girls going off to college were from the lower classes or from left-leaning middle class families and were judged politically advanced. For them academic achievement was secondary. Their college entrance tests were passed without scrutiny, as were later exams, until they would get their degrees. What mattered was their continued political development. The Party needed people with degrees who were first and foremost dedicated to Communist principles, trusted people who could be put in high positions as future leaders. Technical knowledge was not important; those tasks could be delegated to the truly knowledgeable.

When Sári found out what criteria universities used in accepting students, she recognized that if she wanted to go to college, which she was determined to do, she must stop being indifferent to current politics. Her grades were the best, her social background passable; she would only have to make an effort to get involved with political issues, not as deeply as Dora, just convincing enough for the school committee to take notice. If that's what it took, then that was what she must do.

She recalled seeing a school posting at the end of May that offered a six-week indoctrination-oriented youth camp starting July 5, where students would be learning the fundamental teachings of Marx, Engels, Lenin and Stalin. At the time she ignored it, and she still could care less about the whole thing, but now it seemed that attending such camp would be a good opportunity to start building some political credits for the future. She signed up and was told that the camp would be held in the northern part of Hungary with all expenses paid, including round-trip transportation.

Her only problem was what to tell her parents, since they would never allow her to go if they knew it was a political camp. They saw what it did to Latzi. Her only way was to lie. She waited until the last minute before telling them a cockamamie story about a summer camp for selected students as a reward for the extra work they did when books were not available. Originally she was not chosen to go, she said, but now they offered her to replace someone who just dropped out. The camp was free, but the group was leaving the next day, and she must have their signed approval, or they won't let her on the train. Her father was skeptical at first, but Ilonka only bristled that Sárika should have been on that original list; surely she deserved consideration for all the scribbling she had done during those post-war years. A change of scenery and a few weeks in a summer camp would be good for her. And the price was right; heaven only knows, they couldn't afford to send her anywhere on their own.

From her class only Dora was going, but altogether about ten girls from her school were boarding the train the next morning. They had a short stopover in Budapest, when the girls were given a few hours for sightseeing before leaving for the camp. This was Sári's first trip away from home since she was a child, and her excitement grew as the train neared the capital. She and Dora were hanging out the window, not to miss the sight of the recently erected famous 14-foot bronze Liberty Statue standing on top of a 25-foot pedestal on the highest hill of Buda. It was a figure of a woman clad in a long floating dress, arms stretched over her head with a single palm leaf placed across her hands, presenting an impressive monument that dominated the city's skyline.

Knowing that Latzi called his parents to meet her at the station and show her around the city, she wore her favorite dress and new platform sandals. When the girls met that morning at the station Dora commented that she was not exactly dressed for camp, but she didn't care. She was not about to wear some shabby camp gear to visit this beautiful and exciting city!

Dr. and Mrs. Kontra were wonderful to her. First she had lunch at their home, a spacious second-floor apartment in the inner city of Pest filled with antique furniture, Persian rugs, and floor-length drapes over the windows, then spent the remaining time sightseeing with them. It was enough to convince her that this was the place where she wanted to live for the rest of her life. It was only a couple of years before she would be back attending college. Which one, she did not care, as long as it was in Budapest!

When they dropped her off at the station at four o'clock, she ran into the restroom to change into shorts and walking shoes, her regulation outfit for the next six weeks. As she had expected, the camp was a bore. Its purpose, besides the socialist indoctrination, was to turn the girls into little political organizers and give them the know-how to carry out certain tasks upon their return. They were to watch their schoolmates for signs of defiance against the regime, question the teachers if they deviated from the prescribed Party-dictated dialog, and most importantly, never forget to emphasize the importance of the Soviet Union in the country's development. At political meetings and demonstrations they were to initiate a "spontaneous" enthusiastic applause whenever Comrade Stalin's name was mentioned and lead the cheering this beloved leader so deserved.

Sári listened attentively to the lectures and wrote papers sprinkled with the political phrases they were learning. She sang the "Communist Internationale" with the right fervor and shouted just loud enough all the propaganda slogans damning the imperialist dogs, the Titoist collaborators, and the American warmongers who were in that very minute preparing the stage for World War III. She cheered with the rest when told how Communism would triumph over the decadent West and how the world would be a better place with the spread of Communist ideals. And she never failed to show the proper gratitude for the Red Army for liberating Hungary at the cost of tremendous sacrifices.

At the end of six weeks she received her Certificate of Completion, officially declaring her a qualified political youth counselor, an impressing sounding title for a junior leftist agitator. Two years later that certificate became her passport to the College of Economics in Budapest.

Leaving the camp, Sári had time on the long train ride to Sopron to brace herself against the confrontation waiting for her when she arrived home. She knew from the angry letters she had received from her parents that shortly after she left they learned what the camp was really all about, and that she was in hot water from that moment on. Lying was bad enough, but to do it to cover up going to a Marxist boot camp was beyond their understanding. They could hardly tolerate to have one Communist in the house; they wouldn't stand having their daughter's head turned into that direction, too. She destroyed the letters as soon as she read them, lest they get into Dora's hands.

Her mother met her at the station, but she held back the tirade until they reached home. “Aren’t you ashamed for lying to us? Did you think you could get away with it? That we were not going to find out? How could you even consider going to this kind of camp? And the embarrassment your lying caused me! You don’t know how awkward it was when friends came up to me on the street and asked how could I possibly allow you to attend a communist indoctrination camp. I just stood there like a dummy, not knowing what on earth they were talking about. A youth camp to reward you, indeed!! What made you do it?”

“I am sorry, Mother, I truly am, but I wanted to go and I knew you and Father would be against it if I told the truth,” Sári tried to justify her lying. “But you don’t have to worry, I am not like Latzi; all that senseless political gibberish went in one ear and out the other. Do you for one second believe that I could parrot all the stupid things they were hammering into our heads in the camp? Honestly, Mother, do you see me standing in front of the class lecturing about the political and economic philosophy of Karl Marx?”

At this, assuming a stiff, formal pose, she let the words of the standard Marxist rhetoric roll off her tongue, how class struggle plays a central role in society’s inevitable development from bourgeois oppression under capitalism to a socialist and ultimately classless society.

“That’s enough,” Ilonka waved a hand, laughing at the comic image her daughter presented. “A truly eloquent speech, I am sure; it’s too bad I couldn’t understand a word of it!” And when Sári opened her mouth again, Ilonka shook her head. “No, please! Spare me the enlightenment! I prefer to stay ignorant.”

It broke the tension and they both fell into fits of laughter. “Good old Karl Marx would be proud of you,” Ilonka sputtered between guffaws. But laugh as she might, she still wanted to know why did Sári bother to go to this camp at all, what purpose did it serve, when she had no intention of using what she learned there?

“It will help me to get into college, Mom, that’s why! It is to demonstrate that I am eager to learn what we must do to build our socialist world, and that I want to be a part of the struggle that eventually gets us to live in that classless society Marx envisioned. Now don’t laugh, Mother, this is not a joke!” She pointed a finger at Ilonka when she started to chuckle again.

“I am sorry I can’t help it,” she laughed, but then went back to the subject at hand. “I still can’t see how attending a camp will do that for you. Why, you are one of the best in your class. That should guarantee your acceptance into any university.”

“No, it does not, not anymore! These days, political awareness counts more than good grades. And the camp is just a start, Mom. Do you think the Party spent all that money to ‘educate’ us without a return on their investment? They expect us to put into practice what they taught us. I still have time before school starts to figure out how to pull a balancing act, do just enough to qualify me as a politically active person without showing too much red. I am lucky that Dora is in my class; she is a true believer, like Latzi, so I know she will do most of the talking and recruiting.”

"What do you mean, recruiting? You are in school, not in the military!"

"Yeah, you're right, it sounds like the army! But what we are supposed to do is sign up everyone to join a new student organization called the Democratic Youth League (*Demokrata Ifjusági Szövetség*), or DISZ, that will be introduced this fall. Like I said, Dora loves to play the leader and will do the speeches and the convincing; I'll probably just work as her secretary, keep the roster and collect the monthly dues, a few forints to cover the paperwork, put up decorations at special meetings, and things like that. Or I could do something on the so-called 'cultural front', like form an acting group to put on shows and recitals—all, of course, reflecting the revolutionary struggle of the proletariat. The Communists only condemn the decadent bourgeois self-serving art for art's sake stuff, but they believe that plays and films used the right way can be an important tool to influence the mind. I'll wait and see how things will go, but I have to tell you, Mother, one way or the other I must get involved politically, otherwise I can forget about going to college. If you hear me recite some poems in public glorifying our dear Comrade Stalin, you must know that it is because it's better than spying on my schoolmates and reporting them to the committee in order to store up political credits."

"So you are only doing this to go to college? But why are you so set on studying four more years, Sárika? Is it that important to you? Eta did not go to college, and she is happy as a wife and mother. You should be thinking along the same lines. Work for a while after graduation; you will have no problem finding a nice office job, then get married, have children, and raise a family—that's what girls should do. Leave college to the boys! I don't have to tell you that we have no money to pay for your college expenses. Your brothers must come first. You are a pretty girl; you'll find a good husband and you'll be set for life!"

"Like Eta and you? No thank you! I want more than just getting married and having babies. I want to get a good education first. And don't worry, I know you can't afford to support me financially during the years I will be studying. I will apply for a scholarship, and with my grades and two years of political activity, I am sure I will get one."

Ilonka knew her headstrong daughter well enough to stop arguing with her for the moment. "I guess it's no use trying to talk you out of going, but do you know what you want to study, what you want to be?" she asked.

"You got me there, Mom! I wish I knew! What I'd most love to do is study acting at the Academy of Fine Arts, but I have to give that up, simply because I can't memorize things. I have some kind of mental deficiency in that department. I could never remember the lines. So, that takes care of acting. But other than that, I don't really know. I only know what I don't want to be. Teaching is out; I know what our poor teachers have to put up with, and my nerves could not stand that kind of abuse! As for being a doctor, I can't stand the sight of blood and I am not thrilled about treating sick people. Besides, it takes too long; with the internship, it could be seven or even eight years before one can start practicing. Lawyers must follow Party dictates, so that's out too. What's left is studying something that involves math, writing, or maybe economics—I'll see. I still have two years to figure it out. And of course, it also depends on which college would accept me right away. Some colleges are more popular than others; they fill their quotas fast, and I just don't want to be put on a long waiting list. I can't afford to skip a year because I am afraid I'd forget all what I learned before, or most of it, and I am not kidding. Anyway, I'll send in a few applications and see what happens. But until then, like I said, I have to be politically demonstrative; so don't be surprised when you hear people saying that I am a 'pinko.' I have to do it, but you know now that it's all in pretense."

"I understand that, but what am I supposed to say when people start asking? Tell them that you are just pretending?"

"Don't be silly Mother! Only Wanda knows that I am faking it. Just ignore what people say or think. Shrug it off, say that you don't know what's going on, times are changing; perhaps I picked up ideas from Latzi. They might even sympathize with you. I expect people will be a little more cautious in front of me now, afraid they might say the wrong thing. So let's just see what happens. Maybe nobody will dare to ask you questions!"

"Well, I'll think of something to say when it comes to it. But Sári, what if things change? I've seen people hanging from lampposts because they jumped on the wrong bandwagon and then the regime changed. It can happen again, you know, and if it does, there will be fingers pointing at you that you were a Communist!"

"I thought about that, Mother, but I think the political situation is here to stay. As long as the Red Army is sitting on our necks, there won't be any change. If anything, what I heard in the camp convinced me that they are here for the long haul."

Sári was enjoying the last days of summer before going back to school and was about to go and see Wanda, when at the door she bumped into Erzsi, their last maid. She had stopped by to say hello and brought them some fresh fruits and produce from her village. Ilonka was not home, so Sári ushered her in with a noisy welcome. They always got along well, perhaps because Erzsi was only five or six years older than she. The girl was from the nearby countryside, but she sure didn't look like a village girl anymore. She wore a smart summer dress, heels, and clutched a matching purse under her arm, looking quite sophisticated. She even smoked now, as during their talk she pulled out a cigarette, lit up, and after inhaling deeply, blew out the smoke through her nostrils.

Noticing that Sári was staring at her, she apologized for not offering her one too, and held out the pack to her. With her mother out of the house, this was Sári's chance to try the forbidden. Taking the cigarette at once and holding it awkwardly, she leaned forward, waiting for Erzsi to flick open her lighter then, instead of inhaling, she swallowed the smoke and immediately succumbed to a horrid, choking cough. Erzsi quickly gave her a glass of water, chiding her for not telling that this was her first cigarette. When Sári could breathe again, the girl demonstrated how to inhale, and after a few tries she was smoking away, waving the cigarette through the air as she saw Bette Davis doing it in the movies.

While Sári was concentrating on Erzsi's lips as she demonstrated how to blow smoke circles, something glittery around the girl's neck caught her eye. Taking a closer look, she suddenly sat up. "Where did you get that necklace?"

Erzsi's hand flew to the beautiful chiseled cross pendant resting on a gold chain. "This? Why, it's from your mother; we exchanged it for food a few years back. I never take it off, not because I am such a good Christian, but I really love its delicate design," she said fingering the cross.

Oh, Mother, you could have told me! I would have understood! Sári thought, half relieved, half angry. All this time she thought she had lost her necklace and lived in fear that her mother would find out! Well, at least the mystery was solved and she didn't have to worry about it any longer.

They were gone when Ilonka came home, but the minute she opened the door she could smell the smoke. Looking at the table, she saw the ashtray with several cigarette butts, and wondered who had been visiting. She was just about to empty it when Sári bounced through the door.

"You'd never guess who was here, Mother! Erzsi brought you some stuff, but you wouldn't recognize her! You should have seen her! She sure changed a lot!"

"Did she now? By any chance, did she wear lipstick?"

"How did you know? Not only that, but her hair is tinted; it is kind of reddish."

"I can see that she also picked up some bad habits. The house is full of smoke! There must be at least six cigarette butts in this ashtray. And strangely, some have lipstick marks, some don't." Ilonka looked Sári in the eye as she held out the ashtray. "Care to explain?"

Sári knew that she was nailed. "OK, I tried to smoke one. Is it such a crime? This was the first time, and I hope you won't make a big deal out of it. Everyone smokes! Father does, and so did Aunt Anna, even you used to when you were playing cards. I remember the next morning when we went looking for fallen coins, the smoke was so thick in the room that you could cut it with a knife!"

"That's true, I used to smoke, but I had the good sense to quit when I realized how bad it is for you. Unfortunately, your father can't break the habit and given time, it will probably kill him. Smoking is very harmful, Sári, and I don't want you to start on it. Look, I'll show you why." With that she took one of the cigarette butts, lit it and blew the smoke through a thin white tissue paper. "See the brown spot the smoke left? That's tar and that's what smoking does to your lungs; chokes them until you can't breathe anymore. Please honey, don't start; it's addictive and once you get into the habit, it's hard to break it. You are a smart girl; you can see how bad smoking is for your health."

"I still see no harm in smoking a cigarette once in a while, when I—"

But Ilonka did not let her finish. "Very few people can smoke only once in a while, Sári. Maybe you could, but I am not taking that chance. And if you can't see my point to stay away from cigarettes, I will make that decision for you: as long as you live in this house, you are not to smoke. Is that understood? Now open the windows and let in some fresh air."

The subject was closed, but only for the time being. She did not smoke at home, but on occasions when temptation came her way, she gave in. She did not even like smoking; it just meant a glamorous thing to do. Her mother was just exaggerating; it could not be as dangerous as she said. In every movie she saw, the stars were never without a cigarette, and they were not stupid, they wouldn't do it if they knew it would kill them.

It took many years before she would admit that her mother was right. Except in one respect. She never developed a craving for cigarettes. To her, it remained a thing to do when sitting in a café sipping an espresso or talking to friends at a party. And eventually she gave it up altogether.

When at the end of summer Eta and Latzi moved to their new apartment, it brought back Ilonka's fears that with only the six of them in the large house, the authorities would be coming around checking for the extra space that might be requisitioned for other people. She calmed down only when Eta assured her that it wouldn't happen, because Latzi took care of the problem. She would not have to share the house with strangers as long as Latzi was around. Ilonka and Jeno had to acknowledge that membership in the Party proved to be very rewarding for their son-in-law. It was astonishing how fast he advanced after he joined the Communist Party. He was now working as secretary to the City Council, a job with a substantial salary, regular office hours, and an apartment near city hall. When he first told them about his promotion, Jeno made a joke, asking if they should address him as Comrade Secretary in the future. He laughed it off, but it was a forced laugh.

With Eta and Latzi gone, Ilonka rearranged the house. She reclaimed the master bedroom; the three boys shared the children's room, and they put Sári in the front room. For the first time in her life, she had a place all to herself, and she was in love with her newfound privacy. She volunteered to keep "her room" clean and neat, which was not a chore for her; she never liked clutter. Even as a young girl she would always keep her things tidy. At night there was no longer lights-out at 9 PM; she could stay up with a book and read as late as she liked. She had just finished reading *Back Street,* Fannie Hurst's bestseller novel, and found it incredible that, as in the story, a young woman in New York City could just walk down the street and rent an apartment, while here such a thing was simply impossible.

Comparing American books and movies to the dreary, boring, politically infused Russian stories the government crammed down on people's throat lately, opened her eyes to the contrast between the depressing life in Hungary and the lighthearted way the Americans seemed to live. People there were not afraid to say whatever they liked and were not forced to mouth stupid propagandist slogans at every turn. There was life outside of politics. The stories told her that in America honest, hard work was enough to get ahead; political affiliation was not the key to advancement. Contrary to the Communist propaganda that ceaselessly trumpeted the merciless exploitation of the American working classes and how they suffered at the hands of the greedy imperialists, she saw that these poor exploited people managed to have fun; they worked hard but also found time to sing and dance.

These books and movies depicting the American way of life made a lasting impression on her young mind and the endless negative propaganda against it only reinforced her admiration for that faraway country. The simple image of that easily accessible apartment in New York City would not let her rest. Here, if it were not for Latzi, they would have to share their home with strangers! Why couldn't she have been born in America? She belonged there, her whole being told her so. She felt a desperate longing to be part of that wonderful new world. She was meant to live there, not here, where old-fashioned traditions pulled her one way, against forces that compelled her to lie and pretend. Frustrated, she buried her head in her pillow and, with nails dug into her palms, pounded her clenched fists onto the mattress, swearing that one day it would be her walking up to that New York apartment! One day she would be free to live life as she pleased and enjoy it to the fullest as people in America did.

This was not just wishful thinking, a fleeting thought that fluttered across her mind for a second and was forgotten in the next, but a fierce demand for fulfillment of her rightful expectations of life. It took her some time to shake off the strange anxiety that momentarily gripped her, but when she finally relaxed and began to drift toward sleep, it was with absolute conviction that someday it would all happen; she would find her way to America.

Sári and Viktor

WHEN THE GIRLS returned to school in the fall of 1948, to their delight school uniforms were gone; wearing them was no longer compulsory, except for hats. It was meant to lift the financial burden that paying for the various mandatory outfits placed on parents.

It was greeted with enthusiastic hurrahs, but if the girls thought they were now free to wear anything they fancied to school, they were wrong. When some of them showed up in tight fitting and low-cut dresses, they were promptly sent home. A new dress code was quickly introduced listing what was acceptable and what was not, which of course produced a round of protest that doing away with uniforms was only a ruse, if they were forced to adhere to new restrictions. Still, the girls had more freedom of choice now, and some of them would come wearing a different outfit every day. Sári, of course, couldn't compete; she only had a few skirts, some shirts and a couple of dresses, but when she began to whine that she didn't have enough variety, Ilonka just reminded her that she could always go back to wearing her still perfectly good uniforms.

As classes began, the rooms were filled with noisy chatter, students greeting each other, telling about their summer, eyeing who grew taller or had noticeably more curves since the last time they were together. Members of old cliques quickly found each other, girls with similar interests, likes and dislikes. Sári and Wanda had their own group, rather small with only three other girls: Mattie, a small, vivacious girl with an adorable pixie face and a most happy disposition; Erzsi, the girl voted to have the best figure, although she readily offered to exchange her curves for a prettier face; and Itza, beautiful and a diva in the literal sense of the word, blessed with a wonderful soprano voice. She was also the drama queen, with enormous blue eyes that were quick to mist over with tears. Wanda, of course, was the sexiest, her every move languid, tossing her long, near-black hair a la Rita Hayward in *Gilda*. She was the only one who had a boyfriend; his family operated the Elite movie theater, where she got to see all the latest movies for free.

By the end of September, the buzz was out that the incoming university freshmen had decided to open their Balek Ball with a choreographed dance performed by fourteen couples. Invitations were sent to the girls chosen to participate, and it didn't surprise anyone that Sári would be one of them. Her friend, Erzsi, was the only other girl picked from their class. Rehearsals began at the Kosztola Studio with assigned partners—the instructor pairing Sári with a blue-eyed, baby-faced young man named Istvan Fodor. He had a shock of curly blond hair and an endearingly shy smile, and turned out to be the brother of Kati Fodor, a senior in Sári's school. Kati was also in the opening dance, and so was her classmate and best friend, Ella.

The group practiced twice a week for six weeks, and Sári soon noticed that Kati and Ella always arrived accompanied by a tall handsome man who sat on the sidelines with other spectators from the university, there to watch the girls. She learned that he was Viktor Fodor, the older brother of Kati and Istvan, and if her hunches were right, the boyfriend of Ella. At least, his solicitous attention to her hinted that his interest was more than casual friendship.

For this ball Sári wouldn't be wearing a hand-me-down, as Ilonka took her to see Sofie about ordering a formal gown. For fabric they selected a sky blue crepe de chine, and chose a pattern with a dropped waistline. It fit her tall, slim figure perfectly, with long white gloves and white heels completing the ensemble. Soft curls framed her face, with a sprig of blue silk flowers pinned to one side. Standing in front of the mirror on the night of the ball, for once she couldn't find anything wrong with the way she looked.

When her partner, Istvan Fodor, came to escort her to the ball, it was the first time her parents met the young man. Ushering him in they spent a pleasant half hour getting acquainted, sipping a glass of sherry, with Istvan telling that he was from a small place about fifty miles south of Sopron, and that he and his brother were studying forest engineering, which was also their father's profession.

Arriving at the ballroom they found it brightly lit, the ceiling decorated with paper garlands, and a scent of autumn flowers wafting through the air. It was already crowded, and in no time the band sounded the first notes to the opening dance. A few minutes later the fourteen couples made their entrance, the men wearing their formal gold-braided university uniforms, leading the girls dressed in colorful gowns. They lined up facing each other and then, after the girls dipped a formal curtsey and the men bowed from the waist, they touched hands and began their well-rehearsed dance called the *Palotás*. It is a traditional Hungarian dance that starts with dignified slow steps, couples circling each other, the girls passing under an arch formed by the high-held arms of the men, now changing partners with intricate palm-to-palm movements, then coming together again, finishing with a faster paced *Csárdás.*

It was a wonderful performance and the applause seemed to go on forever, until the musicians finally ended it by launching into everyone's favorite waltz, the "Blue Danube." In a minute the dance floor was crowded with swirling couples, while the chaperones settled down, ready to discuss the opening dance, which couple was the most graceful, whose gown showed too much skin, and so forth, down gossip lane.

At one end of the ballroom a large double door opened to a terrace overlooking Szechenyi Square, and since the weather was mild for early November, whenever the music stopped, couples were spilling out to take a breath of fresh air. Flushed from continuous dancing Sári, too, wanted to go outside and cool off a bit, so holding on to Istvan's hand she followed him as he edged his way through the crowd. He was trying to find a quiet spot when suddenly he heard someone calling his name, and turning in that direction saw his brother waving his arm to come and join his party. They crossed over to where he stood with his sister Kati, her friend Ella, and a couple of other young men. Although Sári had seen Viktor at the rehearsals, this was the first time she stood face to face with him, and as he smiled down at her, making complimentary remarks about the opening dance and how much he had heard about her from Istvan, she realized just how handsome he was. Taller than his brother, he had broad shoulders, dark wavy hair perfectly combed, gleaming white teeth, and even in the dim light she could see the amazing green of his eyes. He was nothing like the image of Rudy, the blond ideal of her dreams, yet she felt color rising in her cheeks as he kept a steady gaze on her. Hoping he did not notice it, she quickly turned to the girls with some meaningless small talk.

She did not see Kati and Ella exchanging glances. Viktor might not have caught her blushing, but they certainly did. Immediately an unmistakable coolness crept into their attitudes, making the conversation rather strained, almost uncomfortable, and soon, claiming a chill, Ella suggested going back inside.

On the crowded dance floor, Sári got an occasional glimpse of Viktor, each time with a different girl on his arm. She couldn't explain why she expected him to ask her for a dance, and why she should feel upset when he didn't. She had almost given up when she finally saw him approaching, just as the first notes of her favorite song, "You know why," sounded. The soulful hum of the alto sax always put her in a dreamy, romantic mood, yet now, as Viktor's arm came around her back, she felt her whole body stiffen. What was happening to her? Why was she acting so awkward? Even her arm refused to bend as he began to lead her.

Viktor, leaning closer and looking straight into her eyes, whispered, "I am not going to bite you Sárika. You'll enjoy this dance so much more if you trust yourself to the music." With that, he drew her a little closer and, feeling her resistance weakening, cupped her hand and held it over his heart. She felt the beat, and in that moment her defenses fell away; she leaned her cheek against his and melted into his arm.

The opening dance was a huge success and as credit went to the Kosztola Studio, the owner noticed a surge in new enrollments. To show her appreciation she invited all members of the opening dance for an "After-Ball" party. It was just a small private get-together, yet school authorities considered it a public dance because it was held at the Studio, and as such, attending required getting their permission. This created a problem for Sári. She knew that if she registered the Kosztola party as one of the three dances she was allowed for the school year, she could only go to one more ball later on. That would be the big Valeta ball in February, but she would have to miss going to one of the popular graduation dances in June, and she was not about to let that happen. *A thousand curses on the stupid rules*, she fumed! Normally she'd easily give up the small dance at the Kosztola's, but not now, when so much depended on her being there!

Ever since that one dance with Viktor at the ball, she could not get him out of her mind, even though he never asked her again, and spent most of the evening with Ella. She fished for answers from Istvan if the two were a couple, but all he would say that it depended on how successful Kati's scheming was to get the two together. *Scheming?* Sári thought sarcastically. It should not take much scheming, since Ella was a beautiful girl; any man could easily fall for her.

She ran into them only once in the Loevers. After the first heavy snowfall Sári and her friend Erzsi headed for the slopes with their skis, when they came across Kati and Ella on sleds with Viktor and another guy pulling them. She felt a pang of jealousy, even though she knew she had no right or reason to be jealous. For heaven's sake, they had one dance together and it was most likely a courtesy to his brother. And he was not even her type! But hard as she tried to deny it, she knew that something happened to her during that dance. And wasn't there a moment when she felt his heart quickening, too? Could the attraction be mutual? Perhaps it was just that song and the saxophone that turned her into a sentimental fool! She must find out, and what better chance for that than at the Kosztola party?

To have her cake and eat it, too, Sári decided to go to the party without getting permission from school. Who would know about it when it was such a small affair? To her mother she said it was just a private get-together; it was not considered a "dance" by school standards, and, believing it, Ilonka let her go without tagging along when Istvan came to pick her up.

When they arrived, the party was already underway. Standing in the doorway, Sári scanned the room and immediately spotted Viktor and some of his buddies at the refreshment stand. Could it be that Ella wasn't here? She quickly checked again but to her disappointment, she saw her dancing at the far end of the room. Everyone else was there, too, except Erzsi from her class, and she knew the reason why. She was recently caught walking with a boy and no chaperone, and as a punishment her dance privilege was taken away.

Sári's cousin Lasko Riedl was playing the piano, and when she went to greet him, she asked if he knew her absolutely most favorite song, "You know why." When he nodded, she made him promise to play it later when she gave him a signal. She then took Istvan's hand and headed for the dance floor, all the while keeping an eye on Viktor. Suddenly, she saw his group was about to break up.

"Do you mind if we stop for a soda? It's so hot in here, and I am dying of thirst," she said to Istvan fanning her face, then, without waiting for an answer and sure that he'd follow, started toward the stand. Viktor was just pulling a cigarette case from his pocket when he glanced up and saw them approaching.

"Well, look who is here. How nice to see you, Sárika. I hear more and more about you from this brother of mine. Every time we talk, it's always Sárika this and Sárika that. You must have put quite a spell on him!"

"Is that right?" she looked at Istvan with a flirtatious little smile. "I didn't think I had such powers, but I am very flattered. It's true though, we do have fun whenever we are together, don't we?"

"I only wish it was more often," Istvan laughed, handing her a drink.

"And how are *you* doing?" Sári asked Viktor, her eyes fixed on his face.

"Oh, getting along, thank you," he said, then, still holding his cigarette case added, "I was just going to have a cigarette out in the anteroom—care to join me?"

"Sounds good," Istvan said, "except Sári does not smoke, so you go ahead, we'll see you later."

"No, no, it's OK with me," Sári protested. "It's too warm in here, anyway. Besides, who said I don't smoke?" She tipped her head demurely, then added, "Well, not regularly, but once in a while on special occasions I have a cigarette. And I think tonight is such an occasion. Aren't we celebrating the success of our opening dance?"

Standing in the anteroom and feeling quite sophisticated, she took a cigarette from Viktor. She held it up, waiting for him to light it, planning to cast a provocative glance at him over the flame as she had seen it done in the movies. After that she was going to tilt her head back and blow the smoke slowly toward him, only if Istvan hadn't ruined it by whipping out his lighter first and holding it for her! She lit the cigarette and inhaled deeply to impress them with her smoking expertise, but that was as far as she could carry the imagined glamour. In the next second, the smoke chocking her lungs, she burst into a violent cough that shook her whole body. Clutching at her throat and eyes bulging from the strain, she vaguely heard Viktor yelling at his brother to get some water, while he held her and patted her on the back. Gasping for air and tears streaming from her eyes, she hung onto his arm until the wretched convulsions slowed and the relentless coughing subsided. Exhausted from the ordeal, she remained half collapsed, unable to move, not even to take the hanky Viktor held out to her. Awkwardly, he began dabbing at her face, comforting her at the same time that she'd be all right.

When she regained her composure, they led her back to the studio and brought a chair for her. Kati and Ella, already looking for Viktor, rushed over, and hearing what happened, they hovered over her, patting her hand and coaxing her to get some fresh air. She knew exactly what they were doing, trying to isolate her from the two brothers, but she didn't mind it; the last thing she wanted was for Viktor to see her now. She was embarrassed and ashamed, feeling messy, and above all, angry at her own stupidity for blowing the chance to find out about Viktor's feelings. She only knew that she liked him more than ever before.

Slowly regaining her strength, she excused herself and went to wash her face and fix her hair. She looked terrible and just wanted to go home. While she was out, Kati didn't waste time ridiculing her behind her back for trying to be worldly, and saying loud enough for others to hear that the stupid girl got what she deserved. Both her brothers found her nasty comments uncalled for, and even Ella chimed in with a few sympathetic words.

When Sári returned, she was wearing her coat, ready to leave. It was still early, but her evening was ruined, and she was going home. Without saying goodbye to anyone she headed for the exit, not even breaking her stride when she saw her cousin at the piano mouthing, "What about the song?" She just flipped her wrist and marched out slamming the door. It almost hit Istvan in the face as he ran after her to see her home.

She was still upset on Monday morning when she walked into her class. Erzsi, having missed the party, peppered her with questions but all she got back was, "Don't even ask." Slunk into her chair and hardly paying attention to the teacher, the last thing Sári wanted was to hear her name called out. But there it came, except it was not a request to address the subject being discussed in class. Instead, she was told to report to the principal's office at once. The alarm went off in her head. It could only mean one thing: they found out about Saturday night.

Walking into Mr. Augusztin's office she found another girl already there, one of the opening dancers from senior class, and looking at her contrite expression, Sári was sure they were summoned for the same reason, going to the party without permission. She struck a casual pose with her hands in her pockets until the principal's thundering voice ordered her to stand straight with arms at the side. The hearing was quick; both girls admitted to violating the rules and were told to leave right now and send in their parents the next morning.

Sári picked up her carrying case and her hat and coat, but when she walked out she did not go home. No need to alert her mother just yet. Wanda had called in sick that day, so she went to her house instead, and returned home at the usual after-school hour. She spent all afternoon thinking of how to break the news to her mother in a way that it would soften the blow she knew was coming, and waited almost until bedtime to tell her that the principal asked to see her.

"What is this about?" Ilonka demanded to know. "What did you do this time? You better tell me now so I'll be prepared."

"It's really nothing, Mother, they're just raising a big hullabaloo about going to that silly dance party. I didn't know they would consider it a ball and that I had to get permission! Besides, I was hardly there; you know how early I came home; I don't really know why I went in the first place. Maybe you could tell Mr. Augusztin that the only reason was because I lost something during the final rehearsal and wanted to ask if anyone found it. He should see the logic that it was easier to catch all the dancers in one place, rather than running around town asking everyone separately."

"You expect me to lie so you can get out of hot water? It's bad enough that you lied to me, but now you dare to suggest that I should bail you out with another lie to justify your wrongdoing? No missy, I will tell Mr. Augusztin the truth, and will agree to whatever punishment he decides to give you. And for good measure, you are also grounded for a month. No Wanda, no movies, no skiing—you go to school and come straight home. Is that understood?"

"A whole month?? And during the holiday season?? Mother, you can't mean it! With Christmas coming, I can't even go window-shopping? I know it was wrong to lie, and I promise it won't happen again, but please don't do this; don't keep me practically locked up for weeks!"

But it was no use. This time no begging or promising would change Ilonka's mind. Her unruly daughter must be taught a lesson; she must learn that lying is unacceptable and that there is a limit to getting her way.

Grounding was awful, but what hit Sári far worse was the principal's decision to bar her from the Valeta Ball. It was the big masquerade ball just before Lent and she already knew what costume she would wear. She planned to be the Queen of Hearts. In her head she had already designed her dress and the accessories to the last detail, and now they wouldn't let her go? The thought alone of all the fun she would be missing made her miserable. The fact that on her midterm report card her behavior was downgraded to D, which automatically reduced her otherwise overall A-level achievement to a lowly C, did not bother her at all. Midterms didn't count. But not be able to go to the ball was such a cruel punishment, so unfair, that she broke into heart-wrenching sobs when she heard the verdict. She would not survive if something did not change that evil man's mind. But nothing did. Mr. Augusztin stuck to his guns; the ball would go on without her.

After classes Wanda and Sári always left school together except one day a week during choir practice, when Wanda, having no ear for music, went home alone. A week before Christmas, leaving rehearsal Sári decided to break her mother's rule about going straight home, and took a detour to see the shops along Varkerulet Boulevard. As store windows were dressed for Christmas, she stopped here and there to admire the displays.

Lost in thought, she stood in front of a window full of gift items vying for the shoppers' attention. There were boxes of candies, a huge basket filled with fruits, jams and cheeses—even a can of goose liver pâté—and on the bottom shelf a variety of fine liquors and imported cigars and cigarettes to satisfy every taste. Looking for ideas of what to give her father for Christmas, she settled on a carton of cigarettes, if she could find one that she could afford. She was looking at the different price tags when she heard a vaguely familiar voice, "Still determined to smoke?"

Startled, she turned to see Viktor smiling down at her.

"Oh, you scared me!"

"I am sorry, I did not mean to. How are you doing? You left the party so suddenly the other night, I only found out from my brother when I got home that you were all right. It was not nice to leave without saying goodbye."

"Oh, you saw what a mess I was; I almost choked to death. It was so embarrassing. But you are right; I should have stopped to thank you for your help. I hope it's not too late."

"There is nothing to thank me for. Just promise to be more careful with that inhale the next time you light up," he winked at Sári then changed the subject. "I see you are window-shopping."

"Actually, I am on my way home, I just stopped to get some ideas for Christmas presents. How about you? Are you ready for the holidays?"

"I tell you all about it if you allow me to escort you. And those books, they look pretty heavy to me. May I?" he asked, reaching for her carrying case before she could answer.

"You are welcome to it, but beware, it weighs a ton," she said as they fell into steps and continued their light banter, talking about everything except his brother Istvan and Ella. By the time they turned into Sári's street, he asked her if he could see her again, perhaps have coffee or tea together or see a movie. Feeling flattered by his obvious interest she would have liked nothing better, but she knew that making a date was out of the question while she was grounded. She was thinking fast. If she told him about the grounding, would his interest hold until the first of the year? Not likely, not with Ella lurking in the background. Besides, admitting to be grounded was too embarrassing.

In the end she blamed it on school restrictions why she couldn't go on a date, but quickly added that with a little caution they still could meet after school and walk home together. He could wait for her at a safe distance from school, at least a couple of blocks away, to avoid being caught without a proper chaperone.

And so, whenever his schedule permitted, Viktor would stand on the corner of Szechenyi Square and Erzsebet Street, a favorite gathering spot for university students to watch the girls on their way from school, where one young man after another would peel off, offering a girl to carry her books. If romance blossomed, she was off-limits to new approaches. And so it was with Sári. As her frequent after-school meetings with Viktor soon made it unmistakably clear that Cupid was at play, others gave up all effort trying to gain favors with her. Everyone knew that she was Viktor's girl, everyone, except his brother Istvan.

Shy by nature and interested only in Sári, he was never part of the girl-watching activities, standing on the corner with the rest of the boys. Only when Sári was grounded and he couldn't call on her did he join them, hoping he could at least see her, maybe walk her home. He was stunned when he saw his brother beat him to it. What did he want with her? Viktor never asked anything about her, what she was like, not a hint that he was interested in her. They never discussed how Istvan felt about Sári, either, but from the way he acted near her, Viktor must have known that he was falling in love.

At first when Istvan saw them together, he thought there must be an explanation, until he found out from the other fellows that they routinely met after school. Seeing his confusion, they teased him ruthlessly. Didn't he know what was going on? What was he going to do, challenge his brother to a duel? He was hurt and angry and could hardly wait for Viktor to come home.

"Nice to hear from others that you are going after Sári! Just what are your intentions with her?" he confronted him the minute he closed the door.

"Intentions? I like this girl and I want to get to know her better, that's all. Why, you are not serious about her, are you?"

"Well no, not exactly, it's too early for that, but I know I like her better than you do! And what about Ella? You were chummy with her all these times; what happened with that? Did she drop you, and now you have nothing better to do than chase after my girl?"

"That's ridiculous. And so is this 'which one of us likes her best' stuff. You sound like a lovesick adolescent. This is not a contest between us, or something we decide by tossing a coin. It's up to her whom she likes better. I won't ask you not to see her. Go ahead, keep dating her, I am not standing in your way. On the other hand, I don't expect you to tell me to stay away from her, either. Let her decide. If she chooses you it's fine with me; I'll be happy for you. Fair enough?"

"No, it's not fair and you know it! What chance do I have? Leave it up to her?? I might as well throw in the towel now! I should have kept my mouth shut instead of gushing about her; I bet that's what aroused your curiosity. It's the same old story; it's my rotten luck to be the second in everything."

"Oh come on, lighten up, you are overdramatic. Now look, we are going home for the holidays and by the time we get back she might have fallen for some other guy and leave us both out in the cold. So what do you say? Let's go down to the Tavern. I'll treat you to a beer."

Istvan went along grudgingly but deep down still blamed his brother for ruining his chances with Sári, not realizing that Viktor had nothing to do with it. She never took him seriously; to her, he could never be more than a nice young man, a good friend to have around. The sparks were not there. Beyond a mild flirtation, she never gave him any encouragement, and whenever he came to visit, it was Ilonka who paid more attention to him than Sári. And he was too shy to be forward; he was just happy to be near her.

On the other hand, right from the start Viktor made her heart skip a beat. He was handsome, tall, and athletic—all that makes any girl notice. Yet it was not his looks that impressed her. He was not her ideal man. He stood out from the rest for other reasons. He was older than the other freshmen and acted more mature, with a certain self-assuredness that stemmed from feeling comfortable within. He possessed a natural easy style, a mannerism that was never affected and made people respond the same way. He was friendly, but not patronizing, aware of his qualities but not conceited, and sophisticated without putting on airs. It added a little mystery that he wouldn't talk much about himself. When Sári tried to find out more about him during their walks, he would only say that he was in the military and served on the Russian front during the war, then steered their conversation toward discovering mutual likes and dislikes or just posed some questions and let her talk. That this attractive, intelligent, and charming man was interested in what she had to say made her feel special and immensely flattered.

Ilonka, of course, noticed the new man regularly accompanying her daughter home, but when she casually asked about him, Sári would only say he was just one of the guys. She didn't press further, knowing that Sári was at an age when a string of young men would come in and out of her life. Not too long ago it was Andor Varszi, then Istvan Fodor for a while and now this one, a handsome man for sure, although judging from a distance, he seemed a bit older than the others. If this new interest should be more lasting, she'd have to make inquiries about him.

Right now, though, she had better things to do. With Christmas approaching, Ilonka was busy getting token gifts for the family, some she made herself. Although life was a little better each year, they could not afford anything lavish. Eta, Latzi, and the baby would be spending Christmas with them, and the Varosys were coming too; it was hard enough to put the traditional Christmas dinner on the table.

This time of the year always put her in a nostalgic mood, remembering the beautiful holidays they used to have before the war and how different their life was then. Sometimes in a rare moment when she was alone, she would look at the family album and let the tears fall. Here were her daughters, only twelve years ago, standing in matching outfits before the Christmas tree with their new dolls, and Gyuszika looking suspiciously at Raro, the rocking horse he was so afraid of. And that one, taken even earlier in 1931, showing her and Jeno sitting with the Varosys at a table, posing with cards in hands, waiting to ring in the New Year. How happy she was, the wife of a hard-working, loving man she adored, surrounded by children she loved more than life itself, and sharing good times with friends. Why did it have to end? She never pined for luxuries or tried to keep up with the Joneses. They always lived within their means; Jeno's salary allowed them to maintain a decent lifestyle, keep the children happy and healthy, even afford to hire a live-in maid. What else could anyone ask for? Then the war came and everything changed, their world crashing down around them. And here they were, almost four years after the war ended, and still struggling. This is what their life had come to, making homemade Christmas gifts and pinching pennies to put together an adequate holiday meal? No wonder that the pressure left its mark on both Jeno and herself; her blood pressure was climbing and Jeno had started complaining about heart palpitations. They needed medication but it was still scarce and very expensive. Would a better day ever come again?

She quickly said a prayer asking God to give them the strength to carry on, then slowly closed the album, leaving the past behind. *Life will go on,* Ilonka sighed. As long as they could celebrate Christmas together with family and friends, she had no right to complain.

She was not alone making self-made gifts for Christmas this year. Having time on her hand during her grounding, Sári decided to paint a picture for her mother. Knowing that she was turning more religious, she looked through Ilonka's prayer book to get ideas for the subject. There were several pictures of saints and the Holy Family but in the end she chose a portrait of Jesus with his hand pointing to his sacred heart. She worked long hours on the 13" x 10" watercolor until finally she was satisfied with her creation. Tears sprang to Ilonka's eyes when she saw the framed picture tucked under the tree. It was a total surprise and she told everyone that it was more precious to her than if Michelangelo himself had painted it.

Eta had another surprise for the family. She was expecting her second baby sometime in July. Her son was now a year and a half and she said she wanted the children to be close in age, hoping they would get along better than she and Sári had. Everyone was happy for them, especially Ilonka. The prospect of another grandchild—perhaps a little girl this time—lifted her spirits. Life goes on, indeed!

As the highly intensified political persecution continued throughout 1948, Rakosi, who called himself Stalin's most devout disciple, fulfilled his ambition to become the supreme ruler of Hungary. Like Stalin, he developed a totalitarian self-aggrandizing dictatorship, and now people stood up and clapped, as they did with Stalin, whenever his name was mentioned at gatherings. He was credited with inventing the phrase "Salami Tactics," a practice he used successfully to eliminate all opposition, slice by slice.

For his first important victim Rakosi chose Cardinal Jozsef Mindszenty, the Prince-Primate of Hungary and a staunch opponent of Communism. If he could remove him from the scene, Rakosi could break the backbone of the Catholic Church and stop its anti-Communist rhetoric. To build up a case, on November 19, 1948 they arrested the Cardinal's secretary for the sole purpose of extracting information that could be used against the Cardinal. Under torture he signed a confession that Mindszenty, during his visit to America in 1947, asked the United States to send troops to Hungary and occupy the country until it could be restored as a Kingdom with Otto Habsburg, the last Austro-Hungarian Crown Prince, as its king. He also "confessed" that the Cardinal urged the Vatican to appeal to the United States to refuse demands from the Communist regime to return Hungary's Holy Crown, currently kept at Fort Knox, Kentucky. It was secreted out of the country at the end of the war to save it from the Russians and handed to the U.S. for safekeeping.[3*] The poor man further testified to the Cardinal's involvement in smuggling U.S. dollars by pocketing $10,000 from the Vatican in 1945, $9,000 from Cardinal Spellman, the Archbishop of New York, during his 1947 trip to America, and another $12,000 from the Swiss legation. Mindszenty immediately issued a pastoral letter in which he absolved his secretary and everyone else who might speak against him, knowing that it was not done of their own free will.

Rakosi knew he had what he needed to arrest the Cardinal, but presented it as if he were only submitting to the people's demand for action against him. On November 27 he spoke at the Central Leadership meeting, emphasizing that the accusations were against Mindszenty as a person, not as the leader of the Church; after all, there was no religious persecution in Hungary. Anticipating his arrest, Mindszenty wrote a declaration of innocence against all charges to come, denying his involvement in any conspiracy and stating that if he should make such confession, it would only be the result of human frailty.

A month later, on the day after Christmas, he was arrested. The chief of the AVO, Gabor Peter, reported to Rakosi that Mindszenty kept repeating during his arrest "My errant children, I am Jozsef, Prince-Primate," until they finally had enough and, yelling at him, "Maybe to your flock, but here you are just a criminal," whacked him a few times until he passed out. It took a little over a month of further beatings and relentless torture to obtain his "confession" for crimes against the State, mainly spying for the imperialists, illegal currency smuggling, and calling all Catholics to boycott the newspapers and radio station because they spread nothing but propaganda and lies. At the end of the trial on February 3, 1949, the judges found him guilty on all charges and handed down a sentence for life imprisonment in solitary confinement. His conviction was a significant victory for the Party: with the leader of the Church in prison, their lands and properties confiscated, and all parochial schools dissolved, the elimination of the Clergy was complete.

As pressure to stop attending religious service increased during Mindszenty's trial, Jeno finally asked Ilonka to stop going to church. He pleaded with her that God would understand; it was not the first time in history when people were forced to withdraw from public worshipping. When Ilonka balked, he explained that he already had some bad marks for repeatedly refusing to make a "voluntary" contribution through payroll deduction toward a new program called "Peace Loan" (*Békekölcsön*). It was introduced to help rebuilding the

---

3 * The crown remained at Fort Knox until President Carter returned it to Hungary on January 6, 1978.

country's ruined economy in form of a lottery system with the notes issued by the Treasury, promising repayment with interest to the few winners, but leaving the rest of the people holding the bag. Everyone who worked was expected to participate by pledging—according to unwritten guidelines—equivalent of one month's gross earnings, but how could Jeno afford it when he needed every cent to support his large family? He got away with his excuse, but sympathetic colleagues subtly warned him that the committee did not take his refusal lightly; they viewed it as a sign of silent resistance. Someone actually saw his kader record with several unfavorable remarks, and told Jeno to be more careful in the future.

Contrary to the committee's belief that claiming financial hardship was just an excuse for Jeno, it was a valid claim. He had real difficulties paying the bills. He hoped, as so many others, that life would slowly improve and reach the prewar standard of living, but it quickly evaporated when salaries were set much too low after the introduction of the new currency in 1946. As a result, more and more women who were homemakers and had never before worked outside the home were now looking for jobs, and even though lack of experience limited them to manual work at minimum wages, it still helped to better their financial situation. This option, however, was not open for Ilonka. Her two younger boys, at six and ten, still needed her, and who would take care of the household? It was a full-time job to do the cleaning, shopping, the cooking, and the laundry for six people, plus all the sewing she did to mend the children's clothing.

She was running her old Singer sewing machine one day when suddenly an idea came to her. She could take in sewing! She would be home and still make some money! With so many women joining the workforce, there ought to be a need for this. Even Sári could pitch in; she'd jump at the chance to have some extra pocket money.

Excited about her plan, Ilonka waited impatiently for her daughter to come home from school, but when she finally showed up, instead of enthusiasm, her response was a blank stare.

"You want me to do what? As it is, I hardly have enough time to do my homework and all the other things, the literary assignments, my rhythmic classes, all the political stuff Dora makes me do, not to mention the various other extra-curricular activities! I already cut down spending time with my friends, and you want me to sit here and help you stitch other peoples' clothes in the little free time I have left?"

"And just what are these extra-curricular activities?" Ilonka shot back at Sári's unanticipated reproach. "Is that what keeps you from coming home at a decent time? Don't think I haven't noticed that young man with you when you round the corner! Is he by chance one of your extra-curricular activities?"

"Can we talk about this later, Mother?" Sári whined. "I just came home for lunch and must get back for basketball practice, which, by the way, is one of my extra-curricular activities."

"So you'll be late a few minutes! And don't be fresh with me! Those things you brought up can't possibly take up all your time, not every single day! I still think this new fellow hanging around you lately has something to do with it."

"No he does not; he just carries my books from school, and we talk, that's all. And for your information, that fellow's name is Viktor Fodor, and he is Istvan's brother. They are both freshmen at the university."

"What do you mean they are both freshmen? They don't seem to be twins; as a matter of fact he seems quite a bit older as much as I could see from behind the curtains."

"That's because he is older; he spent years in the military before."

"Before what? If you mean the war, that would make him at least twenty-three or twenty-four!"

"You are off by a year; he is twenty-five. He is a graduate of the old Ludovika Military Academy and fought on the Russian front as an artillery officer. Anything else you want to know you will have to ask him, because that's all he told me."

"What on earth are you doing with a man so much older than you, Sári? You are only seventeen!" Ilonka exploded. "I can see Istvan courting you, but what can you possibly have in common with his brother? I have no doubt why he is hanging around you, even if you don't, but I won't get into that with you now." She paused for a moment scrutinizing Sári's face to see if she understood the implied meaning of her words before she continued. "Of course, you are to stop seeing him. You tell him that he is wasting his time and to leave you alone. That should be the end of it if he has any decency, but if not, you tell your father, he will take it from there."

"Mom, you are overreacting! How can you talk like this about someone you never met? Viktor is not like that at all; he is a gentleman, just like Istvan. They are from the same family, so what if he is a few years older?" she protested angrily, but then she stopped. With a sudden change in her attitude she tilted her head and looked at Ilonka through narrowed eyes. "Frankly, I am surprised about your outburst. I thought you would be pleased to see me going out with a more mature man, since you were about fifteen or so when you and Dad met. And if I am not mistaken, he is more than ten years older than you and he also fought in the war, but it didn't matter, did it? So why should you be so upset about Viktor? You ought to give him a chance, Mother. At least meet him before you pass judgment and order me to stop seeing him."

Reminded of her own situation when she met Jeno, Ilonka had to admit to herself that Sári was right, the similarities were there about the age gap and war experience, and suddenly she remembered the arguments she used to have with her own mother, and that none of it—not the sermons, the threats, not even cuffing her ears or banishing her to her aunt—could stop them from seeing each other. It took a while to wear down her mother's resistance, but in the end Angela truly came to love Jeno. Was she making the same mistake with her daughter now? Perhaps they should meet this Viktor; after all, they liked his younger brother, and if he turned out to be anything like Istvan, perhaps it would be wrong to forbid Sári to see him.

"You are right about your father and me," Ilonka conceded, "but we lived in a different time, a gentler time. Things have changed since then. We were not in such a hurry as young people are today." She knew she had lost some ground and was slipping into the defensive, so she quickly closed the subject. "Well, anyway, I'll talk to your father and see what he says. Now eat your lunch before it gets cold."

Sári grabbed her mother and planted a great big kiss on her cheek. "I know you will like him, Mom; he is really a wonderful guy! And tell Dad he won't be disappointed either." With that she twirled around and sashayed away, knowing that she had won a small victory. In a way she was glad they had this talk about Viktor; hopefully it would lead to his acceptance, and he could come to the house instead of meeting on street corners.

When she told her mother that walking home with Viktor was all there was between them, it was not quite the truth. They also managed to meet here and there, although not alone; some of her friends would always be around. He would come by during dance classes she had been taking lately at the Kosztola studio, and they would sit in the anteroom talking a little, or she would let Viktor know when and where she and Wanda planned to have coffee and he would come and join them. Going to an afternoon movie was another way to spend time together. Again, they couldn't go openly as a couple, it was totally against school regulations, so Viktor always bought three tickets to assigned seats, gave two to Sári and waited until she and Wanda were seated. Then after the lights dimmed, he would walk in and take his place beside Sári.

How much better it would be if Viktor could call on her at home, rather than sneaking around, scared and nervous that they would be found out. A couple of times they came close to it, once when Eta and Latzi were in the same movie theater, but luckily they were seated in the loges and couldn't see Sári and Viktor in the back of the balcony. Another time Gyuszi came upon them sitting on a half-hidden bench in the Loevers with Viktor's arm around her shoulder, but there was no problem in silencing him; Sári just threatened to take away her Latin translations that her brother still managed to pass as his own, even under Mr. Agusztin's Argos-like watchful eyes. All this would be over if her parents agreed to meet Viktor. After that talk with her mother, she knew she had made headways with her; she just had to keep her fingers crossed about her father.

She didn't have to wait long. Her parents didn't see eye to eye at first, with Jeno arguing that Sári was too young and immature to get entangled in any relationship. What if this Viktor was just a temporary thing, he was just toying with her, or wanted to prove something to his brother? Then she would be in for a heartache. He still held back when Ilonka reminded him that at the beginning of their own courtship she was even younger than Sári, and how it didn't make any difference. Then she brought up another point that tipped the scales in Sári's favor.

"What if she is right and Viktor is really a good man? He would be a good catch for her. It would be a shame to lose him to some other girl, if we forbid her to see him. He is certainly a very attractive man and it wouldn't take long before a girl snags him for a husband. At his age he is much more of a marriage prospect than his younger brother. In no time Sári will be the same age as Eta was when she got married. And there is another point. Before this Viktor appeared on the scene, Sári made it clear that she didn't want to get married and settle down at nineteen like Eta and I did. She is hell-bound on going to college in Budapest. Well, falling in love can change all that! I'd much rather see her married to a decent man from a good family than let her go to Budapest. She is an impulsive girl and can be foolish at times, and I am worried how she will handle herself, all alone for the first time in that big city. I think we should meet this young man; it'll give us a clearer picture."

Jeno had to agree that her reasoning was sound, and only asked Ilonka to let him know the day the young man would be coming. He'd make sure to be home to meet him.

By the time the date was set, Ilonka knew quite a lot about Viktor. Sári didn't let up talking about him—how they met, the rivalry between him and his brother over her, his sister Kati's manipulation to bring her best girlfriend and Viktor together, and because that did not work out, Kati did not like her very much, but who cared? She told Ilonka that Viktor played the violin, and although she'd never heard him playing she was sure he was very good at it. But that was not all: he was also an outstanding athlete; the university's track and field team couldn't do without him; he was winning all the races for them. And of course he was so handsome, as Ilonka could see even from a distance, that all the girls at school were jealous of her.

The day before his visit she voluntarily cleaned the house, especially the front room where they would receive him, and that included washing all four windows there and waxing the parquet floor. Seeing it, Ilonka had to laugh. For Sári to do this, it must really be love!

When Viktor arrived and introductions were made, Ilonka knew instantly that they had made the right decision. It was not because Viktor bent to kiss her hand, an old-fashioned custom to express respect that very few young men followed these days. Call it a mother's instinct, but the way he carried himself, the open smile, the eyes that looked straight into hers when speaking—all told her that he could be trusted the same way as his younger brother. And how handsome he was! He reminded her of a movie actor she saw in an American film a few years back. "*Till we meet again*" was the title, but the actor's name eluded her.

Glancing at Jeno, she could tell from his broad smile and the way he was ushering Viktor into the house that he, too, approved of him. While Ilonka served tea and some horse d'oeuvres, the talk centered on Viktor, his years in the military academy, the war, his choice of study, and his general interests. Watching him, it dawned on Ilonka who did he resemble. It was Ray Milland! He played a pilot. What a wonderful movie it was, too. Why the government stopped showing those American movies, she'd never understand. The stupid Russian films they played these days were not worth the price of the ticket. Oh well, did she miss anything in the conversation?

Jeno was talking now, telling a little about their family, about the war and how it altered their life. Sári chimed in occasionally, but kept quiet most of the time, letting her parents and Viktor get acquainted. When he finally stood up to leave, Ilonka invited him to visit again and asked that perhaps next time he'd bring his violin and they could try for an impromptu concert, her at the piano and Viktor on the strings.

The three boys in the children's room got up to meet Viktor on his way out. They shook his hand politely, but as soon as they heard the front door closing they rushed at Sári, jumping around her, blocking her way, chanting, "Sári has a boyfriend!" Embarrassed that Viktor might hear their singsong teasing, she tried to stop them, but it was useless. It was too much fun to give up, just when they finally found a way to mock their standoffish sister.

Although her parents highly approved of Viktor, they made it clear to Sári that certain rules must be obeyed. He could carry her books after school, but she was not to run around with him openly. He was welcome to visit her at home on Saturdays, and if they wanted to go somewhere, to the movies or a play, Ilonka would gladly go with them. With her chaperoning, the school could not raise any objection.

What? Only one Saturday?? Sári was about to protest but she held her tongue. It was better than nothing, even though one visit a week didn't make much difference for them. If they wanted to see each other more, they still had to meet secretly, squeezing in a few stolen moments, sometimes even without help from friends. And as time went by without being caught, Sári got a little bolder and more daring. One evening she was going over to her godparents, but first she stopped at a nearby park where Viktor was waiting. She meant to stay only a short while, just to hold hands, but it must have gotten a bit more intense, because she forgot all about the time. When she realized that it was almost nine o'clock she ran all the way to the Varosys' place, apologizing for coming so late. After giving some excuse and asking not to tell her mother about it, she stayed only for fifteen minutes.

Proud of herself for taking care of the situation, Sári was just stepping into the street, when suddenly her father appeared out of nowhere and blocked her way. Ilonka sent him to find out what was keeping their daughter when she was not home by nine.

"Dad! You scared me! What are you doing here?" she cried out, with her heart beating in her throat.

"Don't you think it's rather late for visiting?" Jeno asked, ignoring her question.

"Oh, you know how it is, Godmother could talk hours about Kurt, and I just forgot to keep track of the time."

Jeno's right arm shot out, his palm landing on Sári's face with a soft impact. "You are lying! You walked in there exactly fifteen minutes ago. And don't try to deny it because I saw you running from that direction. Just where were you and what were you doing all that time? No, let me guess! You were with Viktor. Aren't you ashamed of yourself? We set a few simple rules, one of them to stay away from meeting him on some back street, but you couldn't do it! I am very disappointed in you."

Stunned for the moment and holding the side of her face, she glowered at her father. "All right, I admit it, but is it such a crime? You let him come to the house only once a week, and with the stupid rules, the only way we can meet more often is behind your back. I hate to do it, but what can I do? I want to see him more, Dad! Is that so terrible? We are not doing anything wrong!"

"We'll talk about this later. Now let's just go home; your mother is worried about you," he said with a hint of apology, while turning his daughter's face to the light to check for an imprint of his hand. Of course, there was none, and they turned to go. Reaching the house he stopped for a second before entering. "We'll keep this business between us," he said looking straight at Sári. "You were at your godparents' all evening. No need to upset your mother."

It came as a surprise to Ilonka when next day Jeno told her they should let Viktor come over more often; otherwise how were they to get to know him better?

"I think he is a very decent young man who sees something in Sári that keeps him hanging around regardless of our restrictions. I want to see if that interest would last with us sitting in the next room and the kids running around. If it does not bother him, I think we can consider taking him more seriously. But if the quasi-chaperoning scares him away, well, then we'll know where we stand with him."

And so as Viktor spent more time in their home and his interest in Sári did not wane but increased, Ilonka smugly told Jeno that she knew all along that Viktor would be a man worth holding on to; it just proved that her first impressions were rarely wrong.

"First impressions can give you an idea about manners and intelligence," Jeno conceded, "but I am glad that he proved himself worthy well beyond that."

And indeed, in a relatively short time they got to know him as a straightforward, trustworthy young man with conservative beliefs and solid values, a man who knew what he wanted in life and was willing to work hard toward his goals. His family background put him a narrow notch higher than theirs on the social scale, but prejudice and snobbery was not in his makeup. That he was Catholic made Ilonka sigh with relief. One Presbyterian-turned-Communist was enough in the family! As for vices, he gladly accepted a glass of wine or a mug of beer, but had no taste for the harsh Hungarian *pálinka*, the strong distilled spirit made of ripe plums, pears, or apricots. If anything could be held against him, it was smoking, but even that, he only smoked with moderation. As a credit to his good manners, he would never drop by unexpectedly even though the door was now open for him without the formalities of invitation. He'd always ask Ilonka what day and hour would be convenient for him to visit.

In a very short time they all felt comfortable having him around; even the boys got used to him and stopped teasing Sári. Everyone liked him, but for Ilonka, Viktor quickly became a mother's dream for an ideal son-in-law.

As the relationship between Sári and Viktor began to deepen, the idea that she would miss the grand ball coming up in February drove her to fits of nervous anxiety. Secretly she wished Viktor would ignore the ball and spent the evening with her, but that was impossible, since he was a member of the organizing committee. She just hated to think of her handsome boyfriend walking alone into that ballroom full of pretty girls. She would feel more secure were it not for his pushy, conniving sister Kati! Even though Viktor made it clear to her that Ella did not interest him, she never gave up trying to play the matchmaker between them. And here was this ball, with Sári removed from the picture, a perfect opportunity to advance her schemes to bring those two together!

There was no reason for her to feel threatened, but she was. Ella was a strikingly attractive girl, but more than that, due to her close friendship with Kati, she got to be around Viktor more than Sári liked. It didn't help either that the girl was always dressed in the latest fashion. *It's easy for her,* Sári thought bitterly, *she is an only child; her parents can afford to spend money on her. Why couldn't I have been born into a family like that*? Well, it was useless to get worked up about something she couldn't change. She stuck out her tongue at the imaginary Ella. She had other things going for her, or Viktor wouldn't have chosen her instead.

If unhappy during the days preceding the ball, Sári was truly miserable when the big day finally arrived. By night she was a nervous wreck. Sitting together with the family, she kept glancing at the clock, chewing her nails as she imagined the scenes unfolding at the Kaszino ballroom. At eight people would be arriving; at eight-thirty the musicians would be seated, tuning their instruments; come nine the music would start with the first dancers heading for the floor. And while all that was going on, here she was, sitting at home!

"Oh stop doing that," Ilonka nudged her knee against Sári's under the table as she was constantly pumping her leg. "It's not the end of the world! And you seem to forget that you brought it all on yourself. You broke the rules and went to that dance without permission. It serves you right that Mr. Augusztin—"

"For goodness' sake, it was only a stupid party," Sári cut her short. "I hardly stayed a few minutes, if you remember. That man blew it all out of proportion, just to show he has the power! Well, he won't have it much longer! If the rumors are true, his days as principal are numbered; he'll be ousted for his noncommittal political attitude, and I for one won't be crying when he goes. I hate that man, I just hate him!"

"You deserve to be punished for going against the rules *and* for lying to us. If I'd known the truth, I certainly wouldn't have let you go. Well, I hope this will be a good lesson for you!" Ilonka glared at her daughter over the fast moving knitting needles in her hands.

"Oh . . . Oh . . . I hate . . ." Sári jumped up, and with the rest of the words stuck in her throat, ran to her room.

"Go ahead and say it! I know that you hate me too!" Ilonka yelled after her as she heard the door slammed. Sári threw herself face down on the bed, sobbing bitterly, feeling that the whole world was against her. It was so unjust! She didn't deserve this! Lots of other girls went against the rules; it was only that she got caught. She couldn't stop crying, not even when she heard the door open softly and felt her father's hand touching her hair.

"Now, now, Sárika, it's not worth your tears to cry over a silly dance," he whispered, bending over her. "So what if you missed it? There will be so many other balls! I know that going meant a lot to you and right now you are hurting, but take my word, soon you'll be laughing at how foolish it was to lose sleep over a trivial thing like this." He patted her back and felt her sobs easing under his gentle touch. "That's a good girl. Now dry your tears and try to get some sleep." He waited a minute or two, then, hearing her muffled "I'll be OK," with a final caress, walked out of the room as quietly as he came in.

He didn't hear her renewed sobs, more heartbreaking than before, nor could he know that the tears now flooding her eyes were not because she missed the ball. She wept for an entirely different reason. How could she ever wish to be in Ella's place when it would have meant growing up without her gentle father, the only one who could soothe her aching heart with one simple touch?

In spite of her misery, Sári survived the night and just as Jeno told her, she lost a good night's sleep for nothing. Viktor came the next day and gave a detailed account of who was there, who escorted whom and all the tidbits she wanted to hear. Not only that, but knowing how downhearted she was when she missed the ball, and perhaps feeling sorry for treating her a little too harsh that night, her mother decided to throw a party for her. All her girlfriends came, and Viktor and his brother brought along some of their fellow students.

The Varosys were also there and although they had met Viktor before, Sári's godmother couldn't praise him high enough, how handsome and talented Viktor was, and what a perfect match he was for her precious godchild. Known to exaggerate and to lapse into German when excited—it being her mother tongue—she dramatically lifted her eyes to heaven and announced that she felt thoroughly *lieb eingeschossen*, totally enamored by the young man, when Viktor stood next to the piano, put his violin under his chin and accompanied Ilonka playing one beautiful Strauss melody after another.

As much as Sári was falling in love, she didn't neglect her studies or slacken her political activities. She was always on time for the morning newspaper readings and continued playing secretary to Dora. She didn't mind doing her bidding within school walls, but hated it when Dora assigned her to lead the girls in organized street marches. There were three politically tainted national holidays a year that called for such public celebration: the upcoming Liberation Day on April 4, the day the Red Army freed the country from German occupation in 1945; the International Workers' Day on May 1, honoring the achievements of the Labour Movement; and November 7, the anniversary of the 1917 Bolshevik revolution in Russia. All were peppered with endless political speeches interrupted only by rapturous hand clapping at every mention of Comrade Stalin or his Hungarian disciple Rakosi.

At times she really had to push herself to do her political chores, so annoying, yet necessary to enhance her chances at college. In contrast, she thoroughly enjoyed going to her rhythmic dance classes, currently in the midst of rehearsals for their annual presentation. She had musicality, a slim body, and long legs, and she gave it all when executing the fluid movements and other refined elements required in this type of dancing. During the planning of the show everyone expected that she'd be chosen for one of the major roles, the only surprise came when the instructor cast her as János Vitéz, the heroic male figure of a poetic story adopted for their show. Written a hundred years ago by Hungary's great poet, Sandor Petofi, the poem tells the adventures of a poor shepherd boy who is forced to flee from his village and must leave his sweetheart, Iluska, behind. Years later he returns home, only to find that his beloved died of heartache. Standing at her grave, he plucks a rose that grew from her ashes and carries it with him as he goes wondering aimlessly in the world. One day he comes upon an enchanted land, the Land of Love, where couples lived in everlasting happiness. Alone and heartbroken, he has no more strength to go on and decides to end his misery by drowning himself in a nearby lake. As a final act before taking his life, he tosses the rose from his beloved's grave into the water, when lo and behold, from the very spot the rose fell, he sees his long lost love, Iluska, emerging more beautiful than ever. They are crowned king and queen of this magical kingdom and live, of course, happily ever after.

Although Sári would have preferred to play the ever so beautiful Iluska, she found consolation in that János Vitéz was a more important role, and the choreography was created almost entirely with him in mind. He was the central figure and as such, was on the stage a lot more than the poor resurrected girl.

The show, presented in the city's theater, was a great success. There was not an empty seat in the house when the curtain rose and Sári stepped onto the stage wearing the traditional Hungarian peasant costume of a wide-sleeved, pure white linen shirt, embroidered vest, and tight black pants tucked into shiny black boots. With her arms crossed and held in front of her chest, she danced around the stage, alternating between high kicks and slow turns to the haunting music that underlined the unhappy mood of the sad shepherd boy. Reaching the lake, Sári took the flower she carried, kissed it reverently, and with a passionate flair tossed it into the water. Then, as Iluska rose, the newly crowned couple danced together, surrounded by a fluttering bevy of pretty chorus girls as the happy inhabitants of the fairyland.

As the curtain fell, the sound of thunderous applause and shouts of "bravo" filled the theater, followed by several curtain calls, during which she was presented with a huge bouquet of flowers. Her act as the dancing János Vitéz—

minus Iluska and the assorted fairies—became much in demand as part of the usual entertainment at public political rallies before the party secretary would plunge into speeches. She was glad to participate, since the acknowledgments she received could possibly mean another step closer to her college acceptance.

Ilonka still couldn't comprehend the importance Sári attached to her political involvement, dilly-dallying, as she called it. She couldn't believe that any college could refuse her daughter's application with such excellent grades, the second best among the thirty-six girls in her class. It embarrassed her as more and more of her friends started making comments about seeing Sári leading the "Viva Stalin" chorus at such and such political gathering, or marching at the head of her schoolmates, waving the red flag and singing the Communist Internationale during some demonstration against the West. What was she to say when they asked how could she and Jeno allow it? She would have to sit down with her again and ask her to tone it down, if not for the family's sake, then for Viktor, who surely found her behavior equally embarrassing.

Being a housewife, she was not directly exposed to the incessant pressures the Communist Party imposed on people at the workplace and in schools. She heard the stories, but with her optimistic nature, she believed that it couldn't be as bad and was convinced that her daughter was overdoing the political shenanigans. The Communists had done away with the other parties, forced the poor peasants into collectives and put Cardinal Mindszenty in jail—what else could they possibly do?

How could she and so many others know that these were only preliminaries to what was to come, that the struggle for total power was just beginning?

The creation of NATO, the North Atlantic Treaty Organization, on April 4, 1949, was the start of the Cold War that gave the excuse for the Party to step up the attacks against the imperialists and thwart their plotting aimed to destroy the Soviet Union and its "friendly" nations. The cry went up alerting everyone to be vigilant against spies working for the West and to look out for traitors who could be hiding anywhere, even inside the innermost circle of the Party. They were hard to spot because they were using clever disguises and crafty methods to infiltrate the ranks so they could do their dirty work from within, causing serious harm to the State.

Matyas Rakosi used this propaganda to set the stage for the show-trial he planned for bringing down a man he perceived to be his rival, the second most prominent member of the Party, Laszlo Rajk. Although born into a middle-class family—his father owned a shoe store—Rajk became a dedicated Communist at an early age. In the late 30s he fought in the Spanish Civil War under the Communist-led XIII International Brigade, before returning to Hungary in 1941 to join the underground movement against the Nazis. At one point he was arrested and marked for execution, but his brother, a member of the fascist government, intervened and saved his life. When the war ended he became one of the leaders in the new government, even though he was not a Muscovite like Rakosi and Gero. Because he had never lived in the USSR and didn't speak

Russian, they viewed him as "too Hungarian" who could not be trusted to offer absolute obedience to Moscow. This contributed to his ultimate downfall, but there were other factors, as well.

As Minister of Interior since March 20, 1946, Rajk was in charge of national security and was credited with creating the AVO, the Party's secret police that put tremendous power in his hands. Many envied his position and to damage his reputation started rumors that he staffed the AVO with his "men," Party members to be sure, but with questionable backgrounds. Jobs went to his old friends, some even from the Horthy regime, when he should have chosen people from the working class. Added to the dislike was his somewhat arrogant attitude, handling subordinates with high-handed superiority. Even his top man at the AVO, Gabor Peter, resented his constant lecturing and the way he treated him in an offhanded manner that bordered on disdain. They also feared him, as it was Rajk who led the vicious attacks on the non-Communist coalition parties, liquidated the clergy, and staged the first show trials against the opposition leaders.

Rakosi himself feared Rajk's increasing power and, with a nod from Moscow, decided to get rid of him before he could become more dangerous. As a preliminary step, on August 5, 1948 Rajk was removed as Minister of Interior and named instead Minister of Foreign Affairs, a lower ranking post he kept until his arrest on May 30, 1949. After the general election on May 15 that ended with 97% in favor of the Party, Rakosi was ready to start proceedings against the man he believed to be a threat to his exalted position. He could have put him away quietly, explaining his disappearance with some made-up excuse, as he had done often before and after, but because Rajk stood so high in the Party hierarchy, it would have created suspicion in the public mind. Instead, he decided on a seemingly lawful court case that would hide the true pre-conceived conceptual nature of the trial with the outcome already decided. Rajk was to be tried as a Titoist spy bent on destroying Hungary's independence and restoring capitalism, a crime that demanded a death sentence. It would also serve to show everyone what happens to traitors.

Rakosi knew perfectly well that Rajk was innocent, but he also knew that he *could* be accused of these crimes, and that he *would* sign the confession needed to convict him. To make it more convincing, the case would be presented as a wide conspiracy; after all, Rajk couldn't have acted alone. They would have half a dozen co-conspirators tried with him as partners, even if some of them, as widely known, hardly spoke to Rajk. To build a strong case, they began to arrest potential witnesses to provide the "evidence" against Rajk and his "gang," putting them in jail and interrogating them, often under torture, to extract the damning confessions. They were promised acquittal in exchange for testifying at the trial, a promise that was never kept. The unfortunate witnesses were kept in prison for years simply because they knew too much and the Party feared they wouldn't keep silent.

Rajk himself was tortured as well, using various ways. First he was subjected to non-violent methods such as sleep deprivation, but when he stubbornly denied guilt, Mihaly Farkas, Minister of National Defense, and Janos Kadar, General Secretary of the Party and an old friend of Rajk, personally took charge of the case. Farkas' son Vladimir, a Lieutenant Colonel in the AVO, had Rajk beaten for days, but when Rajk still wouldn't break, they changed tactics again. They called in Russian experts, so-called advisors, with General Byelkin at the lead, who took Janos Kadar off the case as ineffective, and suggested appealing to Rajk's sense of loyalty to the Party.

They told him that it was possible that in the beginning he was unaware that he was being used in a Titoist plot, but by allowing himself to be drawn into their conspiracy against the Soviet bloc and agreeing to put certain men—their trained infiltrators—into important government positions, he committed a crime. They could see why Tito picked him to do his dirty work: as Foreign Minister making frequent visits to Yugoslavia he was easily accessible. In a way he became a victim, but in view of the overwhelming evidence he must surely see that getting involved and going along with their scheme was a treasonable betrayal, a criminal act that must be punished. The only way he could help his situation, and at the same time serve the Party, was to confess and submit to a public trial. He would be convicted, but his sentence would be more lenient. In the name of the Party, his interrogators promised that he wouldn't be executed, and Rajk apparently trusted their word, since he signed the forced confession put in front of him. His steady voice and calm demeanor during the subsequent trial also indicated that he sincerely believed them.

The hearing started on September 16 and lasted six days, charging Rajk with espionage, conspiracy, treason, and plots again Rakosi and Gero. Seven other co-conspirators faced the same accusations and many more were implicated. Even Janos Kadar, whom the Soviet advisors dismissed earlier for failure to extract a confession, fell under suspicion for involvement in the plotting. At his arrest a few months later he was charged with trying to help Rajk by intentionally hindering the investigation, and that he himself was a Titoist agent. During torture, his fingernails were torn out one by one.

Court proceedings began with establishing Rajk's identity. When asked to state his date of birth, without the slightest hesitation he said it was March 8, 1909. This, however, was wrong; he was born on *May* 8, 1909. Did he make the error on purpose to raise doubt in the public mind that everything else he said during the trial would also be false? His wife was convinced of it, since how could any man, even if tortured, ever forget his own birthday?

He pleaded guilty to acting as an agent of the counter-revolution, and denied, when asked, if he was in any way coerced into admitting his guilt. He said he confessed of his own free will in sincere repentance for his crimes. Then he calmly proceeded to describe in every detail, how he carried out those crimes. Accordingly, his contact was the Yugoslav Minister of Interior, whom he met regularly in a guard's field hut near Paks, a port of call on the Danube, some seventy miles south of Budapest. He stated that Tito himself got involved in the plotting, working hand-in-hand with the American intelligence agencies to organize an armed force that was to include the fascist émigrés. Their aim was to overthrow the Hungarian people's democracy and bring the country into Tito's camp. Absurdly, he kept praising the superior vigilance of the Party and the diligence of the AVO for foiling the plot and ferreting out his carefully planted people, while portraying himself as a degenerate criminal.

The "public" in the courtroom consisted mostly of carefully chosen trusted party people who frequently gave voice to their disbelief and rightful indignation with shouts of "hang the mad dog!" and the like. The entire trial was carried live on the radio; in factories workers heard the broadcast through piped in loudspeakers, while in offices people gathered around the radio to listen collectively. No one dared to stay away and risk denunciation as a Rajk sympathizer, or worse, be accused of complicity. Finally, on September 24 the prosecutor began his summing up, ending it by demanding the death penalty for Rajk and two co-defendants. In the name of protecting the State and its citizens from such dangerous traitors, it was quickly granted, along with lengthy prison terms for the rest. On a special note, the judge pointed out that not one among the convicted was from the working class or the peasantry.

Asked if he had a last word in his defense, Rajk continued his bizarre dialog about the invincibility and correctness of the Party and asked no mercy. And he got none. The promise that his life would be saved was forgotten and he went to the gallows on October 15, 1949, shouting, "Long live the Party, Long live Stalin and Rakosi." Considering the great wrong done to him, his strange behavior is debated to this day as to why he chose to accept his role in the trial in such a way as to give testimony even to the very end to the Stalinist dogma that the Party could never be wrong. His two co-defendants were also hanged, but unlike Rajk, one of them was heard muttering, "I am not a traitor, I was tortured, this can't be true, they promised . . ."

To see Rajk, an important political figure, go so fast from being second in command to the chained dog of Tito was a terrifying awakening for the nation. Somehow people could accept the downfall of Cardinal Mindszenty; after all, the Church and the Communist regime were lethal enemies, but if it could happen to Rajk, if the Party could bring down the creator of the AVO, make him confess to far-fetched crimes and put him to death, then no one was safe. It drove home that innocent people could be arrested and hanged at the whim of a controlling few.

The Rajk trial broke the people's spirit; it pushed them into silence, to accept the unacceptable. After his execution there was no more reluctance to join the endless hand clapping and rhythmic chanting at the mention of Stalin and Rakosi's name. From now on they would obediently attend political seminars and willingly swallow the ideological rubbish. The satirical cartoons were gone, too, such as one published not long before the trial with two clerks decorating an office, one holding a framed picture of Rakosi and asking, "Where should we hang him?" All the snickering jokes referring to his thick-necked, bald dome as the lower part of his anatomy stopped. With Rajk's trial, Rakosi achieved his goal in terrorizing the people into absolute submission. From now on they would think and act not as individuals, but according to the dictates of the Party.

CHAPTER FIVE

1950 - 1956

Coping

AROUND THE TIME of Rajk's arrest, students everywhere were busy preparing for year-end exams, but their minds were already fixed on the day when schools closed their doors and vacation began. For most children in Sopron, summer meant going swimming in the Lake Tomalom or hanging out at the public pools, hiking in the Loevers, or simply having fun kicking balls on a soccer field. Some lucky ones got to spend time camping around Lake Balaton or, if their families could afford it, going to one of the better vacation resorts.

But for Sári and Gyuszi, quite a different summer was in store. To help paying household bills, they went to work. Gyuszi got a job at a construction site, while Sári started working in a tool-making factory. She did it willingly, not only because she could keep half of what she earned, but also because nothing could be more impressive on her college application than listing her summer job at the factory. How could they turn her down after reading that she spent her vacation working shoulder-to-shoulder with the workers as one, striving together to bring the country a step closer to achieving socialism? She would embellish it by adding how much she learned from the experience, what valuable insight she gained from witnessing the determination and dedication of today's workers, men and women driven by a single-minded, front-line mentality to transform Hungary into a strong industrial nation, no longer dependent on outside resources. Or something to that effect . . . Any university would be hard put to deny acceptance with this kind of reference.

Three of her classmates were also working at the factory and when the local newspaper heard about it, they interviewed the girls and published the article under the title "The barrier-breaking summer of four high school girls." This was more than Sári could have wished for, hard evidence she could attach to her application! The article was written in glowing terms of how these girls, by doing hard physical labor, proved that the difference between the working class and the intelligentsia was a thing of the past. It went on to say:

> . . . It is the sign of our time that these young schoolgirls, representatives of the politically conscious youth of the new Hungary, recognized almost instinctively the importance of showing solidarity with the laboring masses not only by words but also by deeds. They gave up their well-deserved summer vacation to gain firsthand knowledge of what it meant to be a worker, a worker yet in the field of iron and steel, the manufacturing of tools and machinery. . . .

The reporter then gave a detailed account of the interviews, first with the floor manager whose face lit up as he expressed his satisfaction at how these young schoolgirls were performing, how they rolled up their sleeves and with their feet firmly planted, took the bull by the horns. He shook his head in disbelief that the products coming from their hands were without rejects. Not only that, but they worked with such obvious joy, singing while they hammered away, prompting others to join in, and soon exuberant voices would fill the room, dulling the noise of the machines. Their upbeat mood was simply infectious; the atmosphere had never been so cheerful.

Then it was the girls' turn, each describing why they decided to work at the factory. One wanted to become a safety engineer, and this gave her hands-on knowledge of working conditions in a factory and the dangers the workers were exposed to. Another aspired to study human resources, and being part of the labor force allowed her the opportunity to observe the relationship between labor and management. At Sári's turn, the reporter smiled at the sight of her face speckled with oil and smudged with dirt—he symbolically described it as the rouge of work—and commented that it made her white teeth sparkle even whiter when she broke into a wide grin. Answering his question about her output, she proudly boasted how she had exceeded her norm the day before by turning in 667 pieces instead of 550. Did she feel tired at the end of the workday? Not at all! Sweating over a math problem in school was more exhausting than handling the press here, she said pointing to her machine. Then she talked of the new friends she had made since she started working and how easy it was to do a better job when imbued with the spirit of camaraderie. "You'd be surprised," she said to the reporter, "how quickly time flies when working in such pleasant surroundings."

After the interview, the article concluded:

> . . . The rhythmic noise of the machines intermingles with the rhythm of songs on the lips of these young girls. It is but the rhythm of life. When school starts in the fall these girls will be entering their senior year, but in real life they already graduated, and they did it with honor. They are graduates of life, of work, and of the appreciation of their fellow man.

The day of the interview Sári rushed home from work to tell Ilonka about it and asked her to buy several copies of the newspaper when the article was published. When Ilonka didn't share her enthusiasm, she assumed it was because the papers would cost extra money and offered to reimburse her on her next payday. But it was not money that bothered Ilonka. Everyone knew that the paper was nothing but trash, full of Communist propaganda, and now Sári was going to be written up in it. It meant further embarrassment for her, but for the time being she didn't say anything; she'd wait and see when the paper came out. She promised to get the extra copies for Sári, although she wouldn't spend a penny on buying them; she'd get them from litter baskets on the streets, where they belonged. People just tossed them away, hardly reading the contents.

The next day when Ilonka read the article she was fuming. Just as she suspected, it was nothing but a bunch of lies! Did these editors really think that anyone would believe this nonsense? Do they take people for such fools? What eighteen-year-old would rather work than spend the summer playing, if she didn't have to? And this foolishness about singing while doing hard work—these idiots must have watched *Snow White and the Seven Dwarfs* too many times! She saw how tired Sári was when she came home after work, bitching about how they raised her quota as soon as she exceeded the previous one.

Ilonka was close to exploding by the time Sári walked through the door. Waving the paper in her hand, she gave went to her indignation.

"What on earth got into you saying stupid things like this? What will our friends think when they read this? It's bad enough that the neighbors think that you've gone over to the left like Latzi, but now the whole town will know! I almost believe it myself!"

"Mother, I only said what they wanted to hear, you know that!"

"If you couldn't tell them the truth, that we needed the money, you could have said nothing. You are smart enough to think of some excuse to avoid the interview altogether. This is really, truly embarrassing, and if you are not, I am embarrassed for you." Disgustedly, Ilonka threw the paper on the table but she was not through yet. "What do you think Viktor will say when he reads this?"

"Viktor will say nothing. He knows what's going on; he feels the pressure like all of us, what we have to do to get ahead."

"I doubt that he went around singing these Communist praises just to get into college!"

"He didn't have to, Mom! He got in before the Party started dictating who has the right to higher education and who does not. It's different now. I tried to explain it to you, but you just don't understand. This article could be the push I need to get accepted, and with a full scholarship."

"What I don't understand is why are you so set on going to Budapest and study for years when you have a serious suitor in Viktor. You could lose him, you know, while you are away. Is it worth taking that chance? You wouldn't have to go through all this lying and pretending if you just—"

"Ah Mom, let's just drop this," Sári held up a hand stopping her mother in mid-sentence. "It's no use. Do you think I do these things because I like it? I do what I have to do, because I am going to college! It's not because I am against marrying, or I want to prove something, or I am selfish. In your days girls married and that was that, but the time is coming fast when husbands alone won't be able to support a family. In a socialist society everyone must work, and the easiest way to enforce that is to keep wages low. And that's exactly what the government is doing. That's why so many women, married or not, are already out there working, and I am afraid even you will live to see the day when you have to get a job. And without an education, what will you do? Work in a factory!"

"I am well aware how tight things are without you telling me! And that's why I told you I was thinking of taking in sewing; it is one thing I know how to do. And I can do that without going to college."

"Right, well anyway, I know I can do better than start clanking on a typewriter in some dusty office, because that's all a high school diploma would get me. And that's why I am willing to do these things, so I can have a decent job with a decent salary and stand on equal footing with an equally educated husband. Viktor knows this, but if he decides not to wait for me, so be it. We are not engaged, unless you know something I don't. Did he say anything to you and Father?"

"No he didn't, but I am not blind; I can tell a man in love when I see one. Viktor wouldn't waste time coming around as often as he does if he was not serious. You are seeing him what, eight or nine months now? He must have said something to you about his feelings, has he not?"

"Well, of course, he tells me that he loves me but no, there is no talk of marriage. And don't you or Dad go around making hints in front of him, or God forbid, ask him what his intentions are. Please, promise you won't, it's such an old-fashioned thing!"

"Old-fashioned or not, there is a limit to expectations," Ilonka said, then raised her voice a notch when she saw Sári making a face and pulling down the corner of her mouth. "I know you think today is so much different, but I am telling you, if I were you, I'd give it another year, but after that I would want to know where I stand!"

Neither Ilonka nor Sári could have guessed that at about the same time marriage was very much on Viktor's mind. After the semester ended and he left Sopron to begin his two months of mandatory field study, he had plenty of time to sort out his feelings for that vivacious, willful, yet warmhearted girl he left behind. He liked her from the very start, but as he saw more of her and in different situations, his feeling grew from like to love. He was over twenty-five and at that age, unlike his younger brother and most of his freshmen buddies, he was past running around chasing girls. He knew that in Sári he had found his ideal girl, intelligent, compassionate, and pretty to boot, who seemed to be capable of long-lasting love beyond the first flush of romance.

He considered her innocence and the age difference, but saw no problem with either. His military upbringing taught him discipline and self-control, and as for the seven-year age gap, he saw her as more mature than an average eighteen-year-old. They suited each other in many ways—in mentality, outlook, and expectations—and had the same understanding that in today's atmosphere one must compromise to get ahead. Submitting his college application over a year ago he also bent the truth a little by downplaying his military background. Knowing that a Horthy-era army officer would have no chance of acceptance, he only stated that he was drafted into the service and fought as an enlisted man during the war.

Viktor respected Sári's ambition to go to college and didn't try to talk her out of it. It was important for her. As for the separation, they would work it out. During the past eight months he had learned that, like himself, she was not flirtatious, or into playing games, so there was no cause for jealousy or doubt on either side. It gave him great peace of mind to know that he could truly trust her, and by the time he completed his summer job and was packing to return home, he knew for certain that he wanted her in his life.

It was mid-afternoon on Saturday, the day after the argument between Sári and her mother that Latzi came with the news that Eta was in labor and that the midwife was at her side. Sári had just came home from work—weekends in Hungary started on Saturday noon, with only Sunday off—so leaving the boys in her care, Ilonka immediately went to be with her older daughter. After asking a few questions about Eta's contractions, she told Latzi to stay put, it would be some time before he would meet his new son or daughter.

When she left, Latzi poured a glass of wine to calm his nerves, picked up the newspaper, and went into the front room to settle down for the wait. He found Sári there, writing a letter—no doubt to Viktor—with a copy of the cutout newspaper article lying on the table. Passing by her chair, he leaned over to give her a peck on the cheek and whispered in her ear, "Writing a love letter?"

When Sári quickly covered her writing he continued to tease her. "It must be true that distance makes the heart grow fonder," he said good-naturedly as he walked around and sat down across from her. But when she only made a face and stuck out the tip of her tongue at him, he laughed and changed the subject. "By the way, that was a nice little write-up on you," he said, pointing to the article. "I am really proud of you for what you are doing. But then, you were always smarter than the rest of the Zachars in regard to accepting changes and having the good sense to make adjustments. I am glad that someone else in this family sees the light besides me."

"See the light? Are you kidding me?" Pressing both forearms on the table, Sári leaned toward Latzi with a contemptuous, sarcastic grimace. "What I see is a system that is raising a bunch of hypocrites and opportunists. You don't think for a minute that I meant a word of what I said in that interview, or that I went to work in that stinking place because I wanted to! I did it to help Mother and to have a better chance at college, since my straight-A grades are not good enough to get me there. And you are telling me that this is better than the old days when even a dirt-poor student could get a scholarship based on intelligence and accomplishment alone, not by selling out to the devil! Because that's what this hateful regime forces us do! Do you have any idea how loathsome it is to be forced to lie and pretend day in and day out?"

"Sári, Sári, how would you know about the old days?" Latzi smiled with patient condescension. "You are too young to remember. There might have been some exceptions, but most poor people sweating in factories or out in the fields were stuck in poverty; they could never climb—"

"And they are still stuck in poverty!" Sári cut him off. "What's more, you don't even have to be a factory worker to sink to that low level! Just look around you. How do you think *we* are living now, huh? It sure is not high off the hog, when mother only had enough money to buy me one pair of shoes this year, and a sensible, practical one at that, not exactly what a young girl would fancy for herself. You know very well that we never had all that much, but we still had a relatively good life before, and look where we are now! Talk about changes! Not one of them for the benefit of the people! The only thing your Party has accomplished is bringing about social equality; they made everyone equally poor! Not to mention what they did to the rich!"

Giving vent to built-up pressures and frustration weighing on her lately, Sári was working herself to a pitch. Her loud voice could be heard in the adjacent room and it drew Jeno's attention. "What's going on in here?" he asked, standing in the doorway.

"Sorry Dad, it's nothing. We had a little disagreement, that's all. I just got carried away."

"Be more careful, Sári. The windows are open and people walking by could hear you," he warned her then withdrew with a disapproving glance in Latzi's direction.

"Your father is right about that, Sári. You should watch yourself better and learn to control that temper, or one of these days it'll get you in trouble," Latzi said rising from the table. He picked up his wineglass and newspaper and was moving to the other end of the room, but could still hear Sári muttering, "Well, if my application is rejected, at least I know who is to blame."

Of course she didn't mean it. She knew her brother-in-law would never do anything harmful, but God, did he have a knack for irritating her with his blind Bolshevik beliefs! She sat there trying to calm down, not to let things ruin her day. She'd just about had it! First her mother accusing her of showing too much red, then Latzi saying it wasn't red enough! And there is that daily drudge at the factory with the stupid cheerful pretense—how long could she keep that up?

She looked down at the half-written letter to Viktor in front of her and tried to concentrate on finishing it, but after staring at it for a while, she gave up. What's the use, she thought and threw down her pen. She was no longer in the mood to write anything romantic; the argument with Latzi saw to that. *I have to get out of this house or I'll go crazy*, she said half-aloud, crumpling the sheet into a ball. She'd go over to Wanda's for a little while and talk about her birthday party tonight. She just turned seventeen and to celebrate it her parents were giving a garden party for her at the Deak restaurant. They even hired a band. Sári had saved enough money to surprise her friend with a bright red Max Factor lipstick and matching nail polish from an American package.

Without a word to Latzi, she left the room, slamming the door. Startled by the stormy entrance, her father, sorting papers at his desk, turned in his chair.

"What's wrong? Is he still bothering you?"

"Not anymore, but I am upset and need to calm down. I'll be at Wanda's, Dad, but I won't be long," she tossed the words over her shoulder without breaking her stride. In her rush she almost ran over her mother at the door with Eta's boy, little Latzi in her arms.

"Watch out!" Ilonka cried out, grabbing Sári's arm to regain her balance. "What's the matter with you? I don't see the house on fire!"

"Sorry Mom, I didn't know you were home already. I had a run-in with Latzi. I just want to get away to clear my head so I am going over to see Wanda for a—"

"No, you are not! You can't leave now!" Ilonka stopped her, still puffing from fright. "Eta is having problems with the delivery and the midwife says she might have to be taken to the hospital. But even if not, I am going to stay with her. I just came to fetch Latzi and brought this little guy to stay for the night. You have to take care of him; here, I brought his things, his pajamas and some toys."

Ilonka put the baby down and called out to Latzi, who was already running, asking if Eta was all right, and if the baby was in any danger. They were half-way out the door when she turned around to give some last-minute instructions to Sári: the leftovers for supper were in the cooler, take the baby to the park so he'd sleep better, and not to forget his bath before putting him down for the night.

Like she didn't know how to take care of babies! She had more than enough practice, first diapering her little brother Ochie, then doing the same with Junior here when Eta was quarantined with scarlet fever after his birth. Dropping her head Sári let out a long, frustrated sigh. The day was definitely not going well for her; she was stuck with the kid and could forget about going to Wanda's party. Couldn't Eta have waited a day longer to have that baby? But then she felt ashamed for being selfish when her sister was going through such a difficult time. For Eta's sake Sári hoped the baby would be a girl; otherwise, knowing her sister, she would try again until she got her wish for a daughter.

What she must be going through in this very minute! It made her shudder to think of the suffering women must endure when giving birth. And they do it voluntarily, when they could easily choose not to have babies. Why would they put themselves through such pain and do it over and over again, she'd never figure out. Didn't women realize that having more children was at the expense of those they already had? Wouldn't she and Gyuszi be better off if there were only the two of them besides Eta? The second the thought entered her mind Sári felt a pang of remorse. This was wrong! She knew she shouldn't feel this way. It was not that she didn't love her younger brothers now that they were here. It's just that life for families with fewer children was easier. Well, it was no use dwelling on it, but one thing was absolutely sure! She would never have more than one child, maybe two, but only if she must! And if it did not happen, that wouldn't kill her, either. She had enough babies constantly crawling under her foot while she was growing up. Of course, she could never tell this to her mother; she would never understand it in a million years. She knew exactly what she would say: "Nonsense! Being a mother is the greatest fulfillment in a woman's life. You might not think so now, but just wait until you have a baby of your own!"

Her little nephew gazing up at her finally got tired of standing there and, raising his arms to be picked up, began to fuss. "OK little buddy, would you like to go to the park?" Sári bent and lifted the boy. "I'll take you, even let you kick off your shoes; I know how much you love to run barefoot in the grass. And you know what? Yesterday I saw a big bushy-tailed squirrel in one of the trees there; let's see if we can catch it." She put him in his stroller, but before leaving, she sent Gyuszi to tell Wanda about her predicament and to give her the present.

Later that night, when the children were in bed, Latzi came by to tell that Eta had a healthy little boy, and although it was a hard struggle, they didn't have to take her to the hospital. She was resting now but she would need care, and Ilonka would be staying with her for a day or so.

The next day, with flowers in hand, the whole family marched to congratulate Eta and meet little Peter. Ilonka had lunch ready but as soon as they ate, Sári asked to be excused to go over to Wanda's. Sunday was her only day off and Ilonka knew how much she wanted to hear about the birthday party she had missed last night.

She found her friend in a somewhat strange mood, acting aloof in an almost haughty manner when Sári asked if she had a good time. Yes, the party was a success, everyone enjoyed it; it was too bad Sári couldn't be there. And the presents, what gifts did she get? Oh, lots of things, and she liked them all, especially the lipstick and nail polish Sári gave her.

There was something wrong with Wanda, Sári thought. The way she acted and talked was not like her at all. Where was her exuberance? When she didn't offer further details about the party, or show her the presents, Sári couldn't stand it any longer.

"What's the matter with you? Are you disappointed about something? You didn't like what your boyfriend gave you, or what?"

"No, I liked his gift; he gave me a beautiful gold chain and a pendant with my initial. Here," she said, holding out a velvet box, "see it yourself."

"Oh Wanda, this is beautiful! That guy really loves you, you know. Did he say anything serious last night? Did he ask you to marry him? Is that why you are kind of floating somewhere? Are you holding back some secret?"

"Don't be silly; everyone knows that he wants to marry me!"

"Well, then, what is it with you?"

"Can't you guess?" Wanda suddenly became animated. With that certain superior aura still about her she leaned closer to Sári. "It's not what he gave me or what he said, but what he did!" She pulled back and with a smirk, waited for the impact of her words.

Sári screwed up her eyes and scrutinized her friend's face. Then it slowly dawned on her. "You did it, didn't you? You went all the way with him. Is that it?"

"Well finally, you figured it out!" Wanda broke into a grin. With her secret out, she was back to her old self. "Can you imagine that? A true 'gift of love,' wouldn't you say, making me a 'Woman' on my birthday!" she giggled, curling her fingers in quotation marks and rolling her eyes. "Although I bet he had an alternative motive to pick my birthday to do it, a selfish one: trying to increase the odds that I'd never forget him. And I have to give it to him; I probably never will. What do you say to all this my virgin friend?"

"Well, you beat me to it, that's for sure! And yes, quite a memorable birthday present! But how did you do it? And where? Did it hurt? Was it as good as they say? Tell me or I'll die!"

With their heads together and whispering, Wanda told her all the details she wanted to know. When she finished, Sári hunched up her shoulders and, with a scowl on her face, spread her hands. "Nice?? All you can say that it was nice? Maybe you were too nervous to notice anything more. Or you were afraid that you'd get pregnant. There must be more to it than just nice!"

All the way home and in her bed that night, she couldn't think of anything else but what Wanda had told her: nice but no big deal! She knew she could believe her friend, she wouldn't lie to her, but then why was lovemaking built up to such a crescendo in all those romance novels she and Wanda liked to read? Nice, to her, was the way she and Viktor kissed, but she would expect something more exciting when their time came to do it. Her mother never talked about this delicate subject, not that Sári would have dared to ask. Like most girls her age, naturally curious about what it really meant to "go all the way," she never knew the details about the act until today. Well, she would have to wait to find out for herself, although now, after what she heard, she wasn't in such a hurry. It was a good thing that Viktor never pressured her in any way. She was never in a situation when she would have to fight him off. He was truly a gentleman; she knew that he loved her and it must not be easy for him to be in control all the time.

Tucked in bed, she felt warm and cozy thinking of him and how very lucky she was to have someone like Viktor. She would have to write him that letter tomorrow.

. . . .

When Sári posted the letter the return address no longer carried their old Flandorffer street name; it had been changed to Mihaly Tancsics Street, after a liberal nineteen-century writer. This was the latest Party mania, renaming boulevards, streets and squares that had German or religious sounding names. Even the names of old Hungarian heroes or famous statesmen and poets were dropped if they had fallen from grace since the Communist takeover. If a major boulevard had a simple descriptive name, such as the Varkerulet (Castle Ring) in the heart of Sopron, it was also changed to the politically more appropriate Lenin or Stalin Boulevard. No city, town, or village escaped this renaming fever. About the same time, almost overnight, statues of Soviet leaders sprang up everywhere across the nation, and war memorials paying tribute to the victorious Red Army appeared in parks, on high hills and at other prominent places. Public buildings were also paying tribute to the great "Liberators." Fixed to the top of every administrative building, factory and school glowed the omnipresent Red Star, while the inside walls were decorated with pictures of Stalin, Rakosi, and Lenin, in that order.

These changes reflected the ever-increasing subjugation of Hungary's traditional values and sentiments to those of the Soviet Union. But these were only external signs. More repulsive enactments were incorporated in the newly promulgated constitution, modeled after its Soviet counterpart, and put into effect on August 20, 1949. As expected, it officially declared Hungary as a People's Democracy, and established the dictatorship of the proletariat within a constitutional framework. At first glance, the new constitution upheld all democratic and liberal principles, including equality for all and the four fundamental freedoms, and even went further, guaranteeing the right to work, to education, and to individual property. It instituted a new criminal code that ensured the impartiality of the courts and the right of the accused to trial and legal counsel. All very nice, alas all only on paper, since in practice the various freedoms, rights, equalities and the courts were all restricted by the Party. Private ownership was as defined by the law; individual and religious freedom was dealt with using fear tactics; and as for equality, only trusted people would be put in key positions. Those declared enemy of the people, even if well qualified, were unable to find work, just as universities would only accept students approved by the Party, with preference given to members of the working class and the toiling peasantry.

These were constitutional violations, but none compared to the abuse suffered by the judicial system. Under Chapter X, Article 46 of the Constitution, to speed up the administration of justice, lay assessors were empowered with the same rights and duties as the professional judges. People were told that the installation of these assessors was necessary to help with the tremendous backlog in the courts, primarily to separate cases on the basis of importance. In practice, however, their real task was to clear the way to conduct secret trials by arbitrarily deciding which case would be tried publicly in open court, or handled *in camera*—a session behind closed doors. These trials sent tens of thousands to prisons or internment camps, or simply had the victim disappear without a trace.

People were well aware of the gaping difference between the principle and practice of the new laws, but no one dared to challenge it. Some grumbled in private about the hypocrisy of the government, and many felt threatened that the worst was yet to come, but most just resigned to mute acceptance and tried to live the best way they could under the circumstances.

There was one other shocking enactment aimed to dull national awareness that became so insulting to Hungarian pride and patriotic sensitivity that it was considered a slap in the face to the country. It involved the date August 20, the day when the constitution went into effect, but which was also a great national holiday named after St. Istvan, Hungary's first king, to commemorate his coronation in the year 1000, and his act of establishing Hungary as a Christian nation. In the preceding nine centuries this much-revered holiday, considered the country's birthday, was celebrated with patriotic speeches and fireworks, and no government, including the current one, had ever dared to do away with it, unless risking a revolution. What Rakosi and his party did, however, was to tinker with its name. In an effort to reduce the importance people attached to St. Istvan and his crowning achievement, and to minimize the national character of the holiday, they first declared August 20 as the day of the harvest, or new bread, then a year later changed it again, officially naming it Constitution Day (*Alkotmány nap*).

But that was not enough to satisfy them. The wound they inflicted on Hungary's national pride was not deep enough; they had to twist the knife to make it bleed by mutilating the Flag. In order to identify Hungary with Russia and other socialist nations in the Soviet bloc, they changed its appearance. Back in 1945, at the end of the war, they had already taken out the old Coat of Arms topped by Hungary's Holy Crown from the white field of the red, white, and green flag, but now they replaced it with one that was practically identical to the Soviet emblem: the hated hammer and sickle encircled in a wreath of wheat and crowned with the red star. It amounted to making Hungarian patriotism, the love of one's own country, secondary to that of the love of Stalinist Russia, a creed that no true Hungarian could ever adopt. This shameful act pitted every Hungarian with an ounce of patriotism against the regime.

As a silent protest, defiant little lapel pins of the old flag tied with a black ribbon were sold secretly, although only a few brave souls dared to wear them, and only on the backs of their lapels. Istvan Fodor wore one, but Viktor with his Horthyist military past couldn't take the risk. He felt the insult just as deeply as his brother, but wearing such pin could draw attention to himself as a patriot and have the committee poke into his background. Istvan had nothing to hide; he went to college straight from high school, whereas Viktor would be expelled, and perhaps his whole future ruined, if his former membership in the military elite came to light.

To increase the difficulty in hiding one's past and to help discover previous lies about an individual's background, a new practice was put into effect: the writing of detailed annual autobiographies for the committees. "Detailed" meant to reveal any connection to the past regime, whether on personal level or through family members; to tell about any exposure to the West, including vacations spent there during or before the war; and to submit the names of relatives and freinds living in western countries, especially in the United States or Canada, even if contact has been lost. By comparing each autobiography to previous ones and to the original records on file, always looking for a slip, a deviation, or omission, they hoped to discover some politically damaging fact people might try to hide.

No one escaped the scrutinizing. Everyone who worked or attended college had to turn in these yearly autobiographies, especially Party members and those in higher positions, to prove that they stood above suspicion and that their past was unquestionably impeccable with nothing overlooked or omitted. The Party justified its need for such intense background checks by pointing to the Rajk trial. If they'd had these confessionals before, the party could have been more vigilant in keeping an eye on the likes of Rajk and his traitorous Titoist gang, and could have prevented them from covertly infiltrating the most trusted rank and file of the Party.

Talking with Ilonka one day about this latest "trapping device" Jeno remarked, not without a hint of sarcasm, that Latzi's hand must be getting tired of writing his life story over and over again. "I can just see him lamenting about the regrettable misfortune of his birth that put him into a middle class family, exposing him to certain privileges, like a higher education, ski vacations in the Swiss Alps and trips to France and Italy."

"And let's not forget the apologies he owes to the Party for his father's sin against the State by taking medical supplies to the West at the end of the war," Ilonka added with equal cynicism. "Or for having a Calvinist Bishop for an uncle who, to make things worse, escaped to the West. That gives him a real good reason to beat his chest with mea culpa!"

"Well, that uncle of his left the country during the Nazi era; that might have some mitigating effect," Jeno said. "Latzi mentioned that he now lives in the United States, but they are not in touch with him."

"I wonder what these revelations will do to his illustrious career in the Party. We both know he is incapable of lying or covering things up, his conscious wouldn't allow it, even if it meant they'd kick him out and he'd be without a job. This whole business of poking into people's pasts is just awful! Do they make you write your life story, too?'

"Of course, we all have to do it, Ilonka, although there's not much they can read into mine. Actually, we make fun of Latzi, but mentioning him as my son-in-law gives me some advantage."

"Well, at least for now! Who knows, on account of his family Latzi has enough bad marks the Party could hold against him, maybe not today, but the day could come. Nobody is safe; just look at what happened to Rajk. These people are like a bunch of crabs or spiders, the only species I know that attack and devour each other."

"That trial was really disgusting. Everyone knows that he was innocent and that he was tortured, but still, the way he confessed to everything so willingly! He sounded as if paying lip service to the Party, mouthing what they wanted to hear all the way to the gallows."

"You are still talking about that criminal, still think that he was innocent, regardless of the evidence we had against him?" Jeno and Ilonka were startled to hear Latzi's voice. They didn't hear him coming into the room and only hoped he didn't hear what they just said about him.

He was pulling up a chair, ready to argue the case. "He was a vicious enemy, an agent of the American imperialists. And there are many more like him still on the loose. But we'll get them; we'll hunt them down and bring them to justice. And when we—"

"No doubt, Latzi, no doubt, you will," Jeno nodded, interrupting the tirade. Then with a put-on confused look on his face he turned to his son-in-law. "But I noticed you keep saying we did this and we did that; do you mind telling me who do you mean by 'we'? Surely you don't include us, after you heard us talking."

"No, Jeno, when I say 'we,' I mean the Party, the State and the masses behind it. It is to indicate the complete unity between the people and the Party, and that the will of the individual is in total harmony with the goal of the Party."

"Ah-ha, now I understand," Jeno said looking deadpan serious. "I thought for a moment you might be using the royal plural."

Latzi was not amused by the obvious scorn, but he let it pass as a joke. Then he got down to business, telling them why he came: he had some good news and some bad. On the positive side, he had just received a big promotion, an appointment as head of the municipal council in the city of Szekszard—a city not far from the Yugoslav border. It came with a large salary increase and the use of a single-family home. However, and this was the bad news, with him gone, it was most likely their house would be inspected for extra living space and they would probably have to share one of the rooms with others.

Ilonka was practically out of her seat. "How long do we have to live with that threat?" she cried out in frustration, then slunk back in the chair just as quickly, knowing that it was not a threat, but a real possibility.

"I am sorry that I had to tell you this. Maybe you'll get lucky and avoid detection, but I thought I warn you, just in case," Latzi said trying to sooth her.

"We shouldn't have to live with this kind of fear, strangers camping out in our home, sneaking around and listening to every word we say, just waiting for the moment when they can denounce us and take over the whole house for themselves! All we want is to live in peace. Is that so much to ask? You helped us so far; with your connections there must be something you could do before you leave!"

"I am afraid not, Ilonka. And let me tell you, it was not easy to keep the authorities away. The housing shortage is still bad and this is a big house, almost

2200 square feet for the three rooms alone. According to current allocations, it could officially accommodate nine to ten people. But like I said, maybe it won't happen."

Latzi truly felt sorry for his in-laws. Yes, they were of the old world, nothing could change that, but they were good and honest people and he genuinely liked and respected them. Unfortunately, he won't be here to help them anymore.

The news upset Ilonka more than it did Jeno. By nature he was more accommodating and he did his best to cheer her, make her see that it didn't mean the end of the world.

"Ilonka, sweetheart, don't take this so much to heart. Even if they should put people in here, it's only a temporary situation; they won't stay forever. No one is happy living under cramped conditions and sooner or later, they'd want to have their own place. There are signs that things are slowly improving; buildings are being repaired and new ones are under construction."

When Ilonka just sat there, staring, as if deaf to his words, he tried another approach.

"We always managed when we had relatives living with us and had to give up a room. Perhaps it won't be so bad to get used to strangers either, if they are decent enough people."

But when nothing he said brought a reaction from Ilonka, he gave up and simply said, "Maybe we are worrying about nothing. Let's just see what happens; with luck we might escape the intrusion altogether." But he himself knew this was unlikely. They might escape it now, but what about next year? Sári would be gone by then and somebody was bound to notice that the Zachars had more room than allowed and run to alert the housing bureau.

Suddenly, with a shake of her head, Ilonka was back in the present, her voice shrill as she lashed out at Jeno. "I heard what you said, every word of it! You can hope all you want, but I just know they are going to put some people in here, and God knows what kind. And don't tell me that living with relatives can be the same as having strangers in the house! You are too optimistic; it would never work! What are we going to do? You know well enough how hard it is for me to keep my mouth shut! I like to speak my mind, and now I have to live in constant fear what I might say in my own home? I can't help it that I have a loud voice; do you expect me to learn in my old age to talk in whispers so we can be safe? I have run this house for over fifteen years and I am set in my ways; I know where everything is in my kitchen or in the pantry, and now I should tolerate it when some people meddle with it? And not get upset about it? Just to think of it makes me a nervous wreck! I tell you, I'd rather be dead than live this way."

She worked herself close to tears, her hands clutching at her heart, eyes pleading. She went on and on, that she knew for sure that it would be the front room they would want to take away and squeeze the six of them into the two smaller ones. And what about the furniture, where could she possibly put everything, because she would not leave any of her good pieces for strangers to ruin them! She must find a place for her precious grand piano, even if it would take up half the space in the children's room! That piano was the last reminder of their once pleasant life! Mother of God, how did they sink this low?

The opening and slamming of the door stopped her lamentation. It was Saturday noon and the children were arriving from school, hungry and ready to eat. She managed to pull herself together, but contrary to her usual self, she went around doing her chores without paying attention to their prattle, how little Ochie jabbered about hating first grade, and Istvan retorting that it was nothing compared to the fourth, where they all wished to be back in the first. Only Sári noticed that their mother, always interested in what the children had to say, was not listening, her mind somewhere else, and so when they sat down at the table she reminded her that Viktor and his brother were coming over later in the afternoon.

The mention of the Fodor boys seemed to have a strange effect on Ilonka. Her hand, lifting the spoon to her mouth, stopped half way, and for a moment she sat staring, as if in the process of digesting some important news or idea. Then she blinked a few times and calmly resumed eating her soup. And suddenly she was alert and smiling, her lethargy flown out the window.

Why, of course! The Fodor brothers, bless their souls, by all means, let them come! Ilonka felt a newfound ease wash over her. They could be the key to solving her problem with that cursed living quota! Since the start of the fall semester they were already here almost all the time, she might as well let them move in! At least they were not strangers, and they would be paying rent! Too bad it didn't occur to her before; she could have saved herself that awful scare earlier.

It was all clear to Ilonka now. Everything was falling in place. When the Fodor brothers returned in September they found that their former room was no longer available. Although their landlady promised to hold it for them, she changed her mind and decided she would rather have girls as tenants. To find another room at such a late date was simply impossible, and they were forced to move into the college dormitory, a gloomy place with cramped quarters and hardly any privacy. They hated it, but they had no other choice. None of their friends stayed there; they were surrounded by strangers, a lot of them freshmen picked by the Party straight out of factories. Most of these newly made college boys had no more than eight years of schooling, if that much, but all of them were quite well versed in Communist ideology. They were sent to get their diplomas, come hell or high water. Anyone with more brains and knowledge at the dorm was expected to help them in their studies, while professors were forced to pass them through exams. The place was also staffed with sentry-like supervisors with sharp eyes and ears to report anyone who, in their judgment, displayed politically offensive behavior. Used to carefree banter and occasional jabs at politicians, especially at the bald-headed Rakosi, Viktor and his brother had to be constantly on their toes not to say or do something that could be held against them.

To escape the restrictive atmosphere, they approached Sári's parents and asked if they would allow them to come over to their house to study. Ilonka pointed out that with her two younger boys running around, their home was often a noisy place, but it didn't matter to them; nothing could be worse than the dorm. All they needed was a corner, and so a few times during the week and always on weekends, the two brothers spent a good part of the day at Ilonka's. How happy they would be to leave that hated campus and move in here, Ilonka thought, especially Viktor, getting the extra bonus of seeing Sári every day! Who knows, this might even lead to a commitment. She certainly couldn't wish for a better husband for her. She would make them a fair offer, and wouldn't that extra money come in handy!

The more she thought about it the better Ilonka felt. She'd let them have the bedroom, like she did with Eta and Latzi. Of course, she must talk to Jeno, and he might balk at first at Viktor and Sári living under the same roof with only a door between them, but she could handle him; she could always make him see things her way.

The only other person Ilonka expected to raise questions about the arrangement was Sári's principal, Mr. Augusztin. Well, she would face that when the time came; after all, it was not like Viktor and his brother were moving in tomorrow. Right now it was just a thought; she'd wait and see; perhaps nothing would happen when Latzi and Eta leave town. For now it was enough to know that there was a way to keep strangers from invading their home. She would sleep better tonight.

An unexpected visit at the end of October, however, set things in motion. When the doorbell rang and Ilonka saw their landlord standing there, she knew instinctively that he was about to tell her some unpleasant news. It couldn't be about the rent; she made sure it was always paid on time. No, what he came to tell was that due to circumstances beyond his control he was forced to sell part of the ownership of the property. His lawyers were in process of negotiating with two interested parties, working out the agreements, but Ilonka had nothing to worry about; her lease would be honored until it expired in 1954, with only minor changes to reflect the new ownership and spell out the terms for the renewal. He was sure his co-owners would be happy to keep them on as tenants, although as Ilonka must know, large families were usually not considered ideal renters. He would do his part to recommend their staying, as he could only say good things about them.

Ilonka didn't worry about the renewal of their lease. The State protected tenants' rights against landlords; they couldn't put them out on the street as long as the rent was paid and the building properly maintained. She only asked about the prospective buyers, and it immediately put her on alert when the man mentioned the name of Anna Sinkovich. It was the woman who came snooping around the house once before, a garrulous and nosy creature who lived with her married daughter's family a few blocks down the street. Everybody had heard of their squabbles; the fights with her son-in-law were the topic of neighborhood gossip. Having her as a landlady, even if she was only a part owner, made Ilonka uneasy. It wouldn't surprise her if this troublesome woman had designs to eventually force them out of the house and move her daughter's family in so she could have their old, smaller apartment to herself.

The landlord was ready to leave when he said that before the sale could be finalized the lawyers insisted on an appraisal and a thorough inspection of the house to satisfy the authorities that everything was in line with the current building codes and other requirements. It was a mere formality; they didn't expect any major drawback, not since Jeno had the structural damage repaired. The inspection should take place in the next few weeks and Ilonka would be notified well ahead of time to make sure someone would be home.

The announcement jarred Ilonka's nerves. That's all she needed, a bunch of inspectors crawling all over the house, poking their noses in every corner. They were sure to discover the extra living space, and although Latzi was still in town, they knew he was no longer in position to help. There was still time, but she better see to it that Viktor and his brother moved in by then. She'd wait until the next time they complained about the dorm, which was almost every time they came, then bring up the idea of renting them a room, as a favor, of course, to help in their disagreeable situation. They need not know the real reason.

Everything worked out with great satisfaction to both parties. The rent was set and an agreement was drawn up regarding conditions. Meals would not be provided and kitchen privileges were limited. The bathroom was to be shared. Their door to the connecting room would be locked, and a large wardrobe closet permanently placed in front of it. As for visitors, no females were allowed, except their sister Kati, of course, and male buddies only during reasonable hours. Since there were minor children in the house, entertainment was to be kept to minimum, with civil behavior maintained at all times. Ilonka and Jeno's main concern, however, was their daughter. Regardless that a lot of people these days were forced to share housing, the known fact that Viktor and Sári were romantically involved will surely set tongues wagging. They pressed that both Viktor and Istvan must do their utmost to protect her reputation, and when they solemnly pledged to conduct themselves as gentlemen, the deal was sealed with a handshake.

The boys moved in the next weekend and were at the police station the following Monday to officially register their new residency. With that Ilonka's fear was put to rest; no inspector could claim that the house could accommodate more people. The brothers were equally happy to leave the crowded conditions at the dorm, especially Viktor, who could hardly believe his luck to be constantly so near to Sári. Their dating consisted of knocking on her door, and that only to keep some degree of formality.

As Ilonka expected, Sári's school principal, Mr. Augusztin, found the cozy setup objectionable. It didn't take long before he summoned her to tell that in his view the arrangement was morally questionable, if not wrong, and expressed surprise that she and Jeno, as responsible parents, would allow their teenage daughter to live in a room next to a suitor. Ilonka, however, came prepared to fend off the not-so-subtle insinuation.

"I appreciate your concern, but I can assure you that renting a room to the Fodor brothers will not change my daughter's behavior regarding school regulations. Sári will abide by all the rules, including the one against appearing unsupervised in public with a young man, but beyond that, I must take exception that school officials should be concerned with private matters within our home. Renting out a room should not reflect on Sári in any way. I am sure you agree that taking in renters is wide-spread, and it is certainly not worse than having the authorities requisition part of our home for other people's use, complete strangers, as in most cases. In fact, the main reason we decided to sublet a room is exactly to avoid such a risk. As to why the Fodor brothers, we chose them because we got to know them well and found both reliable and one hundred percent trustworthy. To ensure that propriety is strictly observed we set up certain rules they both agreed to follow. You must take my word that having them in our home presents absolutely no danger to my daughter's reputation. That Viktor is courting Sári is secondary in this, although I couldn't be happier if something serious should develop between them."

Ilonka paused for a moment, then, looking straight at Mr. Augusztin, continued.

"My older daughter Eta was eighteen when she got married right out of school, and to tell the truth, I wish with all my heart that Sári would do the same, rather than run off to some college in Budapest, as she is hell-bent to do. You might think me old-fashioned when I want her to stay home, get married, and settle down, but that's how I feel. Quite frankly, if the day should ever come that Viktor asks us for her hand, it would make my dream come true."

She waited again for a response but when none was forthcoming she cleared her throat, ready to bring the subject to a close. "Anyway, having said that, I hope you have a clearer picture of our situation." With that she rose to leave, then added in a lighter tone, "You might not admit it, but this town would have fewer happily married couples, were it not for parents with marriageable daughters taking college students into their homes."

Mr. Augusztin smiled at the remark and seemed to be in a more agreeable mood, yet not quite convinced that Ilonka was right. "I can see the point you made," he nodded as he opened the door for her, "although I still have reservations."

Ilonka turned to face him one more time. "If you are concerned that people will talk, let them. It does not bother us. Sári is over eighteen, an adult, and Viktor is a true gentleman in every respect. Besides, I am home all the time; I know their every move, and isn't this better than having them meet somewhere on the sly?"

That evening Ilonka told Sári about her conversation with the principal and about the promise she made in her name that she wouldn't be seen in public alone with Viktor.

"What? You want me to walk steps behind him, like in some Muslim countries?" Sári balked, her voice full of sarcasm. "It would be ridiculous when everybody knows that he is living here. No, I am not going to do that! What can they do, deny me going to another ball?"

But it never came to that. For some reason, after Ilonka's talk with the principal not one among the school staff made a report of seeing the couple without an escort.

When Viktor's parents learned about the move they decided to visit the boys in their new place, and at the same time meet the girl they had heard so much about. They knew already how serious Viktor felt about Sári, but curiously, their daughter kept telling them that she was the wrong girl for him. She didn't deny that she was intelligent, but everyone knew in school that she was a Communist. And she was not even all that pretty, and had absolutely no taste in clothing.

"Imagine wearing sky blue ankle socks with that hideous green coat she has! I just can't understand what Viktor sees in her when he could have Ella," Kati complained to them. "And now he's moved into their home! I've never been there, but it is common knowledge that they are quite poor. The truth is, Viktor would be a good catch for Sári; that's why her folks kept inviting him all the time. He was always at their house, and now he is living there!"

From the beginning Kati's parents were well aware of her prejudice against Sári, and they told her outright that what the girl wore was none of their business; they were more concerned about her character. But what Kati said about the family trying to catch Viktor as a husband might be true. They wanted to meet them to form their own opinion.

The upcoming Balek Ball in November was the perfect occasion to spend a long weekend in Sopron, see the children, find out about the situation with Sári and her parents, and do a little dancing, which they had not done for quite a while. At the ball Viktor made the introductions, nothing more than a brief exchange of pleasantries and to arrange his parents' visit for the following afternoon.

Before the appointed hour Sári made sure that everything was in perfect order in the front room, that the crystal glasses sparkled, none of the porcelain serving pieces were chipped, and the silverware gleamed as she arranged them on a lace covered side table. She was quite nervous when Viktor's parents arrived, and after the greetings, she was more than glad to withdraw with Viktor and Istvan to give their parents time to get acquainted.

As often when strangers first meet, the talk between them started out with casual conversation, but it soon turned to the subject of the boys moving in.

"We are truly grateful that you let Viktor and Istvan have one of your rooms," Mrs. Fodor said. "We know how much they hated living on that campus. Hope their presence is not much of an inconvenience for your family."

"Not at all, we are glad to have them; they are both exceptionally fine young men," Ilonka replied. "You did a wonderful job raising them! It's never an easy task, I know. We have five of our own, two girls and three boys; our eldest, Sári's older sister, is married and living in Szekszard, but we still have the others at home."

Meanwhile, Jeno saw to it that glasses were filled, then after sitting down turned to Viktor's father. "I understand that you are a forest engineer and attended the university in Selmec. My brothers and I were all students there until Trianon."

"Why yes, I graduated there before that tragedy," Mr. Fodor warmed to the subject. "And I do remember having a classmate named Gyula Zachar. Is he your brother?"

At once they were on common ground, discovering mutual acquaintances, and when Mr. Fodor found out that Jeno participated in the rescue of their university from the Slovaks, his initial congeniality turned to warm regard.

As the talk between the two men drifted toward shared memories of a beloved town and time, Ilonka and Mrs. Fodor stayed closer to current topics, mainly difficulties with shortages and the increasing restrictions one had to bear today. They took turns talking about the war and what came after, and how it all changed their lives. At one point Ilonka paused for a moment and, without being dramatic, swept an arm over the room and its rather worn-looking furniture.

"This is not the way we used to live," she said with a tone of regret. "We had a comfortable life, nothing luxurious, but pleasant. We had no problem raising five children, I had live-in help, even a German nanny for a while when Sári and Gyuszi were small. Then the war came, and this is where we ended up. We hoped that in time things would improve and little by little we'd recover, but with the direction the country is going, God knows if it will ever happen. All we can do is salvage some of our dignity."

She was not trying to elicit sympathy or sound apologetic, only to convey that their present diminished standing was due to events and circumstances beyond their control. "The air attacks did an awful lot of damage in Sopron," she continued, "but luckily, our house withstood the bombing. It had some structural damage though, and paying for the costly repairs left us without further resources to make improvements inside the house. As you can see the furniture is in various stages of wear and tear, the Persian rug is getting threadbare, and sadly, given the way things are, I don't see when we can start replacing things."

But then she stopped. She had said enough for Mrs. Fodor to understand their reduced circumstances and quickly changed the subject. "Of course, there are many others in worse situations. Our children are healthy and thriving and that's all that matters. They all do well in school, especially Sári. She was a straight-A student in first grade and still is. I don't know if Viktor told you, but she is determined to continue her education. And if you heard rumors floating around that she is involved in politics, please ignore them; it's just to help her get accepted in college. It's a shame that her grades are not enough. She is a smart girl, a little willful at times, quite competitive, but that's understandable with four siblings. We'll just have to wait and see what happens with college. I heard Kati did well when she graduated in June; what are her plans for the future?"

With that she tossed the ball into Mrs. Fodor's court. It was her turn to talk about her family. The war affected them too, but living in the country made things a little easier. There was no bombing, and the food shortage was not as severe. Cities always suffered more during upheavals. Then she talked about Viktor, how he was set for a military career, and how losing the war destroyed it all. Now he was forced to hide that part of his life, like it was a shame to serve one's country! He had to start anew, but he seemed to handle it well.

"You know what he said?" Mrs. Fodor leaned closer with a confidential smile. "He told me that it was all for the best, or he might have never met Sári. He is very fond of her, you know. The last time we talked, he sounded quite serious about their relationship. It's too bad that we live so far from here, because we'd love to get to know her better. Perhaps you and Jeno would allow her to visit us sometime during the summer. We would love to have her; she could share Kati's room and you can rest assured, she would be well chaperoned."

This came as a surprise to Ilonka. She knew that things were humming along quite nicely between her daughter and Viktor, but that he was seemingly this close to making a decision was news to her. Turning to Mrs. Fodor, she said she would have to discuss it with Jeno, but saw no reason to oppose the visit. Perhaps Sári could spend a week with them after graduation, and that she was not worried, she knew she would be in good hands.

A little later, after the two brothers had joined them and Sári served some coffee and sweets, the visit ended. Mr. and Mrs. Fodor left satisfied that Kati's opinion was biased, and that while the family had obviously suffered a considerable setback during the war, they were solid middle class, not above nor below their own social standing.

As 1949 was fast coming to an end, Eta was packing in preparation for their move. She felt sad to leave but at the same time excited. She would have a large house and Szekszard, being a smaller town, would be a good place to bring up children. She only wished the city was closer to Sopron; being so far apart, they won't be visiting very often.

On Christmas day—probably the last such holiday spent with her parents for a long time to come—sitting after dinner Jeno asked Latzi what exactly would he be doing in his new job.

"Primarily, I am to oversee that work is carried out according to our new Five Year Plan. It kicks in on January 1, five months ahead of its schedule, because the Three Year Plan was completed that much earlier, thanks to the workers' dedication and determination," Latzi said with immense pride. "It's true, it required sacrifices, and we all had to skimp, but what we accomplished in less than three years is amazing. And that's just the beginning. From now on we can expect a vast improvement in the economy. The standard of living will increase; the new Plan will see to that. It will clearly demonstrate to the worst skeptics that carefully planned centralized commercial management is superior to that of the unrestrained free-market system controlled entirely by profit-making and trumpeted by the capitalist propaganda to be the only effective form of economy."

Jeno nodded and let him talk without making any remarks. After all, it was Christmas, and who knew when they would see them again. But he couldn't resist asking about his unfinished studies.

"It sounds like you will have your hands full, Latzi, and won't have much time to finish your remaining final semester. Have you given up on getting your diploma?"

"No, Jeno, I didn't forget my promise about that, and I already made arrangements to complete that last leg via correspondence courses. No matter how busy I get, I will find time to study."

Jeno raised his glass to that and offered a toast wishing Latzi good luck and success in his new position as well as getting his engineering degree.

A few more toasts later, as they said goodbye, Jeno jovially poked him in the ribs. "Just watch out for all those Titoist gangsters lurking around the Yugoslav border, waiting to ensnare you and drag you into their traitorous camp, like they did with Rajk."

It was Latzi's turn to say nothing. He smiled, but told Jeno that in his place he would be more careful with this kind of cynicism; others might not appreciate his sense of humor.

They hardly left Sopron when a few days later Lasko Riedl stopped by unexpectedly. His visit came as a surprise, leaving Ilonka wondering why would he leave home during the holidays? After he got his diploma he said goodbye and moved back to his parents' home in Esztergom, even worked at the same forestry estate as his father, so what was he doing here?

Of course she didn't ask. Always glad to see him, they welcomed him heartily, eager to hear the latest news from his family. He said everyone was doing relatively well, but the best of it all was that his brother Erno was home! The Red Cross was able to locate him in one of the Russian work camps, and through connections and bribes, they successfully negotiated his release. When his untreated, festering leg injury rendered him useless, the Russians agreed to let him go, provided they were "reimbursed" for the cost of his keep and care while he was their "guest." Now that he was home, they were doing everything possible to make him well again. He still had problems, both physical and psychological, and while the doctors said that with surgery his knee eventually would be as good as new, erasing the memories of the gulag—the subhuman treatment and humiliation suffered as a slave worker—would take longer.

Lasko also talked about his sister Liza, now studying architecture in Budapest, and how she found herself sitting in the same class with a newly discovered second cousin, Ferenc Callmeyer. His mother, Ilona Zachar, was a cousin to both Jeno and Lasko's father, but somehow no one seemed to know much about that branch of the family. Only now that Ferenc was attending college in

Budapest, did he pick up the threads and took to visiting the Riedls and also Uncle Sandor's family.

When Lasko left, he was strangely subdued and acted almost sentimental when saying goodbye. They had no idea that it was the last time they would ever see this talented, fun-loving young man. They learned later that he and a girl he courted since his college days were in Austria. They waited until a heavy snowstorm dumped several feet of snow that was deep enough to cover the barbed wire fence and the minefield beyond, then tied on their skis and schussed over to the other side. They were on their way to immigrate to Australia.

With Eta and her family already in Szekszard, and the Fodor brothers gone home for the holidays, Ilonka and Jeno were getting ready for a quiet celebration to ring in 1950, when out of the blue Viktor showed up. After telling his parents of his intention to marry Sári, he returned with their blessings to propose to her on New Year's Eve. She could hardly believe it when he dropped to one knee and uttered the magic words, "Will you marry me?" There was no hesitation as she answered with an ecstatic "Yes, Yes, Yes," but then, remembering how upset her parents were about Latzi neglecting to ask them first when he and Eta got engaged, she asked Viktor to go to them and do the proper thing. Of course, they happily accepted him as a son-in-law, but insisted keeping the news confidential until after Sári graduated. It was for the best, since there was no precedent to have a student engaged to be married sitting in the classroom. She would also forgo wearing his ring until then, since jewelry, real or trinkets, was outlawed in school.

Needless to say, Sári could hardly wait to break the news to her friends when classes resumed. She first swore them to secrecy, knowing all too well that not one would keep from telling. The next day the entire school talked of nothing else, but after some furtive glances at her ring finger with no evidence of a sparkler, the gossip died down as mere rumor. And just as well. Entering the homestretch before graduation the girls, including Sári, needed to concentrate on their studies. She easily passed the written tests at the end of May and was well prepared for the oral presentations scheduled for the first week in June. The students, seven each day, would be called to demonstrate their knowledge in Hungarian literature, history, Latin, mathematics, and physics. For each subject they were given an index card showing two topics to be presented, supposedly in the same order as listed.

Sári and Wanda were in the same group, and when Sári arrived on the morning of June 14, she found her friend standing on the front steps with fat tears rolling down her cheeks. There was no trace of her usual nonchalance; she could hardly manage to say between sobs that she knew she would flunk in all subjects. Unfortunately, this time Sári could do nothing to help her other than saying a few encouraging words. Even she got into a little trouble with physics, always her weakest subject, when she glanced at the topics listed on the card her teacher handed her. She had no problem with the second item, the Law of Induction, she had it in her little finger; however, she had no idea about the primary subject, something about forces and acceleration. Up to now there was no doubt her overall performance would be judged as one of the best in her class, but she could easily fall flat on her face now. If only she had more time to think, perhaps that damn force and its acceleration would break through the haze that momentarily clouded her brain. When she could no longer wait, ignoring the order of the topics, she plunged into a lengthy explanation on how induction occurs, and hoped nobody noticed the switch. It didn't fool her teacher; she knew exactly what Sári was doing, and why, but mercifully didn't stop her. Then, when Sári ran out of words about induction, she came to her rescue. "Thank you; that will be enough" she said. "We are quite satisfied with your knowledge, so unless my colleagues have further questions, you may return to your seat." Immensely relieved, Sári sank into her chair, silently blessing the kindhearted woman for her compassion that saved her from humiliation.

On graduation day she received her diploma declaring her sufficiently ready for higher learning. The school also gave her a letter of recommendation to include with her college application, and with that in hand, she sat down to write the required bio, carefully minimizing her middle class background and placing lots of emphasis on her political involvement:

> I was born on September 30, 1931 in Sopron, second of five children. My father is a customs officer. Originally he studied engineering but during the oppressive Horthy regime, lacking adequate financial aid, he was forced to quit. My mother works inside the home. My older sister is married to Laszlo Kontra, who joined the Communist Party in 1946 and is now the head of the city council in Szekszard.
>
> Our family became suspect during the Arrow Cross regime for speaking out against the Nazis, but escaped arrest. We didn't leave the country during the last days of the war but waited until the victorious Red Army reached the city and a few days later liberated our entire country.
>
> After elementary school, from 1942 to 1950 I was a student at the Jozsef Attila Gimnazium for Girls. In the summer of 1948 I attended a six-week indoctrination-oriented youth camp learning the ideologies of Marx, Engels, Lenin, and Comrade Stalin (see attached Certificate of Completion). It was there that I became truly aware of the importance of the Party's leadership in building our social democracy and learned to appreciate the tremendous help and guidance our country continuously receives from the Soviet Union.
>
> Upon my return, I was involved in organizing and expanding the newly created Democratic Youth Alliance in our school and was elected as its secretary, a position I held until graduation. I was also active in our cultural group and was frequently invited to participate in the entertainment program preceding political rallies in our city and surrounding villages. A letter of appreciation I received from Party Secretary Comrade Kovacs is enclosed.
>
> In the summer of 1949 I went to work in a tool-manufacturing factory, and learned to handle one of the press machines. Although it was only a summer job, it gave me the opportunity to work hand-in-hand with the workers, sharing their pride, enthusiasm, and determination to help our country to be-

> come a fully industrialized nation. The newspaper published and article about it, of which a copy is attached.
>
> I graduated with honor this year and now I hope to continue my education in the field of . . . [*here she inserted what she wished to study and the reason why*] Upon my acceptance, with deep appreciation for the opportunity given to me to study, I would do my best to gain the knowledge that will enable me to become a highly productive member of our society. Armed with that knowledge, I am confident, that through hard work and sincere dedication I could contribute to building that solid base on which our new social order will stand.

Putting on paper such absurd driveling almost made her gag, but it had to be done. She sent it out to two colleges, both in Budapest—she was not interested in going anywhere else—one to the University of Economics, the other to University of Arts and Science, then she sat back to wait for a reply.

She tried to relax and enjoy the summer, as it would be the last one she was free to do as she pleased. If her applications were rejected, she'd have to start working soon, but even if accepted, she wouldn't have much leisure time during summer breaks. In order to build up hands-on experience, students were required to complete eight weeks of work in the field related to their studies, severely curtailing their vacation. That they were getting paid eased the pain, but only to some degree.

Viktor already received his assignment in the southern part of the country and had only two weeks to spend at home before reporting to work. Now would be a perfect time for Sári to come for a visit, and when he brought up the subject, Jeno and Ilonka raised no objection; they had already agreed to it in principle when they met Viktor's parents. And so, Sári began packing her suitcase, just some casual clothing for a few days in the country with not much else to do but enjoy the fresh air, go for walks, or swim in a nearby creek. For that she didn't need fancy outfits.

After they left Ilonka found the house suddenly very quiet. Sári would be gone only for a week, but she felt her throat tighten thinking of September, when she would be leaving the nest. With Eta, letting go was easier; it came gradually as she and Latzi still lived at home after they got married. She had time to prepare before they moved away, and even after that she still had her boisterous, excitable younger daughter, by nature so much like herself. It would not be the same once she left.

Oh well, perhaps she was worrying about nothing. Perhaps after spending time with Viktor she'd chuck the idea of college, or maybe her applications were rejected. But if not, if she did leave, Ilonka had no doubt she'd be gone for good. She knew in her heart that after leaving Sopron, Sári would never be satisfied to settle back into the confines of their simple small-town life.

Mr. and Mrs. Fodor were waiting at the station when the train pulled in depositing Sári and Viktor. Although Sári knew that they lived in the country, she didn't know what to expect. A village could be tiny, while others could pass as small towns. Viktor never talked much about their place, only kidded her not to expect any glamour, and she didn't want to press him further. She'll have to wait to find out when they got there.

Viktor and his father picked up the suitcases and headed for the exit, while Mrs. Fodor asked if she would like to visit the restroom before they get on the road. Well, that told her something! If they had a way to go, the Fodors must have a car, even though Viktor never mentioned it before. Intrigued, she followed Mrs. Fodor to the street, but instead of a car, she only saw an open horse-drawn carriage with Viktor standing in front, affectionately patting the horses, while a local lad fastened the suitcases to the back. *They must be kidding! A horse and buggy?* she laughed to herself, although she had to admit, the idea of a carriage ride added a touch of romance to the whole scene. Riding in one—a first for her—had an old-world charm about it. In the old days these carriages used to be the mode of transportation for the gentry living on country estates, but she didn't think they survived and still existed in places like this.

Once seated, Mrs. Fodor pulled out two silk scarves, offered one to Sári, and tied the other over her head, saying it would help keeping their hair in place during the forty-minute ride to the house. Viktor laughed when he saw Sári with the kerchief knotted under her chin and kidded that she was beginning to look like one of the locals already. She laughed, too, but didn't find it funny. She always hated scarves and hats, and his remark put her in a defiant mood. Just where were they going? So far she only saw endless farmland and some rolling hills farther back, but not one house, not even a barn.

After about half an hour, the landscape started to change. The hills were considerably higher and greener with patches of dark leafy trees, even the air was cleaner as the horses now kicked up clumps of earth instead of dust.

"We are almost there," Viktor said, patting Sári's hand as the carriage turned off the main road and into a tree-lined lane leading to a large rambling country house with several smaller homes and other buildings around it. Kati and Istvan were waiting for them on the porch with cold refreshments, after which Mrs. Fodor took her to acquaint her with the house. It was quite large with six rooms, all filled with comfortable furniture, and a huge kitchen that took up half of a wing. She then left her in Kati's room to unpack and freshen up before lunch. Sári expected Kati to resent sharing her domain with her, but surprisingly she acted friendly. Perhaps she had finally given up the idea of making Ella her sister-in-law.

Later in the afternoon it was Viktor's turn to show her around the ranch. One building was his father's office, others housed his rangers and clerks and their families, and there were quarters for the farmhands. Farther back stood the stable, a barn, a storage building, and behind them in the open some pieces of machinery. They had electricity, and telephone was installed, but still, the isolation was beyond what she had imagined. The house was impressive, but it was in the middle of nowhere, a good distance from the village, with nothing to do for the week ahead.

As it turned out, her days were filled with activities. For starters, Viktor taught her to ride a horse. She was not afraid of the animals, and after a few lessons she was right at home in the saddle. Most mornings the four of them would ride down to a nearby creek, find a spot where the water was deep enough to swim and then, after a refreshing dip, they would spread a blanket and unpack the picnic basket Mrs. Fodor prepared for them. If the weather was too cool for swimming, they brought along fishing poles, and considering that she never touched a rod in her life, she quickly caught on how to cast for trout. Another day they handed her a shotgun to teach her shoot clay pigeons, but she gave it up after a few tries; skeet shooting, she found, was not for her. Some afternoons the boys teamed up with others from the ranch to play soccer, with the girls cheering them on. There was also a basketball board fastened to the side of the barn, where every hour of the day someone was shooting ball.

On Sunday everyone rode back to the village to attend church, then walked around the little stalls the peasants set up to sell their produce and homemade wares. They'd have lunch in an open eatery, drinking the local wine and listening to a group of musicians playing old gipsy songs. Party functionaries were nowhere to be seen; they stayed behind closed doors, pretending not to see the people celebrating Sunday the old traditional way. Yes, Sári could see that life could be rather pleasant in a small place, if one was old enough, like Viktor's parents. The men would go hunting—there was an abundance of deer, rabbit, and pheasant in the forest, even a young boar would turn up on a lucky day—while the ladies got together playing bridge, gave small dinner parties, and did volunteer work in the village. But at her age she had a lot of living to do before she'd be ready, if ever, to settle into a life such rural surroundings offered.

Sári and Viktor usually took a walk after dinner to get away and spend a little time alone. They talked about the future and what it held for them, but more than talk, they were getting to know each other more intimately. During these walks with no one but the stars watching, their playful, hurriedly exchanged daytime kisses became highly passionate, more ardent and demanding, each leading a step closer to an inevitable surrender. Their moment came on a bright sunny afternoon when just the two of them rode out to their usual picnic place at the creek. They spread a blanket under a tree, and emptying her tote bag Sári began piling towels, magazines, and suntan lotions on it. Finally, kicking off her shoes and ready to change, she pulled out their swimsuits, handing his to Viktor.

Suddenly, her movements slowed and they both grew quiet. It was the first time they were completely alone, not a soul around, and while other times nobody gave a second thought of stripping down to change behind the bushes, now they just stood, hesitant, almost ill at ease. Breaking the awkward moment, Sári nervously turned and started toward the shrubs when she felt Viktor's hand catching hers, pulling her back. Feeling shy and rigidly tense, she kept her eyes downcast, watching as his fingers went to the top of her shirt, working slowly down each button until it fell open. She didn't make a move to pull it together, but stood motionless, and when she looked up into Viktor's face she knew, this would be their time; there was no turning back. And in that instant the crippling discomfort that gripped her until now fell away. She might not know what to do, but she could trust this man. He would be patient, he would teach her. And when Viktor reached for her and pulled her close, she came into his arms, willingly and unafraid.

Shortly after Sári returned home she received the first reply to her college applications, a rejection from the University of Fine Arts. Ilonka saw how disappointed she was, yet secretly hoped that the other one would turn her down, too. Since their last talk, she had given up dissuading her daughter from leaving, but the rejection gave her another chance to bring up the subject one more time.

"I know you feel let down, but it's not the end of the world, Sári; maybe it's for the best. I know we talked about this before, that you want prestige and a better paying job, and I can see it would be important for a single woman, but you will be married to Viktor, a forest engineer with a good future. Isn't that prestigious enough for you? I just can't see why you would want to put yourself through years of studying for something you won't be using. Viktor's job is not going to be in Budapest; you will be living in the country, just like his parents, running the household and raising your children. What would you do with your diploma in a place like that, except hang it on the wall?"

"Oh Mom, not again! We've been through this before," Sári sighed wearily. "I know you want what you think is the best for me, but you just don't understand, it's a different world today. Being married is no longer a main goal in life for women, at least not for me. I want more than to cook and clean house and have a bunch of babies. It made your generation and even Eta happy, but it's not enough for me. I don't want to be entirely dependent on a husband, and only an education could give me that."

"Well, it's true, you always liked to be on your own, doing things your way," Ilonka admitted. She had to smile, thinking of the time when Sári at age eleven went against her wishes and enrolled herself in the gimnazium; perhaps if she had stopped her then, they wouldn't be having this conversation now. "I know I can't change your mind about college, but tell me, why do you have to go to Budapest? Don't they have correspondence courses you could take? You could work here and be with Viktor while you are studying."

"Working to do what? Slinging the power looms at the textile factory like Wanda, or going back to the tool factory? No thank you."

"Now you are being over dramatic! Of course you could find a nice office job; people here know your capabilities. Wanda is a lazy and irresponsible girl, flunking all her subjects; she is not smart enough to get a better job. You can't compare yourself to her!"

"She only flunked Latin and math Mother, not all subjects."

"It makes no difference. You could find a good job here if you wanted to, and earn your degree through correspondence. I even thought that since you don't have a clear vision of what you want to be, why not study forest engineering right here at our university? Wouldn't it be interesting to have the same job, working side by side with Viktor? He could even help you with your studies."

"No, that won't work. Companies don't allow couples to work at the same place. Besides, it does not appeal to me to make a living by looking at a bunch of trees in some godforsaken backcountry. We talked about this with Viktor and I told him, I want to live in Budapest, and he is willing to look for a job there in the Ministry of Agriculture. They need engineers, too."

"Is he doing this just to make you happy?"

"No, it's not just that. He said the reason he went in the military was because he didn't want to live in the country for the rest of his life. Neither of us is crazy about waking up to a rooster crowing. We want to live in the city, where there are things to do and places to go."

"Well, if you have talked about this, and if you both want the same thing, that's a good start. I hope it will all work out for you," Ilonka sighed in final resignation that nothing could keep her daughter home. She just wanted to get away. But what was driving her? There got to be a reason! And as she searched for an answer it occurred to her that insisting to study in Budapest might be just her way to escape. But from what? Is it from home, their small-town life, the city? Looking at Sári with profound sadness, she took her hands in hers.

"You know honey, we always tried our best to provide a loving home for you, and I always thought we were lucky to live in Sopron, a wonderful little city, not too small, not too big, with beautiful surroundings, but the way you are so set on leaving makes me think that you must be very unhappy with your life here, otherwise how could you walk away so easily? It's your birthplace, where you grew up, where your family and friends live. Don't these things mean anything to you?"

"Don't say that, Mom, you are making me cry!" Sudden tears sprang into Sári's eyes as she fell into her mother's arms. Ilonka held her, rocking her gently and patting her back until her sobs subsided.

Still sniffling and brushing away her tears she blurted out, "How can you think that I was unhappy living at home? Or in Sopron; it was a perfect place to grow up." Another wave of sobs rolled over her before she could go on. "I don't really know why I want to leave; maybe the urge to fly the coop is stronger in me than in others, but I want to see what is out there. From here it all seems so exciting, so different, and I want to be a part of that! It's almost like a challenge, like poking an elephant in the ribs to see if I can get away with it." She was smiling though her tears now. "Most likely it's gonna kick me in the head and I'll be crawling back with all my teeth missing, with no more bite left in me!"

Ilonka broke into a smile, too. "Never! Not you, sweetheart! That elephant would probably beg you to poke him again!"

Laughing and hugging they both felt that something was now settled between them. It was here, in her mother's arms, and not in Viktor's embrace near the water's edge that sunny afternoon, that Sári left her childhood behind. And it was also the moment when slowly, painfully Ilonka started to say goodbye to her restless, high-strung girl, so intent on discovering the world, and accept it that she must let her go.

A week later when the postman handed Ilonka a letter from the University of Economics, she took it with mixed feelings: deep inside she still wished for a rejection, yet it would sadden her to see her daughter's hopes and plans come to nothing. Handing it to Sári she watched anxiously for her reaction as she tore open the envelope. But it was neither an acceptance nor a rejection, only an invitation for a personal interview. A decision would be made afterwards.

Sári took the train to Budapest, staying with Latzi's parents. On the day of her appointment she was nervous but everything went smoothly, with most questions aimed at discovering whether she was a good candidate for further ideological development. They knew she had the academic qualifications, but they wanted to be sure she would live up to their political expectations. Dressed plainly, almost dowdy, with hair pulled back, and not even a touch of makeup, she appeared in front of the panel and did her best acting job to convince them that she deserved their trust and was worthy of their investment. It apparently worked, because a few weeks after she returned home she received their congratulatory letter saying she was accepted and with full scholarship at 750 forints a month. It was granted for one year, with renewal pending on the evaluation of her achievements. They also offered lodging on campus, four girls sharing a dormitory room for 300 forints each per month that also included meals, but since space was limited, she was to notify them of her decision within ten days.

It was the farthest thing from Sári's mind to live in a dorm; she knew it from Viktor that it was stacked with quasi-illiterates and spies. Besides, 300 forints was not such a bargain for sharing a room with three others. While she was in Budapest she already asked Mrs. Kontra what were the chances for renting a room somewhere around the college. It would not be easy, she was told, as the shortage in apartments was even more acute in Budapest than in the provinces. Rent for a furnished room ran minimum 300 forints or more, depending on the the size and district, but of course, providing food was never a part of it. Mrs. Kontra promised to keep her eyes open and let her know, but until something turned up, she also offered a couch for Sári to sleep on.

The remaining days of summer were winding down fast, and as the time for her departure approached Sári made the rounds to say goodbye to her friends. Wanda said she was also moving to Budapest the first chance she got, but until then Sári was to write her about everything that made living in the big city interesting and exciting.

"What about your boyfriend? I thought you were serious about him," Sári asked.

"Well, what about him? We are not engaged! And who are you to talk? You and Viktor are practically married, but that does not stop you from leaving."

"That's different; I am going to school, and he'll follow me later when he is finished here."

"So? My boyfriend can do the same if he wants to, or rather if I want him to. Anyway, just make sure you write me as soon as you get there!"

With only three days left Viktor came back to spend the last few days with her. They were together every waking hour, roaming the Loevers in search of secluded places where they could be alone, making bittersweet love under the sky and vowing that distance would never come between them. To make love at home was too risky; they were hardly ever alone, and even then the possibility of someone coming home unexpectedly made them both nervous. They did it only once or twice, but neither of them could relax, and with nerves on edge the comfort of a soft bed was largely diminished.

The last night before leaving Sári started to pack, with Ilonka hovering near to make sure she was taking the right stuff. Already thinking of the colder days to follow, she put a stack of warm, fuzzy underwear in the suitcase, which, of course, Sári put right back in the drawer as soon as her mother left the room. She was almost done when her father walked in. Unlike Ilonka, he had never tried to talk her out of leaving; he thought it wonderful that his daughter wanted to study; ambition and pursuing a goal attested to a strong character. Remembering his own financial struggles when he was in college, he had only admiration for her that she was able to secure a scholarship. But when he saw her packing, he found himself overwhelmed by emotions. It hit home that she was really going and wouldn't be around anymore.

"You don't have to do this, Sári, you know. You can put your clothes back in the closet and put away that suitcase and I would be just as proud of you as if you came home with a PhD."

It touched her deeply, but of course she couldn't stay. She had come this far, how could she give it up now? She cried a little on Jeno's shoulder, her adored, gentle father with his quiet, loving ways that always told her that she was special, that she was cherished.

The next morning Viktor took her to the station to see her off and even got on the train to be with her a little while longer, at least until the next stop. They didn't talk much; they had already made their promises. She sat holding his hand, stubbornly resisting the tears gathering behind her eyelids. What was there to cry about? They both would be busy studying, and then it would be Christmas and she'd be home again to spend the holidays together. She only started to cry in earnest after Viktor got off the train and stood there, waving goodbye until his handsome figure vanished in the rapidly growing distance.

When Sári arrived at Dr. and Mrs. Kontra's, they had good news for her. One of their friends, an elderly couple who had fallen on hard times, had a small room that used to be the maid's in their better days, and they were willing to rent it to her for relatively little money. It was just a tiny room, but the apartment was in a very desirable part of the city.

Their story was sad, but not unique: a once socially prominent military family, now labeled "enemy of the people" by the new regime. The old gentleman held the rank of brigadier general when he retired before the war, while his only son, also a career officer, fought against the Russians until Hungary fell. He knew better than to stay in the country, and eventually found his way to the United States. His parents, getting old and unwilling to abandon their home and some land and a vineyard they owned around lake Balaton, chose to remain—a decision they sorely regretted. To start with, in the spring of 1945 they lost their land to the massive land redistribution, confiscated without compensation. Next, the general's military pension was taken away, and finally the inflation wiped out the couple's bank account. They were in their seventies, unemployable, left without any kind of income, and no one to turn to for help. The only way to survive was to rent out a part of their spacious five-room second story apartment. They already had two medical students living there when they offered Sári the little room at the end of the hall. It had just enough space for a twin size bed, a nightstand with two drawers and a small table and chair, but no room for a closet; she was to use the one out in the hallway. This didn't bother her as long as she had privacy. The rent was reasonable, and when she saw the room she immediately took it.

The location was indeed excellent, near the central part of Pest with easy access to trams, busses, and the metro. To get to the university she only had to transfer once. She quickly learned her way around the city, especially how to get to Vaci Street, where the best shops and intimate bars and cafés were located. Of course, the pre-war glitter and elegance was long gone, but it was still exciting to walk around and window-shop there. Looking didn't cost anything, because that's all she could afford in those inner-city shops; to buy something, she went to the cheap state-owned department stores.

When classes started she soon settled into a quiet routine. Lectures were held from morning till 1 PM, but instead of going home she remained in the library, studying until the mess hall opened for dinner at five. They served three meals a day seven days a week, and staying in saved her from shuttling back and forth just for the evening meal. Food was very simple and cheap. Breakfast consisted of black coffee or tea and a slice of dense dark bread with a piece of pressed jam. Mid-day dinner was always a hearty soup and some pasta, or a casserole made of potatoes and sausage, and a piece of fruit for dessert. Meat was served only twice a week. For supper there were sandwiches with cold cuts and cheese or occasionally wieners. No milk, juice, or soft drinks were available at the time. On Sundays she only went in for the mid-day meal, or skipped even that if Mrs. Kontra invited her to spend the day with them.

She loved every minute of her newfound independence and while she missed her family and Viktor, she never had pangs of remorse for leaving home. If anything, the total lack of feeling homesick made her feel a little guilty. As she promised her parents, she often visited Uncle Sandor's mother, Aunt Mariska, and her daughter Margit, and it was there that she met her second cousin Ferenc Callmeyer, Feri for short, now in his senior year at the Jozsef Nandor Academy of Science. He was from Miskolc, a city northeast of Budapest, the only child of adoring parents. His father, a colonel, died in July 1944, but his widow was left well provided for until they lost all their money to the horrendous inflation after the war. Mrs. Callmeyer managed to survive by selling their furniture, the piano, Persian rugs, artwork, and jewelry—everything they owned—with Feri helping by working during summer vacations. By 1948 she had nothing more to sell and was forced to move into a rented room, while at the same time Feri left for Budapest to study architecture. Because in those earlier years talent and academic excellence were still considered prime requirements to get into college, he was accepted with full scholarship in spite of his unfavorable bourgeois family background. His entry exam was among the best, and he also carried high recommendation from the architectural firm where he had worked during the past two summers.

In 1950, however, as the political scene shifted to the left, his refusal to participate in any form of political activity cost him his scholarship. According to the school committee, his ideological development lagged far beyond expectations, and although he might become a good architect, in their view he would never absorb the Marxist-Leninist-Stalinist ideals, so essential in building socialism. But then, what else to expect of him, coming from an elitist family, a son of a high-ranking officer of the fascist Horthy regime!

Losing financial help hurt him, but at least he was not kicked out altogether, as were several of his equally talented colleagues. One of his friends was expelled when it came to the attention of the committee officials that he falsified his application. He first presented himself as a son of a miner and that he was born in the USSR. This, of course, put him on top of the eligibility list for everything under the sun in 1949-1950 Hungary. Unfortunately, a little digging revealed later that his father was actually the owner of the mine and his birthplace, now a Ukrainian town, was part of Hungary at the time he was born.

Considering that it was an intentional deceit, his expulsion could be viewed justified, but Feri's best friend suffered the same fate for pulling a silly joke. Sitting in the back of the lecture hall, a rather safe spot to go unnoticed, Feri made a ten-forint bet, daring his friend to sit through the class with a thick Stalinist mustache painted under his nose. His friend won, but with dire consequences. The innocent prank was made into a capital offense against the Generalissimo, an unforgivable insult grievous enough to get him kicked out of the university.

The two of them rented a small room and set out to make the best of their pitiful financial situation. In previous summers they both had worked at various architectural firms and now they turned to them for help, Feri looking for part-time work to get him through until he finished his final semester, and his friend hoping to find full-time employment. Feri had no problem; he made enough money to complete his studies and on July 16, 1951 received his diploma. He was promptly offered an adjutant position by one of his professors, but during the approval process the Party stepped in and barred him from teaching. They objected on the ground that with his well-documented apolitical attitude and anti-Soviet sentiments, he would have a corrupting influence on Hungary's future architects. The professor had no choice but to withdraw the invitation, although not before giving him an excellent referral that secured Feri a position elsewhere.

His friend, however, had a tougher time. When it came to light that he was ousted from the university for political reasons, nobody dared to hire him. It took a courageous and kindhearted professor to find a way to circumvent the official Party denunciation that employers were forced to observe, and with his help he was able to get a job. Later, after a turn in the regime in 1953, he was allowed to return to the university and continue his studies, although they didn't make it easy for him. The same people who voted to oust him two years earlier were sitting on the panel to decide whether or not his technical knowledge was adequate to let him back as a senior. Otherwise, he'd lose a year. They informed him that it depended on whether he passed the exams on several new subjects that were added to the curriculum since he left. The start of the new semester was less than a month away and they were certain that he couldn't possibly succeed. But he proved them wrong and a year later proudly received his diploma.

Through Feri, Sári discovered another long lost second cousin, Gabriella, or Gabi. Her mother, Maria Zachar, was the sister of Feri's mother, both of them first cousins to Jeno. Gabi's father, Alajos Posch, the editor of the local newspaper in Ungvar in eastern Hungary (now part of the Ukraine), fell victim to a tragic event at the end of WWI when the city was annexed to Czechoslovakia. On the day the armed Czech occupational units were entering the city, he happened to be in the vicinity where some people started shouting insults at the troops. The soldiers fell on the unfortunate innocent man and left him bleeding to death from more than a dozen bayonet wounds. He was thirty-five years old, his death a senseless killing for being in the wrong place at the wrong time.

His wife, crushed and her heart broken, died shortly afterwards, leaving little Gabi, their only child, in the care of her grandfather. Spoiled, beautiful, and headstrong, she spent most of her summer vacations with the Callmeyer family in Miskolc, until at age sixteen she eloped to marry a Jewish doctor in Prague. The marriage didn't last and they were divorced, but she remained in Czechoslovakia. Only after Reinhard Heydrich, the German Deputy Protector of the country (officially of Bohemia and Moravia) was assassinated on May 27, 1942 and the Jewish persecution began in earnest, did she decide it was easier to return to Hungary than submitting to lengthy procedures to prove to the Czech authorities that she was not Jewish. After arriving in Budapest, it didn't take long for the exceptionally gorgeous woman with cornflower blue eyes and golden hair to find a new husband in Tibor Kalmar, Jr., a well-known composer of popular music.

After Sári met them, she became a frequent visitor in their home. They had a large circle of friends, many of them from the music business. On weekends there were always people at their apartment, listening to record albums smuggled in from the West that Hungarian stores were not allowed to carry. During these get-togethers, Sári heard long discussions about the various American recording artists and jazz musicians, their sound and style all new to her ears since back home her family listened mostly to the music of Strauss and Lehar.

Although she knew of Glenn Miller from the movies, she had never heard of the other famous big-band leaders like Benny Goodman, Tommy Dorsey, or Harry James. It was at Gabi's parties that she became familiar with the voices of Frank Sinatra, June Christy, Ella Fitzgerald and Peggy Lee, although the Four Freshmen and the fabulous Annie Ross quickly became her favorites. She learned some of the songs by heart, such as "The Gypsy," "Sentimental Journey," and "You Belong to Me," hoping that perhaps she could be part of a vocal group Tibor Kalmar was planning to organize. Unfortunately, after testing her, he suggested she'd better stick to studying economics.

The people she met at Gabi's place patronized the small espresso café bars that dotted the inner city, and sometimes they invited her to tag along. These places, like the Paradiso, Anna Bar, and Kedves, offered small-scale entertainment in the evenings, usually a singer backed by a trio. A popular redheaded singer, Ida Boros, drew a large audience singing American songs, mostly in Hungarian translation, among them "Mr. Sandman," "Oh My Papa" and "Autumn Leaves," until someone denounced her as an admirer of decadent music from America and the West. It ended her career; she was never heard singing again.

Years of terror

AS THE YEARS advanced, so did the Stalinization of Hungary. With the totalitarian subjugation of society completed, the early 50s became the darkest period of terror and despotism since the war. Cloaked in the highly developed Stalinist "Cult of Personality," Rakosi now embarked on the systematic removal of people branded as politically undesirable, whose only "crime" was belonging to the wrong social classes. It unleashed an avalanche of deportations that uprooted so many decent people and caused endless suffering and humiliation for the unfortunate victims.

It always began with the dreaded knock on the door in the middle of the night, as Sári witnessed one night in November. She saw firsthand the brutal process of how the Party dealt with those they called "outsiders." Everyone in the house was in bed when they heard the knock and three civilian AVO detectives wearing identical leather coats entered the apartment. They came to conduct a search of the premises, never showing a warrant, although if there was one, no one dared to ask for it. They rounded all of them up in the living room with strict orders to stay put. Numbed by fear and whispering back and forth, they had no idea what the men were searching for. And search they did! They went through every room, methodically opening drawers, cabinets, and closets, shaking out books on the shelves and emptying desk drawers. They took several letters and documents before going to the kitchen to search the cabinets there and check under the sink. They worked without talking much, but that changed when one of them reached the pantry and opened its door. Calling out to the other two, they all became excited; it seemed they found what they were looking for. It was obvious now that the axe would fall on the old couple. After much discussion, one of the detectives came in the living room, ordered Sári and the two medical students to return to their rooms and took the terrified landlords to the pantry.

Then the shouting began.

What they found was a few rods of winter salami hanging from a beam, half a sack of flour on the floor, and a container of lard and a bag of sugar sitting on the shelves.

"Explain this, you black-marketing scoundrels! Oh, you didn't know that hording food is against the law! It's because of criminals like you that we have shortages in this country, why the poor workers still have to live with rationing! But don't worry! The AVO is prepared to deal with people like you! Mindszenty and Rajk were big fish, but the Hungarian people won't tolerate your kind of criminals, either. The evidence here will bring down the wrath of the people on your miserable heads. And it's about time! We have had enough of people like you, an old reactionary Horthyist colonel, and his good-for-nothing wife, who never did a day of decent work in her life! Just wait and see if that war criminal son of yours hiding under the skirt of the imperialist West will come to help you now! You'll get your lessons, rest assured, we'll see to that!"

Sári and the others could hear every threatening word hurled against the poor defenseless couple. What would they do to them? They soon found out. When the yelling finally stopped, the detectives wrote up a report, padlocked the pantry, and told the couple to pack two suitcases each, and be ready by eleven o'clock the next evening. They would be picked up for a little trip to the country, they added with a sarcastic undertone, then left.

Nobody was able to sleep a wink that night. The frightened couple just sat crying. "What is to become of us? Where are they taking us?" was all they could say between sobs. They had no one who could help. All their friends were like themselves, old and from the same rank of "outsiders," most likely facing the same fate, if not already deported. It was pitiful to see them so helpless, but what could Sári and the others do? Offering a few comforting words for sure, but no matter how heartfelt, that didn't bring any consolation.

The next day the old lady told the girls to look through the closets and drawers when they were gone and take whatever they could use; they knew that once they left, they would never see their home again. Then they sat with their four suitcases and waited for the knock on the door. As thousands before and after them, these poor forcibly removed people were taken to remote villages and placed in the homes of the other class enemies, the kulaks—the formerly "rich" peasants made landless and denounced in the 1945 land distribution. If taking away their land was not enough, to have these unfortunate homeless people foisted on them was another form of punishment.

The abandoned apartment didn't stay empty for long. Within the week after the deportation another couple, both in AVO uniforms, moved in with their four suitcases. So this was the reason for ousting the old couple! The AVO needed a nice apartment, most likely to reward one of their men for some extra meritorious service rendered. The AVO officer, judged to be in his mid-30s with a very young wife, immediately gave notice to the two medical students but allowed Sári to stay, for what reason, she didn't know. They even let her have the vacated room, which was much larger and had windows to the street.

As the new landlords settled in, Sári noted that the man often worked at night, while his wife, Vali, had regular office hours. She was a pleasant looking young woman close to Sári's age, a rather shy small-town girl, new in the big city and obviously looking for a friendship with her. At first it was just casual talks, sitting together with a cup of coffee, Vali telling her that she and her husband were practically newlyweds, but when she started to divulge some very personal things about their married life, it made Sári very uncomfortable. Wanting nothing more than a tenant-landlord relationship, she was not about to get involved with problems of such intimate nature and started to make up excuses whenever Vali came knocking on her door to talk. It worked most of the time, except when a few weeks later Vali invited her to their house-warming party that was impossible to refuse. It would be an insult, and they might even ask her to move. While at the party, Sári could observe the couple interact socially, and when she noticed the man downing glass after glass of the fiery Hungarian pálinka, she had no doubt that all was not well between the two. She was more sympathetic to Vali now, but after another outburst of complaints against her husband, Sári simply told her that since she had never been married, she wasn't the right person Vali should talk to. After that her attitude changed; she remained cordial, but the coffee klatches were over.

A few months passed when one evening, studying in her room, Sári heard some moaning, and a minute later Vali staggered through the door, doubled up in obvious pain.

"What's the matter Vali, are you hurt?" She jumped up to help her to the bed.

"I think you better call an ambulance, I am in real trouble," Vali managed to say, her face distorted and drenched in sweat. She crawled on top of the bed and curled up, panting and groaning, holding her knees to her chest.

"Please, go, call the ambulance before I die!" she managed to say through clenched teeth as a new wave of unimaginable pain ripped through her body. Then Sári saw the blood.

"Oh my God, what's happening to you? Shouldn't I call your husband first?"

"No, no, just do as I ask! And hurry!"

By the time the ambulance came she was burning up with fever, her teeth chattering, barely conscious. They checked her into the hospital as having suffered a miscarriage, but the doctors were not fooled. It was an obviously induced abortion; they'd seen it many times before.

The next day Sári went to see her, and after some prodding Vali told her what had happened. Unhappy in her marriage, literally afraid of her husband, she was about to leave him when she found herself pregnant. Keeping the baby was out of the question; she would be stuck in the marriage, and so she never told her husband about it. The problem was finding a doctor willing to perform the abortion, as it was illegal and very few would risk going to jail and losing their license to practice. Even referring to a doctor was punishable. She had to be careful when fishing for information, never at work, and always pretending that it was to help a "friend." Still, whenever she approached the subject, she met with blank refusal.

She was getting desperate when one evening, returning home after a get-together with three of her girlfriends in a café, she found a note tucked in her coat pocket with a phone number and a scribbled message to call regarding her "friend." She knew instantly what it meant, although she had no idea which of the girls slipped it to her. The next day she dialed the number from a public phone booth, and without mentioning specifics, she and the man on the line agreed to meet in an out-of-the-way bar. A young man greeted her and after some cautious preliminaries they turned to discuss her so-called friend's problem. He said he knew someone, a young doctor currently serving his last year of internship, who was willing to cooperate. The fee was 2,000 forints, it would be safe, and if her friend was interested, let him know, he'd set up the appointment. When Vali asked if he could give him some references, the young man spread his hands with a "you can't be serious" expression on his face. No, that was not possible. There must be mutual trust in such matters. They had no guarantee, either, that she was not acting as an informant.

Since there was not much to think over, she confessed there was no "friend," and told him to make the appointment. Two days later they met at the same bar and the man took her to the young doctor's apartment in one of the suburbs. They led her to the kitchen, where she saw a sheet-covered table and next to it on a tray, an assortment of gleaming instruments. Visibly nervous, she handed them the money, then the intern gave her an injection and put her in an adjacent room to relax. She was hardly aware of what happened afterwards, only that they helped her up on the kitchen table. She remembered hearing the sound of instruments clinking but felt nothing more than mild cramps.

It was soon over and with a sigh of relief she got down and finished dressing. They told her to go home and rest; there might be some discharge, but it was nothing to worry about. Feeling woozy and lightheaded she took a taxi home and went straight to bed. Of what happened next, Sári knew already.

Hearing the story, she was just as adamant as Vali that she had been duped, that those two unscrupulous men took her money and set her up for the abortive miscarriage, knowing that she had no recourse whatsoever against them. By going to the police she would have to admit wanting to terminate her pregnancy, which was a crime equal to performing the abortion. She couldn't even confront the girl who slipped her the information, because she didn't know which one did it. She probably got a kickback, and was laughing at her expense! The whole situation was deplorable; she could have bled to death, and the scoundrels would be safe. Vali was just as angry with the law that allowed this to happen! No one should have to go through the ordeal she was made to endure at the hands of such crooks, and Sári agreed wholeheartedly.

Vali swore her to secrecy never to tell her husband what really happened. He only knew that she had an unfortunate miscarriage, and believed Vali when she said she didn't tell him that she was pregnant, because she herself didn't know. He was very grateful for Sári's help, and so was Vali. She knew how lucky she was to find her home when she became ill.

It took a week before she was released from the hospital, and another two before she returned to work. Her emotional healing took longer. It seemed the trauma she experienced left a mark on her. Talking to Sári, she said it taught her to see her marriage in a different light, and she was willing to give it another try. It apparently worked, because while Sári lived there she never heard Vali complaining against her husband again.

Life at college kept Sári busy attending lectures, participating in study groups, doing homework, and going to meetings. She was also compelled to continue the charade of demonstrating her socialist "fervor" by either joining the literary club to discuss and promote the work of current Soviet writers and poets, becoming a member of the "Sunday Brigade," a group of students who "volunteered" to help building new schools or pick fruits in nearby villages, or to participate in cultural activities, such as folk dancing or acting in the amateur drama club. She chose the latter, perhaps for no other reason than to satisfy her frustrated ambition to act. The group produced only highly politicized plays written by a new crop of flatterers, always aimed at glorifying the Soviet Union as the shining example to follow on the road to socialism. They had no entertainment value whatsoever; not even a trace of the old artistic freedom and creativity remained by then. Theaters could only produce dreadfully boring Party-approved plays, which no one was interested in seeing. To fill the empty seats, the Party brought in truckloads of workers, but even they lasted only until the first intermission before slipping away.

The scholarship money Sári received covered her basic expenses—rent, food, books, some college fees, transportation—but not much more. The grant was supposed to help her gain the knowledge necessary to become an educated member of Hungary's new socialist society, and not to buy trendy clothes or pay for fancy hair salons. To buy small personal things, she sometimes sold her meal ticket, either lunch or supper, just enough to buy a pack of cigarettes or treat herself to an espresso in one of the little cafés along Vaci Street. She only smoked when out with friends or at Gabi's parties, but then she could easily finish half a pack. It made her feel more sophisticated to light up and puff on a cigarette, but she never craved smoking.

What bothered her most about not having money was that she couldn't dress the way she would have liked. She didn't have a lot of things in Sopron either, but it was different there. She had to do with fewer dresses and shoes than her friends, but the style and mode they wore was the same. She never felt deprived, or not at par with the current fashion; what she lacked was only a matter of degree. But in Budapest she felt poor and shabbily dressed compared to students who could afford the latest trends, those she wanted to emulate. She saw herself as a provincial country bumpkin wearing her outdated things that no amount of accessorizing could improve. Not that anyone dared to show up in classes in some garishly trendy garb, or God forbid, wearing makeup, and risk denunciation for mimicking the decadent West, but when she heard that some of these fashionably dressed girls, and guys, too, were making comments about her appearance, that she was overdoing her efforts to prove her solidarity with the proletariat, it hurt her feelings. Her only consolation was that from their comments she knew that although she might seem to them like a *proli*—a derogatory expression for someone from the proletariat—she was not thought of as being one.

When Sári returned to Budapest after spending Christmas at home, she took with her a warm comforter to keep from freezing; winter was in full force and she was shivering in her unheated room. Like so many buildings in the city, there was no central heating in the apartment, and those tall, old-fashioned ceramic tile stoves needed substantial amounts of wood or coal that she couldn't afford. She stayed at school until closing time, but when she was home she put on her rabbit fur jacket, pulled a cap over her ears, and wore gloves to keep warm while studying for the upcoming exams.

On one such evening a girl she had befriended at school named Alexa came by to borrow a book and, seeing the Siberian conditions of her room, suggested they could study together at her place. She lived with her parents near the shopping district of Pest and though their apartment was small, it was thoroughly heated, and she had her own room. Since Alexa needed help with her studies, her parents more than welcomed Sári's presence and tutoring in exchange for a warm spot and an occasional dinner. Of course, the girls didn't spend every minute with their noses buried in books; at times they would go down to one of the local espresso café bars and sit with a cappuccino gossiping, watching people and listening to the piano player. In time they became close friends, sharing not just fun, but profound experiences that bound them together throughout the highs and lows of the coming years.

Knowing that only ice-cold sheets were waiting for her at home, Sári stayed with Alexa until late in the evenings. She never slept more than six or seven hours anyway, so going to bed late never bothered her. Still, she tried to get home before 11 PM, the hour when, according to a long established city rule, the main entrance door to every apartment building had to be locked. Only the caretaker had the key, and latecomers had to ring the bell and wait until the grumpy old man, or woman, as in Sári's case, would get out of bed and shuffle to the door to let them in. To compensate for the inconvenience a tip was in order, some small change slipped into the outstretched hand. And this was where Sári usually ran into trouble if she didn't make it home before the door was locked. More often than not, reaching into her pocket, she came up empty-handed, much to the resentful scowl and indignant huffing of the janitor. She had a stack of excuses: missed the tram, her watch stopped, someone needed help, she lost something and had to go back, and so on, but she didn't fool her.

And so, as the cold weather lingered on, Sári's confrontations with the concierge continued until one day it came to a showdown. It started with an unexpected visit from Eta. When Sári saw her sister standing at the door, her first reaction was that something bad had happened in the family, but Eta assured her that everyone was fine; the reason she came was to find out what was going on with her.

"What do you mean, what is going on with me?" Sári was taken aback.

"Well, Mother is very concerned about you and wanted me to check on you."

"I don't understand; they know I am fine. I write home regularly; why should she be concerned? About what?"

"See it for yourself," Eta said opening her purse and pulling out a letter addressed to their parents. It was unsigned and badly written, a warning about the immoral life their daughter was leading, coming home all hours of the night. It was left to their imagination what she must be doing staying out until the wee hours.

Sári knew immediately who wrote it. It had to be the disgruntled janitor, although how the woman got her parents' address was a mystery to her. She told Eta about the reason why she was coming home late and to prove it, she took her to meet Alexa and her family, who backed everything she said. She then took Eta to meet Vali, and when she showed her the letter she laughed out loud, saying that it could only come from the old witch downstairs. Next Sári dragged her sister to confront the janitor herself, demanding to know if she wrote the despicable letter. She denied it but grumbled on about how some people should make the effort to get in before closing time if they didn't have the "appreciation" for the trouble a janitor must go through to let them in.

Eta was relieved, but Sári was upset and before her sister left, she gave her a piece of her mind.

"What really makes me angry is that you and Mother could believe such vicious innuendos. She should have thrown that letter in the trash where it belonged! I think I have the right to expect my family to do that. She should know me better! But if not, why didn't she just ask me? I would have known right away what was this about. Spending money to have you run up here was a total waste. I just hope she had the good sense not to tell father and Viktor about that stupid letter!" She was livid and she let it show.

"No, she didn't and there is no need to get excited," Eta countered. "You can't blame Mother; she worries about you living all by yourself, with the awful thing that happened to your poor landlords and all. It's understandable. And the trip didn't cost anything; she asked me to come by and see you the next time I was up here visiting my in-laws." Then, with a hurt look on her face, she added, "At least you could say that you are glad to see me now that I am here." Hugs and kisses took care of the rest, and realizing that Sári was so short on money that she couldn't tip the porter, Eta tucked a few bills in her pocket, just a little insurance against getting another nasty letter.

This was only a mild example of what power these janitors had over tenants, how they could taint reputations because they carried a grudge for not tipping enough, or held some other grievances against them. This situation became truly frightening when on April 17, 1951 the government issued a decree that made surveillance of tenants a *specific duty* for janitors. In addition to the web of informants spread over the entire country, infesting every city, village, and workplace, even prison cells, now the caretakers became de facto members of the Party's spy ring. Being empowered to report on people living in their apartment building put every tenant at the mercy of the janitors. They could denounce anyone at will; even mere suspicion of listening to Radio Free Europe, a broadcast from the West, in the privacy of one's home was enough to bring about the dreaded knock on the door. And from that day forward the tips grew, and tenants went out of their way to gain the janitors' goodwill and stay in their favor. Whereas in the past most people would hardly bother to talk to a porter unless it was necessary, now they were practically paying court to them. Men tipped their hats with deference and women greeted them with the friendliest of smiles, making idle conversation about their health and well-being.

With fear dominating every aspect of people's lives, nobody dared to complain that rationing was still in effect. It was not due to failed crops, but because of the peasants' reluctance to work in the collectives. When they were forced to give up their land, rather than joining the state-owned co-operatives, they left their villages and went looking for a job in the city. As a result, the output of agricultural production fell; it couldn't supply the government with the amount they needed in foreign exchange—mostly to import machinery to support their vast industrialization effort—and feed the people at the same time.

This rush to develop heavy industry was the pet project of Erno Gero, Rakosi's right-hand man. Following in the footsteps of his Soviet idol, Kaganovich, he swore to transform agricultural Hungary into a country of iron and steel, a process that couldn't be hindered by such trivialities as people going hungry. Let them. Hungary was not France and the year was not 1800. In 1951, revolution was outlawed in Hungary.

And so people ate less but didn't raise their voices in protest. Men and women disappeared for lesser "crimes" in ever increasing numbers, simply vanished without a trace. There was something in almost everyone's background that could be made into a capital case if the Party so desired. Their methods were ruthless and applied without distinctions from ordinary people to ministers and generals, or even those within the Party and the secret police, if they became suspect. It went around in hushed circles that there were only three types of people in Hungary: those waiting to be arrested, being arrested, or sitting in jail. The cells of the notorious political prison at Andrassy Avenue 60 were getting so overcrowded that in order to make room for other victims, the AVO had to create several new concentration camps. Among these Hungarian gulags, where thousands labored under conditions similar to the infamous Nazi death camps, Recsk, a rock quarry in northern Hungary, was the most notorious.

Upon arrival at the camps, the AVO greeted the inmates with the warning not to talk about their arrest, or risk tagging fifteen additional years to their sentence, provided they survived the beating they would get for not keeping their mouth shut in the first place. Yet what absurd stories these prisoners could tell! One man was arrested on mistaken identity, but instead of an apology, the AVO sent him to Recsk to "recuperate" from the treatment he received during interrogation. Another spent two years there on the mere assumption that although he didn't do anything, he would have, given the opportunity. A factory worker was in the camp simply because after listening to speeches about the hard struggle required to build socialism he innocently asked whether they were living in socialism already, or would it get worse?

There were many other victims: former social democrats whom Rakosi never forgave for deserting the short-lived Soviet type regime in 1919; the ex-leaders of the labor movement for insisting on serving the interest of the workers rather than of the State; those army officers who in 1944 had gone over to the Russians to fight the Nazis, only to be accused of being sent to spy; members of the old underground party activists for their nationalistic sentiments and refusing to kowtow to Moscow; the kulaks, so their lands could be taken; factory workers hauled in for some minor deviation only to set an example and intimidate the others by showing what would happen if they got out of line; and countless others with connections to the West sentenced for espionage.

Beatings for the slightest infraction were the order of the day at these camps. For sheer entertainment the guards sometimes picked one prisoner and subjected him to some special humiliation, or another one for regular and systematic beatings that went on for days without any reason. Daily rations consisted of one can of beans with a piece of bread and half a can of water. Hygiene was non-existent; there were no showers since water shouldn't be wasted on rotten traitors, stinking fascists, and Titoist or Zionist pigs. They were forbidden to talk, to keep photographs or books, and to write or receive letters. They were there to work and see if they would survive. The prisoners were allowed twice daily, in the morning and before bedtime, to relieve themselves at the outside latrine, nothing more than a felled log on the side of an open trench, but even there they were watched and poked if they spent more time than the guards deemed necessary.

There was a "health clinic" run by a doctor and an assistant medic, with a clerk assigned to take notes, all of them prisoners. The clerk was planted there as an informer to report any irregularities, such as caring for prisoners who didn't look sick enough, or if he thought the doctor gave preference in treating those accused of being a fascist or having committed acts against the Russians. Medical supplies were at a bare minimum, and in case of a serious illness or injury, the prisoner had to wait to see the visiting doctor, who usually came twice a week. For these outside "specialists," the assignment to serve at a labor camp was itself a form of punishment for some minor offense against the Party, perhaps as simple as showing more interest in the latest achievement in the field of medicine than in the progress of the Five Year Plan. Some of these doctors took their resentment out on the poor patients that sometimes included denying treatment. If the resident prisoner doctor dared to open his mouth to object, he was threatened to have his sentence extended. One time an extremely frustrated visiting doctor lost control and started to scream at the prisoner doctor, who happened to be Jewish: "It's easy for you to talk! You will serve your sentence and sooner or later be out of here, free to go to Israel, but me? I have to stay put, with nowhere to go but hell!" He must have gone just there, because it was the last time he was seen at the camp.

Using informants for a little extra rations, a few cigarettes, or small privileges was widespread in the camps, even though everyone knew who they were. If they were rather harmless, prisoners ignored them, but there were retaliations against those whose reporting brought on severe punishment. It was nothing drastic, a shove at the top of a staircase, perhaps a foot furtively extended to trip them up, all but "regrettable accidents." If an informant had enough and tried to quit, the guards would make his life miserable, and they wound up as pariahs, not to be trusted either by the officials or the prisoners.

At the end of her freshman year, with the exams behind, Sári went home again for a well-deserved few weeks' rest before reporting for her summer work assignment in Budapest. She spent the first week with Viktor at his parents' place, where everyone treated her with the same love and affection as always. Viktor had eyes only for her, yet somehow she felt their time together had lost some of its excitement. She expected the same sparks that flew a year ago and couldn't understand when this time they only sputtered. Viktor was the same loving, caring, handsome self, and she didn't get involved with anyone either, so why the change?

Was it the yearlong separation, or perhaps the way Viktor asked if she had any regrets leaving Sopron, such a wonderful place, he said, compared to the hustle and bustle of Budapest? Was he changing his mind about moving there after he got his diploma? Deep down she knew with absolute certainty that after living in Budapest, village life or even a place like Sopron would never be enough for her. She loved the sophistication of the city and the excitement it offered, and although she loved Viktor, her uncomplicated, down-to-earth man, when she watched him riding through the open fields during her stay, in the back of her mind there was another image, that of the smoke filled cafés full of people sipping espressos, talking in hushed voices, while soft music played in the background. She missed that bohemian atmosphere and the get-togethers at Gabi's house, where they listened to the sound of jazz and discussed the poetry of Francois Villon.

Whenever such opposing images emerged, she tried to suppress them. She'd find a balance between her disturbingly conflicting feelings, she was sure of it. All she needed was another year, until the newness of the big city wore off.

Her mother was right; Viktor was a true treasure, he'd make a wonderful husband, and when she went home she said so to Ilonka. Seeing her commitment to Viktor unchanged, the lingering doubts Ilonka had harbored ever since Sári left, that she would fall for someone whose worldly ways she'd find irresistible, vanished. She knew that sophisticated sort of things always impressed her daughter—for what reason Ilonka could never explain—but after their talk she felt reassured that she had no cause to worry.

During her stay Sári was glad to see that all her brothers were doing well in school. Gyuszi just graduated from the gimnazium with summa cum laude and confidentially was told already that his application to study geology at the local university was assured; written confirmation was a mere formality. Next fall Istvan, at thirteen, would start his third year in secondary school, and Ochie would be in third grade. None of them ever caused any trouble at home or in school, and Sári could see why both Ilonka and Jeno felt so proud of them.

In the evenings everyone played gin rummy, her parents' favorite game, and it was then that Sári noticed that her father's hand, holding the cards, trembled slightly. At times he would also quit the table and head for the bedroom, even though it was much too early to call it a day. Whenever this happened, she detected a faint smell of ether drifting from his room, telling her that not all was well with him. Confronting her mother about it she admitted it was true, although the problem was not his old ulcer now, but the stress he was under, and what it did to his heart. It was the relentless political pressure at the office, the constant demand to politicize everything that was hard on him. He was forced to attend Marxist-Leninist seminars and show enthusiasm to serve the Communist regime, when his whole being hated what they were doing to the people and to the country. Never one to pretend, it was hard for him to live in a world full of lies. When he started complaining about heart palpitations, tests showed that thank God, his heart was fine; it was stress affecting his nerves that caused it. To make Jeno feel better, the doctor gave him some medication that contained ether, and that was what made the whole house stink. Ilonka only hoped and prayed that it would help him to keep calm and in control. The Party was not likely to tolerate it if he didn't learn to adjust. She feared that if he got into some conflict with them, they would just let him go.

Blinking away tears, Ilonka tried not to show how worried she really was about what would happen to them if Jeno, now in his mid-fifties, should lose his job. Struggling with health problems and marked with unfavorable political attitude, he would be unemployable, and she would have to go out and find a job to survive. How did they get to this? What kind of upside-down world did they live in, where hard working people with years of experience and inbred work ethics must live in fear of dismissal?

Sári knew the answer but kept it to herself. She had tried for years to explain to her mother that in order to live in the coming world one must compromise, or at least adapt. Throughout history social changes usually occurred slowly, through the passing of generations, but the Communists had no patience. They wanted their shiny new world now, and those too slow to understand this, had to go. They belonged to another world and as that world disappeared, so must they.

To keep her mother's spirits up, she tried to console her that things couldn't get much worse, and if Jeno could just put up with the prevailing politics for a few more years until he was sixty and could retire, he would be home free. By then she'd be finished with college and would be able to help them with a little money, then Gyuszi would get his diploma and he, too, could contribute something to their finances. Things would work out, just don't lose heart.

When Sári returned to Budapest to start her summer job in the bookkeeping department of an industrial milling company, she couldn't shake the uneasy feeling about what could happen to her father. Every time she opened a letter from home she expected the worst: that the axe had fallen. Instead, it came as an utter surprise when a few weeks later she read that her father was going to be transferred to headquarters in Budapest! This didn't make any sense to her. It certainly was not a promotion; the main office of the customs department was stacked with young politicos. There must be a reason!

And there was. When the Korean War broke out in July 1951, and the government once again launched a campaign asking for "voluntary" contributions to aid the friendly nation of North Korea, attacked by the warmonger imperialists in their quest for world domination, Jeno again declined to make the pledge. He used the same family obligation as an excuse, even colored it with some politically correct-sounding words that he needed the money to ensure that his three sons received a proper education to become productive members of the next generation of workers to serve the country, but this time it didn't work. For party officials striving to achieve 100% participation and collect the highest possible amount of money, any rejection meant a setback, and they were no longer willing to accept his refusal. His case was brought up at the next committee meeting, and while they admitted that he was well liked and his family situation was understandable—one could sympathize with his difficulties—it was quite obvious that he could never be won over to the new ideology. Something had to be done before someone from the higher hierarchy looked at his kader record and asked why he was still working there. What would they say? That none of them had the heart to kick him out with a young family to support and with thirty years of service behind him?

Looking for a solution, someone suggested to transfer him to headquarters; let them deal with the problem and decide what to do with him.

And so, on September 2, the day after Jeno arrived in Budapest, he knocked on Sári's door, bitter and unforgiving for what they did to him. To uproot the whole family and bring them to Budapest was out of the question, but then how was he to maintain two separate households when his salary was hardly enough to pay the bills at home? For the time being he was lodged at the Customs building, but their guestrooms were only for short stays, and soon he must find a place to live.

Sitting down to talk about ways how to lessen the added burden, they quickly came to the conclusion that moving together was the only sensible solution. Although Sári's room was large enough for both of them, and Vali and her husband were willing to let him in without raising the rent, it was not a good idea for Jeno to live there. After all, they were AVO officers, and with only a door in between, they could easily overhear his constant grumbling about the regime. They needed to find another place, but where to start? Jeno called on Latzi's parents and also asked his aunt Mariska for help, and soon she put him in contact with a friend who was willing to rent them a room. The house with a beautiful garden was located in a quiet neighborhood in the suburbs, a bit in the outskirts, but it had good connection to the inner city. Transportation was not a problem; it would just take a little longer to get to the office and to school.

The fact that Sári paid for the room from her summer savings and her scholarship money made Jeno feel angry and humiliated. It seemed he had reached the lowest point in his life, accepting help from one of his children to be able to feed the others. It gnawed at him day and night, especially when he knew how little money Sári herself had. This was not right; she deserved better, but it couldn't be helped. On November 11 he spent his fifty-sixth birthday alone with her, the first time away from Ilonka and the rest of the family. He worried constantly, slept badly, and could hardly eat the food served at the office cafeteria. It was no wonder that he began losing weight. He was always slim, partially due to his ulcer, but now his jacket just hung on him. By the middle of December he was forced to see a doctor, who wrote up a recommendation for a month-long medical leave. When it was granted, Jeno took the train back to Sopron.

During the first two weeks of an illness, employees were entitled to receive their full salary, but after that it was gradually reduced to 50% of earnings. Universal health insurance covered 100% of all medical expenses, but to show one's "appreciation," it was customary to slip an envelope under the table to the attending physician. The same was expected if more than one doctor was involved, or even by nurses, if the patient was hospitalized. Jeno was entitled to check into a healthcare facility for treatment, but he preferred staying home. He knew that the root of his problems was being separated from his family; their mere presence was therapeutic for him. Besides, he didn't care to wake up every morning in his hospital bed with the pictures of Stalin and Rakosi staring down at him.

Ilonka tried not to complain about money, that Istvan and Ochie were fast outgrowing their clothes, and that starting in December food prices were increased across the board. Instead she put on a cheerful face, cooked the dishes the doctor recommended for Jeno, and baked his favorite custard-filled desert. They had a quiet Christmas, just the five of them and the Varosys—Sári didn't come home to save money—and by the first of the year Jeno was noticeably better, gaining some weight, his spirits much improved. All he needed was to be with his family, away from the stress at the office.

. . . .

Unfortunately, time was flying and soon he would have to go back, knowing that his problems would start over again. And when after hardly a month he was home again, Ilonka knew the day would come when he wouldn't be able to work at all. It was a vicious cycle, and sooner or later it would be up to her to provide for the family. Thank God, the boys were old enough now to get by without her constant attention. And as she thought about the day she'd be forced to work outside the home, it suddenly occurred to her, why wait? She might as well look for a job now! With the extra money, Jeno could pay for the room in Budapest; she knew how much it bothered him to rely on Sári for that.

The ideal workplace would be the garment factory only a few blocks from the house, and she was sure she'd qualify as a seamstress. God only knows, all the patching up she did for the children gave her enough experience. And so, right after New Year's, she put in an application, passed the test on the machines, and was told by the manager that pending approval by the committee, she'd be hired. Ilonka went home full of confidence. Her prospects were good; those Party people couldn't find anything objectionable in her past. This would be her first job, she was well liked in town, got along with people, and had learned long ago to keep her opinions private. Also, at age forty-four, she still had eleven years of good work ahead before retirement—fifty-five for women—so there was no reason why she shouldn't get the job.

But she did not. When she went back the next day, the woman on the committee who had the last word in hiring told her that she was rejected as a "class alien"—the newest term describing undesirable elements, only slightly better than "enemy of the classes." When Ilonka asked for a better explanation she said a spoiled wife who never worked a day in her life and whose husband once served the rotten Horthy regime did not deserve a cushy job at their factory. If Madam wanted to work, go and clean toilets, it was about time she learned what real work was all about.

There was nothing Ilonka could say or do, but she knew there must be something more to the rude and spiteful way she was treated. How could she be labeled a class alien when Jeno was still allowed to work? She could hardly wait to get home and tell him what happened. And sure enough, as soon as she mentioned the woman's name, Jeno had the answer. She held an old grudge against him for catching her smuggling something into the country during the war, and this was her perfect moment to take personal revenge.

When her aunt Mitzie heard the story she came to warn Ilonka that from now on she had very little hope of finding a job in the city. Working at the textile factory for years had taught her how things were done these days. That vicious woman had the power to make sure she was not hired anywhere around here. Her best chance would be to try the foundry near Banfalva; it wasn't that far, only a couple of miles from the city, and her son Franz was a foreman there; he could put in a good word for her.

But Jeno wouldn't hear of it. That kind of work was not for women, not for his wife. Let the dust settle, he said, then after a while Ilonka could look for something else. Perhaps Latzi could help; he still had a lot of connections in the city. Besides, there was no real urgency that she would have to start working right now. Things were not that bad; he still had a job to go back to.

But after he returned to Budapest, Ilonka decided to check out the job at the foundry anyway. She knew in her heart that it was only a matter of time before he'd be sent home permanently, and by then the job might not be available. On Franz's recommendation she was hired on the spot; her job would be removing the casting from molds after the metal had solidified and cooled. The next morning she was given a uniform, protective goggles and a hammer, and led to the main floor, where the foreman showed her how to break up the molding material and clean the sand from the metal product.

At the end of the day, with her fingers blistered, dirty all over and smelling of sulfur, she went home crying all the way, a sharp wind whipping at her tear-soaked face. There were times during and since the war when she was down-hearted and felt disappointed in life, but never before did she know humiliation and degradation as she did on that first day at the foundry. She didn't know it then, but that day marked the beginning of a dark journey that ultimately led to her destruction.

Ilonka's foresight about Jeno's situation proved to be correct. Living away from home and with the same worries and under the same pressures, Jeno's symptoms always reappeared and it was inevitable that after repeated medical leaves they would let him go. He was no longer a viable contributor to the great task of building the new Hungary. Had he shown a more positive attitude toward re-education, they could have tolerated his weakened physical condition for the few years left until retirement—age sixty for men—and give him something to do, updating manuals, or training new people, but he was hopeless. With his stubborn refusal to accept changes, any further attempt to indoctrinate him was a waste of time and effort. His mentality was stuck in a lost era, and the party had no use for such people. In view of his age and length of service, instead of firing him, they put him on permanent disability, which entitled him to medical benefits, and after turning sixty a reduced pension.

Sári packed his father's suitcase and said goodbye to him as he left Budapest for the last time. In spite of his dismissal, he was in an optimistic mood. He was going home, he'd be reunited with his family, and once he got better, he would find a way to earn some money. Things would work out, as they always did. If they made it through the misery of the war, they could climb out of this hole too.

Of course, for the time being they would need help. What little money Ilonka made could never pay the bills, so Eta and Latzi stepped in offering financial help. Sári, too, insisted on chipping in as soon as she found a cheaper room and a roommate to share the rent. As before, accepting money from her was hard on Jeno, but it was unavoidable. He swore that once he got on his feet he'd pay her back to the last penny. Living together, he saw how little she had; that the old fur jacket she wore was almost embarrassing with bald spots showing around the shoulders and cuffs. She could buy a decent coat if she kept the money for herself.

As euphoric Jeno felt at first to be back home, his spirits soon sank at seeing how disheartened Ilonka was working in the foundry. She got up before five o'clock in the morning six days a week, walked the miles to work come rain or shine, and after eight hours of hard work came home exhausted and depressed. She usually took a nap, but then she had to start preparing next day's meal for Jeno and the children. On Sundays, her only day off, she cleaned the house, did the laundry and whatever mending that needed to be done. She was always in bed by nine o'clock, secretly crying herself to sleep to spare Jeno from seeing how despondent she was. He could feel a deepening sadness, a hopelessness that spread through the house like a massive poisonous presence, dulling the senses and wilting the smiles even on the children's faces. He blamed himself for loosing his job and not being able to provide for his family as he always have, a feeling that left him angry, made worse by knowing that he could do nothing to change their deplorable situation.

Viktor and his brother were also aware of the prevailing gloom, but aside from sympathizing, there was very little they could do to help. The few times they went home to visit their parents, they always brought back something from the farm, a dozen eggs, a slab of bacon or smoked meat, for which Ilonka was most grateful. Regardless of the help from Eta and Sári, and the rent from the Fodor boys, it became increasingly difficult to pay their bills on time, and when she had to ask the grocer for credit and he refused, Ilonka knew something must be done. And so the day came when, sobbing her heart out, she was forced to say goodbye to her beloved grand piano. They sold it for enough money to pay off what they owed and buy some much needed clothing for the boys, then used the rest to live a little better for a while.

Able to breathe a little easier helped Jeno both physically and mentally to get back on his feet, and by the fall of 1952 he was strong enough to look for work. He made the rounds but sadly, there were no jobs for a fifty-seven-year-old man with medical problems. As so many times before, it was Aunt Mitzie who came to the rescue. She tipped off Ilonka that the old man handling the freight elevator at the foundry was going to retire soon and Jeno should apply for the job. It was easy work, anybody could push those buttons, and wouldn't it be nice that Ilonka wouldn't have to walk to work and back all by herself? And so, when Jeno was hired, the two of them began making the daily trek together, with Ilonka complaining a little less about working in what she called that awful sulfur-smelling hellhole.

The day Jeno received his first pay they stopped accepting money from Sári. Eta was different; they were doing very well and wouldn't miss the few hundred forints they sent every month, but he knew how Sári was struggling. He remembered from his days in Budapest how she turned her head away from looking at window displays. Now she wouldn't have to do without the little things young girls love to have, especially his Sári, always aspiring to look fashionable.

By now she was living with a roommate, a girl she didn't care much about, but the room was cheap and it was closer to school. She wrote home regularly, even though there was not much to write about besides studying, visiting relatives, and seeing her friends in her free time. She wrote about Alexa, that she dropped out of college and was now working as a bookkeeper, and that she was going out with Oszkar Teleki, the goalie of Hungary's most famous soccer team. Amongst the relatives she often visited Aunt Mariska, who tenaciously clung to the hope of seeing her son Sandor someday, even though there was no word of his whereabouts in Russia. She also kept in close touch with her cousin Feri and his girlfriend Eva. They worked at the same place, and it looked like he was getting quite serious about her. Her other cousin Gabi and her husband still held small get-togethers, always full of interesting people. But just who these people were, Sári never mentioned in her letters. Not a word about a certain young man, a musician with a popular band playing at the elegant Bristol Hotel.

Letters to Viktor were similar in content with added sentimentalities typical of lovers separated. Since she didn't come home for Christmas, Viktor decided to take the train and spend a few days with her during Easter break. To his surprise a red-haired Sári greeted him at the train station, although it was not flaming red, only a discreet light auburn shade, just a rinse to give her hair some color. It took him back for a second, but he had to admit that it went well with her eyes of undefined green.

According to house rules, Sári couldn't bring Viktor to her place, even if he was her fiancé, eliminating any possibility for physical intimacy. To his great disappointment they could only meet on dates. She showed him the university and introduced him to Alexa—sporting the same hair color as Sári—who took them to see Oszkar playing at the Fradi Stadium. One evening the four of them had dinner at the Bristol Hotel, where they were seated at a choice table near the bandstand. Well, Viktor thought, sport stars like Oszkar had that kind of clout. Dancing cheek-to-cheek, he held Sári close to his heart, never noticing the subtle eye contact between the handsome blond clarinet player and the girl in his arms.

Viktor had no idea what was in store for him when they said goodbye. A few days after returning to Sopron he received a "Dear John" letter from Sári, breaking their engagement, blaming the distance between them, and how it made her realize that she couldn't make him happy.

It simply broke his heart. He was inconsolable. The betrayal cut to his very soul. Devastated, he stayed in his room, lying in bed, refusing to eat or go out, given to crying as he mourned the loss of the love he held sacred, inspiring, binding. That letter crushed his spirit and destroyed his dreams for the life he planned with her and couldn't imagine without her.

When his brother took the letter and showed it to Ilonka, she almost screamed out loud, *I knew this was going to happen! That silly, irresponsible girl! I just knew she would do something like this once she left home!* She wanted to rush to Viktor, this wonderful, sensitive man, to comfort him, to tell him he deserved better than that heartless, misguided daughter of hers, but Istvan held her back. Viktor needed to be alone. He couldn't face anyone at the moment, and even days later he could hardly talk about the rejection without a mist clouding his eyes. He was deeply wounded and it would take him a long time to overcome his self-doubt and regain the sense of trust Sári so cruelly crushed.

Ilonka's immediate reaction was to take the next train and try talking some sense into her reckless daughter. "I have to find out what happened!" she said to Jeno. "There must be someone she met, or she got mixed up with a wrong crowd that made her change her mind. Perhaps it's not too late to make her realize what a mistake she is making by tossing a man like Viktor aside. You know as well as I what an exceptional young man he is, solid as a rock in his feelings for her. He never once stayed out since Sári left home; she just doesn't realize what a wonderful husband she would have in Viktor! He does not run around chasing skirts, doesn't drink; he is loyal, an educated man—simply a picture of a perfect family man that is the dream of every woman! And she throws it out of the window!"

She thought about the time when they first met Viktor's parents, how she made an almost humiliating effort to excuse the rather shabby look of their home, trying to convey that regardless of their current setbacks, Sári was a well-brought-up girl. There was no doubt in her mind that Viktor could easily marry a girl whose parents were better off than they were, who could provide a dowry, or at least more than what they were able to give Sári. Yet, he wanted her, and she couldn't appreciate it.

"I just can't get over what she has done," she kept repeating to Jeno. "She was always impulsive, rash at times, doing things without considering the consequences, but I never thought she would let Viktor go! Didn't you notice any signs that this was coming when you two were living together in Budapest? She must have talked about Viktor; didn't you catch a word here and there that would hint at the change in her feelings?"

But Jeno said there was no indication whatsoever. The breakup surprised him just as much, affecting him as deeply as it did Ilonka. He genuinely liked Viktor and greatly regretted losing him. He discreetly waited a few days before knocking on his door, not to try to console him with banalities, that he was better off that this happened now and not after they were married, but to apologize for the way Sári behaved. That she had a change of heart and broke off the engagement was regrettable, but it could happen in any relationship, he told him. What made it inexcusable was the cowardly way she chose to handle it. She should have told Viktor face-to-face when he visited her recently; she must have known her feelings already then. Writing a letter was callous, insensitive, and cruel, and for that he was deeply sorry.

Ilonka was still determined to go and see Sári immediately and try to turn her head around, but Jeno talked her out of it. "What would a dressing down accomplish, Ilonka? We both know that once Sári has made up her mind it is useless trying to change it."

In the end she gave up the idea. "You are right," she admitted, "she won't listen to me. She never did, so why would it be different now? Let's just hope that given time she'd realize what a mistake she made, and that it wouldn't be too late."

But the letter they received a day later confirmed what they feared, that Sári's decision was final. She didn't explain a lot, only that during Viktor's visit he admitted that he didn't want to live in Budapest. He said the pressure was much higher working in the central planning office, he would have to sit in endless meetings, and he'd much rather live in the country, working in his profession with less stress and decidedly less politics. He also thought that for a newly married couple it would be easier to start life in a smaller place, which would also be better for raising children. All true, Sári admitted, except she would never be happy tucked away somewhere in the middle of nowhere. She loved Viktor, but their preferences in lifestyle turned out to be so different that to ignore it would be a major mistake. The question of children also came into play. She could see having one, maybe two, for his sake, but definitely not more, while he wanted a bigger family. Staying together would have meant compromising, one of them giving up dreams, and in the end neither of them would be happy.

She didn't act impulsively, she wrote, but weighed all the pros and cons before deciding. She knew that writing the letter was insensitive, but she was afraid that if she told him face-to-face Viktor would have been able to sway her, make her back down. And that by itself would have cast a shadow over their marriage; it would have left a lingering doubt in him, that if she were ready to leave him once, she would do it again.

What Sári said was entirely true, but there was more to it. She never mentioned that the young clarinet player she met at Gabi's had become a part of her life, not physically at first, but shortly after she made up her mind to break up with Viktor. The attraction was there from the start, especially for Sári. She never forgot Rudi Somogyi, the beautiful young boy who once, when she was fifteen, taught her to dance the swing but never bothered to ask her again. His image was forever imprinted on her adolescent mind, and while the picture might have faded during the passing years, it never truly disappeared. It all came back, the chiseled face, the blond hair and blue eyes, the certain aloofness, when she first set eyes on Adam Koltay.

Just as Ilonka got over the shock of Sári's breakup, the postman put another letter in her hand. It brought sad news: Erno Riedl, only twenty-four years old, had died in a tragic accident. After several operations and lengthy physical therapy he had completely recovered from his leg injury and was back at the local swimming pool, doing what he always loved best: swimming and diving. It's ironic, that after surviving the war and the gulags, he would meet his ultimate fate where no one imagined anything could harm him. Enjoying his recovered athletic prowess he was diving from a five-meter platform and by misfortune landed on someone swimming underwater. Swimming pools in small towns like the Riedls' didn't have chlorinated water in the 1950s, making it impossible to see below the surface. The impact broke his neck, leaving him paralyzed for life. Perhaps it was for the best when a week later he suffered a coronary thrombosis that killed him. Devastating as it was, even his parents agreed that had he lived tied to a wheelchair, such life for this once vigorous, athletic young man would have been no life at all.

Ilonka was almost afraid to open the third letter she received, this time from Eta. She was not superstitious, but the old saying about bad things come in threes put her on alert. As it turned out, what Eta wrote could be interpreted either good or bad, depending on one's political perception. From Latzi's point of view it was painful: he was ousted from the Party and was told to render his resignation. He was a good Communist yesterday, but overnight had turned into a class enemy. Someone—probably a co-worker envious of his job—started digging into his background and came up with the accusation that he deliberately misled the Party by hiding the fact that he had an uncle who had been a colonel in the old gendarmerie. Nothing could be more damaging in the eye of the Party than having a relative who belonged to that quasi-military force, a small mounted and armed peacekeeping unit during the Horthy era with the primary duty of maintaining order in the rural parts of the country. They put down noisy disturbances, subdued drunkards, and settled petty disputes between peasants so fights wouldn't get out of hand. Although respected by the peace loving and disciplined members of the community, they were feared by those on the other end of the stick. Condemned by the Communists as sadistic peasant-beaters, the worst kind of chauvinist and fascist pigs, their unit was abolished after the war and any gendarme caught was sent to concentration camps, where the guards were encouraged to treat them with exceptional cruelty.

This high-ranking fascist relative of Latzi was only a distant family member who disappeared when the war ended. It was all news to Latzi when the Party confronted him with details about his whereabouts: that he lived in Toronto, Canada, what his address was, where he worked and in what capacity. Considering that hiding such a relation was enough to pin some far-fetched conspiracy charge on him, Latzi was lucky that they only stripped him of his party membership and kicked him out of his job. They had to get out of the house, too, and until they could figure out what to do next, they put their belongings in storage and moved in with Latzi's parents in Budapest.

As for Jeno and Ilonka, they felt sorry for them, but in a way they hoped that perhaps this would sober him up and make him see the ways of his beloved Party. Free of political involvement, he could now concentrate on finishing his studies and getting his degree. He could easily do it if they came back to Sopron. Ilonka even offered to make room for them, but Eta wrote that Latzi had already gotten his diploma a year ago and was now looking for work in the field of his profession. The next time they moved, it would be where his job was. And when Ilonka offered to send some money, the same way they helped Jeno when he was out of work, they declined that, too; they would manage on what savings they had.

When Sári heard what happened, she went to see them right away. She expected to find them bitterly disappointed, but to her surprise, Eta was almost relieved and Latzi quite resigned. During their talk Eta, who nurtured socialist sentiments but was never fully comfortable with her husband's total dedication to communist ideology, willingly admitted that to her it was a blessing in disguise that Latzi was out of the Party. Now he could start doing what he set out to do ten years ago, plant trees and manage woodlands. But Sári's jaw dropped when instead resenting what the Party did to him, her brother-in-law said they had all the right to kick him out.

Was he crazy? His family could be on the street, and he found excuses for those party fanatics who branded him a class enemy after picking his brain for years! She couldn't believe that Latzi could justify their action, insisting that it was all his fault; he was to blame. It didn't matter that he was not trying to hide anything, he simply forgot mentioning his uncle when writing the required annual bios. He was always a distant figure, and for years no one even knew if he was dead or alive; it's no wonder that he overlooked to include him as a family member. Regardless, he could see why the party viewed it as a deliberate deception; it was understandable that they lost faith in him and could not trust him any longer.

Luckily, within a month he found a job working as a forest engineer in Debrecen, a large city in the eastern part of the country. It didn't come with a house like in Szekszard; the bombing of Debrecen during the war was very destructive and the housing shortage was still acute, making it hard to find a suitable place for them. They had to settle for a small flat, but it was close to the school where little Latzi would be starting kindergarten in the coming fall.

Sári finished her sophomore year and learned before she went home for her customary two weeks' vacation that her scholarship would be extended for the next year. Viktor and his brother were gone by the time she arrived, and as expected, they gave up the room; they wouldn't be back in the fall. The day-to-day contact with Sári's family after the breakup became too strained for them to stay. Ilonka and Jeno couldn't blame them, but they were truly sorry to see them go. They were ideal tenants, quiet, reliable, never late with the rent. They would be sorely missed.

Their departure also resurrected Ilonka's fears about sharing the house with strangers, and she knew, in order to avoid it, they would have to find new renters come September. Talking about it, Sári suggested why not take in girls this time around, and why students? Ilonka wouldn't have to wait until the fall; there were plenty of girls from the countryside who worked in Sopron and would love to rent the room right now. These girls usually went home on weekends, and wouldn't that give her parents a little more privacy? The more Ilonka toyed with the idea, the more she warmed up to it. Then she went a step further. What if she changed the rooms around? If she reclaimed their old bedroom and rented out the large front room, she could take in several girls. With the grand piano gone, she had enough space there to accommodate four people, instead of just two.

And so once again, she rearranged the furniture, set up four small beds without overcrowding the room, and in no time she had all of them rented. It was an excellent idea, not only for collecting twice as much rent, but on weekends the girls brought back from their villages things she needed, fresh produce, eggs, fruits and other items for half what they cost in the stores. She had to give them kitchen privileges, although they used it very little; they ate their main meal of the day where they worked, and if they did cook occasionally, she saw to it that they cleaned up afterward.

Before Sári returned to Budapest to start her summer job, Ilonka couldn't resist bringing up once more her breakup with Viktor. It was not to reproach her anymore; the affair was over, but she told Sári how hard it was to see him suffer, how much he must have really loved her.

"You know, Sári, I always had the feeling that you were never head-over-heels in love with him. I think you were more impressed by his attention. You were too young when the two of you met and couldn't appreciate what he had to offer. You will live your life as you wish, but one day you might look back and realize what you lost when you wrote him that letter. I believe that everything people do, good or bad, has an impact on their life. I just hope you'll be spared the same kind of heartache you caused that poor man."

"Was he really that distraught? I never thought it would affect him so much, and I am really sorry for it. But I think you are right, I was impressed that he picked me over his sister's best friend. I mistook that for love, and perhaps was in love only with the idea of love itself."

"I still think it would have worked if you had stayed home. I prayed you wouldn't leave. That's why I didn't interfere with your carrying on with him right here in the house."

"What do you mean carrying on?"

"Oh, come on, you think I didn't know what went on between the two of you? And that is something that worries me now. You say you didn't get involved with anyone since you left Viktor, but I am sure you don't live like a nun, either." She raised a hand when Sári opened her mouth to protest. "I know what you are going to say, that it's none of my business how you live your life. And it's true, you are on your own, but just don't show up here one day with a baby in tow!"

"Why, Mother, I thought you loved babies," Sári gave a chuckle. "But fear not, that won't happen. I had enough of looking after babies while I was growing up. Settling down is the farthest things from my mind right now. I am only twenty-one, Mom! I am not ready for that. I see you believe in karma, and if it's true, and I have to pay for my mistakes, well, that's part of life. I only hope I will learn something from it. You must have made some mistakes, too, didn't you? Do you ever have regrets?"

"Regrets? No, not really, I was lucky to find a husband as wonderful as your father. I loved him from the moment we met, and I still do. It's a miracle that being as quiet as he is, he has put up with my loud mouth and impatient nature for all these years. But he did, bless his heart. I'll never stop thanking God for putting him in my life. And I was blessed again to have such good children. All of you—there was hardly a time when we had to make you stand in the corner. Well, that was that one time when you and Gyuszi jumped on the piano and scratched it up pretty good. I do regret punishing you so harshly, though you deserved a good spanking."

"That we did. I should have listened to Eta; she said we were gonna get it!"

They laughed over that long ago incident and kept on reminiscing about days gone by, but then Ilonka grew quiet. "Ah, we had such a nice life. If I had to do it over again, I wouldn't do anything different. No, I take that back, we had such nice life until the war, and even then, it was not so bad until the December bombing. But from there on everything went downhill. Look at us now, your poor father and I working in that stinking hellhole. We didn't deserve that . . ."

Her voice trailed away and she stopped talking altogether. She sat there, staring at nothing, hearing Sári's soothing, encouraging words but unable to respond. Taking her mother's hand, Sári, too, lapsed into silence. What could she say? The old world her mother clung to was gone, and although she herself was also born into that era, luckily it passed while she was too young to be left with the same sense of loss. She would always remember the warm days of her childhood, the happy laughter, the glow of Christmas trees. She would forever cherish the memory of those early days, but unlike her mother, she didn't dwell on what once was, or mourn the passing of that old world. Hers was a new world, a different world with different challenges.

It never occurred to her then that someday her new world would also become old, that the day would come when she, too, would look back, feeling the same nostalgia and longing for the past as her mother did now.

The last thing Sári did before returning to Budapest was to go to the police and change her residency status. Until now, she had kept Sopron as her permanent address because it allowed her to come and go freely, while non-residents were denied unrestricted entrance to the city and its surrounding area as the government's latest effort to seal off the western border. It seemed that barbed fences, watchtowers, and minefields were not enough deterrents to keep people from attempting to flee the country, so they created these restricted buffer zones where people from outside areas could only enter with special permits. Requests for entry were scrutinized and issued on a per visit basis, with the applicants closely watched during their stay.

The reason she was willing to submit to such annoying procedure was to obtain permanent residency in Budapest. That is where she lived and wanted to stay when she finished her studies, but the city was getting overcrowded with thousands of new people pouring into the capital, and rumors circulated that it wouldn't be long before residency would be curtailed. Budapest was the most desirable place to live for many. For the workers the lure was the big factories, and the same for the peasants deserting the collectives. The best office jobs and the most prestigious universities were all there, and generally life seemed less dull than in the provinces. Young people were especially drawn to the excitement the big city offered. The problem was where to house all these newcomers? Apartments vacated by the political deportees went only to Party members and to the AVO. The uncontrolled influx couldn't go on forever. Sooner or later the authorities were bound to set up preferential quotas, listing certain categories of people they'd allow to settle in Budapest, and when they finally did it, and the list included full-time college students, Sári was ready to rush and formally register.

She loved Budapest, both sides of the city, for different reasons. There was romantic Buda in all its historical grandeur, dominated by the Royal Palace, the ancient Coronation Church, and the Fishermen Bastion that offered a peek-a-boo view of the Pest side through lace-trimmed arches and turret windows. Two thousand years ago the city was called Acquincum, the capital of Pannonia, a small frontier Roman province, enclosed by the remnants of the Alps on the West, the Danube on the north and east as the river makes its ninety-degree turn to the south, while the Sava river formed the southern border between Pannonia and another Roman province called Dalmatia. The Roman occupation lasted from 20 AD through the middle of the 5th century, when the Huns and other diverse nomads from the East began pouring over the borders of this distant outpost of the Empire. These invasions, however, couldn't dim the vivid picture the Romans left behind of their rich life and culture: an amphitheater, artifacts to fill a museum, and a Roman bath fed by the natural hot springs bubbling up from the deep and still feeding many of the city's current spas. There were other historical remnants from subsequent foreign conquests, most notable a Turkish mosque and minaret from the ruinous Ottoman occupation that lasted from 1526 to the end of the 17th century. One of their thermal bathhouses was still in use, known as the Rudas bath. Not all was old in Buda, however. There was the elegant new Gellert Hotel with its Olympic size indoor swimming pool, a spa, and a huge outdoor pool with artificial waves that in the summer delighted children and adults alike.

Pest, across the Danube, also had its attractions: the famous Parliament Building, the Chain Bridge, and Heroes' Square with its impressive Millennium Monument. It was erected in 1896 to commemorate the founding of Hungary ten centuries ago in the year 896, and consisted of several components all merging into one imposing unit. At the center rose a 118-foot high obelisk, topped by the statue of the winged Archangel Gabriel holding Hungary's Holy Crown. At its base, mounted on a large pedestal, stood the equestrian statues of Chief Arpad and his seven Chieftains, portrayed as Conquistadors arriving at the Carpathian border to take possession of the land that became Hungary. The base was then flanked on each side by semi-circular colonnades with statues of Hungary's most outstanding kings, princes, and national heroes.

And there were the museums and theaters, the opera house, and all those splendid shops on Vaci Street that were truly Sári's favorites. Now that her parents no longer needed financial help, she could keep the money she earned on her summer job, and when she strolled along the shops, instead of just window-shopping, she could actually walk in and spend a little on herself.

Adam liked flashy looks in women, like the singers he worked with and the girls working as bartenders, wearing lots of makeup, and alluring dresses. She, of course, couldn't keep up with them on her budget, but to avoid wearing the same outfits, from time to time she borrowed some of Alexa's. They were the same height and had similar skin tone and hair color, so much so that people on meeting them assumed they were sisters. The only thing that didn't fit her was Alexa's shoes—a size and a half smaller than hers—and so, no matter how careful she was with her money, when it came to shoes, she spent more than she could afford.

At work, of course, she only wore plain skirts and shirts and no makeup, looking the same dowdy self as in school, since there were other students from her class working in the same office. Still, it was unavoidable that some of them would see her sitting near the bandstand at the popular Grand Hotel on Margit Island where Adam's band played that summer, looking glamorous sipping a cocktail and holding a long cigarette holder, as she waited for him to finish work. Naturally, gossip spread about the changes in her appearance, and while some thought that dressing a little showy outside the office was her business, others found it unbefitting for a young college student, especially when supported by financial aid.

Sure enough, when classes started in the fall, she heard rumors circulating about her leading a "double life": that while she presented herself at school as a struggling student trying to get by on scholarship, on the outside she masqueraded wearing garish makeup and gaudy clothing mimicking the decadent West. It all came to a head after a weekend spent with Adam, when she woke up Monday morning and realized that she was out of nail polish remover and had to attend classes with her nails painted bright red. She tried to be inconspicuous, but as her luck would have it, she was called to the blackboard where everyone could see the damning evidence of her duplicity.

The next day, while sitting in the large lecture hall, several members of the student council, all Party people, marched in and, interrupting the professor, announced that they had received angry protests from students who had witnessed a disgusting display of decadent behavior.

"Comrades, there is among you someone who deceitfully pretends to have embraced the ideals adherent to building our new society, free of degenerate Western culture. Her mask fell, however, revealing the truth that instead of rejecting it, she admires and imitates the shameful and corrupting ways of the West. It became apparent when she showed up in class with her fingernails painted red and proceeded to flaunt them frivolously, without regard to how offensive her Western mimicry was to the others. In their rightful indignation, they are adamant that such a two-faced hypocrite has no place among them, especially in view that this person is a recipient of generous grant from our government. It was given to her in the belief that upon graduation she would join the ranks of the hard-working ideologically conscious millions, and would take her place in the struggle to strengthen our still vulnerable young People's Democracy, but instead of appreciating the opportunity, she repays it by such inexcusably repulsive behavior."

An immediate grumbling broke out with intermittent shouts demanding to know who this brazen, despicable opportunist was. To Sári's horror, sitting in the back with her shoulders hunched, she heard her name, a voice calling for Comrade Zachar to come to the podium. She stood there amid indignant exclamations, pilloried in front of the entire class, damning her—and for what? Putting on nail polish? This was insane! She was twenty-one years old, for heaven's sake, and yes, she loved to wear makeup and nail polish; it shouldn't be a crime! They expected her to make a tearful public confession and plunge into the typical chest-beating, guilt-ridden self-criticism that everyone practiced, even if they had to invent some misdeed to apologize for in order to demonstrate remorse and submission to the Party.

But she robbed them of the satisfaction. Anticipating a confrontation—although nothing of this proportion—she was ready with a concocted story.

"There is an explanation for this unfortunate incident that hopefully will make it clear to the Comrades that any offense I might have caused them was unintentional. I am a member of an amateur theatrical group, acting just as I do here in our own cultural group, and I was appearing in a play on Sunday night portraying a decadent American girl, a role that called for wearing makeup and nail polish. Only when I got home did I realize that I forgot to remove the polish, and for that I am sorry. Since I am not in the habit of painting my fingernails, I didn't have polish remover at home, and no stores were open at that late hour to buy some. In the morning I had two choices: either wait until a drugstore opened and be late for an important class, or come in with the hideous lacquered nails. What was more important? I chose the latter, and that is the truth. I hope the Comrades now have a better understanding of what caused this regrettable mishap for which I apologize. I promise, it will not happen again."

She doubted that anyone believed her, but the boos and heckling died down and finally the ordeal was over. The committee left, Sári went back to her seat and the lecture continued. Yet she knew that the incident would have further consequences. There was more to come. And she was right: later in the afternoon she was summoned by the committee to be told that regardless of her excuses, her behavior was a great disappointment to them, and that since she apparently had an acting job, starting November 1 her scholarship would be reduced to 250 forints a month. When she protested that she was not paid anything for performing, they said she should consider herself lucky to be allowed to stay at all. She was dismissed with a warning to mend her ways.

They need not have worried. With her scholarship cut and savings from her summer earnings fast disappearing, she had no money to spend on foolish cosmetics. She could stretch her finances until January, but after the mid-term exams she was left with empty pockets. She knew she had no choice but to quit and start working if she didn't want to starve, and so even before the exams, she began looking for a job. She approached the office where she had worked during the summer and when they offered her a position in accounting, she requested a six months extension at school. It was granted without objection; she could come back in the fall, but her scholarship would remain reduced.

Her parents took the news with regret, but Ilonka wrote that they, too, had noticed the change in her appearance during her visit in June. They didn't mention it then, but they thought it projected the wrong image, and perhaps it was time to tone down the makeup, forgo tinting her hair and stop wearing tight skirts with slits a bit too high. On the other hand, they consoled her that at least she could continue her studies in the fall semester, not like poor Viktor, who was kicked out in the middle of his final year, just a few months before getting his diploma. They discovered that he lied on his college application about his military background: that instead of being a private, drafted into the army during the war, he was a graduate of the fascist Ludovika Military Academy, and was commanding troops on the Eastern front. Who could tell how many heroic Russian soldiers had to die because of him? By his deceitful and cunning cover-up he had managed to defraud the State and usurp the trust the People's Republic placed in him. His shameful and deliberate lie deprived a more deserving comrade the opportunity to get a higher education, and for this he was no longer tolerated at the university.

Sári was truly sorry about Viktor's expulsion but at the same time she was glad that she had broken up with him before it happened. What if she had waited until now? Everyone would think that his ousting made her change her mind. At least he knew it was not the case.

The day she read Ilonka's letter about Viktor's misfortune, coming on the heels of her own incident with the nail polish and its consequences, was the first time she began to feel real hatred toward the system that forced people to lie so they have a chance for a better existence. She felt a deep disgust for a regime that would punish people like Viktor for their background, or having the "wrong" relatives as in Latzi's case, and dismiss breadwinners like her father because they had no more use for them. And the way they treated her mother, denying her the opportunity to work in a decent place, was simply unforgivable. They didn't care what happened to people, to their families, to the children, when they condemned them to a lesser quality life from which there was no escape.

By using discriminatory practices against what the regime regarded as unwanted segments of society, the Party meant to widen the wedge between the working classes and the old intelligentsia, and there was no end in sight when they would be satisfied to have purged the country from all such "harmful" elements. In fact, they kept discovering newer channels by which, through treachery and espionage, the enemy was able to penetrate the Party. According to the latest rumors, Gabor Peter, the head of the dreaded AVO, fell under suspicion for involvement in a plot against Rakosi. He was to play a major part in a new trial, this time in the framework of a Zionist conspiracy, and in preparation to collect evidence against him they began taking into custody a score of his fellow officers, many of them Jews like Peter.

His arrest came on January 2, 1953, with Stalin's personal go-ahead. The Generalissimo himself was building a similar case in the USSR that involved doctors plotting in concert with the CIA-financed international Jewish Zionist organizations to poison him, the members of the top Soviet politburo, and the leaders of the military. Stalin by then was so paranoid about physicians that he would only consult veterinarians about his health. Originally, thirty-seven of the most prestigious and prominent Russian doctors were charged as depraved "saboteurs" plotting under the mask of caregiving, but hundreds of others were arrested to extract confessions and line up potential witnesses. One of them was Fyodor Byelkin, a former Soviet expert in staging show trials, who in 1949 was sent to help Gabor Peter in organizing the case against Rajk, and was now hauled in jail to testify against him. According to Byelkin, while working together Peter tried to recruit him into an espionage ring in the service of the British and Zionist intelligence. The former AVO chief was further incriminated when during the search of his home the detectives discovered a photo of him together with Allen W. Dulles of the CIA. It was taken in 1945 in Switzerland, where he was a member of the Party delegation negotiating the extradition of war criminals, but now the purpose of his participation there suddenly became a covert ruse to establish contact with the CIA.

And so the relentless hunt, the senseless accusations, the widespread terror of Rakosi continued. Since June 1951 tens of thousands under various labels had been exiled to internment camps on the assumption that it was better to sacrifice a hundred innocent people than to let one of the "enemy of the people" escape. Everyone lived in fear of something or someone, terrified by the threat that hung over everyday people as well as high Party officials. Men and women rose in the morning with dread and went to bed fearing the next day. Added to the gloom was the bitterness and frustration that all must be endured in silence. There was no venue to lodge the slightest protest, to speak up against the cruelties, the rising prices, lack of consumer goods, or the increasing poverty. To raise one's voice was not permissible.

No one escaped the pressures to conform to Party dictates, not even musicians, including Sári's boyfriend Adam and his band. They were accused of playing decadent Western music, but when they switched to old-fashioned waltzes it brought another charge, that of trying to bring back the Horthy-era music. Such sentimental schmaltz, they were told, had long lost touch with the masses; it only played to the petty bourgeois, stirring up their nostalgic longing for a past that was better left forgotten! It had no redeeming value in socialist society, thus had no right to exist. They were given a list of Party-approved music, while singers were forced to use songs with stupid lyrics about young lovers happily working side-by-side and dreaming of the wonderful life awaiting them in the future socialist world.

That's when Adam started to talk about wanting to escape to the West. He had enough of living in a country where every step must be considered and every word chewed over twice, or risk taking the consequences. Sári must know the forest trails around Sopron that led to the border, and didn't she say her cousin skied over the fence and minefields and made it to Austria? With a good plan they could do the same! But Sári wouldn't hear of it, although she said she would be the first to leave if it was possible. She explained the difficulties in getting to Sopron, let alone the area near the border. Faced with reality, Adam reluctantly gave up the idea, but after that seemed to carry a chip on his shoulder, a resentment against Sári, as if it was her fault, not the system's, that he was stuck in this godforsaken country.

And then, in this atmosphere of fear, frustration and distrust came the news on March 5, 1953 that Joseph Stalin, the great leader of the Soviet Union and the beloved father of all socialist countries under his wing, was dead. All work stopped as Party officials, with grim expressions, some with tears in their eyes, appeared in factories, offices, in every kolkhoz and school to announce his death, which was decried as the greatest loss of the 20th century. During the five minutes of silence that followed, intermittent sobs could be heard, but soon a buzz of subdued denial rose, people asking if it was really true, or was it just another diversionary tactic of the enemy? How could he be dead, when there was no prior sign of illness? The speculations ceased only when it was officially confirmed that Stalin had suffered a cerebral hemorrhage, a stroke that paralyzed the right side of his body and ended his life a few days later at the age of seventy-four.

Although work was suspended and people were dismissed for the day, free to go home and listen to the radio for further announcements, the committees didn't disperse those seemingly grief-stricken people who stayed on to lament over Stalin's death, or stood around in stunned disbelief, discussing what repercussions his passing would have on the country. At the same time the committee duly noted those leaving, an indication of lacking interest to participate in such public display of sorrow.

By the time Stalin was embalmed on March 9 and put to rest beside Lenin in a transparent enclosure in the Lenin Mausoleum, rumors were flying that the great leader was poisoned. Although it was never confirmed, suspicion shifted to Lavrentiy Beria, the feared chief of the Soviet secret police. It was well known that after Molotov was disposed of in a previous purge, next in line to fall from grace was Beria, along with Khrushchev and other high-ranking members of the Politburo. Stalin, in his schizophrenic mind, felt threatened by Beria's increasing power and planned to remove him by making him part of the Jewish Doctors' Plot. Many believed that to prevent this, Beria used a certain undetectable, flavorless rat poison that induced a hemorrhagic stroke. He was alleged to have boasted after Stalin's death, saying, "I took him out." If it was true, he didn't live much longer to gloat about it. A few months later Khrushchev denounced him, charging Beria with the usual assortment of crimes against the

Party and the State—treason, terrorism and conspiracy with the British intelligence—that brought about his execution on December 23, 1953.

When Stalin died, the excesses of the so-called "personal cult" he practiced died with him. With Khrushchev taking over the Soviet leadership, there were encouraging signs of loosening the old Stalinist dictatorship. The new leaders embarked on a round of reforms and half-hearted concessions to take terror out of totalitarianism, at the same time making sure to keep the Party system intact. They also opened the way to re-establish diplomatic relations with Yugoslavia and its leader, Tito, the former archenemy of the Soviet Union.

These changes, however, went unnoticed in Hungary. Rakosi mourned the passing of his idol, but when the memorials were over he resumed his bloody reign over the much-suffering country. His endless orders for arrests continued and the AVO, his apparatus of terror, kept on carrying out the punishments to his exact instructions. His cruelty stemmed from an absolute belief in his infallibility, his complete disregard of scruples, and the one hundred percent backing of the AVO and Party autocracy. They acted at his will, knowing that they must stand or fall with him.

Stalin might be dead, but Stalinism survived in Hungary. Nothing had changed; the rhythmic applauding and stupefying repetitive chanting of Rakosi's name whenever it was mentioned during political speeches lasted even longer than before. Obeying his orders, thousands of people marched on the American Embassy for an organized protest against Julius and Ethel Rosenberg's execution, scheduled for June 19, for espionage and passing secret information to the Soviets about developing the atomic bomb.

Rakosi's supremacy was cemented when the Parliamentary elections held on May 17, 1953 gave his government a sweeping victory, with over 98% of votes cast in favor of a single list of candidates presented by the Party. The only choice was "For" or "Against" the list. This "rubber stamp" election would have secured Rakosi's dictatorship for the next five years, were it not for the events that took place a month later in Russian-occupied East Germany. On June 16 disgruntled steel workers, unhappy over recent wage cuts, went on strike and began demonstrating on the streets of East Berlin. The crowd swelled and by the next day the movement had turned into a widespread uprising, with demands for political changes and the resignation of the government. It took sixteen Soviet divisions and an avalanche of executions that followed to suppress the revolt and discourage similar "Western instigated disturbances."

Rakosi first ignored what was to be the first crack within the Soviet-dominated Eastern bloc, but the Russians did not. Khrushchev could not afford the luxury of sitting back and closing his eyes and ears to what had happened in East Germany. An example was set, and if no steps were taken, others would surely follow. The Russians knew the history of the rebellious Hungarians and were well aware of the prevailing general pessimism in the country caused by Rakosi's oppressive Stalinist methods. They feared that it would only take a spark to ignite the passion of this highly disillusioned people and decided to take preventive measures.

As Khrushchev was leading the de-Stalinization process in Russia, he clearly saw the similarities between Stalin and Rakosi and identified him as the source of all problems in Hungary. The "Beloved Leader of the People"—a name Rakosi gave himself, as if mocking the people he knew bore nothing but hatred for him—was summoned to Moscow for a strong dressing down. He was highly criticized for the dismal economic performance of the country and for using excessive force against the people. They called upon him to account for the endless purges, the over 2,000 executions, the 100,000 political prisoners and internees crowding the jails and labor camps, and the more than 200,000 Communist comrades expelled from the party organization during his few years in power. They reminded him that he had managed to kill more dedicated members of the Communist Party than Horthy did during his twenty-five years as head of the country. When he tried to make excuses that he was strictly following Party dictates, he was quickly reprimanded that the fault was his alone; the Party never made mistakes, only its members!

As a result, Rakosi was forced to step down as Prime Minister and Imre Nagy, the former Minister of Agriculture, who was also in Moscow with Rakosi, was appointed to replace him. Returning home, between June 27 and 28 the Central Committee held a two-day session where Rakosi gave a report on the Moscow talks and made a moderate self-criticism over his activities during the past years, ending it with his resignation as Prime Minister. The resolution was adopted, and with it came a devastating critique directed at him and his clique. The Central Committee chastised him for bringing the country to the brink of bankruptcy by using unrealistic economic policies, which, in direct violation of Leninist principles, worked against the interests of the people. His errors and unlawful excesses caused immeasurable suffering to the citizenry and did great harm to the Party itself.

Although the session closed with retaining Rakosi as General Secretary of the Party, to be forced to step down as the leader of the country and be made the scapegoat of all failures must have been painfully humiliating for a man with such a tremendous ego.

The outcome of the meeting, however, was kept under cover. According to the official announcement on July 2, 1953, Rakosi resigned, claiming recurring health problems that required him to leave the country for "treatment and prolonged recuperation" available only in the Soviet Union. It took over three decades before the public learned the true details of the resolution.

Hopeful changes

WHEN THE SOVIETS ousted Rakosi, their main concern was to stabilize the situation in Hungary and avert another East German type crisis caused by the general fear and distrust of the government. They realized that the Party had become divorced from the workers and peasants, and they picked Imre Nagy to restore contact between the masses and the ruling Party. They were particularly anxious to change the deep distrust and hostility of the peasants that had existed ever since they were forced into the collectives, and due to his rural background, Nagy seemed to be the ideal man to deal with this problem and bring the disgruntled farm workers around.

Nagy was born into a landless peasant family but after eight years of schooling he left his village and worked in a factory as a locksmith. During WWI he served in the army and fought on the Eastern Front until he was taken prisoner by the Tsarist Russian Army and sent to Siberia. When the 1917 Bolshevik revolution broke out he managed to escape and immediately joined the Red Army to fight on their side until the war ended. By 1919 he was back in Hungary as a member of the newly formed but short-lived Communist government. After their defeat he spent some time in prison and later lived undercover until 1929, when he found a way to flee to the USSR. There he joined the Russian Communist Party and became an informant for the Soviet secret police, the NKVD, the forerunner of the KGB. His exile ended in 1945 when he and the other Muscovites returned to Hungary to form the new government. Appointed as Minister of Agriculture, it was Nagy who introduced the historic 1945 land reform, but when he later opposed Rakosi's drastic agricultural collectivization, he fell out of favor, and from 1948 to 1951 was expelled from the Party on charges of advocating counter-revolutionary ideas. Eventually he was reinstated and held the post of Minister of Interior, but still maintained his criticism of the economic policies of the Rakosi regime. For this he could never regain the trust of Rakosi and was excluded from his inner circle.

At first the announcement of Nagy's appointment as Prime Minister was met with caution, if not with distrust. What worked in his favor was his image as an honest man, his widely known pro-Hungarian attitude, and that he was judged to be more sensitive to the voice of the people than the ideologue Rakosi. In time public sentiment turned into confidence, even though it was clear that Nagy was not cutting ties with the Party. Both leaders were deeply committed to keep the Party firmly in power; they only differed in their approach: Rakosi ruled by terror, while Nagy wanted the support of the people.

On July 4, the day after Rakosi left for the Soviet Union, Nagy made his inaugural speech, a declaration that caused a sensation. He referred to past mistakes but did it without pointing a finger to the person responsible for them; it was not necessary, everyone knew who it was. People hung on his every word when he announced his plans for changing the country's economic development through a program he called the "New Course." The core of its objective was to halt the forced march toward industrialization and put more emphasis on consumer-oriented industries, which would raise the standard of living.

He then outlined in details how his revisionist program would affect every segment of society and all aspects of democratic process:

Workers: The quota system was to be abolished, for it was a violation of the workers' right by forcing them to work on Sundays and overtime to achieve unrealistic compulsory production quotas.

Peasants: To correct the overly rapid development of the cooperatives, the peasants would be allowed to leave the co-ops, but still guaranteed access to tools, seeds, and fertilizers. Delivery quotas would be fixed to let them know their obligations in advance.

Intellectuals: Discriminatory and unjustified purges against them would cease. Competent and experienced intellectuals would no longer be deprived of opportunities to serve the country.

Education: Only achievement, not background or political attitude, would be considered for acceptance into the nation's great halls of learning. Organizing students to perform "voluntary" brigade work on Sundays would be abandoned.

Religion: In the principle of greater tolerance, freedom of religion would be observed. Coercive measures against practicing religion would not be tolerated.

Legal System: The government would adhere in all its activities to the legal order as set down in the constitution, with focus on safeguarding the security and inviolable rights of the people. As a constitutional guardian of the law, a Supreme Court should be created.

Power of the Police: Police jurisdiction is incompatible with the principles of a people's democracy, and for an investigative body to act also as judge would not be permitted. His new program would radically correct the previous abuses that shook the people's confidence in the law.

Internment Camps: Institutional internment would be abolished, and all detention camps would be liquidated. Political prisoners whose release would not imperil the security of the State would be immediately pardoned, discharged and permitted to choose their place of residence.

Nagy closed his speech stating that the previous government confused the roles between the Party and the State, and that from now on concentration of power in the hands of a controlling few would not be allowed.

Needless to say, his statement stunned the nation that someone in the Party dared to stand up and publicly condemn the policies of the hated previous administration. There was no precedent for this, not without risking the wrath of the Party. Immediately a sense of liberation set in, but perhaps more than any other promise, the closing of the camps brought the greatest relief for the people. To live without fear of being hauled off into these gulags for the slightest infraction created an almost euphoric atmosphere and the instant acceptance of Imre Nagy. No wonder—there was hardly a family who didn't have a relative or friend serving time for some fabricated crime. By August, more and more inmates began to arrive home, among them Jeno's colleague Mr. Jakab, a devoutly religious man, who served time at Recsk on trumped-up smuggling charges. At first no one said much about life in the camp; they were told upon release to keep silent, but eventually stories began to emerge of the abuses and suffering these victims endured at the hands of the AVO.

Living in the camps prisoners knew nothing about the world outside, as newspapers and radios were not allowed, but they did learn about Stalin's death from newly arrived inmates, a word dropped here and there in covert whispers that the monster from Gori—Stalin's birthplace in Georgia—was no more. Immediately rumors started that the regime was about to collapse, but when nothing happened and the brutalities continued, they lost hope again. Then suddenly in early July, they noticed subtle changes in the guards' behavior. They seemed nervous and jumpy, their eyes shifty, with an almost apologetic glint. The beatings stopped, rations were increased, the sick were treated better, but nobody knew why. They could only guess that the AVO had received orders not to mistreat the prisoners. Then a current newspaper "carelessly" left where the inmates could easily find it finally shed light on the mystery: Rakosi was gone, Imre Nagy was the new Prime Minister and the camps were to be closed.

New AVO men appeared, with insignias identifying them as attorneys. They were going through files, reviewing records, putting inmates in groups, and soon the releasing process began. Ten, twenty, thirty prisoners a day started to leave, first the politically insignificant elements, the likes of those who spat on Rakosi's picture, or stood up and began singing the Hungarian National Anthem during an April 4th parade celebrating the "liberation" of Hungary by the Red Army. The release of certain publicly known figures—parliamentary deputies, leading intellectuals and famous actors—came next, their cases handled on an individual basis, although the final interview for each was the same. Typically, the inmate was put at ease by a cheerful, smiling lieutenant who informed him that it had come to light recently that he confessed to crimes he did not commit. Did he lie to deliberately mislead the AVO, which is a punishable offense and his incarceration would be justified, or was it the result of physical or psychological coercion, in which case they wanted the names of those forcing him to sign the incriminating confession. They explained that these were imperialist saboteurs who wormed their way into the AVO and would need to be punished to make sure this sort of error wouldn't happen again. Of course no prisoner dared to accuse the AVO, not while still in their hands! They only signed papers stating that the confession was extracted under duress, but claimed to have forgotten the name of the investigative detectives.

Mr. Jakab talked about the doubts and anxieties he and other internees felt when suddenly allowed to leave. Was this some kind of trick? Alarm set in when on several occasions after a group left, machine gun fire was heard in the distance. Were they killing the freed inmates? The notion was dismissed by the argument that the AVO wouldn't go through the elaborate process of providing civilian clothes and handing out train tickets, only to shoot them dead. It would be simpler to lock them in the barracks and burn down the camp. But there were other doubts. Could they be arrested again? Imre Nagy spoke about limiting the power of the police, but he left intact the AVO's right to have the final word in cases where release was doubtful. All inmates were told before the gate opened that they were forbidden to talk about the camp and that they would remain under surveillance to make sure they kept quiet. One word about their confinement meant six to ten years of imprisonment. They were to tell some excuse if asked about their absence, and report anyone probing for a better answer. With such restrictions how safe could they be?

And there was the worst fear: would the families they hadn't heard from for years still be waiting for them? Would friends have the courage to see them? Would they have a job?

By the end of September the camps were emptied. Upon release an AVO attorney stood at the gate reciting apologies to each prisoner as they passed into freedom, asking forgiveness in the name of the Hungarian People's Republic for the wrong and indignity they were subjected to.

Individuals judged dangerous by the Security Forces were not released but rounded up, taken back to Budapest, tried again for the same alleged crimes, found guilty and thrown into jail. Although treatment in jails also improved and a few inmates close to having their sentence completed were given amnesty, most stayed locked up, among them Gabor Peter, the former AVO chief.

Nagy's "New Course" ushered in a more flexible period in Hungarian politics that alleviated the terror-induced fear of everyday life under Rakosi. The relief was palpable and it left its mark on everyone. Workers in factories, peasants toiling their own plot, office managers and newspaper editors, all walked around with more confidence in the future. The projected moderations had a remarkably invigorating effect; people started their workday with a smile and were still smiling on their way home. Suddenly prices seemed fair, and if stores were still half empty, well, it would not be long before merchandise would fill the shelves. Give Imre Nagy a chance to carry out his proposals.

Even for Ilonka and Jeno the walk to the foundry seemed a few steps shorter. They had hope now that the change would lessen the tension between neighboring countries and Jeno could go back to Losonc to visit his ailing mother. She was eighty-six years old and in declining health. Unfortunately, the Slovaks refused to grant him a visa and she died before mother and son could see each other for a last time.

For Sári the passing of her grandmother was sad news, but since she had only vague, early childhood memories of her, she put her death quickly behind her. Like most everyone in the country, she focused on the political changes taking place and hoped that perhaps the label the college pinned on her as an admirer of the decadent Western culture would now be lifted and she might regain her full scholarship. In any case she was going back to college, but first she needed to pass certain exams on subjects she missed when she dropped out. If she concentrated on studying for the prescribed courses, she could make it; she had already learned a lot by working in accounting in the past seven months. But staying home in the evenings and weekends and burying her nose in her books cut the time she usually spent with Adam, and it didn't surprise her when she heard from Alexa that another girl was now sitting next to the bandstand where Adam was playing. Their breakup was tearful but without bitter scenes, and although it hurt her when she first found out that the new affair was turning serious, she took it calmly when Adam and the girl got engaged.

It helped to cheer her when Wanda wrote she was soon coming to Budapest. She broke off with her boyfriend and after that nothing could hold her back. She would be staying with her sister Tessa and her husband—she married an attorney in Budapest—and she already had a job lined up in the textile factory where Tessa was a buyer. She would be doing the same thing as in Sopron, working the looms, except here she'd be on a rotating three-shift system. It meant that besides Sundays they could only get together every third week when she worked the morning shift, at least until something better came along.

Sári had missed her childhood chum and her quirky humor; it was exactly what she needed now that Adam was out of her life. Her Sundays were especially lonely but now, with Wanda in town, she could look forward to having some fun again. With the warm Indian summer lingering on, the two of them would go to the popular beaches along the banks of the Danube to spend the day with other beach-going sun worshipers. Unfortunately, it only lasted until the day a tall and handsome young man with a perfect physique appeared, walking along the water's edge, causing noticeable excitement. He was the well-known and best looking member of the country's water polo team, the winners of the 1952 Helsinki Olympics, who immediately aroused Wanda's interest. Knowing full well what an eye-catching picture she could make, she slowly stood up stretching a bit, just as the young Adonis looked in her direction. Adjusting the straps of her well-stuffed bikini top, she walked down to the water, testing it with her toes, as if undecided about taking the plunge. She only had to wait a minute before he was standing next to her, ready with a quick line about the water temperature. By the time they climbed out of the water and sat down beside Sári, they were in the first stage of an apparently budding romance.

With Wanda just embarking on her next liaison with the gorgeous water polo player, and Alexa in a steady relationship with her soccer-playing champ, Sári began to wonder if there was something wrong with her. Her only boyfriend since she broke up with Viktor was about to marry someone else, and she saw no sign of another prince on the horizon, galloping in to carry her off. Not that she was less attractive; she was just as pretty, perhaps in a different way than her friends, definitely not as voluptuous as Wanda, but still pretty. Wanda, with her dark sultry look, could easily pull off the kind of stunt she used on her new boyfriend, displaying her assets in an enticing way that drew the attention of every male within a mile. She was very good at this, but it would never work for Sári. What was there to show? She had a nice slender, athletic body, but assets? And even if she did, somehow she wouldn't know how to use it. She had no talent to play the vixen, acting in a sexy, teasing way. It was just not in her. She also lacked the easy charm and quiet magnetism of Alexa—an appreciative smile, a sincere-sounding compliment, the effortless way she could shine importance on others—that was part of her allure that made men, as well as women, gravitate toward her. Sári tried to imitate her a few times when talking to people: "Oh, you are so right" or "I wish I could do it as well as you," and the like, but she stopped doing it. It sounded phony coming from her, and the pretense made her uncomfortable. She could praise someone's accomplishment, but never merely for flattery.

So it was back to visiting her aunt, calling on Latzi's parents, and occasionally seeing her two cousins, although she dropped going to Gabi's parties, knowing that Adam and his fiancée would be there. They might think she was still pining after him, and they wouldn't be too far from the truth. There were men buzzing around her in the office, as well as guys from her college, asking to meet for a cappuccino or go to a movie, but these were dates totally lacking romance. Just as well, Sári thought. Working and studying, she probably couldn't maintain a steady relationship, anyway. That was the reason she had lost her lighthearted bohemian boyfriend in the first place.

Her insecurity about not being able to dress like Alexa and Wanda also haunted her. With both girls working and living at home free of charge with meals provided, it was no wonder they could spend money on trendy clothes. She, on the other hand, had to put away every penny she earned to supplement her reduced scholarship when she resumed her classes in the fall. She would barely have enough to cover her living expenses and would have to go on skimping and wearing the same old outfits until she was through with college.

No doubt, financially she was at a great disadvantage, but there was one thing Sári had over Wanda and Alexa to make up for what she felt was lacking: she was smarter, better educated, more independent and had definite goals. These were her hidden assets, and she knew that eventually they would give her the means to make up for what she was forced to do without at the present.

Spending time with her books paid off when in September she passed all the required exams to start her junior year. As expected, her request to reinstate her full scholarship was rejected, but when she wrote home about it, to her great surprise her parents offered to send her 250 forints each month, at least for the coming year. She could thank her brother Gyuszi for it. The money he earned working part time at the university while studying geology made it possible.

By November Wanda moved out of her sister's apartment into a rented room with central heating and most importantly, access to a telephone, a luxury very few ordinary people enjoyed. It was a privilege extended mostly to sports stars, famous actors, doctors, and lawyers in the private sector, and of course to Party members, although a well-stuffed envelope slipped under the table to the right people could magically put a phone in one's home. Wanda's landlady, a woman in her late fifties, must have done just that or had powerful connections, since she didn't work and still had a two-party line phone. She lived alone in a two-bedroom apartment and rented out one room to meet the occupancy quota. The rent she charged was high, but Wanda could afford it, and without sharing it with someone, for which Sári truly envied her. She never liked her roommate, a nosy girl who loved to talk, mostly about things that were no interest to her. She also knew that the girl went through her personal things, read her letters, and swiped her cigarettes. She only tolerated it because renting a room on her own was out of reach.

Now that Wanda had a warm and cozy room, whenever she worked the afternoon shift she let Sári bring her books and study at her place. But during those weeks when she was free in the evenings, they often met for an espresso in one of the little bars along Vaci Street. Their favorite was the Paradiso, a vastly popular place with a full bar and a small dance floor with a trio playing after seven. On one of their dates in November Sári got there early, when the place was still half empty, and took a seat on the padded bench that ran along the wall facing the entrance. It offered the best spot to observe the entire room, follow the interaction between the tables and see who was coming or leaving and with whom.

She put her jacket next to her seat to reserve a place for Wanda, then ordered an espresso and lit a cigarette. With her eye on the door she waited for her friend, late as usual, and kept refusing to surrender the spot she held for her as the room began to fill with people. She was on her second cigarette, annoyed at Wanda's tardiness, when she saw two men in their late 30s or so entering the room. They stood for a moment, looking over the place, then started threading their way among the tables in her direction. A minute later they stood in front of her, politely asking in German if the empty seat next to her was free. Apparently they were foreigners, but even before speaking Sári could tell they were not Hungarians. Their complexion was darker, their hair pitch black, and both wore exquisite tailor-made suits. The one who addressed her had a full mustache, and while he pointed at the empty seat, she noticed that his nails were coated with clear lacquer.

"Sorry, but I am waiting for a friend," Sári told them and pushed the jacket a little further to mark a wider space. They nodded and sat down at the next table. Where was Wanda? She should be here by now! Irritated, she glanced at her watch and decided, if she didn't show up in the next ten minutes, she'd leave. She pulled out another cigarette and was reaching for her matches when a gold cigarette lighter flashed in front of her face.

"Permit me," she heard the man with the mustache say, reaching over and holding the lighter for her. She thanked him with a nod, then immediately turned away, making it clear that she was not interested in starting a conversation. She had almost finished her cigarette when finally, through the curling smoke, she saw Wanda at the door. She took her time checking her coat and made a grand show of twisting and turning as she skirted the chairs on her way to the table. The mustachioed man got out of his chair to let Wanda slip into her seat, a gesture she returned with an appreciative smile. Turning to Sári, she gave her excuses for being late, and at the same time quickly appraised the two obviously foreign looking men at the next table.

Before they would get into their usual girl-to-girl talk, drinking too much coffee and soda water while waiting for her friend sent Sári to the powder room. On her way back she stopped at a table to chat for a few minutes with people she knew.

"Who are those gentlemen talking to Wanda," one of them asked, "I never saw them here before."

Sári's head snapped in Wanda's direction and sure enough, there she was engaged in a seemingly lively conversation with the two strangers. "I have no idea who they are," she said, "but I have a feeling I am about to find out."

"Ah, there you are," Wanda looked up, smiling, when Sári got back to their table and with the greatest of ease proceeded to introduce Ali, the man with the mustache, and his friend Hassan. They were from Cairo, working at the Egyptian Embassy in Budapest, she said, and what interesting stories they were telling her about the land of the Pharaohs!

Yeah, Sári thought, *the only reason these characters are trying to talk to us is to tell about the tomb of Tutankhamen!* But she sat down and listened as Wanda and her newly acquired friends kept chatting in German, a language both men spoke fluently. With nothing better to do she reached into her purse for a cigarette when Wanda, puffing on an American filter tip cigarette, waved it in front of her face.

"You should try one of these, Sári, or you'll never know what you are missing!" she said, but even before she could finish the sentence, Ali grabbed his box of Tareytons and held it out for Sári, apologizing for not offering it sooner. It was a temptation she couldn't resist, but flatly refused to accept the brandy the men had ordered while she was in the restroom.

Seeing that Wanda was not in the mood for their regular gossiping tonight, she decided to leave as soon as she finished smoking her cigarette. Although the two men were polite and obviously eager to keep them engaged, she was not interested. She almost felt embarrassed to see Wanda laughing a little too loud at Ali's stories, tossing her dark hair, and incessantly lighting cigarette after cigarette, as if she would miss out by turning one down. Sári was collecting her things and was about to tell Wanda that she was leaving, when half-way across the room she saw a young man with a shock of dark hair and amazing blue eyes coming toward their table. The next minute he was shaking hands with the two Egyptians, and all thoughts of leaving flew right out of her head. He was obviously not one of them, but they seemed to know each other well. After inviting him to join their table, Ali turned and introduced him to Wanda and Sári. His name was Harold Lombardo, and contrary to his looks and his name, he was not from Italy, but from America. Like his friends, he spoke German and when Wanda asked if he was visiting in Budapest, he said no, he was working at the U.S. Legation.

Immediately Wanda took control of the conversation. Ignoring the Egyptians, all her attention was now focused on him.

"How interesting! And how do you like our fair city?"

"Budapest is beautiful, although I am still trying to find my way around. I only arrived a couple of weeks ago."

"Well, if you need a guide, look no further! I would be more than happy to show you the sights. If you have any special interest, the history of the city, a particular area you'd like to explore, or perhaps the nightlife, we could make up a plan to see everything in order of your preference."

Sári looked at her friend with a quizzical frown. This was not the way Wanda usually talked! She sat listening as her friend bombarded the American with questions: how did he become a diplomat? He said he was not a diplomat, just an employee. Very well, then which city in America did he come from? Oh, New York, from Brooklyn? She had relatives, not exactly in Brooklyn, but in Princeton, New Jersey, which couldn't be all that far! Did he have his family with him here? No, he was alone, unattached.

As she carried on, trying hard to impress him, Sári almost felt sorry for Ali and Hassan sitting there mute, excluded, dropped from Wanda's graces. As a gesture she asked a few casual questions from Ali, who sat closest to her: how long had he been in Budapest and how did he meet his American friend?

"The American friend has a name; please call me Hal," Harold leaned toward her, smiling, catching her eye and holding it. She smiled back with a slight nod, and suddenly the conversation shifted. Now it was Hal's turn to ask questions, but not from Wanda. What was Sári doing? College? What was she studying? Just then the piano player came back from a break and, sitting down, softly ran his fingers over the keyboard, sounding the first chords of "Autumn Leaves." Hal reached out his hand and asked Sári if she would like to dance. Getting up, she caught Wanda's resentful stare, but she didn't care. Of course, it added to his appeal that he was American, but even before she knew it, the mere sight of him made her heart skip a beat.

The tiny floor was crowded and dancing any other way but close was impossible. And Sári was glad for it. Feeling his arm around her and resting her cheek against his felt wonderful. Then slowly he pulled his head back and, looking down into her eyes, smiled. "You look lovely, Sári, and feel lovely, too. Would you like to go to some other place, perhaps a bite to eat, to talk a little, just the two of us?"

"I'd love nothing more, and I mean it, but I don't think it's fair to leave my friend here alone."

"She won't be alone. Our Egyptian friends will gladly keep her company. Besides, I think you are overly concerned. Do you think she'd hesitate for a moment in your place?"

"I know, but still, she gets upset easily."

"Well, OK, I understand. But I would like to see you again, alone, without your friend if possible. Is there a way I can reach you? A phone number?"

"Sorry, but I don't have a telephone. You forget that you are in Hungary! Not everyone has a phone here, you know. But Wanda has one, or rather her landlady. I could give you that number and you can leave a message with her."

"No, I'd rather not call Wanda. It's better if I give you my phone number. But why don't we make a date right now? Are you free next Friday for dinner? Yes? How about the Bristol? Great, the Bristol it is, at eight o'clock."

He pulled her to the side and jotted down his phone number on a napkin that she tucked into her pocket. They danced a little longer, until the song ended, then he led her back to the table and after ten minutes or so made his excuse and left the Paradiso.

Wanda was quick to tell her that Ali had invited them for dinner at the Gundel, and they had a car, too, but Sári declined. "I am not interested in going out with these guys, to sit and smile and make nice the whole evening for what? Just to eat at Gundel's?" she whispered in Hungarian.

Wanda gave her that "are you crazy?" look. "It's the best restaurant in the country! You've probably never even been there! Come on, do you have anything better to do? These two are very interesting to talk to!"

"I know, the pyramids and the Sphinx, and whatnot, but I'd rather go home, Wanda."

"Have it your way, but I think you are going to miss out on a very nice evening."

Wanda didn't know it, but at that moment her uncooperative friend could only think of that other dinner next Friday at the Hotel Bristol.

Sári had a few days to get ready for her date with Hal. Alexa lent her a dark blue dress suit with a white silk crepe blouse and her good wool overcoat; she had her hair and nails done, but made sure that this time she had a bottle of polish remover handy at home. Wearing light makeup, she walked in the hotel lobby, where Hal was already waiting for her. He asked for a table away from the band so they could talk and get to know each other. They had a lovely evening. She translated the menu for him while he chose the wine; they talked, danced a little and talked some more, and by the time he ordered an after-dinner drink she felt at ease enough to ask the question that was on her mind ever since he first asked her to dance at the Paradiso: "Why me?"

"Very simple," Hal laughed. "You made me feel like I was back home with a real American girl!" Teasingly, he tapped the tip of her nose. "You look and act like them, the type of girl I was always drawn to, starting with my pretty red-haired kindergarten teacher. As for Wanda, you said she is exotic? In my neighborhood back in Brooklyn people would think she is Puerto Rican. This might fit the image as exotic in Hungary, but believe me, that's not the case in New York!" Smiling, he shook his head slightly, then added, "But even if she looked like Betty Grable, for me she is too aggressive. She was trying to dominate the entire conversation with an obvious effort to show herself in the best possible light, but instead she came across as pushy and pretentious, if not phony, at least for my taste. It might be just a first impression, but I don't think I am too far off in my judgment."

"She is a little forward, you are right, but she is a real nice girl, Hal. I've known her since our early school days. You'll see when you get to know her a little better."

"I knew you would say that, and of course, I could be wrong. But enough of Wanda, let's talk about you. I know so little about what you like to do when you are not sitting in lecture halls. Do you like movies?"

"All my life! Although not lately. There is nothing worthwhile to see now. Besides, you wouldn't understand the dialog; there are no English subtitles here, as you can guess. And if you expect to find American movies playing here, you are out of luck!"

"No, of course not, I've learned a few things already since I arrived. What I meant, we could watch some American movies at my place. The embassy has some fairly recent films and I can have the projection man come out and set it up for us, if you'd like. I think a movie called *Quo Vadis* just came in, a story in Nero's time. It doesn't have subtitles, either, but you would be able to follow the story, or I could narrate it for you."

"Oh, I read the book; it's a great story. I'd love to see it, if it's not too much trouble."

"Not at all, just name the day."

They agreed on next Wednesday and after finishing the evening with a little slow dancing, headed for the lobby. Although Hal offered to drive her home—he had a 1950 Chevrolet coupe—Sári insisted on taking a taxi. For Wednesday, too, she thought it better if she would just come to his apartment. Things had eased up since Imre Nagy took over, but certain misgivings lingered on. The street address he had given her was familiar, just a few blocks off the central boulevard near the Hotel West End. A Metro station was nearby, she'd only have a short way to walk.

His place was on the second floor with a wide staircase leading up to it. As she mounted the steps she felt both tense and excited: here she was, just a girl from Sopron, on her way to a rendezvous with a handsome American! She still didn't see what he liked in her; why, he could have his pick from a dozen more beautiful, certainly more sophisticated women in the city. There was Julie, for example, a gorgeous redhead working as a bartender at the Hotel Arizona. She spoke English, too, and even looked a bit like Sári. This whole thing seemed so unreal, like she was playing a part in a movie.

She hardly touched the bell when the door opened and Hal ushered her into the spacious living room furnished with casual elegance. Glancing around, she noticed that a small dining table was set for two in the adjacent room.

"I hope you are hungry! My housekeeper prepared a light supper for us. She is a very good cook, although I usually eat outside or at the embassy; she only comes twice a week to keep the house running."

The middle-aged woman serving the dinner was polite and discreetly attentive, and left soon after the dishes were done, but Sári didn't trust her for one moment. There was no question in her mind that she was planted in the household as an informer, to report the comings and goings of people in the house. Her mere presence made her uneasy, and if Hal invited her again, she'd prefer a day when the woman was not around.

They were finishing their coffee when a man arrived bringing the film, and after he set up the projector and a large screen, they sat down and watched the movie. As the story played out, with Deborah Kerr and Robert Taylor in the title roles, she just couldn't understand why such a wonderful picture would be so damned in the socialist camp. Oh, she knew the Party used films as a propaganda tool, the best ever devised to shape the mind of man, according to Lenin, but why must every movie be directed to glorify socialism? Use it if they must, but leave room for entertainment!

Seeing her obvious delight, Hal promised to reserve the next film to arrive at the embassy. They usually received at least one new movie a month he said, but until then he hoped she'd come again without the allure of watching another film. They made a date for Saturday the coming week to have dinner at one of the quaint little restaurants Buda was famous for. Then, when they were finally alone, Hal put on a stack of Nat King Cole records, and as that wonderfully soft voice filled the room, he drew her close, swaying slowly to the music with his arms around her. Caught in the magic of the moment he bent to kiss her, and yielding to his passion she responded with all the promises of a first kiss.

It was not easy to stop before the rising sexual tension would carry them further, but they did, knowing that there would be another day. Calling it a night, Sári gathered her coat and purse, ready to catch the subway, except this time Hal wouldn't let her leave alone; he insisted on driving her home, or at least to the corner where she lived. She said it was to avoid drawing the neighbors' attention to an American car on their street, and then pointed out a nearby café where he could pick her up on their next date. With a lingering kiss he wished her goodnight, but remained in the car and waited until she was safely inside the house before driving away.

She could hardly wait to tell her friends about the evening. Alexa was genuinely happy for her, already planning which of her dresses would be perfect for her Saturday date, an offer Sári gratefully accepted. Wanda, on the other hand, played down Sári's obvious excitement over watching a movie with her new boyfriend.

"I don't see what's the big deal about that," she said with a wry smile. "If Hal's idea for a first date is staying home, eating a home-cooked meal and watching a movie, it just shows that he has no class. Was he too cheap to take you out to a good restaurant, then to a nightclub or a show? It's too bad that you didn't stick with the Egyptians; they sure know how to entertain a girl. Maybe it's not too late. I could try to arrange a date for you with Hassan for next weekend."

Sári just let the remarks pass. She knew exactly what her friend was doing. It all started with that long ago ice-skating incident in Sopron, and by now she had plenty of time to get used to her subtle stings and slides.

Wearing Alexa's dress, she looked beautiful when Hal picked her up on Saturday. The date ended at his place, the first time they spent the night together, each taking and giving in equal measure, passionately, lovingly, and unselfishly. The glow of their first lovemaking didn't diminish with the morning sun climbing to a cloudless sky, as they remained unaware of the radiant day unfolding outside the closed shutters. There would be times to enjoy the sun, but for that first weekend they cared only for the splendor of their togetherness.

From that day on the pattern was set. They saw each other once during the week and always on weekends. As soon as classes were over on Saturday noon, she hurried to spend the rest of the weekend with him. The only exception was when occasionally he had to leave the country on business, mostly to Vienna or Zurich. He spoke several languages, including Swiss-German and Italian, both official languages of Switzerland besides French. He always returned with small gifts for her, a box of candy, fresh oranges—and that still in the cold of winter—or a pair of nylons, the first she ever had. As the season turned warmer he once came back with some bananas, a fruit Sári had never seen before. Handing her one, Hal watched in disbelief as she proceeded to bite into it, peel and all. He couldn't help but laugh out loud, and she laughed with him when Hal showed her the proper way to eat a banana.

During their time together, Hal made all their plans: where to go for dinner, see a nightclub act or go dancing; he got tickets for the opera, and took her to the Davis Cup in the spring. They stayed pretty much within city limits, since Embassy employees were advised against taking side trips. She saw several more movies at his apartment, the best among them *The Snows of Kilimanjaro*, *Moulin Rouge*, and *Singing in the Rain.* Wanda started to nag her if she could come over the next time Harold had a movie, and when Sári asked, he agreed, if only because the girls were such close friends. It turned out to be the first and last time she was invited. She made such a spectacle of herself by flirting openly with him that he told Sári never to bring her again. He didn't have to tell her twice. She was quite resentful herself about her best friend's obvious attempt to steal her boyfriend, which, of course, Wanda denied, putting a spin on it that it was Hal who did the flirting.

"You are too naïve if you believe that Hal has no other girls on the side! Behind your back he was giving me all kinds of signals; I had a hard time ignoring it. I am telling you this because I don't want you to get hurt, Sári."

"You don't have to worry; I know well enough what I am doing. So just do me a favor and stay out of my affairs," Sári said quite bluntly.

"No problem, just remember what I told you!" Wanda said and walked away. When Sári didn't see her for a couple of weeks, she was sure she got the message that she was no longer welcome at Hal's. But not Wanda! A little while later she nonchalantly asked when was Hal planning the next movie, so she could arrange to be free to come. Sári simply ignored the question and stopped talking about the films she saw. She knew that if she told her outright what Harold said, Wanda would only turn it around and accuse her of being jealous. Thinking that she finally gave up, Sári could hardly believe it when Hal told her that Wanda called him directly about the movies, and turned quite nasty when he made it clear to her that the movies constituted a date with Sári and her presence would be an intrusion. Wanda never mentioned this to Sári, but her jabs at Harold became meaner and more constant.

She didn't need Wanda to tell her that the affair would not last; she knew from the start that one day it must end. When, she didn't know, because she and

Hal never talked about it. She didn't ask and he never mentioned how long his assignment would keep him in Budapest. Although he said he loved her, they both knew there could never be a commitment.

That day came toward the end of May, but only he knew that it would be the last time they'd see each other. To avoid the painful scene of saying good-bye, Hal told her that he was leaving on one of his short business trips and would be back soon. He acted touchingly sweet and loving in the days before he was to leave, and noticing it, Sári teased him about growing sentimental in an old-fashioned way. She also took it as a sign of his deepening affection when after driving her home on the night of his departure, instead of letting her out at the usual corner, he insisted on walking with her to the door. Standing at the entrance he kept her from going in, holding her with great tenderness, his eyes misting over as he looked at her. Seeing him so emotional, she kidded him again that she wouldn't disappear into the thin air; she'd be right here waiting for him, if he'd just hurry up and get back. Her light-hearted tone seemed to draw him out of his melancholy mood; with a last kiss he turned, raised his hand in a vague gesture of farewell, and walked away, leaving her still wondering, *What was that all about?* He looked back one more time, but by then she was gone, and never saw the silent tear rolling down his face.

The day when Hal was supposed to return, Sári called him but there was no answer. Making sure she didn't make a mistake, she dialed the number more carefully, but again, no one picked up the phone. First she assumed his business took a little longer than expected, which had happened before, but then he usually sent a postcard saying when he would be back. She waited a few days, but when no mail arrived and the calls still went unanswered, an uneasy feeling stirred in her. What if something had happened to him? There were increasingly more cars on the road these days, what if he got into an accident? Fully alert by now, she had to find a way to learn what happened to him. To call the Embassy was out of the question. For her own protection, Harold never gave her his number there. Regardless of the regime change, the dreaded AVO was still keeping tag on calls made to the American Legation.

Then she remembered the maid who always came to clean his place on Wednesdays. When she rang the bell and the door opened, the woman recognized her and immediately said that Mr. Lombardo was gone.

"Gone where?" Sári pressed her.

"I don't know, I am just the housekeeper here, but I was told to do a thorough cleaning because someone else will be moving in."

"Who told you? The Embassy?"

"Well yes, another American is moving here, but that's all I know. Now if you'll excuse me, I have work to do." She was ready to shut the door but Sári blocked it with her foot.

"Just one more question! Is it possible that Mr. Lombardo moved to another apartment? Do you still have any of his personal belongings here? If so, do you have instructions where to forward them?"

"No I don't. And he left nothing behind. Whatever else you want to know, you have to ask the new gentlemen moving here next week."

And that's what Sári did. The man answered the telephone and simply told her that Harold was transferred to another country and wouldn't be returning. He made it clear that he was not allowed to give out his address or take a message for him, not now and not in the future, so it was useless to call again.

So that was it. Now she understood the reason for his sadness when they said goodbye; he knew it meant forever. She didn't blame him for keeping it a secret; it was better this way. She didn't feel betrayed, nor did she have regrets about the relationship; it was wonderful while it lasted. She would miss him, his gentle ways, and the fun times they had together, and admittedly, she would also miss the unique position of parading on the arm of a handsome American boyfriend. She cried a little, and while she couldn't deny it that his sudden disappearance hurt, she knew that it was nothing compared to what Viktor must have felt receiving her Dear John letter. She didn't suffer the pain that rejections and broken promises always inflict.

And so she was back to her dull pre-Harold days, once again the fifth wheel when Alexa and Wanda and their boyfriends invited her out. They felt sorry for her and tried to cheer her, although Wanda couldn't resist rubbing it in gleefully, "I told you so, but you wouldn't listen."

At the end of summer, before her senior year kicked into gear, Sári had time to spend a couple of weeks with her family in Sopron. Her parents had no idea about her American affair and she was not about to tell them either. No need to let her mother discover that she had lied to cover up an incident that happened last spring during her carefree days with Hal. One weekend Ilonka took the train to Budapest for a quick visit, but because Sári didn't receive her note in time before she took off to be with her boyfriend, she never got to see her. When she realized what had happened she felt an overwhelming guilt at how her mother must have felt arriving at the busy train station to find no one waiting for her. Ilonka was staying at Aunt Mariska's, and Sári could imagine her mother's state of mind when told that they hadn't seen her daughter for months, or worse yet, when she rang Sári's doorbell and the landlady said she was never home on Saturdays and Sundays.

Ilonka had to return to Sopron before Sári got home late Sunday night, and although she immediately wrote to apologize, the guilty feeling gnawed at her. In her letter she made up an excuse that she usually spent her weekends with either Alexa or Wanda because she couldn't stand her roommate; she hated to be cooped up with her in that crammed place they shared with the landlady's family. Her mother must have seen the conditions there and hopefully would understand her wanting to get away. She would move out in a beat if she could afford it.

As a renewed plea for forgiveness, she brought up the painful subject again during her stay. She used the same excuses but added another. "As sorry as I am to have missed you, Mom, such a thing could never happen in a more civilized country, where most people had a telephone or at least easy access to one. It's really a shame that this country is so backward! They boast to have built that ugly new city, Sztalinvaros almost overnight, but they can't put a phone in people's home! By next summer I'll be through with college and once I start working, at least in the office I will have a phone where I can be reached."

With that she put the incident behind her and turned the conversation around, asking how things were at home. "You seem to be in better spirits, Mother, than the last time I was here, though you said in your recent letter that nothing has changed."

"That's true, I am still stuck in that godforsaken factory," Ilonka said with a sigh. "I am only a little more resigned to it now, and it's always better in the summer when walking to work is easier. At least your father won't have to do it too much longer. He'll be sixty next November and will start receiving his pension from his old job instead of that paltry medical subsidy. He'll quit working, but he promised he'd come and get me in the afternoons so I don't have to walk home alone. I don't put much faith in it, though. You know him. If it were up to him he'd just sit home and read or listen to the radio. He doesn't even go to an occasional soccer game anymore. I'd like to take a trip together now and then, just somewhere around here, but he won't hear of it, not even when we get special discounts for working in the foundry. He still plays gin rummy, but only with the Varosys. He says the old card-playing crowd at the coffeehouse is long gone and the place is empty. No one could drag him to a movie or the theatre if something decent is playing. I have to ask Mitzie or Mrs. Beyer across the street to come with me. And if I invite some of my women friends over, he says hello and disappears; staying even for a few minutes is too much for him. It's quite embarrassing, you know. True enough, he was never a social creature, but now he is getting to be a real recluse."

Sári didn't expect such a barrage of complaints; it was the first time she had heard her mother talk this way about her father. Her immediate reaction was to hear Jeno's side, what he had to say about the criticism. She waited until Ilonka left for Sunday Mass, then sat down with him, expecting a denial. To her surprise, Jeno acknowledged everything Ilonka said, except he couldn't see why she would bring it up now.

"She knew from the start how I am, that our personalities are different," Jeno reflected. "Perhaps it didn't become an issue while she was preoccupied with raising the children and I was out of the house a great deal working. It's only now that I am constantly around and the boys can look after themselves that she has more time to find faults with me. I always preferred books to movies, let alone the stupid politicized films playing these days. And few could blame me for staying away from your mother's coffee klatches. As for going to places, in the past I could never take time off for vacations, because to pay for it I had to take on extra work, filling in for others. It was almost a joke, when someone in the office needed covering, they just said, ask Jeno! I never stood in her way to take you and the children somewhere, but she wouldn't go without me. And now, that I have time, I am not feeling all that well, Sári. She thinks the thermal spa near Bükk would help and wants to take me there, but six oxen couldn't drag me to just sit in some sulfuric hot spring and be plastered with mudpacks. And that's just how things are, always were, and since neither of us going to change, I am afraid always will be."

Realizing for the first time the vast difference between her parents, Sári wondered how they ever wound up together, her mother being outspoken, willful, devoutly religious, and her father the opposite, soft-spoken, keeping everything inside, a man who hardly went to church, though always held to high principles. She acted on impulse while he wouldn't take a step without due consideration. For Ilonka, people were either with or against her, while Jeno, at his own choosing, had a few life-long friends, but had everyone's respect and no enemies. Her world was rosy one day, turned black the next; Jeno could blend the colors and they didn't fade. Even during card games, Jeno could lose graciously, while Ilonka always had to win. If not, there were times when cards flew across the table, and the game was suddenly over.

Comparing the two, the old adage that opposites attract must have worked for them, but still, with their basic interests so out of sync, it seemed almost a miracle that disagreements never got out of hand. Knowing her mother's quick temper and lack of patience, she had to admire her father's ability to keep arguments from escalating. There must be no squabbling in front of the children! It couldn't have been easy for him to hold their polarized personalities in balance, and it was to his credit that the children were not aware of any underlying tension in the home while they were growing up.

After listening to both her parents she could see the point each made, but deep in her heart she could thoroughly understand her mother. She couldn't blame her for wanting a little more out of life after the many setbacks she suffered. Even her childhood was difficult, facing prejudice for her illegitimate birth, growing up without a father, and coping with her mother's health problems. The only real happiness she knew was the time after she married Jeno until the final year of WWII. Only then did she enjoy true bliss and contentment, raising her children and living a well-rounded middle-class life. 1944, with all its devastation, put an end to that, and what came after was but mere survival with no hope for betterment. She never regained her foothold, and now, condemned to work in that foundry, is it any wonder that she longed to squeeze a little enjoyment into her dreary existence?

And yet, Sári knew, unmatched as they were, they loved each other regardless. They stood fiercely committed to hold onto each other for "better or worse," as they promised almost thirty years ago. To see that such bond could be sustained against odds was awe-inspiring, and for the first time she felt an uneasy doubt nagging at the back of her mind: did she make a mistake in letting Viktor go? She was so convinced before that the difference in the way they wanted to live was too great to overcome, but now something told her that with Viktor at her side they would have had the same sort of marriage as her parents have. He would have been the kind of husband her mother was fortunate to find: patient, considerate, loyal.

Well, it was too late to dwell on what was lost, but from now on she would concentrate on what still might be, if given another chance. With luck, a good man would come along again to offer her a solid partnership, and she would now be wiser to look beyond the selfish, immature concepts of her early years on how her life should be.

It was with a greater understanding that she said goodbye to her parents and took the train back to Budapest. As Sopron faded from sight, she was also leaving behind her childish notion that life would be perfect if she willed it so. Such idealistic expectations were better left for the very young with time on their hands to learn how to brush off disappointments and step over broken dreams without losing hope to dream again.

Rakosi returns

BY THE TIME Sári started her final year at college in the fall of 1954, there were visible signs of national disappointments in the performance of Imre Nagy's "New Course," the program that held such broad promises for the country when first introduced a year ago. After the euphoria died down people came to realize that it might take a long time before they'd see a real improvement in their daily existence.

In order to succeed, he needed the support of the Party, but because of his radical proposals for changes, the higher hierarchy refused to side with him. Only a narrow circle accepted his bold new ideas, while the rest felt he overstepped the limit in policy reforms that Moscow had in mind for him when they put him in power. He was chosen because the new post-Stalinist Russian leaders believed that under his leadership people would be more willing to submit to party control than under the hated Rakosi, but they expected a strict adherence to their bidding. Nagy was to act according to their dictates, and to ensure it, Moscow left intact two very important government positions: Rakosi remained vice premier and Gero, the second man in command, was still the Minister of Interior. They were to sit back and let Imre Nagy do the necessary Leninist dance of giving in a little in order to advance.

When he jumped the gun with his radically reformist speech on July 4, 1953, the Party turned against him and did everything in their power to prove him wrong. Rakosi led the attack after he returned from the USSR in November 1954, calling Nagy a "rightist deviationist," and blaming him for the dismal economy. Before he left the country in 1953 he grudgingly admitted that mistakes were made, especially in the aggressive agricultural collectivization, and that corrections were necessary, but he stubbornly maintained that industrialization must remain the ultimate goal, and the new policies must not threaten the Party's supremacy and prestige. He relentlessly criticized Nagy's every move, attacking his performance and sending negative reports to his Russian bosses in an effort to undermine his rival's authority.

Gero did his part as well to help erode Nagy's political position. Development of heavy industry being his pet project, he focused his criticism on Nagy's proposal to curb the country's industrialization, and emphasized the problems it would create, primarily widespread unemployment, especially among the steelworkers, miners and foundry men, who together formed the backbone of the socialist system. If they were weakened, so would the proletarian political power, and to this, the Party would never submit.

The press and radio also remained under the control of the Communist Party and by publishing only the negative side of Nagy's program, they helped to influence the general public opinion. Two years had passed since his proposals, yet what had he accomplished? Nagy needed more time, and more importantly the Party's help, to implement his people-friendly comprehensive program, something he couldn't possibly do alone, and when they deserted him and sabotaged all his reforms, he was doomed to failure.

On March 9, 1955 the Central Committee publicly condemned Nagy, making him a scapegoat for Hungary's economic decline and, ignoring Nagy's rejection of the accusations, the National Assembly stripped him of power by a unanimous vote. He was forced to resign on April 18, and on the same day Rakosi was back in the saddle. He did not, however, regain the same power or the full Soviet support he commanded while Stalin was alive. The nightmarish terror, the purges and the slave camps remained things of the past, and he was not allowed to continue his personality cult by which he dictated who would be arrested on what charges, and what punishment his victims would receive. The days of secret trials, merciless beatings to obtain submission, and summary executions were over, along with the paranoia about imperialist and Titoist spying rings.

Perhaps it was for this reason that Sári didn't panic when in late May she was summoned to appear at the local branch of the AVO. That it was not at the dreaded headquarters at Andrassy Avenue helped to keep her nerves in check. There was no doubt in her mind why she was called in: they wanted to talk about her American boyfriend. But why now? As apprehensive as she was, she was curious why they waited this long and what aspect of her relationship interested them most.

She was nervous when she was led into an office where three civilian detectives greeted her. They tried to create a relaxed atmosphere by starting with small talk and offering cigarettes and coffee, easing slowly toward the subject at hand, her relationship with Harold Lombardo. It surprised her how much they knew about their activities: how often they saw each other, places they frequented, that they spoke German. Then the interrogation began. Their first question was what would an American possibly want with her, a college student with no access to any important information or connection to the government? What was the attraction?

It was something Sári herself often asked.

She simply told them the truth that their relationship was strictly romantic. "We met by chance and fell in love, and that was all. He told me that he was not like his co-workers, socializing exclusively with each other, but would rather spend his free time with me. Is this so hard to believe?"

"Did you discuss his work?" they wanted to know ignoring her remark.

"No, he never told me what he did at the embassy. From little hints, like he knew how to type, I assumed that he had a clerical job, but I never knew for sure."

"Did you talk about politics, or about his life in the USA, his family back home?"

"No, only that he was from Brooklyn, New York."

"Nothing else?"

"Nothing else."

They went on questioning: were any promises made? No, nothing was said about the future; they both knew there would be an end. Well then, did she receive any material things from him, either money or gifts? Other than small gifts, nothing ever exchanged hands. When they suggested that it would be understandable if she accepted help, after all, as a student she must be short on money, she simply said that the nature of their affair was not like that. It never came into play. She suspected that he had no idea how poor she really was because she constantly borrowed clothes from friends to appear to be better off than she really was.

Then she had a question for the detectives. Why did they wait almost a year to question her? It was obvious that they were aware of the relationship at the time it was going on; why the interest now, when it was long over? They made some vague comments about certain slackening of awareness and lack of vigilance in the past couple of years, and that they were now following up on cases to see whether any of them involved serious neglect. In her case there were other reasons, as well. They were curious to see if perhaps her friend would return, and if he did, would he have contacted her again? And also, they were watching if she would try to seek out other foreigners, maybe attract another American? Now that it was apparent that neither was happening, and that her case was strictly a personal affair, they were satisfied to close her file.

It was over! She was free to go. She gave a huge sigh of relief as she left the building and thanked her lucky stars that she met Hal after Imre Nagy came into power. Even now that Rakosi was back, his secret police seemed to have lost much of its old bite; otherwise she could have been easily labeled an imperialist spy and as such, wouldn't be going home.

She quickly scanned the street, hoping that nobody she knew saw her coming out of the AVO and think that she had anything to do with them! She was not going to tell anyone about her interview and create such suspicion. Not even to her two best friends. Distrust and fear still lingered on.

The day in June finally arrived when years of studying paid off and Sári received her diploma, not just any kind, but a "Red Diploma," granted only to the highest achievers. She now had a degree in business administration, specialized in industrial planning. The university also worked with major corporations to find suitable placements for their graduates, and of course, the best jobs went to those with Red Diplomas. They offered her a position at the Hungarian Steel Works, one of the largest in the country whose performance had vital importance in achieving the goals of the Five Year Plan. In a hurry to begin making money, she started working right after graduation, without taking any time off. The location was not ideal, a good forty-minute tram ride with two transfers from where she lived, but the salary was good, 1,200 forints a month to start as compared to the average 950 for office workers, and now, with emphasis again on heavy industry, her prospects for advancement were promising.

To celebrate, Alexa and Wanda with their boyfriends took her out for dinner at the Grand Hotel on Margit Island and, looking for a quiet spot to talk, they took a table at the back of the open terrace. They were engrossed in conversation when during a break in the music Alexa suddenly stiffened and stared at something beyond Sári's back. "Don't turn around but, guess who is coming this way," she managed to whisper before Sári heard the familiar voice.

"Well, well, it's nice to see old friends again! How are you all doing?" It was her old boyfriend Adam, smiling down at her, handsome as ever with his tousled blond hair and usual bohemian ease.

"It's good to see you too," Sári smiled back but didn't invite him to sit down.

"What about you?" Alexa chimed in. "We heard you got married. How is married life? Is your wife treating you nice?"

"She did for a while, until she gave up on me," he laughed and pulled a shoulder.

"Gave up on you in what way?" Wanda's voice was full of sarcasm. "Kicking you out?"

"It's a long story. Let's just say we are no longer together." Then, changing the subject, he turned to Sári. "And how are things with you? You look great!"

Before she could answer, Alexa raised her glass. "You bet! And she has good reason to look so radiant. She just graduated and is on her way to a great career!" She leaned across the table, clinking her glass to Sári's, with the others following in a round of cheers.

"Why, that's wonderful! I know it was not easy, but you did it! And look at you now, an independent woman to take all that life has to offer!" He bowed his head and, taking her hand, raised it to his lips. "I wish you the best, Sári; you deserve nothing less." As their eyes met and held, Wanda and Alexa exchanged glances and rolled their eyes. It was obvious that sparks still flew and things were not quite over between these two.

And they guessed right. The very next day Adam was calling her to say how much he missed her, wanting her back in his life if she was willing to give him another chance. He was sorry, he made a mistake, he said, but without it he would not have found out how much she really meant to him. And of course, she forgave him and agreed to resume their relationship, except it would not be like the old days when they spent practically every free moment together. That was a mistake she won't make again.

When they wound up in bed that night, his renewed demand to possess her chased away any lingering doubts she still held against him. The years they spent apart never happened, all was new again, and this time nothing ever would come between them.

Her friends were not overly enthusiastic about the reconciliation and openly questioned how she could trust him when he abandoned her once, married someone else, and then couldn't hold on to his marriage. Wanda was especially against it. Adam would never change! He couldn't help himself; he was too good looking, a popular musician, the type of man women are always attracted to. She personally would never have anything to do with entertainers, she said, but then Sári never listened to her, so what was the use trying to talk sense into her. To hear Wanda downplaying her boyfriends was nothing new to Sári; she was used to it and just ignored her disparaging remarks.

As Sári settled into her new job she could finally start looking for a place of her own. Of course it could only be a rented room; the housing shortage had not improved since the war ended ten years ago. The rush to heavy industry did not leave room for rebuilding bombed out buildings; they still stood pockmarked, with boarded up doors and windows.

It was sheer luck that through one of her new co-workers she found a nice room in the garden-like Pasaret district. Her colleague's sister, Rene—recently separated, not working, and raising her three-year-old daughter—was looking for a renter who would baby-sit occasionally, not too often, only on special evenings when she had a social engagement, and for that she was willing to lower the rent. It was a perfect arrangement for both parties. The house had central heating, a nice garden, even a telephone, and good bus connections to the inner city, and so, after the rules were set about kitchen and phone privileges and barring boyfriends, Sári moved in.

She wrote her new address to her parents and to Eta, who surprised her with news of her own: she was expecting again, a final try for a little girl. She was also packing to move. The apartment in the city was getting too small for their growing family, and when they found a nice house in the suburbs with a big backyard, they took it. It even had a plot to plant vegetables and perhaps raise some chickens; at least she could put into practice what the nuns taught her in school.

Visiting her Aunt Mariska, Sári received yet more good news; her uncle Sandor was coming home from Russia! Her aunt didn't know the details of his release, only that it had something to do with the German Chancellor Konrad Adenauer's negotiations with the new Soviet leadership. As the hard stance of Russia's international policies began to soften and Khrushchev was making conciliatory gestures toward Tito, he also accepted an invitation from Konrad Adenauer to reopen diplomatic relationship. As part of the negotiations, Adenauer demanded the release of the 9,000 German war prisoners still held in the Lubyanka prison or in the Siberian gulags, a claim loudly rejected by Nikolay Bulganin, the Premier of the Soviet Union, on the basis that there were no German prisoners of war in Russia! They were immediately let go when the war ended. The mentioned 9,000 were all war criminals, duly tried in courts, and sentenced under Soviet and international laws. But when Adenauer dangled the economic carrot in front of Khrushchev's nose—something the Russians must have sorely needed—the proposal was accepted and on September 28, 1955 most of the German prisoners were given amnesty and were let go. Since a number of Hungarian officers, among them Sandor, were kept together with the Germans, they were also set free.

They were all taken to Moscow, given papers, and loaded into wagons for transport to their homeland. At the Hungarian border the AVO took over. With machine guns drawn they separated the Germans, sending them on their way to Germany, where they were greeted as heroes, but the Hungarians were retained and sent to a collection center at nearby Nyiregyhaza. They arrived there in mid-November to undergo a screening process that included questions about their imprisonment in Russia. The fact that the Russian release papers didn't indicate the original crime or sentence, only that the man was free to return to his country, created a problem for the AVO. What if some of them were really dangerous war criminals? In order to check the background of these returning ex-officers they were ordered to write several in-depth autobiographies, which would be checked against old AVO records. If nothing turned up after thorough scrutinizing, they were let go; others, including Sandor, still under suspicion, were transferred to a prison in Jaszbereny for further investigation. Should an existing charge against them come to light, they wouldn't slip through the AVO's fingers this time! They'd get their punishment, even if the AVO had to wait ten years before catching them!

And so Sandor was kept locked up, still a prisoner, to the great disappointment of his mother and sister. Their only consolation was that at least he was back in the country and would be treated better than in Russia.

It took another turn of events before he was freed in the fall of 1956.

At her new job Sári went through a long interview with the personnel department. They had already received her kader record form the university and, noting that she was involved in cultural activities there, invited her to join a similar group at the company. They also urged her to apply for membership in their trade union, explaining how it represented the workers' interests, created better working conditions, improved productivity, and ensured opportunities for workers to acquire greater technical knowledge.

Of course nothing was further from the truth. Everyone knew that since the Communist takeover, the unions had ceased to represent the workers and it was no longer possible to voice genuine grievances. The unions were nothing more than a Party tool, where management set contracts and production quotas without workers' representation. Forced to submit to whatever the Party dictated, workers lost confidence in their union leaders and regarded them Party lackeys no longer serving their own interests.

Naturally, Sári signed up, and like everyone else, kept paying the monthly dues, but whenever union meetings were called, she had urgent deadlines to meet. She also neglected to attend the phony sessions held each morning to read the newspaper. What was the use of discussing Cardinal Mindszenty's release from prison on July 17, 1955, when everyone knew that he was only transferred from jail to house arrest somewhere in northern Hungary? She was equally uninterested why so many of her co-workers got excited about some "Memorandum" written by prominent communist writers in November 1955, in which they condemned the return of the rule of force after Rakosi's reinstatement. What difference did it make? It was no concern of hers either that Imre Nagy was kicked out of the Party in December; membership decision was strictly Party business. And what did she have to do with Hungary's admittance to the United Nations when it was announced on December 14?

Inevitably, her passive political attitude drew the attention of the office committee and, not waiting for her annual evaluation, they called her in for a review at the beginning of 1956. Not mincing words, they told her that although her participation in cultural activities was appreciated, more was expected of her; after all, she owed her education to the State. They needed young educated people like her to help paving the way to socialism, and she must be more willing to participate in that struggle. They made it clear that getting involved on the political front was essential, at the same time hinting that such commitment wouldn't go without reward.

Sári thanked them for the insight their discussion had given her and pleaded that she was just learning to function in the workplace. She would do better in the future. It was an eye-opener for her that even in a large industrial company no individual escaped the vigilance of the Party and she slowly convinced herself that it would be better working at a smaller place where pressure was less, and good work valued more than political attitude.

She was not actively looking, and keeping her promise, dutifully attended union meetings and other political gatherings, but when one of her colleagues changed jobs and called her later to tell about an opening in their accounting, she didn't hesitate to give notice. Management tried to talk her out of leaving by offering a salary increase, but she declined. It was not worth it. The new pay was a little lower, but the reduced pressure made up for it, plus the place was much closer to her home. She started working on April 2nd and found the political atmosphere far more relaxed. There was no forced newspaper reading, everyone concentrated on working hard, and she noticed that some of the women even talked openly about problems in the country—the high prices and still existing food shortages—without any fear of being reported.

Happy in her new job and more than content with her improved living conditions, Sári felt that her life was finally heading in the right direction. Her relationship with Adam was better than ever. Because Adam worked at nights, they saw each other on Monday evenings, his night off, and Saturdays and Sundays before he left for work. They both liked the outdoors, especially Adam after working in smoked filled rooms, and often took small excursions around the hills surrounding Budapest. Going to soccer games was another Sunday afternoon favorite, but when the weather cooled, they were just as happy to stay home or take in an early movie.

Perhaps because of the ongoing debates in the press demanding more freedom of expression, the quality of movies and plays improved. They were showing good foreign films, and live theaters were bringing back the old pre-war standards. When the National Theater went so far as daring to include in its repertoire one of Hungary's most beloved plays, the hitherto banned *Tragedy of Man*, people flocked to see it, with tickets sold out far in advance. It was written in 1861 by Imre Madach to give people hope for a better tomorrow during the time the country withered under Habsburg oppression. He used the framework of man's struggle from the day of Creation through subsequent ages to justify mankind's existence on earth. The story starts with Adam and Eve, but as civilization advances, every time society seems to be on the brink of achieving some noble goal, Evil strikes to prove that mankind is doomed, and God's experiment with the human race was a failure. It ends somewhere far in the future when people appear to have lost all purpose to go on, but then, on the brink of losing faith, a divine command is heard from above that they must continue the struggle even if unsure of rewards. The play's final message, *Ember küzdj és bizva bizzál*—loosely translated: Strive on and never lose faith—always had a special meaning for Hungarians, who had suffered so much throughout history under foreign rulers. It urged them never to give up, and now, just as in 1861, people sat in the theater with tears in their eyes, clinging to the hope to be free again even if the outlook seemed hopeless. It was due to this final message that the government banned the play. Up to that point the story actually played into the hand of Communist ideology, that all the different social structures in history failed to advance the human race. They only found fault in that it didn't end with the victorious triumph of Communism, the perfect social structure where humanity finally ceases its endless struggle and begins to live happily ever after in a faultless world, the workers' paradise. But then with such ending the play would be nothing more than a fairy tale, playing to empty houses.

With the subtle cultural changes and the writers' ever-increasing demands for freedom of the press, people began to breathe more freely, as if suddenly a vent opened allowing fresh air to circulate. Music was changing too; radios nixed the likes of the Russian *Ochin Chornaya* ("Dark Eyes") and were playing songs popular in the West. Whenever people danced, it was to the sound of Glenn Miller, not the monotonous, boring tunes musicians were compelled to play before. Youngsters began to jump and twirl as American teenagers were seen in movies, seemingly forgetting years and years of indoctrination against such decadent behavior. It was new and exciting and they embraced it with the fervor typical of youth everywhere in the free world. They were rejecting the cultural boundaries the Party imposed on them and were pushing for the right to be free to make choices.

The Hungarian film industry was making adjustments, too, dropping the production of boring politically themed movies that aimed to re-educate the masses but failed miserably. They realized that after seeing the newly imported lighthearted Italian films with gorgeous stars, people no longer swallowed the Party-approved stories of proletarian boy meets confused middle class girl, rescues her from her petty bourgeois self, and once awakened to the truth, she and her hero find happiness in toiling together, pledging to build socialism 'till death do them part. And when the story came to light about how Carlo Ponti discovered Sophia Loren, it set off a search in Budapest for a new face that the film studio could develop as the first Hungarian movie star since the 1930s. Agents were scouting amateur plays and student productions; they were approaching pretty girls sitting in cafés or even stopping them on the streets to offer a screen test.

Alexa and Sári, coming out of a movie theater one evening, were also handed a card inviting them to come in for a film test. At first they just laughed about it and discarded the notion, but later, talking it over, they decided to give it a try. Why not? What was there to lose? If nothing else, they might have fun seeing the inside of a movie studio. The next day they called the number on the card and made their appointments. Sári was scheduled for a Saturday afternoon session, where they took a series of headshots at different angles, looking into the camera, over her shoulder, pulling her hair up, letting it fall, changing expression from serious to smiling, and so on. When it was over they thanked her with the promise to let her know the results.

After testing hundreds of hopefuls the studio ended up choosing a well-known actress for their next movie but kept the tests on file. Both girls received periodic calls for work as extras, but of course, Sári had to decline; she couldn't take time off from her new job. She didn't even dare to ask for a Saturday morning off—their short workday—so she could get to Sopron on time for her mother's 50th birthday party. She had to rush to catch the train in the afternoon, but made it home just in time to see Ilonka blowing out the candles. Everyone was there—the children, grandchildren, the Varosys, Mitzie, and other friends—all congratulating her for reaching this important milestone.

The lack of vacation time created another problem for Sári when at the beginning of July Adam invited her to spend a week with him in Siofok, the most popular summer resort on the shores of Lake Balaton, where his band was playing in one of the hotels. When he asked her to come, it was not only because he missed her; he just received his final divorce papers and wanted to celebrate his newly gained freedom with her.

It had been six weeks since they'd last seen each other, and Sári was dying to go, if only she could figure out a way without jeopardizing her work!

She still had a long way before she'd be eligible for vacation, two weeks after one year of service, but until then only an emergency situation would get her time off. Unfortunately, a week spent in blissful togetherness with her boyfriend did not qualify as an emergency, but that didn't deter her. She would just have to invent one. And so, with a sad look on her face, she told management that her father was seriously ill and she must go home at once. There was no objection; they only asked her to notify them when she would be back.

With that accomplished, she sat down and wrote two notes. The first one was to management, postdated a few days into the following week, saying that she'd return on Monday, July 23. She put this into a stamped envelope addressed to her employer, sealed it, then slipped it into another envelope she sent to her mother with a note asking her to drop the enclosed sealed letter in the mail the day after she received it; she would explain the strange request in her next letter.

Her friends knew where she was going, but she said nothing about the devious way she got the week off. It was her business alone. Proud of her clever scheme and confident that all would work out, she packed her bag and on Saturday, July 14, took the train to Siofok. Regrettably though, not all went as planned. The company received her note from Sopron all right, and that would have been fine, but in the middle of the week they also got a phone call from Alexa asking when Sári would be back from Siofok. When the manager cautiously asked why Comrade Zachar would be in Siofok, she innocently told the truth, visiting her boyfriend.

The following Monday morning Sári walked in the office with a somber face befitting someone who just returned from the bedside of a gravely ill parent. Strangely though, nobody asked about her father; even her friend who brought her into the company avoided looking at her. *Why all the long faces?* she thought with a touch of guilt. Could it be that they didn't get her note? She put down her purse and went to see the manager, but before she could open her mouth he raised a hand and stopped her. "We know everything, Comrade Zachar," he said and picking up her work record book, handed it to her. "We accept your voluntary resignation over family emergency. Due to circumstances, we have no other choice but to say goodbye to you."

And with that Sári was out of her job with no one to blame but herself. It was very generous of management to indicate voluntary resignation as reason for leaving, and she was truly grateful for that. They could have easily marked her walking papers as dismissed for unethical conduct, which would automatically draw an inquiry from any future employer and jeopardize, if not ruin, her prospects of finding another job.

Since her one-week "leave of absence" went without pay, her last paycheck was pitifully small, just enough to cover the rent for August, leaving very little to live on. Her small savings were tied up in the bank, with penalties for early withdrawal, and although she applied for unemployment benefits, her payments would only start after a three-week waiting period. What was she to do in the meantime? She sent out résumés and made calls to let people know that she was looking for work but only got negative responses. She was sitting at home hoping for callbacks, but when the phone rang it was only her sister on the line. She was in town visiting her in-laws for a few days, and when she learned that Sári was out of work—although not the reason why—and was short on cash, she suggested to come and stay with them in Debrecen until a job came along. She could use a little help around the children.

Sári was more than glad to go; she wouldn't have to worry about money while there, and also could spend a little time with her nephews. It was hard to believe that Eta's new baby, a little boy named Istvan, was already seven months old, an adorable child, although with everyone expecting a girl, his sex was a small disappointment to his parents and grandparents. It was Eta's last chance for a daughter, since she gave up on trying a fourth time and resigned to wait until a granddaughter came along.

Their old arguments forgotten, Sári was happy to see Latzi too. Aside from politics, they always got along well, and she knew he loved Eta and was a good father to the boys. During one of their talks she asked her sister about him and how he was doing in his job now that he was no longer involved with the Party.

"Well, Latzi is Latzi, you know how he is," Eta pulled a shoulder.

"Don't tell me that he still clings to his leftist theories!"

"That never changed; he still believes that living in a world according to Marx is the guarantee to a better life. No, what I meant was his Calvinist stubbornness. There is no give and take in his way of thinking. We could have it so much easier if he'd just bend the rules a bit."

"What do you mean? What rules? Is it about money?"

"No, no, it has nothing to do with that; he is a good provider and the kids never lack anything. He just doesn't know how to handle his employees, the men working under him. He is in charge of managing the forest estates, and it is common practice that the rangers come sometimes offering things in exchange for wood; everyone does it, but not him! God forbid he'd let people chop up some old fallen trees! Or let them shoot a pheasant or quail when they were not supposed to. They are property of the State! In return we could have all the fresh vegetables and fruits or whatnot free, but no, he won't hear of it. I have to grow my own and raise chickens to save money for other things. And not only that; he could turn down the requests for favors with a smile, make some excuse for not going along with the suggestions, and the men would get the message without feeling rejected, but that wouldn't do for him; he has to put them in their places! He must give the poor devils a lecture and rub their noses in it that what they ask of him is against the law. His underlings all hate him! I know how they talk behind his back: who does he think he is, and things like that. At times I am scared that one of these days he'll have an 'accident'."

"Don't be silly; nobody would dare. But can't you tell him to act with a little more finesse, to be more diplomatic?"

"I tried but it's no use. He just gives me that 'I am surprised that you side with these people' look and then gives me a lecture to boot. Do I need that?"

Sári believed every word her sister said about Latzi. She knew firsthand how infuriating his righteousness could be from the time when her scholarship was so drastically reduced. He had no sympathy; it must have been something she had done! It was futile to argue with him; he always had to have the last word.

It was perhaps the first time that the two sisters had a grown-up heart-to-heart talk and felt a stronger connection. It made it a little harder to say goodbye when after three weeks Sári returned to Budapest hoping to have some positive responses to her job applications. She felt optimistic; things would soon be better. That buoyant mood, however, turned sour as soon as she reached home. There were no job offers waiting, but worse than that, Rene's husband was back in the house, the two blissfully reconciled, and now she'd have to find another place to live. As reality set in, that she had no job, very little money, and no place to live, her soaring spirits plummeted. Talk about bad luck! Did someone put a jinx on her?

Rene felt sorry for her and, feeling a little guilty over the situation, returned her August rent money. She also had a suggestion that until Sári got on her feet she could stay at her parents' apartment. They had a tiny room next to the kitchen, which they let her have for practically nothing. The location was very good, close to the business district in the center of the city, which should help making the rounds easier while job hunting. It would also come handy that they had a telephone.

So once again, Sári packed her belongings and moved into what turned out to be a cubbyhole with a cot, a small table and chair, and nothing more. But Rene's parents were very kind; they practically apologized for the room, and since they both worked, they let her use their living room during the day.

The minute she settled in, she stepped up her efforts to find work. She dropped off more resumes, made cold calls, and followed up with friends about job openings. When offers wouldn't start pouring in, she called the movie studio to let them know she was available and got called in occasionally to act as an extra. The pay was good, 50 forints for a day's work, which was half of what she paid for her room in a month. The money helped, but aside that, she had fun being part of the movie making business, and hoped that not all her scenes ended up on the cutting floor.

Whether she made it to the big screen or not, she never found out. Events unfolding that fall in Hungary prevented it.

CHAPTER SIX

1956 - 1970

Fight for freedom

ALL THROUGH THE summer of 1956 the writers and journalists, most of them card-holding Party members, continued their battle to push for the right of free expression. What began with refusing to write rapturous articles about false achievements and sing exaggerated praises for the Soviet Union now has reached the point where they felt compelled to report nothing less than the truth. It was a reflection of the country's general mood, and sensing the discontent, Moscow realized that allowing Rakosi back in power was a mistake. They sent Anastas Mikoyan, the second most powerful man after Khrushchev, to assess the situation and do what was necessary to keep the Hungarians in check. Arriving in Budapest in the middle of July, he decided that Rakosi must go, and acting upon his recommendation the Central Committee removed him as First Party Secretary during a three-day session, replacing him with Erno Gero. Hoping to placate the people, the reshuffled party leadership promised to speed up liberalization and asked the restless writers to end their daily criticism, write some good books, and leave politics to the professionals.

When this pathetic appeal didn't change the writers' attitude or lift the prevailing pessimism, making it clear that stripping Rakosi of power was not enough, the Soviets went ahead and removed him from the national scene altogether. He left Hungary on October 15, once more claiming recurring "illness" that required medical treatment available only in the USSR, but this time his exit was final; he would never return to the country again. He remained in Russia, living out his days in Gorky in the Kirghiz Soviet Socialist Republic until his death on February 5, 1971.

He was still in power when on March 27, 1956 he announced the rehabilitation of Rajk and his co-defendants by acknowledging that their trial was a miscarriage of justice, their execution a grave error. They were victims of criminal excess committed by the AVO and its then chief Gabor Peter, now sitting in jail. Trying to explain away his part in staging the bloody trial fooled no one; people knew he was to blame, and he was advised to stay away from attending the state funeral for Rajk and the two other victims planned for October 6.

That date was chosen symbolically by Rajk's widow, unbroken by six years of imprisonment and released only in July 1955 by Imre Nagy. The 6th of October was Martyrs' Day in Hungary, a revered national holiday commemorating the hanging of thirteen leading generals of Hungary's failed attempt for independence from Austria in 1848. Dark clouds and light rain added to the solemnity of the interment as over 200,000 mourners gathered to say goodbye to Rajk and pay their respects to his widow. She was standing by his casket holding the hand of her eight-year-old son, born in the year of his father's execution. Amid a sea of flowers, Rajk was eulogized by speaker after speaker as a great martyr of the working class, all proclaiming that although the dead cannot be resurrected, such "criminal excesses" and "killings by error" would never be repeated. The AVO feared that with nerves tense and the atmosphere overheated, it could take a single word from Mrs. Rajk to turn the funeral into a mass unrest, but it did not happen. The crowd remained solemn and, as if determined not to tarnish the memorial, kept its discontent under control.

Near the end of ceremonies Imre Nagy, the former premier recently forced out of office and expelled from the Party, emerged from the crowd, and as a now-private citizen embraced the sobbing widow. The simple expression of sympathy evoked a spontaneous emotional reaction from the crowd that didn't go unnoticed by the Party. It brought into focus that regardless of falling from grace, Nagy's popularity continued. Perhaps expelling him from the Party was wrong! They hastily corrected it by declaring that Rakosi's personal hatred for Nagy played a large part in their decision to expel him, and offered to reinstate his membership. First they insisted that he admit to making "mistakes" during his short-lived leadership, but when he steadfastly refused, they dropped the demands and on October 14 readmitted him anyway. This was tantamount to accepting his 1953 revisionist policies as correct, forcing them to endure his renewed attacks on the Politburo. They had no choice but to stand by as he lectured that ruling by terror destroyed the most noble of human virtues, those of courage, sincerity, loyalty, and the adherence to principles, and instead promoted cowardice, falsehood, hypocrisy, and opportunism. As before, his sharpest criticism was directed against the power of the AVO, how it rose above society and the law.

For the moment it didn't matter what he preached, the Party looked the other way because they saw him as less of a threat than the growing tide of discontent. He was the people's favorite and perhaps given a chance, he might be the man who could appeal to the masses and keep them calm. And it might have worked, if not for events that started unfolding in Poland on October 19, four months after the bloody summer riots in Poznan. In that June workers there staged massive protests demanding better wages and working conditions. During a violent confrontation with soldiers and the police shots were fired into a crowd, leaving behind scores of dead and injured. In retaliation the people attacked the Party Headquarters, ransacked the Security Offices and other government buildings, and opened the prison doors. The Soviets interfered and, taking control of the situation, quickly put down the protest. Arrests followed and by mid-August over 700 demonstrators were in prison as "provocateurs."

That was in the summer, but by October the Polish government realized that some changes were inevitable to stabilize the workers and elected Wladyslaw Gomulka, considered a moderate, as their new leader. He began to turn the regime around to accept some of the workers' demands and carry out reconciliatory reforms. Moscow viewed the new developments with renewed alarm, but another conflict was avoided because of the strong leadership of Gomulka. He was able to placate the Russians and at the same time persuade his countrymen to have more patience. When he took power on October 19, it was without opposition from the USSR.

Writers and university students, closely following Gomulka's political maneuverings, were emboldened by his success. Inevitably a question rose in their minds: why can't we do the same? Members of the newly formed Petofi Circle, a Communist youth organization made up mostly of students and backed by the Writers Union, held a series of meetings to discuss conditions in Hungary. The writers acknowledged that since Rakosi's removal as First Secretary, they were allowed to write about his wrongdoings, but suddenly they wanted more. Claiming the right to criticize anybody, including the current leaders, and to uphold the truth at all cost, they rejected all interference with the writers' freedom of expression and stopped praising the regime and printing false success stories that everyone knew to be a lie.

These proclamations had a powerful effect on the popular sentiment. It was common knowledge that the men and women of the press were the voice of the Party, and now they were making a drastic turnabout, demanding changes without showing any fear of the consequences. Following their example, the university students also came out with their own resolutions compiling their grievances in a fifteen-point program. Among others they called for abolition of compulsory courses of Marxism-Leninism, dropping the Russian language classes and to exempt students from mandatory military training. They also listed freedom of speech, the right to self-government, revised work quotas, the withdrawal of Soviet troops, reinstatement of multi-party elections with Imre Nagy as Premier, and publication of trade agreements with Russia, especially those involving Hungary's uranium deposits. The root of resentment against trade agreements was the Soviet control of Hungary's economy by operating mixed companies, manipulating prices, imposing heavy military expenditures and generally keeping the trade balance unfavorable to Hungary. As for the uranium—recently discovered in southern Hungary and considered a national treasure—people expected it would provide cheap power for the country, freeing it from dependency on foreign imports, but instead, according to persistent rumors, Rakosi concluded a secret pact with Russia, granting them exclusive rights not only to the new deposits, but also to exploit any similar future discoveries in exchange for a ridiculously small compensation.

And so, as the Petofi Circle became the forum to voice objections and attendance to their meeting swelled to the thousands, a plan began to emerge for a great demonstration. It was planned for October 23, partially to express sympathy with Gomulka's goals and the Polish people's struggle to improve their political situation, but also to publish their list of demands. Copies were printed for distribution during the demonstration, along with banners and signs with slogans such as "Independence for Hungary!" "Bring Rakosi to justice!" and "Solidarity with the Polish people!"

The writers were also going to participate in the march but withdrew when they learned that the government refused to grant permission. It would create clashes with the police and they proposed finding other ways to present the demands. Only when the authorities reversed their decision and lifted the ban did they agree to join the students. And so on the bright and sunny morning of October 23 streets began to fill with students heading for the gathering point at the Petofi statue in the center of Pest. They carried stacks of the printouts of their proposals, handing them out along the way, noisily inviting others to join.

Most people heading for work had no idea what was going on, but after catching some phrases from the highly excited youngsters on the streets and glancing at their list of demands, word quickly spread that what happened in Poland was happening here!

In no time offices and shops were abuzz with the news. As more and more people arrived at work, they brought further news about the students' march and of their plan to broadcast their program over the radio. Work virtually stopped as employees gathered in groups to read the printouts, most of them with unabashed enthusiasm, some with cautious reserve. Everyone had an opinion. It was about time that someone dared to speak up! Twelve years of Russian occupation was twelve years too long! Out with them! People had the right to know what happened with the nation's uranium! Hungary had paid war reparations to the Russians long enough! How about the people the Russkies dragged to Siberia? How many were still alive? Bring them home! Let's get some answers! If we all stand up as one, they can't silence an entire nation!

Foolish talk, countered the pessimists. There was no sense getting exited over something that had no chance to succeed. This nation no longer had the guts to rise up. For one thing, it was too divided. What do these young kids think? Playing David against the Russian Goliath? Even if organized, sooner or later someone would alert the AVO and that would be the end of it. So why bother?

But the doomsayers were in the minority and their voices were fast silenced into shame. And so it was at the office of the Institute of Industrial Planning, where Sári began working on October 1. It took her a while to find a job, but finally she landed there, working in statistics. As everyone else, she was caught up in the highly charged debate whether to leave and join the demonstration, or wait and see what developed. The place resembled an overturned beehive and pulsated with excitement as suddenly the door opened and in marched the office manager, Mrs. Steiner, a staunch member of the Party and in charge of political education. Raising her hand, she announced on good authority that the Party was already in contact with the student leaders regarding their legitimate proposals to correct some of the errors of the previous government. Comrades Gero and Kadar were at that very moment on their way back from a constructive meeting with Marshal Tito in Yugoslavia, and would sit down to confer with the student delegates later in the day.

"Stay calm and return to your work," she said. "The Party will see to it that, within reason, all requests will be granted."

"We've heard that before and nothing ever happens! It's just another lie!" someone shouted.

"It's too late for promises! People have lost all confidence in the leadership!" another voice claimed.

"And just what do you consider 'within reason'? Does it include the withdrawal of the Russian troops?"

"The Soviets are here for security reasons in agreement with the Warsaw Pact," Mrs. Steiner retorted. "Their removal would upset the unity of the socialist bloc; everyone can understand that!"

"Not everyone, Comrade Steiner! The truth is that the Party is afraid that without the Russians they'd be ousted, kicked out, as they should be! Let them pack up and leave with their Big Brothers so we can be free to build a true democracy, as we started in 1945!"

"That is nonsense! It's true that the Rakosi regime made grave mistakes, but no one can deny the tremendous improvements the Party has made in the past seven years! And with the new leadership the country is heading for even greater achievements, but you must have patience. You are risking the future by rocking the boat."

She was practically shouted down with that last remark. Rocking the boat? If people were so happy with those "tremendous improvements," they wouldn't take to the streets and demand changes. With shouts fired at her from every direction, Mrs. Steiner had enough. With a final warning against recklessly joining the demonstrators, she turned on her heel and walked out, slamming the door behind her. But she was not finished. In no time she returned with the district party representative, a heavyset woman seemingly confident in the authority of her office.

"Comrades! I come as the representative of the 5th District Party Committee to inform the Comrades about the Party's standing on today's demonstration. It has come to light that fascist provocateurs and agitators are among the demonstrators and for that reason the Interior Ministry has revoked the permission to continue the march and ordered the crowd to disperse. Those who refuse will have to take the consequences. And to ensure that these fascist elements, when they begin to run, would not find refuge in nearby buildings such as this, we gave strict orders to your director to lock all the entrance doors."

Her arrogant stance and smugly chosen words were like adding oil to fire. Shouting back that they were not little children to be ordered around, and that locked doors were intended to keep them inside, not to keep the "fascists" out, everyone, even the skeptics, turned away, and grabbing coats and purses headed for the exit. Sári was swept along with the rest, but once outside the building she stood hesitantly, not knowing what to do next. Then someone caught her by the arm, shouting, "Come on, you don't want to miss a day like this!" With that she soon found herself standing in the midst of an ever-swelling crowd in Petofi Square, mostly students, waiting to start the march. Their intention was to go to the statue of Jozef Bem, a 19th century Polish general revered in Hungary as a symbolic figure of freedom for fighting on the side of Hungary during the 1848 revolt against the Habsburgs. The statue stood on the Buda side, where they were to lay a wreath as a tribute to the Polish people and to Gomulka for his brave action to expand freedom in Poland.

The crowd milled around peacefully, cheering loudly every time a new truckload of factory workers arrived to join the march in spite of attempts by party officials to keep them from leaving. But everyone grew quiet when a well-known actor was seen climbing onto the platform that held the statue of Petofi, the young poet who always and forever represented the free spirit of Hungary and the country's fierce resistance to foreign oppressions. Emotions ran high as the man, standing still and holding the flag, began reciting Petofi's "National Song," a patriotic call for independence he wrote on the eve of that other revolution more than a hundred years ago:

RISE, Magyars! Answer the call,
The time is now, or never at all.
Shall we be slaves or shall we be free?
This is the question! Which will it be?
God of Magyars! To you we swear,
Swear to cast off the chains we wear.
(Author's translation)

By the time he finished all six verses of the poem, the crowd picked up the refrain and chanted in unison, "God of Magyars! To you we swear, swear to cast off the chains we wear!" Flags appeared everywhere, and when people saw several with the hated sickle and red star emblem cut from the middle, the rush was on to do the same. Just then, someone somewhere intoned the National Anthem, and as voice after voice joined in, the square soon echoed with the soaring prayer of this much-suffering people:

GOD bless us, these Magyars,
With plenty and good grace,
Stand with us, protecting us
If enemies we face.
Torn and battered by ages past
Grant us better years,
We had suffered much too long
For our past and future sins.
(Author's translation)

In the passion of the moment, the thunderous applause and shouts of "Long Live Freedom" and "Long live Hungary" seemed to go on forever. Then finally, at one o'clock a loudspeaker called for the march to begin, and people started to line up, ready to move. Carrying flags and banners, they marched in orderly fashion across the Margit Bridge, where busses and streetcars stopped to let them pass. Curious passengers stared in disbelief: look at the slogans and those cutout flags! This was not one of those organized demonstrations that everyone loathed to attend! And when the demonstrators waved and shouted to come and join the march, many got off and fell into step with them.

By the time they reached the Jozef Bem statue the crowd had swelled well over 20,0000 and still more were coming. A large number of people were forced into side streets, but amazingly, nobody complained, no one pushed or tried to elbow their way closer to witness the ceremonies. It was enough to be part of the excitement, to share in the prevailing spirit of patriotism and solidarity. As the crowd grew quiet, a pair of students holding Polish and Hungarian flags marched up to the imposing monument and stood at stiff attention, while a delegation of young men placed a wreath at the foot of the statue. After singing the National Anthem and "La Marseillaise"—the French national anthem that the Hungarians always considered a song of international solidarity—someone stepped forward to speak, keeping it short since there was no microphone and only those standing close could hear.

Then suddenly, blowing its horn and causing a commotion, a car from the Budapest TV station pushed its way through the crowd. Several reporters jumped out and rushed to the front, while a cameraman with equipment mounted on his shoulder started recording. Although they were late for the main ceremony, the president of the Writers' Union was still to speak. Earlier in the day the writers had modified the original proclamation drawn up by the students and reduced their fifteen points to seven by dropping several and consolidating others. Wisely, they saw that some of the demands were unattainable for the present time, foremost among them the immediate withdrawal of the Red Army. The government was bound by various agreements to accept the continuous presence of the Russians, and to expect that this could be undone by youthful demands was nothing more than wishful thinking. To insist could lead to a bloody confrontation.

A member of the TV crew put a microphone in the speaker's hand as the crowd listened, intent on not to miss a word of what he had to say:

> Dear friends! We have arrived at a turning point in our history. We all agree that the party and the government leaders have so far failed to give us an acceptable and efficient program, and that the responsibility for this failure falls on those who purposely neglected to create conditions that are required to build a true Socialist Democracy.

His words draw a tremendous response from the crowd, shouts of approval that seemed to go on forever. When the patriotic outburst finally subsided, he continued to enumerate the demands of the Hungarian Writers as formulated in complete solidarity with the people:

1) We demand an independent national policy based on the principle of socialism. Relations, including treaties and economic agreements with the USSR and other counties must be based on equality.

2) End the national minority policies that disturb friendships between peoples.

3) The government must disclose the true economic situation of the country and include workers, peasants, and intellectuals in the political, social, and economic administration of the country.

4) In factories the workers and specialists must be included in management; wages, norms, quotas must be reformed and the trade unions must represent the true interests of the workers.

5) Agricultural policies must be revised, and the peasants must be granted the right to determine their participation in cooperatives.

6) The Rakosi clique must be eliminated from all public life. Imre Nagy must be appointed to a high post he so deserves. At the same time, we must stand against the emergence of counter-revolutionary attempts and aspirations.

7) Our electoral system must reflect the demands of socialist democracy. Election must be free and by secret ballot.

He concluded by calling for calm and discipline, encouraging everyone to have confidence in the government that after receiving and reviewing the demands, it would do its utmost to validate them. With a final praise for the Polish government and the leadership of Gomulka for restoring order and stabilizing a potentially explosive situation, he brought the ceremonies to an end and urged people to disperse and return peacefully to their homes.

But the people were not willing to move. Voices demanded to know when the proposals would be presented and to whom. Not to Gero! Down with that traitor! We want Imre Nagy! He would listen to us! Let's go the Parliament! And by the sheer force of the mounting excitement, the crowd began to turn and push its way back toward Pest. People broke into groups as they crossed the Danube by different bridges, then headed toward three main locations: the Parliament building, where most of them went, expecting to hear from Nagy; the radio station, hoping to air the students/writers' proclamation; and the official newspaper building to demand publication of their points.

It was still light, about four-thirty in the afternoon, and everywhere the crowd passed more people joined, increasing the number of demonstrators to over 100,000. Windows flew open and people, leaning out, shouted encouragements, some displaying flags with the Communist emblem cut out from the middle. Seeing the enthusiastic responses, the massive crowd grew louder, more daring as they shouted their slogans and called out their demands. Just as a riverbank gives way to the rush of an oncoming flood, the repressed frustration of the past years burst open with the sweeping power of some elemental force that also brought forth all the anger and spite against those who robbed them of a future so promising in 1945. They remembered the fear that pressed them into submission; the loss of their voice, be it in the factories, farms, offices or the art and media; the forced adulation of anything Soviet; the senseless mandatory rhythmic applause at the mention of Stalin and Rakosi's name; and the subordination of national pride to Soviet superiority with ridicule, even retribution for expressing the slightest patriotism. And all this in the name of falsely glorified achievements, when in reality, due to blatant exploitation and the grandiose over-extension of the five-year plan, the standard of living had steadily declined. Only the privileged party officials prospered, those in the higher ranks living like aristocrats in villas staffed with servants, driven in American armored cars, and vacationing in exclusive foreign resorts.

To the disappointment of those arriving at the Parliament, they found the building deserted and the doors locked. When shouting for Imre Nagy went unanswered some people began to disperse, while others still milled around aimlessly. Then suddenly a truck drove by loaded with people shouting, "Down with the Stalin statue," a cry that the crowd picked up with an enthusiastic uproar. Immediately, a large group set out in the direction of Varosliget, the vast city Park, where the gigantic 26-foot bronze statue of Stalin stood on a 13-foot base. Spurred on by the challenge of tearing down that hated symbol of the terrorist regime, the tree-lined Dozsa Gyorgy Avenue leading to the park was soon crowded with noisy, unruly masses dragging steel cables and blowtorch cutters, all bent on pulling down the image of the despised Soviet tyrant.

It took hours of strenuous work before the bronze colossus fell to the triumphant, almost intoxicated cheers that rose from the jubilant onlookers. Only the boots remained standing and someone quickly climbed up and stuck a pair of Hungarian flags in them, while those below took out their pent-up anger on the downed giant. Spitting in its face, kicking the loathsome head, and trampling the body with unleashed hatred, they proceeded to tie the mutilated statue to a truck, dragging it down the boulevard amid joyous shouts of approval over its demise, stopping here and there to let people rush at it with curses and raised fists.

Back at the Parliament building, where a sizeable crowd still waited, the windows remained dark as evening slowly descended on the city. With streetlights coming on, the enormous, brightly lit red star on the top of the building drew the people's attention. Already agitated for not being able to present their proposal, the sight had an infuriating effect on them. Shouts of "Down with the red star" filled the air, when suddenly all the lights went out, leaving the square in total darkness. If it was meant to frighten the crowd, it didn't work. In no time the entire place was ablaze with torches made of discarded newspapers. Still, it was a relief when a few minutes later the lights came back on, with the exception of the red star. Its wires disconnected, it was no longer visible.

But this also meant there were people inside the building! And sure enough, the door to the balcony opened and someone with a loudspeaker stepped out and began to speak. With his face half-hidden by the loudspeaker, it was impossible to tell who the man was, and several people cried out, asking to identify himself. The minute he told his name, Ferenc Erdei, the current Minister of State, a storm of protest went up: "Down with you! We are not interested in what you have to say! We heard you before, and it was all lies! We want Imre Nagy! Where is Imre Nagy?"

Someone pushed Erdei back and told the crowd that they only wanted to announce that Nagy had arrived in the building and was ready to speak. Amidst thundering applause and more clamoring for their man, Nagy appeared on the balcony to address the people. "Dear Comrades!" he began, but in an instant his words were drowned out in a round of stormy protest:

"We are not Comrades! There are no Comrades here!"

"My dear countrymen!" he started over but was stopped again, this time by wild cheering and shouts of "Long Live Nagy."

He started for the third time:

> My dear friends! I am told, the youth of Hungary voiced a desire for a national renewal. I agree with their sentiments, but since I hold no position whatsoever in the government, I have no power or authority to act upon their rightful proposals. I can only promise that as soon as possible I will seek out the officials and present your demands to them. Until then, I implore you all to keep calm and return peacefully to your homes. For now that is all I can say but be assured, I will be in contact with your leaders to advise them of the outcome of my discussion with the government. It's been a long and difficult day and I wish you all good night.

His words had a calming effect on the people. It was getting late, a long time since they had left home in the morning. Since very few people had telephones, contact with families was very limited, and folks at home were getting worried after hearing the news about the unrest in the streets. From late afternoon, radio programs were interrupted by bulletins that demonstrators were turning into unruly mobs, the voice cautioning civilians to remain calm. Then at 8 PM Erno Gero, the First Party Secretary, went on the radio vehemently denouncing the demonstrators as provocateurs, gangs of bandits who were attacking public buildings and security units and were bent on destroying democracy, undermining the power of the working class and disrupting the country's friendship with the Soviet Union. He vowed to do everything necessary to repel the dastardly attack and ended with summoning the workers to exert "the greatest vigilance to prevent our enemies from breaking the unity of the Party."

Earlier in the day, sensing the mounting excitement of the people and noting their call for Imre Nagy, the government suggested to Gero to let Nagy deliver a speech. They all knew that people hated Gero as much as they hated Rakosi, both Soviet citizens and staunch Stalinists who felt nothing but contempt for the Hungarian people, but he stubbornly insisted that it was his duty to address the nation, and failure to do so would be taken as a sign of weakness. Anticipating an angry reaction to the planned speech, the government ordered a large detachment of armed AVO men into the radio building, making it a virtual fortress. For further protection, they also lined up several fire trucks to block the entrance.

The people still at the Parliament building knew nothing about the speech and its disastrous effect on those gathered in front of the radio station. The crowd there was already frustrated and angry at being denied entrance to the building and broadcast their demands, but to hear Gero calling them saboteurs and fascist gangs truly infuriated them. It was his blatant disregard of the situation and his brutal rejection of their program that transformed the day's peaceful demonstration into a bloody revolution, as the students, provoked beyond restrain, began storming the station. Trying to hold them back, the firemen turned on the hoses but that did not deter anyone. Drenched with water, they stood their ground, and in fierce determination to gain entrance to the building, cut the hoses and overturned the fire trucks. In response, the AVO first attacked them with teargas, and when that did not stop them either, opened fire into the crowd.

This marked the moment of no return that made all reconciliation and peaceful ending impossible. People began to fall, while the rest scattered in all directions, running for their lives in a wild stampede. The momentary retreat allowed ambulances to pick up the wounded and the dead, but soon the crowd roared back. Strangely, under the impact of those first shots, these young people suddenly ceased to be afraid, as if suddenly recognizing the power their unity represented.

The sound of shooting stopped everyone around the Parliament building from dispersing. Wondering what it was they heard, they stood in confusion until a pickup truck jammed with students made its way into the square with a loudspeaker blaring the horrifying news: "The police are shooting into the crowd at the radio station! There are scores of dead and wounded! We need your help!"

Responding to the call, those rushing to the scene found themselves in the middle of a battlefield, as young men and women without weapons tried to fight their way into the building, while well-armed AVO men crouching inside fired at them indiscriminately. If they thought that shooting would scare the people away, they were wrong. It seemed nothing would stop them, not even when the military appeared. Learning about the seriousness of the situation the government dispatched truckloads of army troops and several tanks to help the AVO, but when they arrived and saw the great disadvantage of the students, they halted and looked around in a confused state. Immediately people ran up to them shouting, “Don’t shoot us! You are Hungarians like us, we are not your enemy!”

In this momentary lull in the fighting, a young officer in the leading tank threw open the hatch and shouted that his orders were to go to the radio station, but nothing else. They would not shoot, and with that, while still standing, he commandeered the tank toward the main entrance. Once there, turning to the crowd with a broad grin on his face, he raised both his hands over his head. Whether he wanted to silence the crowd to say something, or gestured to convey that he kept his promise not to shoot, will never be known, for in the next instant he slumped over, killed instantly by a bullet coming from inside the radio building.

The other tanks, about seven, remained standing with hatches closed, but the soldiers, stunned and enraged by what they just witnessed, abandoned their trucks and joined the crowd. They were instantly bombarded with demands for guns the student so desperately needed. As a response, the soldiers who drove the lifeless body of the dead officer back to the barracks returned bringing weapons, machine guns and ammunition, including hand grenades. Other help also arrived, factory workers pulling up with truckloads of guns taken from the Lampada munitions plant, where they found the usually heavily guarded gate unattended. Was it a miracle, or was the door left open intentionally?

No longer unarmed and defenseless and with trained soldiers among them, the demonstrators took up the fight. The bloody battle raged all night, with mounting casualties, but as more and more workers coming from the industrial region of Csepel joined the ranks, the outcome slowly began to shift in favor of the insurgents. It was almost daybreak when the rioters succeeded breaking into the building, where a man-to-man fight continued until the last AVO man was dead or in flight, escaping through a secured underground tunnel.

Sári knew nothing of the events unfolding in Pest. After the demonstration at the Jozef Bem statue, she had just about enough of marching and listening to inflamed speeches and decided to stop by her cousin Feri’s place on nearby Nogradi Street. This area called Svabhegy was one of the most beautiful sections of old Buda where the rich and famous built their stately estates between the two wars—Eichman lived in one of the grand villas during the Nazi occupation—and now it was the choice location for the elite Red aristocracy to take up residence there. The house Feri and Eva lived in since their marriage in 1952 was built by her parents in the 1930s, and although it was big and spacious enough for the young couple and their two children, it was no match for the mansions around them.

When Sári knocked on the door Eva greeted her, visibly upset that even though they had a telephone, Feri hadn't called all day. She heard about the demonstrations and knowing her husband, she was sure he would be in the midst of it all. She calmed down a bit when Sári told her about the orderly march to the Bem statue and how restrained people behaved there. But she herself began to worry about her boyfriend when she tried to call him and there was no answer. On the last try before she was ready to go home, Adam picked up the phone and told her to come to his place, he won't be working that night with all the turmoil everywhere. He urged her to leave right away, but to be careful, streetcars and busses were standing abandoned, and there were people roaming the streets. There was no telling how the day would end.

Sári found the busses still running on the Buda side but only to the Chain Bridge; from there all traffic stopped, and she had to walk the rest of the way to her boyfriend's flat on Vaci Street. She bypassed the main boulevards and squares to avoid getting caught in the crowd and was glad when she finally reached his apartment. It was there, listening to the radio, that they heard Gero's disastrous speech. Disgusted with his lies, they looked at each other in astonished disbelief. How could the government allow this man to go on the air when the crowd wanted nothing to do with him?

It was a question everyone who listened to the broadcast asked. Is this how the leaders of the country handle an explosive situation? Didn't they learn anything from their Polish counterpart, that to avoid a potential crisis the government must keep calm at all cost, listen to the people's demands, talk to them, offer to work with them, but not insult and aggravate them!

Evidently some from the Party also realized this and, sobered by the virtual siege of the radio station, called members of the Central Committee to come to the Parliament for an urgent meeting. They gathered together and behind heavily guarded doors began to debate what to do next. As they argued back and forth how best to restore order, two factions emerged: the moderate reformists led by Janos Kadar, a member of the Politburo, and the old Stalinists on Gero's side. Kadar proposed reshuffling the party leadership and insisted on Gero's immediate resignation as the only way to avert further bloodshed, but Gero stood his ground, and instead wanted to appeal to the Soviets for help. He said their intervention was indispensable since it was obvious that the Party could not rely on the Army, and the AVO was overwhelmingly outnumbered.

Their tumultuous argument was interrupted by the sounds of firing from the outside as some students tried to battle their way in. During the shooting and in the ensuing confusion, Gero abruptly left the meeting. When he returned after midnight he announced that he, as First Party Secretary, had gone ahead and asked for and obtained the fraternal assistance of the Red Army. In the same breath he proposed replacing Prime Minister Andras Hegedus with Imre Nagy. After a moment of stunned silence, most members, even among Gero's supporters, broke into loud protestation. Several got up and left the meeting, others demanded his resignation, which he again refused. As for Imre Nagy, although he was not present, the Central Committee agreed to elect him as Premier and summoned him to come immediately. They also appointed several of his friends, including Kadar, to be part of the new government, a step in the right direction, except they also made Andras Hegedus, the most prominent among Gero's partisans, as deputy premier. With Gero and Hegedus still in power, what Imre Nagy and his friends could do was drastically reduced.

When Nagy arrived at dawn he was told of the Committee's decision. He was not asked to accept the position under said conditions; it had been decided for him. After that they kept him a virtual prisoner, guarded by the AVO and the Russians in complete isolation from his friends and supporters, while at the same time, around 3 AM on the morning of October 24th, the Russian tanks rolled onto the streets of Budapest. Half an hour later, Gero again went on the air from a new radio station set up inside the Parliament building and told the country that, unprepared against the bloody attack of the armed fascist, reactionary elements and counter-revolutionary gangs, the government, in accordance with the terms of the Warsaw Treaty, appealed for help to the Soviet units stationed in Hungary. He then urged everyone to welcome ". . . our friends and allies as they are now hurrying to our help . . . "

This was followed by conflicting communiqués issued in the name of either Nagy or Kadar, some ordering the insurgents to capitulate, others issuing ultimatums with deadlines to lay down their arms, yet another announcing the defeat of the counter-revolutionists. All this time not one government or Party official appeared to face the sizeable crowd still outside the Parliament building. No one seemed to be firmly in charge, and without leadership, the Party machinery simply fell apart, presenting a lamentable spectacle of confusion and dissension while sitting in the cellars of the Parliament, holding meetings and pointing fingers at each other.

The news that the Red Army was now brought into the action added a new dimension to the outrage of the people. As soon as the radio station was in the hands of the students, they began giving out reports on the movements of the enemy tanks and directed reinforcements where the revolutionary fighters needed it the most. Surprisingly, the most violent clashes between the Russians and Hungarians occurred in the industrial district of Csepel. Many from these factories fought at the radio station and after returning, they convinced the others to disregard the conflicting news coming from the Parliament. As a result, whenever Russian infantrymen backed by heavy T-54 tanks appeared at the Ganz railroad-car factory, at the Red Star tractor plant and numerous other large facilities, they met with fierce resistance. These workers, completely unorganized, without serious weaponry and vastly outnumbered, rushed against the rattling machine guns with not much more than hand-made gasoline bombs they christened "Molotov cocktails."

This immediate solidarity of the proletariat with the cause of the insurgents surprised Gero and the Soviet leaders. They assumed that the revolt was confined to the students and writers, and if they send in the Red Army, it would be quickly crushed. They could understand the intellectuals constantly harping about the truth and freedom of speech, nothing but bourgeois slogans they loved to use, and the students, always rebellious by nature, but they were counting on the fidelity of the coddled proletariat. As the battles continued all day, with casualties growing on both sides, it became obvious to the Russians that Gero was wrong in assessing the situation and they dispatched their two specialists in Hungarian affairs, Anastas Mikoyan and Mikhail Suslov. They arrived in Budapest on the morning of October 25 to announce over the radio that Gero had been replaced as first party secretary by Janos Kadar and gave assurances that as soon as order was restored, the Russian troops would be withdrawn. With that the two Russians flew back to Moscow taking Gero and also Hegedus with them for further discussions.

With Gero out of the picture, Nagy immediately sought to resume contact with his supporters. His main concern was to put an end to the bloodshed, but when in his radio address that same day—later claimed to have been made under duress while still in the hands of the AVO—he proclaimed that the intervention of the Red Army was necessary for the sake of preserving the socialist order, people began to wonder if he was betraying them, especially when, referring to the uprising, he used the term "counter-revolution." Even his faithful friends couldn't understand why he kept Hegedus, an old left-wing Stalinist, as his deputy premier and entrust him, of all people, with negotiations in Moscow. It didn't help his image, either, when Kadar went on the radio, calling on all "Comrades" to join the fight against the enemy, and issuing summons to the insurgents to capitulate. Proclaiming martial law and setting curfew hours also fed the people's distrust, reinforcing the general belief that there was no real change in the government, merely a reshuffle with Nagy put in the leadership, and only because the people demanded it. As a result, they refused to obey orders issued by the new regime and decided to follow their own logic to create a new social and economic organization that would represent their genuine interests.

The revolt rapidly spread to the provinces, especially in the larger industrial cities, but in Sopron the city remained relatively calm. Caught up in the spirit of the incredible turn of events, there were demonstrations—a group of students smashed some of the infamous Red Stars, and factory workers formed a few revolutionary committees with similar proclamations as published in Budapest—but there was no fighting in the streets and the situation never got out of hand.

Regardless of the relative calm, Ilonka and Jeno were frantic, not knowing what was happening to Gyuszi in Miskolc, where he now worked as a geologist engineer, Eta in Debrecen, and Sári in Budapest, all hotbeds of the rebellion. With the telephone service and mail delivery interrupted, there was no way to find out if they were all right. The best they could do was to hope and pray that all three had the good sense to stay away from the demonstrations and not get involved in the ruckus.

Hearing the terrifying news that Russian tanks were shooting into crowds of civilians, Jeno rushed to the post office when the telephone lines were reopened a few days later. After standing in line for hours waiting for his turn, he finally reached Eta and learned that they were fine, but had no such luck with the other two children. Gyuszi only had an office number, and of course no one answered with all work suspended, and when he called Sári, her landlady could only say that they had not seen her since the morning of the 23rd.

Perhaps at the very same time Gyuszi, a resolute patriot just like his father, could be seen with three other men on top of the Miskolc Mining Institute building trying to knock down the Red Star to the wild chanting of a large crowd below, many among them miners. They were on strike and were the loudest to yell "Down with the Star!" until finally the hated symbol crashed to the ground and broke into pieces. Looking down and waving triumphantly to the people, Gyuszi noticed several reporters from the local TV station just arriving on the scene, one of them already panning his camera over the crowd and upward to where he and his buddies stood. He quickly turned away and, stepping through an open widow, disappeared inside the building. He was glad that the news crew came late, but a sense of uneasiness left him wondering if someone else might have recorded what he did.

Sári and Adam, on the other hand, stayed away from all activities; they left home only to buy some food or, if it seemed safe, walk around to survey the damage the street fighting left behind. They also stopped by Alexa's place, a few blocks from Adam's, and found her nervously chewing her nails. Her boyfriend and his soccer team were out of the country competing in some championship, and she was sure that after hearing what was happening in the country, he was not coming back.

"I know Oszkar, he had already flirted with defecting before this happened, but I tell you, I am not going to sit here either! I am going to leave, too, the first chance I get," she said with firm determination. "It was bad enough before, but now with the Russians shooting everything in sight, there is nothing left for us here. Only a fool would stay. I am just waiting for the opportunity to get out. What about you two?"

"We'll see. Perhaps with the new government and the negotiations in Moscow, the future is not that bleak. If the Russians leave, better days might come," Adam said, speaking both for himself and Sári, but back at his place, talking it over, they agreed that if the situation did not improve, they would also leave. As a musician, Adam could always find work, and Sári had her mother's cousin, Uncle Guido in Vienna, who would help her to get started. They'd wait and see what the next few days would bring.

During these turbulent days Sári only went home once to change, pick up a few things and to let her landlady know where she could be reached in case her parents called again. She also called her cousin Feri to tell him the same thing, and during their talk she learned that he was present at the bloody scene that took place on Thursday the 25th at the Parliament. A mass protest was building up and soon several Russian tanks appeared around the edges with guns aimed at the crowd. The AVO also took up position on top of the surrounding buildings, their machine guns pointing down to the square. At one point one of them opened fire, and the Russians, perhaps in the mistaken belief that they were under attack, started firing at random. In the ensuing mayhem some 200 people, women and children among them, were killed and Feri barely escaped when a bullet struck a man next to him. With the brain of the victim splattered over his jacket, he was able to climb to safety through a window of the nearby Ministry of Agriculture. Forty-two years later in 1998, a decade after the demise of Communism in Hungary, he was commissioned to create a memorial to the terrible events of that day. His simple design consists of bronze bullets fitted into the bullet pockmarks still existing on the walls of that ministry.

A few days later Wanda came by saying that like Alexa, she, too, wanted to leave the country, regardless of how things turned out. No matter what, Hungary would still be a Communist country, and she'd had enough living under such a stupid, restrictive system. Being single without family obligations, stuck in a job without prospects to earn more than the necessary, and owning nothing of value, what was there to hold her back? She was leaving as soon as the shooting stopped and would go to Austria where she had relatives. And Sári should do the same, she said; she had nothing to lose either. When Sári seemed to hesitate, Wanda couldn't understand why. Didn't they always talk about how much better life was in the West? Well, this was their chance to get out!

Yes, it was true, but there was one thing Sári *would* lose: her hard-earned diploma would become useless if she left the country. Her education was geared to the operation of a state-controlled, planned economy, and she knew nothing of the capitalist, consumer-driven free market system of the West. It meant that all her years of studying and doing without would be for naught; she'd have to start all over again in Austria, from the bottom up. And even if she did qualify to work in an office, there was also the language problem. Her German, although fluent on a conversational level, would fall far short in the business world, where dealings required a language more specific than just casual. She would be handicapped as a foreigner without experience, money, or connections, not the most promising outlook for a twenty-five-year-old woman, alone to support herself.

She would have to think long and hard, because whatever she decided now would affect her whole life. The only problem was, she might not have all that much time to vacillate. Every day brought new twists and turns; it all depended on what the Russians would do. If they crushed the revolt, the current government had no chance to stay in power; they'd bring back Rakosi or Gero, and bloody reprisals would surely follow. She had no desire to live through another Rakosi era with all its excesses, but by then it might be too late to find a safe way to escape, and she'd miss the opportunity that might never come again.

The days that followed saw no let-up in the fighting; it continued without either side winning, while another type of movement was taking place inside the factories: the rapid nationwide expansion of the so-called Workers' Councils. These were small, autonomous cells of proletarian power born out of a spontaneous popular movement, which later, when banded together, formed the basis of a new authority. Their goal was to abolish centralized state control, give the workers active participation in factory management, and eventually replace the collapsed administration. They emerged as a virtual Republic of Councils, a powerful force capable of pressuring Nagy into concession and ultimately into accepting all their demands, even those incompatible with his ideology. Their first act was to sweep aside the Communist-controlled factory managers and the Stalinist trade unions, and most importantly, to reclaim the workers' right to strike. They rejected the one-party system, where the election outcome was decided in advance, making it impossible to vote for representatives trusted to act in the workers' interest. Next, they created an armed workers' militia to replace the regular police, which by then was completely disbanded, either keeping their distance or joining the insurrection. It was to the credit of these Revolutionary Guards that subsequent angry acts directed against the AVO, the hated secret police, were kept in moderation and the spread of lynching and disorder was eventually stopped.

Intellectuals, technicians, and students soon followed the workers in forming similar organizations, and together a new state began to emerge over the ruins of the former totalitarian system. It rejected the Stalinist form of government but didn't plan to restore capitalism, either. Their new society would be clearly based on social principles with free elections and multi-party participation that included the Communist Party, but not in its former Stalinist-controlled form. Their country would be free of oppression by the hand of a privileged few, who could maintain power only with the backing of a secret police and foreign troops.

The young people who set foot to a peaceful march just a few days ago were now on their way on a new path to create their own kind of socialism: national independence and a popular democracy, freed from Soviet control. And for that they were prepared to make the ultimate sacrifice.

Defeat

DURING THE BLOODY fighting it greatly helped the young insurgents that the Hungarian army refused to fire at them, and in many cases switched sides and joined them. The High Command, realizing that their orders were largely ignored, decided to neutralize the troops. With a nod from the Russians, the soldiers were quickly disarmed and told to go home. If they joined the uprising as civilians, they couldn't be charged with desertion or insubordination.

There was one gifted officer, however, Pal Maleter, who didn't shed his uniform but openly and wholeheartedly went over to the side of the freedom fighters. He was a thirty-seven-year-old handsome and charismatic professional military man captured by the Russians early in the war, who during his captivity became a Communist. Returning to Hungary in 1945, he kept a low profile, which saved him from the 1949 purges that decimated the officer corps. On October 24 he received orders to dislodge a large group of "fascist rebels," but when he pulled up his armored units and allowed a delegation from the other side to approach under a flag of truce, he became convinced that they were patriots fighting to oust the Stalinist government and restore the country's independence. He set up a formidable stronghold in the Kilian Barracks in the center of Budapest, and from there led a fierce battle against the Russians that forced them to withdraw. People celebrated him as a liberator when on October 31 the Soviet troops began leaving the city.

It was not an easy victory, and other factors also contributed to its success. While the fighting raged on in the streets, inside the Parliament urgent negotiations took place, trying to convince the Russians to halt the attack. Mikoyan returned from Moscow on October 27 to evaluate the situation, with Nagy desperately trying to make him see that the intervention was a terrible mistake and that it did nothing but compromise the chances to find a peaceful solution. Mikoyan shot back that it was the Hungarian government, after all, who requested the Red Army's help to restore order. It was only when he saw the erupting battle scenes and the horrific effect of the Russian tanks shooting point-blank into crowds that he became more conciliatory and agreed to the withdrawal.

The increasing presence of foreign correspondents might have influenced him further to soften his stance. During the first days of fighting young rebels rushed to the border to take down the barbed wire fences—the minefields were cleared by Nagy's order before he lost power a year ago—and secure safe entry for Western reporters to come and witness that Moscow's report of a fascist reactionary rebellion was but a lie. These reporters and TV crews poured in from Austria to record the events, sending pictures of Russian tanks and troops roaming the streets of Budapest, shooting people and demolishing apartment buildings and military compounds without distinction. Perhaps this was not the image Mikoyan wanted the West to see.

And there was also the threat of intervention by the United Nations. The day before his arrival a group of freedom fighters seeking Western Diplomatic assistance called on the British Embassy and asked to submit the Hungarian situation to the United Nations. The confidence that the UN would not tolerate such blatant intervention was boosted by Western broadcasts, especially by the U.S. funded Radio Free Europe, giving daily assurances that the Western Powers were strongly supportive of Hungary's fight for independence.

To ward off Western involvement, the Russians immediately took precautionary measures. Before a Security Council meeting could be called, and without consulting Imre Nagy, they instructed Karoly Kos, the Moscow-appointed Hungarian delegate to the United Nations, to warn against foreign interference in Hungary's domestic affairs. Kos, whose real name was Leo Kondutorov, was a Russian citizen who spoke Hungarian and was recently granted Hungarian citizenship to fill a post in the Ministry of Foreign Affairs.

Considering all the factors currently at play, the Russians reluctantly agreed to announce a cease-fire, then sat back to see what Nagy would do to bring the rebels to reason. But when the guns finally grew silent, Nagy found himself the head of a government in name only, and holding very limited power. He was left alone with no army, the AVO in hiding, and the party machinery virtually disintegrated. With no other options, his new government, with the approval of First Party Secretary Janos Kadar, gave in and announced the acceptance of all proposals. Yet doubt remained in the people's minds: would he be able to keep his promises when his cabinet included many of the previous communist leaders? As a guarantee they demanded to reinstate the 1945-48 multi-party system, then appoint representatives from them to the new government. Nagy again bowed to their wishes and agreed to constitute a new coalition government. Within three days there were forty different parties in the country.

On October 28 Nagy addressed the nation over the newly named free Kossuth Radio, stating that the government rejected to view the formidable popular movement as a counter-revolution and declared it an indisputable great national and democratic movement that expressed the unanimous will of the nation. He further talked about the progress being made with the Soviet government to withdraw its troops, and that all was done in the spirit of friendship and in the principle of mutual equality and national independence. He ended with promising amnesty to all who fought in the uprising and to abolish the AVO.

As broad as this program was, it failed to satisfy the revolutionary authorities. Emboldened by their success, they stepped up their demands, foremost among them an immediate free election, the declaration of Hungary's neutrality in the mold of Austria, Sweden, and Finland, and the withdrawal from the Warsaw Pact. They reasoned that since the Warsaw Pact guaranteed national independence and mutual non-interference in the internal affairs of its participants, the Russian intervention violated the treaty, and Hungary was justified in withdrawing its membership. Unfortunately, they didn't know that the Treaty contained a secret clause Rakosi signed in May 1955, which gave the right to the Soviet Army to come to the "aid" of its signatory nations if threatened by a popular movement that was capable of endangering the existing system. It was a misleading concept of independence and formed the basis for the presence of the Red Army in the satellite nations.

Faced by these latest demands, Nagy found himself in a perilous dilemma. How could he possibly yield to these new wishes without risking a Russian retaliation? So far Moscow had shown tolerance, but how long would their patience last? The Russians expected a quick return to discipline when they yielded control to him, but instead they only saw mounting disorder. The workers got more aggressive in their demands, they refused to return to work, and reports were coming in about attacks on AVO headquarters. In one incident several AVO men were hanged after a group of insurgents stormed the prisons and freed some 5,500 political prisoners. The horror stories these victims told sent the enraged crowd hunting for members of the AVO. When caught, there was no mercy; they were beaten to death or hanged and spat upon in retaliation for the terror they carried out in Rakosi's name.

There were other acts of vengeance, mostly against anything Russian, smashing Soviet monuments, burning Russian books and pulling down the

Red Stars, all symbols of Stalinist oppression. In factories, schools and offices, people broke into the personnel departments, ripping open files in search of the hated kader records to see the secret notes written about them. Sári's cousin Feri found the following record the office committee kept on him:

> Budapest, March 31, 1952
> Ferenc Callmeyer:
> Obtained his architectural diploma on July 16, 1951
> Monthly salary 1,000 forints
> Was granted 500 forints for exceeding his first quarter quota by 205%
> His Peace Loan pledge for the year was 900 forints
> Young architect, professionally talented
> Has good technical knowledge; stands out in design work
> Already completed several small projects
> Willing to aid his co-workers and part-time employees
> Unwilling to participate in any form of political activity
> Stepped-up political indoctrination is recommended
> NOTE: According to Comrade Sebo's report, he keeps a close friendship with a certain Laszlo Papp. Suggestion: find out who this Laszlo Papp is.

These were relatively favorable comments; the road for advancement was left open for Feri, provided he was willing to submit to political re-education. Other reports were more damaging, as people would find out that a well-deserved promotion was blocked perhaps for no other reason than some politically compromising remark. It could be a ridiculous joke, like what is the difference between capitalism and socialism? The capitalists manufacture ropes and sell them to the socialists to hang themselves, while the socialists make their own ropes. But more than anything, everyone wanted to find out who the spies were, who reported them?

Tossed from office windows, thousands of these reports and personal files landed on the streets, adding to the rubbish below, where overturned streetcars and burned-out vehicles blocked every intersection. Nothing was moved out of the way, sending a message to Nagy that unless he acceded to the people's demands, these makeshift barricades would remain, the mess would not be cleaned up, and work would not resume. He felt control slipping from his hands and knew that he must act fast, before time ran out. Still, Nagy hesitated. He was faced with a tragic choice: remain faithful to the Soviet Union, or pledge his loyalty to his country. Could he put Russian interests above those of his own people? After a few anxiety-ridden days, on October 31 he finally took the plunge, "My country right or wrong!" That afternoon he appeared before an immense crowd gathered in front of the Parliament Building and declared his intention to denounce the Warsaw Pact and proclaim Hungary's neutrality.

This, of course, could never be accepted by Moscow. The USSR couldn't be expected to allow the secession of Hungary and set a precedent for the rest of the satellite countries. Mikoyan and Suslov, for the third time within a week, immediately flew back to Budapest and told Nagy that Hungary must adhere to the Warsaw Pact or face the consequences. Nagy's reply was that considering the general atmosphere of the country and the deep resentment the Soviet intervention aroused in the people, it was simply impossible to reject the demands. His hands were tied; should he back down on his promise, the government would be swept out of office.

When the delegates left, in spite of the scarcely veiled Soviet threats, the Hungarian leaders refused to believe that the Russians would risk alienating world opinion by continuing their repressive measures. They were confident that given a little more time, a compromise could be reached.

They should have known better. Whatever time there was to negotiate, the Russians used it to reorganize and be ready to teach the rebellious Hungarians a lesson they'd never forget.

Cardinal Mindszenty was still under house arrest in a northern province when on October 30 a group of military guards arrived and set him free. On his way back to Budapest church bells rang out and people rushed to greet him as their much-suffered martyr. His vast popularity and immense prestige could have given him the power to tilt the scale either in favor of moderation or revenge, but he remained reserved, keeping his ardent hatred for the Russians and Communism under control. When asked to speak, he pleaded for time so he could assess the situation in the country, but promised to address the public after the Russians left Hungary.

As if an answer to his prayers the next day, October 31, all fighting stopped and the Russians began to pull out. And as the Red Army retreated, Budapest exploded in a wild victory celebration. Exuberant young people, overtaken by patriotic enthusiasm, filled the streets, giddy over their hard-won triumph. Yet, in the midst of jubilation, they did not forget their fallen heroes. Collection boxes full of cash to help the victims' families appeared on street corners, left unguarded without fear of theft. There was no looting; goods were left intact behind broken store windows, as if to discredit Gero's allegations that the insurgents were nothing but roving gangs and bandits. This was the indoctrinated youth the Party regarded as the mainstay and future of Communism, not infected by the capitalist rot of the older generation. So much for Lenin's quote: "Give us a child for eight years, and it will be a Bolshevik forever!" Their defection stood as clear proof that his theory was false; it would never work.

These young freedom fighters filled with revolutionary zeal, focused on doing away with the present system of lies and deceit, and create a better, more just world for themselves. They were not fascists and reactionaries aiming to restore the old Horthy regime; they only wished to rid the country of the Stalinist dictatorship and return to the 1945-48 parliamentary system, a cause so many had died for in the past few days.

And as the first day of November dawned on Hungary, it became evident that the dead heroes of the revolution did not die in vain. The Russians were gone and that same evening Nagy delivered a speech declaring the neutrality of Hungary and praising the people for their courageous fight that carried the cause of freedom and independence to victory. He went on to say that the newly organized Hungarian National Guards stood ready to defend the State and safeguard the transitional period until free elections could be held to form a new government. He closed by calling on the people to help protect and strengthen the now free, independent, democratic, and neutral Hungary.

Cardinal Mindszenty also spoke, focusing on the importance of peace and mutual respect amongst the neighboring nations, and calling for a general election free from abuses. Next came representatives of the Jewish citizenry, saluting the achievements of the revolution and confirming that they stood firmly aligned with the now independent and free People's Republic.

In the meantime Janos Kadar, as First Secretary of the Party, was busy trying to reconstruct the Party by reshuffling its leadership. The pre-revolutionary Party membership of 800,000 had dwindled down to a pitiful 100,000 and, to attract more people, he changed the Party's name from the old Communist-affiliated Hungarian Workers' Party to the better-sounding Hungarian Socialist Workers' Party (*Magyar Socialista Dolgozók Pártja*, or MSDP). After Nagy spoke, he also took to the air, this time addressing the nation as "Hungarian workers, peasants, and intellectuals," instead of the customary "Dear Comrades." He no longer referred to the October events as a counter-revolution, and in the name of the Party accepted the proposed changes. Then, using a more cautious tone than Nagy, he added:

> . . . In a glorious uprising our people succeeded in shaking off the Rakosi regime. We have won freedom for the people and independence for the country, and without freedom and independence there can be no socialism . . . Communists, who had been persecuted by Rakosi, fought in the front lines against his political tyranny and despotism, and we are proud of our active participation in the armed uprising. . . . [1*]

He then closed with a solemn promise that the party would never return to its former criminal ways.

After the speech he left to attend a meeting with his newly named party, but he never arrived there. His car was driven in the direction of the Soviet embassy and he was not seen after that. Whether Kadar went of his own free will or was kidnapped was anyone's guess. About the same time Russian armored units surrounded the airfields of Budapest. When Nagy protested in the sharpest terms, loudly demanding to halt the Russian forces, Yuri Andropov, the Soviet ambassador gave the explanation that the presence of their military was necessary to ensure the peaceful evacuation of the families of the departing Russian soldiers. In truth, they were there for one reason only, to cripple the Hungarian Air Force.

By the morning of November 2, the entire city of Budapest was encircled and additional armored columns were converging from all directions around

1 * Melvin J. Lasky: *The Hungarian Revolution*

the capital. Alarmed, Nagy called for an immediate Soviet-Hungarian meeting to discuss the situation and arrange the details of troop withdrawals. He appointed a delegate with Pal Maleter's lead, the popular military commander he just named Minister of Defense. The Russians agreed to the meeting, although the troop movements continued. To obtain the goodwill of the Russians, Zoltan Tildy, former President and current Minister of State, told them that while politically Hungary wished to become independent, with a parliamentary democracy after the Western model, the reforms instituted since 1945 would not be abrogated. The collective farms would be abolished but the peasants would retain the land gained by the agrarian reform; banks and mines would stay nationalized and workers would continue to own and operate the factories. All the newly created parties agreed to uphold socialist principles and the country would never consider joining NATO, the Western rival of the Warsaw Pact.

Hoping that the United Nations would put diplomatic pressure on the Soviets, Nagy made a formal appeal to them, to which the Russians replied that Nagy's allegations were absolutely baseless, and that the two countries were in the process of negotiating for an agreement. This time they told the truth. During the morning of November 3, in a cordial atmosphere, the Soviet-Hungarian talks began at Russian headquarters. At noon the meeting adjourned, but the Hungarian delegates were asked to return at 9 PM to continue the discussions.

Nagy and Maleter were confident. With the end of street violence the city seemed calm, students were back in school, and people resumed working at their jobs. And above all, the Russian withdrawal was no longer a question since during the meeting they agreed to it in principle. In the evening the delegates returned to the conference to work out the details, but then everything changed when they were not allowed to leave. Nagy and his government waited in vain inside the Parliament with a sense of foreboding that rose to the level of acute danger as they received reports of more Soviet reinforcements pouring over the border. A night of anguish followed, with one question on everyone's mind: would the Russians intervene again?

The answer came at 5 AM on November 4 with MIG fighters roaring overhead and Soviet tanks opening fire on the city with a brutal force. And so, after all the promises of the Soviet 20th Party Congress a mere eight months ago, Khrushchev returned to the harsh punitive measures Stalin used against those who refused to toe the line.

At 5:20 AM Imre Nagy, his voice breaking, issued an emotional statement on the radio:

> This is Premier Imre Nagy speaking. Today at daybreak Soviet troops began an attack on our capital with the obvious intent of overthrowing the lawful and democratic government of Hungary. Our troops are engaged in battle. The government is in place. I am informing the country and the entire world of this fact.

His statement was repeated in English, Russian, and French.

At the same time, through his newly appointed delegate, Nagy formally informed the United Nations of the attack, and in response they agreed to put the matter on the agenda as soon as the delegate's credentials were established. The process, however, was deliberately delayed and the voting didn't take place until the November 10th session. The resolution passed with 53 votes for, 9 against, and 8 abstaining, but by then it was too late to do anything effectively.

Desperate appeals were broadcast to the Soviet military command to stop the bombardment and avoid bloodshed, with assurances that the Russians were and would remain the friends of Hungary. When these were ignored, the Writers' Union aired a moving statement at 7:56 AM:

> . . . We appeal to every writer in the world, to all scientists, to all writers' federations, scientific academies, and intellectuals the world over! We ask for your help and support! There is but little time! You know the facts without giving you special reports. Help Hungary! Help the writers, scientists, workers, peasants, and intellectuals of our country! Help us! Help us . . .

But the world kept its distance and no one answered. A small Central European country was of little interest to the big powers when at the same moment they were facing a crisis of their own involving the Suez Canal. It erupted over the Anglo-French-Israel invasion of Egypt, and while the UN was quick to adopt a resolution calling for cessation of hostilities there, it didn't see fit to apply the same principles to the Soviet intervention in Hungary. Their peacekeeping troops were sent to Egypt, but not to Hungary. The West chose to avoid criticizing the Russians in order to stay clear of being criticized for the action they took against Egypt for nationalizing the Suez Canal. The double standard was a bitter and sobering lesson for the Hungarians who believed that the conduct of United Nations was guided by the principles of international morality.

The writers' SOS message was repeated three times, the last one at 8:24 AM. After that the radio fell silent, and when broadcasting resumed at 9 PM, it was under Soviet control. During a temporary lull in the firing, Imre Nagy received a Russian ultimatum that unless the Hungarian forces capitulated by noon, the bombardment of the city would continue. When no response came, the Soviets threw in 6000 tanks and 17 armored divisions to subdue the Hungarians, with more than one quarter of the forces used against Budapest alone. And so the fighting picked up where it had stalled a few days before, an uneven contest with Molotov cocktails against tanks and well-equipped Russian troops. Some soldiers, many from Asia, when forced to abandon their destroyed tanks mistook the Danube for the Suez Canal in the belief that they were sent to fight in Egypt. There were instances when after being told the truth, some troops refused to fire at the workers and students, and some even hoisted the Hungarian flag, but their numbers were few. Most continued to follow orders to quell the rebellion.

Poised to storm the Parliament, the Red Army found no one but Zoltan Tildy and two other Cabinet members there. Imre Nagy and several of his partisans took refuge in the Yugoslav Embassy, while on the same day Cardinal Mindszenty sought and was granted asylum at the American Legation. The leaders were in flight, but regardless, the stubborn resistance continued as workers began building barricades in a desperate effort to stop the tanks. Late in the afternoon a free radio station from somewhere was still heard appealing for help:

> Civilized people of the world! Listen to our plea and come to our aid! We need your help! Send us your soldiers! Send us arms! Pious expressions of sympathetic words are of little help against the Russian tanks! . . . We implore you to help us in the name of justice, freedom, and fraternal solidarity. Our ship is sinking, the light is fading, and the shadows grow darker every hour over our beloved country. People of the free world, extend your hand, act now, come to our help!

It all fell on deaf ears.

After three days of hopeless struggle, the fighting finally came to an end on November 7. Although the Csepel workers held out until the 14th, and sporadic guerilla activities were still reported in the northern regions of the country almost until Christmas, the revolution was dead. But the strong resistance surprised the Russians. With their tremendous force they expected an easy triumph, overlooking the intensity of hatred the people held against them. They suffered considerable losses both in troops and armored cars, with 720 killed, 1,540 wounded and about 100 tanks destroyed. On the Hungarian side there were over 2,652 lives lost and 19,226 wounded, not to mention the significant damage to property in Budapest, where buildings along the main boulevards stood half destroyed, and the torn-up streets were littered with burned out cars, busses, and trolleys. The area around the Kilian Barracks, where the heaviest fighting took place under Pal Maleter's command was totally demolished. It was reminiscent of the aftermath of the Allied bomb attacks in 1944.

And so as the bright days of October faded, so did the exhilarating hope of the Hungarian people for a better tomorrow. The promise of October 23 that shined but a few thrilling days had vanished, its voice proudly proclaiming freedom drowned by the rattle of the Russian guns.

About the same time as Imre Nagy appealed to the world for help, the voice of Janos Kadar was also heard coming from a provincial radio station in Szolnok, a city roughly thirty-seven miles southeast of Budapest. In a seemingly coordinated act he announced that he and seven others, including several from the former Nagy Cabinet, had decided to break with Imre Nagy and form a new "Revolutionary" workers-peasants government. He gave as the main reason for their defection Nagy's weakness and inability to control the situation. He claimed that Nagy became paralyzed under pressure by the counter-revolutionary forces, those elements that, under the cover of democracy, were dragging the country toward anarchy. He further stated that in the interest of the workers and peasants, and to safeguard the achievements of the people's democracy, they had requested the help of the Soviet army to crush the black forces of reaction and restore peace and order to the country.

The reason behind Kadar's defection could only be speculated. He was known as a stern but sincere Communist, incapable of duplicity, who at one time was dragged though Rakosi's torture chambers—accused of conspiracy with Rajk in 1949, his fingernails were torn out—and it was feasible that his sudden about-face was the result of coercion and terror-induced fear. This would support the theory that the Soviets succeeded in breaking his spirit and forced his hand.

But whatever his motives were, most Hungarians took his declaration as an act of treachery. With typical gallows humor they said that in Kadar and his supporters the Russians finally found at least eight genuine Hungarians to defend the country against nine million fascist counter-revolutionary imperialist agents. In spite of all the misery and suffering, posters full of sarcasm appeared overnight, saying, "Come and see our beautiful city during the ongoing Soviet-Hungarian friendship month!" or "Warning! Former aristocrats, landowners, capitalists, cardinals and other supporters of the old Horthy regime, now disguised as factory workers and peasants, are spewing propaganda against our Russian friends!"

On November 9 Kadar returned to Budapest and the next day formally announced that aside from his justification for the temporary Soviet intervention, and with the exception of neutrality, withdrawal from the Warsaw Pact, and immediate free elections, he had taken over Nagy's program. He sharply denounced the crimes of the Rakosi-Gero clique, promised a democratic government, freedom of speech, revision of the economy, higher standard of living, assistance to small businesses, acceptance of the workers' councils, full pardon to the insurgents, and even the withdrawal of the Soviet troops after order was restored.

On the subject of dissolving the AVO, however, Kadar said nothing. No sooner did the Russian troops occupy a city quarter than these members of the loathed secret police came out of hiding and began rounding up students, writers and other young patriots. Driven by vengeance, it was now their turn to retaliate, as freedom fighters were being hanged from bridges and on lampposts. And those brave young men and women, so unafraid of death when facing T-54 tanks, now locked in prison cells, were relearning fear at the hands of their tormentors. When Kadar did nothing to stop it, it set off an exodus to the West in which two percent of the total population, nearly 200,000 Hungarians, most of them educated, chose self-exile rather than accept the return to the past. If compared to the U.S. population as of the 2010 census, this would equal to over six million people.

The fight was over, but the people found other ways to show their defiance. They stubbornly sported small red-white-and-green rosettes, the color of Hungary's flag, sabotaged the government's efforts to restore order, and adhered to the general strike proclaimed on November 4th. In a large-scale passive resistance movement that followed factories remained closed, traffic stood crippled, newspaper editors declined to print distorted news, and the workers' councils refused to surrender the power they held. Faced with such rejection and complete distrust, Kadar even went so far as promising to include Imre Nagy in his government. Of course, he could do nothing, he said, while Nagy was at the Yugoslav Embassy, on foreign territory, but once he returned he would offer him the premiership. This was certainly a false promise, since by November 14 he was already negotiating with the Yugoslavs to deport Nagy and his companions to Romania.

In contrition Kadar also promised that once order returned, there would be clean and honest elections with the participation of several parties, and added that although with all likelihood his party would be defeated, he hoped that, given time, it would regain the workers' confidence. Hiding behind such a conciliatory attitude, Kadar gained time to neutralize the resistance and restore the one-party dictatorship, albeit in a somewhat milder form. On advice from the Russians, he continued in Nagy's path, acknowledging the legitimacy of the insurrection, but with one difference, by dividing it into two stages: from October 23 to 28, the just and glorious uprising, and the period after the 28th, when counter-revolutionist and fascist groups made the Soviet intervention inevitable. A mere three months later, by slurring that dividing line, the heroic revolt became a counter-revolution from the very start, but for that Kadar first needed to consolidate his position.

It helped him that the workers slowly came to realize that the strike could not go on forever. How were they to live without money? The workers' councils knew that some sort of *modus vivendi* must be reached and on November 16 ordered a general resumption of work. There were dissenting voices, arguing that they should hold out until the government began to carry out its promises, but these clashes between the differing parties only helped Kadar to achieve his main objective, to break the unity of the resistance. And from that moment on his attitude stiffened. On November 19 he threatened to dismiss all strikers, and two days later reduced the power of the workers' councils to nothing more than to supervise working conditions, ordering them not to interfere with the newly appointed state-approved managers and union leaders.

In response, the Central Workers' Assembly called for a 48-hour general strike starting on November 23 and threatened to continue it indefinitely if Kadar refused to reverse the orders. They argued that it was unacceptable to hoist a bureaucratic Party control over tens of thousands of workers when only a few of them belonged to the Party. At Csepel only 360 out of 30,000 workers were registered members and most of them were office employees. Kadar reluctantly backed down and the strike was called off. It seemed the difficulties had been cleared away, except the question of Imre Nagy.

On November 23 the Hungarian radio announced that as the asylum for Nagy and his friends at the Yugoslav Embassy had expired the day before, the group had requested to be allowed to leave the country and seek refuge in the Romanian People's Republic. Not one person believed that Nagy and his compatriots had made such a request, and they were correct. When the subject was discussed earlier at the embassy as to what to do in case they were not welcomed back into Hungary, Nagy explicitly refused to go to Romania, and said he would then wish to go to Yugoslavia. Tito himself conducted the negotiations with Kadar about the situation and insisted on a written guarantee for the personal safety of the refugees in his care. Kadar was willing to comply under the condition that Nagy and his men would go to another socialist country until Hungary was stabilized, after which they would be allowed to return but only if they publicly admitted their errors, renounced their posts, and expressed support for Kadar. Hearing the proposal, Nagy and the others outright rejected it.

Kadar then withdrew his demands and submitted a written guarantee for the safe conduct of the refugees, promising they could leave the embassy without fear of punishment for past activities. The next day, while two Yugoslav diplomats escorted Nagy and his companions out of the embassy and into a waiting motor coach, a Soviet officer appeared out of nowhere to join them. Pulling away, they were surrounded by patrol cars and driven to Russian military headquarters. When the Yugoslav diplomats protested, accusing the Soviets of violating the Hungarian government's signed agreement, they were unceremoniously ejected, while Nagy's party was transferred to two armored vehicles and drove toward an unknown destination.

Nagy's blatant abduction prompted another call for general strike unless he was returned and installed in the new government. This time, however, the decision was not unanimous. Moderate voices advocated patience. Perhaps Kadar was prevented from helping Nagy, they said; the Russians must have forced him not to interfere with the abduction. And what if Nagy really wanted to leave until he could decide what role he wanted to play when he returned? Didn't Kadar say that it was his intention to include Nagy in the Cabinet, but what could he do if Nagy chose to go into exile? They must wait and see if he would be willing to return at all.

Although the majority of the people firmly believed that Nagy was forcefully deported and they quickly stifled the moderators, the dissension further helped solidify Kadar's position. He even injected the possibility that Nagy was afraid to stay in the country because he was at risk of being attacked, even murdered, by the marauding counter-revolutionary gangsters. Incredibly, in his growing arrogance it took only a few weeks for Kadar to change his rhetoric when talking about the insurgents. First they were glorious heroes of the revolution, then misguided counter-revolutionists, and now murderous gangsters.

Slowly and deliberately Kadar was creating doubts in people's mind aiming to demoralize the workers' councils by proving them to be hesitant and ineffectual. When they brought up the question of free elections, he practically laughed in their faces. What good would it do, he told them, when the Party with its 900,000 members would come out as the winner, anyway. His boldness stunned the councils. In a free election it would be lucky if Kadar could gather a few thousand votes above the 100,000 from his current Party members.

But Kadar's tactics, however devious, seemed to work. The councils started losing ground and by November 27 they dropped mentioning Nagy's return and saw their other demands left ignored. When within a week Kadar decreed the dissolution of the revolutionary committees, in their last effort the insurgents took to the streets again to protest. This time, though, they were not the only demonstrators. Hastily organized pro-Kadar groups marched against them shouting, "Peace! Order!" and "Long live the workers-peasants government!" Violent clashes erupted between the two factions, and on one occasion at Octagon Square, shots rang out from both sides, causing casualties, while Hungarian and Soviet police stood by taking notes. Large-scale arrests followed and two workers' council leaders were arrested on charges of counter-revolutionary provocations. A week later, on December 12, after putting martial law in effect Kadar empowered summary courts to pass the automatic death sentence for those declared "guilty." He warned everyone to stop making foolish demands and threatened to extend the death penalty for strikers.

The answer was another 24-hour retaliatory strike, followed by a series of arrests, as the tug-of-war continued for the rest of the year. By the beginning of 1957 Kadar had the upper hand. Firmly in control, he quickly dismissed the workers' councils, reopened the Party offices in the factories and other establishments, and reinstated the previously dismissed Party-picked factory managers as the sole authority to act in matters concerning the workers. With all resistance muted, the arrest of anyone with the slightest hint of revolutionary activities now began in earnest. The first to fall were two leaders of the uprising, Jozsef Dudas and Janos Szabo, paraded as "ringleaders." They were put through a hastily conducted five-day trial, found guilty of subversion, sentenced to death and swiftly executed on January 10 and 19 respectively. It was only the start, with forty death sentences handed down and carried out by February 23, followed by the conviction and hanging of three of Dudas' followers on May 7. Together with numerous other secretly conducted summary executions, the killings totaled eighty-nine by June 11, 1957.

The refugees caught while trying to escape to the West were treated less severely, at least for the time being. They were kept in prison for a relatively short time, partly because of their sheer number—there were not enough cells to hold them—and also to demonstrate the government's goodwill in accepting the explanation that they were fleeing from counter-revolutionary terrorists. The fear of these "counter-revolutionists" must have been truly deep-seated though, because once released, many headed for the West again with the full knowledge that if caught the second time, they wouldn't be treated with such leniency. Day after day, thousands crossed the border to Austria, young students, writers, those in the professions, sports stars, and in some cases entire sports teams. They represented the vitality and brainpower the nation greatly needed, and in order to entice them to come back, the government set the date of March 31, 1957 to return without reprisal. Surprisingly, no one came running back. The exodus stopped only after the Iron Curtain descended once again, plugging the drainage to the West by bringing back the old barbed wire fences, elevated lookout towers and armed patrols with guard dogs.

And so this man, Kadar, who during the glory days of the revolution solemnly pledged never to return to "the crimes of the past" and promised socialism "on a democratic basis in conformity with the Hungarian national character and tradition," now at the end could not remain faithful to his word, but veered back to follow in the path of his predecessors, Rakosi and Gero. Later he explained that people do not always know what is good for them; therefore it is the duty of the leadership to act, not necessarily according to the will of the people, but what it deemed to be in their best interest. This apparently meant that if someone was not in agreement with the Party leadership, the use of bullets was acceptable to make him see the errors of his ways.

By the end of February the workers' councils had all but disappeared, the undesirables were removed and the Red Star was restored on all public buildings. Kadar's success could be credited to a cunning ability in giving assurances then breaking what he promised, and to the skillful way he used first persuasion, then intimidation, and finally repression to cement his power. In just three months he disarmed all opposition and managed to degrade the patriotic national revolution by declaring it a mere temporary setback on the road to Communism.

Flight to the West

WHEN SÁRI AND Adam woke up on Sunday morning, November 4, and heard the gunfire and Imre Nagy's pathetic broadcast along with other desperate appeals for help, it brought an end to their earlier dithering whether to stay or get out of the country. The sound of the Russian artillery made the decision for them; they would leave. The only question was how to get safely to the border. Because of the general strike, trains stood idle, the bus depots were closed, and only some cars and trucks were moving in and out of the city.

By the time the fighting ceased and the exodus to the West began in earnest, with people hitching rides and latching on to anything that moved, the government had set up checkpoints along the road leading toward the western borders. Russian and Hungarian soldiers stopped every vehicle jammed with people to check IDs, and anyone without proper documents or a legitimate reason to head that way was pulled off and sent home. Large families—parents, children, grandparents, uncles, aunts—riding together were especially suspect; why was it necessary for the entire family to visit an allegedly gravely ill relative living in Sopron or some other border town? It seemed that suddenly everyone had loved ones in the western zone who urgently needed help and looking after!

In time truck drivers found a way to help those without papers by letting them off before the checkpoints to walk through the fields, then picking them up after passing the guards. But then the soldiers caught on to the scheme; one of them would jump on the half empty truck to ride along, making the rendezvous impossible. It was a game of cat and mouse, and many of the refugees wound up walking a good part of the hundred and fifty-five miles between Budapest and the border.

Sári now wished she had kept Sopron as her permanent residency; it would get her through the checkpoints without a problem. But she could try the next best thing: prove that she was from Sopron, and that her parents were still living there. To start, she returned to her cubbyhole to pick up her birth certificate and a few recent letters from her parents, each with the postmark clearly visible on the envelope to show they came from Sopron. She also collected her high school and college diplomas, packed a small canvas bag with a change of clothes, put in an extra sweater and a few of her favorite photos, then told her landlady that while the strike was on she wanted to go home and check on her parents.

The documents that tied her to Sopron were probably enough to pass her through inspections, but she wanted to be sure. Weighing several possibilities, she decided that nothing would beat a road pass from Russian headquarters. At least it was worth a try to obtain one. And so, with her broken school-learned Russian, she went to plead her case why she must go back to Sopron. She told the two Russian officers willing to listen that completely cut off from her "sick and elderly" parents, she had no way of knowing if their caretaker, a woman paid to look after them, was still with them. She was afraid that with all the turmoil going on, she might have abandoned them.

She was sure the Russians didn't believe a word she said, or even that they understood her well enough, but seeing them turning away and talking in low voices gave her hope that they might be inclined to grant her the pass. Perhaps they were amused by her audacity to come in and ask for their blessings to leave the country, or were just in a good mood that day, but when they turned around she perceived a hint of a smile on their faces. Adam was with her, and one of them, nodding toward him, asked what he had to do with her problem. She readily explained that he was her fiancé, and he wouldn't let her go alone. Surely, they could see that it was not without risk for a lone young woman trying to hitch a ride on the open road.

The officer who seemed to be in charge asked for identification papers and when Sári saw him pull out a pad and start scribbling, she was certain they would get their passes. Elated, it was not easy to maintain the woeful expression on her face and she had to bite her inner cheeks to keep from smiling while they waited until the papers were signed and stamped with a huge official red star. It was written in Russian, and after thanking them profusely and turning to leave, she quickly read it to make sure it was not an order for their arrest.

With the papers in hand, they planned to leave on Wednesday the 14th. They would go to the road leading to Vienna, where people lined up from early dawn waiting for the opportunity to catch a ride, a slight chance since most trucks heading west were already full of people and didn't even bother to slow down. For some larger families it could take days before they would be picked up. Then, once in Sopron, they would hire a guide to take them over the border; it was much safer than trying to do it on their own. These smugglers knew the safest points to cross, kept track of the patrols' schedule, found out which of the guards could be bribed, and how much it took to persuade them to look the other way. All in all, it was quite a lucrative business, charging 1,000 forints for adults—about Sári's monthly salary before deductions—with different rates for family groups and children, and whether a bribe was involved. People willingly paid the fees since the Hungarian forint was useless outside the country.

The weather on Wednesday, however, made it impossible to leave, with wet snow falling and making the roads unsafe to drive. Nervous and apprehensive, they waited two days before the skies cleared enough to allow a ray of sunshine to break through, and even though the forecast was not promising, they decided to put their luck to the test. The doubtful weather might even work to their advantage; it might deter others from flocking to the road.

Armed with their road passes and carrying all their worldly possessions in a tote bag, they set out Saturday morning at eight o'clock for the Vienna Road. The city streets, still littered with debris, were crowded with young people milling around, while here and there an ambulance could be seen, or a farm truck bringing potatoes and apples to the city. They only walked a few blocks when a black car pulled up to the curb and a man, who turned out to be Adam's friend, leaned out yelling to get in, he'd give them ride. Not all the way to Austria, he laughed when Adam told him where they were heading, but still, the lift saved them at least an hour walking.

Sári was sitting in the back seat between Adam and his friend, quietly listening to the three men boasting about what they did during the fighting, when suddenly she saw a handgun lying beside the driver and froze. These men were all keyed up; what if they get caught in some kind of skirmish on the streets? She and Adam could be stranded or worse; their entire plan could go up in smoke! Trying to direct Adam's attention to the revolver, she gave him a small kick and raising her eyebrows, flicked her eyes toward the front seat. The driver, glancing at the rear view mirror, apparently saw her nervous signaling and turned around with a broad grin. "Oh, don't worry about the gun; everybody has one," he said. "We are just cruising around, not looking for trouble." Still, she was glad when he finally deposited them on the open road and drove away yelling loudly for everyone to hear, "Say hello to the Viennese!"

Stepping out of the car and standing on the roadside with a smarting wind whipping at her face, Sári soon pulled out a cap and scarf from her bag; the last thing she wanted was to catch a cold now. People lined both sides of the road, shuffling their feet to keep the circulation going and breathing into cupped hands to warm their faces. Craning their necks they stared down the empty road, always on the alert to pick up the distant sound of approaching vehicles. Then, if a truck came into view, everyone began to move, grabbing bundles and herding families as they rushed forward, not knowing if the truck would make a stop or simply drive on.

Adam and Sári did as everyone else, stood in the cold waiting, ran to the trucks, tried to get on, got left off, turned back to wait some more, until after several hours luck finally smiled on them. An open truck already filled with people stopped near the spot where they stood and let off a middle-aged couple. With one foot on the tailgate and grabbing several outstretched hands, Sári hoisted herself onto the bed of the truck, followed by Adam and a young boy about twelve. The next minute they were moving, the driver tooting his horn and people on the truck waving and shouting to the others still on the road, "See you in Vienna!"

At the first checkpoint, just outside the city limits two soldiers, a Hungarian and a Russian, standing in the middle of the road with machine guns strapped to their backs, called for a halt. After checking the driver's papers the Hungarian guard ordered half of the people off the truck and asked for IDs. He separated those without proper documents then climbed up to check on the rest, but didn't bother with the IDs anymore. He just looked at the people's faces for a few minutes and was ready to jump off when he spotted the young lad who got on the truck with Adam and was now huddling in the back, trying to become invisible. "You, come over here," the guard crooked a finger and motioned him to come forward. "Just where are you going, son?" he asked, but continued without waiting for an answer, "Well, let me see, you want to check on your grandmother, is that right?" Shaking his head he tweaked the boy's ear. "You are going home, young man, to your mother! I am sure she doesn't give a fig about that supposed grandmother of yours but is worried sick, wondering where you are!"

He took him down and shortly after, the truck was back on the road. By then it started to drizzle, turning the weather wet and nasty. Packed shoulder-to-shoulder it was impossible to crouch down for protection; the best Sári could do was to turn up the wide collar of her coat and hold it tightly around her head. Hats pulled low and heads bent they stood against the wind and rain, but no one complained or wanted to get off and return home.

When they reached the second road check about fifty miles from Budapest the guards there were less congenial. Everyone had to climb down and show papers, and those without acceptable documents were not allowed back. The Russian-issued pass Sári and Adam presented worked like a charm, but it drew suspicious glances from their fellow travelers when the Russian soldier, smiling and nodding approvingly, handed back the papers. Once the truck pulled out, Adam was quick to dispel the obvious distrust, boasting that the pass was such good fake that he could have fooled Comrade Stalin himself, were he alive, which, God be thanked, he was not.

It was almost dark by the time the driver stopped near Gyor and warned that the road check here would be very strict, and people without good papers would be better off walking through the fields the rest of the way to the city. He also said that Gyor was his destination; he wouldn't be driving any farther, but from here trains were running to the south and west. He then wished everyone good luck and safe crossing, and drove the few remaining people through the checkpoint straight to the train station.

When at five o'clock Sári and Adam walked inside the station they didn't know how soon they'd be able to catch a train to Sopron. Luckily, one was scheduled to leave at 7 PM that left them enough time to freshen up and order a light meal at the canteen, even after standing in line almost an hour to buy their tickets. So far all went well; the rest of the way should even be easier, with no more gun-toting guards asking for IDs.

The train pulled out on time with standing room only. Looking around, Sári couldn't recognize one person from Sopron. These were not the regular commuters returning home, reading the newspaper, or dozing off, heads lolling to the rhythm of the motion. People were very much awake, highly alert, talking excitedly, some visibly nervous. Tension was in the air, and it only increased when the door opened and the conductor stepped in, asking to have the tickets ready. His friendly face and jovial demeanor failed to bring on the usual smiles; perhaps the mere sight of someone in uniform—a sign of authority—made people more edgy. Sensing the mood, he tried to inject a little humor, saying that as the day's special, the tickets to Sopron would be valid all the way to Vienna, but only a group of young men in the back broke out in a rowdy cheer. The rest would only respond with a self-conscious chuckle, their furtive glances conveying that the insinuation applied only to others.

It was about nine o'clock when Sári and Adam reached her parents' home, finding it completely dark, the family already asleep. She stopped for a moment to think how to slip into the house without causing a commotion. She knew that if she rang the bell at the street entrance facing the casern, her mother's surprised cries to see her would draw attention from the sentry, the very thing she wanted to avoid. She must try to wake them up first. Keeping to the side street, where the guards couldn't see them, she led Adam to her parents' bedroom window and had him lift her high enough to tap on the glass. As soon as the light came on and the window cracked open she whispered, "Mother, its me, keep quiet and open the door."

Lowered to the ground, she could still see her father coming up to the window and heard him gasp, "My God, it's Sári!" By the time they rounded the corner the entrance door was ajar, her mother standing behind it, pulling her inside and into her arms. Adam stood quietly in the background until the hugging and kissing subsided and Sári could introduce him as her friend.

Walking into the house, Ilonka led them toward Istvan and Ochie's room.

"No, don't wake up the boys, Mother, let's just go in the kitchen. We can talk there, and I could use some tea," Sári said in a hushed voice, but the moment she said it Ilonka burst into such pitiful sobs that it truly frightened her. For a moment the picture of young boys about the same age as her brothers sprang into her mind as they fought on the streets of Budapest, but the next instant she remembered where she was. Sopron was safe; there were no Russian tanks here and no gasoline bombs to throw at them!

Baffled by her mother's obvious anguish, she grasped her by the shoulders. "What's the matter, Mom, what's wrong?" By then Jeno was at their side and, throwing an uneasy glance at Sári, gently guided Ilonka inside the room, where she collapsed into a chair, crying inconsolably.

Following them closely, Sári's eyes wandered over her brothers' empty beds, and an understanding began to flicker. "Where are the boys?" she asked in a low voice.

But she already knew the answer before she heard her mother's voice choked with tears. "They are gone, both of them, they are gone!"

"Gone? But where? she asked with alarm bells ringing in her head. Seeing her mother near collapse, she pleaded with her softly, "Please Mother, don't cry." Standing behind her chair she put her arms around her heaving shoulders, and pressing her cheek against the tear-soaked face began rocking her gently from side to side, as mothers often do to soothe a child. She only stopped when she felt the spasms beginning to ease.

"Now, now, that's better" she kissed the top of her mother's head. "I'll bring you some water, then you can tell me what happened."

Adam followed her into the kitchen and when the door closed, it was his turn to calm Sári as she exploded. "My God, Adam, if my brothers left the country, as I think that's what this is all about, how am I going to tell her that I am leaving too?" She stared at him with a bewildered look. "You don't know my mother; her children are her life! You saw how distraught she is!" Turning on her heel she punched the air with her fist. "Those stupid kids! How could they do this to her? For God's sake, Ochie is only thirteen; he is her baby!"

Angry, upset, and afraid of her mother's reaction when she told her that she was here to say goodbye and nothing could keep her from going, she dreaded to go back. Still groping for the right words to break the news, she was handing the glass of water to her mother when, as if reading her mind, she looked up and said with a voice full of resignation, "You don't have to say it Sári, I know why you came; you want to leave, too."

It took Sári a second before the words registered, bringing relief. "Thank you, Mother, I really didn't know how am I going to tell you, but yes, I am going, and I guess that's what the boys did, too, gone over the border, didn't they?"

Tears flooding back, Ilonka nodded. "Istvan left on Friday the 9th and three days later, on Monday, Ochie disappeared, too. And they left without saying goodbye . . . they just walked out . . ." The words came between wrenching sobs, her hands spread in a pleading gesture that almost made Sári cry too. It took Ilonka a minute before she could continue. "Of course, they were afraid to say anything, knowing full well that I would not let them go. If only I had an inkling! But I had no idea what was to come. At least Istvan had a plan; he was smart, he knew what he wanted to do. But poor Ochie, who knows where he is, all alone, no one to look after him . . ."

Seeing Ilonka relapsing into tears Jeno took over telling her the details.

"The day Istvan didn't show up for supper I went looking for him in the school gym—that's where he liked to hang out with his buddies—and there I ran into other parents frantically looking for their sons. We figured that they must have left the country together. They actually made a good team: the father of one of the boys was helping refugees to get over the border and his son knew the safest route to Austria; the second boy spoke German, which Istvan and the other boy did not; and there was Istvan, armed with an address in Vienna. He must have gotten it from my desk, judged by the disarray I found among my papers later."

"I'd say that was clever, organizing their escape like that," Sári tried to sound encouraging. "So many people just blindly head for the border without any idea how to get there and what to do once they made it across. The boys must be at Uncle Guido's by now, the poor man, with three *spitzbuben*, runaway rascals on his hands. Is there any word from him yet?"

"Nothing, but of course we still have no mail delivery. I am sure though they are in Austria, because if Istvan was caught and brought back, we'd know it by now. He is still under eighteen, not yet an adult, and parents are hauled in when children are apprehended."

"What about Ochie? How did he get out?" Sári was sorry to have asked when she heard her mother's renewed sobs, her hand pressing a crumpled handkerchief to her mouth.

"Your mother was standing in line for bread at the corner bakery when she saw Ochie and a couple of kids meandering along Selmec Street," Jeno continued. "He didn't notice her until she called after him, asking where they were going when he was not allowed to leave the house without permission. He knew he was in trouble, especially for being caught on a street leading in the direction of the border. To save face in front of his friends he acted nonchalantly, yelling back that it was no big deal, they were just out for a walk. Only when Ilonka insisted that he return home and stay put, did he do as told. Dragging his feet, he turned around and went inside the house, and that's the last he was seen."

"Can you imagine? He climbed out the back window and with his buddies headed straight for the border," Ilonka cut in finding her voice. "We know this since one of them, the little Szabo boy, got scared at the last minute and ran home. After he told his parents about it, they immediately came over and made him repeat the story, how he saw his friends cut a hole in the wire fence and crawl through it. So they all made it safely to Austria, but how could Ochie do this to us?" The tears were coming again, although this time she fought them back. "I know you will leave, Sári; you've always done what you wanted and we won't try to talk you out of it. I'll even help you. I know people who can get you out risk free, but you must promise me, when you get to Vienna, you'll find your brothers and send them home. At least Ochie, I won't survive without him. Promise me you won't rest until you find them; you must do that much for me!"

"Of course I will, I promise. Look, he might even be with Guido already. Even if he didn't have the address, he knew his name; you always talked about him. And I heard that the Austrians are well organized in helping refugees; it would be easy for them to locate Guido—after all there couldn't be that many Guido Guerinis in Vienna."

Just the thought made Ilonka feel better. She even managed a wan smile. "Ah, Sári, you don't know what it was like here in these past few weeks. First your Uncle Sandor knocked on the door on his way to Vienna. He was so—"

"Uncle Sandor was here? When?" Sári cried out in surprise before Ilonka could finish. "The last time I saw his mother she told me that after the Russians sent him home, the Hungarians put him back in prison. How did he wind up here? I bet he got out when the people freed all the political prisoners during the revolt!"

"Exactly. And he told us that once he saw the Russians shooting up the streets, he swore he was not going to wait around this time to be dispatched again to Siberia! He said as long as he lived he would never trust a Russian. He showed up here at the end of October—I can't remember the exact date—but only stayed one night, then left. The border was wide open in those days so he just walked across. I gave him Guido's address, but he said he also had a few contacts in Vienna from his military days. I hope he made it, but you know Sári, as much as I love that man, I think if he hadn't come, Istvan and Ochie would be still home. They hung on his every word as he talked about his captivity and said that even if the Russians left the country, he would never stay. He would never feel safe, and even if he were to sweep the streets in Vienna for a living, he would be better off than here."

"I believe that, but what will happen to his poor mother and sister? They waited so long for him to come back, and now he is gone again." Sári grew quiet, thinking of the two women alone in their little flat. "It must have been awfully hard to say goodbye knowing that this time he won't be coming back, and they might never see him again."

She pushed the depressing thought out of her head and turned to ask about Eta and Gyuszi. Had they heard from them?

"Eta is fine, but not a word from your brother," Ilonka said, then remembering something she added, "But we saw your friend Alexa."

"Alexa? She is here in Sopron?"

"Not anymore. She came about a week ago but left the next day, after I got her a guide to help her over the border. She was a nervous wreck and wouldn't stop cussing at Wanda, swearing up and down that she never wanted to see that bitch again."

"What on earth happened? They were best friends! And how did she find you? I never gave her this address."

"Wanda's mother sent her here. The way she told me, she found out back in Budapest that Wanda got a ride to Sopron with some friends, and although she begged them to take her along, they refused, saying there was no room in the car, not even in the trunk. A couple of days later she found some other way to get out of the city—she said something about an ambulance driver picking her up, then another truck—so anyway, she made it to Sopron. It was late at night when she got here, scared out of her wits, a stranger without any idea how to find Wanda's house. I still don't know how she got there with so few people on the streets after dark. Now can you imagine how she felt when she finally rang the bell and Wanda's mother wouldn't let her in? She kept her at the door, saying it was too dangerous to let her stay; they could be accused of helping refugees escape. When Alexa pleaded that she had nowhere to go, Wanda's mother shut the door in her face, saying 'Go to the Zachars'."

"That's terrible, how could they do that to her? I wouldn't have the heart to treat a dog like that! It's a miracle that she found our house in the middle of the night."

"Well, she didn't. She said she was too afraid of being picked up wandering alone, so she spent the night on a park bench, hiding behind the bushes whenever she heard someone approaching. She said she was cold and hungry and scared to death, a night she'd never forget as long as she lived. By the morning she was able to get directions and that's how she knocked on our door."

"Poor girl, I don't blame her for cursing at Wanda, though I can't believe that she would have turned Alexa away. It was all her mother's doing. So what happened next?"

"Like I said, I found a man to help her escape, and I know she made it across all right because I spoke to the guy next day. What happened to her in Austria, I don't know. I helped her as much as I could, but I didn't give her Guido's address; she must look after herself once out of the country."

"Oh don't worry about Alexa; she'll find a way. She is a survivor; she'd manage even if floating on top of an iceberg alone in the middle of the ocean. Isn't that the truth, Adam?"

The poor man was sitting quietly all through the commotion until Sári finally remembered that he was there. It was getting late and they'd both had a long day. They made up a bed for him in the boys' room, and while he was getting ready in the bathroom, Jeno and Ilonka naturally asked if they were more than just friends. It would be comforting to know that Sári had someone in Vienna besides Guido, but she evaded a direct answer: yes and no, and who knows what will happen.

She slept in her parents' room, but as exhausted as she was, her nerves kept her awake for a long time. She tossed and turned, not knowing what tomorrow would bring, if she'd ever be back in this house that held so many memories for her.

Next day, the 18th of November, dawned cold and damp with slate-colored skies threatening rain. Sári thought to go and see Wanda, but thinking of what she heard yesterday, she changed her mind. After breakfast she took Adam to show him a little bit of the city, then, it being Sunday, they stopped at the beautiful Dominican Church on Szechenyi Square, where High Mass was in progress. They were not churchgoers, but this time they gladly sat through the service, praying for St. Christopher's help during the fateful days ahead.

When they got home Ilonka greeted them with the news that she had already lined up two men to take them over the border, and they would be here to pick them up around three in the afternoon. So this was it! And as reality began to sink in, the thought that they'd be leaving everything behind, perhaps forever, hit Sári harder than she expected. Too nervous to eat the special meal Ilonka prepared for them, she sat at the table, forcing down a few bites, her eyes following her mother as she moved around, then settling on her father's beloved face, all the while wondering if she would ever see them again. By nature she was not overly sentimental; she left home for college six years ago without an afterthought, never feeling homesick, so why was she quivering with emotion now?

Hot tears were building up behind her lids but she held them back until she heard the doorbell a little before three. For once, couldn't they be late? Adam got up to fetch their belongings, leaving Sári alone with her parents to say goodbye. Holding on to each other, the three of them stood in a desperate embrace; only the sound of their muffled sobs told of the pain tearing at their hearts. After a long moment, it was Ilonka who pulled away first, blotting her tears as she ran to the kitchen and returned with a couple of sandwiches and a few apples to take along. She also forced on Sári a hooded plastic cover; they predicted rain, and it could come handy.

With a final hug and repeated promises to find her brothers, Sári turned to Adam, ready to go. Still teary-eyed, her parents didn't dare come out to see them off. It would be a clear giveaway to the guards across that this was not a simple family visit. All they could do was watch from behind closed curtains as Sári slipped out the door and into the waiting pickup, waving a final farewell as the driver pulled out and quickly drove away.

It took less than twenty minutes to reach Kophaza, a small village right on the border. Stepping inside the house the man asked to see the pre-agreed fee, counted the bills, but pocketed only half of the 2,000 forints, saying he'll take the rest at the border.

"You might as well get comfortable, we can't do anything until it gets dark," he said showing them into a small room with the curtains drawn. "And try to relax, you'll need your strength once you are over the border; you will have to walk a good four or five miles through rugged open fields before you get to the nearest village."

While he spoke his friend went to the kitchen and returned with a plate of cheese, some bread and a bottle of *Kékfrankos*, a good red wine known for the region. "Here, this might help you to unwind," he said putting down the tray and filling two glasses to the rim. "We'll leave you alone for a spell while we check on things and make sure everything is fine, but we'll be back as soon as it gets dark."

Suggesting Sári to relax was easier said than done. Nerves stretched thin, ready to snap at the slightest noise, she sat on the edge of her chair, thinking of nothing but what the next few hours would bring. Would they make it safely to the other side or find themselves in front of an interrogator?

Adam was more at ease and raising his glass winked at Sári. "Well, here it is, to a safe crossing!"

"I drink to that!" She clinked her glass to Adam's, her voice a notch too loud, as if releasing some of that inner tension.

"So what are we going to do once we are in Austria?" he asked. "We never really talked about it before."

"I suppose the village people will have a place for us to stay the night. They'd been dealing with refuges for weeks. We'll see, provided we make it through."

"What kind of talk is that? Of course we'll make it through! Don't let this waiting get to you! Soon it'll be dark, and we'll be on our way."

Jittery, Sári looked at her watch. "I wish these guys would hurry up! What if they just took the money and left us here to rot? We don't even know their names! I bet they are sitting in a tavern, getting drunk. What if they forget to come back? "

"That's absurd. They are gone only ten minutes. Your mother wouldn't have trusted them if they were crooks. But getting back to my question. What I meant to ask is what about us, you and me, not where we will spend the night after we got out."

"Well, I don't know about you, but I am going to my uncle. I wonder what his face will be when he sees another Zachar on his doorstep. And I thought you have your parents' friends where you could stay."

"I'll find that out when I knock on their door, even though I am not overly concerned whether they'd take me in or not. With all these people from Budapest, I am bound to find friends I can hook up with. Musicians are a tightly knit bunch; some of them even owe me a favor or two. It's just a matter of time before I'll be working and on my way. But you are not listening! This is not what I was thinking when I said let's talk about us. It's more like how do you see us from now on? Do you want to stay together? I thought we could even say we are married; in this chaos nobody will ask us to produce a marriage certificate. We could just register as man and wife and say we were married in a rush before we left Budapest. It's a good enough reason why your documents still show your maiden name."

"Why Adam, is this a roundabout proposal? If it is, it's very tempting and I am flattered, but no thank you. I don't want to start a new life with a lie. As they say, it only invites trouble."

"Not necessarily. We would get married later of course. This pretending would just make it easier to stay together, to get through the chaos."

"It sounds that you paid a lot of thought to this, but as I said, it still would be a lie. No Adam, this is not the way to go. Let's just leave things as they are until we catch our breath. We have enough drama right now, I don't want to complicate things more."

"Have it your way; it was only a suggestion. And you are right; it's not worth the chance getting caught in a lie. What's the rush anyway, right?"

His words hung in the air as they listened to sudden noises on the outside. When it came to nothing, they sat silently, each with their own thoughts.

As promised, the two men returned when it got dark, saying that all was in order, the arrangements were in place, and they could leave after six o'clock. This left Sári and Adam plenty of time to make a quick trip to the outhouse, zip up their duffel bags, and be ready for the door. The driver also warned them that it was quite cold outside and to dress warmly, so Sári, wearing a wool skirt and a turtleneck sweater put on the extra cardigan and a pair of legging she brought along. Bundling up was one thing, she thought, but with all the layers under her coat, she felt like a stuffed teddy bear.

Tense with heightened anticipation, they all got in the truck parked in front of the house. It was pitch dark but the man drove without headlights, hitting some rough spots on the bumpy dirt-packed country road. A few minutes later he pulled to the side and cut the engine. "We are almost there," he said. "My friend is staying with the truck but I'll walk you right to the spot. It's not far, maybe a hundred yards or so. It should be safe there tonight, so just follow me."

Nervous and oblivious to the cold wind that picked up and brought a whiff of dampness, they walked along the newly reinstalled wire fence that for so many refugees meant the dividing line between dragging limitations and bright shiny opportunities. The guide ahead was examining a section and when he stopped, they knew they had reached the crossroad where their next step would crucially alter their lives. In that moment it was still in their power to turn back; no one would know that they came this far, except for them there was no second thought, no hesitation.

After giving the man the rest of the money, he told them they'd have to crawl under the fence, then crouch down and run across the strip of land roughly sixty feet wide that separated the two countries. "At the other side of the clearance there are no fences to keep the Austrians from trying to sneak into Hungary," he chuckled. "You'll be safe there on Austrian soil. Once you are in the clear, just keep walking until you see the village lights in the distance. Head in that direction and when you get there, knock on the first door you come to; they will tell you what to do and where to go."

They thanked him with a hearty handshake then, with adrenaline surging, waited until he pulled up the fence high enough to squeeze through. He watched them scrambling across the clearance, a quick dash, and they were safely on the other side, drawing the first breath of that invigorating, dizzying fresh air of true freedom, for which so many had died in the preceding tragic days.

"Good luck, and no need to send a postcard," the man called after them, then touching his fingers to the brim of his hat turned and went on his way.

The earth beneath their feet, a plowed-under cornfield, felt lumpy but solid, trouble-free enough to walk at a brisk pace. Lucky for them, the rain that would have transformed it into a slippery quagmire did not come. Although the night temperature hovered around 40 degrees Fahrenheit, they soon felt hot and sweaty from the sheer excitement and the vigorous tempo they kept. They only stopped to shed a layer of clothing before charging ahead, anxious to spot a twinkle of light to guide them in the right direction.

Exhilarated and almost giddy, Sári kept up a recount of the day's events, as if to confirm that what they'd been through really happened. "It was really hard to say goodbye to Mother and Dad; I wish I'd had little more time with them . . . Wasn't that stupid of me to think that these guys would pull a trick on us when they stayed out a little longer . . . They were probably fiddling with the fence, he had no problem pulling it up . . . You know, one day when I tell my children about tonight, I will have to embellish our escape, make it more daring and dangerous. It was almost too easy . . ."

She finally stopped when her throat ran dry and her tongue felt twice its size. Adam, too, was dehydrated, wishing they had some water. Then Sári remembered the apples; their sweet juice worked just as well at quenching their thirst. By then they had been walking about thirty-five minutes and Adam calculated that if the man was right, they had another hour and half to go before reaching the village. But where were the lights? The terrain was flat; they should be able to see something in the distance, yet the horizon remained dark.

"Could it be that we lost direction? That we'll find ourselves back at the fence?" Sári asked, half serious, half joking.

"You are talking nonsense! It's the visibility, you little dummy! The dampness hanging in the air makes it hard to see. Trust me, lights or no lights, we are going to get to that what's-its-name village."

"Pick your choice, Deutschkreuz, or Nemetkeresztur in Hungarian, when it still belonged to us. And I was just kidding, I know we are safe; but perhaps we should wait until some other people come this way. I am sure we are not the only ones crossing the border here tonight."

"Will you just stop being silly, Sári? We are not going to stop; we'll get to the village on our own, unless you are tired. Are you? We could rest a few minutes if you want to; last time I looked back nobody was chasing us and it's not like we are going to be late for some royal reception."

"Are you kidding? Me tired? I can't wait to get there! You want to race?" She challenged him with a small jerk of her head and took off running. She didn't get far before Adam heard her cry out, "Oh no, I don't believe this! And you won't either! Come quick!"

She was standing at the edge of a shallow but fast-flowing creek, no more than three feet wide, an easy jump, were it not for its slippery banks.

"You wanted a better story for your children, well, you got one now," Adam stood there laughing.

"This is no time for witty remarks!" Sári stared at him with an icy look.

"Well, what do you want me to do? I am a musician, for Pete's sake, do you expect me to build bridges?"

"A pontoon would do! You said you were in the Boy Scouts—well, didn't they teach you how to make one from matchsticks?"

"Very funny! But if they did, I was not listening."

In the meantime Adam was looking over the ground to see if he could find some broken branches, or something to put down as stepping-stones, but without a flashlight it was hopeless.

"I am afraid, there is not much we can do but wade in," he finally said. "I'll go first and see what it's like, then figure out how to get you across."

She waited until he took off his shoes and socks, rolled up his slacks and stepped into the cold water. "It's not that bad, not even a foot deep," he yelled back when he reached the other side. "But the bottom is pretty muddy and slippery, I don't think I can carry you; we both could wind up with our butts in the water. Do you think you can jump, and I try to catch you?"

"There is not much Sir Galahad in you, is there? And no, I am not going to jump, I'll just wade through like you did; it looked easy enough." And so, carrying her shoes and lifting the edge of her coat, Sári plodded through the water, even managed to scoop up and drink a handful. They used her scarf to dry their feet then, hoping that this was the last obstacle for the night, resumed their walk. Without talking much, they kept at a steady pace to make up for the time lost at the creek, when finally they noticed some lights beginning to break through the fog.

They reached the village close to nine o'clock but found most of the homes dark, the shutters closed, the occupants either sleeping or still out. Turning the corner they finally saw one with the lights on and when they rang the bell a little girl of about eleven opened the door. Not to scare her off Sári quickly began to apologize, but the girl just turned her head and shouted over her shoulder, "Mama, two more from Hungary!" Her mother, a friendly and sympathetic woman, greeted them, saying that this day was the busiest for refugees since they started coming, then sent her daughter to escort them to the school, where people would take care of them.

The school auditorium had been set up as a temporary daytime shelter for the new arrivals, offering a warm place to rest and a bite to eat. Volunteers welcomed the refugees as they stumbled in, doling out sandwiches, strong black coffee, and cookies and milk for the children. They listened with much empathy to the stories the refugees told about their escapes, some exciting enough to fill a book, all a testimony to bravery and courage that would endure the passage of time.

When Sári and Adam came through the door they saw a roomful of noisy, animated people standing in groups talking and laughing, still in the first flush of exhilaration. A sense of relief mixed with hopeful expectations filled the air. Considering what they had been through in the past twenty-four hours, it was incredible that no one was tired; even the children were fully alert, forgetting that it was long past their bedtime. Perhaps they, too, sensed the importance of the day and how their lives changed forever because of it.

Sitting with a cup of coffee Sári and Adam scanned the crowded room hoping to see a familiar face, but finding none. They were in the middle of strangers, just the two of them, holding hands in a reflective mood, knowing that the worst was over and they were safe. Yet for a moment, faced with the reality that they were entirely alone, without a home or country to call their own, Sári found herself seized by a touch of sadness. By wading into that creek today they crossed their own Rubicon, the point of no return, and while there was no regret, she couldn't help but wonder if they'd be strong enough to conquer the world that now lay open before them.

The shrill voice of a volunteer brought her back to the present. The woman called for attention and announced that a bus was on its way to take them to the nearest refugee center, a well-equipped camp set up to help them start a new life in Austria. A few minutes later, just before ten o'clock, they heard the bus pulling up. The driver gave a brief orientation on what would happen next: everyone, including those with relatives or friends in Austria, would be required to spend the first few days at the camp to undergo registration. In a day or so they would be given temporary identification cards, which they needed to move about. It also entitled them to receive various aids and benefits the government made available to the refugees. He stressed the importance of the registration for another reason: the information collected would be fed into a database, which would help people searching for missing loved ones. When the refugees bombarded him with questions he raised a hand, saying that they'd have to wait until they got to the camp. People there knew more than he did.

It was drizzling when people boarded the bus, only a light sprinkle at first, but by the time they turned onto the road it was raining hard. Even with the windshield wipers going triple speed the driver had difficulty seeing and decided it would be too dangerous to continue. Stopping in the next village, local volunteers quickly set about making arrangements for the refugees to spend the night at the school gym, and while there were not enough cots for everyone, nobody complained about sleeping one night on mats spread out on the floor.

Only some of the younger people, including Sári and Adam, opted out of staying after they saw the conditions, babies crying, people lolling about on the floor, and a long line queued in front of the restroom with a single toilet. Instead, they decided to look for an all-night café and soon found one on the main square only a block away. Crowded with Hungarians, they stood in line waiting to be seated, when suddenly Adam heard someone calling his name. It was one of his close musician friend, Karoly Nemet, motioning vigorously to come and join his group of several young men and women. He had fled Hungary a week before and was now living in Vienna; he just came back to the village to visit a girl he met in this same café on the night of his escape.

He turned out to be a great source of information. Hearing that they had places to go in Vienna, he told them to forget about going to the camp; conditions were terrible there, men, women, families, all thrown together in the same room, people getting irritated, fights breaking out, and the food was awful. Instead, get on a public bus heading for Vienna—one stops at 6 AM right across from the café—and go directly to the city's central registry; they could get their papers there just the same. He said the main reason for sending everyone to these camps was to decentralize registration and ease the burden on the headquarters in Vienna, where thousands lined up each morning as early as five o'clock, their line stretching three blocks even before the doors opened.

He also told them that once they received their papers, they could get a little money from the Austrian government. Religious organization also helped, although Catholics couldn't expect much; there were just too many of them and the Catholic charity, Caritas, was running short of funds. Protestants and Jews were better off; they were put up in hotels—not a Hilton, to be sure, but still a hundred times better than the camps—and they also got meal tickets to certain restaurants. Some clever rascals among the non-Jews were learning to recite Hebrew prayers, hoping to pass as Jews, until it came to present physical proof.

Otherwise, he said, the Austrians were friendly and sympathetic toward the plight of the refugees fleeing from the Russians, remembering what it was like when part of their country was occupied by the Soviets before Austria became neutral only a year ago. Still on the path of recovery, it was truly commendable how a small country, smaller than Hungary, was able to handle the sudden influx of so many refugees. Their economy, with hardly any industry other than international tourism, was rather weak, yet they didn't shut their doors when these people started pouring over their borders with nothing but the clothes on their backs. Other countries were stepping in offering help—Germany, England, France, Sweden, Canada, all taking in thousands of Hungarians—but Austria still bore most of the burden. Interestingly, the United States, where most of the refugees hoped to go, only accepted a few hundreds, claiming that their immigration quota for both 1956 and 1957 was already filled. This outraged the Europeans, where even Switzerland, a country notorious for its closed-door policy, was willing to take in four thousand Hungarians. Backing down, the number of U.S. visas was then raised to 6,500, a figure increased again to 35,000 by September 1957.

Sári and Adam were thankful to their friend for all the information, and taking his advice decided to skip going to the camp. When he left around midnight they promised to look him up in Vienna, then spent the rest of the night at the café drinking strong coffee and listening to other refugees. Aside from talking about their escapes, the main topic among them was where to go from here, which country offered the best future for immigrants. The winner was undoubtedly the United States, with Canada and Australia a close second and third. It was amazing to hear how many of these people suddenly recalled having long-lost aunts and uncles, or even one-time friends living in these countries, and how they expected them to come forward, open their homes and take them, virtual strangers, into the bosom of their families. That they didn't speak the language was a minor obstacle. Learning would come later. There was simply no limit to their optimism; their only concern was to get a visa before the quota was filled.

Hearing all this wishful talk about going to America, Sári remembered how she, as a young girl reading the book *Back Street,* made a vow that one day she would have an apartment in New York City, just like the heroine in that story. How enamored she became with the way Americans lived as seen in their movies, and more so later, when she caught a real glimpse during her relationship with her American boyfriend. Could it be possible that he still cared for her, that they could meet again? She'd never know unless she, too, would go to America.

The idea was but a fleeting thought, and she dismissed it as totally absurd. What was she thinking? These people in the café had no reason to stay in Austria, but she did. She spoke the language well enough, had her uncle to support her until she could get on her feet, and Vienna was close to her parents. When things got settled in Hungary, she could go home for visits. But most importantly, she had her promise to fulfill, to find her two young brothers.

When the bus came in the morning and Sári and Adam got on board, they could only offer Hungarian forints to pay for their tickets, but the driver waved it aside. It had no value in Austria, not even in these border towns. He had been picking up refugees ever since they started coming, he said, and giving them a free ride was his contribution to the cause. Once they had their papers they would ride free, anyway. Sári asked if by chance the bus would be passing near where her uncle lived, but the driver shook his head. The central police headquarters, however, was along his route, and he would gladly drop them off there. Those officers were all trained to handle the refugee situation; they should be able to put them on the right track.

And he was right. When they walked into the police station and Sári said they came over the border that night, they were greeted warmly and were told that they came to the right place. Central Registration was part of police operations, the building only a couple of blocks down the street. As they talked, noticing that Sári spoke German, one of the officers suggested she could help interviewing refugees. They always needed interpreters, and in return for a few hours' work, they'd rush through her papers, and of course, Adam's too. It would save them endless hours standing in line just to get near the office.

Sári could hardly believe their luck, especially when she saw the long line queued around the block. Inside the courtyard was no different; it was jam-packed with standing room only. The officer who accompanied them had to elbow his way through the crowd, and regardless of his uniform, there were angry shouts that the line formed outside. Other nasty remarks and mean-spirited innuendos were directed at Sári, as to how she earned the privilege of being allowed ahead of everyone else. Only a stern warning from the policeman put a stop to it.

Once inside, Sári and Adam went through a quick interview, then she sat down beside a typist and started translating personal information, name, date, birthplace, and occupation for each refugee questioned. Within one hour Adam got his ID—the Hungarians called it the "Gray Card," after its color—and with that in hand left to find his parents' friends. Sári stayed until one o'clock, then walked out with her card stamped November 19, 1956, granting her political asylum in Austria. It also entitled her to free transportation, emergency medical treatment, and limited monetary aid.

Before she left she got directions as to which streetcar to take to her uncle's apartment on Seidl Gasse 10 in the first district of Vienna, and, using her new card, cashed in on her first free ride. She had never met her uncle but knew him and his family from photographs: Aunt Rosa, and the children, Guido, Jr., and Inge, both in their teens. They were wonderful to her when she showed up, the third Zachar in the past three weeks, as Guido told her with a broad smile.

"What, both my brothers are here? Where are they?" Sári asked, relieved that she found them already.

"Well no, Istvan was here for a short while, until he was sent to a school near Saltzburg. But we know nothing about Ochie. Did he escape too?"

"He did a few days after Istvan left, and I must find him. They both sneaked away without a word to Mother, and she is frantic not knowing what happened to them. I promised to find them and send them home."

"Oh, she need not worry about Istvan, he is in good hands in that school run by Piarist monks! They took in a bunch of Hungarian boys, then recruited Hungarian-speaking teachers to ensure their continued education. I already heard from him, and he is very happy there."

"That's good news, but then who is the third Zachar you mentioned?" Sári asked.

"That was your uncle Sandor. He is here in Vienna; we'll call him tomorrow. But that poor Ochie, he couldn't be much older than my son. Why didn't he come here too?"

"I don't know, Uncle Guido, he is just a kid. I guess he didn't have your address and didn't dare to ask Mother about it."

"Don't worry, we'll find him, I'll ask around where to start searching. But you must be tired, girl, let Aunt Rosa get you settled. You'll share Inge's room."

Soaking in the hot tub felt like sheer luxury, except it made her sleepy; she could hardly keep her eyes open. All the excitement and going without sleep for over twenty-four hours caught up with her, and although the family had a hundred questions about her escape, it would have to wait until tomorrow. It was only mid-afternoon, but she knew she wouldn't last until supper, so after grabbing a quick bite she put on the nightgown Inge laid out for her and crawled into bed, sleeping well until noon the next day.

When Aunt Rosa took her to the central registry to start the search for Ochie, she filled out the required form, then, thinking of Alexa, she submitted one for her, as well. That done, they stopped at the Hungarian Refugee Aid center, where she collected 120 schillings, roughly 12 dollars, for basic personal expenditures. As for a change of clothing, Inge would have been happy to share some of hers, except they were not the same size. Instead, she organized a collection among her friends and schoolmates to help her poor refugee cousin.

Guido called Uncle Sandor and he came immediately. The last time he was in Sopron Sári was about eleven years old, and when he looked at her now, his eyes grew misty. Holding her at arm's length, he said she was undeniably a Zachar girl, resembling the aunt she was named after. Sári also could see a little bit of her father in Sandor, especially the eyes and the shape of the mouth. During the following weeks he came to visit her regularly, and although he had very little money, occasionally treated her for coffee or a movie. Together they saw *Rebel without a Cause* and *The Tender Trap*, her first American films since she dated Harold. They talked about his years in the military, the war, but not of the time he spent in Siberia and in the notorious Butyrka and Ljubljanka prisons in Moscow. He would only say that the Russians robbed him a decade of living, and he'd never forgive them for that.

When Sári asked him why he never married, he simply said that the woman he admired was not free, and after that he didn't find anyone who could compare. Then, with a mischievous wink, he added that he might still get lucky and find someone who was willing to share the little room he was renting. He never complained about his circumstances; he said he was getting by on a meager pension Austria set up for officers of the former general staff who served under Horthy's regency. Old colleagues who left Hungary at the end of the war and lived in Vienna were also helping him, not so much with money but with referrals to find a job. As a result he was just hired as an agent to promote tourism. He was contented with his life, but constantly worried about his mother and sister all alone back in Budapest.

After settling in, Adam also came to see her a few times. He had a room in the home of his parents' friends, but it was only temporary, because he was not going to stay in Austria. He found out from talking to his friend Karoly that chances of finding work as jazz musicians were slim here, since the local music was still in the "ump-pa-pa" stage, playing S*chrammelmusic*, the maudlin tunes that was so popular in the little wine taverns tourists flocked to in Vienna's Grinzing district. They'd be better off going to Germany where music was more sophisticated and opportunities were far better. Emigration was no problem, Germany had an open door policy in accepting refugees, and once he settled down, Sári could follow. What did she think about his plan? Of course, Sári was in no position to tell him whether he should stay or leave. All she would say that if things didn't work out in Germany, he could always come back, but when they said goodbye, she had a feeling that it was for a long time, if not forever.

Her immediate concern was to earn some money, and see if she could land an office job. She sat down with Uncle Guido and told him about her background and work experience, but when he found out that she couldn't type or use shorthand, he shook his head. Without those skills and with her average German it would be a miracle if someone would hire her. She would be better off looking for a job as a sales clerk or waitress; neither paid much, but living with them rent-free, she could manage. Mulling it over, it didn't take long before she made up her mind that waitressing was not for her; she had no experience and no patience to deal with fussy customers. Selling was a better choice, especially if she could get into a boutique, where she could buy items on discount. She would start making the rounds soon, while there was still much sympathy in Vienna for the refugees.

A week went by, but she heard nothing from the registry; they couldn't locate either her younger brother or Alexa. Ironically, it was Alexa who found her. After spending a miserable week in a camp, she was transferred to Vienna and immediately began looking for her. Central registration found Sári's record right away, probably because she got her papers there. It was a noisy and joyful reunion when she showed up at Uncle Guido's one day, both girls totally surprised that they had found each other in the current chaotic situation. They spent hours talking, each telling about how they got out, with Alexa heaping praises on Sári's mother for helping her. She was a saint, willing to help a total stranger, and that if it was not for her, she could easily be back in Budapest, or worse. Then, in the same breath, she wished all hell on Wanda and her mother for the way they treated her in Sopron. Although Sári knew what had happened, she listened patiently as Alexa recounted her ordeal in minute detail and then continued describing how she crossed the border through an abandoned coal mine. Once in Austria, soldiers picked her up and took her and other refugees to a camp in Eisenstadt, a place that was far short of her expectations. After a week there, being a Lutheran, the Protestant Charities took over her case, brought her to Vienna, and put her up in a hotel off the Ring Strasse. It's a tiny room, but it's all hers, she didn't have to share it with anyone. Anyway, it was only for a short while, she said, because she was going to America; she was only waiting to find Sári so they could go together.

"What are you talking about, Alexa? I am not going to America! I have a place here with my uncle and I have to find my little brother. I am staying right here in Vienna."

"No you are not! You are coming with me! This is what we've been waiting for all these years, to go to America! And since we are both alone, we should stick together. I don't see why you would want to stay here. Austria is nice, but not nice enough! So stop talking nonsense. And we better hurry and get started pronto! I heard the quota is very low and it's filling up fast. Tomorrow we'll go to the U.S. Embassy and put in our application for an immigrant visa."

"You are really serious about this? It's a huge step, Alexa. I know we talked about this kind of thing back home, but it was more like wishful thinking; we never thought that we actually get out one day. And why do you say that you are alone? Where is Oszkar? Didn't you find him yet?"

"I found him all right. He is in Spain, where they were playing when the revolution broke out and that is where he wants to stay. He loves Spain; they are treated like stars there. He asked me to come, too, but for what? He said nothing about marriage, and I won't go just to be his little senorita. If I have to start new somewhere in this world, I want it to be the best place on earth, and that's America! Frankly, I am surprised that you want to settle here. You even have a foothold in New York! You actually know somebody there, your old boyfriend. Didn't you think about that?"

"Only for a second, but it's ridiculous. How do I start looking for him? All I know that he is from Brooklyn. It's useless checking the phone book; Lombardo is not exactly a unique Italian name, there must be hundreds of them. And even if I find him after dialing every Lombardo listed, it would probably be his wife who answers."

"All right, so Harold is out, but there are lots of other reasons you should come with me. What do you have to lose? If you don't like it, you can always come back. I heard that if within two years someone is unable to adjust to the American way of life, they get a one-way ticket back to Vienna. So there, you have no more excuses. I just don't understand why you'd hesitate. You would have given an arm and a leg for such an opportunity back in Budapest."

Sári couldn't deny it, it was true; in her heart she always dreamed of living in America if ever given a chance. So why was she dithering now, when that big "if" turned into a real possibility? Aside from the promise to her mother to find Ochie, there was not much else to keep her here. It wouldn't hurt to put in an application. The process must take time, and it's no guarantee that she'd be accepted. In the interim she would continue looking for her little brother and see what develops. If they turned her down, or if she got her visa but couldn't find Ochie, that would be the end of it. On the other hand, if she was granted admittance *after* she located her brother, then she had fulfilled her promise and was free to go.

And so the next morning found Alexa and Sári standing in line in front of the U.S. Consulate, and by early afternoon they were inside filling out papers. Within a few days they were both called in for a personal interview that included questions regarding membership in the Communist Party and whether they participated in the uprising. They also went through a medical examination, mainly eyes and lungs, and at the end of the day, on December 5, 1956, their Austrian ID card was stamped with a temporary "Non-quota" immigration visa number. They were sent home to wait for further notice.

Three days later Sári received information about Ochie. Like Istvan, he too was placed in a parochial school for boys, but much closer, only a twenty-five-minute drive from Vienna. He looked fine when Guido and Sári went to see him, but wouldn't hear of returning to Sopron, and no amount of pleading would change his mind. The school was a prestigious private school, and it was easy to see why he liked it there. They attended classes where history was not distorted to glorify everything Russian, and there was no mandatory Russian language, either. No one was forcing them to go marching in stupid demonstrations against the imperialist warmongers and yell idiotic anti-Western slogans; he said he's had enough of that. When Sári told him that he'd break his mother's heart, he just shrugged. If he went back, he wouldn't be home for long anyway; he'd be drafted into the Army in a few years, so why bother?

In a way Sári could understand him. It was not for pure adventure that these young boys left the country. The political pressure on them was tremendous. From first grade on, they were pressed into joining the Pioneers, an organization that directed the indoctrination process both in the classrooms and during summer camping trips. Later, as they advanced to the Communist Youth Organization (*Kommunista Ifjusági Szövetség* or KISZ), applied propaganda led their young minds further into Communist activism. Geography books accorded 75% of the pages to Russia, history downplayed everything the West achieved, and all teaching emphasized the glories of Communism and the weakness of Western democracy. Children were intensively trained to love Russia and defend Communism, all in an effort to counteract the opposite they might hear at home from their parents.

Sári's conscience was clear; she did what she promised. Her mother must understand that she could not grab Ochie by the ear and force him to go home. He was in good hands and he also had Guido to look after him; he could always count on him. Before they left she told her brother about her intention to immigrate to America, and that if she was granted admission, they might not see each other for a long time to come.

She was hardly back in Vienna when she received the good news that her visa was approved and that she was scheduled to leave for the United States on Saturday, December 15th. The gathering place was Stephansplatz, the main square in downtown Vienna, and she was instructed to be there at 10 AM with her papers and one suitcase, ready to board one of the waiting busses. She couldn't believe how fast her girlhood dream was becoming a reality. She jokingly told her uncles that it took a revolution to bring it about, and everything that happened was for one reason, to fulfill that dream. In a way, she almost believed it.

She immediately went to see Alexa and found out that she also got her visa, except she was called to report a day earlier. It seemed that all their planning to leave together was for nothing. Sári accompanied her to the bus station, where they learned that for a few days the refugees would be taken to a place outside Vienna already under American authority to wait until final transportation could be arranged either by plane, weather permitting, or by ship. Disappointed about their separation and not knowing whether they would land in the same place in America or end up in different parts of the country, the girls made a solemn promise to find each other again no matter what. And so, when it was time to board the busses, they only said a temporary goodbye.

The next morning, it was Sári's turn to head for the American holding camp. After a tearful leave-taking from Uncle Guido and his family, her other uncle, Sandor, took her to the bus station carrying her small suitcase that contained only a little more than what she had when she arrived in Vienna three weeks ago. He whole-heartedly approved her decision to immigrate and predicted that being smart and adaptable, she would do well, although it didn't hurt, he added with a smile, that she was also a pretty girl. When the call came to get on board he wished her good luck and a safe journey, then with a final hug stepped back and waited until the wheels began to turn. He wouldn't see her again.

Sári's home for the next couple of days was a former military compound, rooms with rows of bunk beds. There was no separation between men and women; people stepping off the busses were assigned in groups to a room and warned not to move anywhere else. The food was also poor, leading to rumors that some greedy Austrians were making money by pocketing American dollars that were meant to provide better meals and accommodations. Well, if it was not exactly cozy, no one minded; people knew it was just a matter of time before they'd be on their way to America.

Sári and Alexa soon found each other again. They were lodged in separate buildings, and while they wished they could be together, they didn't dare breaking the rule against changing one's place. The purpose for ordering people to stay put was to eliminate confusion when departures were called. Daily transfers were scheduled according to rooms, and only the occupants were allowed to leave. Anyone missing was left behind, as were those present but not on the room's roster. Not to cause trouble, the girls stayed where they were and said goodbye once more when the bus with Alexa's group rolled out of the compound.

Regardless of weather conditions, these transports were leaving the collection center regularly to make room for the newly arriving refugees and avoid the possibility of overcrowding. On clear days the busses went to Schwechat, Vienna's airport, for flight to the United States; otherwise they were sent to Germany. If the weather cleared along the way, the refugees would be flown out of a German airport; if not, they would be driven to the docks at Bremerhaven and transported to New York by ship. When Alexa's bus left the sky was overcast, but since the forecast for the next day was good, they were taken to Schwechat.

The following morning, although visibility was still poor with limited take-offs, hoping that the fog would soon clear, another busload of refugees—Sári among them—was sent to the same airport. For lack of space her group spent the night sleeping on cots in an unheated storage room, yet everyone remained in a euphoric mood thinking that planes would start flying soon. They could be in the United States within a day or so! Unfortunately, the prediction was wrong; if anything, the weather got worse. During the night it began to snow and by morning the airport was completely shut down. The outlook was dismal and the authorities knew something must be done to start moving the refugees.

At breakfast Alexa spotted Sári, and this time they became determined to stay together. Marching into the office in charge of organizing the departures they pleaded not to be separated. They presented their situation as two "helpless" young women alone, without family or relatives, only each other to rely on. Alexa, already scheduled for the next available transport, told them with just enough drama that she would not leave unless they found a way to keep them together.

The staff was sympathetic but they said the passenger list could only be changed if somebody canceled. Otherwise, their hands were tied. They were already two days behind schedule, and because the airport could not handle this many people for another day, transportation would begin that very afternoon. Should something come up they would let them know, but that was all they could promise.

The two girls sat on pins and needles with their fingers crossed, and it must have helped, because they received word that someone did get sick, and they would be leaving on the same transport later in the day. Not by plane, however. It was impossible to fly, but according to reports the Stuttgart airport in Germany was open, and that's where they would be heading. Staying together brought great comfort to Sári and Alexa, but to say that they were two poor helpless females, was a slight exaggeration.

It was still snowing when about five o'clock the busses pulled onto the autobahn starting on a six-hundred-plus-mile ride across Austria and Germany. Around eleven, as they stopped at a roadhouse inn for dinner, the snow let up and the sky began to clear. By the time they reached Stuttgart and the sleepy passengers got off in front of the international air terminal, the sun was shining in a cloudless blue sky. No doubt, they would be flying out today; it was only a matter of time to get the plane—a military prop—ready for take-off later in the afternoon. They were served breakfast and lunch and had plenty of time to stretch their legs before the long flight. Some even took a nap, until word finally came around four o'clock to get ready for boarding.

None of the refugees had flown before, and excitement mixed with apprehension grew as they were led out to the plane. Everyone had heard of airsickness and some felt woozy already from sheer nerves, but conquering their angst, they climbed the steps and entered the cabin, where several handsome young men smartly dressed in Air Force uniforms welcomed them to the United States of America. After a smooth takeoff the sensation to see the city below and later the lights coming on at nightfall was an experience that Sári and Alexa would never forget, no matter how many times they flew in later years.

It was completely dark by the time they've made a stop at Shannon, Ireland, to prepare the plane for the long flight over the Atlantic. The crossing was bumpy at times, but they landed safely in Newfoundland, Canada, the last stop before entering the United States. After a bite at the airport cafeteria they were handed small packets of toiletries to use when freshening up, as men were shaving and women were putting on makeup to look their best when arriving in their new homeland.

It was still pitch dark and freezing cold when the plane took off for the last leg of their long trip. As they headed toward their final destination, Newark, New Jersey, they watched the sun rise over the horizon to a brilliant, sunny morning. The plane touched down at noon, with several Hungarian-speaking Army personnel waiting to take the refugees through immigration. Handing their Austrian ID cards to the immigration officer, Sári and Alexa got them back with a stamp that read: "U.S. Department of Justice, Admitted Dec.21, 1956, Newark, N.J., Immigration & Naturalization Service." They were in America, scarcely two months after the first shots rang out in the streets of Budapest.

. . . .

Outside the terminal Army busses waited to take them to nearby Camp Kilmer, an old military camp built during WWII for troops heading for deployment in Europe. It was closed in 1949 but now reopened for the Hungarian refugees. The 1573-acre camp was under the command of Major General Sidney C. Wooten of the U.S. Army and was staffed with soldiers with Hungarian backgrounds or at least some knowledge or familiarity with the language to help bridge the difficulties in communicating with the refugees.

During the drive a sergeant fluent in Hungarian welcomed everyone, then handed out a two-page typewritten note on what to expect upon arrival. A hand-drawn map of the camp with emergency telephone numbers was also attached. Most of the refugees, however, were too busy to bother with reading rules and regulations; they were watching the countryside and small towns drifting by. It was their first glimpse of America, or at least that part of America where picket-fenced homes with whitewashed sidings and sloping shingle rooftops, so different from their European counterparts, dotted the tree covered wooded landscape.

Turning off the multilane turnpike—an object of much admiration—the busses drove through the entrance to the camp, a large area divided into two sections: rows and rows of wooden barracks to the right, and a group of larger buildings on the left side. Checking the map, these buildings were designated as reception hall, entertainment hall, mess hall, medical facility, and a convenience store. Behind them stood several chapels, one for each faith. There were also a few barracks there, one designated as Red Cross, sharing space with other faith-based charity organizations.

The refugees were ushered into the large entertainment hall for orientation. They learned that for the first three days they would be confined to this side of the camp and no one would be allowed to leave, not even if they counted the Rockefellers as relatives waiting anxiously to take them home.

This "quarantine" was necessary to check the admission papers, go through a medical examination and most of all, have the all-important Alien Registration cards issued. These were commonly known as Green Cards that were to be carried on the person at all times. The Red Cross also interviewed the refugees to evaluate their personal situation. For those who had relatives or friends to go to in the United States, they helped to establish contact, verify the sponsorship, and clear the way for the release of the refugee. For the rest in need of sponsors, the interview served to evaluate their status in regard to family situation, education, and capabilities, so they could be matched with people offering jobs and willing to assume responsibility for them.

After the briefing ended with warning to listen carefully to loudspeaker announcements and check the bulletin boards in the mess hall for daily postings, the refugees were sent to the barracks behind the buildings for their temporary three-day stay. They found them lined with cots in typical military fashion, without any sort of partitioning. There were only two small rooms in the back, one reserved for the sergeant in charge, the other left to his discretion to assign as he saw fit. Immediately a fierce competition broke out, with everyone scrambling to prove entitlement to the room, but the sergeant had the last word, and when he chose Sári and Alexa, two unattached young ladies in need of protection from prying eyes, the mood turned downright mean against the poor girls, with unkind remarks trailing them as they closed their door.

At the end of the three days the refugees with sponsors were released, while everyone else was transferred to the secondary camp to wait until someone would sponsor them. Sári and Alexa were sent to barracks No. 655 and assigned to cots D-4 and D-5 near the entrance door. To maintain some degree of privacy, the occupants—families and single women—were allowed to hang up sheets between cots, which helped but only at night. During daytime children used them to play hide-and-seek or pulled them down to make play tents.

True to military tradition, a long list of rules was posted in each barracks, detailing all aspects of what to do and what was prohibited. Every person was responsible for making up his or her bed and maintaining order around it, with broom, bucket, and soap available to clean the floors. No cooking and laundering were allowed inside the rooms. Smoking in bed was forbidden. Visitors were restricted to the reception hall and were barred from entering the barracks.

Receiving meals and making small purchases were also regulated. Meal tickets were issued to individuals by name, and an ID was required for redemption. Three meals were served cafeteria style, with repeats allowed, but not leftover carry-outs. Warnings were also posted not to remove plates and silverware when leaving the mess hall. As for buying cigarettes, candy, writing papers, or items of hygienic nature sold at the canteen, everyone over age ten received coupons worth $2.50 per week. These, too, were non-transferable, imprinted with the refugee's name and checked against IDs. When the flint in Sári's cigarette lighter gave out, she went to buy a replacement but drew a strange look from the English-only speaking soldier at the counter after asking for a "firestone"—the literal translation of the Hungarian word for flint, *tüzkö*. His scowl turned to a knowing laughter when she pulled out her lighter to demonstrate the lack of spark.

For recreation the camp offered movies, a library, and a place to socialize and play cards. The favorite place for women, however, was a room with donated clothing the charities collected, some new, some used, put in piles for the ladies to rummage through. There was also a long table stacked with white cotton bras in every size. Although in Europe well-endowed women usually, although not necessarily, wore bras, shapely young ladies rarely had use for them. Nevertheless, if America dictated such delicate encasement, so be it, they were ready to oblige and hide their pretty assets, were it not for the problem of finding the right size. American sizes A-32, B-36, C-38 and D-42 or a truly formidable DD-48, didn't compute easily to European centimeters. Since there was no dressing room, a great deal of guesswork went into deciding which would suit what figure. It seemed that the best way to choose the right bra was to cup a hand—or two—around one's breast, then stiffly maintaining the shape, find a bra that would fit over it.

Like most of the refugees without relatives to welcome them, Sári and Alexa went through the required interview aimed at matching them with sponsors. After an initial evaluation by the Red Cross, the girls were assigned to their respective faith-based charity organizations to wait for their ultimate placement. It soon brought about their separation: Alexa, a Lutheran, left the camp within days, while Sári, a Catholic, stayed behind. Because the powerful Protestant charities could do a lot more for the relatively fewer number of refugees belonging to that faith, it took less than a week to find a middle-aged Lutheran couple in Omaha, Nebraska, willing to take Alexa into their home. After signing a sponsorship agreement—a three-year pledge for her support—her "adoption" was finalized and she was on her way to join her new family. Sári, on the other hand, had no such prospect. The Catholic relief organization was vastly overwhelmed handling thousands of cases, some quite difficult, especially when it involved large families unwilling to separate. These people were destined to linger in the camp for weeks and, in many cases, for months to come.

And so, after saying goodbye to her longtime friend, Sári hunkered down to a lengthy wait. She underwent a deeper probing interview about her education, and as expected, was told that her diploma in economics was of little use without speaking the language. Her counselor suggested she put in an application for college, first to learn English fast and efficiently, then later to take courses studying the way the American business world operated. With so many colleges and universities opening their doors to refugees with generous financial aid, he thought she had a good chance to be accepted.

It seemed a sound advice and Sári took it, even if it meant an extended stay in the camp. The earliest she could hope to leave was around the end of August, before the start of the fall semester. In the meantime, she decided to use her time wisely by attending English classes offered in the camp. She spent hours memorizing words and also watching television to hear them pronounced correctly. For recreation she played bridge, and in the evenings there was always a movie to see, mostly musicals with no lengthy dialog that no one could understand. It was standing room only when they showed *Rock around the Clock* with Bill Haley and the Platters, the first time these Hungarians had ever heard of rock music.

During one of these evenings she met a pretty girl, Andrea Seres, a few years younger than herself, also alone in the camp. She was from Budapest and although she looked vaguely familiar, Sári was sure they had never met before. Talking about their escapes, Andrea said she and her brother left the country on November 6 and were among the earliest arrivals in Camp Kilmer. Coming off the plane, they were interviewed by reporters—they both spoke English fairly well—and she proudly showed Sári the article with her picture published in *The New York Times.* After the first three days in the camp her brother was sent to study at the prestigious Brown University in New York, and to be closer to him she was determined to find a sponsor in New York City. She was in a good position to spot one, too, since she was helping out in the Caritas office where she could see the incoming sponsorship offers.

When Sári complained about her situation, that she might be stuck in the camp for who knows how long, just waiting to see if some college would grant her a scholarship, Andrea had a suggestion.

"You shouldn't be sitting here twiddling your thumbs, wasting time until something turns up! Get a sponsor and leave; the camp will notify you about the college when and if you are accepted. Why don't you come with me to New York? We could stay together! I will keep an eye on the list of sponsors; surely there must be someone willing to take us both."

Sári's ears perked up, but only for a minute. "It sounds wonderful, but it wouldn't work," she said, deflated. "People expect years of work in return for the sponsorship, and it's not fair to leave after only a few months. Here in the camp I am the guest of the U.S. Government; they pay for my keep until they find a college that would take me with full financial support. Besides, what could I do in New York without speaking the language? Work in some factory, or get stuck as a maid to a Hungarian family?"

"Not necessarily, there are other things you could do where the lack of English is not a major problem, and the pay is good," Andrea said, looking Sári up and down and scrutinizing her face. "You have good features and you are slim, a couple of inches taller would be better, but still good enough to get into modeling. That's what I am going to do. That's what I did in Budapest. I'll show you later some of the magazines I brought with me that carried my ads. Modeling is great work; you might even give up going to college. Just sit tight, sooner or later something will turn up."

Ah-ha, that's why Andrea looked so familiar, Sári thought later in the day when looking at her ads. And she might be right; this is something she could do. The photographer at the film studio when she made her screen tests liked the angles of her face. So why not give it a chance if—and this was a big if—a sponsor could be found.

She knew it wouldn't be easy. Regardless of how hard the charities worked, it was a monumental task to find sponsors for all these refugees. It required a generosity of the heart to become a sponsor, to take in total strangers who only spoke their native tongue, and assume total financial and moral responsibility for them for a three-year period. It was especially hard to place large extended families. A man could be well-educated, may have a PhD degree, yet it was lucky if a farmer somewhere in Iowa or Kentucky signed on to take him with a family that also included elderly parents, grandparents, cousins, aunts and uncles. For many, the camp became a long-term residence where they lingered waiting and hoping, yet no one gave up; no one wanted to go back to Austria. America was still the best place to live; they just needed to be patient.

As 1956 was winding down, news spread in the camp that Robert Wagner, the mayor of New York City, was hosting a special televised New Year's Eve party for 150 refugees at the grand ballroom of the Sheraton Hotel on Times Square. The event aimed to solicit sponsorships, hoping that perhaps seeing the refugees on TV and hearing about their plight would touch people's hearts and encourage more Americans to come forward and sign on as sponsors.

Andrea got two invitations, one of them for Sári, even though they wouldn't be sitting together at the banquet. As an interpreter, she'd have a place at the VIP table, while Sári was assigned to seat No. 72 at table No. 9. On the back of every invitation a message was printed: "If this Hungarian refugee is lost, please phone KILMER 5-7200 Extension 522."

Expectations to see New York ran high, but nothing prepared the refugees for what greeted them as the busses rolled into Manhattan. To see the city on New Year's Eve, ablaze with lights and thousands of people converging on Times Square, is an exciting experience for any American, but for these refugees, some from remote villages of a country that was still struggling to catch up with the 20th century, it was the thrill of a lifetime. Driven through the city they marveled amidst oohs and aahs at the sights of the tall skyscrapers, the famed Empire State Building, and the line of brightly lit theaters along Broadway and 42nd street.

Arriving at the Sheraton, they were welcomed by the Mayor himself and several other dignitaries. After the speeches and interviews with representatives from the camp and English-speaking refugees, among them Andrea, the waiters began serving the first course of the festive dinner, a dish utterly strange looking to Hungarians. They saw small pieces of white something with pink tails placed over the rim of a stemmed glass bowl that was filled with crushed ice and held a tiny cup of red sauce. It drew hesitant stares and raised murmured speculations about what it could be. Of course, none of the refugees had ever heard of shrimp cocktails, and when word spread from table to table that it was some kind of a snail, no amount of persuasion could make them taste it. The astonished waiters, with expressions of unmistakable contempt for these barbarians, had to collect and carry away the untouched delicacies.

After dinner was over, the younger people took to the dance floor, while others stood around the windows, looking down at the ongoing celebration in the square below. It was fascinating to see the crowd outside noisily waiting to ring in the New Year, then turning around and see the same scene on television. Soon the moment arrived when everyone stood with champagne glass in hand, watching the traditional ball slowly descending over Times Square, ready to join in the boisterous countdown during the last ten seconds of 1956.

And as the noise erupted at midnight, people hugging and kissing each other, wishing good luck, the refugees raised their glasses not only to welcome the brand new year, but also in remembrance of the fateful events of the old year that brought them to this place, to their new home, America.

Worlds apart

FROM THE MOMENT Ilonka said goodbye to Sári, her mood alternated between hope and despair. Alone with only Jeno in the suddenly empty house she could think of nothing but her missing children. What this revolution did was tore the family apart; it brought the worst nightmare a mother could have: not knowing where her children were.

As much as she hated the foundry, it would have helped to go to work and keep her mind on other things, but the general strike was still in effect and there was nothing to distract her from worrying. She knew from the two guides that Sári was safe in Austria, but did she find Istvan and Ochie? With the flood of refugees, the situation must be chaotic in that poor country. She even heard that to help, other countries were offering to take in refugees. What if her boys left Austria and wound up in some place where they could never be found? She didn't dare to think of that possibility without risking her sanity. She blamed herself for not watching them closer, not seeing the signs that they were planning to leave. Oh, why couldn't they have gone together? At least Istvan could have looked after Ochie, but every time she thought of her younger son, still a child, lost in some refugee camp, she broke down and wept. All alone, so handsome and so innocent, he could easily fall prey to some pervert, and she could do nothing to protect him. The thought terrified her and while in the past she always found solace in prayers, this time it did not bring her peace.

Jeno tried to calm her but nothing could ease the pain in her heart. Perhaps he was not convincing enough, because deep down he worried just the same. He felt better about Istvan; at eighteen he was more mature, he knew how to conduct himself, evaluate his situation and make the best of it, and most of all, he was not alone; he had Guido to help. But young Ochie was entirely another matter. He was the baby in the family, always indulged, looked after, his friends and activities closely monitored to keep him safe from bad influence, all making him extremely vulnerable when thrown into such a muddled, disorderly situation that must exist in the camps. He was as desperately concerned about him as Ilonka, and she sensed it.

And there was still the uncertainty about Gyuszi, not a word from him since the start of the turmoil. They worried about Eta, too; who knows what had happened to them since Jeno called? With her husband's crazy idealism, to fight for a socialist Hungary without Stalinism must be highly appealing to his overheated political senses. They could only hope that now with three children he had better judgment than taking to the streets shouting, "Russians go home."

In the early evening of December 6, St. Nicholas day, they were sitting in the kitchen with a cup of tea, Ilonka reminiscing about events that occurred on this very day back in 1943 and 1944.

"Remember, Jeno, when Sári was playing Santa Clause, and how she made the boys kneel and kiss her hand, then a year later when during the bombing she and Ochie were stuck in the neighbors' cellar? I thought we were never going to see them! Just like now. They are all gone. What would I give to have them back, to be together again!"

Their quiet talk was suddenly interrupted by the shrill sound of the doorbell. Ilonka's heart leaped, could it be that Istvan and Ochie were already back? But when almost simultaneously they heard the front door opening, they knew instantly who it was; only Gyuszi had a key to the house! Ilonka was on her feet, spilling her tea as she ran to meet him. "My God, it's you!" She hugged him, covering his face with kisses. "Are you all right? We were worried sick about you."

With Ilonka clinging to Gyuszi, Jeno had to wait his turn to welcome him. "It's good to have you home, son!" he said, holding him in a tight embrace for a long moment, just enough to blink away an insistent tear. Releasing him, he patted him on both shoulders. "Thank God you are safe. We heard Miskolc was a hotbed during the revolt, with the miners threatening to blow up the mine when the AVO came to arrest some of their men."

"He can tell about that later, Jeno, let him sit down first!" Ilonka said nudging Gyuszi toward the kitchen. "You must be hungry, come, and have something to eat."

She was busily setting the table, momentarily forgetting her worries about the other children, when suddenly she heard Gyuszi asking the same question as Sári did when she came home: where were the boys? In an instant she froze, her face the color of chalk as she turned to Gyuszi.

"You are not here to tell me that you want to leave?"

"Why yes, I have to, Mother, it's too dangerous for me to stay. They are arresting every other person in Miskolc, I could be—"

There was no time to finish the sentence; if he hadn't jumped to catch his mother, she would have collapsed in a heap.

With Jeno's help, they eased her limp body into a chair and tried to bring her around. "The boys and Sári are all gone, and we have not heard from any of them since," Jeno quickly told Gyuszi, before Ilonka started to stir. Within a minute she regained consciousness but she just sat there, slunk in the chair, staring vacantly, silent tears rolling down her cheeks without an attempt to wipe them away.

Jeno was bringing her a glass of water while Gyuszi, pulling out his handkerchief, dabbed at her face. "Please Mother, you must not let it upset you this much. I heard from Dad what happened, but I am sure Istvan and Ochie are fine. I know first hand from a friend who escaped but came back for his wife that the Austrians are very well organized. Everything will be fine, you'll see."

"Fine? How could it be when I don't know where my children are?" she said, her voice breaking into sobs. "And now you want to leave, too . . ."

Her words, spoken with such deep sadness, stabbed Gyuszi in the heart, shaking his hitherto solid determination to flee the country. It was not on a whim that he decided to join the exodus; staying could put him in real danger. The AVO had been picking up suspects ever since the roundups began a week ago, and he could very well be the next one. How could he make her understand that his freedom was at stake? He pulled a chair close to Ilonka and, taking both her hands into his, told her the brutal truth about the ongoing retaliations, how several of his colleagues were in jail already, accused of having a leading role in the demonstrations when they were only innocent bystanders. One of them was not even in town at the time, but the AVO just shrugged saying there were plenty of other charges they could pin on provocateurs.

"And I did a lot more than just demonstrate," Gyuszi went on. "I helped to knock down the Red Star from our building in front of a large crowd. Everyone saw me, and what's worse, the AVO might have a recording of me doing it. A TV crew was at the scene—what if they caught me in action? With proof like that they can put me away until my hair turns white. Even without the tape, there's a good chance that I'll end up in jail."

"In jail I can still visit you, I'd still have you," Ilonka's voice rang out, now shrill and challenging. She had snapped out of her lethargy and was fully alert, fighting to keep her son from leaving. "If you really believe that you'd be arrested, then leave Miskolc, come home, or better yet, go to some other place in the country, where you can hold out until this craziness is over. You must know some girl from a small town; marry her and you'd be safe. She can hide you! You'll get through this! Sooner or later things will have to get back to normal, then you can come back to Sopron; you can easily get a teaching job here at the university. Just don't leave, don't go, because if you do, you'd be signing my death sentence. I won't survive if you, too, desert me! You are all I have left! I can't go on losing four of my children all at the same time, not knowing where they are, what became of them. I'd rather die . . ."

She couldn't go on. And in that moment, with her words drowned by sobs and her face buried in her hands, Gyuszi knew his fate was sealed; he could never leave, even if it meant risking his freedom. To see his mother consumed by such despair and hear her pathetic pleading was more than he could withstand. It had a more profound effect on him than any hysterical outburst, or bringing up the sacrifices she made for him. He would stay and hope for the best, and when the smoke cleared he would come back to be close to her. It wouldn't bring his brothers back, but his presence perhaps could help her bear the loss with a little less sorrow.

He remained for a week, but when word came that Kadar had threatened to impose the death sentence on strikers, he had no choice but return to Miskolc. He came to Sopron with firm resolve to leave the country, his hopes pinned on a future free of fear somewhere in Canada—the place most of his colleagues were heading—but instead, here he was, giving it all up and going back to face danger and uncertainty. With bitter disappointment, he thought of what might have been, his opportunities lost forever, and pondered whether it would have made a difference if he had come earlier, when his brothers were still at home. Would his mother have let him go then? The question remained unanswered to haunt him for the rest of his life.

When the general strike was called off Ilonka, too, went back to work. The resistance was broken, and life was slowly returning to its old pre-October days. The post office started to deliver mail, but there was no reply from Guido to Ilonka's desperate letters. She called on the parents of the boys who escaped with Istvan and Ochie to see if they had heard anything, but it was the same.

Apparently, mail from the West was blocked. For a moment Jeno thought of asking some of the conductors working on the trains to Vienna to contact Guido, but dropped the idea. Even though he knew most of them from his working days, he was not sure anymore who could be trusted. The days of suspicion and the fear of denunciation were back in full force.

At least they received a letter from Eta, just a few lines that all was fine, and Gyuszi also wrote that so far he was safe. These were reassuring to read, yet every afternoon when Ilonka returned from work Jeno saw the same hopeful glint in her eyes, expecting news from Vienna, and then the disappointment when there was none. Christmas without the boys was especially hard on her; it was the first time she didn't put up a tree, or prepare in any way for Christmas.

The opportunity to learn what had happened to the boys and Sári finally came in February, not by courtesy of the post office but through the help of her aunt, Mitzie. She came to say that her son Franz, who was now in charge of sales and distribution at the foundry, would be going to Bratislava on business, and from Slovakia he would have no problem calling Guido without someone monitoring the conversation. The day he returned and told Ilonka that both boys were safe and in good hands was the first time Ilonka felt her nightmarish fears subside. Tears still filled her eyes, but now they glistened with relief, as she learned that no harm came to them, and while they were not together, both were in highly prestigious parochial schools. She only felt remorseful that in her despair she had lost faith in God and blamed him for allowing her children to be taken from her, while all the time God was protecting them, guiding them, delivering them safely into the bosom of his blessed Church.

"And what about Sári? Is she with Guido?" she asked her cousin.

"Not anymore, she is in America," Franz said, handing Ilonka an envelope he received from Guido while still in Bratislava. "He told me on the phone that everything is in there, a letter she wrote you from New York but was returned to her, which she then mailed back to Guido, hoping he'll get it to you someway or another. I don't know about that girl; she could never stay put in one place long enough to warm her seat," he said, shaking his head. "Going from Sopron to Budapest to Vienna, and now to America! What on earth is she after?"

Ilonka didn't even hear his muttering. Tearing at the envelope, first she found Guido's letter about the boys, and that he visited Ochie regularly. Then she took out the other letter with Sári's handwriting, staring at the return address: 126 West 73rd St., New York, NY, care of Marylou Briggs. Impatient, and at the same time half scared of what it would say, she waited until Fanz left before she opened the letter and began to read:

Dearest Mother and Father!

I can imagine your stunned disbelief as you read my letter from halfway across the globe, but that is where I am, where this whirlwind that swept through our country has landed me. When we said goodbye I had no idea that in three short weeks I'd be in America. That was never my intention when I left you. Everything happened so fast that it's hard to pinpoint what exactly made me change my mind and leave Austria, when at first I wouldn't even go to Germany with Adam. His decision to move there ended our friendship.

Let me just say that as wonderful as Uncle Guido's family was to me, I couldn't burden them with a prolonged stay. I wanted to be on my own as soon as possible, but when I asked him about job opportunities, I found out that they were very limited for refugees. Then Alexa showed up, and when she could talk of nothing else but going to America, and that we should go together, I said to myself, why not? This was a chance of a lifetime. If I have to start all over, there is no better place for it than the land where everything is possible. I discussed it with Uncle Sandor, and he said if he were younger, he'd do the same thing.

Ilonka had to stop. Her heart began to race and she felt faint just thinking about her daughter alone in that far away country. She *must* relax, or the anxiety might kill her! Taking a deep breath and blowing it out slowly she calmed down enough to glance at the next lines about Sári's flight to the States, her days in the refugee camp, and meeting Andrea there after Alexa got a sponsor and left the camp.

It is on account of Andrea that I wound up in New York. She is the one who found our sponsor, a wonderful young woman named Marylou Briggs from New York City, who was willing to take us under her wing and help us to get started. We left the camp with her on January 5, and although her apartment is small—the kitchen is part of the living room—we love it here and get along fine. We were very lucky to have found her, not only because we wanted to live in New York—Oh Mom, if you could see this great city with all the skyscrapers!—but also because she helped us start working right away. As part owner of a modeling agency she got us jobs as fashion models, or what you'd call mannequins in Hungary. I work for a company by the name of Rainshedder on 42nd Street in the heart of Manhattan. Their showroom is on the 34th floor, and all we do is prance around in front of buyers showing the new line of raincoats for the upcoming season. It's an easy job and kind of glamorous, and the best part is that speaking English is not crucial; in fact we are not allowed to say anything to the buyers, other than the item number of the coat we are presenting. If they have a question, they have to ask the sales people. None of that 'What's your number honey?' business. We work from nine to five, Monday to Friday, and get paid $78 a week after deductions, which is very good money compared to what the girls make in the office. Out of that we each give Marylou $20 a week to help with our keep, even though she didn't want to take it at first; the rest is ours to spend as we please.

You can see how lucky we are when so many of the refugees are still lingering in the camp, or if sponsored, girls like us work as housemaids, nannies, or in some factory, getting paid a fraction of what we earn. I could go on about how happy I am to be here, that my life is truly a dream come true, even though my decision to immigrate created such a great distance between us. I only hope you won't hold it against me, but be happy for me.

I know that while living in Budapest during the past six years I didn't visit you very often, but I always knew I could hop on a train and be home whenever I wanted. Sadly, I can no longer do that, and not only because of the distance. Even from Vienna I couldn't come home to see you, and you know the reason why.

Although I can't even guess when we'll see each other again, I am sure the time will come. Until then, know that I miss you very much, and that not one day goes by without thinking of you. Take care and write me as soon as you can.

Your loving daughter, Sári

P.S. I am sure you know by now from Guido that I located Istvan and Ochie before I left; more than that I could not do. I am also sending here a photo of Andrea and me taken in Central Park, not far from where we live.

When Jeno came home that day he found Ilonka sitting at the table, a handkerchief pressed to her mouth, gazing at some letters spread in front of her. But when she looked up she was smiling. "The boys are safe, and Sári is in America," she said, her voice choked by emotion as she handed him the letters. They sat together at the table, looking at the photograph, relieved and sad at the same time over the news, not noticing that the sun was going down, while somewhere on the other side of the world it was just beginning to rise.

Learning the whereabouts of her three missing children, Ilonka was now resigned to accept losing Istvan and Sári, but would never give up on bringing Ochie home. When toward the end of 1956 the government announced that refugees who returned to Hungary by March 31, 1957 would be granted full amnesty, she bombarded her young son with pleading letters to come back. She also begged Guido to do everything he could to talk him into coming home, and after a while it seemed she'd get her wish. The way Guido saw it after talking with Ochie, once the first flush of excitement died down, he and his buddies came to realize that "freedom" was not exactly as they imagined it would be. To escape was a great big adventure for them; they were off to see the world, a world without restrictions, no parents to obey, or strict school rules to follow, but instead they found themselves living under the thumbs of the monks. Ochie also said that one of the priests started to pay more attention to him than he liked. Frequent late night visits to his bedside in the dormitory and certain unmistakable hints of an intimate nature made him extremely uncomfortable and he wanted out. He was willing to go home.

A written parental request and his consent to return was all the authorities needed to release him, and so on February 16, on his fourteenth birthday, Guido picked him up and drove him to the border where Aunt Mitzie and Franz waited for him with a borrowed company car. Parents were not permitted anywhere near the border in fear that somehow they would manage to slip through and join their children on the Austrian side.

The reunion was a family celebration, with aunts, uncles, friends, and schoolmates, all noisily singing happy birthday to him while Ilonka carried in a cake with fourteen candles to blow out. Once again the sound of laughter echoed throughout the house, with all the gloom and doom of the past four months flown out the window. Ilonka clung to her son with obstinate obsession and from that day on, he could do no wrong.

Jeno, too, felt overwhelmed with emotion when he embraced Ochie. The boy's disappearance was as hard on him as on Ilonka, but while she never for one moment gave up on getting him back, he would have understood if Ochie had chosen not to return. Like himself, he was the youngest of three boys, growing up in the shadow of his older brothers; he knew what it was like being under constant pressure to compete, to be compared to them, to their achievements, or to live up to expectations the others failed to fulfill. He viewed his escape as an attempt at emancipation and he could understand and forgive him for trying to find a way to be on his own. Nevertheless, now that he was home, holding him made his heart overflow with happiness and when he looked at him, his eyes shone with unabashed love and joy.

Ochie was readmitted to school without any disadvantage for having missed a semester. Actually, he was ahead of the others, since during the general strike schools were closed in Hungary, while in Austria he regularly attended classes. Most of his classmates looked at him as a daring adventurer, someone with courage to leave the country, but there were also those who taunted him for coming back.

As much as Ilonka and Jeno rejoiced to have him home, some nights a troubling question kept them awake: would Kadar keep his promise of amnesty for returning refugees, or was it just a ruse to lure them back so he could punish them? It didn't bode well that jails were full of people caught trying to escape to the West, so why should those who left but came back be treated differently?

They had good reason to worry. Kadar didn't keep his given word to forgive all who fought during the revolt. Swift and vicious retaliation followed, ruthless reprisals against all who dared to rise against the status quo. There was no mercy, no clemency. And there was worse to come. When Kadar came back from Moscow on March 20, 1957, he had their permission to reintroduce the old Stalinist conceptual trials for all anti-government activities during the uprising and also to reopen the labor camps. Regardless how minor the "crime," it carried the charge of "organized armed seditious act aimed to overthrow the social system of the State." In many cases, being caught in the vicinity of a battle without any participation was sufficient to fit the charge and bring a conviction. As in the past, these trials were conducted without the slightest regard to lawful proceedings; their aim was not to discover the truth, but to prove guilt at all cost. They were a parody of justice, mere formalities, where the prosecutor's opening statement consisted of an over-dramatized, lengthy description of the anti-governmental atmosphere that prevailed during the revolt. Great emphasis was placed on presenting the uprising as a carefully planned conspiracy, even though it was totally spontaneous. Sadly, it was the tragedy of the revolution that the freedom fighters were unorganized, unprepared, ill-equipped, and without strong leadership.

As for the defense, the accused was denied legal representation during the pre-trial period, with a public defender assigned right before the trial and with only a vague knowledge of the charges in the case. Not that it mattered. Attempts to clear the victim, including testimony of witnesses on his behalf, were all ignored since the verdict had been pre-determined by those outside the court. All verdicts were subject to appeal; however, the outcome often increased the severity of the original punishment, rather than mitigating it.

Such was the fate of Ilona Toth, a twenty-five-year-old young doctor serving her internship in a hospital where the wounded were brought in from nearby street fighting. It was also a gathering place for revolutionists to use the hospital's copying machine for printing announcements and other flyers. On November 21, 1956, Dr. Toth and several others at the hospital were arrested and charged with distributing anti-state propaganda leaflets. Later, on December 4, it came to light that a wounded AVO man was brought to the hospital on November 18 and died there on the same day. When the trial opened, the charges against Dr. Toth included murdering the AVO man by piercing his heart with a knife, this according to the minutes supposedly taken at her arrest, thirteen days *before* the death of the AVO man was discovered. This was such a blatantly fraudulent attempt to pin the murder charge on her, such a proof of the pre-conceived nature of her trial, that in spite of her confession, obviously made under torture, the penalty handed down on March 8 was a life sentence, instead of the usual automatic death penalty. Upon appeal, however, the higher court changed it to death by hanging, which was carried out on June 28, 1957. It took over four decades and the defeat of Communism before Dr. Toth was rehabilitated, when in 2001 her trial was declared unlawful, and the verdict nullified. The autopsy of the dead AVO man showed no wound caused by piercing of the heart, a fact carefully concealed at the trial.

With the avalanche of arrests and reintroduction of the showcase trials, it was a relief to Ilonka and Jeno that Gyuszi's "criminal" act went undetected; no one denounced him, and it seems the TV crew didn't catch him in the act, either. Knowing that Istvan was happy and well treated at his school also kept their spirits high; he would be graduating in June, and after that would immediately go into a compulsory nine-month military service.

As for Sári, her letters arrived regularly; she was in love with America, the people were friendly and she had no problem adjusting to life there. The revolution was still very much in the news; *Time* magazine chose a picture of a Hungarian freedom fighter as the "Man of the Year" for its January 7, 1957 cover. The only resentment against the refugees came from earlier Hungarian immigrants, those who left the country shortly before or during the war. And it was understandable. For the newly arriving refugees the U.S. government eased the otherwise strict immigration rules, granting them permanent visas in days, waiving sponsorship requirements prior to admittance, and paid for their transportation, while the others had to wait long periods, sometimes years, lingering in some miserable refugee camp in Europe before gaining entry, and then had to reimburse the sponsoring charity organization for sending them third-class boat tickets.

Her enthusiasm was boundless. To go to America was the best thing she could have done. Living in New York was an adventure, she loved her work, and Marylou was like an older sister to her and Andrea. They got along great, but regardless, they felt Marylou deserved more privacy, and they were saving money to eventually rent an apartment near her place.

The only one Ilonka had not heard from lately was Eta. Oh well, she thought, she had her hands full raising her three boys. But when a letter finally came in the middle of May, it shattered their relative tranquility with the news that Latzi had been arrested for counter-revolutionary activities! The charge against him was the usual: participation in the unlawful organized armed uprising against the People's Democracy. It was all lies, nothing but false accusations, as Eta described Latzi's involvement in the revolution. When the fighting broke out he was elected to the local workers' council and was a member of the delegation entrusted to negotiate with the government until Kadar dissolved the councils on December 8. When four days later, in retaliation, the workers of Csepel called for a general strike, he supposedly rallied the workers in Debrecen to follow suit and go on strike, a ridiculous charge, since they would have joined the strike without Latzi or anyone else urging them to do so.

They also accused him of distributing guns, which again was totally made up. In fact, the exact opposite happened. Some people came to his office asking for rifles the forestry kept as a fully authorized part of their business, and he refused. Angry for the rebuff, these people started rumors that he was not really representing them, especially when they found out that while the Party secretary was in hiding Latzi delivered the man's bi-weekly earnings to his wife, saying that Party or no Party, the man had to feed his family. Eta lamented that Latzi could never strike the right note when dealing with people, and was sure that making the workers feel rejected had a lot to do with his arrest: either they denounced him out of vengeance, or from fear that he would implicate them. It was widespread these days to point fingers at others to divert suspicion from one's own anti-government activities during the revolt.

Eta wrote that Latzi was not yet home when the AVO came for him late in the afternoon. They searched the house looking for weapons, but when they didn't find any, they took his collection of medals he had won as a long-distance runner during his college days. These were all imprinted with the Horthy-era Holy Crown emblem, a sure sign, they said with sardonic satisfaction, that he was a dedicated fascist reactionary who fought to bring back the old pre-war capitalist system that sucked the blood of the working classes. During the search Eta, huddling with the children, prayed for some miracle that would keep Latzi from returning home, but as usual, he arrived on time right after leaving his office. Hearing his motorbike pulling up, the AVO men rushed outside and took him away without giving him a chance to say goodbye to his family.

It was days before Eta found out that he was taken to a jail in Budapest and kept in a large overcrowded cell until formal charges could be drawn up against him. No contact with family was allowed; she only received a court notice indicating the date of the trial. She and Latzi's brother Gyorgy, a doctor working in the Ministry of Health, attended the hearings, a typical prearranged procedure where witnesses were put on parade against him, while the judge ignored testimonies brought in his defense. The shock came when taking the stand Latzi began to speak: all his front teeth were missing. Eta bit down hard on her inner lip to stifle her cry, knowing full well what that gaping mouth meant. She was beyond consolation when she thought of the senseless beatings her husband must have endured, and for what? To make him one of the tiny nails that held together the rickety structure on which Russia's attack on Hungary could stand justified?

The trial didn't last long, and the judge handed down the standard verdict prescribed for similar cases, a seven-year jail sentence. Gyorgy led half-dazed Eta out of the courtroom, assuring her that he had some connections and would hire a good attorney to handle the appeal. Eta was a strong woman who could always take life's adversities in stride and would never feel sorry for herself, and now again, she found the courage to pull herself together to face the years ahead alone with her boys. How, she didn't know, but she and her children would make it through.

Although Latzi's salary stopped when he was arrested, the subsidy the state paid to families with more than one child continued while the trial lasted. Once the sentence was handed down, however, that, too, was suspended. Eta was notified that it would be reinstated if she agreed to divorce her husband, and she would also be allowed to stay in their house, otherwise face eviction. They gave her thirty days to prove that she had started divorce proceedings, but typically, Eta flatly refused to accept the offer. Everyone pleaded with her that Latzi would understand if she took advantage of the divorce; it would only be a piece of paper to save the children from further trauma. It was the sensible thing to do. After his release, they could get married again; it was as simple as that. Except Eta wouldn't budge, not even when Latzi himself urged her to file for divorce. He might say so, but it was only human that deep down he would feel abandoned, and she was not about to add to her husband's misery.

She started packing to be ready for the day when they must leave their home. She knew that according to her deportation order they would be taken to some village in the eastern region, but when they got there she was thoroughly shocked. The place was an abandoned farmhouse, slightly better than a shack, in the middle of nowhere, with no electricity or plumbing, only a well with a bucket to draw water, and a couple of gypsy campers for neighbors. This time Eta sat down and cried. She looked at her young children and didn't know how they were to live under such primitive conditions.

She didn't have much time for self-pity, however, as the driver and his helper needed direction to unload her small belongings. She only brought the most necessary furnishings and stored the rest with friends. While the men worked, she quickly made a survey of the place and knew that to survive the first few days she must get to the village before dark to bring back some basic supplies. She needed a kerosene lamp, an axe to chop wood, groceries, and some food for her animals, a dog, a few chickens, and two piglets. Paying the driver extra money, he drove her and the children to the village some five miles away, while the other man stayed behind to ward off the gypsies.

They were back in no time, but it would be another matter to make the trip alone without any kind of transportation. She would have to walk to the store, and almost every other day, since in the warm weather food didn't last. It would take at least one hour to the village if she went alone, but she had to take the children with her; she couldn't possibly leave them home alone. And so several times a week she set out with her boys, Latzi, almost ten, helping to pull the little cart with the baby propped up in it, and seven-year-old Peter pushing from behind. Seeing her struggle, the grocer took pity on them and offered a helping hand. His son was driving a truck for the collectives, he said, and would gladly deliver what Eta needed if she gave him the list. He also told her that the gypsies were harmless and were probably more afraid of her than the other way around; they were just hiding from the authorities to avoid work.

A few weeks later Eta's brother-in-law came with the news that his family had hired a lawyer to work on the appeal, although he warned them not to expect much. They also found out that once a month prisoners were allowed a half-hour visit from relatives, and a food parcel not exceeding five pounds. Before leaving, Gyorgy gave her some money with the promise she'd get the same every month.

On the day Eta went to see her husband, she left young Latzi in charge to look after his siblings. Forced to grow up fast, he showed a remarkable understanding of their situation, and Eta knew she could trust him to keep the younger boys inside while she was gone.

The package she took for Latzi was filled with items he could chew easily, but whether he received it or not, she didn't know, for after arriving at the jail it was taken away for later distribution. For an hour she and other visitors stood in line for inspection and to sign papers promising to observe the rules, until finally at ten o'clock the door to the visiting room was opened and they were led inside. The prisoners were already lined up in the back of a cage-like enclosure, waiting until the guard called out their names to step forward and sit opposite their loved ones already seated outside the wire partition. Everyone was warned to keep their hands folded; touching through the divider was strictly forbidden.

It broke Eta's heart to see Latzi in prison garb hanging loose on his thin frame and trying to cover his toothless mouth when talking, yet he didn't complain. The food was passable and his cell was comfortable compared to the crowded community jail where he spent weeks prior to his sentencing. He even landed a famous cellmate, a well-known actor condemned for "inciting" the crowd with his recital of the patriotic Petofy poem on the day of the October 23 demonstration. He said they did not work, at least not yet; the prison had some kind of system in deciding who would work and who would not. Eta brought him pictures of the boys, lied that they were reasonably well in their new place, and asked him what she should bring the next time. Too soon the visit was over; it was time to put on a brave face as she said goodbye.

Latzi's first appeal took place in front of a judge who seemed to be more lenient and reduced the sentence to five years. According to the attorney, however, it had nothing to do with leniency, but more with the jails getting seriously overcrowded. People were being arrested and brought in by the thousands without enough room to hold them all, giving hope that Latzi's final appeal would result in further reduction.

With summer limping toward fall and Eta barred from moving closer to the village, she had to face another problem. The two older boys were supposed to attend school, but to get there on time with the days getting shorter, they would have to leave home while it was still dark, something Eta wouldn't allow. When Ilonka offered to take the children so they wouldn't miss a year, Eta let Peter go, but not Latzi; she needed him in their great isolation. She would just tutor him at home and hope he wouldn't fall too far behind in his studies.

It took her brother-in-law to pull some strings, but through connections he succeeded in lifting the restrictions that tied Eta to that godforsaken farmhouse. Before the year ended, she was allowed to move into a small cottage on the outskirts of the village, where she had neighbors to talk to, could walk to the stores, and little Latzi had no problem getting to school. What luxury it seemed to just flip a switch to turn on the light and open a faucet to get water! And when it came time to visit her husband she had someone to watch the baby until Latzi came home from school to take over the task. She even had a fenced-in yard where she could plant vegetables in the spring. Luckily, she knew how to, thanks to switching schools from her Latin- and math-heavy gimnazium to that agricultural school her parents enrolled her when she was fourteen. Academics wouldn't be much help to her now!

Their situation further improved when she made a little money by taking in finishing work from a seamstress. She was seriously considering bringing Peter home; she missed her quiet little boy, but at the end she let him stay in Sopron where schools were far superior to that in the village.

At Christmas, she put up a small tree and tucked a few presents under it for the two boys, but in her heart there was no room for festive celebration. Her thoughts were with her husband, sitting in his cell, alone on this day that was meant more than any other to be shared with loved ones. Looking at her young sons, thriving in spite of all the setbacks, she gave thanks for the small blessings she had received, but when she thought of the next four years, all those Christmases spent without him, it took all her strength to still the ache in her heart and keep the smile on her face in front of the children.

The news about Latzi's arrest in May reached Sári in the new apartment she and Andrea had rented in April. Her heart went out to her sister when she read her mother's letter describing what happened, but of course she could do nothing to help. Not that they asked for anything. The last thing poor Latzi needed was money or packages sent from America and have a spy charge thrown on top of what he was already accused of. As for Eta's hardship in coping with the situation, she couldn't understand why she refused to go through the formality of a divorce; it is what she should have done, what anyone with common sense would have done. Big deal, a piece of paper was all it would have taken to avoid being kicked out to some gypsy campsite. She could have saved all that trouble, but no, she had to "stand by her man"! Divorcing didn't mean that she abandoned him. She could have continued to visit him and support him in every way; Latzi would have understood that she did it for the children's sake.

What they did to Latzi and Eta proved to her that nothing had changed in Hungary. Here she was, barely five months in America, a country that welcomed her, where she was living free of harassment, working, earning enough money to have a nice apartment, and there was her brother-in-law in jail like a criminal, and her sister thrown to the wolves to fend for herself and her sons, struggling to survive under primitive conditions. The thought that she could easily be in the same situation if she had married Viktor, made her shudder. She knew that as a staunch patriot, it would have been unthinkable for him to sit on the sidelines during the revolution or leave the country after the defeat. Perhaps it was fate that guided her hand when she wrote that Dear John letter, otherwise she would be stuck in Hungary, denied the chance for a better life, bitterly disappointed.

She loved everything about her new country, but most of all, the security of living without fear that someone was watching, waiting to hear a wrong word that could be reported. As long as people observed the law, they were left in peace, free to enjoy life, their "pursuit of happiness" protected by sacred right.

For the moment, pursuing happiness for Sári meant acquiring the material things she was denied when living in Hungary. There she worked only to exist. In all her years spent in Budapest what did she have? A tiny rented room, a few outfits, nothing more. And here, coming only with a small suitcase, in a few months she already had a closet full of clothes. It was true, her best dresses were solicited by Marylou from her garment-district clients who used her models, and the rest were bought second-hand from a Goodwill store, but they were in good condition, so who cared if someone wore them before! She spent her money carefully but still managed to have her hair and nails done regularly. These were small luxuries but working as a showroom model, she needed to look her best. How ridiculous it all seemed now that back in Budapest she was condemned as a depraved decadent, her opportunities curtailed, all for wearing red nail polish!

Having their own place, a spacious, nicely furnished flat, made Sári and Andrea feel more independent, but they kept very close contact with Marylou. They lived only a few blocks apart and got together often. It was also on account of her that Sári met her first boyfriend in America, not by personal introduction, but through a roundabout way. As at the start of 1957 the public interest about the Hungarian revolt and the plight of the refugees was still high, Marylou arranged for an interview with Barry Gray, the talk show host of a popular radio program that aired at late night from a nightclub. He was told that only Andrea spoke English well, so after introducing the girls, he directed his questions to her: how did they escape, what was life in Hungary compared to America, and was it hard to adjust life in their new country?

Sári's English of three months was definitely not at a level where she could carry on a lively conversation, so she just sat there, smiling prettily. At one point Mr. Gray, probably feeling sorry for her, decided to pose a few simple questions to her as well: did she like America and was the food very different here? When she had no problem answering—she even elaborated beyond a plain "Yes"—he pressed a little further, asking what she liked most about New York.

"The big houses," she announced, and to be sure they understood that she meant skyscrapers, she stretched an arm toward the ceiling. It drew a good-natured laughter from the audience, and when her host asked if she had yet a chance to visit the Empire State Building, the tallest "house" in New York, she said no, but proudly added that the place she worked at, a company called Rainshedder on 42nd Street, was on the 34th floor.

The next morning arriving at work the receptionist told her the boss wanted to see her. Not knowing what to expect, she was nervous walking into his office, and when he asked if she was a guest on *The Barry Gray Show* last night, her immediate thought was that mentioning the company name must have been a mistake. She needn't have worried. Instead of chastising her, he said they had several calls from clients talking about her appearance, and to show management's appreciation for the free plug, she was free to choose one of the coats from the line.

Then a few days later when she and two other girls from work were having lunch at the bistro in the building, a handsome young man approached them to say that he saw her on the show, and knowing where she worked, he staked out her "big house" hoping to meet her. By the time lunch was over he had her phone number.

As they began dating Sári discovered the fun side of living in New York. Her new friend, an advertising executive, took her to parties, to Broadway musicals and to see the show at Radio City Music Hall and other nightclub acts. It was a thrill for her to watch Harry Belafonte, the Mills Brothers, and other entertainers perform, most notably Frank Sinatra at the Copacabana, where her boyfriend even arranged with Sinatra's manager to take her backstage and meet the famous singer. On casual dates they went ice-skating at Rockefeller Center, and when the weather turned warm, spent weekends at the beach or visiting Greenwich Village. And there were the intimate little bars of New York, where he taught her to dance the cha-cha-cha, the latest import from Cuba that was fast gaining popularity. Perhaps the only thing she found missing was the small European-style cafés where people would sit with a demitasse, just relaxing or talking with friends, letting time slip by.

. . . .

Her life was perfect, even when in the spring she lost her job and was out of work, although only for a week. She quickly learned that modeling work was seasonal. Once the manufacturers presented their new line and took the orders, they went into production and let the models go. The girls, however, could almost immediately start on another job, even in the same building, if they knew which company would be showing clothes for the next season. After building up a connection to manufacturers with lines for the various seasons, they could work pretty much all year around.

In the beginning of summer Sári ended her second round of modeling jobs and was looking around where to work next, when she received an important letter from the World University Service. It stated that the application she submitted in Camp Kilmer for a scholarship had been reviewed and approved, and she was accepted at California Western University in San Diego. She was granted full tuition and a place on campus with guaranteed part-time work to cover her personal expenses. A train ticket to California would also be provided.

She accepted the offer at once, and for several reasons. For one, modeling was a fun way to earn good money but she knew it was not something to build a future on. She had a degree in economics, a good basis to work in the business world, but for that she needed to be proficient in English. It was her key to a better job. Living with Andrea had the disadvantage of always speaking Hungarian at home, which hindered her from picking up the language. A year or two spent at the university would make all the difference; it would give her a chance to find a solid job, perhaps in statistics or accounting, with good potential to make a fair living. Then there was the weather in New York. Winter and early spring were pretty much the same as in Hungary, but it was another matter when temperatures began to climb toward the end of May and humidity set in. They had an air-conditioner installed in their living room window, but in the bedroom at night she was miserable, tossing and turning between damp sheets and looking haggard in the morning. Leaving for work, it took less than a block to the subway before she felt sweat trickling down her back. How was she supposed to look good when she arrived at work with her makeup melting and her hair limp?

While many in New York City could afford to escape the summer heat and retreat to the country, it was beyond her means; with her college admittance and scholarship, however, she could move to California, the land of eternal sunshine! Everyone envied their glorious weather, the easy lifestyle, where everyone drove a car and people routinely ran into movie stars, as she heard it firsthand from Marylou, who came from Oceanside, California, and also from one of the girls at work who lived in Hollywood for a short while and came back only because she missed the excitement of New York City. Another reliable source was an old classmate from Sopron, Eva Pataki, and her husband Endre. She ran into them in Camp Kilmer shortly before they left to join Eva's uncle in Los Angeles, and they, too, wrote later that they wouldn't live anywhere else in the world.

Describing her situation Sári immediately asked them if she could stay with them for a few weeks before going to San Diego. Their answer was yes and no. Yes, she was welcome to stay, but not for weeks. Their place was too small, she would have to sleep on a sofa as it was, but they would help her find a little studio apartment nearby; they had already checked one out, and the rent was very reasonable.

So far Sári said nothing to Andrea about her plan to leave, but with all the arrangements now in place, it was time to let her know. She hated the moment because she knew Andrea couldn't afford to pay the rent alone and would either have to find a new roommate or move out. To her surprise, she didn't get upset; in fact, she was quite relieved. She had a secret of her own. Her brother would be through studying at Brown University soon and they planned to move together, leaving Sári to cope with the situation. With her going, however, they could stay in the flat; it spared them the headache of looking for a new place.

Sári had a month to prepare for her trip. She knew that in San Diego she wouldn't need her heavy sweaters, the wool skirts and her winter coat, so she packed them up and sent them to her parents as her first "care package" from America. Things would fit her sister, or her mother could sell the pieces and use the money. She remembered how eagerly girls in Hungary waited to buy clothes from American packages, as she herself did in the not-so-distant past.

By the time she received the government voucher for her one-way train ticket, she had already said goodbye to her friends, including her boyfriend. There were no tears. With their easy, fun-filled relationship, he even gave her the phone number of his friend in Los Angeles who would gladly show her the sights there. And so on the day of her departure, Marylou took her to Grand Central Station, sending her off with some last words of wisdom. She also slipped her the address of her parents in Oceanside, a small town near San Diego, so she'd have a place to visit whenever she felt lonely.

With a final round of promises to write, Sári boarded the train at noon carrying two suitcases and $150 in her pocket, and quickly settled into a window seat, in coach of course, where she would spend the next three days and two nights. It was far from luxury, but it didn't matter; with all the frequent stops, the lurching and the whistle blowing, nobody could sleep much, anyway.

For her long ride Sári brought along some fruit, a packet of mixed nuts, and a bottle of water, which she often refilled at train stations during stops. If there was time she also grabbed a bite in the station's canteen; it was cheaper than the sandwiches sold on board. Along the way she bought postcards—Chicago, Kansas City, scenic Colorado, Santa Fe, Albuquerque, and Las Vegas—and kept a journal, jutting down her impressions of the places the train passed through during the day.

On Sunday at one o'clock in the afternoon the train finally pulled into Union Station downtown Los Angeles. The weather was hot but dry, without a trace of the humidity of New York. She gave the taxi driver her friends' address in the Highland Park area, and although the ride was short, she got an eyeful of the tall skinny palm trees lining the streets along the way.

Eva and Endre greeted her warmly, and after a much-needed shower and change, treated her to an old-fashioned home-cooked meal. In the afternoon they took her sightseeing in Endre's pride and joy, a red and white Ford Fairlane convertible. It was truly impressive to see how much they had achieved in seven months, but they readily admitted that even with both of them working, Endre as a draftsman and Eva waitressing in a cafeteria, they could never have done it without help from Eva's relatives who came to America in the 1930s.

The drive through Los Angeles, Hollywood, and Beverly Hills, all the way to the beach, was more than Sári could ever imagined. Although entirely different from New York, with not even one skyscraper in sight, she loved the garden-like atmosphere of the city, the wide boulevards, the swaying palm trees, and manicured lawns, all under never-ending, cloudless blue skies. With the top down, they cruised along Wilshire Boulevard that stretched eleven miles from downtown L.A. to the beach at Santa Monica.

That evening they sat down to discuss Sári's immediate plans. Since school wouldn't start until mid-September, it was obvious that she wanted to find some temporary work. Showroom modeling was non-existent in Los Angeles, and to get into photo modeling was impossible without an agent and with thousands of beautiful girls competing.

"You could work as a waitress, like me," Eva offered. "The cafeteria is downtown; they only pay minimum wages but it's not hard work. All we do is dole out food from behind the counter. We could ride together; Endre drops me off and picks me up every day. Do you want me to see if they are hiring?"

"It's very sweet of you, and considering that I don't have a car, it would be ideal if I could ride with you to work, but what I really want to do is try to get into one of those office buildings I saw along Wilshire Boulevard. There must be something I could do there, work in the mailroom opening and distributing mail, making copies, that sort of thing, and if I am hired I would look for a room nearby where I can walk or take the bus to work. I thought I'd check with an employment agency; perhaps you can recommend one?"

"Well yes, there is one right on Wilshire and Vermont Ave, the Nancy Nolan Agency," Endre said. "They handle placements for all kinds of office work. It's easy to get there; you only have to change busses once. But how good is your English? Can you fill out an application when they send you out on an interview?"

"I don't really know. I never had to submit one while I was modeling. I have no idea what an application looks like."

"The first part is about personal information, your education and experience, but the rest is a test, quite easy, if you speak English. Anyone with eight grades could sail through it, but for us some of the multiple-choice questions are tricky, because you really have to understand what is being asked, and know the meaning of each sentence to pick the right answer, especially if a proverb is involved."

"Well, I've been studying English for seven months now, but not in school, just on my own by reading a lot and memorizing words, so I probably won't pass the test. Still, I want to give it a try, and if I can't cut it, I can always learn to dish out food, right?"

And so on Monday morning Sári took the bus to the agency for a consultation. All went well, except for a minor objection to the dress she was wearing. They thought her white spaghetti strapped dress with red polka dots would be hard put to meet the current office dress code and suggested to wear a simple skirt and blouse on job interviews; perhaps put on white cotton gloves, or better yet, wear one of those popular little flat hats that lent such a refined look to aspiring young ladies.

The next day the agency already called to say that they had two appointments for her. Wearing a nice shirtwaist dress, though without the hat and gloves, she reported back to pick up the addresses. Both were in the downtown area, one a small advertising office on 6th Street in need of a file clerk, the other a dry cleaning store, where the job involved light bookkeeping and also helping out at the counter. Although she was armed with an English-Hungarian dictionary to help her fill out the applications, neither place required one; they only conducted a personal evaluation.

She knew right away that the job at the laundry was not for her. Her English was not good enough to deal with customers, especially if there were problems and complaints. The clerical job was fine, except it required light typing, a skill she lacked. The agency should have known better! She told them during her interview that she couldn't type. The next morning she called to remind them of it, but they said not to worry, they were working on other possibilities, just have patience; something would come up. *Easy for them to say*, Sári thought, when she needed a job as soon as possible. She didn't want to be a burden to Eva and Endre for too long.

When the phone remained silent for the next few days her initial confidence began to evaporate. Her limited English and not being able to type presented a real handicap, reducing her chances for working in an office. Sitting at home, the job at the Ontra Cafeteria began to look better by the minute. It would only be a temporary job anyway, and if nothing happened in a day or so, she'd talk to Eva about it.

Fortunately, it didn't come to that. Later in the same afternoon the agency called, saying they had another appointment lined up for her, this time with an insurance company. They were looking for rating clerks, a job that didn't require typing. The interview was at ten o'clock next morning, if she could make it. No problem, Sári said, it seemed a great opportunity, if she only knew what a rating clerk was. The agent told her that the work involved calculating premiums, easy to handle with a little training by the company.

Zurich American Insurance was located on Wilshire Boulevard, a block west of Perino's where the bus dropped her off. She knew she was in the right neighborhood because Endre pointed out during their Sunday excursion that

Perino's was one of the best restaurants in Los Angeles, frequented by the rich and famous. Promptly at ten she walked into the lobby of the two-story building bearing the company name and was directed to a room with four other applicants already there. As she sat down she heard them complaining that judged by the time it took to interview the girl who just left, they could be sitting there for hours. Sure enough, at noon she and the girl next to her were still waiting, until finally someone came apologizing for the delay and asking them to come back after lunch.

They left together and found a coffee shop a few blocks up the street. During their talk Sári learned that the girl, Nina, was from Flint, Michigan, and like her, was also new in town. She had a studio apartment near McArthur Park, only four bus stops away, and was looking for a roommate to share expenses. She could only offer a sofa bed to sleep on, but would Sári be interested? What a question! Of course she would be interested, Sári said, if she were lucky enough to get the job. She already saw that to get around in Los Angeles without a car was not easy; the city was spread out and didn't have a metro like New York. She would need a place close to work, and living only four bus stops from the office was better than ideal!

She was now doubly anxious to pass the interview. At her turn the receptionist took her to see Mr. Wolfschmitz, the man in charge of hiring. It was undoubtedly a German name, and when she saw him, a pleasant looking blond man with a broad face, she knew he couldn't be anything but German. The accent confirmed it as he greeted her, offering a chair. She almost slipped into German with an automatic *danke*, but caught herself in time and "senked" him in English.

"Is that accent by any chance Hungarian?" he smiled, peering over his glasses. He could see she was tense, and to put her at ease he talked about his own experience as an immigrant. He knew the plight of refugees and the problems they faced, since he, too, came to the United States at the end of the war without good command of the language and with very little money in his pocket. And although he was a university-educated businessman from Hamburg, without speaking English he worked loading cargo on the docks of Long Beach for the first year or two. He also expressed great sympathy toward the failure of the Hungarian revolution, so similar to the fate of the East German uprising in 1953.

After a few questions about her education and work experience, he handed her an application that she needed to complete in thirty minutes, and then, wishing her good luck, directed her to an empty cubicle. *So, this is the famous application,* Sári thought looking at the four-page questionnaire. The first page asking for personal information was a breeze to fill out, but when she saw the next two pages full of questions to test English grammar and language proficiency, she came to a halt. With the help of her dictionary she might be able to answer some, but as Endre suggested, she had problems with multiple choices, and drew an absolute blank when she had to pick the correct sentence out of three that best matched the meaning of a given proverb. She could spend the entire time trying to make sense of what "A bird in a hand is worth two in a bush" meant, so instead of struggling further, she skipped both pages and went straight to the last one to work on the math problems. Within fifteen minutes she was finished and handed the application back to Mr. Wolfschmitz without saying a word.

He read the first page with obvious interest, but when he turned to the blank midsection his eyebrows went up and he made a small "hmm" sound. After checking the last page he shook his head slightly and spread the application on the table. "This has happened more than once in the past few weeks," he said pointing at the blank pages with an annoyed scowl.

Another Hungarian refugee? Sári thought wryly, bracing herself for a sure rejection. Instead, she could hardly believe what she heard next.

"For some reason these pages tend to stick together, and I apologize for it. I'll have the supply clerk look into the problem, but it's OK, I see you solved all the math problems and without mistakes. It tells me that you are good at calculation, and that's exactly what we need, someone who can work well with figures; that is the most important requirement for raters."

It was not easy for Sári to keep to her chair. She wanted to jump up, dance around, and hug this kind-hearted man for taking pity on her. Whether she'll get the job or not, she would never forget him. Nevertheless, she managed to keep calm and businesslike, and asked what the job would entail.

"Rating involves calculating the premium we charge to insure an applicant's automobile," Mr. Wolschmitz explained. "The clerks use a manual and certain information from prospective clients, but they don't talk directly to them. They don't even have a telephone on their desk. If they need clarification, our underwriters will handle that. I think with the training we provide, you will do well in this job. Of course, management would have to approve, but if you were to come aboard, initially it would be for a two-months trial period at a $240 starting salary. Upon acceptable performance your status would become permanent with a slight pay increase and two weeks paid vacation after the first year. We will let the placement agency know about the decision, but if all goes well, I look forward seeing you here next Monday morning."

Sári was practically walking on air when she saw Nina waiting for her in the lobby. Her luck was holding; in one day she had gotten a job—she was sure of it—and found a roommate. Nina showed her the flat on Bonnie Brae Street just off Wilshire past Alvarado, a furnished studio apartment with a pull-down Murphy bed, and a sofa sleeper. The place had a kitchen with a small dining table, a full bathroom with tub and shower, and a dressing area with a built-in closet. The neighborhood had a grocery store, a laundromat, two coffee shops, and a movie theatre, with the bus stop on Wilshire right across from their building.

The next day, not quite a week after arriving in Los Angeles, Sári learned from the agency that she got the job. So did Nina. That evening she thanked Eva and Endre for letting her stay, then packed her things and moved into her new friend's apartment to begin the next phase of her life in America.

. . . .

"Is that girl ever going to stop moving?" was Ilonka's first reaction when she read Sári's letter from Los Angeles. Jeno got hold of a map of the United States and they traced her journey across the country. It was hard for them to imagine the enormous distance between New York and Los Angeles that took a train three days to cross, when they thought traveling the one hundred and fifty-five miles to Budapest was a long trip.

"Sári knows what she is doing," Jeno countered. "I think she is right about going back to school, and if she is accepted in San Diego, that's where she will have to go."

"Still, it's hard to keep track of her ever-changing addresses! Perhaps that's how people live in America: they just pick up and go whenever expectations fall short. I've heard they moved around a lot, not like here, where some people die in the same place where they were born. Regardless, I wish she had stayed in Vienna, close to us and to Istvan. She spoke the language, too, and could always rely on Guido. It just doesn't make sense why she wanted to go to America, but then, she has always done things her way."

Their own life continued pretty much the same since the October revolution was defeated. They felt sorry for what happened to Latzi and Eta, but Ochie was home and seemingly safe; no one bothered him in spite of the abounding rumors that people who returned from Austria on promise of safety were disappearing one by one. It hit them so much the harder when toward the middle of August Ochie was summoned to appear at AVO headquarters in Gyor. Ilonka was in a panic. If anything happened to her son, she would never forgive herself for insisting that he come back.

On the day of the appointment Jeno accompanied him but was not allowed to be present at the questioning. The poor boy was scared when they started asking why he left the country, and with whom, and what he did in Austria, but when they suggested that he came back because he was solicited as a spy, he almost laughed in their faces. Were these people serious? What idiot would want to recruit a fourteen-year-old schoolboy to spy—on what? But he managed to deny the accusation with convincing sincerity, and remained contrite when he said that running away was just an adventure for him; he only wanted to get away from his controlling mother, until he found out that the discipline the monks maintained was a lot worse. The police slapped him around a bit but let him go with a warning that he wouldn't get away so easily should he be foolish enough to try it again.

They returned home, relieved that the AVO was satisfied with his excuses and this would be the end of it. Unfortunately, they were not yet finished punishing him; they were going to limit his future, prevent him from reaching his full potential. When Ochie finished his fourth year at the gimnazium with very good grades, he was told not to come back in the fall. Adamant, Jeno went to see the principal, but he would only say that they had no room for him; classes were full with boys more deserving than his son.

That foolish excursion to Austria marked him with a political stigma and destroyed his chances for higher education and a better life. Bright as he was, with his path to college blocked, he wouldn't be graduating. He was forced to learn a trade, and even that was not easy; it took several rejections until finally the Electric Power Plant accepted him as an apprentice. Jeno was more depressed about the setback than Ochie; he actually liked it there. The boys had to attend regular classes in addition to the technical training, but there was no Latin, no Russian, or higher mathematics.

Now Jeno and Ilonka were glad that Istvan decided to stay in Austria. He was happy there, currently serving his stint in the Army. He sent them some photos wearing a uniform, looking quite grown up and apparently in very good shape. He wrote that after finishing his service he would be working with Guido, an engineer at Phillips Electronics, and taking evening classes toward an engineering degree.

Gyuszi, too, was doing well in Miskolc. In his latest letter he wrote that he was seeing a girl he met during one of his field trips to Acs, a small town near Gyor. Named Itzu, a nickname for Ilona, she was a third grade teacher and the daughter of the former mayor of Acs. Although he was ousted in 1945 and the family barely escaped deportation when the Communists came to power, he was "allowed" to work as a field hand in the agrarian co-op. To help make ends meet, his wife also went to work as a kindergarten teacher. It was a far cry from how they lived before, but at least they could stay in their home, a rambling house with a small vineyard and fruit orchard behind it.

Ilonka's greatest concern now was Eta and how she was coping alone, living in that godforsaken backcountry. The day she heard of their eviction she offered to take them in, but Eta were forbidden to leave the place. To keep them isolated must have been part of the punishment; putting the breadwinner in jail was not enough, they made the wife and children suffer, too. Ilonka's heart ached for them, but other than taking Peter under her wing there was not much else she could do to help.

As for her own situation at the factory, it had improved slightly since they discovered that she could sing and play the piano. They invited her to join the cultural group, where she made new friends, some from management, and through them she got a better job assignment. It involved going around the floor to record the daily production, and then, based on the output, compute the earnings for each worker. It was not hard to learn, but if she got stuck, she just took the paperwork home for Jeno to finish the calculations.

The lighter work and knowing that Ochie was now safe made her feel more relaxed, quicker to smile. She even stopped wondering about Sári and her ever-changing situation. First it was New York, the most wonderful place to live, but then the weather got too hot; she loved her modeling job, but it was not steady enough. And now, this letter! A few weeks earlier she could hardly wait to start college, but now she had reservation about going back to school. She just learned, she wrote, that her scholarship was guaranteed only for the first year, and to renew it she must earn a grade point average of 3.0 or better. How could she attain such high level with her beginner English? And there was her age. She was almost twenty-six years old, hardly the usual age for a college freshman. Was it worth giving up her job and go back to scrimping and living on campus for a year without much hope to receive further financial aid? Losing the scholarship meant she would have to quit and start over again looking for a job. She liked her work, she was getting regular paychecks, and she was happy living in Los Angeles, so why give it all up?

It didn't surprise Ilonka to read in Sári's next letter that she had decided to stay in Los Angeles when Mr. Wolfschmitz told her confidentially before her trial period ended that her employment would be made permanent. With a steady job she could start making long term plans, mainly saving money for a car. She could always take evening classes to improve her English. Good Lord, Ilonka thought, another thing to worry about, that girl driving a car! She should concentrate on finding a husband, and all her problems would be solved.

What her mother didn't understand was that driving a car was a necessity if one lived in Los Angeles. And Sári was determined to get one. She had already taken driving lessons and studied the rules to obtain her license. She had no problem passing the written test, but she flunked the road test even before the car left the curbside. First she had to demonstrate various hand signals, which was no problem until the examiner asked her to turn on the beam she would use while driving at night on a backward country road. Beam?? What beam?? Unfortunately, all her behind-the-wheel training sessions took place in daytime, never at night, and only on city streets, not even close to a deserted country road. She had no idea how to switch on the high beam, so she fumbled around with the buttons, making some lame excuse that the car she borrowed for the test drive was unfamiliar to her. It didn't save her from failing. She was asked to return in three weeks, and by then she made sure she knew how to use every button and switch on a dashboard.

With her brand new license and money put aside for a down payment, she started looking for a car to buy. The opportunity came in April 1958 when a girl in the office put her 1954 Oldsmobile up for sale, asking $1,000. Sári put down $400—all the savings she had—and Bank of America trusted her with a two-year loan for the balance, paying it off in monthly installments. It was one of the most exciting moments in her life when she sat behind the wheel of that big white-and-turquoise all-power 98 Olds! With Nina in the passenger seat, she drove off from the office parking lot, down Wilshire Boulevard, all the way to the ocean, where her friend took pictures of her at the wheel, standing in front of the car, then with the door open to show off the interior. Laughing, she predicted that when her mother's friends back in Sopron saw the photos, they'd say she was just showing off, posing with someone else's automobile. They would not believe that the car was hers, that after a mere sixteen months in America she could already have one.

Her parents hardly had time getting used to her driving, when there came another address change. Once she had a car it was no longer vital to live close to work; they could give up their tiny flat and move to a more comfortable place.

So, the girls went apartment hunting and on August 15 moved to Grace Avenue in Hollywood, a few blocks above the famous Hollywood Boulevard. It was a beautifully furnished one-bedroom apartment with a view of the hills, and an easy twenty-minute drive to the office. She enclosed some pictures of their new place and wrote that although this wouldn't be a permanent address, either, hopefully it would be a longer-lasting one.

Goulash Communism

THE BEST CHRISTMAS present Eta received in 1958 was the Supreme Court's decision to further reduce Latzi's sentence to a final three-year term. It was unexpected, when the year was marked with increased retaliation against freedom fighters and stepped-up executions. It started with the hanging of the commander who led the attack at the radio station, followed in March by the execution of two former members of the Csepel national guards. Next came the death sentences of several "counter-revolutionary" leaders, carried out in May; then on June 16, 1958, Imre Nagy himself, the military leader Pal Maleter, and two others were led to the gallows. They were brought back from Romania in April 1957, put on trial before the Council of People's Court, found guilty of treason for initiating and leading a conspiracy, and sentenced to death by hanging, a verdict that had been sanctioned by Kadar before the trial even began. When Nagy was asked if he had anything to say in his defense he staunchly rejected all charges, and in a short speech placed judgment over his actions into the hands of a future generation. He expressed the belief that with the passage of time, in a more impartial atmosphere the truth would emerge to show that he was the victim of a gravely mistaken court. With his very last words he refused to ask for clemency.

He was hanged in secret, his death made public only a day later. It didn't matter that Nagy was a Soviet citizen and worked as an NKVD agent—later changed to KGB—while living in exile in Russia between 1930 and 1945, or that without seeking the leadership of the country he was thrust twice into power by Moscow, first in 1953, then in 1956. Once he crossed the line and became useless to them, his former merits were not enough to save him. He was liquidated, his body dumped in a common grave in parcel No. 301 of a municipal cemetery in the outskirts of Budapest, the gravesite that held the remains of many other victims of these political trials.

Before Nagy died he predicted in private that like Rajk, he would also be rehabilitated, and he was right. On June 16, 1989, thirty-one year to the date of his execution, he was given an honorary burial as a symbolic figure of the 1956 revolution with 100,000 people attending his reinterment. Nagy also believed that the people putting him on the gallows would likely be the same ones saying his eulogies at his honorary funeral, but that never happened. By then these henchmen of a terror-driven system were no longer around, as Communism itself was in the throes of collapse.

In the two years since the crushing of the revolution, fear was once again the dominant factor in people's lives. The AVO was busier than ever, and Kadar ruled supreme. He succeeded in re-establishing his Party that had collapsed under the first blows of the insurrection, when even the nucleus of the Politburo and the old high-ranking government officials were in flight. Not that there was a rush to return to the folds of the Party; former card-holding members of the labor force were distrustful to rejoin in spite of promised incentives and privileges. To help the Party becoming more acceptable to the people, Moscow agreed early in 1958 to withdraw a small detachment of its troops from Hungary, and consequently on March 15, the popular national holiday celebrating the outbreak of Hungary's 1848 revolution, 17,000 Russian soldiers left the country. It was to prove that Kadar was a man who kept his promises.

The Soviets also came to his aid on the economic front. The uprising caused considerable destruction, with 40,000 dwellings in ruins—mostly by Russian bombardment—and transportation heavily damaged. The national income dropped drastically due to the strikes; exports of Hungarian goods were 10% of the normal figure; and at the same time the need to import consumer goods increased dramatically. Hungary badly needed foreign loans to begin the immensely difficult task of rebuilding its economy, but couldn't possibly look to the West since it was not a member of the International Banking institution. To cement Kadar's position the Soviets were willing to grant a credit of one billion Rubles, 20% in currencies and the rest in goods, a sum approximately fifty million in U.S. dollars at the then-existing rate of exchange.

With the loan and a new three-year plan introduced on July 19, 1958, the economy began limping toward recovery.

By then, people were back working under the old depressing conditions of pre-revolutionary days, as if October 23 never happened. Factory management was taken out of the hands of the workers, who were once again forced to work under the old quota system and for the same low wages. Peasants were back in the collectives, intellectuals either kept silent or resorted to mouthing Party propaganda, and students once more were learning Russian. Shortly after Nagy's execution Kadar published his so-called "White Book" that officially declared the uprising as a criminal counter-revolutionary conspiracy, thus validating the 26,000 political trials that followed, the condemnation of 13,000 victims to prisons or labor camps and the execution of 300 innocent people. This sad chapter in the history of Hungary was closed when the general election held on November 16 returned 99.6% yes votes for a single list of candidates called the "People's Patriotic Front."

In years to come with Russia's tolerance—if only to avoid another upheaval—the country evolved into a sort of consumer socialism, or "Goulash Communism," that became the envy of the Eastern bloc countries. But what price the Hungarians paid for it was by then systematically erased.

By the beginning of 1959, the government felt secure enough to announce the end of trials for participation in the revolution and ordered the review of lighter sentences on the theory that perhaps the judges acted too severely toward those individuals who "genuinely erred" or were simply "misled" during the revolt. And so, as April 4 drew close, the date when the government customarily granted a wide amnesty in honor of the anniversary of Hungary's liberation by the Red Army, hope of gaining their freedom rose among the thousands of political prisoners. Unfortunately, it excluded those convicted for taking a more active part in the uprising, and hearing it, Eta's heart sank. It meant her husband would not be coming home.

Her spirits revived, however, when three weeks later, with credit to his attorney, Latzi was granted a special review, and on April 30, after serving a little less than two years, he was set free. The nightmare was over; his family would be together again and he could start rebuilding his life. In view of the leniency the court extended to him, he was reinstated in his job but not in Debrecen. He was transferred to the city of Kecskemet on Hungary's Great Plain and given the important task of finding a way to bind the sandy, ever-shifting soil of the surrounding area known as Bugac.

More happy news was in store for Ilonka and Jeno as the year wound to a close: in December both Gyuszi and Sári got engaged. From the pictures Sári had sent them and the letter she wrote about her fiancé Philip, he seemed to be a nice young man with a broad smile, looking at Sári with obvious love. They learned that he was originally from Boston with his family roots reaching back to Ireland, and to Ilonka's delight, he was a devout Catholic. He first came to Los Angeles to attend the University of Southern California, and as so many others, stayed to take advantage of the mild weather and casual lifestyle. He was thirty-four years old, never married, and ran his own advertising business. Sári met him at a party in November, and now, after short six weeks, they were already planning their wedding. It was set for Saturday, January 30, 1960, with Phil making all the arrangements for about fifty guests. He lost his father, a doctor, some years ago, and his mother more recently, but his sister and brother would be attending as part of the wedding party, Claire as maid of honor and Ted as best man.

When Ilonka received a copy of the wedding album with pictures of her daughter, radiant in a white gown, standing at the altar, she could not help but cry. This time her tears were tears of joy, her prayers finally answered. Their free-running, restless girl was finally settling down, married, ready to become a wife and mother. In photo after photo she was seen smiling happily, receiving congratulations, cutting the cake, getting into a limousine, and in the last one lifted off her feet as her husband carried her over the threshold. If only she and Jeno could have been there to share her happiness on that special day!

As expected from a new bride, her letters to Ilonka were full of chatter about their honeymoon on the Mexican Riviera, and about settling into married life. She moved into her husband's home on Doheny Drive, a quaint little house just a block from the famous Sunset Strip, and at his insistence she quit working. Married women in America stayed home to keep house and look after their family, and that's what she was doing, too, although she had a cleaning lady once a week to help with the bigger chores. Phil bought her a new Chrysler Valiant, not as big as her Oldsmobile was, but driving around in a brand new car made up for it. She was learning to cook, even though they often ate out since they had an active social life with Phil's many friends and business associates. His best and closest friend was Doc, nicknamed after his profession as a doctor, an older man, divorced and quite lonely, who came by almost every day to watch TV, or play cards. Another frequent visitor to their home was their parish priest. She hinted that married life was a huge adjustment, and perhaps she should have waited a little longer, but then, as they say, the first year was always the hardest. And no, she was not expecting a baby.

Well, Ilonka knew all about married life and the proverbial "period of adjustment" most newlyweds go through. Personally, she thought six weeks was too short to plunge into marriage, but on the other hand, if Sári waited too long she might have changed her mind, as had happened before.

Gyuszi and Itzu also set the date for their wedding. It took place on October 8, 1960 in her hometown, a large provincial wedding with over one hundred guests. After a short honeymoon he took his bride to Pecs, his home since the previous fall, when he accepted a position there at one of the largest coal mines in the country. A year later, on October 31, 1961, they presented Ilonka with her fourth grandchild, a little boy named Zsolt, the first grandson to carry the Zachar family name. Ilonka only wished they lived closer, for what was the use of having grandchildren when she could hardly ever see them, watch them grow? Take Eta's boys for instance: the eldest, Latzi Jr., already fourteen, was growing by leaps and bounds, some six inches since they last saw him three years ago, and Istvan, the youngest, no longer a baby at six, was fast becoming a sweet-natured, handsome boy.

Strangely, there was still no baby news from Sári, as Ilonka surely expected after the year and a half she has been married. Come to think, she hardly mentioned Phil anymore, and stopped sending photos like she used to. Oh well, Ilonka thought, they were no longer newlyweds. It was only natural that once the honeymoon was over, young couples would have a few spats now and then. Phil would be back in the picture as soon as they made up. What mattered most to Ilonka was that Sári was not alone in the world. She even shrugged off yet another address change, this time to Palm Avenue in Beverly Hills; by now she took it for granted that moving often was part of life in America.

The letter said nothing about the new place, not a word that it was just a small, furnished flat Sári rented on the day she moved out of their home. The marriage was over, but she kept it from her parents, knowing how much they would worry. She went back to work at Zurich American and filed for divorce, claiming mental cruelty, the standard grounds for divorce in the 1960s that required two witnesses testifying that her husband mistreated her. The truth was quite different, but she wouldn't disclose it publicly that Phil had problems in the marriage bed. He had seen several doctors but nothing much helped. The fact that he did not tell her about it before they got married bothered Sári more than the physical aspect of the problem. She refused to accept his excuse that he was afraid she would have turned him down if he confided in her before he proposed. To her it was a question of trust, the most important thing in any relationship.

Only after her interlocutory decree was granted did she tell her parents about the divorce. Eva Pataki was one of her witnesses, and she was afraid that if she'd write about it to her mother in Sopron, soon the whole city would know. It was better if they learned the truth from her instead of through the grapevine, even though it was not easy to put it in a letter that her husband was impotent. She knew what their reaction would be: didn't she know it before they got married? After all, she was not a blushing bride without any experience. Granted, six weeks was a short time to get to know each other but still, she should have had some inkling of what to expect in bed. Once engaged, men usually asked for a little in advance; didn't she find it peculiar that Phil made no such demands? Yes, she admitted, it sounded strange when Phil told her that he wanted to wait until they were married, but then, he was Catholic and deeply religious, and she took it that he simply adhered to the teaching of the Church. She even thought it showed strength and character.

The news explained the odd silence about Phil in her past letters. It shocked her parents but they didn't blame her; she had a valid reason for divorcing him. She was thirty years old, and if she wanted children, it made no sense trying to stay in a marriage that would deny her that chance.

To Ilonka's joy, in August, before the start of school Eta brought her boys for a two-week visit, a stay too short before they had to leave again. Their departure made the house painfully quiet again, perhaps more noticeable since lately Ochie started to stay out longer, sometimes coming home long after midnight. He was eighteen last February, a handsome young man with strong resemblance to his father. No wonder, Ilonka thought, that girls began to chase him; even one of her renters, a year or so older than Ochie, seemed to be taken with him, finding excuses not to go home on the weekend and hanging around the house, hoping to rouse his interest.

At first they ignored the signs that he might be getting involved with the opposite sex. Ochie was much too young! They were convinced of it even when he brought home a girl, Marika, a year younger than himself, and introduced her as his steady girlfriend. But they were wrong. By the spring of 1962 he told them that he was going to marry her; they loved each other and why should they wait? They both had jobs—he worked at the Electric Plant and Marika at a daycare center—but more than that, if they were married, as a young couple they had a better chance to qualify for a state-approved apartment. And if Ilonka worried about Marika moving in, she shouldn't; they meant to rent a room someplace else until they get their own place.

Jeno was adamantly against the marriage. They were too young, still children in the throes of first love, without any notion about married life. He reminded Ochie that he was facing a two-year stint in the military, so why not wait until he was through with the service? If they still felt the same way after his discharge, he'd give his full blessing. Rush into marriage now, and most likely she'd have a baby while he was still in the army, and how was she going to support herself and the child on what little she earned?

Ilonka, however, sided wholeheartedly with the young couple. Was not she also eighteen when they got married? Yes, Jeno argued, but he was thirty years old, the military behind him, and holding a steady job, two completely different scenarios! True enough, Ilonka shot back, but had he been nineteen and in Ochie's shoes, wouldn't he have wanted to marry her, anyway?

What could Jeno say to this kind of logic? In the end he lost out against the three. The wedding took place on July 14, 1962, with Marika moving in. Ilonka wouldn't hear of letting Ochie move out. Not her baby, not after what she went through to get him back! Nothing would really change by having Marika around, Ilonka argued. As a matter of fact, she could use a little help with the household chores, so everything would work out just fine.

Although she did not say it, Ilonka secretly hoped that in a year there would be another addition to the family, a new baby she could spoil—girl or boy, it wouldn't matter. Others at her age, fifty-seven next May, might not welcome caring for babies, but she would never get tired of it. The joy of holding another grandchild in her arms, to see that first smile, was always a gift to her, the gift of witnessing a miracle unfold.

As Jeno predicted, Ochie was drafted early in 1963 and as Ilonka hoped for, two months later Marika broke the news that she was expecting. All looked bright in Ilonka's world, and so she decided she would quit working when the baby arrived. With retirement age for women set at fifty-five, and the ten years' required service behind her, she was already eligible for pension; she only kept working because her job was easier now and the money came handy. She actually enjoyed participating in their cultural club and having three weeks paid vacation each year. As a foundry worker she also received deep discounts at resorts, among them nearby Bükk, where she loved to soak in the healing waters of the bubbling hot springs.

Unfortunately, just as she happily started counting the days to retirement, her life took a near fatal turn: she suffered an accident at work that almost took her life. She was making her rounds on the factory floor when the overhead conveyor carrying empty buckets malfunctioned, dropping down dangerously low. One of the buckets struck Ilonka in the back, knocking her unconscious and sending her to the hospital.

Jeno and the Varosys waited anxiously in the lobby, hoping to take her home, when they learned that she had suffered a trauma-induced stroke, leaving her paralyzed on one side and unable to speak. She was off the critical list, but the doctors wanted to keep her in intensive care for the night. No one knew at the time that the decision would save her life. At one point the chart monitoring her heart triggered an alarm, alerting the nurses that she was undergoing cardiac arrest. She suffered a myocardial infarction that was considered fatal unless treated immediately; luckily, being in the hospital at the crucial moment, the quick response helped her pull through. According to the doctors, the stroke most likely brought on the heart attack, but in a strange twist, by putting her in the hospital where help was near, it also saved her life. Had she been home at the onset of the attack, she probably wouldn't be alive now, a likelihood not far-fetched considering that she was overweight, plagued with high blood pressure and was poorly suited to handle pressures well. She could have been struck down anytime. It was a miracle that it didn't happen in 1956 when three of her children left and she was threatened with losing the fourth.

After her condition was stabilized, Ilonka was transferred from intensive care to a ten-bed ward, where each bed had a nightstand but no hook-up to a central unit to signal for assistance. A nurse was in the room 24 hours a day, periodically checking on the patients, but most of the time sitting in the back corner doing paperwork or reading. During her first night in the ward Ilonka woke up feeling excruciatingly thirsty, her tongue clinging to the roof of her mouth, desperate for water, but being half paralyzed and unable to speak, how was she to get the nurse's attention? She had to wait until the woman in the next bed stirred then, using her good hand and pointing toward the nurse's station, she gestured to her that she needed help.

Apparently annoyed for being jarred out of her nap, the nurse approached Ilonka's bed, snapping at her rudely, "Well, what is it? What do you want?"

With a pitiful appeal in her eyes, Ilonka curled her fingers as if holding a glass and brought it to her mouth, trying to convey that she needed water.

"Where is your cup?" the nurse asked looking at the empty nightstand. Ilonka motioned that she didn't have one.

"No cup, no water!" the woman said and turned on her heel.

"For heaven's sake, she was just brought in a couple of hours ago!" the lady in the next bed called after her. "Take my cup, I am sure she wouldn't mind drinking from it!"

When Jeno came to visit the next day he was told to bring certain items his wife would need, including a cup, but Ilonka never told him how cruelly the night nurse treated her. She didn't dare. He would certainly make a complaint that would only alienate the mean woman, and she needed to be in her good graces for the long stay ahead.

It took months of therapy before Ilonka regained her speech and mobility. When released she was told to avoid physical exertion, but more importantly, guard against stress, her worst enemy; otherwise, if she kept to a healthy diet and did some walking, she could expect a complete recovery. During her recuperation Marika looked after Jeno and took over the running of the household, not an easy job when working full-time and with her pregnancy advancing. But she did it gladly, never forgetting how Ilonka stood by them when she and Ochie wanted to get married.

She always tried to please her, and they did get along well, until the birth of her little boy Sanyi. Then everything changed. The baby instantly became the center of his grandmother's life, but when she practically took charge of caring for him, problems quickly erupted. Angrily resenting her mother-in-law's interference, Marika made it clear that while Ilonka was welcome to hold her son from time to time, she should leave the rest to her. Arguments between the two grew sharper by the day with Ilonka finding fault in everything her daughter-in-law did around the child. Nothing was good enough. She knew everything better; after all, she brought five children into this world, and they all turned out well, didn't they? There was no end to her criticism: Marika didn't hold the baby's head firmly enough; the bathwater was too warm or too cold; or the baby was not bundled up enough when she took him out in his pram. Both women bombarded Ochie with complaints, and it created further tension that he sided with his wife.

The situation eased somewhat when Marika's six-month paid maternity leave ended and she had to return to work. At first they clashed again over her decision to take the baby with her to the nursery where she worked, with Ilonka lashing out that it was an insult to her and a crime against the child, when she was at home and fully capable of taking care of him. But later, tired of listening to her mother-in-law's endless tirades how thousands, nay, millions of young mothers would be eternally grateful if their children could stay in the home and receive the kind of care only family can give, Marika finally relented. It was also a question of money. Keeping the baby in the nursery was not free, as she first believed; she would have to pay the regular fees regardless that she worked there.

After admitting that basically Ilonka was right, the two women came to an amicable truce and put a stop to their constant bickering. Ochie was greatly relieved when he came home on a short leave and saw his wife and mother getting along better. And so was Jeno. To keep out of the ongoing feud and withstand pressure to take sides was hard on his nerves, and to escape he often went over to the Varosys. He could also smoke there, which was not allowed at home around the baby. He knew the doctor had warned him to give up smoking but how could he when Sári kept sending those wonderful filter-tip American cigarettes?

Her gift packages arrived regularly, filled with items that were not available in stores and were highly sought after. It created an opportunity for Ilonka to cash in on the old capitalist theory of supply and demand, as she began selling items she didn't use or could do without. Her "goods" included jars of Nescafe, cocoa mix, cartons of American cigarettes, nylon stockings, and cosmetics, mostly pancake make-up, eye shadows, and lipsticks. Injector razors, the latest American invention in shaving, were her best sellers for men; it also kept them coming back for the refill cartridges. In no time she had a clientele clamoring to buy her wares, proving on a small scale the superiority of the free market principle.

At first she paid the required duty on the content—items the government considered "foreign imports" instead of gifts, and taxed high as such—but when it cut into her profit she asked Sári to send the parcels to Istvan in Vienna. As all refugees, he was barred from entering the country and bringing in the packages, but he could easily enlist his Austrian friends to take them to Ilonka whenever they drove into Sopron looking for cheap bargains. Food and services cost half of what people paid for them in Austria, luring the ladies to do their grocery shopping and getting their hair done in Sopron, not to mention the scores of dental patients coming over the border to have their teeth fixed.

Sári was also sending money for her parents through Istvan, because Hungarian banks used unfavorably low exchange rates in foreign transactions. He could get a lot more forints for U.S. dollars in Vienna, but his Austrian friends were less willing to carry the money across the border. If caught, they would be charged with smuggling currency, and the money would be confiscated. Putting their heads together, Ilonka and Istvan then came up with a better system. Hungarians traveling to the West could only take a ridiculously low amount of spending money with them, or risk hefty penalties for hiding more than allowed, but with Ilonka's new plan they could get their hands safely on more money by making a quick stop in Vienna. The transaction involved two simple steps: Ilonka collected forints from people needing foreign money while traveling, and they would pick up a comparable amount of either dollars or Austrian schillings from Istvan in Vienna. It required trust on all sides, but it worked, and as a result, Ilonka was able to buy a refrigerator, a television set and had her kitchen remodeled with a gas-burning stove.

Sári was glad that she could make life a little easier for her parents. She could do even more for them when in 1963 she changed to a better paying job at Johnson and Higgins, a large international insurance brokerage firm in the Wilshire business district. With the higher salary she also decided to move to a bigger place, and rented a nice unfurnished one-bedroom apartment a block from Sunset Boulevard. Excited at the prospect of choosing her own furniture—the first time in her life—she applied for a loan and set out to make the apartment a cozy nest that reflected her personal taste.

By now her divorce was final, and she was dating several men but no one seriously. She took up tennis and skiing and spent her vacations in San Francisco, Las Vegas, Lake Taho, and other popular places. Looking at the postcards and photos she sent home, Ilonka admitted they had no reason to worry about her; at age thirty-two she looked better than ever, but she couldn't help wondering why she was still single. All this traveling was fine, but what about finding a husband and starting a family before time ran out? If only she could sit down, and have a heart-to-heart talk with her!

Surprisingly, as 1964 rolled around, it seemed that this might become a reality. For the first time since the revolt the government began to ease restrictions placed on visiting those who escaped to the West by granting exit visas to elderly relatives. While this allowed Eva Pataki's mother, Mrs. Balog to come for a six-month stay, such a trip was too risky for Ilonka after her recent heart attack; the sheer excitement of flying and seeing Sári might be too much for her. They would have to wait and see what Kadar would do next. Would he also open the door for the refugees to come?

In the eight years since the uprising, most of these ex-patriots were well settled in their new homelands and had money to spend, all in hard foreign currency. It didn't take a genius to figure out that by lifting restrictions and allowing them to visit the old country, the government could easily channel some of that much-needed money into their own coffers. The result was a quick amnesty for all; only the most notorious ex-freedom fighters were denied entrance to the country. And as expected, the refugees began to arrive, first only a few to test the waters, but once it proved safe, by the thousands, bringing German marks, Swiss francs or Austrian schillings, all a boon to Hungary's economy.

Since the U.S. was the archenemy of Communism, the Hungarian immigrants in America were a bit more cautious about venturing back to their abandoned homeland. Would they be free of harassment while in Hungary, and would they be allowed to leave at the end of their visit? But when it became clear that their European, Canadian, and Australian brethren suffered no harm, they too began taking out visas.

Upon entering the country, they were asked to respect the rules and regulations, with subtle hints to refrain from expressing opinions when comparing Hungary to their country. Going through customs they learned that certain items were not allowed to bring in or take out of the country, and many others were subject to import duties. Travelers also had to comply with registration requirements, go to the police within twenty-four hours of arrival and fill out forms, and do the same before departure. This was mandatory at each place they stayed for more than one day. Hotels usually offered to handle the task for their guests, but it was burdensome for individuals staying with various relatives or friends when each lived in different parts of the country.

There were also restrictions. Exchanging money other than in banks was illegal, and taking pictures in certain areas was prohibited. Other than that the refugees were not bothered, unless of course someone was crazy enough to stand on a street corner and shout: "Down with Communism!"

Sári got a firsthand report on travel into Hungary from her brother Istvan, who drove into Sopron in 1965 for the first time since his escape. He had no problems while there—well, almost no problems. They gave him a hard time at the border for bringing a small TV, but after paying a rather hefty duty he was allowed to take it in. It was a gift for Ochie's wife to stop her complaining about having to watch the programs Ilonka liked on the family's only set. Then, when he took a picture of his parents posing at the side of their house, a soldier from the casern across ran over and confiscated the film from his camera, saying it was taken at an angle that showed their military compound. He learned his lesson, and his next visit went without a hitch.

Still, it took a few more years before Sári applied for a visa. She waited until Eva and Endre Pataky returned from their trip to Hungary in 1967 with assurances that there was nothing to fear, especially since by then they were all U.S. citizens traveling under the protection of the prestigious U.S. passport. Letters from home also urged her to come; her visit was long overdue.

And it was true, it had been much too long—over ten years—since she said goodbye to her family, which by now included two sisters-in-law she had never met, two new nephews and the latest, a little niece, Nora, born on September 15 to Ochie and Marika. But more importantly, she realized that time was marching on, and while new members were added to the family, others were slowly leaving. First she lost her uncle Sandor in 1962 at age sixty-one. To Sári, it always seemed a miracle that he survived the torturous years he spent in captivity in Russia. Then Eta wrote about the passing of her mother-in-law last year, and just this year in June her uncle Laszlo Riedl died. Her godfather, Jozsef Varosy could be the next; he was in the hospital with a perforated stomach ulcer, and according to Ilonka, his prognosis was grim.

And there were her beloved parents! What if she waited too long to visit them? Her mother was now sixty-one, and although she had survived a heart attack, would she be as lucky if she suffered another? And what about her father, that quiet, gentle man she loved with all her heart? He would be seventy-two on November 11, and according to her mother, there was cause for concern about his health. He was never strong physically and often complained about health problems, mostly imagined in Ilonka's opinion, but lately even she admitted that something was not right with him. She didn't like that he slept so much; it made him visibly weaker. He'd sleep late, get up for a few hours, then lie down again, and she would have to wake him up to eat something. He was always a fussy eater but now he just picked at his food and hardly drank anything. He never left the house except to see Dr. Torday with one ailment or another, most recently a recurring temperature and an insistent cough. But what really scared Ilonka was when lying in bed on a beautiful warm summer day Jeno complained that it was chilly and asked her to shut the window to keep out the cold wind. A few days later he went to Dr.Torday again, and this time he detected some respiratory irregularity and ordered Jeno to stop smoking, which he finally did. Dr. Torday also referred him to a specialist, but Jeno refused to make an appointment. Going against doctor's orders suggested to Sári that her father was afraid to hear the diagnosis.

Reading his latest letters, she also noticed that his handwriting had lost its firmness, and instead of filling the usual page or two, he only added a few lines to what Ilonka wrote. It nudged her a step closer to take a plane and spend a little time with her parents before it was too late. And so in the spring of 1968 she began to plan for her trip. First she asked for a two-month leave of absence at work, and when it was granted, she made her flight reservation for June 27. Then she sent ahead to Istvan several parcels filled with gifts: outfits for Ilonka, shirts, a robe and slippers for her father, toys for all the children, and down the line, something for everyone on her list, careful not to show favor to one over another. Her plan was to fly to Vienna, stay a few days with her brother, then loading the packages in his car drive together to Sopron.

Her stay in Hungary was not going to be a vacation. Although she'd spend most of her time with her parents, she was also going to visit her sister in Kecskemet, her brother Gyuszi in Pecs, and her two cousins, Feri and Gabi, in Budapest. Traveling from one place to the other and constantly packing and unpacking would be tiring. And there was Istvan's upcoming wedding on July

13 in Pecs, planned so she could attend. He met his fiancée, a neighbor of Gyuszi and Itzu, while visiting them a year earlier. Ochie and his family still lived in Sopron, but not for long. Much to Ilonka's regret, they were also moving to Pecs, where he was hired as an electrician at the same place his brother Gyuszi worked as an engineer. She'd miss them, already lamenting about losing *her* babies, but she couldn't blame Ochie for taking the job. The pay was considerably higher, and it allowed Marika to stay home with the children.

The day Sári and Istvan drove into Hungary the border guard pulled them over and ordered the trunk opened for inspection. Seeing the many packages, he pointed to one in the back and demanded to see it. Scattered on top were a dozen injector razors, and the way he picked one up and turned it this way and that, Sári knew he had never seen one before and had no idea what it was.

"Oh, this is a new type of razor, it's for my father," she said casually. "He is getting old, you know, and his hands shake, but with this he can't cut himself accidentally. The blade is hidden in this protective cartridge, you see, and you just slide it into the razor." With that, she quickly held out another one. "Here, you should try it and see for yourself how easy it is."

She didn't have to tell him twice; he understood the offer and in a flash the razor disappeared in his pocket. He spent a little more time pretending to look into the other bags before waving them on.

"Now that was easy enough," Sári laughed as they drove away. "That two-dollar razor saved me a bunch of money they could have collected as duty on all that stuff in the trunk!" But her mood dampened when on their way to Sopron Istvan warned her not to be shocked upon seeing their father. He was visibly ill and Dr. Torday suspected lung cancer.

She was glad for the warning. The minute they pulled up to the house Ilonka was running to greet her, shouting for Jeno to come, Sári was here, but the poor man could hardly make it halfway through the hall by the time she stepped inside the house. Seeing him so frail, his arms outstretched and calling her name, she broke into great big sobs, burying her face in his shoulder. And when a moment later she felt her mother's hand stroking her hair, she reached out to her and without breaking away pulled her, too, into her embrace. The three of them stood there for the longest time, clinging to each other without words, just like on that rainy November afternoon in 1956 when she last said goodbye to them.

It took days before the excitement over seeing each other again subsided and they could sit down and catch up on all the changes without getting emotional. Since this was their first chance to talk face-to-face after she left the country, everyone wanted to hear the details of her escape, how she made it to Vienna and on to America. Ilonka brought out the photo albums she put together with the pictures Sári sent over the years and, looking at them together, she would regale them with stories, what happened here and there. When they came to the wedding album, Ilonka naturally asked about her failed marriage, and whether her bad experience was the reason she didn't marry again.

"Perhaps it was at first, but not anymore," Sári said. "I would like to get married but it's not that easy at my age. Most men I know are either married, or divorced with obligations; others are not up to my expectations, and I would never marry just for the sake of being married."

"Oh, you are just too choosy," Ilonka retorted. "There must be someone in Los Angeles who would live up to your 'expectations.' If you wait too long time will run out to have a family; have you thought about that?"

"Being thirty-seven is not that old Mother! You were that age when you had Ochie!"

"Yes, but I had the four of you before him! There is a big difference having the first baby when a woman is older."

"I know that, but Mom, it wouldn't be the end of the world if I remained single! I am very happy with my life—really, you must believe me when I say that I won't miss it if I never have children."

"You are just saying that because you don't know how it feels to hold your child in your arms!"

"Of course I don't, you are right in that, but to me it's not all that important. It's not a tragedy that I don have a husband and children."

"Well, maybe not a tragedy, but I think in time you would have regrets."

"Ilonka, leave Sári alone. It's her life, don't try to tell her how to live it," Jeno finally interrupted them. And so they dropped the subject; there were better things to do than argue. Sári wouldn't let Ilonka cook every day, they would often go out to eat. They took long walks in the Loever, even her father seemed to rally and go along a few times. And when the annual Art Festival of Sopron opened in July, they visited the exhibits and attended concerts, including the traditional choir competition at the former Eszterhazy Palace—now a museum—in nearby Fertod. It featured the music of the composer Haydn, known as the "Father of the String Quartet," who spent nearly 30 years starting in 1761 as court musician to the princely Eszterhazy family. The highlight of the festival, however, was the weeklong presentation of several operas staged inside the great caverns of Sopron-Kohida that resembled the ancient rock temples of Egypt. Its superb natural acoustics enhanced the sound, making the productions highly interesting and very popular. Tickets were sold out far in advance, but through one of her old schoolmates with connections, Sári was able to take her mother to see *La Bohame*.

When at home, there was a constant flow of people coming to see her, mostly friends of her mother, Mrs. Balog, Aunt Mitzie and her family, and of course her godmother, Grety Varosy. Her godfather unfortunately passed away; he never made it out of the hospital, and as a widow with nothing but time on her hand, Grety stopped by every day, so much so that Ilonka began to resent her insistent presence. It was not so much for the intrusion, but because of the exaggerated praises she heaped on Sári, how beautiful she looked, how fashionable her clothes were, the confident way she carried herself, and so on. Everyone knew that her godmother was a little-over dramatic, but this was becoming almost embarrassing even for Sári. As for Ilonka, she could never get used to her friend's theatrical ways, not even after forty years of friendship.

Old schoolmates of Sári dropped by, too. Even Wanda took the train from Budapest to spend a day together. Through the years they had kept in touch but only loosely, and it took them hours to fill in the gaps. Looking back, they wondered about how differently their lives turned out. With all her talk in 1956 about leaving the country, Wanda never did. She got married, went back to school to get a degree in electronics, and was working full-time. They had no children, only a dog. She wanted to know everything about Sári's life, and whether she and Alexa were still friends. Sári couldn't say much about her though, only that she now lived in Chicago with her husband and two kids. They had seen each other only once in ten years, and were left with exchanging birthday cards and Christmas greetings.

Then on July 10 Istvan came from Vienna to take his parents and Sári to Pecs for the wedding. The ride was hard on Jeno, the roads being what they were, and he was feverish by the time they arrived. The day of the wedding he was still too weak to get up, but Ilonka wouldn't have any of it. How many chances he'd have to be together with his five children and six grandchildren all in one place? Yielding to her prodding, he forced himself to go, but he barely lasted through the ceremony, a long nuptial Mass officiated by the bishop in the great eleventh-century Cathedral of Pecs. As soon as it was over Gyuszi and Sári took him home, but when she wanted to stay Jeno wouldn't allow it. He insisted he would be fine; he was just going to sleep anyway, and sent them back to enjoy the reception. He rested a few days and by the time they took the train back to Sopron, he felt better. He slept through most of the five-hour ride lying down in their private compartment, his head cradled in Sári's lap.

At the wedding Sári took rolls and rolls of pictures and whenever she looked at them later in life she could see just how sick her father really was by then, his eyes feverish and sunken, spittle sitting in the corner of his mouth. But apart from Jeno's illness, the wedding was lovely and it was wonderful to see everyone. She promised to visit all her relatives, and after spending a couple of weeks in Sopron, she set out to fulfill that promise. She first went back to Pecs, splitting her time between her two brothers and also getting acquainted with the city and its rich history, going back to 2nd century Roman times, when it was known as Sopianae. Centuries later, in 1526 it was at nearby Mohacs where Suleiman the Magnificent defeated the Hungarians and added one third of the country to his vast Ottoman Empire. Forty years later, at age seventy-two, he was leading another campaign through Hungary when he died suddenly of unknown causes. He was buried there until his body could be moved to his permanent tomb in Istanbul. As one of the well-preserved remnants of the Turkish occupation, a beautiful mosque still stood in the center of Pecs, although it was now converted to a church.

For a few days Gyuszi and Itzu took her to Lake Balaton where a year before they had built a small vacation cabin. From there they made several boat excursions, one to Badacsony, famous for its vineyards, and another to Tihany with its ancient Benedictine Abbey founded in 1055 by King Endre I, whose body lay entombed in a crypt underneath the church.

At the end of her stay Gyuszi drove her to see Eta in Kecskemet. To spend more time together, her sister took a week's vacation from her job at the little museum and souvenir shop at Bugac, the nearby prairie where loads of tourists came from Budapest to see the daring horse show put on by Hungarian cowboys. Sári never knew much about horses, but it was impressive to watch these horsemen demonstrate their riding skills. They could ride three horses at the same time, standing on their backs and jumping from one to the other at a fast gallop. Other riders clad in colorful costumes, cracking whips and emitting high-pitched rebel yells, were busy rounding up a group of wild running horses with expert ease.

Kecskemet was also the birthplace of Zoltan Kodaly, the prominent and much honored composer who collected old songs from remote villages and incorporated them into his compositions. He was also known for developing a unique method of teaching choral music to young children, instilling in them the love and appreciation of music.

Sári was there when on August 20, 1968 the news about a Czech uprising hit the airwaves. People everywhere sat with ears glued to their radios as Russian tanks rumbled through the streets of Prague. It seemed nothing had changed in the preceding twelve years in Moscow's attitude toward its satellites: any ideas of liberalization would still be crushed. Although the reforms proposed by the Czech leader Alexander Dubcek were far from radical—he merely planned to put a human face on socialism and never made demands for the withdrawal of the Red Army—Leonid Brezhnev sent 200,000 troops and 2000 of his T-55 tanks to silence him. That it didn't turn into a bloodbath as in Hungary could be credited to Dubcek's levelheaded leadership and his ability to keep people from putting up resistance.

That day Sári noticed that while listening to reports of the unfolding events in Prague, Eta's husband took a bottle of pálinka, the strong Hungarian brandy, and sat drinking until he nearly finished it. He kept mumbling about the stupidity of the people wanting political changes when socialism was still better than the oppressive and exploitative capitalist system.

"I see, even you finally agree," he nudged his head toward Sári, "otherwise why should you come back at the first chance the government allowed the likes of you to return. I never understood why you left in the first place; now you have to start again from square one."

At first Sári ignored him and his jabbering nonsense, but by now she had enough. "What on earth are you talking about? You are drunk and don't know what you are saying. I am here to visit, not to stay! I wouldn't live in this country if you paid me! And frankly, except for the family, I don't care if I ever see Hungary again!"

"You just say that to save face. Deep inside all you refugees regret that you left. That's why so many of you are crawling back."

"Are you crazy? We come back to see relatives, and because we can afford it. When was the last time you could go anywhere?"

"It's always the money with you people, isn't it? The capitalist greed!"

"And what of it? That capitalist 'greed' gave us the greatest economic system in the world, while yours is teetering on bankruptcy; I studied economics, I know the difference. And you are wrong, it's not just the money, it's the total freedom we have! I can stand up in the middle of a crowd in Los Angeles and yell 'Out with the President' and nobody would arrest me. I'd like to see you try that with Kadar! I don't have to remind you how you lost your teeth! To be honest, I am surprised that after what they did to you, you are still mouthing their stupid propaganda. But then, you are drunk, and you've never been in America, so what is there to expect?"

Still upset, she got up and found Eta in her vegetable garden. "What's wrong with Latzi?" she confronted her. "He never used to drink, not like this! He drank himself to a stupor and is talking nonsense that I came back to live here—as if I wanted to! Imagine that!" She made an indignant sound, but a warning glance from her sister stopped her from saying another word.

Eta picked up her bowl of tomatoes and motioned for Sári to follow her inside.

"I know it's over ten years since you left, but it's still not safe to make remarks like that in the open," she warned her. "People might hear it, and we had enough trouble with Latzi as it is."

"What remark? All I said was that—"

"I know, I know, it's hard for you to understand, but those women in the parcel behind me could take your words as derogatory to the regime, and people still get hauled in for things like that. That's just the way it is here."

"It's that bad? Maybe I shouldn't have opened my mouth in front of Latzi, either! I gave him a piece of my mind when he started making noises as a die-hard Communist," she said sarcastically, but quickly apologized when she saw the hurt in Eta's eyes.

"You don't know what I have to go through with him, Sári. He is a conflicted, deeply disappointed man, and that's the reason he took to drinking. You know that he is a born idealist, and he is truly convinced that socialism is the best social system, but he also believes that it shouldn't be tied to rigid rules, that adjustments are needed on the road to socialism. That is why he got involved with the revolution. And he can't reconcile with the fact that they punished him for that. It slowly drove him to drinking to realize that idealism has nothing to do with socialism."

"I am so sorry to hear it, Eta. I had no idea. Mother didn't talk much about him; she mentioned nothing about his drinking. How bad is it?"

"It's bad enough, but it's worse today. The news from Prague got him upset."

"Can't you do something to keep him off the booze?"

"Not much. He stops every day on the way home to have a drink or two. I tried reducing his spending money—he gives me all what he earns, you know—but it didn't help; he drank on credit and I had to go around paying his liquor bills. It's plain embarrassing, not to mention what the drinking does to his health. He is thin as a rail, because when he comes home after drinking he is not hungry and refuses to eat a decent meal."

A nice example he is setting for his young sons! Sári thought, but she held her tongue. Her poor sister had enough trouble. How could she stand it? She herself would never put up with a husband like Latzi! But then, Eta was Eta; she would stick by him no matter what. She had proved that when he was sitting in jail.

She felt sorry for her sister and the boys, but she knew she could do nothing to help. After saying goodbye to them she had one more stop to visit her cousins in Budapest, then she returned to Sopron to spend the rest of her time with her parents. During her stay she noticed the house needed repairs: too many tiles were cracked in the hallway and kitchen, and on rainy days water was seeping through under the windowsills. Everything seemed worn out and backward; they still had to fire up the water tank for a bath, and do the laundry by hand. Even if she bought them a washing machine, what good would it do without a hot water hook-up? She would have to do something to improve their condition, and it would take money, but somehow she'd find a way.

The last remaining days passed quietly, each bringing them closer to the moment of her inevitable departure. Jeno held up surprisingly well until the last evening, when he became feverish again. Still, he insisted on staying up after dinner and Sári had to trick him into retiring by pretending that she had packing to do. She waited until both her parents were in bed before going in to say goodnight. Seeing her father so frail lying on his pillow she gave another try to persuade him to see the specialist.

"Promise you'll make an appointment," she said pulling up a chair. "I am sure it's nothing serious, probably a stubborn infection that a prescription could easily clear up. I can send you the best medicine if you just let me know what you need."

"I know you would, although you have done too much for us already. You shouldn't worry about us; we have enough of everything for the time we have left. We'll manage."

"Of course you will, you always have, just look what we've been through—the war and what came after—and you always kept us going. Now it's time you enjoy your life, but you must get well. Just do what the doctor says and go for a thorough checkup, OK?"

"I know I should, Sári, and I will, but I know I will not last long." The resignation in his voice made her want to cry and she turned her face to hide her emotion. Then she felt her father's hand patting hers. "I know it's hard to talk about these things, but I want you to know, I am not afraid of dying. I had a long life, most of it good, but even in times of trouble you were always a ray of sunshine to us. I don't want you to feel sad; I will be at peace as long as I know you will remember me."

Sári couldn't bear it any longer. Fighting tears, her throat too tight to speak, she bent to embrace her father, then quickly turned and walked toward the door. She needed to get out, to be alone to give free vent to her grief. She was halfway there when she heard her mother's soft voice. "Don't I get a goodnight kiss, too?"

The words stabbed her in the heart. How could she forget her mother when she was right there, her bed next to Jeno's! The guilt! Leaving the room without so much as a glance in her direction! Sári ran back, sobbing, muttering that she didn't want to cry in front of them, that she would have come back. But there was no need for apologies. Ilonka understood. She knew her daughter adored her father, but she loved her just as much.

The next day, after a restless night and some last minute repacking, they sat waiting for a taxi to take them to the train station. Her godmother joined them there, and this time Ilonka welcomed her presence; her constant prattling helped to keep the tears at bay as time to say goodbye drew ever closer. Jeno stepped away for a moment to find out how much time they had before Sári must go through customs in an area at the back of the platform restricted to travelers only. When he returned, assured that there was still a good half hour left—an officer even promised to alert them in time—he took Sári out to the street and led her to a wrought iron gate, a side entrance to customs. It was locked, but he told her to come there after she checked her luggage; they could have a few minutes more together until it was time for her to leave.

Finally, the dreaded moment arrived as the officer was signaling for her to come. To say goodbye was heartbreaking, but Sári held up admirably as she opened her suitcases for inspection. They quickly passed her through then nudged her toward the gate, where her parents were waiting.

"Have a safe trip and come back soon!" Ilonka said, then reaching through the bars grabbed Sári's hands, holding on to her if only for a moment longer. Her father also urged her, "Take care and don't stay away too long!" Hearing it filled her heart with an infinite sadness, not so much the words—spoken a thousand times at scenes of parting—but the way he said it, pleading, his tone anxious. Would this be the last time she hears his voice?

A minute later the shrill sound of a whistle reminded them that their time was up. Choked with emotion, unable to say another word, she kissed her fingertips and thrusting her hands through the iron bars touched them to her parents' lips. With tears running freely she climbed the steps to the waiting train, then stood at the window blowing a last kiss as the wheels began to turn. She remained standing there, watching her parents slowly fading into the distance, never imagining that it was to be her final glimpse of them. In her heart and mind she halfway accepted that her father might be gone by the next time she came, but never that this was also the last time she would see her mother alive.

To keep his promise, Jeno finally agreed to see a specialist. Tests showed signs of emphysema and bronchitis in the lower lobe of the left lung. The doctor suspected that the persistent low-grade fever was a sign of walking pneumonia and put him on antibiotics with bed rest for the next five days. It made him feel better, but when he got up the fever returned.

He also complained of acute pain in his hands; writing was difficult, at times he could hardly separate his fingers. The diagnosis was rheumatoid arthritis and the doctor sent him for a series of electric heat treatments that didn't help at all.

By June 1969 his legs started to swell and walking became painful. He was taking three prescription drugs, but they made him nervous and edgy. Little things bothered him, especially noises. He found the television too loud when Ilonka turned it on—he himself didn't care to watch TV—or her voice was too shrill, the laughter too raucous when her friends visited, all grating on his nerves. Ilonka shot back that if she was forced to listen to the TV with her ears pressed to the screen and was criticized for laughing in her own house, then she'd rather go to her friends, where nobody protested. And so she did, but then Jeno became anxious, accusing her of leaving him alone too long.

The bickering about the TV stopped for a day when on July 20, 1969, they both watched in utter disbelief as Neil Armstrong made his historic first step on the moon. Ilonka remarked that as awesome as the landing was, it was more amazing that they had lived long enough to see such an astounding feat.

At that same moment Sári watched the moon landing amid a wildly cheering crowd in the lobby of the Hilton hotel in Honolulu. She was there on vacation with a girlfriend, going to the beach, seeing all the sights, and learning a bit about the history of Hawaii. They were on a four-island tour, including three days on Oahu and overnight stays on Maui, Kauai, and the Big Island of Hawaii.

The photos she sent home were all beautiful, but it was not the picture of Sári standing on an outcrop over Kilauea Volcano that captured Ilonka's interest. It was her mentioning that she met someone during the trip. He was from Los Angeles and worked in sales at a Porsche dealership. They had a few dates, and although he was a few years younger, she thought that in time the relationship could become more than casual. Not that she was going to rush into anything; her first marriage taught her to give it time, but she really liked the man.

And when she added that he was originally from Vienna and perhaps sharing common European roots played a part in the attraction, Ilonka, always fond of anything Viennese, was overjoyed. "Let's hope he lives up to her 'expectations' and that he knows how to use that Viennese charm," she laughed handing the letter to Jeno. "I am keeping my fingers crossed! If they get married, at least we can talk to him. I was always afraid, how were we to understand each other with an American husband."

Jeno, too, perked up at the news. Whenever something positive reached his ears, his spirit rallied, he would make an effort to stay up longer, even go out for a short walk. Noticing it, how his emotional state of mind affected his physical well-being, Ilonka tried to shield him from anything sad or upsetting. Unfortunately, there were times when the truth had to be told. She dreaded to show him the announcement she received in mid-September that his beloved sister Sári died of pancreatic cancer. They knew she was not feeling well during the past few months, and that the doctors couldn't agree on the cause of her illness, but they were not prepared to lose her. She died within two months after surgery revealed the inoperable cancer.

A few weeks later they received another sad news; Jeno's elderly aunt Mariska and her daughter Margit were found dead at home, lying side-by-side, fully dressed, their death deemed suicide. Apparently, they had reached the point when life lost its meaning for them, and they decided to put an end to their pitiful existence. They were victims of a regime that stigmatized them for the sheltered life they once led, for having a family member raised high in the ranks of the despised former military, and later condemned as a war criminal by the Russians. After Sandor was taken to the Siberian gulags in 1945, his mother and sister, left to the mercy of the new rulers, struggled to survive by cleaning houses and taking in sewing, but they never gave up hope of seeing him again. That ended when he escaped to Austria in 1956, and subsequently with his death in 1962. They kept on a few more years, until their life became no longer worth living.

Distraught by the death of his sister, his aunt, and cousin, Jeno's condition, both mental and physical, worsened. Trying to shake him out of his depression Ilonka suggested they spend the winter with Eta in Kecskemet; they had room for them now that the two older boys were in the Army. Fourteen-year-old Istvan, who spent the summer with them the year before, was always a joy to Jeno, and Ilonka thought being around the boy would cheer him up. With the cold weather coming, it would also spare them from chopping wood to heat the house, but Jeno wouldn't hear of leaving.

So they stayed, a decision they regretted later when winter set in, the coldest since 1929. Storms dumped mountains of snow and with Jeno too weak to clean the street in front of the house, Ilonka had to grab the shovel and do it herself. The severe weather affected transportation and caused widespread power outages, but the worst came when they both caught a vicious form of influenza. Sick in bed with high fever and a never-ending cough, Ochie's wife Marika came up from Pecs for a week to look after them.

Jeno never really recovered after that. He was weak and his emotional ups and downs worsened, too. When Sári's letters stopped for a while during March 1970 he constantly worried, imagining the worst—perhaps she had a car accident; he heard how recklessly people drove in America. It didn't help to tell him that there was a postal strike in the United States. The only thing that perked him up and made him forget for a moment how ill he was when a telegram arrived on May 10 with the news that Itzu had given birth to a healthy baby girl they named Orsolya. Nicknamed Orsi, she was their eighth grandchild.

Young Istvan came again for the summer, and he was there when on July 11 Jeno collapsed. Lifting him onto the bed, Ilonka could feel that he was burning up with fever, and even though he was conscious and talking, what he said didn't make sense. The boy ran for Dr. Torday who, seeing his condition, immediately called for an ambulance. Arriving at the hospital, they gave him a transfusion and put him on life support; he was completely dehydrated, his whole system nearing collapse.

Ilonka was devastated; she couldn't stop crying, and it was a blessing that her grandson was there to keep her spirits up. They went to see Jeno every day, bringing him food she knew he liked, even if he wouldn't touch it, saying it didn't matter anymore. He was kept on life support and received additional transfusions, but it was clear that he was wasting away. Regardless of all the care, his legs remained swollen and his lungs kept filling up with fluid; they had to drain him four times in five weeks, removing three quarts of water each time. He was down to skin and bones, his eyes sunken, the face skull-like, and as hard as it was to lose him, Ilonka came to believe that it would be better if God would take him and end his suffering. In the middle of August she arranged for a priest to come and hear his confession, a great comfort to her that Jeno, who was not a practicing Catholic, finally made his peace with God.

Sári's get-well cards arrived almost daily and Ilonka wrote her that even though Jeno protested that it was not necessary, these fancy cards cost too much money, his eyes lit up every time the nurse put one in his hand. Ilonka tried to keep a cheerful facade, but she broke down sobbing during her visit on August 16, when Jeno for the first time spoke to her of dying. He knew there was no hope; he would never leave the hospital. He talked about their life, the memories of the forty-five years they'd been married, how he never forgot the moment when he first saw her at the edge of the forest with wild cyclamens in her hair fifty years ago.

Ilonka was close to collapse when during the final days he told her not to bring his grandson again, he was too young to witness his dying, then asked the boy to say goodbye for the last time; he would not see him again.

The end came three days later. When Ilonka arrived in the morning, he no longer recognized her. He just lay there quietly while she sat on his bed, crying softly, holding his hand, covering his face and eyes with kisses. Then at eleven o'clock he stirred, and soon the final struggle for his last breath took over his emaciated body. The doctor took Ilonka by the hand and led her out of the room; with her damaged heart she should not watch him suffer through the agony of death throes. He consoled her that they did everything possible, but Jeno was at a stage where the best doctors in the world couldn't save him; there was nothing they could do anymore.

The cause of death was pneumonia, hemorrhaging in both sides of the lung, pleurisy, and sarcoma, a form of lung cancer. In the doctor's opinion it was amazing that he lived as long as he did; many patients even stronger and younger than Jeno would have succumbed sooner to this kind of lethal attack on the system.

His words were not much comfort to Ilonka. All she knew that Jeno was gone, and she couldn't imagine life without him. Grief-stricken, she left it to the children to make the funeral arrangements, choose the casket and order the flowers. Knowing that Ilonka was not prepared to cover the cost, the five of them pooled the money together and paid for a first class funeral. All the family came, except Sári. During her visit she had already discussed with her mother that when her father died, she wouldn't come back for the burial. Getting a visa, even in an emergency, took time, and by then it might be too late to book a flight. Still, when Sári tore open the telegram with the news of her father's death, her first reaction was to get on a plane and go. Then she looked at the calendar. Due to the slow transatlantic wire service from Hungary on top of the nine-hour time difference, it was already August 21, a day away from the funeral.

Next she reached for the phone, ready to dial, when she realized she couldn't even call her mother in this hour of sadness. She didn't have a telephone! The best she could do was to call Ochie's in-laws, Marton and Maria Brody—she met them only once but knew their number—and arrange for a time when her mother would be there to receive her call. Talking to her was very emotional, a teary-eyed conversation, yet it brought acceptance of the irreversible truth that her father was gone forever.

It touched Ilonka deeply how many people came to say goodbye to Jeno. The grave was a mountain of flowers and even days after the funeral people still stopped her on the street—some she hardly knew—just to say a few kind words about him. It brought her to tears when Mr. Jakab, a close friend and former colleague of Jeno, presented her with a letter written collectively by people at the customs department, expressing their condolences in profoundly moving words:

> . . . *We believe that God in his everlasting love prepared a place for Jeno and that our prayers will help to carry him there. His passing fills our heart with sadness, but let it be a consolation that after life's journey, his gentle soul now rests in the all-encompassing embrace of the Heavenly Father. May the Lord grant him grace and eternal peace*. . . .

With Jeno gone, Ilonka next had to deal with the authorities. Right away there were problems with his pension; it stopped immediately, and when Ilonka complained that as his widow she was entitled to twenty percent, they said it would take time to make the adjustment, and to have patience. And how was she supposed to pay the bills in the meantime? What savings she had was locked in a three-year bank deposit earning high interest with penalties for early withdrawal, and the money from the children went toward funeral expenses and down payment for the headstone. At the present she only had her own pension, some pitiful 600 forints a month. The rent on the house was low, only 200 forints, but the utilities ate up as much, and if it were not for the rent she collected from subletting, she would be in dire straits.

To tide her over, Sári transferred some additional money directly to her, even though the amount she received at the official low rate was only half of what it would be if exchanged through Vienna or sold on the black market. It helped Ilonka to breathe a little easier, even go without tranquilizers, but that didn't last long. Soon her old nightmare about sharing the house with strangers reappeared in full force in the person of Anna Sinkovich. The funeral was hardly over when this woman, who pestered her before and now owned one-third of the house, was at her door again with renewed demands to move in. That earlier time, when she made overtures to take over a portion of the house, she couldn't do anything because the occupancy quota was filled; the children then were living at home, but now, with only Ilonka and the renters in the house, her claim posed a real threat. She even had a new weapon. According to a new ruling that made subletting rooms subject to the owner's approval, she had the right to force the girls out from the front room, and with the law on her side, Ilonka knew that the pushy woman was going to do just that; it was only a matter of time before she'd move in.

Just thinking of it made Ilonka distraught. How could she live with a person known in the whole neighborhood for her controlling and quarrelsome nature? It was typical of her scheming and calculating ways that she waited until Jeno was out of the picture and could catch Ilonka at her most vulnerable moment, when she was in deep mourning and couldn't even think straight.

Ochie and Marika stayed with her for a week after the funeral and when they saw how upset she was about the dismal prospect of sharing the house with Mrs. Sinkovich, Ochie approached the woman and suggested a deal: his mother would give up the house and move to an apartment, provided Mrs. Sinkovich found her a suitable one. Of course, it must have electricity and gas, not like some rundown coldwater flat in the periphery of the city. The landlady seemed to be agreeable to the exchange, at least in principle. She had no objection, she said, and would start looking for an acceptable place.

The thought alone had a calming effect on Ilonka, and when Ochie and Marika went back to Pecs, they left her in a hopeful and positive state of mind. Unfortunately, it was only momentary. Finding herself completely alone for the first time in her life, she relapsed into the disheartening pessimism that overtook her since Jeno's death. The highlight of her days was the trip to the cemetery, where she spent hours at his grave, coming home depressed and crying over her great loss.

Grety Varosy came to see her a few times, but stayed only for short periods, since she was busy getting ready for a trip to visit her son in Buenos Aires. It was faithful Aunt Mitzie who was at the house every day, keeping her company, trying to ease Ilonka's anguish. She, too, had lost her husband a few years ago and knew what it meant to be suddenly alone. She sat with Ilonka, sometimes crying with her if that was what she needed, always consoling that all would soon be better and the pain would ease. Life would go on, regardless of the devastating loss she suffered and the overwhelming loneliness she felt.

"You might feel alone, Ilonka, but you are not," she encouraged her. "Not like some poor old widow without any family; you have your children and grandchildren to cheer you up."

"Yes, but where are they? Yours are all here in Sopron, but my children are scattered in all directions," Ilonka lamented.

"So, you go and visit them! Just think of it, going to visit Sári and spend time in America! I wish I had the opportunity to globetrot like that. You have options, Ilonka, so pick up your life, and make the best of it. You are alone only if you choose to be."

With the genuinely heartfelt concern of her aunt and the constant attention she showered on her, Ilonka at least made an effort to adjust to her lonely life. Her hope that the problems with the landlady would be solved soon also helped, and she started to feel better, sleeping without pills, if only for a time being.

CHAPTER SEVEN

1970 - 1971

Ilonka's birthday

BY OCTOBER THE weather turned cold as the winds swept down from the foot of the Alps, but it made no difference. Ilonka made her daily trips to the cemetery, staying at Jeno's grave and often checking with the stonemason about the marble headstone she ordered. Would it be ready, as promised, by November 2, All Souls' Day, when the children would be coming to light a candle at their father's grave?

They all came, bringing flowers and visiting the grave, but back at the house sitting together in the evening, Eta had a proposal for her mother.

"Why don't you give up this old house and come to live with us in Kecskemet? It would end your problems with this Sinkovich woman, and you'd be closer to Gyuszi and Ochie, too."

But Ilonka wouldn't hear of it. This house was her home for almost four decades, and that's where she'd stay.

"Well, maybe you change your mind later, but at least spend the winter with us," Eta said. "You wouldn't have to bother with heating the house, and a long rest would be good for you after what you've been through."

Still, Ilonka refused. "How could you ask me to leave your father alone in the cemetery? And what would happen to the house while I am away? What if Anna Sinkovich found an apartment for me and I missed the opportunity? Besides, Jeno's pension is still not settled; I simply couldn't go."

As determined as she was at first, when the freezing weather set in by the middle of December and she found herself sitting alone in the kitchen, the only place she kept heated because she had no strength to chop wood or carry buckets of coal from the cellar, she finally gave in and packed her bags. She was ready to go. First she spent the holidays in Pecs, where Gyuszi and Ochie planned a big Christmas celebration for her. Surrounded by family and seeing her four grandchildren, wide-eyed and wonderstruck as they stood before the glittering Christmas tree, seemed to have a healing effect on her. She doted on little Orsi, taking her along on her walks, as they were often seen together in the neighborhood with Ilonka pushing the baby's stroller. She enjoyed the excellent air quality around Pecs, the product of the surrounding forests that did wonders for her increasingly bothersome asthma. And so, as two weeks went by without her renters reporting any harassment at home, and knowing that Grety Varosy, back from her travel, would look after Jeno's grave, she began to relax.

With the anxiety of the past few months fading, she felt at peace when after the holidays she left to stay with Eta for the rest of the winter. She was there for the January wedding of her first grandchild, Latzi, Jr., now an arborist technician working with his father. His brother Peter was in the army, only young Istvan was still at home. Everything seemed fine until the middle of February, when Ilonka began complaining about abdominal cramps, nausea, and diarrhea. Eta took it as some bug or the stomach flu, but when the pain increased and fever set in, she took her to the doctor. Tests revealed that she was suffering from inflammation of the lower colon, not a life-threatening disease, but hard to treat. According to the doctor the recent stress and depression might have brought it on. He prescribed some antibiotics and another drug, Azulfadin, and when she complained that the medication kept her awake all night, he also gave her some sleeping pills.

Eta took good care of her, but she worried about how the new medications—in addition to the other pills Ilonka was taking for her asthma and blood pressure—would affect her heart. On top of everything, she was coughing more lately, often gasping for air, a sure sign that her asthma was getting worse. The doctor told her that Kecskemet, sitting in the middle of the dust bowl of Bugac, was the worst place in the entire country for people with respiratory problems, and he urged Ilonka to return to Sopron. Of course, Eta wouldn't let her leave when she was ill and needed looking after. Even though she worked full time, she cooked the special meals the doctor recommended for her mother, made sure she took her pills, and that Istvan went straight home from school so she wouldn't be left alone but a few hours in the morning.

With plenty of rest, medication, and diet, Ilonka's intestinal problems improved somewhat by April, but the asthma attacks wouldn't let up. She talked more and more about going home, but became truly restless when the government announced a large-scale rent increase planned for June 1, 1971. Until now the state kept rents deliberately low in exchange for making tenants responsible for paying for repairs, but as neglects became widespread, they decided to switch the burden from tenants to owners, and at the same time put through the rent increase. New rules also forced the owners to use the extra income strictly for the maintenance and improvement of the property.

Hearing the news, Ilonka wouldn't wait a moment longer. All her former worries came flooding back. It was bad enough before, but now with the rent increase the woman was sure to put even more pressure on her to share the house. So far there was not one word from her about finding an apartment for Ilonka, making it clear that the exchange was off. What if she had already moved in? It wouldn't surprise her; she knew what that cunning, malicious woman was capable of! She didn't dare to bother them while Jeno was alive, but the minute he was buried, she started badgering her. There was no time to waste; she must go home, and go home now!

Nothing could hold her back. Gyuszi drove up from Pecs trying to convince her to give up Sopron and move in with them permanently. It was a sensible solution: they had room for her, she had her grandchildren there, and Pecs had clean air, yet Ilonka was unyielding. "That's how I am to live in my old age, bounced from one of you to the other?" she snapped angrily, and hearing it, both Eta and Gyuszi threw up their hands. They stopped pressing, afraid that with Ilonka's nervous state of mind, arguing further might bring on another heart attack. And so Eta packed her mother's suitcase and on Friday, April 17, took her home to Sopron. Before they left, she wrote a note to Mrs. Sinkovich asking her to come to see them during the weekend to discuss her intentions regarding the house. When the woman never showed up, Ilonka broke into tears, her nerves raw from the uncertainty of what to expect.

Sunday evening Eta took the train back to Kecskemet, and the next morning the landlady was at Ilonka's door with excuses why she couldn't come the day before. Then she handed her a piece of paper from the housing authority that truly stunned Ilonka: come June 1, her rent would go from 200 forints a month to 600, a shocking three-fold increase! It made her speechless; she sat there numb to the world, with another figure throbbing in the back of her mind: her 800 forint readjusted pension.

"I know it's a shock," she heard Anna's voice, dripping with honey. "It's an awful lot of money to pay for having a roof over your head, especially when living on a pension. But Mrs. Zachar, now that you are by yourself, do you really need such a big place? The apartment exchange your son suggested is out of the question. I couldn't find anything that would satisfy the conditions you set, but I think we can find a solution that will work for both of us. This house can easily split into two separate living quarters. I already talked to a contractor who said the storage room at the end of the hallway has a common wall with the bathroom and could be converted to a second bathroom. The plumbing is there; it can be done. Your bedroom would be partitioned off, you'd keep that with the existing bathroom, and I'd take the other two rooms and the converted bathroom. We'd have to share the kitchen and the toilet, but I don't see any problem with that, do you? Now what do you think of it?"

When her question went unanswered and the offer failed to elicit a response, the woman realized that momentarily Ilonka was almost beyond comprehension. She just sat there dazed, staring at the paper in front of her. Leaning forward, Mrs. Sinkovich immediately began to press the issue. “This is a good offer, Mrs. Zachar, you can stay right here and have your privacy; we will work out an arrangement to stay out of each other’s way. I would pay for the remodeling; the only thing I ask is that you sign an agreement that after you are gone, God forbid, your children will not claim the right to occupy your apartment. We could go to my lawyer even now, and as soon as the papers are drawn up, the contractor can come in and start the work.”

Something in what she said finally penetrated Ilonka’s mind and with a slight nod she handed the notice back to her. “I heard your offer, but of course I can’t do anything without talking to my children. My son is coming on the 30th, so let’s sit together then and talk about it. Please make sure that you come this time; he will be here only for the weekend.”

“Well, of course, if you want to think it over, go ahead,” the woman’s voice hardened as she straightened her back, “but I don’t have to tell you that this is not the only way I can move in here. I have the law on my side. Legally you are not entitled to three large rooms. When your children moved out you got around it by subletting the front room, but the girls are not family members and they can’t claim primary residency here. I am sure you have heard about the new rules; as a part owner I will have no problem evicting them. What’s more, the government is considering proposals to restore even more rights the landlords used to have, and I expect eventually we will have significantly more say in choosing our tenants. I wouldn’t like to be in your place then, Mrs. Zachar. So I suggest, go ahead and talk to your children if you must, but I wouldn’t stall too long!”

With that, she marched out of the house, leaving Ilonka in a state of despair. She knew that the woman was right, she had no choice but to accept her offer, no matter how much she dreaded the thought of living with her. Losing all hope for a quiet existence, she went to bed crying every night. Everyone was taking advantage of her! It was not enough that she suffered the loss of her husband and that she had health problems, now her nerves were giving out, too, because of all the harassment from this troublesome, domineering woman. All she wanted was to live out her remaining days in peace in the house that held so many memories for her. Was that too much to ask? Surely Eta or Gyuszi would take her in, but young people had their own lives to live, and putting up with elderly parents always created friction. Visiting was one thing, but being dependent on them was an entirely different matter.

She couldn’t think anymore; it hurt too much. She closed her eyes and thought of Jeno; he would know what to do, how to handle this problem. But he was gone, sleeping in eternal peace in that other world, where there were no more worries, no more pain.

And in that anguished moment the thought began to form in her mind: there was a third choice. She could be with him, resting safely by his side, where nothing could hurt her anymore.

When Sári read her mother's latest letter, full of pessimism, bitterly complaining about the landlady, and telling her to enjoy life to the fullest while she was still young because old age was nothing but misery, she became truly alarmed. She had to talk to somebody in the family! First she dialed her sister's number, but when no one answered she called Gyuszi at work, the only phone he had, and asked how he saw the situation. Was there a way to solve the dilemma with the house? She was relieved to hear that he and Ochie were going to Sopron the following weekend to settle the matter one way or another. There was no question, their mother would have to accept the offer to divide the house, but to make sure that she gets a fair deal they would hire a lawyer. They hung up with Gyuszi promising to write as soon as he had a clearer picture.

The two brothers arrived in Sopron on Friday evening, the last day of April, and stayed up late into the night talking with Ilonka. When they saw how overstressed she was—the mere mention of Anna Sinkovich's name started her crying—they decided it would be best if she stayed out of the negotiations tomorrow; she could be present but should leave the talking to them.

The next day, however, her intention to keep quiet flew out the window when sitting together to work out the details on the remodeling the woman announced that she changed her mind about paying for it.

"Why should I foot the bill? I am not bothered living in the same house with your mother," she said to Gyuszi. "If Mrs. Zachar wants more privacy, let her pay for the convenience."

"You see how she is?" Ilonka shrieked in a hysterical outburst. "How am I to live with such a two-faced woman who changes her mind on a whim? I know what she is doing! By constant vexation she is trying to hasten my death so she can have the whole house to herself!"

When she wouldn't stop crying and kept up with her tirade, Gyuszi led her out of the room, but secretly he had to agree, the woman was manipulative enough to count on the vulnerability of Ilonka. She knew that her irritable presence would drive Ilonka to the point where she'd give up the fight and go to live with one of her children, or perhaps drop dead of a heart attack.

Left alone with the landlady, Ochie turned to her and calmly said that perhaps she should reconsider, because there was a way he could stop her altogether from moving into the house. Anna's ears perked up as she listened with sudden interest.

"You see, if we don't come to an agreement today, I will move my family back here, and that will be the end of all this harassment. It will stop you from putting your foot in this house for a very long time to come. I don't have to tell you that with us here, my mother, my wife, two small children, and a new baby on the way, you could kiss goodbye to your schemes and any hope of moving in for the next twenty years."

The prospect made her sit up, but in a minute she was ready with an answer. "And you call *me* a schemer? Nice try, but you don't scare me! Perhaps it would work for a little while, but twenty years? Don't be ridiculous!" she huffed and puffed. "Everyone knows that you moved away because your wife couldn't get along with your mother. Sooner or later they'll be at each other's throats again, the same as before; I only have to sit and wait until you've had enough and pack up again."

That moment Gyuszi came back and calmly asked them to put aside threats and arguments; he had a new proposal. For the sake of Ilonka's peace of mind the family would pay for the alteration, except they'd use their own contractor. They would also waive their right to the apartment after Ilonka's death, and if the attorneys could draw up the contract during the week, he would come back next Friday to look it over and get it signed and notarized.

There was no objection from Mrs. Sinkovich, and after promising to discuss it with her attorney, they parted with a handshake. The minute the door closed behind her Ochie brought over a friend who worked in construction to give them an estimate. The man said he could do the job for far less than Anna quoted, and working on weekends and evenings with his buddy, a plumber, they could be finished by the end of summer.

The day ended with Ilonka feeling happier than she had been in a long time. She couldn't stop the Sinkovich woman from moving in, but at least she would have enough privacy to avoid her. The problem seemed to be solved, and to celebrate Gyuszi and Ochie took her out for a nice dinner; at last they could relax and enjoy a worry-free evening. With a good bottle of wine and listening to gypsy music playing in the background, it was wonderful to see their mother in a cheerful mood, the smile back on her face. And that night when she put her head down on the pillow, sleep came softly, without the help of her little pills.

Returning to Pecs on Sunday afternoon the boys left her in the same happy frame of mind, but were hardly home when on Wednesday they both received a letter from her, bitterly complaining that as soon as their train left, Anna was back, telling her that the only reason she agreed to the remodeling was to get them off her back. There would be no partitioning because, as Ilonka knew, she was not the sole owner, there were two others involved, and when they heard what she was planning to do with the house, they refused to give consent. This setback was the last straw, Ilonka wrote; she might as well give up, since finding an acceptable solution was clearly impossible.

She went on to say that a day later one of the other co-owners, Mrs. Bender, came to see her and asked if Gyuszi by chance planned to be back on the weekend. They were also having problems with Anna, a long drawn-out dispute that was heading for the courts, and it would help their case if Gyuszi could make a deposition regarding difficulties in dealing with her. Their appointment with the attorney was for Saturday morning at nine o'clock.

He immediately wired back that he would be arriving late Friday evening and was more than glad to give evidence. Ochie also wrote Ilonka a four-page letter saying that after talking it over with Marika, they had definitely decided to move back home. It was not just to ward off the landlady and put an end to her machinations, but because Marika felt homesick. She just never got used to living in Pecs. They would be back as soon as he lined up a job in Sopron, although Marika and the children might come earlier.

Friday at work Gyuszi was about to leave to catch the train to Sopron when he was handed a telegram from Ilonka that said, "Mrs. Bender's attorney can handle everything. No need to come. Letter to follow." He could only guess that perhaps Ilonka would make the deposition instead. In any case, there was not much he could do at this point but wait for her letter with more details, but it upset him that with his trip cancelled, his plan for his mother's 65th birthday tomorrow went up in smoke. He wanted to take her and her friends out to her favorite restaurant, but now it was too late even to send a birthday card; a telegram would have to do. He couldn't even call her, since she didn't have a phone.

Feeling out of sorts, he walked down to the post office to send the wire, dumping his resentment on the clerk, why couldn't a man in this country just pick up the phone to wish his mother a happy birthday? He carried on—not that the poor woman could do anything about it—that while everywhere else in the civilized world homes had telephones, in Hungary you must be a politician, a sports star, or a doctor to have the privilege.

His black mood stuck to him throughout the next day. The smallest things irritated him, the noise from the children, and especially the continuous chitchat between Itzu and her mother, who was there for a month-long visit. It had never bothered him before, so why was he so edgy today? He blamed it on the frustration over the failure to deal with the troublesome landlady and wondered how his mother was able to cope with that mess, if it could upset him this much.

He was glad when evening came; tomorrow would be a better day. Lying in bed he was half asleep when around eleven the shrill sound of the doorbell jolted him upright. "I guess the day is not over yet," he mumbled to Itzu as he put on his robe and shuffled to the door. But he became wide-awake when he saw one of the miners standing there; it could only mean that something bad happened down at the mine! The night crew could handle minor problems; they would only send for him in case of emergency.

But the man didn't seem to be in a hurry. He was shifting his weight from one foot to the other, looking down, then to the side, in obvious discomfort.

"Well, what is it?" Gyuszi prompted him, "An explosion? A collapse?"

"No, Comrade Zachar, nothing happened at the mine. Everything is fine there. I only came to give you a message, a sad one I am sorry to say." He was shaking his head as he handed a piece of paper to Gyuszi. "This man called to tell you that your mother is dead. His name and number is there; he wants you to call him right away. I can drive you back to the office."

It was lucky that by then Itzu was standing next to Gyuszi and could steady him as he staggered at hearing the news. "Did he say what happened to her?"

she asked the man, but he knew nothing more. Glancing at the note, they saw it was Marton Brody, Ochie's father-in-law in Sopron, who called.

When Gyuszi dialed the number he answered at the first ring. With a voice full of emotion he could only say that they found Ilonka dead. She killed herself.

Marton was waiting for them at the station when Gyuszi and Ochie arrived in Sopron late Sunday afternoon. He said the police had sealed the house and they wouldn't be able to get in until Monday morning, but he had room for them for the night. Eta and her husband and Istvan from Vienna were already here at Aunt Mitzi, waiting for them. Grety Varosy, who was the last one to see Ilonka alive, was also there, and so was another couple, Rudi and Panni Balazs, close friends and distant Bohaczek relations.

Walking into their aunt's house they found Eta disconsolate, her eyes swollen, slumped in her chair in a haze of shock and disbelief. Overcome by raw emotions, the four siblings clung to each other, unable to speak except one word, the desperate question that could never be answered now: Why? It took minutes before they regained a measure of calm and found the inner strength to listen as their friends recounted how their mother spent her last days, the meticulous way she prepared for her suicide, and how her body was discovered.

Thursday afternoon Mitzie went to see her and invited her for Friday evening to celebrate her birthday, but Ilonka declined, saying she was expecting Gyuszi from Pecs that night. It was a lie, of course, but no one knew at the time that she had called off his visit.

That same Thursday evening she went over to Panni and Rudy's place for dinner, complete with a birthday cake and toasts for good health and happiness. She seemed fine, complaining a little about her ongoing battle with the landlady, but mostly talking about the children and grandchildren. Later they watched an old Laurel and Hardy movie televised from Vienna, and Panni recalled how much they all laughed at the comics' hilarious antics. There was no indication whatsoever of Ilonka being depressed or dispirited, nor did they notice anything out of the ordinary when she said goodbye. As always, she hugged and kissed them, but they didn't see any sign of sadness or finality, a tighter hug, or a lingering backward glance.

The following day, on the eve of Ilonka's birthday, Grety Varosy went to congratulate her. Ilonka was showing her the birthday card and photographs she just received that day from Sári, but Grety sensed that the usual joy and enthusiasm when Ilonka talked about her daughter was missing. She vividly recalled their conversation, what Ilonka said when Grety asked if Sári had any plans to come for another visit.

"It's a big trip to come all the way here, and for what, to sit with me in this old house? You know how young people are, your Kurt, too, when he was here with his wife, they were constantly on the go."

"Well then, why don't you go and visit her? You always loved to travel and the restrictions for older folks like us are completely lifted now; they let you stay as long as the Americans allow it. I got my exit visa to Argentina without any problems."

"I know I could get a visa, it's not that, but my health. I wouldn't dare to go with my bad heart; the excitement alone might kill me. I can't take the risk of another heart attack while I am over there. Nobody will insure me, and doctors and hospitals are very expensive in America. How is Sári going to pay for it if anything should happen to me? She is not a millionaire, you know, she is a girl living alone, working in an office."

There was nothing Grety could say that would brighten Ilonka's mood. Most of the time she just talked about Jeno's passing, how much she missed him, and how her entire life had taken a downturn ever since he died. Their whole talk was downhearted, making Grety feel that her friend was losing the will to go on. She took both of Ilonka's hands in hers and, speaking softly, reminded her of her strong religious beliefs, how she always found consolation in prayers and never questioned God's will.

Grety's voice faltered and she had to stop. Should she continue and reveal what Ilonka said when she knew it would be heartbreaking for the children to hear? Did they need to know the depth of her despair, the total hopelessness she felt before she ended her life? But then, it might help them to understand one aspect of what drove her to her desperate act: her loss of faith. And so in a voice chocked with sadness she repeated Ilonka's words: "I tried to pray, but God has abandoned me. He no longer hears my prayers."

The heart-wrenching sobs that erupted stopped her from continuing; she too was in tears and had to wait before she could collect herself and return to describing the remaining final minutes she spent with Ilonka. She told that as darkness approached in that late afternoon, she felt a chill and asked why Ilonka didn't heat the room.

"I would have if I had known you were coming," she said. "I was going to light the fire just before Gyuszi arrives, and stay in the kitchen until then. Anyway, I don't think it's that cold in here, but I don't want you to catch a cold, so perhaps it's best if you go home."

Grety detected a strange urgency in Ilonka's voice, and so with a final hug and best wishes for her birthday she left, never guessing that it was the last time she'd see her alive.

The abrupt way she suggested to her friend to leave was not polite, but Ilonka needed time. With her gone, she was now assured that she would be alone the rest of the evening and most of the next day to prepare for what she must do. Her renters, as usual, would be leaving at noon to spend the weekend with their families, but to be sure, she asked them repeatedly during the week if that's what they planned to do. Mitzie heard this from the girls today when, after returning from their village, they couldn't get into the house and came to see her. They also said that before they left on Saturday Ilonka asked them to drop six or seven letters at the post office. One of them recalled teasing her that she must have been up all night writing this many letters. She didn't know it, but that's exactly how Ilonka spent her last night on earth.

At that point Marton Brody took over to describe what happened next.

Toward the evening on Saturday, he and his wife Maria went to wish Ilonka a happy birthday, but found the house dark, the door locked and all windows closed. They thought it strange. She was usually home by eight o'clock; that's why they came late, to be sure to find her there. Well, perhaps she was visiting with relatives or friends, Marton said, and was ready to turn around and go home, but his wife insisted they try to track her down; she was probably at Mitzie's or Mrs. Varosy's. She didn't want Ilonka to think that they forgot her birthday.

They couldn't find her at either place, but when they learned that Ilonka was expecting Gyuszi for the weekend—no one knew that she called it off—they checked several restaurants in case he took her out to celebrate. Again, there was no trace of Ilonka, and by then the Brodys began to worry; it was not like her to stay out without telling someone where she would be.

Their last hope was Rudi and Panni Balazs but they had not seen her, either, since she was there two days ago. Rudi then volunteered to go back to the house with them and look into the situation. If they still found no sign of Ilonka, they would go in. He knew a secret place where she kept a spare key.

By the time they reached the house it was pitch dark with no light from inside. They rang the doorbell several times and Rudi went around banging on the windows, making enough noise to wake her up if she was asleep. When there was still no answer, they all agreed that something was drastically wrong and began to debate what to do next. Marton brought up the possibility that with all her recent troubles Ilonka could have suffered another heart attack, and they should call the hospital, or perhaps the police before they do anything. Rudi, however, insisted on going in first and make the calls depending on what they found. As a distant relative—his name was Bohaczek before changing it to Balazs—he had the right to enter the house and with that, he went to look for the hidden key. It always hung on a nail inside a tiny window high in the back wall that could only be reached by standing on a chair. Climbing up and poking his fingers through the opening, he could feel that the key was there. Careful not to let it drop on the inside, he retrieved it and after opening the door, turned on the light in the foyer and loudly called out to Ilonka. Getting no response, they cautiously went into the bedroom but found the bed with the cover neatly in place. Could it be, Mrs. Brody suggested, that one of her children had an emergency and she had no time to tell anyone before leaving? But there was no sign of hurried packing, a torn-open telegram, or a written note that she would have surely left for them.

With dark foreboding, they walked to the next room and stood in the doorway while Rudi was trying to find the light switch. From the dim glow of the hallway they could only make out the table in the middle of the room and on top the vague outline of a vase filled with flowers. When the light came on they could also see some packages with little notes, a plate of homemade cookies and a box of chocolates laid out on the table.

"Why, it looks like Ilonka was preparing for a birthday party, but at this hour?" Maria blurted out, stepping closer to the table. "And look at these gifts—they are not for her! She is giving them instead! They all have little notes, this one is for Orsi . . ." Picking it up she began to read it, but Rudi's voice stopped her in mid-sentence. "Hush, there she is, sleeping over here," he pointed to a couch partially hidden by the open door, with Ilonka lying on top, fully dressed.

"She must have gotten tired of waiting," Marton said, keeping his voice low, "It's strange, though, that she didn't wake up at the banging, or hear us coming in."

Maria started toward the couch but froze midway. Her hand flew to her mouth as she whispered through her fingers, "She is not sleeping; look at her hands, clasped together, entwined with a rosary. She is dead!"

Crossing herself, her breath coming in short bursts, she backed away and let her husband and Rudi confirm what she already knew with utter certainty. They didn't have to tell her about the two empty pill bottles they found nearby.

Rudi immediately rushed to the police to report their finding, while the Brodys waited with great uneasiness, hardly able to move, until he returned with two officers. After making a short statement they hurried home to make the sad calls to the children. They reached Eta and Istvan, the only ones with a phone at home, and left a message at the mine for Gyuszi and Ochie, then spent the rest of the night traumatized, speculating what it was that drove Ilonka to such a desperate act. Even now, talking about it, they could only speak haltingly as they recalled the scene last night.

Rudi finished the story, how the police called the hospital asking to send a doctor. When he arrived he established the cause of death as suicide by overdose of sleeping pills, but just how many she took could only be determined by autopsy. He wrote up his preliminary report, estimating the time of death between three and six in the afternoon, then went back to the hospital to send the ambulance. They pulled up around two-thirty in the morning and left fifteen minutes later with Ilonka's sheet-covered body.

In the meanwhile, the police took some notes from Rudi, checked the table setting and took the letter propped against the vase, but left everything else untouched. They waited until the ambulance was gone, then taking the key sealed the house until Monday morning, when relatives could retrieve both the key and the letter.

Exhausted from crying and from the shock of learning the details, Eta and her brothers were beyond consolation. They knew that the image of their mother methodically preparing to end her life, swallowing the pills and lying down to wait for death to take her, would haunt them for the rest of their lives. To think of her state of mind, what she must have felt as she made sure no one would interfere with her plans, that she would be left undisturbed to write her letters and set the table with her little gifts, was devastatingly painful. What were her last thoughts? Why did she do it? Could they have done anything to prevent it? They asked themselves these questions over and over, trying to find an explanation for her final act, when to the rational mind there was none.

Although no one would be able to sleep that night, it was time to get at least some rest they all needed to face the difficult days ahead. Gyuszi was almost at the door when he asked if anyone thought of sending Sári a telegram. Eta, whose presence of mind never failed her, said that she took care of it earlier, although she didn't tell her sister everything. Remembering her anguished letters after the death of their father, she decided to keep silent about the suicide, at least for the time being. It would be better if she didn't know, and everyone agreed. However, shielding her from the truth meant they needed to keep her from coming to the funeral, and to ensure it, Eta delayed sending the wire until later in the afternoon. Even without it, they doubted if she could arrange for a visa and book a flight in time.

Knowing what a tremendous shock it would be for Sári to read the tragic news of her mother's unexpected death, keeping her in the dark was perhaps indeed a kind act. If hiding the true circumstances spared her additional heartache, it justified the cover-up.

The truth would come out soon enough.

One of the hardest moments for the distraught children came on Monday morning when they entered the house, realizing that their mother would no longer be there to greet them with her welcoming embrace. She was gone forever; they'd never see her smiling face or hear her laughter again.

Feeling numb and emotionally exhausted from the drama of the past two days, they still made an effort to maintain some degree of composure as they walked down the long hallway. It only lasted until they stepped inside the room where their mother died and saw the scene their friends had so vividly described the night before. The sight of the pillow with a slight indent of her head still visible, the table set with her gifts and the smell of the now wilting flowers broke all their restraint, and they just stood there grief-stricken, weeping like children.

After some long, agonizing moments they finally found the courage to open the letter the police handed them when they picked up the key. Hoping it would shed some light on why she chose to end her life, Eta, hardly able to control her emotions, began to read their mother's final words. She wrote that she was worn out and reached the point where physically every breath was a struggle, and mentally could think of nothing but Jeno. The harassment over the house made her feel threatened and helpless, and if her lot was to live under constant stress and aggravation, she knew her heart would give out sooner or later, and she didn't want to wait. Sick, tired, and alone, and feeling totally defenseless, she was simply at the end of her endurance; she had no more strength to face life. Closing her letter she wrote, "I'll be with your father; that's where I belong. Be happy, live your life to the fullest, and love your children as I have loved you, and will love you always and forever, Mother"

"She was not left alone!" Eta blurted out between sobs. "I begged her to stay with us. The hell with this old house! The hell with Sopron! But no, she was bent on coming back; she kept saying that's where father was put to rest, where her mother was buried. Who would look after their graves?"

"Well, Kecskemet was not good for her asthma, but she liked Pecs," Gyuszi said, his voice breaking as he turned to Eta. "You heard me when I asked her to come and live with us, and I repeated it again when I was in Sopron the week before she died, but she just didn't want to live anywhere else."

"All right, she wanted to stay in Sopron, but why cling to this house? It was like an obsession with her," Ochie was shaking his head. Living with his parents longer than the others, he knew more about Ilonka's growing fixation to remain in the house. "Why, she almost felt relieved when the apartment exchange fell through and she could stay here," he told them. "Still, I think if she had moved in with Aunt Mitzie it would have worked; she had room in her house and they always loved each other."

Istvan said nothing. They all knew how Ilonka refused even to consider moving to Vienna, although he and his wife asked her repeatedly.

They all agreed that most likely she didn't want to be a burden to anyone. If only she had talked about her feelings! Now it was too late; they could only speculate. They must accept it that she fell into a deep depression, lost her will to live and this was her way to end it all.

The task of sorting out the little gifts on the table was still waiting, but no one was willing to go through the painful process. Just then the doorbell rang, the once familiar ring now jarring their nerves. The woman from the apartment in the backyard came to offer her condolences and asked if she could be of any help. She was cooking and perhaps they would join her for lunch? None of them could even think of food in their anxiety-ridden state; instead, they gave her the cookies and the box of candy from the table to give to her young daughter.

Back in the room, it was Eta who finally had the strength to open the gifts. It seemed that Ilonka divided her small trinkets of rings, bracelets and watches between her granddaughters, while the boys got her gold Cross pen, and small pieces of jewelry Jeno had. She left her little necklace with a heart shape pendant, Jeno's first gift to her, to Eta; a package for Itzu contained her priced crystal stemware and decanter; Istvan and his wife got her beautiful Herendy porcelain demitasse set; and Ochie his father's gold watch. As for Sári, noting that there was nothing of value she could give her, she wrapped up a decorative pillowcase she embroidered herself with a popular native Hungarian motive she knew Sári liked.

They also found a list of items from the house she wanted them to have: Jeno's writing desk; a full leather-bound edition of classic Hungarian literature; the color TV; and her beautiful antique wall clock, but she left it up to them to decide who should keep them.

In a separate envelope they found her papers and a savings book with instructions that the money was for her funeral. Added to her small death benefit, it should cover the expenses. Her last wish was to keep everything simple; there was no need to go into debt for her; they had spent a lot of money already on their father's funeral a mere nine months ago.

Of course, this part of her instructions was completely ignored. They selected the best casket, arranged for a first class service, and ordered Holy Mass in each of the three churches she frequented. Everything was ready for the funeral to be held at noon on Wednesday the 12th.

Sári got home from work on Monday afternoon to find an attempted delivery note from Western Union on her door. With deep foreboding she rushed to pick up the telegram; to her, they usually meant bad news. The last one she received was when her father died, and she remembered the overwhelming sadness she felt then, but it was nothing compared to the shock that numbed her now as she stared at the words: "Mother died Saturday. Her poor heart gave out. Funeral on Wednesday; letter to follow."

She just stood there, stunned. Another heart attack? Of course it was possible; the doctors had warned them about it, but somehow in her mind it always remained just that, a distant possibility, a vague threat that hung in the future. Yet here it was, the telegram in her hand telling that the warning was real!

With tears welling in her eyes she glanced at her watch. It was close to 6 PM, already 3 AM Tuesday in Hungary. No use trying to call any of her siblings at home when they were all in Sopron by now, and there was no telephone there. The only way she could reach them was through the Brodys, and she dreaded it, recalling how Mrs. Brody kept her on the line the one time she called to speak with Ilonka after Jeno's death. No doubt, she'd do the same, telling her what happened, details she didn't want to hear from her, nearly a stranger. No, she'd rather send a telegram to Eta and ask her to call her collect as soon as possible. According to Western Union, considering the nine-hour time difference, it would take about twenty-four hours before they'd receive the telegram in Sopron. If she sent it right away, she could expect her sister's call after she got home from work tomorrow.

She slept badly, but went to work in the morning, thinking it would keep her mind occupied. At least she wouldn't be sitting home alone, imagining how her mother died, or dwell on the funeral that she knew she was unable to attend. Somehow though, that didn't bother her. Even if it were not too late to go, what good would it do to travel thousands of miles just to be in the middle of all that grief, all that crying, everyone in such a state of utter devastation? Her mother had said the same thing when they talked about what she should do when her father died. She didn't go to his funeral then, and so she would again stay home and mourn her mother's passing in private.

Coming home from work next day, she sat by the phone, chewing her nails, waiting for her sister's call. In the ensuing tearful exchange Eta told her how devastating it was to find their mother dead, to lose her yet on her birthday! She said they knew it was too late for her to come to the funeral, but not to worry; they had made all the arrangements. They ordered the flowers and several wreaths, one in her name, and they would send her pictures so she could see it placed on the grave. Eta admitted that paying for two funerals within the same year put a financial strain on all of them, but they would manage. Like before, they'd split the cost five ways and she'd let Sári know her share.

It was a difficult conversation, both of them crying, unable to stay composed. Overpowered by sadness and torn by immense grief, the tears kept falling long after Sári hung up the phone. Strangely, she had held up well until now, perhaps the result of shock from reading the telegram, but after talking with Eta the reality hit her with full force. She was simply unprepared to lose her mother so unexpectedly.

After spending a sleepless night, she was unable to bring herself to go to the office in the morning, and stayed home to mourn her mother's passing in tearful solitude. She spent the day, the day of the funeral, remembering her selfless loving care that guided her through her happy childhood, the patience and tolerance she showed during her teenage years, and her generous heart that forgave her foolish mistakes.

The sun was at its zenith when the bells of old St. Mihaly Church began to toll on Wednesday, May 12, as family and friends gathered around an open grave that was destined to become Ilonka's final resting place. Just like ten months ago, at the same spot where they buried their father, Eta, Gyuszi, Istvan and Ochie once again stood in silent sorrow, listening to the priest's prayers, watching through tears as he sprinkled holy water over their mother's slowly descending casket. A final thud of falling earth brought home the absolute finality that she was gone. The grave was closed, the mound covered with flowers, gladioli, roses, and carnations, a wreath from Sári interwoven with cyclamens propped against the double headstone. The carving already had her mother's name and year of birth, only the year of her death was yet to be added. She was now home where she longed to be, at peace, together with her husband, for all eternity.

The day after the funeral, her senses still blunted, Sári went back to work, or rather to spend an unfocused, utterly useless day in the office. At 5:30 PM she pulled into her garage, parked the car, and walked to check her mail. She opened the mailbox and stood frozen, staring in total disbelief at the blue Hungarian airmail envelope addressed in her mother's familiar handwriting. She could hear the pounding of her heart as she looked at the letter, knowing full well that her mother was already dead and buried.

Dazed as if afraid to touch it, she lifted the letter and carried it to her apartment. Once inside she put it on the coffee table, then picked it up, only to put it down again. Her nerves stretched to the limit, it took a long time before she finally found the strength to open the envelope and read her mother's final words to her:

My dearest Sári,

Thank you with all my heart for your birthday wishes and the photographs you sent me. As always, seeing you so radiant and happy fills my heart with gladness. Stay as young and beautiful as you are now, and try to fill your days with laughter and joy, because old age is not pleasant.

I wish I could tell you that I am getting better, but I am not. Unfortunately, there is no cure for my illnesses. My asthma is almost as bad as my mother's was, and I remember well how much she suffered at the end.

The trouble with the house is also wearing me down. We couldn't come to a decent agreement with the Sinkovich woman, and I am certain it's only a matter of time before she'd be living here. No one can get along with her, not even her family, and now I am forced to share my home with her, the house where I lived for forty years. Just thinking of it drives me to despair. It will ruin my chances to spend my remaining days in peace, and I am helpless to do anything to prevent it.

I am left without hope, and feel tired to exhaustion. It would be better to put an end to it all. My only consolation is that your father didn't live to see my misery; he is at peace, and my only wish is to be with him.

My dearest Sári, I won't burden you further with my problems. I stop now, but before I do, I want you to know that even though you are an ocean away and I can't hold you, you are with me the same as when I carried you under my heart. And when I close my eyes tonight, and forever after, you will never be far from me again.

With all my love and blessings, Mother

From time to time in the passing years Sári would take out her mother's last letter and remember the shock when she first read it, realizing with certainty that it was not her heart, but her own doing that killed her. Could she have done anything to prevent it? No, there was no feeling of guilt, only a profound sadness over her mother's desperate act, and a deep compassion that she had the courage to carry it out.

That her siblings tried to cover up the truth made her upset at first, but she could understand their motive. And it didn't really matter. Even if she had been able to attend her mother's funeral, or her father's for that matter, to see them lying in a casket was not how she wanted to remember them. When she thought of her parents, it was as she last saw them, standing together behind that iron gate at the railroad station, their hands reaching through the bars for a last touch, smiling through tears and waving goodbye as she boarded her train to Vienna.

It was that precious image, frozen in time, that she would forever carry in her heart as their living, breathing memory, cherished and treasured, never to fade away . . .

CPSIA information can be obtained at www.ICGtesting.com
Printed in the USA
BVOW070046050713

325084BV00003B/6/P

9 781938 223235